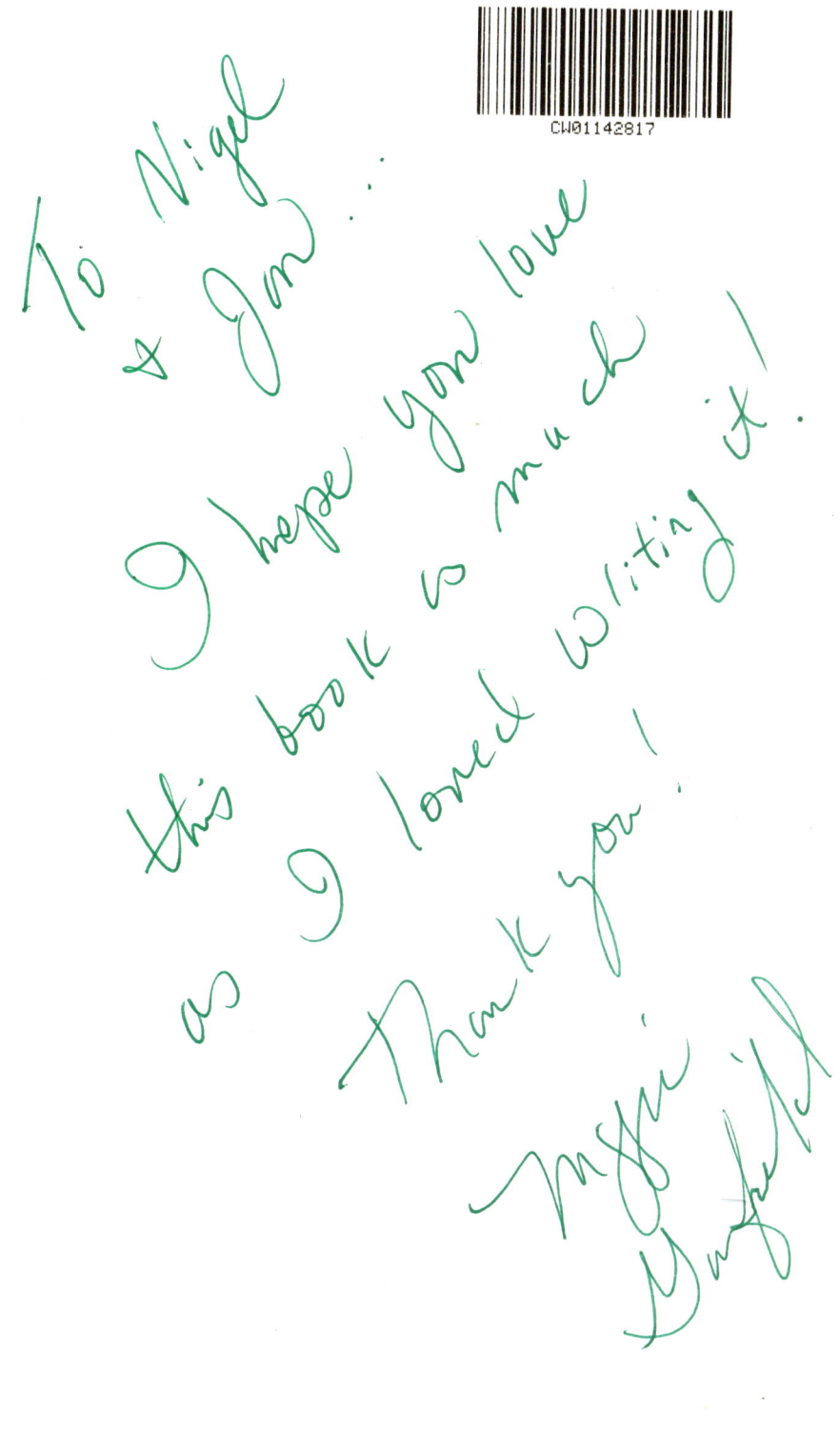

ALSO BY M. GARFIELD

FICTION – YOUNG ADULT

To Beg Our Cousin the King

A DOMESDAY TALE

BY

M. GARFIELD

Pennaeth Publishing
San Francisco

Although this work is based on actual historical characters and events, A Domesday Tale is a product of the author's imagination.

A DOMESDAY TALE. Copyright © 2015 by M. Garfield. All rights reserved. This book may not be used or reproduced in any way without the author's permission. For information, write to m.garfield@comcast.net

Cover designed by Evren Bilgihan

The cover is inspired by *The Bayeux Tapestry* which hangs in the Musée de la Tapisserie de Bayeux, 13 Rue de Nesmond, 14400, Bayeux, France. www.tapisserie-bayeux.fr/

Family Tree and Map designed by Virginia Ruths, touchstonepubs@gmail.com, www.touchstonepubs.com

contact@pennaethpublishing.com
Pennaeth Publishing
P.O. Box 2448
San Francisco 94126

ISBN 978-1517303990

For My Family

ACKNOWLEDGEMENTS

I am eternally grateful to my family for their undying love and support throughout the entire process of writing and publishing this book.

Additionally, I wholeheartedly thank Eric Levine, my husband, and Rachel Garfield-Levine, my daughter, for being the strictest and finest editors I know.

Evren Bilgihan, my illustrator and nephew, has drawn for me the most exquisite cover for my novel, and has managed beautifully to preserve the integrity of *The Bayeux Tapestry*.

To Susan Walls—you were with me from the start, telling stories to each other, writing stories, reading and editing our books together. I could never have achieved the publication of this book without you and I thank you with my whole heart and soul.

The writers' group that I have worked with for almost twenty years have provided me with endless inspiration and motivation.

Ginny Ruths, it took quite a long time, and I'm so proud to have the family tree and map you designed for me gracing the pages of my book.

I am grateful to the authors and editors of all of my reference books for teaching me, sometimes contrarily, all about the Conqueror's family, and the history, both political and social, of the late eleventh century.

My extended family showed continual interest in my writing, especially Terry, my sister-in-law, and Aryn, my niece, by suggesting edits and furtive ideas for storylines.

My extraordinary parents, Wayne and Mary Garfield, both who have passed, never lost faith in my ability to succeed as a published author. My father's dream was to write a historical fiction novel, which he started, but was not able to finish. This book is for him.

Thank you again to everyone above who has help me create my great joy, A Domesday Tale, and who will join with me in continuing the process with its sequel, A Plague of Devils. I love you all.

A DOMESDAY TALE

The Family of William the Conqueror

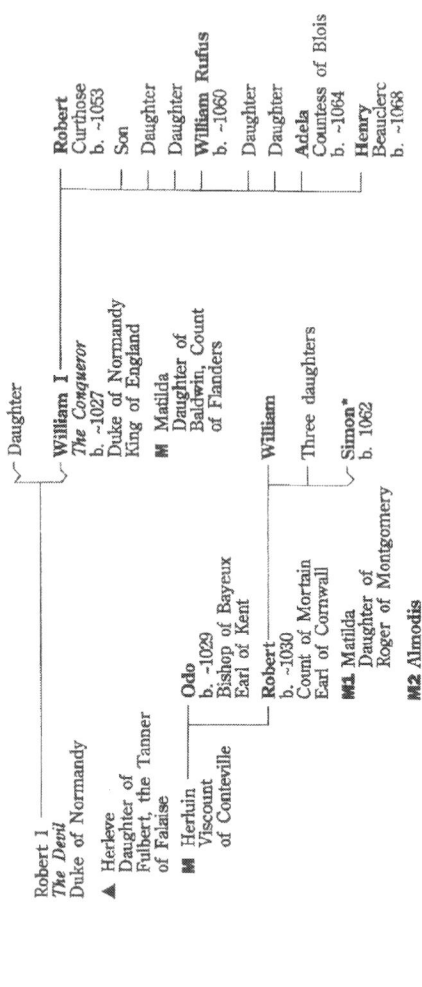

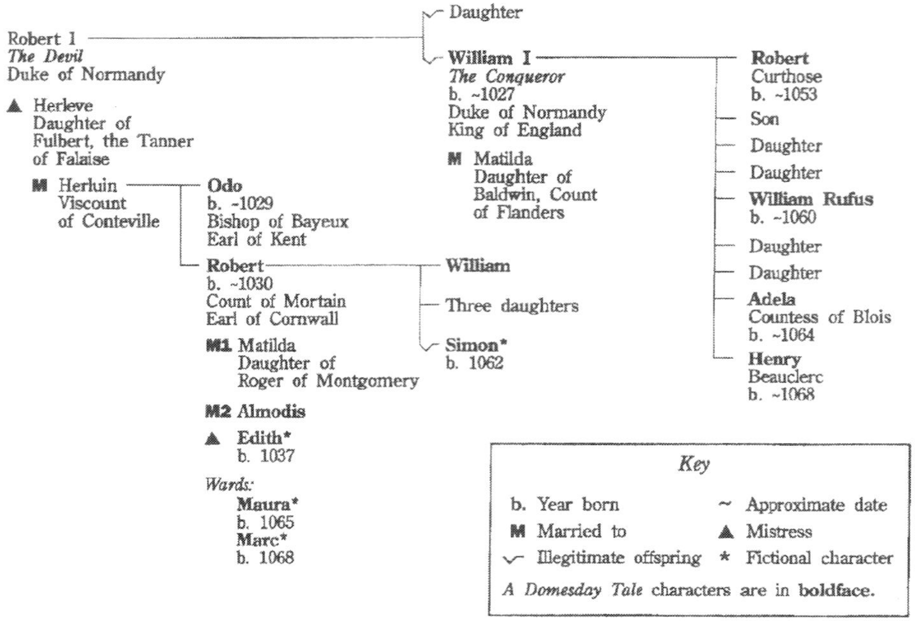

England and Normandy
Principal Locations in *A Domesday Tale*

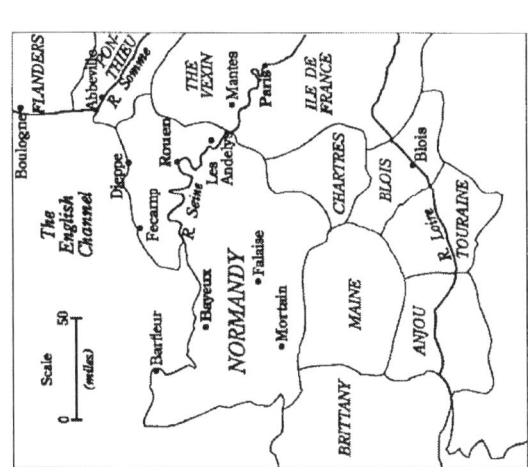
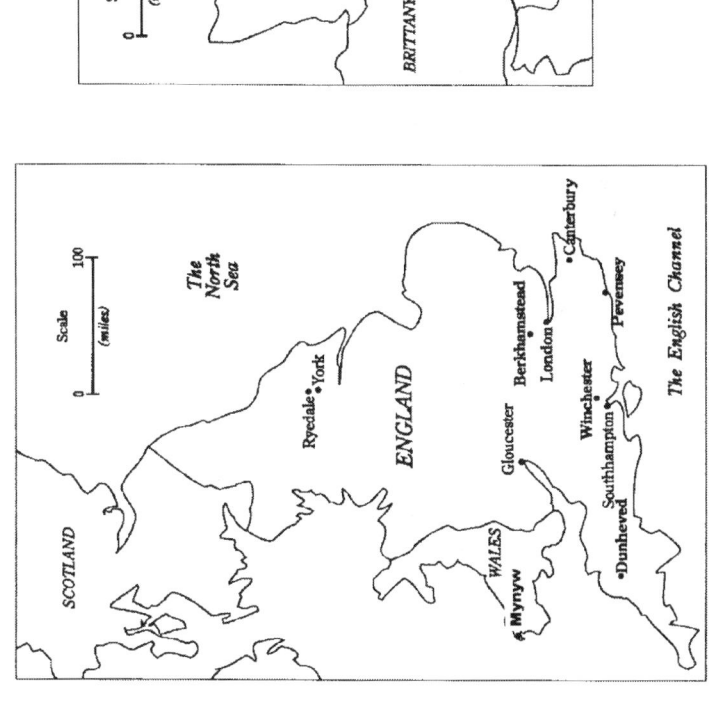

CHAPTER ONE - A REUNION

𝔚ithin the dank, cavernous ruins of Winchester Minster, Maura tossed fitfully in her bed and dreamt a dream more treacherous than the storm outside…

The nightmare raged round Maura's tiny crouched figure, huddling in the corner of a blazing hut and shielding a sleeping child in her clutch. Flames raced up the timbered walls, leapt from thatch above her head, licked at rushes beneath her feet. An unseen force bound her ankle; she strained for freedom, batted smoke, and choked, "Hel...help us! Please, help—"

Flaming darts exploding from a tumbling wall gagged her plea and briefly parted the smoke. Close before her, a man and woman thrashed in brutal combat—the man's shimmering armor mirrored the flames; the woman's hair shone gold as the inferno. Maura heaved up from the floor and kicked at her shackle, wailing, "Here! We're here! Save us!" The woman spun to the squall and, at her lapse, the man unsheathed his weapon. "No! The man!" cried Maura, but the crackling pyre drowned her shriek, and the sword neatly severed the woman's head.

The man charged for Maura. She bundled the child and shrank deeper into the recess. The man drew himself to an ominous height, his reddened sword poised to strike. She challenged his smoke-veiled glower and dropped over the child. The blade plummeted…

With a tortured scream, Maura bolted from her bed. She flailed wildly through the blackness and collided with Rose, who tackled her to the ground inches from a circle of still live coals. "Wake up!" Rose shouted. "Maura, wake up!"

Rose's firm shake woke Maura fully and she gasped, "He'll kill me, Rose! Kill me!"

"No, no, my angel," soothed Rose, clasping Maura to her breast. "It's the dream, only the dream. You're safe here with me. I'll let no one harm you." Maura raised desperate eyes to her aged guardian's silhouette, framed by the glow of the smoldering fire. Limply, she accepted Rose's helping hand, and staggered on her own the short distance back to her bed.

Rose soon settled by her, armed with a soaked rag and a candle lit by the coals. The breadth of wavering light illuminated two crude boxes packed with straw, bracing the moldering, timber and stone walls of the Minster. Maura shuddered beneath her frayed coverlet and reached a trembling touch to a rickety table linking the beds. The simple act drew from her a long quivered sigh of relief, and the realization that this was *her* chamber—there was no smoke, no sword, no man.

Rose passed her the rag. "Cool your face, angel." Then, cautiously, she pressed, "The dream comes to you more often. Was the man clearer to you this time?" Maura shunned the much repeated question by burying her face in the cloth and breathing deep its coolness. Rose forced a grin and sweetly urged, "Lie back down, angel, and try to sleep more."

"How can I sleep?!" The cloth dropped from Maura's fumbling grasp, exposing an expression stark with dread. "I'll only dream again!"

"And what will you do besides?" asked Rose, neatening a mussed lock of Maura's hair.

"Think us a way out of—this stinking hovel!"

With a desolate wag of her head, Rose crawled stiffly beneath her patched woolen blanket. "All the thinking in the world won't rid us of our hunger, angel."

"*I'm* the cause of our troubles!" Maura fiercely returned. "Why should you be forced to suffer when I'm the one Rufus hates?" A loose thread dangling from her worn chemise snapped off in her balled fist, and the cold rocks of the wall stabbed at her back. The sight of Rose's frail figure trembling under her scrap of a blanket swelled Maura's upset and grief cramped her belly. Rose grew weaker by the day; there was little chance she would survive another harsh winter.

"Rufus isn't particular, he hates every—" Rose paused to hack convulsively into her palm, then croaked on, "If only King William or Lord Robert would answer your letters."

"How can they answer letters they've never received?" said Maura. A groaning gust of frigid wind roared its way through the tiny shuttered window heading her bed, blanching her freckled skin and flaring her sapphire eyes. She vigorously chafed her arms and cursed, "One of these blasted gales will topple these rotted walls! Then where will we go?"

Rose neglected Maura's gripes to grouse her own. "Whatever did we do to rile him so? Rufus treats us like slaves. No worse, like sows." A violent image worsened her anguish. "And it's November—the slaughtering month! He'll do away with us! Why shouldn't he, there's no one to stop him, no one to care...no one..." She shifted away from Maura, her lament fading with the taper's light. "Maybe, if we escaped the castle and..."

Maura's expression wrenched with fury while she yanked on a lock of flame red hair and racked her mind for a cure for their oppression. For the past two hard years, each night had ended with the same mental ritual, and still the solution eluded them. This night proved no different. Exasperated, she flopped to her side, and watched helplessly Rose continue to shake. Her troubled gaze drifted off Rose and came to rest upon the coals shimmering meagerly just beyond the chamber's door. If only she could bring their healing warmth closer, but the tiny chamber had no proper venting for smoke. She supposed she should offer thanks to God for the crumbling wall facing the door; it allowed a bit of heat to leak into their room while drawing the bulk of fumes out to the castle's bailey. She recalled tales of Saxon priests being housed in these tumbled remains; thick-skinned priests she imagined, as she buried her head under the cover. Clenching shut her eyes, she struggled to imagine something cheering, yet her belly's rumblings scattered her hopes, and she drifted away to a deep, blessedly dreamless sleep.

Dawn's first rays sifted through the window and crept upon Maura's face, coaxing her from her slumber; a pounding on the door completed the task. She rose, wrapped clumsily in her blanket, and stumbled to answer the summons.

A burly guard clad in rusted chain mail loomed in the doorway, commanding, "I would speak to the Lady Maura."

Maura steeled herself taller and answered, "I am Maura."

"William FitzRoy orders you and your servant to vacate this chamber by midday."

"No, he can't!" she fiercely objected, gripping the door's latch to steady her shock.

The sentry ignored her protest and ordered on, "The Prince's servants will arrive shortly to remove you, your servant, and your possessions."

"Where are we to go?!" she implored.

"The FitzRoy has left that decision to you. This chamber is required to quarter the King's soldiers. I will return within the hour to see that the Prince's orders have been carried out to his *complete* satisfaction. My Lady..." He cracked a smug grin, kicked away dead coals, and departed.

"Oh my God!" anguished Rose, hobbling near and hugging Maura's arm. "What are we to do?!"

Maura gestured for calm and was quiet. Suddenly, she let out a tight gasp, dashed from the chamber, and sidled the damaged wall into the bailey. The sun's radiance, too often absent, teared her eyes as she peered intently up to Winchester Castle's battlements, and searched amongst the many pennants flapping in the brusque wind. One partly-colored banner waved above all—King William's banner. "He's here!" she cried out, spilling back into the chamber. "Rose! Oh Rose, the King is in residence!"

"Will you speak to him?" asked Rose.

"I shall see him!" Maura replied with force. "No one will dare stop me...though—" Her resolve faltered as she frowned down at her tattered, soiled chemise. "Do I have anything besides *this* to wear?"

"It certainly would help our cause if you didn't," muttered Rose. "I do believe you have one somewhat decent gown left. I've traded all the others for food."

They dragged a battered trunk from a shadowed corner, Maura excitedly urging, "Rose, please fetch the candle! I can't see a thing." She flung back the cracked lid and began rooting furiously through the rags. Rose returned with the light, and Maura soon yanked forth a fairly clean and intact gown. She climbed swiftly into the russet frock and smoothed its worn and wrinkled wool over her sylphlike figure. Rose deftly laced the dress, cinched a matching girdle round Maura's waist, then attacked her tousled tresses with a wooden comb owning too few teeth.

Maura felt her cheeks flush hot at the tremulous notion of confronting the King, then again she'd eagerly confront God or the Devil to plead for release from Rufus' tyranny. She scraped her teeth with the end of a rush, stumbled into her moth-eaten slippers, then fashioned a stained linen coif over her hair, securing it with a braided leather circlet. With a twirl, she called out in hope to Rose, "Am I presentable?"

Rose squeezed her gnarled fingers together and gushed with pride, "Oh yes, angel! It's been ages since I've seen you so lovely." Then she darkened with despair. "Maura, what if the King refuses you? It's a long way to Dunheved. I don't know if—"

"*Please*, Rose, no doubts, no tears!" begged Maura, grasping hold her hands. "I need your strength. If the King has called a meeting of his Curia Regis, Lord Robert will be a member of that council. The King and Robert will rescue us from Rufus."

Rose gripped back, her fear blatant. "Take me with you. Don't leave me here alone!"

"I swear to return shortly with good news," Maura gently assured. "Bolt the door and let no one inside—no one!" Swift kisses broke their hold, and Maura whisked herself away.

Rose, her gaunt face chiseled with worry, stared a long while after Maura, then listlessly took up a shapeless woolen garment from the foot of her bed. Once a robust, stately figure, Rose now winced as she wriggled her cold and aching bones into her only tunic. Of course she would never willingly leave Maura. She'd seen to her care ever since Lord Robert had delivered the wild, copper-haired waif to Dunheved Castle sixteen years past. Rose considered Maura her true daughter and cherished her wholly. If she were to die soon, she'd prefer to meet God cradled in Maura's loving embrace. Rose swabbed at tears welling in her brilliant black eyes and knelt to pray for deliverance.

Maura hiked up her skirts, sprinted past the tumbled wall, across the green bailey, up the stairs to the keep, then down squat dank halls, and halted abruptly before the lofty doors of the great hall. Her heart thudded painfully as she spotted two surly, hulking guards barring the entrance. She lay her hand upon her chest to calm her breath and braved one step forward. A sudden flurry of servants bustled past, jostling her and ruffling her courage. One sentry regarded her scornfully, "What is it you want?"

Maura dropped her eyes and, after a dry swallow, stammered, "I...I would see the King."

Both men sniggered at her request and rumpled appearance. "And who might *you* be?" mocked her interrogator.

She raised defiant eyes and challenged, "I am Maura, ward to Lord Robert, who claims the titles Count of Mortain and Earl of Cornwall, and—" she frankly finished, "he is the King's brother!"

The guards started to her pronouncement; the rude one fumbled with the door's latch, sputtering, "I'll announce you at...at once, my...my Lady."

While Maura's foot tapped her impatience, her eyes darted about, taking in the surrounding chaos. The air was thick with excitement, and she wondered if it was due to the King's presence, the feast of Martinmas, or perhaps both. The creaking doors of the hall interrupted her pondering, and the guard reappeared, bowing low, and gesturing. "King William will see you now, my Lady."

Maura stepped gingerly inside Winchester's great hall. Awed by its grandeur, she hesitated a moment and let her wide gaze wander. Timbered arches bolstered the towering stone walls; birds dove and flitted between nests in the rafters; a great roaring fire greeted her, its dense smoke swirling up and out a gaping hole in the roof. She tread cautiously by the fire pit and beheld the King's massive bulk slouched at the dais, mulling over a steep stack of parchments. A balding clerk at his side read to William. Maura waited for a pause in the clerk's discourse, drew a bracing breath, and addressed the King with the familiar, "Uncle?"

William the Conqueror, King of England and Duke of Normandy, raised his beleaguered face to the faint greeting. He squinted curiously through drifting smoke and, upon spotting Maura, his dark eyes lit in fond remembrance. He shoved up from the table and loudly beckoned, "Maura! Come!"

A strangled cry of relief propelled Maura round the long raised table. In her haste she bruised her hip on its sharp edge and tumbled against William's portly body. He caught her easily in his strong arms, chuckled at her awkwardness, and stepped back to take her small, soft face in his huge, coarse hands. Maura's pallor betrayed her despair, and her raspy sigh, "At...at last you've come," told her struggle.

William motioned for his clerk to leave. He draped a comforting arm round her shoulders, helped her sit, and offered his cup of wine. "What is it, Maura?" he wondered tensely. "What *ails* you?"

"Your son Rufus ails me, my Lord!" She instantly regretted her rashness and clamped shut her mouth.

He pried away her fingers, demanding, "Speak up! What has he done?"

Her voice and body quaked with rage and fear. "No! I can't say. I—"

"You needn't fear *me*," he stressed. She strained to escape; his hold and voice sharpened. "You won't go till you confess his crime!"

She stared down at their clenched hands, and her chest heaved as she quavered, "Shortly after the Queen's—" Again, she hesitated.

"The Queen's *death*," he firmly assisted. "Go on, child."

"Rufus banished Rose and me to the old Minster. He robbed us of most of our possessions, all of our coins, and denied us food and fuel!" The King's eyes bulged to her dire tale, and she meekly met his glare. "I confess, my Lord, I stole herbs from your physician's room, and blankets and wood. I had no choice! Rose fell ill and I had to help her. She's yet to regain her strength. The cook snuck us leftovers and seeds to grow our own vegetables. We reaped little harvest. What we managed to save, we've bartered. And just this morn Rufus ordered us from our chamber. Uncle," she anguished, "it's been two days since we've eaten. We've nothing left! I don't know what—"

"No more!" William's fist shook the table, and his roar, "Guards!" rocked Maura from her seat. The two sentries raced in from the outside hall and dropped to their knees before the dais. "Fetch my son," William ordered. "Bring him to me! Now!"

Maura's panic stuck in her throat, cracking her plea, "I...I beg of you, Uncle, don't do this. Please don't punish him! He'll only seek—"

"Silence!" he thundered back. Her paleness tempered his rage and he asked, more gently, "Why didn't you let me know? I was here this past Easter."

"No one told us," mourned Maura. "Rose took ill at Easter and Rufus refused us a physician. I couldn't leave her. I've scripted hundreds of letters to you and to Lord Robert. I'm certain Rufus destroyed them."

"Damn the fiend!" William flailed and barked, "I leave my family, my castle, and my country in what I believe to be capable hands! Now I hear this—"

"Father..." The gruff voice drifted from the shadowed doors and, to Maura, seemed to fan the fire. William Rufus, the King's middle son, stepped begrudgingly into the light, and asked with innocence, "You called for me?"

The King pointed rigidly to a spot before the dais. As Rufus dallied in his approach, his hueless eyes shifted warily between Maura and the King. He pried his collar from his thick neck, straightened his stout, mighty body, then cringed to his father's sneering insult, "You brutal beast!"

Rufus knew exactly what had sparked his father's wrath and quickly countered, "The witch lies!"

"How dare you abuse my niece?!"

"She's *not* your niece," scorned Rufus. "She's a honey-tongued leech who's wormed her way into our family to steal—"

"Enough!" William flared, storming round the dais.

Rufus foolishly firmed his stance, yet floundered his retort, "Bu...But it's true! She... she's always lurking about, moaning and nagging. She deserves abuse!"

The King seized the neck of Rufus' tunic and yanked him close. "Every member of our family deserves your respect!"

Rufus reeked sarcasm. "Is...is that so? What strange respect you've shown your dear brother, Odo. He's been locked away how long now? Has it...it truly been four years, Father?"

William's swift blow to Rufus' jaw knocked him on his broad bottom. While the Prince blubbered shock, Maura warily scrutinized her tormentor. A yellow nest of grimy hair crowned his head and hung in matted clumps from his blotched, ruddy chin. His fat lips trembled into a pout as he knelt and touched his prominent brow to the rushes. "Forgive me, Father," he sniveled. "After Mother's death I...I was upset...confused. I only had her moved. And then...then...I forgot—"

"Forgot!" bellowed the King. The tip of his boot cuffed Rufus' shoulder and sent him sprawling. "You won't easily forget this, you filthy brute!" William raged on, kicking his son across the room. "I swear, I'll toss you in with Odo and melt the blasted key!"

"No, Father! Stop! Stop!" howled Rufus as he rolled to his hands and knees and scuttled for escape.

William's tirade chased close behind. "Get from my sight, you...you despicable toad!" At the door, he planted one last sound boot to Rufus' backside and threatened, "If you so much as belch in Maura's presence, I'll have you thrashed! Now, get out!"

Rufus shot a seething glare Maura's way and, hissing broken curses, crawled away in defeat.

Her eyes bulged with terror, Maura stood stiffly at the dais, anticipating Rufus' reprisal, but it didn't come. She heard the doors latch shut and sank, limp with relief, back into her chair. The King's wine cup sat close by. She snatched it up and swiftly downed the numbing claret, then blearily watched her adoptive uncle lumber his way back to his throne. William's decline was appalling. The past three mettlesome years had hunched his once intrepid figure; his belly had grown huge, a very few strands of gray hair crisscrossed his freckled pate, and his once woolly red beard was now sparse and white. Deep crevasses, forged by a lifetime of worry, wrath, and toil gouged his face. She felt guilt for this newest fluster, and strove to soothe. "I'm so sorry, Uncle. I didn't mean to cause you more bother."

"Nonsense, I should have been more vigilant. I—" Gravely, he gazed at his niece and cupped her hands between his own. "Maura," he spoke tentatively, "Robert will arrive soon with news regarding your...marriage."

Maura blinked in disbelief and echoed dreamily, "Marriage?" Her face twitched with confusion, then beamed with hope. "I'm to be *married*?"

"Yes," he sadly sighed. "Robert will announce his plans at the grand feast this evening."

Her zeal made her stand and stammer, "I...I believed Lord Robert had forsaken me! When...when's it to be? Who will I wed?! Is he a baron, a soldier, a seneschal? *Please* tell me, Uncle!"

"No, Maura. That's for Robert to say. For the remainder of your sojourn here, you and Rose may reside in my daughter Adela's rooms. My personal servants will see to your comfort. I'll call for a tray of food to be prepared and sent immediately." He grew more somber and, with a caress to her cheek, added, "Remember Maura—no matter what Robert utters, *don't* despair."

She cocked her head in question, though didn't comment on his odd request; instead, she kissed his fingers and burbled, "Thank...thank you, Your Grace!" Her spirits sank to his continuing upset, and she fretted, "Are you well, my Lord?"

"I'm dreadfully tired..." he confessed in a hoarse whisper, "And I heartily apologize for my son's cruelty."

Maura kissed his scratchy cheek in forgiveness, and suggested with strained cheer, "We will talk more at the feast."

"Yes, I would love that. Maura?"

"Yes, my Lord."

"Did Rufus ever strike you?"

She faltered at the question, then tenderly lied, "No, my Lord."

He pressed her fingers and spoke in earnest, "If he should ever try...never attempt to fight him alone. You run and find help." His final words trembled, "For...for when Rufus is enraged, even *I* cannot defeat him. Swear, you'll do as I say."

Maura's paleness returned as she wriggled her hand from his, wavered a short bow, and left him brooding. The King's caution evoked heinous memories of her countless frays with the FitzRoy. She hesitated at the door and wagged her head at William's instruction to 'run and find help'. No one runs from Rufus, she argued inwardly, and battling him had enabled her to survive, though barely, her four tumultuous years at Winchester. Surely he'd not attempt an assault now, not with his father so near. Yet her knees still knocked as she peered tentatively down both lengths of hall. Seeing no one menacing, she mustered confidence and speed, and raced the long distance from the great hall back to the Minster and Rose.

*****

Maura tugged Rose into Adela's chamber, twittering, "You can look now."

Rose lowered her hand from her eyes and gasped, "Adela's chamber! Oh angel, you've performed a miracle and tamed the grumpy old bull. Amazing is what you are, simply amazing!"

"Rose," Maura laughed, "don't go on so. It was hunger, not bravery that drove me to the King, and also the sight of you so miserable. If he hadn't returned, I would have found us food...somehow."

"I've no doubt," said Rose. "It's the *somehow* that had me worried."

"Well, that worry has vanished. Look!" Maura turned Rose to a silver tray set upon a vanity, adorned with cheese, bread, fruit and wine. They almost tripped each other rushing to their lavish repast. Maura bit off a fat hunk of cheese and instantly began coughing.

"No angel!" Rose scolded, plucking it from between her teeth. "Little pieces first. You don't want to shock your empty belly." She pinched off a tiny chunk and popped it between Maura's eager lips.

Thrilled by the exquisite flavor of the cheese, the luscious warmth of the fire, and her solacing surroundings, Maura twirled a blissful dance across the carpet of fragrant rushes. She flopped upon the broad feather bed piled high with pelts, and sank with an indulgent sigh into its cushiony folds. And as she tangled herself in the shimmery gauze bed curtains, a brief image of a gentler time came to her—she and her spirited cousin Adela, tucked snug beneath these pelts, gossiping and giggling the night through.

Rose chuckled at Maura's antics. "You'll get crumbs everywhere."

"Crumbs!" Maura exclaimed. "What an exquisite word. There will be an endless supply of crumbs once I'm wed!"

Overwhelmed by their sudden windfall, Rose lowered herself into a padded chair set alongside the tiled fire pit, and whispered in awe, "Married..."

"I was afraid Lord Robert had forgotten me," said Maura, pushing upright. "I'm a bit old to be bargained for, and feared I'd end up cloistered." The thought forced her stutter, "Rose, if...if it had come to that, I'd have run—"

"No angel, the nunnery is no longer a threat. Lord Robert has at last found you a husband, and I'm certain he's a fine, gentle man. And," she said teasingly, "if you're old at twenty-one, what does that make me at seventy?"

Maura scrambled up from between the curtains, and knelt reverently before Rose. She hugged her waist, and raised sparkling eyes to beam, "Wonderful! Even now you look stronger."

At Rose's tender kiss, Maura sprang to her feet and flitted about the opulent room, humming to herself, and munching bread. Delicately, she fingered the jeweled toiletries gracing the vanity, then bent to dig through Adela's trunk of treasures. Luxurious undergarments soared through the air. Off came Maura's rags and she hurriedly squirmed into a silk chemise, sporting a tall embroidered collar and long, clinging sleeves. She jerked a royal blue woolen tunic from the garment cord tied behind the door, tugged its neck hole over her head, and girdled the frock with a braided rope. Once she'd secured a pair of linen hose with garters, she stood stately before Rose, hands clasped firmly at her back, eagerly awaiting approval.

Rose, her cheeks plump with bread, grunted her approval. Maura disappeared into the adjoining chamber and swiftly returned, ladened with a stack of sensible, thickly woven, drably dyed tunics. And as Maura expected, when they were set upon Rose's lap, she practically ruptured with glee.

Maura squeezed her feet into a pair of short, cured leathered boots, swallowed the last bit of cheese, and announced, "And now, something I've dreamt of doing for years!" She dragged their trunk close to the hearth and tossed each piece of spoiled clothing into the flames. As the fire blazed higher, their laughter blared louder. Maura stumbled to the vanity, threw back a gulp of wine, and headed for the door, spouting, "I'm off."

Rose stood to ask, "Where?"

"To catch the excitement and the sun!"

"Don't be long. We'll need time to prepare you for the feast." Rose hung out the door and called worriedly, "Maura, wait! Take a cloak, mind what you eat, and please—stay shy of Rufus!"

Maura flew down the spiral staircase, stopping once to clear her whirling head. She struggled along the crowded passageway, shoved wide the keep's ponderous door, and tumbled out into the crisp November air. A chilling breeze whipped her hair and blushed her cheeks as she peered out over the snow-kissed bailey from high atop the keep's sheer, wooden steps. The expansive courtyard, dotted with thatched huts and shielded by a steep stone curtain wall, lay nestled between the rectangular keep and the village of Winchester. Today, it swarmed with gaily clad visitors, disgruntled livestock, roisterous soldiers, and overburdened tradesmen. Maura shivered at leaden clouds tumbling toward the castle and raised the fur-lined hood of her cloak. She raced down the steps and, at their base, was swept up by a turbulent sea of bodies. She flowed with them past the forge, the stables, and a towering shelter housing the wine press. When the kitchen hut came into view, she squirmed free of the horde, and sprinted to the door of the thatched cottage. The entrance was densely packed with servants, so she hustled round to the rear, passing on her way recently slaughtered hog carcasses dangling from the jutting roof. She held her breath to their pungent smell, while leaping curdled pools of blood.

Maura squeezed herself through the rear door and stood agape at the frenzied preparations. A huge iron cauldron, linked by a thick chain to the timbered roof, topped a sputtering fire, and spewed voluminous clouds of odorous steam. Suddenly giddy, Maura escaped the grisly sights and sounds of swine being butchered, and resumed her search from a deserted corner. She spotted the rotund cook and waved. Cook acknowledged her with a wide smile and sly wink as she barreled her way to Maura's side. She planted a sloppy kiss on each cheek. "Oh, Maura!" she bubbled. "Your happy news reached us this morning. We're so pleased for you!"

Maura grasped Cook's flour-dusted hands. "And I see I've picked the wrong time to thank you for your help."

"We are a bit flustered—the feast, you know. Come back after and tell me who it's to be!"

"I will," Maura yelled above the din, "and I'll bring Rose!"

"Yes, do! I must go. Enjoy yourself!" Cook bustled back into the chaos, baying orders and complaints.

Maura licked her lips and whisked a finger across the top of each custard pie lining the table nearest the rear door. As if waiting for her, one lone pie sat at the end of the table, flanked by a spoon and empty wooden bowl. She shoveled gobs of custard into the bowl and, licking the spoon, stole away. A short while later, a young servant tested each pie with a sniff and a taste. The girl reached the disturbed pie and cringed to its acrid odor. Promptly, she emptied the gelatinous mixture upon a pile of refuse.

As Maura spied Rufus and his cronies storming their way across the bailey, she abruptly halted her trek and ducked behind the kitchen hut. Their crude guffaws and snickers rumbled past and faded beneath the merry chattering of the crowd. To ensure her safety, she waited till her pulse had slowed, then crept to the fore of the kitchen. The devils had gone. She sighed relief and leant up against the hut's wall to relish its warmth and her custard, and view a lively parade of knights and soldiers. It seemed ages since she'd entertained thoughts of a man. Then again, she'd been raised with males, and sorely missed their company—excepting a few. So each handsome face and figure that sauntered by, she intently examined, while her mind toyed with idyllic fancies of her betrothed.

From the corner of her eye, Maura caught a streak of movement. She focused on a groom racing from the stables and her curiosity followed him to the side of a mounted man shrouded in black. Piqued, she walked a few steps forward to better her view. The mysterious man dismounted, appeared to listen to the groom, then strode on to the keep. There was something disturbingly familiar in his proud, determined gait. Maura squinted to see his face. His hood obscured his features; the only clue of identity was an escaped lock of golden hair. As she watched him enter the keep, fat drops of icy rain plopped upon her hood and spattered her nose. She shivered to a queasiness that stole her mirth and cramped her belly. The empty bowl and spoon tumbled from her grasp, and she hastened back to the safety of Adela's chamber.

*****

Simon hurried up the steps to Winchester's keep, his mind pounding with expectation and abundant confusion. Inside the entry hall, he waited for the King's page while pondering his latest mission. The King's messenger had arrived at Canterbury Cathedral the past night, interrupting Simon's studies with scant news—William needed Simon's discreet skills for a mission of utmost importance and urgency. Intrigued, Simon lost little time, but much sleep rushing to Winchester.

"This way, my Lord." A young page ushered Simon down a slim passageway off the entry hall and under an arched doorway. "King William will arrive shortly," the boy blurted as he bowed and left.

Simon doffed his cloak and turned to the startled faces of a short line of seated clerks. He felt his cheeks flush scarlet and, with a shy smile, nodded. They continued their intense gaping, so he lowered his eyes and retreated to a shadowed corner. It had been years since he'd last entered a royal residence, and the awkwardness he felt was almost painful. He hugged himself and crouched closer into the dim recess, silently pleading, *Hurry Uncle.*

Hours passed and, in the stifling heat of the tiny chamber, Simon's belly rumbled, his tired limbs sprawled, and his eyelids drooped. The King's strident call, "Simon! Simon, where have you gone to?" jerked him awake.

He scrambled up, rubbed his sleepy, limpid blue eyes, and shuffled over to the King, yawning, "I'm...I'm here, my Lord."

William, clad regally in a scarlet floor-length tunic and fox fur cloak to discourage the chill, beamed with affection as he delightedly watched his favorite nephew drop to one knee. William patted Simon's thick blond hair and mumbled, "Rise." Simon stood, to be instantly engulfed in the King's effusive hug. "My boy!" William boomed, slapping Simon's back. "It's marvelous to see you. How was your journey?"

"Long and wet," mumbled Simon.

"Then come and sit. We'll have wine." William's wrapped one arm around Simon's shoulders, the other dismissed his clerks with a wave. "Off with the lot of you," he grunted. "Go prepare for the feast." The clerks slipped their quills into wells, and obediently filed from the chamber.

Simon lifted a sheet of penned parchment, pondered it a moment, and asked, "What's this?"

"My census. The final scripting," said William. "Handsomely done, don't you think?"

"Yes, quite," Simon agreed and set the sheet back upon the neatly cropped stack.

"I'm grateful for your help with the translations," added William. "But tell me lad, do my people truly refer to the census as '*The Domesday Book*'?"

Simon arched a slim brow and answered cautiously, "So I've heard."

"Then I suppose that means they view me as a God?"

Simon smirked at William's proud grin. "That they do, my Lord."

"Yet, alas, clearly not a benevolent God," teased William. "And how do *you* view me, lad?"

After a formative pause, Simon cleverly replied, "As my benevolent uncle...and King."

While William laughed, Simon raked his fingers through his shaggy mane and restlessly took in the chamber. Hooded sconces jutted from the walls, casting quivering shadows; trestle tables, draped in linen and arranged in the shape of a horseshoe, faced a circular tiled hearth, its coals aflame; and dozens of piles of parchment, each flanked by a candle and quill, graced the tables.

"Sit," the King directed, noticing his nephew's disquiet. Simon rounded the tables and rested his long wiry frame in the rushes before the fire. William grimaced, "No, not on the floor!" Simon started to rise, but William relented, "If you'll be more comfortable, you may stay."

William forced his corpulence into a too skinny chair and poured wine. Simon politely accepted a cup with a smile and the reminder, "Your messenger mentioned your request was urgent."

"Yes," answered the King, "indeed it is, though before we discuss business tell me what I've taken you from."

"I was at Canterbury."

"Oh? And how fares the Archbishop?"

"Lanfranc's as jolly as ever."

"Good. Why were you there?"

"I was tending to the hospitals and studying—" Simon sipped and winced at the potent wine; he gasped, coughed, then stammered, "Lan...Lanfranc allows me access to his medical volumes and writings from Salerno."

William chuckled at his difficulty. "Fascinating. I'm afraid your studies will have to wait. However, while we're on the topic—Simon, lately my belly fights me mercilessly, I'm forgetful, and I often feel sluggish. What advice do you have for this very old man?"

Simon wagged his head at the King's constant complaints and duly prescribed, "Dilute your wine, avoid rich foods, and stop battling."

"I'd hoped you would suggest an *easier* cure," William argued with petulance.

"If the symptoms never change, why should the remedy?"

"You're too shrewd for me, lad. I long to have you as my personal physician. You wouldn't coddle me. And I do appreciate your frankness—"

"And?" Simon prompted.

William took a long draught of wine and wiped his lips to admit, "It's rather late for me to change."

"Then why ask?" ruffled Simon.

"My, aren't we peppery," William chortled. "And speaking of change, why haven't you addressed my request that you smarten yourself up?" He clicked his tongue at Simon's rugged appearance and admonished, "God's teeth, lad, you dress like a Saxon rogue!" Simon struck a wounded look, and the King softened. "I'm sorry for the insult. I only wish you'd show more pride in your *Norman* heritage."

Simon swatted a nagging lock of hair from his eyes, and cast his uncle a narrow glare. "My pride shows in the work I do for you, not in the state of my clothes."

"Yes, well, I can't fault you there," said William. "This evening, at the feast, I plan to reveal our pact and brag of your success as my chief mediator. I'd prefer you looked the part instead of like a...a..." William paused to locate the perfect comparison and finally blurted, "...a peasant farmer!"

Simon hated their recurring argument; he frowned and tugged at the frayed skirt strings of his coarsely woven, unbleached tunic, carping, "Why make our work known? Why risk confrontation? I have enough enemies as is, Uncle. I pray that's not the only reason you've called me here."

"No..." William took another swig of wine and a moment to ponder his contrary nephew. The King considered Simon, in relation to the rest of his nettling family, a jewel in a pile of coals. Simon, the bastard son of William's brother Robert, was a veritable wonder—innately wise, overly impetuous, and brutally honest. His dogged boldness tickled William, for only Simon had the gall to wrangle with him face-to-face, and he cherished their skirmishes. The lad's scruffy appearance was irking, yet endearing. Mostly, his comely face held the dark brooding air of an outcast, which he was, his father having disowned him four years past. Yet William never tired of Simon's capricious expressions; he likened chatting with Simon to conversing with a multitude of individuals, and nothing heartened William more than Simon's dazzling smile.

Simon squirmed and poked impatiently at the fire with a long rush. It seemed each time they met, the King's reflective moods lengthened, which was fine, but if his need was urgent—Simon started to his Uncle's touch. "What is it, my Lord?"

"I want you to stop a marriage," stated William bluntly. "It seems I've made a dreadful error and you must make it right."

Simon rubbed thoughtfully at his shaven chin and muttered, "Explain."

"At Sarum this past August, I had my entire vassalage declare homage to me," said William, stretching his bulk nearer to the flames. "It was there that your father convinced me to sign a betrothal contract."

"Concerning?"

"Rufus and Maura, Robert's ward."

Simon dropped his jaw and his wine, snapped the rush, and sputtered, "Ma...Maura?"

"Yes and I—"

"And Rufus!" he vehemently intruded, floundering up from the floor.

"I don't know what came over me—"

"Betrothal!" Simon cut in again.

William glowered. "Yes, Maura and Rufus' betrothal! When did you last wash your ears? Now stop your riddles and listen—"

"It can't be!"

"What can't be?" smoldered William, prying himself from his seat. "I've just told you—"

"Maura's *already* married!" Simon returned with equal harshness.

"No!" shouted William.

"Yes, she's married and living in Normandy!"

"Simon!" William clasped his shoulders and shook him gently. "Stop this nonsense. I need your help, not your hysterics. Maura has resided here at Winchester for years. Why, I spoke to her just this morning."

Simon's eyes bulged as he choked, "You...you spoke to her?"

His nephew's volatile manner alarmed William and he strode a safe distance round the table. "Yes...I told her of the betrothal, not the name of her intended."

Simon lunged after him and swiped hold of William's cloak, demanding, "Tell me where she is!"

"Are you mad?!" William batted Simon's hand away and yelled, "Sit! Now!"

"No! I will see her!" fiercely parried Simon. William swung his fist to strike; Simon easily blocked his blow, and softened his posture to implore, "Let me see her. *Please Uncle*, let me speak to her!"

William retreated one step. "You *will* see her," he said with fragile calm. "After our meeting, we'll go to the great hall. You may talk with her there. Robert's to make the betrothal announcement—"

"My *father*!" Simon groaned, slumping into a nearby chair.

"Yes. You need not fret," William swiftly affirmed. "I'll ensure he causes you no grief. After his proclamation, I wish to make known our work...I know I should have made a provision for Rufus' marriage. I never seemed to have the time, but not Maura, it can't be Maura, and I must..."

While his uncle jabbered his plans, Simon heaved at a spitting torch and silently raved, *How can she be here at Winchester? I've searched everywhere, everywhere for her! She couldn't have been this close to me—all these years—so close. And my father? Why confront him, why face the hate? Why?!* He turned crazed eyes on William and flared, "Why do you need *me* to stop this...this atrocity?! Tell Father no!"

"I've signed the blasted papers!" retorted William. "I choose you to find the impediment to this cursed union because I've no finer scout!" Simon's furor entered the King, and he lumbered round the table to probe and incite. "Think Simon, think! What will you do? Tell me!"

Simon cradled his throbbing head and struggled for a course of action. Only an instant passed before he raised a tenacious face to declare, "I'll travel to Dunheved and question Avenal, Father's seneschal. If the impediment isn't to be found there, I'll visit Trematon, Tintagel, Montecute, Berkhamstead, Pevensey—Hell, I'll ride to Mortain if I need to! There has to be an error somewhere and I will find it!"

"Excellent!" exclaimed William. "I don't know what madness has claimed you, lad, but whatever—it's been most effective. Now, I'll need any information you manage to obtain by Christmas Court."

"That's only five weeks away!" Simon's fingers strangled the chair's arms; he cringed and stammered, "I...I don't believe I can—"

"Of course you *can*," bolstered William. "I have complete faith in you and we mustn't let the Lady Maura suffer more. Her time with Rufus has been riddled with turmoil and I expect she'll be quite disturbed to hear—"

Simon leapt up to insist, "What has Rufus done to her?!"

A page halted William's reply by shrilly announcing, "Sire, your vassals await you in the great hall."

They spun to the report, and William ordered, "Fill their cups and caution them I'm on my way." A firm grip to Simon's shoulder accompanied William's explanation, "If I don't show soon, there's liable to be a riot. We'll go."

The King prodded Simon toward the door; Simon dodged his poking and asked, "Go where?"

"To the feast."

"No!" Simon chafed madly at his wine-stained braies. "I can't go like this!"

"I've never seen you so twitchy," chuckled William. "If you had listened to me and preened a bit, you wouldn't be having this problem. Now make haste!"

Simon scowled, then realizing he had no recourse but to obey, he combed his mussed hair with dirty fingers; swatted mud from his tunic, shirt sleeves, and braies; and wiped his damp brow with his soiled cuff. He tripped after his uncle, struggling to keep pace with William's broad brisk strides; then the thought of seeing Maura spurred him to a run and he overtook his uncle. William's resounding warning, "Hold up, lad!" reached Simon too late. He burst through the hall's doors, and stumbled directly into his father's path.

Robert, Count of Mortain, Earl of Cornwall, and the King's half-brother, froze aghast, blinked furiously in disbelief, then stuttered his command, "Gu...Guard! Throw this traitor from the hall!"

Robert's guard charged the doors with brandished sword. Simon yanked his dagger from his belt and steeled for attack. Guests and servants scuttled for cover as the sentry balked to the deft swipe of Simon's blade.

"Stinking coward!" Robert raged to his man. He drew his own dagger, and thrust it in his son's face, gritting, "How dare you show yourself in this hall! You'll leave here now, or I swear I'll—"

"You'll what, Robert?!" hollered William, barging through the doors.

Robert whipped his head to William's shout, and shock and confusion tumbled from his lips, "Brother...uhm...I mean to say, Your Grace, how dare you allow this...this..."

William strolled casually to Robert's side and clapped his shoulder with affection. "He's not a *this*, Robert, he's your son. And Simon has as much right to be here as you or I. Now," William said as he cautiously lowered his brother's weapon, "let us sit, enjoy a fine meal, and strive to act a bit more civilly." A brittle moment lingered, then Robert bowed his head, belted his dagger, and slouched on to the dais.

Nervous expressions eased, and the crowd thrust up their cups in a lusty cheer to their Monarch's arrival. The adulation swelled William's chest and he glided majestically to the raised table.

Lord Robert's only legitimate son, William, called Will to avoid confusion, stood at the dais and smugly considered the disorder below. He too was astounded, and more than a little miffed, to see his half-brother, Simon. How unfortunate, he lamented, that during their time apart, Simon hadn't graciously gotten himself killed. However, Will's spirits rose as his father approached the dais. He thrilled to the ire in Robert's eyes—his hate for Simon was still fervid and, thank the Lord, healthily growing. Then again, as Will noticed

Simon trailing the King, he pondered the cause of his visit. He knew his brother to be exceedingly headstrong and stupidly brave, though he'd never taken him for a fool.

Tempers simmered, throats cleared, and bodies shifted to Simon's unexpected presence. With a surly huff and mumbled curses, Robert planted himself in a chair. Simon purposely rounded the opposite end of the dais and gingerly took a seat, separated from his father by only the King's ornate throne. Robert strangled his cup and glared into the blood-red liquor. His loathing for his youngest son was all consuming, blinding and dizzying. He quaked, focused his fury on the horde below, and silently screamed, *Where is Maura?! This night is to be my most illustrious moment! The profitable alliance I've long dreamt of will soon come to pass. Simon's foul presence has already spoiled my joy, Maura had best not consider ruining the remainder of the evening.*

Rufus entered the hall and, spying Simon, burst out a loud guffaw. Then, he noted his cousin occupied his own seat, and grew sour and withdrawn. He sagged into the chair next to Will's and groused, "What's that *mongrel* doing here?"

Will's icy blue eyes gleamed mischief. "An intriguing question, dearest Cousin. Our fickle King seems perturbed with you. Perhaps your father plans to disinherit you and adopt my little brother as his one true and deserving heir."

Rufus bristled, threw back his wine in one long, loud gulp, and snapped, "More!" to a nearby servant.

"Now, now, Rufus," chided Will. "Check your intake of that deadly potion. If you succeed in making a spectacle of yourself this grand evening, your downfall is assured." Will briefly scanned the crowd, and asked lightly, "And where, pray tell, is your sweet, doting bride-to-be?"

A snide, contented smile curled Rufus' lips as he too hunted the hall for Maura. How tickled he'd be watching her squirm in agony to their betrothal's announcement.

The King wedged himself into his throne, patted Simon's arm, and smiled at his nephew's obvious distress. "Have some wine, lad, and try to enjoy yourself." Simon tensed a grin William's way, then glimpsed the trestle tables below and witnessed there a boisterous, obscene circus—barons, knights, and soldiers slurping copious quantities of wine, inciting quarrels, and groping at serving wenches. His anxious eyes abandoned the chaos to sweep the length of the dais, as he asked himself, *When? When will Maura come?!* He felt about to burst with anticipation and jumped as a servant loudly dropped a trencher down before him. A huge slice of meat was slopped atop a plate of thick, spongy bread; a dense sauce hid the putrid fare, mingling and congealing with the pig's blood. His father's seething manner, and the cramping suspense of seeing Maura combined to steal away Simon's appetite. He sucked a saving breath, gulped it dryly, and shoved the platter aside.

Throughout her bathing and dressing, Maura's pain and trepidation swelled. She grew silent, afraid to admit even to herself her fear—a daunting sense that the gaiety and triumph of this day soon would be dashed. She attributed her upset belly to nervousness, yet a stabbing nausea now joined the ache and fiercely fed her dread.

Their hands tightly clasped, Rose and Maura cautiously descended the open staircase to the great hall. They reached the base of the steps, passed by the King's bedchamber, and approached the rear of the dais. Rose strode tall and proud in her new slate gray tunic; her silver and black braid, shrouded by a linen wimple, dangled low down her back, and a silver crucifix glimmered upon her chest. She protectively led her charge, glancing back several times at Maura's blanched face and furrowed brow. Rose couldn't fathom what had besieged Maura in the short time they'd been apart, but whatever the crippling ailment, its effect worsened by the moment.

Maura stopped short, hugged her waist, and blurted in a broken whisper, "I...I can't go on, Rose. I'll be sick."

"No...no, angel," Rose soothed, "it's only the excitement that flutters your belly. Wine will surely put you right."

As they drew nearer the revelry, the pungent odors and grating sounds struck Maura, making her break from Rose's hold and gasp, "The smells, the noise! Rose, I can't go on."

"What you can't do is risk your future!" Rose strictly countered. "We'll stay for the betrothal announcement, then return to Adela's room. I won't allow you to turn back, not when our liberty is so near!" Maura grudgingly followed and Rose anguished inwardly—Maura was never ill and rarely mentioned pain. Something was terribly amiss, and Rose prayed the wicked offense wasn't sitting and waiting for them at the dais. She motioned a quick sign of the cross, and gallantly strode ahead, tugging Maura behind.

Maura forced her eyes on her feet as she passed behind Simon, the King, and Robert. Simon, his attention stuck on the crowd, didn't notice William twist to the sound of swishing skirts, though heard clearly his command, "We'll stand for the Ladies."

None of the striking aspects of Maura's appearance—her copper silk gown, her lustrous, flame red hair hanging free in lush waves, nor the silver circlet adorning her brow—could mask her torment. Simon gaped unabashedly at her wan beauty and felt his body instinctively drawn to hers.

Robert's face lit to her fine image; he was pleased, quite pleased, nevertheless, her pallid countenance was annoying. He reached over and nudged her shoulder, gruffly instructing, "Look bright, Maura. Happy news awaits you."

At Rose's whispered cue, both women bowed lowly to their Liege. They obeyed Robert's bid to stand, and when Maura raised her eyes to his noble figure, she noticed little about him had changed over their long separation. For a man approaching sixty years, his attractive face held few wrinkles; his skin, bronzed and taut, covered bones structurally sharp, a closely cropped band of white hair circled low on his bald pate, and his rarely seen grin sparkled his pale blue eyes.

Maura chanced a look past Robert and the King to the far end of the dais where Rufus and Will sat chattering. Rufus' garish grin heightened Maura's malaise, and she shifted her narrow gaze to Will. Foppishly handsome, Will exuded charm as his gaze roamed her body. Yet his styled black curls, expertly-cropped mustache, and impeccably embroidered black tunic seemed overly perfect, and stirred in Maura a vague upset that only intensified her nausea.

Her interest in Will was quickly vanquished by a stealthy movement at Robert's shoulder. Gasping horror, Maura sagged forward, halting her fall on rigid arms. She wagged her head and viciously gritted, "Get him away! Get Simon away from me!"

As if struck, Simon recoiled from Maura's livid glare; he recovered quickly and boldly advanced. His brashness hiked Maura's agony and Rose's wail, "Please, Lord Robert, *stop* him!"

Robert struck out, his elbow stabbing Simon's chest and knocking him breathless to the rushes. Maura bolted. Robert caught and wrenched her arm, commanding, "You'll stay!"

Maura's howl of pain drove Rose to her knees with an agonized plea, "I beg you, my Lord, Maura's ill! Please release her and allow her to return to her chamber."

"No!" railed Robert, thrusting Maura into the chair by his. "She will remain for the proclamation!"

William jerked Simon up by his collar and shoved him into his seat, demanding, "What have you done?!"

"I've...I've done...I don't..." sputtered his dazed nephew.

"Robert!" blared William. "Get on with your cursed speech and be quick about it! Then let Maura leave."

"My Lord," Simon jumped up to protest, "you swore I could speak to her!"

"Enough!" the King shouted. "Be still and keep silent!"

Simon sat and hid his tumult behind splayed fingers. What had he done? How could she hate him?! He lowered his hands and risked a look, praying her expression would betray a clue.

Simon's stare bore through Maura, twisting her already tender insides. Bile burned and crept up her throat. She gasped distress, and clung to Rose for strength.

Will and Rufus chuckled at the festering melee. At times, it shamed Will to be a member of this ill-bred tribe but, then again, their antics could be quite entertaining. The fracas spread rapidly to the tables below, rousing the crowd to a sonorous frenzy.

His vise-like hold on Maura held firm as Robert, in a feeble attempt to capture attention, stood and tapped the table with his cup.

The thunderous din, the snarling hounds clashing for scraps, and Robert's rattling cup convulsed Maura's mind. She squeezed shut her eyes, and the ensuing blackness flashed raging visions—Robert's fierce grimace, Rufus' mocking leer, Simon's gaze full of grim wonder. Her misery and pain peaked, offering a brief respite of peace, and she slumped onto her crossed arms.

"God's blood!" William exploded to the ever-banging cup. "Give me that blasted thing!" He stole the tankard from Robert and hurled it at the fire, roaring, "Quiet!" The clamor instantly hushed.

Alarmed by Maura's stillness, Simon leapt up again, only to be knocked back into his seat by William, who flared, "I swear I'll have my guards toss you from the battlements! Now behave!" William turned his glower on the crowd, further taming the revelers. "Now that we have some sanity," he growled, "my brother Robert has an announcement to make and we will all listen quietly and politely!"

Robert, wearing his usual stoic expression, straightened his floor length moss green tunic, and began, "It pleases me greatly to announce my ward, Maura's betrothal to our beloved King's son, William Rufus. The wedding will be celebrated the day following the Feast of the Resurrection." Robert paused for a reaction to his revelation. This union, if indeed Rufus succeeded to the throne of England, would render Robert the wealthiest landowner in England. He surmised many of his fellow vassals not being overly pleased with this prospect, and a spattering of jeers in the applause confirmed his judgment.

Rufus swaggered to Maura's side. Rose hovered protectively over her charge, blubbering tears of revulsion. Surely, she'd heard wrong! The King would never allow such an abomination!

Maura stirred to Rose's wretched weeping, and heard an odious voice suggest, "My sweet Lady, rise with me and show our company how overjoyed we are with our merry news."

She didn't need to look, Rufus' stinging spittle and foul stench told her curse—Robert hadn't announced a betrothal, he'd condemned her to death! Whatever burned her belly surged swiftly upward and groaning, "No!" she lurched from the table.

Alas, she was not fast enough. Rufus grabbed hold of her arm, yanked her back and swung her around. Vomit splattered his face and beard and dripped thickly from his tunic. "Wha...what—" he sputtered in shock, then exploded, "Bleeding Jesus, you flaming bitch! What have you done?!"

Maura took advantage of his distress to escape and raced crazily for the door to the inner garden.

Rose charged after; Robert barred her way, fuming, "I said you'll stay! And—" he cruelly cautioned, "Maura had best return quickly!"

"Let me go to her!" raved Simon, thrashing dementedly at William's grip. "*Please*, let me go!"

The King grasped the scruff of his neck, and roughly yanked him close. "Are you blind? Can't you see she doesn't want you near? God's blood, leave her be!"

Rufus stormed back to his seat, grabbed up a serviette and mopped frenziedly at his face and clothes. "She's made a fool of me!" he raged to Will.

"Yes, indeed she has, and she's done it with such flair," laughed Will, then sternly he waved his cousin away, demanding, "and don't get near me! You stink!"

"She'll cause me no more strife this day!" seethed Rufus, as he plopped himself into the last chair at the dais and guzzled his fifth cup of wine.

The coarse wooden door slammed against Maura's back, pitching her to her knees. She gagged and retched violently into the virgin snow, then sprawled to her back and coiled in anguish. Her fevered cheek melted the snow as she struggled to quiet her mind. To survive she must think rationally! She swiped wet from her eyes and peered through the spitting sleet. Not far away was a door, the door to the rear stairs. If she could reach her chamber, she'd take the jewelry and a dagger, then steal a steed and run. Pain tore at her belly as she raised up on quaking arms and groped her way forward.

The King rose, cleared his throat, and then spoke with a calm that belied the surrounding melee. "Now I would like all to acknowledge with a salute the excellent work of my nephew and emissary, Simon." William's fingers bit into Simon's shoulder and hoisted him weightlessly up from his seat, as the King pleasantly continued, "Without Simon's critical help many a quarrel would have resulted in war."

From the crowd below, a drunkenly bold soldier risked a slur. "Si...Sire, perhaps he... he could aide your grouchy clan!"

The horde exploded with laughter, and the King nodded and smiled, "I admit we are sorely in need of a lesson in court etiquette. Now, let us raise our cups in Simon's honor."

Simon ignored the flattery as his eyes shifted narrowly amongst his kin, striving to deduce their plans, sense their motives.

The cheers of the first salute died, and Lord Roger of Montgomery, a member of the King's elite council, stood and brightly addressed the crowd. "I believe a drink to the twentieth anniversary of England's conquest would be fitting."

"Twentieth!" exclaimed a beaming William. "Is it '86 already? God's breath, the time does slip away!"

The entire party rose to their feet in a pious salute to William. With the King distracted, Simon wriggled from his grasp and snuck to the far end of the dais where, to his chagrin, he discovered Rufus missing. "Where's Rufus gone?" he whispered sharply to Will.

"He left by the main doors awhile back," offered Will, then patting Simon's cheek, he added fondly, "It's a delight to see you well, Brother, and I'm highly impressed with your secret profession. When you have an opportunity, come visit me at Berkhamstead. Father won't be there. We'll have fun!" Simon snorted in response, ducked behind Will, and slunk through the dense crowd to the exit.

The liberating door at last loomed above Maura. She grasped the iron handle and, with great effort, hauled herself to her feet. Her last vestige of strength pried open the door just enough for her to squeeze through. She rested back against the coarse wood, trying vainly to still her trembling, and groaned as she beheld the steep and lengthy staircase that blocked her flight. How, she anguished, how could she possibly climb—

Beyond her labored breaths, she heard boot steps. Panic seized her. She pressed fast to the door and gaped in terror at a towering shadow recklessly descending the stairs. The steps broke their forbidding rhythm and stumbled to the landing. Rufus, his squinty eyes red from drink, face purple with rage, and tunic stained with vomit, regained his balance and stammered, "I...I wondered where you'd gone...and...and was wor...worried."

Maura shoved from the door and strained to crack it back open, but Rufus leapt the last few steps. He threw his body against hers, slamming the door shut, and crushing her to the wood. Her struggling and muffled moans amused him as he fingered her damp hair, and chillingly murmured, "No one abandons me, my Lady, least of all—you!"

*****

CHAPTER TWO - SECRETS

Rufus' grinding weight smothered Maura, and splinters dug and stabbed her cheek. He squeezed closer, his fingers circled her neck and paralyzed as he stuttered, "Damn you, bitch! Father hates me, wo...won't speak to me. It's all your do...doing!" He eased his lethal grip to caress, and sweetly slurred, "I'm thrilled we'll wed. I want you by me always—"

Maura drove her elbow into his gut and arched violently, knocking him off balance. Ducking under his flailing arm, she lunged for the stairs, yet his sweeping hand grabbed her shoulder. He whipped her around; she cowered, shielding her head to his monstrous roar, "You'll pay for your sin!" His swift and savage blow shattered her arm.

Maura screamed and crashed her body to his, tumbling him back against the door. While Rufus wavered and drooled curses, Maura hugged her splintered limb, whirled round, and floundered up the steps. Her mind swirled with pain; she groaned puffing breaths. The landing—only one more step and she'd reach the landing! She thrust her body upward, and her fingers groped at the polished stone above, madly scratching for a hold.

Rufus jolted to her escape and hissed, "You won't get away...ever!" He sprang from the door, clamped hold of her ankle, and yanked back. The chiseled rock slammed her brow, gouging, and scraping as he dragged her to the floor and flipped her to her back. He sank giddily to his knees. Maura's lashes fluttered open to his plunging fist, then all was black.

Trapped in a maze, Simon raced from chamber to chamber, his frantic call, "Maura!" ever spiraling. He heard her scream and froze.

Beads of Rufus' sweat dropped off the tip of his nose and splattered Maura's ravaged face. She lay so still, so peaceful; she'd never betray him again. He wiped his bloodied hand distastefully on her gown and placed a cold kiss on her cheek. Then from somewhere beyond his wheezing, someone yelled her name. Terror gripped him. Rufus shrank from the desperate squall and snuck into the garden.

Simon darted past the staircase and halted to a glimpse of copper at its base. He flew down the steps and dropped to his knees by Maura's side, panting, "Maura? Maura! God's breath! No!" Blood coursed from between her lips, shredded skin hung from her brow, and her forearm jutted obscenely beneath the stained silk. His hands hovered over her body as he battled a ferocious urge to grab her up and crush her to him. Instead, he ground his palms together and moaned in anguish. Help, he must get help! But he couldn't leave her! Her attacker might return!

In the great hall the gathering had dispersed, leaving those too drunk to walk lolling in the littered rushes. Hounds had claimed the tables, crunching bones and lapping up a reeking mix of spilt food, ale, and vomit. Rufus stumbled through the postern door. He gathered snow from his shoulders, chafed it on his heated cheeks, then straightened and ambled casually to the dais.

Of Rufus' family, only Robert and Will remained. Rufus approached from behind and whispered in Robert's ear, "Uncle, I'm concerned over Maura's long absence. She seemed ill and upset by Simon's presence. I...I stepped outside for air and heard a scream, and...and now Simon's gone."

Robert bolted from his seat, blaring, "Rufus, guards, come! I swear if Simon's touched her, he'll die!"

The raging troop skidded across the garden. Robert flung wide the door and caught his son crouched and gathering Maura in his arms. Simon snapped his head to Robert's bellow, "Take him!"

The guards pounced and ripped Simon from Maura's side. He thrashed from their hold, surged rabidly for his father, and seized his tunic's neck. "No!" he cried. "It wasn't me! I'd never hurt—"

Robert's silencing fist drubbed Simon's ear, then hammered his belly, hurtling him back into the guards' clinch. They wrenched his arms to his back and dragged him, convulsed and groaning, away.

Rufus, keeping close to the garden door, cracked a smug grin and snickered at Simon's defeat. Yet as Rose's gray, flapping figure suddenly appeared, his bravado faltered and he ducked once again out into the garden.

Rose knelt by Maura's head and spoke tersely, "Fetch the physician." Will rushed to obey, while Robert gingerly offered his handkerchief. Rose dabbed at the stream of blood leaving Maura's lips and quavered to Robert, "Who...who's done this?"

"I found Simon with her—"

"No. Not Simon! Find where Rufus was when this happened."

"He's here—" Robert turned to find Rufus gone; confused, he threatened, "Rose, you speak treason!"

"Perhaps," she answered, dampening the cloth with spit, "it's long past time someone did. Have your guard carry her to Adela's bed and send the physician. Then leave us. You've caused her enough grief this night."

Robert tensely paused, wondering why he should obey this harridan. Then with a deep sigh, he gestured to his guard. Rose supervised every inch of Maura's transport and, once she was abed, motioned for all save the doctor to go. He, Rose held at bay, till she'd carefully peeled the spoiled gown from Maura's body, leaving on her dry chemise.

During the course of his brief exam, the physician's sour expression revealed nothing. He covered Maura with pelts, hiked up the sleeves of his long robe, and stroked his scraggly beard while dully diagnosing, "Her arm is cracked between the elbow and wrist and, apart from the blows to her face, I can find no other damage. I'll return shortly with a brace and ointment for her cuts. You may cleanse her face."

The guards wrestled Simon, bucking and howling, down the hall. King William rounded a corner, stopped short of the violence, and hollered, "Set him free!" Simon broke from the fuddled bunch and scurried to the safety of the King's side. William grabbed and shook him, coarsely insisting, "Now what have you done?!"

"Nothing!" Simon jerked from William's grip. "I found Maura beaten. Father blames me!"

William's tone turned frantic. "Where is she?!"

"At the base of the garden stairs. Come!"

They reached the red-stained site and chased a spattered trail of blood up the curling steps to Adela's chamber door. Simon raised his fist to pound. William stopped his hand and encouraged, "No, Simon, wait. I won't come inside, my council awaits me. You see to her care, find her a guard then begin your journey. I have a peculiar sense I was tricked into agreeing to this marriage." Ruefully, William continued, "I love my son, but I also know that any woman will suffer horribly as his wife. I care too dearly for Maura to allow her further harm, and it's clear you feel for her as well. Use that affection to drive you, Simon—find a cause to break this betrothal and find it quickly!"

"I will, my Lord!" Simon passionately pledged.

He started to bow, but William took his arms, pulled him close, and sadly kissed his cheeks. "Take care, lad. Stay safe and shy of your father, he's not to know of our plans. And accept this gift." The King pressed a money pouch to Simon's palm. "Please, don't give all to your sweet mother, keep a few coins for yourself. If God allows, I'll meet you at Gloucester for Christmas Court."

Simon glumly watched his sole ally disappear down the stairs. He absently tied the pouch to his belt and rapped softly on the door. Rose, believing the physician had returned, peeked out only to be startled and repelled by Simon's figure. He blocked the slamming door with his boot. "Let me in, Rose, let me help her!" Rose strained against Simon's push, then weakened to his curious statement, "The King has ordered me to tend Maura!"

"Why you?" Rose asked, askance.

"I'm trained as a physician. *Please*," he begged, "let me help her!"

For a long moment Rose battled furious doubts, then grudgingly opened the door. Simon hesitated at the threshold and Rose carped, "What is it now?"

"I'll see your palms and belt first."

Rose vigorously wagged her head. "No games, Simon. Maura—"

"I agree," he retorted. "no games!" Despite Rose's sputtered objections, Simon swiftly flattened her empty palms; his hand smoothed the length of her girdle, found her weapon, and stuck the dagger in his own belt. He left her fuming, and hastened to Maura's side.

Rose circled the bed, hands on hips, scowling at Simon's every move. His fingers rested lightly on Maura's brow, brushed over her cheek, and walked the length of her neck. They dipped inside her torn lips, stroked her jaw, then traveled her arm to examine the bone. He fought to appear unmoved by Maura's closeness and chanted silently— *Calm, I must stay calm.* If not, he risked being tossed out, leaving Maura at the mercy of a bumbling charlatan!

He shifted thoughtfully to Rose, yet before he had a chance to speak, she stated, "The physician has gone to fetch a brace."

Simon nodded, adding, "She's feverish. Was she ill before the beating?"

"What makes you say beating?" piqued Rose. "Did you see anything? Anyone? Do you know who—"

"Rose!" he snapped. "Was she ill?"

"Yes."

"Her complaints?"

"Pains in her belly."

"What had she eaten?"

"Cheese, fruit, wine," said Rose. "After that I've no idea."

"The person who did this—" Simon paused and gulped to finish, "does he want her dead?"

"My God!" Rose wrung her hands; her voice cracked, "Simon, I...I don't—"

"You do know! Would he poison her, then beat her to quicken the deed? Answer me!"

"He...he might have."

"Then fetch milk. Be quick!"

Rose started to his order, though stayed where she stood, bewildered.

In his most trustworthy voice, Simon explained, "The wounds won't claim her, the poison will. Do you *want* her to die?"

"No!" moaned Rose.

"Then *please* hurry!"

Rose heaved sobs in her rush from the chamber, and Simon reluctantly left Maura's side. The chamber's fire pit was clear of ash, so he snatched up the silver tray from the vanity, cast back a fretful glance, and hurried to search the neighboring chamber for coals.

Maura pried one eye open to shimmering candlelight. She bolted up in bed, stifling a moan as she hunted the room for movement. All seemed too tranquil; could it have been a dream? No, her searing pain proved the nightmare true and Rufus would soon come to finish her! Clattering sounds drifted from the adjoining chamber. She couldn't risk endangering Rose and must flee now! She rose shakily, took a quick moment to try to clear her splitting head, then staggered to the vanity. Beneath the lid of the jewel case rested a dagger. Her good hand plucked it from the box, and lodged it snugly up the taut sleeve of her damaged arm. She scooped rings and necklaces, then a cramping in her belly spilled them from her grasp. Whimpering, she snatched her cloak and ran. Each time her hurt threatened to stop her, the horror of Rufus drove her on, down the stairs, and along the trellised walkway to the stables. Two grooms slept soundly beneath the stable's lone torch. She snuck by them, unlatched the outer door, slipped inside and, donning her cloak and hood, gingerly scaled the last stall's fence. Maura grasped the horse's mane, and forced her diffident body astride his broad back. Her head spun and sight dimmed at the exertion; a deep breath set her right, and she tentatively urged the steed from the stall and into the bailey.

Like a dozen suns, huge torches illuminated the courtyard. Maura hid in the shadows and squinted through the dense, twinkling snow at a party of mounted soldiers sauntering toward the main gates. As the ponderous doors groaned opened for them, she waited till the last horse began its exit, then sharply kicked her steed.

Simon returned to Maura's chamber and, discovering her gone, promptly dropped the ash-laden tray to the floor. Rose rushed in from the hall and sloshed milk from her pitcher, crying, "He's taken her!"

"No!" Simon froze, his mind racing. "He wouldn't, not so soon after—" He glimpsed the scattered baubles and blurted, "She's run off!"

"How dare you leave her!" lashed out Rose.

"I only...I had to...I—" With a crazed groan, Simon streaked out the door.

Rose chased him to the top of the stairs and shouted after, "Simon, stop her! Don't let her reach the guards!"

Maura galloped across the slick bailey, her mount struggling with his footing. Three guards, alarmed by her rapid approach, hustled to shut the gates. Not deterred, Maura forged her steed ahead toward the rapidly shrinking exit, praying for luck and time. The stallion reared to a halt just feet before the closed gates; his back hoof clipped a slick of ice, crashing him and Maura to the frozen ground. He swiftly rocked to his feet and, shying away, left her alone to suffer the sentries' wrath. They hauled her up from the ground, one snidely taunting, "My, my, aren't we in a rush. It appears you've had a lively evening. Come, my beauty, we'll take a walk to the gatehouse and find out who's missing you." She wrenched from his grip, whipped out her dagger, and slashed wildly at his face. He barely dodged her swipe and yelled out, "She's armed!"

Maura hissed through bared teeth, lunging again and again at the flocking guards. Baffled by her ferocity and skill, they fumbled with faint attempts to disarm her. Her name, she heard someone shout her name! Footsteps rushed her back; she whirled round and sliced.

Simon shielded his face and gasped as the blade dug the length of his forearm. He thudded the dagger from Maura's grip, and lunged to steal her from the sentries. The guards' capture was quicker; they wrestled Maura's arms to her back, forcing from her a long tortured wail. Simon's deafening roar, "Let her be!" drowned her cry and scattered the sentries.

She stood alone, bent and wavering. Her mind screamed, *Run! The guards are gone, the road is clear, not far is the village, someone will take me in, hide me!* Yet her conquered body refused to budge. In a small trembling voice she begged to Simon, "Help me..."

He spread his arms to embrace; she shrank from the gesture. Then, using great care, he offered one hand and sighed as her fingers at last mingled with his.

Maura smiled in blissful illusion as she floated numbly along behind Simon. They were always together, strolling home to Dunheved as they had so many times before. Simon hadn't gone, he loved her and had sworn never to leave. She stopped to nuzzle her fevered cheek into his palm, then stumbled her next few steps. He caught her collapse, and swept her up and back to the keep.

At the base of the keep's stairs, a milling crowd hushed and parted for Simon and Maura. Rose rushed down the steps, shoving gawkers aside. "What happened?! Where was she?" She gasped at fresh blood smearing Maura's sleeve. "You've hurt her!"

"I found her..." grunted Simon, "battling the guards at the main gates."

Rose panicked to Maura's dull stare and prodded Simon upward. "Make haste! The doctor awaits her."

In Adela's chamber, the physician, irked by the King's decision to snub him in favor of an inept, snotty-nosed boy, paced an ever-widening path through the rushes. Simon struggled through the door, brushed by the doctor, and carefully laid Maura on the bed. His adoring gaze never left hers as he reached out to the doctor and muttered, "I'll have the brace."

The doctor made no move to oblige. Rose huffed disgust at them both, snatched the cast of crudely fashioned wood and gauze from the physician's grip, and tossed it on the bed.

Simon ripped the sleeve of Maura's chemise, gently straightened the splintered bone, and positioned her forearm between the slabs of wood. He snapped his fingers. "Now, the bandage." Again he was ignored. "Give me the blasted bandage!" he yelled to the doctor, then to Rose, he directed in a kinder tone, "Mix the ash in the milk and pass the cup."

Encroaching blackness stole Simon from Maura's sight. She groped through the dark, found and caressed his warm cheek. He stopped his wrapping to press his hand over hers, and felt his fragile control crumbling to her sweet touch. The tender act sparked Rose's fury. She pried away Maura's hand, shoved the acrid mixture under Simon nose, and gritted, "Get on with it."

Simon again faded from Maura's view. Her head lolled, her muffled moans strengthened, growing clearer, more frantic, "Simon, Simon, don't...don't leave me! Don't go!"

"I *will* return, Maura," calmed Simon. "Believe that I'll be back."

Yet as he supported her head to offer the milk, she gagged, spat, and exploded in a fevered rage. Maura batted the cup, drenching him with gray cream. Simon caught and forced her good hand to the bed. Her wounded one clamped hold of his slashed arm, and pain made him flinch away. She flew up from the bed to keep him, the bandage unraveling as she clung to his chest and cried, "No! Stay with me!"

Simon's resolve shattered and he clutched her as passionately, swearing, "I won't go—"

"Get away!" Rose attacked, pummeling Simon's head and shoulders, screaming, "You won't—I won't let you torture her again!" She pleaded to the doctor, "Help me! She's delirious, he's too strong! Help me!"

The physician joined Rose's struggle and, together, they barely managed to break Simon and Maura's clench. The doctor promptly stripped Simon of his weapons and flung him at the door, gritting, "You'll go quietly or I'll have you imprisoned for attempted murder and the King will never know what became of you. Now—get out!"

Maura's wail ripped through Simon's skull; his howl rattled the walls as he lurched from the chamber and punched the door closed. Hugging his bruised hand, he groaned and slumped in defeat to the rushes. Advancing boot steps cut short his misery. He fumbled along his belt for his absent dagger, and scrambled back to his feet.

As if sent from Heaven, Maura's younger brother Marc, clad in a rusty hauberk, loped toward Simon, and met him with a fierce embrace. They hugged in anguished silence, then Simon stepped back to search Marc's cherubic face. As always it shone comfort as Marc swore, "I've met with the King and he told me all. I'll stay with Maura while you're away."

"Marc!" raved Simon. "If I go, the doctor will kill her with quackery! She ran from me, fought me, then begged me to stay. How can I leave her this way?! How?"

"I won't let him, or anyone else harm her, Simon," vowed Marc. He winced at Simon's bloodied shirt, and carefully urged, "There's no time to waste. I must go to Maura. You must fetch us a guard and be on your way." He grasped the door's latch, and added with hope, "Meet us at Christmas Court. We need you, she needs you!"

Simon grabbed Marc's metal sleeve to implore, "Don't let him purge or bleed her! After the milk and ash, force her to drink a brew of bruised rue. If the broth doesn't help, feed her the herbs. Swear, Marc, swear you'll do what I ask!"

"Those are treatments for—poison!" Shock tripped Marc's speech, "Who...who would—"

"I can't say, not now. Never leave her side, never!"

"I swear, Simon, I'll stay close, always!" Marc patted Simon's hand and disappeared into the chamber. Simon waited, his ear pressed to the door. He heard squabbling, and his anxiety eased slightly as Maura's cries ebbed. Simon knew Marc spoke the truth, what choice did he have but to go? Here, enemies surrounded him, eager to pounce, and with the King closeted with his council, he could easily be apprehended and stashed away forever. At least, before he left, he would attempt to secure Maura's safety at Winchester. As Simon forced himself from her door and toward the great hall, he envisioned his next encounter and shuddered with revulsion.

*****

The elite visitors had long since retired and the great hall was now dark; embers glowed in the fire pit, a lone candelabra lit the dais, and hounds sniffed for scraps. Simon hid behind a wooden pillar and stealthily took in the peculiar drama being played out before him. Drunken cackling drifted from the raised table, where Rufus and his cronies clustered round a terrified young page, plying him with port, taunting him with slaps and pinches. Simon boldly approached and startled the revelers with his demand, "Release the boy!"

Rufus whipped his head to the intrusion and dully replied, "I thought Uncle Robert's guards locked you away."

"Your father changed their minds."

"Pity..." Rufus released one hand from the boy and pointed rigidly to the doors. "You have no power here. Now, get—"

Simon lunged across the table, eyes raging. He gagged Rufus' order with a quick twist of his collar and shouted, "I said let him go!" Then quieter, he added, "There's a matter we need discuss—in private."

Pouting, Rufus scratched at a festering boil on his cheek, swatted Simon's grip away, and gestured to his men. "Release the boy and leave me...for a short while." His friends plodded from the dais, glaring at Simon and rumbling discontent. The huge doors groaned shut behind them, and Rufus said, "This had best be quick."

"That is my intent, Cousin," said Simon. "If further harm comes to Maura, I will personally crush your hopes for the crown."

"What? How?" blustered Rufus, springing up from his father's chair and wielding a fist. "Why, you stinking dunghill! How dare you accuse me—" Simon grabbed Rufus' hand, and slammed it palm up on the table, revealing the damning copper stain smudging his cuff. Rufus quickly buried his hand beneath the skirt of his tunic and stammered, "It...it's only...spill...spilt wine."

"Everyone, including your father, suspects you of Maura's beating, and I add poisoning to your offense," said Simon with deliberate smoothness. "The King may not know all your putrid secrets, Rufus, but trust me, if Maura receives another scratch, I'll happily betray every one of them to him. I doubt he'd be comfortable handing his crown to someone with your *excesses*. So take yourself off somewhere—far from Maura."

Rufus dropped his jaw to rail, but instead he slumped back on the throne. His eyes shifted maliciously about, avoiding Simon's relentless glower as he sneered, "Sod off—you hideous little man."

"With pleasure," Simon returned with a snort. He reached the door, turned to issue a final threat, and ducked as a hurled wine cup exploded above his head, raining burgundy on his hair and shoulders. Maniacal laughter echoed through the rafters. The doors flew open, and Rufus' companions aped his hysterics as they gamboled by Simon back to their mentor. Simon ignored them, ruffled drips from his hair, and hurried to the clerks' room to fetch his cloak and satchel.

Rufus greeted his men with caresses and guffaws, then recalling Simon's threat, he turned grim and pensive. His father was already irked with him and Simon wasn't the sort to bluff. It mattered not that he'd been caught. What perplexed him most was the blame of poison. As best as his wine-fogged mind could recall, Maura had seemed tame during their squabble and lacked her usual plucky challenge; she really hadn't been much fun. Only, he'd never *poisoned* her—that wasn't his forte—warring was his greatest skill. Perhaps he should take his cousin's advice and get away, at least till the furor faded. Yes, he'd take himself off to Normandy and join his father in battle against King Philip of France. Rufus sighed dreamily at his decision, and smiled as his thoughts journeyed back seven years earlier to his Uncle Odo's castle in Rochester. There, unseen, he'd spied on his younger brother Henry and Simon clashing in mock battle...

Rufus had felt a bit smug, for at nineteen he'd finished his schooling and had recently been awarded knighthood. Simon, only seventeen, still had two years of training to suffer. Yet as Rufus witnessed Simon's sleek body dance about, he cringed with envy and desire. His cousin already owned the makings of a masterful warrior, and Rufus couldn't tolerate anyone showing prowess equal to his own. The whole next year he'd constantly nagged Simon for the chance to fight and beat him, only Simon, perhaps aware of the true motive behind Rufus' advances, spurned his pleas. Rufus eventually abandoned his chase, and the lustful admiration he'd felt for his cousin rotted to loathing...

Rufus shook from the dismal memory and, refilling his cup, wondered why he always felt awkward, tongue-tied, and flushed in Simon's presence. Perhaps it was because the man was so damn beautiful! He shrugged, downed his wine, and wiped the oozing liquid from his lips with his sleeve. Tomorrow he'd leave for the battlefield—his haven of contentment, and whack away his frustrations on some marauding Frenchman.

*****

Snoring men blanketed the guards' hut floor. Simon tiptoed between them, searching for his friend and, spotting him, crouched to whisper, "Alan...Alan, wake up."

Alan, a guard in the King's service, stirred, pushed up from the floor, and peered through the dim light. He beamed with affection and squeezed Simon's shoulder. "Simon! Why are you here? It's dangerous for you to be inside—"

"I haven't time to explain. I need your help."

"What is it?" asked Alan.

"Would you guard my father's ward, Maura, at least till Christmas Court?"

"I'd gladly watch over her, but the King has stationed me—"

"The King ordered me to find Maura a guard. I trust only you."

Alan raked rushes from his thick black hair, smoothed his bushy brown beard, and answered, "Then it's settled. Where is she?"

"In Adela's chamber. Do you know Marc, Lord Roger's squire?"

"Yes, I'm familiar with him."

"He's Maura's brother and will explain more. I, though, must leave at once."

They crept from the hut and entered the stables. Alan stilled E'dain while Simon mounted. "Keep Maura safe, Alan," Simon said wearily.

"I will," pledged Alan. "You needn't fret."

Simon quickly checked his belongings, and ashamedly asked, "May I borrow your dagger? I seem to have misplaced mine."

"Of course," grinned Alan as he relinquished his knife. "Where does this mission take you?"

"Dunheved—beyond there, I don't know. With luck and God's grace, I'll meet you at Gloucester. Tell Rose and Maura that the King has posted you at their door. You needn't mention my name."

Alan nodded and muttered, "Take care," as he sloshed away through the snow. Simon steered E'dain out of the stables toward the main gates and paused to search the keep's wall for Adela's chamber. He quickly spotted the shuttered window framed by candlelight, and offered a silent prayer for Maura's recovery, and a meek wish to speak with her at Gloucester. He swiped at an anxious tear, and galloped through the parted gates onto the high road to Dunheved.

*****

For the last two years, Simon had traveled constantly for the King, and knew intimately every road in England, especially this route to his father's central stronghold in his domain of Cornwall. Spurred by the hellish vision of Maura's torment, Simon rode hard and steady, stopping only for respites and food. To pass the time over the long miles, he devised his strategy and rehearsed his appeal to his father's seneschal, Avenal, though he knew his severest obstacle lay in simply gaining entrance to the castle.

It was late afternoon on the second day of his journey when Simon entered the walled village of Dunheved. He rode at a canter straight to his mother's cottage in the heart of the borough. Six months had passed since his last visit and he felt a familiar twinge of concern, which he swiftly shrugged off as absurd. After all, she was the most capable person he knew. He dismounted, settled E'dain with oats and ale in the two-stalled stable and, taking his satchel, entered the adjoining hut. His mother's absence didn't surprise him, for at this time of day she'd be selling baked goods at market. Smells of spice and dough perfumed the air and worried his belly. He drank in the luscious aroma and rested his sore backside on one of two stools. His frigid hands he chafed over the smoldering coals as he fondly took in the meager, yet comforting surroundings. Soon he began to fidget. The searing emotions upturned by the Winchester debacle threatened to erupt and, craving solace, he tossed his satchel on the trestle table, and went to find his mother.

Simon skirted potholes topped with icy slush and hugged himself against the biting wind as he hurried down the main road to the market stalls. Threading his way through the bustling crowd, he glimpsed hooded stalls flanked by livestock, hung with carcasses, stacked and draped with cloth, and adorned with rare herbs, perfumes and jewelry. On tiptoe, he searched the swarming bodies, spotted Edith bartering with a customer, and smiled. She never seemed to change; her stature was small and slender, her skin bronzed by the sun, and smooth of wrinkles. The only clue to her forty-nine years was the silver glistening the thick, honey-brown plait that peeked from beneath her wimple. Simon watched amused, as her dark eyes flared in response to a wrangling client. A fellow burgher spied Simon, called to Edith, and she turned to Simon's wave. Her smile radiant, she promptly abandoned her sale, and shoved through the throng to engulf her only child in an abundant embrace. Edith covered his cold cheeks with her warm hands and beamed with pride. "Each time I see you, you're more gorgeous than before!" She kissed him and laughed at his pink rush of embarrassment. "Help me pack my loaves and I'll cook you a scrumptious supper." While Edith lowered the awning shading her stall, Simon crammed two burlap sacks with bread, and swung them over his shoulder.

On their stroll to her cottage, Edith studied her brooding son. He seemed distracted, and she wondered aloud, "You look well, Simon, though tired."

"I've been riding for two days straight," said he.

"Why ever for?"

"A mission for the King." That was all he was prepared to share for now, so he asked, "And how have you been, Mother?"

"Time changes little here, Son. I'm fine, I do, though, worry about you."

"You needn't."

His response seemed stilted. She wrapped her arm round his and pressed on, "Where have you come from?"

"Winchester."

"Winchester! Oh, Simon I envy you. While there, did you happen to see—"

"I had no time for visits. The King needed me."

His curt interruption puzzled and irked her, yet noticing a shudder rack his body, she sensed trouble and urged him into the hut, muttering, "There's wood in the stable. Feed the fire and I'll mix the stew. Then—we'll talk."

Edith keenly watched her son work his task and, with a light voice, attempted to cheer. "Tell me the gossip from Winchester. How is the King?"

"He seems fine, though his sons trouble him."

"Don't they always?" She smiled and passed him a cup of ale. "When you're done with the fire, rest."

As Simon watched the flames grow, he felt his tension slacken, and lounged back upon a pelt-strewn pallet cushioned with pillows. Above the fire, Edith hooked a pot to a chain dangling from a beam in the roof, stirred the mixture once, and settled by Simon to resume her inquiry. "Did you enjoy your time at Winchester? Was there a feast?" At his prolonged silence, she tapped the spoon impatiently on the pot and followed his stare up the pillar of smoke to the vented, soot-stained ceiling. She dropped her forced gaiety and the spoon to demand, "What's happened, Simon?"

"The King insisted I go to the feast," Simon burst out, "and...I ran into Father!"

Edith swallowed tightly; her fingers strangled her braid, and she asked with a hardened expression, "And how is your *father*?"

Simon yanked off his boots, and jabbered with heavy sarcasm, "Oh, he's *very* well, hasn't changed a bit in four years—still despises me."

"Keep away from him, Simon!"

"Gladly! But my mission concerns Father."

Edith's eyes grew large as she haltingly prodded, "Tell...tell me the details."

"The King mistakenly signed a betrothal contract and he wants me to find a reason to stop the marriage."

"Whose marriage?"

"You needn't know," he shrugged.

Her face darkened. "Don't coddle me, Simon! Whose marriage?"

"William Rufus'."

Befuddled, she squirmed and muttered with relief, "Well it's time he married. Though I'm amazed anyone would have him. And?"

Simon tensed and spilled, "Maura."

"Maura..." sighed Edith with scant surprise. She'd known the answer before he'd spoken; his fawning look had betrayed him from the start. "Surely, she's already wed," she said, then nudged closer and squeezed his hands. "Did you see her?"

He nodded vaguely.

"Speak to her?" she continued.

He returned the pressure of her grip and mumbled with rising upset, "Barely. She...she's been beaten and poisoned."

"By whom?"

"I suspect Rufus."

"Will she live?"

Simon shot up from the floor; his scraped knuckles slammed his cupped hand as he raved, "I was forced to leave before I could tell! Bleeding Jesus! If she dies, I'll search him out and tear him—"

"Simon, stop!" Edith jumped up, blocked his pacing, and wrestled still his flailing. "Refuse this mission! Let Robert do what he pleases with Maura. You must avoid them all! Can't you see the risks, the danger?"

"No!" He jerked away; his crazed look returned and he cried, "She held me, begged me to stay!"

Edith groaned and slumped onto a stool, her mind swimming with dread. "Who...who was with her?"

Simon turned suspiciously to Edith. There was an odd lilt to her voice, a curious pinch in her ashen expression. She shrank from his piercing stare as he questioned, "Why do you ask?"

"I...I only pray she's not alone."

"Rose is with her, and I left them with Marc and Alan."

Edith strangled the skirt of her patched tunic and fumbled for a reply; when it came, its coldness startled her, "Then she doesn't need *you*." She met his stunned, wounded expression and instantly regretted her callousness. "Simon, I didn't—" Too late came her apology; he slipped out the door and she lapsed into tears.

Edith stifled her guilt-laden sobs and wiped her cheeks with her sleeve. This crisis needed no hysterics, but rather clear, rational thought. The dreaded day had come at last—Simon and Robert had been reunited. She wondered why the King had recklessly assigned Simon this mission. Surely William knew the dire consequences of such a command. It was only through William's loving protection that Simon had remained safe these past hard years. And Maura—with her involvement Simon would lose all sense of detachment and caution. Edith's heart ached at Maura's trouble, yet she knew if Simon continued this quest and defied his father, he could die! It was useless trying to alter his tenacity. Instead he needed someone to curb his rashness, offer sane advice, and she would strive to be that person. Edith spotted his boots sitting in the rushes by the fire; he couldn't have gone far. As she rose to find him, a gnawing dread stabbed at her—what if Rose and Maura betrayed her deeply-buried secret? No, Simon said only Rose, Marc and Alan were with Maura, no one else. Four long years Edith had prayed her suspicion about Maura was false, for if it was real and Simon discovered the truth, he'd *never* forgive her.

Edith found him crouched by the door, his fingers absently tugging the leather thong that gartered his hose. She laid a comforting hand on his shoulder and heard his somber vow, "Even if Maura doesn't need me, I'll carry out the King's orders. Robert *won't* succeed, Maura won't marry Rufus."

"I'm sorry," she said tenderly. "My harshness came from fear, not anger. I respect your decision, Simon, only—*please* take care." She squatted beside him and rested her tear-stained cheek on his hair. His hand covered and patted hers.

For the remainder of the evening, they avoided volatile talk, ate a filling meal, and chatted on the more convivial events of the past six months. Simon scrubbed three days of grime from his body; Edith snipped his hair and helped mend his tattered clothes. Neither slept. Simon, unable to vent his wrenching emotions, found it impossible to quiet his mind, and Edith's fears came alive in the dark, vexing her.

*****

Early next morning, Simon halted at the base of the hill leading to the gatehouse of Dunheved Castle, and raised wistful eyes to the towering keep. The castle, stark and foreboding, had been built shortly after the Norman invasion to serve as Earl Robert's chief defensive seat in the west, and was barely habitable. Then again, for a young boy growing up after the Conquest, it had been Heaven on earth. Simon tightened his cloak against stinging sleet, and ruffled at the clump of guards loitering on the drawbridge. There was no chance of entry here and he pondered his next move. When it struck, he was off in a shot, eyes bright and gait quick, up the hill, across the ice-packed ditch, and round to the side of the circular curtain wall. To his great relief, there were no guards about as he carefully examined the patterns in the stone barrier and whispered his count. A slim smile curled his lips as he dropped to his knees, and crawled on his belly under the dense hedgerows hugging the wall. He emerged before three stones, their cement long ago chiseled away. Carefully working them free, he wriggled through the skinny opening into the bailey, and replaced the stones. The bailey seemed oddly hushed. Between the prickled branches of a rose bush, Simon watched a chattering group of tradesmen ramble by. He slyly slipped in step behind them and roamed the courtyard. As far as he could surmise, nothing had changed since the harrowing day he'd been forced to escape his father. Memories both glorious and malignant jumbled his mind. He shook his head to rid it of distraction and focused instead on the swiftest, safest route to Avenal. Briskly, he crept up the steep stairs to the keep and stole along dark, smoky hallways, pressing into recesses as guards idly sauntered by. At last he came upon Avenal's chamber door. There seemed little chance he'd be there, but Simon knocked anyway and heartened to stirrings inside.

The door opened a slim crack. "Simon?!" Avenal gasped as he pulled Simon into his cramped cubicle and sputtered, "I can't believe...I...I didn't believe I'd ever see you again! How did you get by the guards?"

Simon gazed affectionately at the aged steward's startled expression. Blue veins and deep wrinkles etched his translucent skin, his white beard and hair hung to his shoulders, and long robes shrouded his stooped body. Simon felt instantly at ease in Avenal's presence and chuckled wryly, "I have my ways."

Avenal returned his smirk. "Yes, I clearly remember *your* ways. Why are you here? Has your father sent you?"

"Heavens no," Simon said with a slight scowl. He took Avenal's gnarled hand, helped him sit on the slim, rumpled bed, then settled beside him.

"Then all is not well between you—still?"

"No, nothing has changed. I'm here at the King's request." Simon took a moment to review his appeal and confidently began, "He wishes me to uncover information concerning Maura—"

"Maura?" cut in Avenal. "Why would the King be concerned about her?"

"Well...he's agreed to her marriage and wants to know more of her background and...uhm, her family's status."

Avenal seemed surprised. "Why?"

Simon considered Avenal's puzzlement. If the union resulted in Maura becoming Queen of England, certainly her family's history would be of crucial importance. Carefully, he delved further, "The King is interested in—He wants to feel sure she's worthy of this marriage."

"Worthy! Maura is from a far more prominent family than she's marrying into!" said Avenal. "I've always felt Robert could have made a better arrangement for her, though he's been distracted of late and seemed willing to take any offer."

"Any offer?" echoed Simon, totally confused. He shifted on the bed and, watching Avenal pour wine, tried a new approach. "Why don't you tell me about Maura's family? What caused Robert to become guardian to Maura and Marc?"

Avenal handed Simon a cup. The steward took a long draught from his own, mused a moment, then began, "Let me see, I believe it was in the winter of 1070. Yes, the Welsh attacked a fellow baron of Lord Robert's on the north border of Wales. Robert rushed to his defense, though, alas, not soon enough—his friend was murdered. So he took responsibility for the baron's two orphaned children and brought them here. That's all I recall."

An odd tale, Simon thought, and queried, "Why would anyone have small children on the border of Wales during the uprisings?"

"I'd wondered that myself," said Avenal. "After he returned, Robert never spoke of the incident. The King can be assured that Maura's father was a highly respected baron. Why all these questions over an insignificant betrothal, Simon?"

"William is having doubts about the union. Do you happen to know where I can find the formal betrothal writ?"

Avenal motioned toward his desk stacked and strewn with parchments. "It's in one of those damned piles. I suppose I should dig it out. We'll need it come spring. Can you stay while I search? Though I warn you, it may take hours."

"Yes, I'll stay." Simon stood and helped Avenal rise. "Do you mind if I wait upstairs?"

"No, not at all. Lord Robert spends little time here and the castle's upkeep is lax. Mind the rats, I expect they're hungry."

"I promise." Simon set his cup on the table and smiled warmly as he offered his hand. "Thank you, Avenal. I'm grateful you didn't toss me out."

"I never had any problems with you and could never fathom what all the fuss was about. But then, your father doesn't accept advice or criticism easily, does he?"

Simon arched a brow in agreement and accepted a passed candle.

At the door, Avenal added, "I'll have someone fetch you when the writ is found. Be careful, lad, there's scant light upstairs." He smiled feebly. "And Simon, you may leave by the main gates. Give my regards to your sweet mother."

Simon ambled across the great hall and paused a pensive moment by his father's bedchamber door. His tentative touch swung the door wide and revealed his parents' bed impeccably draped with its familiar pelts, one corner of the blanket folded down as if awaiting their arrival. He gingerly stepped inside to see better the austere chamber and his eyes were instantly pulled to a spot beside the fire pit—the spot where his father had lain that terrible morning, unconscious and bleeding. Simon bolted from the memory and the chamber, and clambered swiftly up an open staircase hugging a sheer rock wall. He batted and flinched from clinging cobwebs as he inched his way down a dank, tunneled hallway. A whipping wind from nowhere snuffed the candle, plunging him into blackness. Despite his thudding heart and the rodents romping at his feet, he pressed onward. His fingertips crept the wall, scratching a search, and he sighed as they finally found and gripped the latch to his bedchamber door. Once inside, his sight faltered to a blinding shaft of sunlight glaring through the wall's loophole. It swirled dust and memories, the wrenching weight of the latter sagging him onto the bed. He tossed the candle stick and rubbed furiously at his stinging eyes, battling an overwhelming urge to turn and run—again. He didn't run; instead he flopped across the bed and squirmed fitfully as torturous images flooded his mind, tensed his body, and beckoned him to a past he'd rather not confront. The pain on his forearm flared to the conjured sight of Maura's face twisted with agony. She screamed at him to remember, share the misery, the guilt, and her torment shattered his resistance. To understand her wrath, he would once more willingly subject himself to their history of bliss, hatred, and terrible violence. Tears threatened as he caressed the dusty worn blanket and reflected back four long, lonely years...

In October 1081, Simon had turned nineteen years old, yet along with the anniversary of his birth came the disgrace of expulsion from his Uncle Odo's castle in Rochester, where he'd spent the first years of his adolescence training for knighthood. His alleged offenses were espionage and treason, the charges arising from a seemingly happy, uneventful late-summer visit with the King. There at Winchester, after being plied with heavy doses of potent port, Simon had innocently divulged to William, his brother Odo's plans to borrow a number of the King's garrisons and travel to Rome. An innocuous trip to seek guidance from the Pope, he'd been told by his wily uncle. It wasn't till much later that Simon had learned of Odo's scurrilous plot to usurp the Pontiff. The King promptly imprisoned Odo for treason and seduction of William's troops.

When Simon had returned to Rochester, he'd found his belongings rifled through and ruined. Odo's seneschal denied Simon knighthood and banished him to Dunheved to await Lord Robert's ruling on the ugly matter. Six months of constant fretting had followed and there was still no word from Robert. Despite that harrowing time, Simon managed to find solace with Maura. He continued to love her as his closest companion, though now he also loved her in a different way. Since they'd parted, she had blossomed into a beautiful young woman and he wanted her terribly, but he dared not confess his want, for fear she might shun him, and he couldn't bear to think of her gone. It was Maura who finally confessed her passion for him one chilly spring evening in March. Edith and Rose were away on extended visits to friends and family, leaving Maura and Simon alone. That wondrous night and its delights would always remain vividly clear to him...

They had spent the afternoon enjoying Shrove Tuesday celebrations in the town. Giddy from the fair, they gamboled back to the castle and built a roaring bonfire in a secluded garden below their rooms. Simon spread his cloak upon the grass and they stretched out upon it, Maura resting her head on his chest. Simon reveled in the silken feel of her hair sifting between his fingers. If only life could always be this blissful, he rued to the threatening dusky clouds; if only there had never been a meeting with the King, and he didn't have to wait for his father's return. Would he *ever* return? That tragic notion flared his woe, for he dearly loved his father, and longed for his comfort and praise. But what praise would he get for shame—shame for being responsible for Odo's downfall, for being denied knighthood?

Suddenly, Maura's pinched face blocked his view of the encroaching storm. To Simon, her expression appeared far too severe, as if she had something disturbing to say. Or perhaps, he panicked, he'd somehow betrayed his desire for her! He tried to rise; she stopped him with firm hand and tender tone, "No, Simon, don't get up. Lie with me awhile longer. Why is it every time I try to get closer to you, you shy away? Why are you so afraid of being alone with me? You needn't be." Her fingers traced his lips, and she blurted, "I...I love you, Simon. Could you possibly love me?"

Simon dropped dizzily back upon the cloak and, as blackened clouds swirled madly above, he clutched the grass to steady himself. He'd dreamt of this moment for months, and now that it had come true, he realized that he *was* petrified, afraid of disappointing, afraid of hurting her!

Maura encouraged his response with rousing caresses and the breathless plea, "Simon, touch me, hold me! I want you so—"

He needed no further urging, grasped her closer and, crushing his lips to hers, swiftly flipped her to her back.

They fumbled feverishly through layers of tangled clothing and when at last their bare skin met, his exuberant entrance into her body made her gasp in what he thought was pain. He froze, fretting, "Maura, I don't want to hurt—"

She faintly assured, "There's no hurt," and, with a swooning kiss, implored, "Don't stop, Simon. *Please*, love me!"

He wantonly obliged and too abruptly found release. Ecstatically light-headed, he slipped limply to her side and thanked God for the light rain that helped cool the unbearable heat he suffered. Maura lay too stiff and silent; he worried again, and pushed up on his elbow to catch her comment or expression. She shifted away and stared vaguely at the smoldering remains of their fire.

Simon's lonely arms clenched her waist. He molded to her back, found and fondled her breasts. His lips explored her neck, urging her to snuggle back against him. He squeezed closer, and felt her heart race and himself stiffen to his wish, "Maura, I want you...again." A chilling breeze joined the drizzle, so he grasped her hand and, rising, suggested with an alluring sigh, "Not here...Come with me to my chamber."

They hastened from the garden and scurried up the winding stairs to his chamber. Spilling inside, he grabbed for her; she escaped his swipe, and whispered, "No, wait..." Maura used the fire of an oil lamp to flare the end of a rush and touched its flame to every wick she could find. The room now luminous, she reached for him, offering with a deep blush, "Do you...do you want to see me?" He vehemently nodded and helped tug off her tunic and, then with the softest touch, he slipped her chemise from her shoulders and watched it drift liquidly to her feet. Simon gaped and blinked, marveling at her bared figure. Her fairness easily surpassed the beauty of his dreams. He drew her near; again she paused and boldly coaxed, "Now you...I want to see you." She helped him out of his tunic and shirt. He stepped from his braies and stood naked and proud before her. She gazed awestruck at his aroused body, and a glint sparked Maura's eyes as her fingertips feathered his chest and strayed down his belly to stroke between his legs. "Is this because of me?" she asked with a blush and beguiling smile.

"You've been the cause of that for the past six months," he admitted in a shivered sigh.

She glowed and wondered, "Why didn't you tell me? Does it hurt?"

His hands roamed her back and gripped her slim hips, urging her closer. "It's more uncomfortable than painful, and I...I was afraid to tell you." He winced and loudly swallowed, "I was afraid that I would disgust you and you would leave me."

"No, Simon, never," she murmured, melding her body and lips to his. "I felt the same way, and was afraid that you'd *shun* me. I'm so happy I was wrong. Are you happy too?"

"Indeed I am!" Lusty laughter broke their ravenous kiss. They tumbled onto his bed, wrestling, and pawing clumsily at each other. Simon nuzzled her neck, making her giggle more, as he murmured, "Has any man touched you?"

Maura's laughter abruptly died to her fervent reply, "A few have tried. I fought them off to wait for...you."

Between nipping kisses, he earnestly confessed, "I've always...loved you."

"Not only as a friend, Simon, as a *woman*. Do you love me as a woman?"

"Oh, yes..." he indulgently affirmed as his eager lips lit upon her breast and lingered awhile to taste and tease.

Maura gasped in delight and burbled, "The servant women tell me there's great pleasure in bedding the *right* man...And I've always believed that *you* were the right man for me, but—" she ventured carefully, "in the garden...that can't be all—" She purposely tangled her fingers in his tawny hair, encouraging his exploration as his thrilling trail of kisses ventured lower. "Oh, Simon," she pleaded, "this time, can we go more slowly, and you will teach me all you know of loving and—"

"Maura—" He lifted a bashful face to confess, "You know as much as I."

She sat aghast. "I'm your first?!" Her surprise humiliated and he turned away his shame. Maura's gentle touch swiftly cooled his flaming cheeks, and she sweetly cooed, "Simon, you mustn't feel embarrassed. I'd be dreadfully jealous if someone else had been first to know you, for I love you so."

"No...no one else dared enter my mind," he fervently stumbled. "I could never love another the way I love you." He surged back into the safety of her stirring embrace, suggesting with a hearty chuckle, "Why don't you tell me all that these servant women told you and then—we'll teach each other."

"They didn't truly *tell* me," she admitted in airy suspense. "If Rose knew I secretly listen to their chattering, she'd kill me! Oh, Simon, they talk of the most amazing wonders—what they do to please their men, and what they ask their men to do to please them. Before you returned, and many times after, I'd go back to my chamber, and imagine us together...umh...doing all those things, and I'd feel a delicious tingling everywhere, and especially here..." She guided his hand between her legs, and breathed her passion, "I crave your touch always, only your touch, Simon! Make...make me sigh and moan with pleasure like the women say they do when they bed the right man!"

Feeling faint, Simon deliriously tripped, "You...you show me all that...that these women say, and I'll do everything I can to make you sigh and moan with all the pleasure you can possibly desire!"

"Oh yes!" she exuberantly agreed, then ardently purred, "And I'll do the same for you." Maura's lustful look blazed anew as she urged him to his back and draped his body with hers. His love swelled to her torrid kisses and tempting vow, "And this time we'll make it last forever..."

After that glorious night, Dunheved Castle became a magically sensual world that belonged solely to them. Oblivious to everything and everyone, they loved fiercely, whenever they could, wherever they were. They escaped the scrutiny of the castle, and spent the summer days and nights cavorting upon the moors and beaches of Cornwall, not returning to the castle for days, sometimes weeks. The summer cooled, yet their love flared to obsession. They vowed never to part even if faced with death, and constantly dreamt of escaping to the wilds of Wales. Autumn arrived, driving their passion indoors, and gossip of their liaison spread like rampaging flames throughout the castle. And when at last it crackled in their ears, they became acutely aware of how horribly reckless they'd been. Adding to their distress came the rumor of Maura's imminent marriage to a son of the illustrious Lord Roger of Montgomery. The daunting news forced them to spend each precious moment together zealously plotting their liberation.

Seven months after Simon and Maura's first night together, Edith's sudden reappearance temporarily staunched their passion and flight. At first, her time was consumed with righting the affairs of the castle and she noticed nothing awry. The lovers, though, fearing her discovery of their secret, attempted living apart. Steeping frustration led them to squabble, and they separated further. And then Maura took ill, vomiting continuously and feeling too wretched to leave her bed. Edith believed Maura's ailment contagious and refused Simon's furious demands to see her. Weeks passed and, crazed with worry, he repeatedly tried to force his way through her locked door. As Simon's furor grew, so did Edith's suspicions.

Robert arrived mid-November, and ordered Simon to appear before his Legal Council. Simon strove valiantly to explain to his father his unwitting role in the Odo affair, that he'd meant no harm, no malice. Robert refused to acknowledge a word of his defense and threatened disinheritance and severe punishment.

That dreadful night, Simon returned to his room, broken in heart and spirit. Just when he was convinced everything was lost, Maura came to him and, cradled in his loving arms, wept bitterly. He tried soothing her with tender words and caresses, but she refused to confess the cause of her woe. They clung together throughout the night and, immersed in their misery, neither heard the footsteps, nor noticed the shadow lurking beneath the door.

Just before dawn, Maura grudgingly left Simon's hug to return to her bed, and moments later he heard her scream. Half-dressed, he burst into her chamber and stared agape at the appalling scene before him—Maura cowering against the wall, a swollen red welt staining her cheek, and Edith looming over her, poised to strike again, screeching, "You stupid whore! We'll all suffer for your lust! How long has this gone on?! How long? Answer me!" Edith swung to slap again; Simon caught her arm. She whirled her fury on him and ranted, "You fool! Do you want to die?! Robert's council is now deciding your punishment. If he had found you with Maura, he'd have murdered you both!" Edith stormed to the door and threatened, "I too have made a decision! This day Maura will be cloistered. You'll never see nor touch her again! No one will!" She slammed the door with a force that rattled its hinges.

Maura clung to Simon, whimpering, "Don't let her send me away. *Please*, Simon, stop her!"

"Edith's frightened for me, that's all. You needn't worry," he shakily assured, swathing her in a blanket.

"You'll never leave me?"

A rustling at the door stalled his answer and sparked their fear. He stilled her sobs with a trembling kiss, rose, and tucked the cover round her, tensely whispering, "Maura, stay here."

"Where are you going?" she asked, her voice and grip rigid. "Simon, I'm afraid!"

"I'll speak to Edith, try to calm her, then I'll return. I *swear* I'll return." He slipped from Maura's hold and the chamber and, pressed tightly to the wall, crept down the stairs. He hadn't descended far before his father's roared curses and his mother's wails reached his shocked ears. Simon leapt the remaining steps, burst into the chamber and barged his way between his wrestling parents. He struck his father with a force that hurtled him backward through the flaming hearth. Robert crashed into the wall. His head soundly thudded the stones and he slumped senseless to the floor, dangerously near the fire. Edith and Simon dragged Robert from the hearth, and swatted madly at sparks glittering his tunic. Blood seeped from Robert's head, dripping between Edith's cradling fingers, and staining the rushes. She moaned her anguish, while Simon clenched at his belly, and groaned in horror, "Is he dead?!"

"No..." Edith sobbed. "He listened at your door and knows you're lovers! He only planned to imprison you. After this, he'll be mad enough to kill! You'll leave! Now!"

"For where?!"

"A...a sanctuary. Do you remember our pilgrimage to Wales, before you left for Odo's?" He stood crazed and trembling, and she had to shout, "Simon! Answer me! Do you remember?" At his uncertain nod, she stressed, "Go to the Cathedral at Menevia. They will hide you."

Robert stirred and moaned. "He's waking!" Edith panicked. "Go, quickly!"

"I won't leave Maura!" Simon swore.

"Don't be a fool, she's ill!" Edith abandoned Robert and roughly shoved her son toward the door, frantically swearing, "I'll protect her, and when all is safe, I'll bring her to you."

His stammering turned hysterical, "How...how will you—"

"Damn you, go! Leave on foot by the postern door!"

Simon stayed rooted in shock till Edith's sharp blow to his cheek rocked him from his trance, and he reeled away to her lethal warning, "If you stay—Maura *dies*! Run!"

Simon vaulted the stairs as Robert hobbled from his chamber, howling for his guards. Maura quaked in the frame of her door, waiting. With no word or look, Simon flew past her and disappeared into his chamber.

She chased after him, demanding, "Simon, what happened?" In his frenzy, he couldn't answer, and her alarm soared as she watched him throw on his shirt and snatch up his cloak. Before he could don his boots, she stole one and held it behind her back. Her terror erupted and she groaned, "What are you doing?! Simon! Answer me!"

He grabbed the shoe away, pinched her shoulders hard enough to hurt, then gritted low and threatening, "Go to your chamber and lock the door. I have to leave. If they question you, tell them I forced you to be with me."

"Leave!" she shrilled. "No...you...you can't leave!"

"I...I—" He froze to the ominous rumble of hollered commands and scuffling boot steps. "Maura! Hurry—the guards—go to your room!"

"Wait for me!" She dashed for the door. "I'll come with you."

"No!"

"But when will you return?!"

"I can't, I won't! When it's safe, Edith will—" Simon halted in the doorway and risked a quick glance back to the stairs.

The sentries' cruel glowers appeared at the landing. Simon sprinted for the opposite door. Maura floundered behind, swiping, clawing at his cloak, squalling, "Don't—don't go! You swore—swore you'd never—" She caught his arm, yanked back, and flung herself against him. Her nails gouged his back as she cried, "I—I can't—won't stay here alone!"

Simon weakened to her wails and clutched her fast, gasping and sputtering, "Edith... Edith will—"

A flurried movement caught his eye. A guard charged, his broadsword aimed at Maura's back. Edith's portent, 'If you stay, Maura dies—she dies!' jolted Simon. His powerful thrust slammed Maura against the wall, saving her from the sword, and hurtling him backwards down a whirling, endless, bruising stairway. Blinded by darkness and tears, he scrambled up and raced away—away from his home, his family, and Maura, her tortured screams shattering his heart, and haunting him forever...

"My Lord?" The page's light call jarred Simon from his reverie. He pushed up to sit and squinted at the dimmed figure in the doorway. The boy cautiously approached and offered a rolled parchment. "Lord Avenal said you're to have this."

Simon nodded and accepted the skin. "I'm grateful. Where's Avenal now?"

"Sleeping, my Lord. He's not been well."

"Then don't wake him. Later, give him my thanks."

"I will, my Lord," replied the page and, with a jerky bow, he vanished.

Simon stayed a moment, twirled the parchment in his dusty fingers, and mused over the end of his tragic tale—but there really was no end. He'd run and escaped only a few miles before heavy doubts and cold had slowed his pace. Then he'd returned to the castle for Maura, only to find that she, Edith and Robert had gone, Maura supposedly to Normandy to wed. Two years passed before Simon and Edith were reunited in Dunheved and, ever since, she'd adamantly refused to speak of the heinous incident. Simon had never insisted. Perhaps now, he thought as he stuck the parchment in his belt, it was time he did insist. He rose with effort, glanced longingly back at the bed, and left.

*****

CHAPTER THREE - UNWELCOME SURPRISES

Vile weather thinned the market crowds, and Edith hastened home to spend the afternoon with her son. She excitedly prepared a hot meaty stew and welcomed Simon with a huge hug and kiss. Brushing snow from his shoulders, she searched his face and felt her hopeful mood sink to his lost look. "Did Avenal see you?" she asked warily.

Simon slung his cloak in a corner, slumped onto a bench by the table, and ripped a hunk of bread from a loaf. "Yes," he muttered, "and he sends his regards."

"He's such a good soul," Edith said mildly, sitting herself, and passing Simon a bowl of stew. "Where did you meet with him?"

"In his room, then...I wandered." His stare pierced; her smile faded. "It's amazing," Simon continued, "nothing has changed...nothing."

She averted her eyes and sighed submissively, "How long can you stay?"

He pressed forward and asked the one question that had never been answered. "What happened the morning after I left the castle?"

"No, Simon!" Edith heaved up from the table and escaped to the far end of the room. "Don't make me think of that time! I won't...I can't remember!"

Two broad steps took him to her; he squeezed hold her shoulders, sorely pleading, "I have to know! Why does Maura hate me? Surely you told her why I had to leave, that she would die if I didn't go! Tell me, Mother, why would she do *this*?" He yanked up his sleeve, revealed the jagged gash, and cried, "Look at me and tell me why!"

Edith spun to face him. One hand stifled her gasp as her other reached tentatively for his wound. "How?" she despaired. "How could I tell Maura? The guards dragged her to her chamber. I ran to help her, then the door slammed shut and locked!" Edith's color drained, she sagged in his arms, and moaned, "Her screams, Simon. I've been haunted four long years by those horrible screams! They are *my* punishment, and they will torture me forever!" He eased her down to the rush-strewn floor and heard more anguish. "Robert's men ripped my hands from her door. I...I fought to reach him, begged for mercy, but he never looked at me or spoke! I don't remember what happened after. When I woke, I was lying outside the main gates. He abandoned me with nothing! A friend in town sheltered me till I felt strong enough to travel to my family in Sussex. *They* refused me." Her wet gaze drifted. "Then something, love or maybe only familiarity, drew me back here."

Simon's guilt raged at his mother's despair, and he faintly rued, "So everyone suffered for my sins, everyone that is, save me."

"No, Simon." Her hands trembled over his brow, through his hair. "You mustn't blame yourself, you were innocent and ran to save her, only to save her!"

"I don't believe Maura remembers it quite that way," Simon gravely replied, and then was silent. Eerily silent, thought Edith, for in his succoring embrace, she could practically hear his mind scheming a plot to confront Maura, discover the truth, and recapture her love—no matter the consequences. She shuddered; he fetched her a pelt, a cup of warm ale and, with a thin appeasing smile, eased their torment. "Why don't I tell you of my last mission for the King? It truly was quite exhilarating."

Edith instantly brightened. "I would love that, son," she sniffled and gushed, "I'm so very proud of you!"

Much later, Simon, unable to sleep, stroked Edith's cat and vacantly watched rain drops dive through swirling smoke to their frizzling death upon the live coals. After one particularly loud hiss, he recalled the writ. Noiselessly, he rooted through his heaped clothing, found the thin skin, and unrolled it facing the fire. The printing was tiny and smudged; he squinted to read the Latin, and its astounding contents dropped his jaw. Once more he read diligently and rechecked the date—the first day of November, 1085. Miraculously the impediment to Maura's marriage lay before him! The document was indeed her formal betrothal writ, though *not* to William Rufus. This had been too easy to find! Did his father suffer from senility, or had the King been correct to suspect trickery?

The rain had ceased by morning, yet a bitter, misty chill lingered. Simon sadly packed his few belongings and the bread, dried meat, and cheese Edith had set aside for him. It was always hard to leave her and seemed especially so after this unsettling visit. She brushed a wisp of hair from her swollen eyes, asking with a gulp and strained cheer, "And now where are you off to?"

"North of York, to a small village called Ryedale," he replied, fastening his cloak with a broach at his shoulder. "I need to validate a document given to me by Avenal."

Wrapped in a blanket, Edith escorted him to the stable, then glumly followed as he led E'dain outside. She watched him mount and, reaching up, received a small pouch instead of his hand. "What's this then?" she asked.

"A gift...from the King."

"To you, not to me. Simon, you shouldn't."

"William clearly mentioned it was for *you*."

"And you're a sweet liar."

"I don't need it, you do. No more arguing." His heart ached to her miserable expression. He grasped her hand, kissed it, and managed a wistful smile. "I'll return soon. Promise to take care of yourself."

"I always do." Before letting go, she squeezed his gloved fingers and whispered, "I love you, Simon."

"And I you, Mother."

He started away, then hesitated to her call. She tugged her blanket tighter and boldly requested, "When you see them, give my love to Rose, Marc and...Maura."

Nodding, Simon kicked E'dain and cantered off down the lane. Edith hid her grief till he was well out of sight, then dissolved in a rash of tears, convinced she'd never see him again.

*****

Monstrous, distorted demons heckled Maura, daggers jabbed her belly, fingers tipped with flames poked and prodded, singeing and melting her skin. She writhed in agony, battled vainly at groping hands, strained to escape the deafening voices. This surely was Hell! The Devil loomed before her and forced a cup of steaming worms to her lips. She clamped shut her mouth. The molten liquid spilled over her cheeks and down her neck, searing...burning...

Rose joined Maura's shrieks, "Let her be! For God's sake, give her some peace!" She shoved Marc from the bed and crushed Maura to her chest, rocking and soothing, "No, angel, no more fighting. You must sleep, sleep." Maura thrashed in Rose's arms and groaned gibberish.

"Rose," insisted Marc, "Simon said I must force the herbs—"

"That fiend knows nothing! He delights in her agony. Four days, Marc, four days of torture!" Rose pointed accusingly to the chamber pot brimming with bloody vomit. "There's nothing left of her. I'll allow no more. Fetch the physician!"

"No!" fought Marc.

"I'll go!" she flared. "You stay and hold her. Do nothing else!"

"Then you bring the Bishop as well," said he. "She'll need him after the doctor's murdered her!"

Their clashing only heightened Maura's frenzy. She beat and scratched her guardian, forcing Rose's plea, "Help me, Marc! She's mad with fever. Help me!"

"We'll wrap her," stressed Marc. "Fetch more blankets, heavy pelts, hurry!" He wrestled hard to restrain his sister, while Rose skittered between the two chambers, snatching up pelts and blankets. Marc forced Maura to her back and draped the blankets; their pressing weight stilled her thrashing, her head lolled, her moans grew fainter.

Smothering, she was smothering! The Devil's heat crushed and strangled. Everyone had deserted her, God, Rose...Simon! So tired, too tired to fight...A soft familiar voice sifted through the choking heat, beckoning, "Maura, look at me, I'm here. You needn't fear, I won't leave you." She gasped to a cooling touch on her brow and frantically sought her rescuer's face.

"Rose! Come near. She sees me! I'm certain of it, she sees." Marc leant closer and begged, "Maura, speak to me. It's Marc...Marc!"

The burning peaked; a violent shudder convulsed Maura's body and fluttered her lashes. The voice called louder, "No, Maura! Stay with me, talk to me!"

She forced her eyes on a face crystallizing before her. Her fingers touched brown hair flecked with gold, brushed across milky white skin flushed with innocence, and came to rest upon full red lips. Maura stared pleadingly into eyes that mirrored her own, and whimpered, "Ma...Marc..." as she lapsed into a profound and curing sleep.

*****

With Maura tucked up in a dry chemise and clean bandages, Marc wearied of Rose's tirade over Simon, and trailed her into the garderobe to defend his friend. He sourly watched her empty the chamber pot's contents down the rank hole, and bristled at her haranguing. "Why do you scorn Simon so? He helped save Maura!"

"I'm not convinced of that!" retorted Rose. She brusquely swished the pot in a pail of soapy water, wiped it with her skirt, and strode back to the bed, harping, "He's a sweet-tongued devil who hides behind the guise of a healer. He won't fool me! When she wakes there will be no kind words of him spoken in this room. Is that clear, Marc?"

"Why? Why do you hate him so?"

Rose stopped fussing with Maura's pelts to cruelly answer, "There was a time I prayed for his death. His crime is not for your young ears. Concern yourself with your sister's care, her feelings, and forget that fiend! If you persist in nagging me about him, I'll have Lord Roger send you elsewhere."

Marc swelled and snorted, "If you haven't noticed, Rose, I'm no longer a child. I say and think what I please!" With that, he spun on his heels and huffed away.

As the door slammed shut, Rose sank to the bed, cradled her head in her hands, and languished. Just the mention of Simon's name wrought so much pain and discord! Of course his treatment had helped Maura. Three kitchen workers stricken with an identical food poisoning had died under the physician's *expert* care. Yet how could she acknowledge Simon's success when a tumult of hate boiled inside her, threatening to explode? She gazed with pity at Maura, sleeping peacefully, patted her hand, and whispered, "Enjoy sweet dreams, angel, for come Easter, you'll never know peace again."

Three laborious days passed and Maura slept, waking only for meals of bread, milk, and boiled rue. When at last she mustered the strength to speak, she requested a bath. The warm water soothed her aching muscles. She rested back against the spongy wood and dangled her braced arm over the tub's wall. Her discolored face held a dull, vacant look that winced periodically as Rose tugged a comb through her sopping hair and babbled incessantly, "We were all horribly worried, especially Lord Robert. I never doubted you'd recover and my prayers were answered. I've offered my thanks to God and you should do the same, Maura. When you feel stronger, you'll accompany me to Mass and—"

"Did I hurt him?" blurted Maura.

Rose faltered to Maura's odd question, then scowled her answer, "You can't hurt someone who has no heart. Don't trouble yourself with Simon's welfare."

"Will he return?"

"Not if I have any say in the matter." Rose's calm evaporated; she tugged harder, and ranted, "That treacherous bastard! He's despised by all save the King, and Simon flaunts their bond, believes he's special because of it. He's nothing but a dirty little spy! I'm certain he purposely picked this time to harass you, knowing how vulnerable you'd be at mention of the betrothal—"

Rose's yammering faded as Maura closed her eyes and saw again Simon's pale, loving gaze. Cupped water splashed away the hurtful image and her tears. She stood shakily, mumbling, "Please, Rose, no more. Help me out."

"I'm not finished."

"I am. Please help, then leave me awhile."

"I don't think that's wise," argued Rose as she assisted Maura from the tub.

"I promise not to run off," Maura said, straining a weak grin and slipping on her robe. She examined Rose's morose expression, realized her fear, and laughed in astonishment. "You think I'll purposely harm myself! Haven't I just proven a very strong will to live? Rufus definitely is not worth *my* life." Maura grasped Rose's hand and begged, "Please, just a moment alone with my thoughts."

"Your thoughts will make you so sad," said Rose.

"Then fetch Marc. He always cheers me."

Rose slumped in surrender. "As you wish, though only for a short while. First we'll get you dressed."

Alone for the first time in seven days, Maura sat before the fire pit, absently twirled a lock of hair, and considered in the dancing flames her doomed future. There was little chance of escape, she hadn't the strength to bolt, and the risk of endangering others was far too great. If only she could return to the time before the feast, those precious few hours when she had truly believed her troubles gone. She even felt a faint twinge of longing for the squalid life she'd lived with Rose. They may have been cold and hungry, but at least they'd been free of Rufus. The disastrous family reunion had dredged up fragments of a past best kept buried...deeply buried. Yet even now, terrible anger, hatred, and fright gnawed at her insides, weakening her feeble control. How fervently she'd prayed for marriage to save her, and she would gladly have accepted anyone of Lord Robert's choosing! Rufus—just the thought of him made her quake with revulsion. To him she was nothing but a battering toy, and he'd soon tire of his plaything and find a discreet way to dispose of her. She'd heard he had joined his father in war against the King of France; still, he was never gone for long. Suddenly a distant memory lit Maura's eyes and brightened her gloom. The King had said, '...don't despair'. Was he speaking of the betrothal? Christmas Court was only four weeks away. There, she'd find the opportunity to plead her case to Uncle William! He must put a halt to this calamity before it was too late.

The chamber door flew open and Maura snapped to Rose's flustered entrance. "Maura!" Rose breathlessly announced, "Lord Robert's coming this way. Here, give me your arm. I'll help you up."

"She needn't stand." The women froze to the stark remark and raised meek faces to their Liege, standing nobly in the doorway, his face set in its perpetual scowl. He swiftly approached and took the chair beside Maura's, grunting, "Rose, leave us. I would speak to Maura alone." Rose squeezed Maura's hand, bowed deeply to Robert, and scurried away. He stared severely at his ward for what seemed a long while, then as always spoke bluntly, "I can't say you look better, you actually look worse. If you had obeyed me and stayed at the feast, none of this would have happened!"

Maura shrank to his scolding, and lowered her eyes to her lap.

"Did Simon beat you?" he asked tersely.

Not sure she'd heard him correctly, Maura met his hooded glare and asked, "Who told you *that*...my Lord?"

"When we found you, he was at your side, looking guilty."

"I never saw him after I left the feast, my Lord."

"Then who was the culprit?" demanded Robert.

Her haunted gaze slipped to the fire and her nails bit the chair's arms as she flatly answered, "No one, my Lord. I was sick, dizzy, lost my balance, and fell down the stairs."

Robert started to argue, then decided it was easier to accept her questionable excuse. "Take care, Maura," he said strictly, crossing his arms and his legs, "I need you well come Easter. You should be proud to have been chosen Rufus' bride." He spoke as if in secret, "It's of course too early to predict, yet I believe, and others do as well, that there's an excellent chance you will become *Queen* of England."

She stared aghast at the supreme ruler of her life, then shook from her trance, and asked, "My Lord, did the King speak to you of Rufus' ill treatment of Rose and myself?"

"Yes...he mentioned something about misuse of my funds and rationing your food," replied Robert casually. "I've spoken to Rufus about the matter. He readily acknowledged his mistakes and begged my pardon. I forgave him, as should you."

Maura heaved at his repugnant order and felt a rush of nausea. She gulped it back to stammer, "I...I will try, my Lord."

Robert stood and rigidly straightened his black tunic. "I must take leave of Winchester. Urgent matters at Dunheved require my attention. You will complete your recovery here, then travel to Gloucester for Christmas Court."

"Will we see you there?" she meekly wondered.

"No, there are too many preparations to be made for the wedding. I'm sorry to miss it for it promises to be a grand affair. Will and my wife, Almodis, will represent our family at Gloucester. You haven't met the Lady Almodis, have you?"

"No, my Lord. I look forward to the occasion and meeting your Lady wife. I was so sorry to hear of the death of your first wife, my Lord."

His stern expression didn't twitch to her comment as he answered, "Well, now I must go." He raised her good hand to his lips just as Marc burst unannounced through the door.

Robert whipped round and watched Marc gibber his embarrassment, "My Lord, forgive me! I didn't know...I'll go—"

"No, stay. I'm leaving." Robert completed his cold kiss, and his eyes and words darted uneasily between his two wards. "I trust both of you to show fitting behavior at Christmas Court and have a joyous holiday." He strode to Marc and soundly clasped his shoulder. "Roger has informed me of your excellent progress. I regret I won't be able to attend your knighthood ceremony, though always know my pride is with you."

"Thank...thank you, My Lord," Marc stuttered.

Marc knelt, received Robert's touch to his head, and remained kneeling till his Liege had departed. Then, lifting anxious eyes, he was greeted by Maura's extended arm and sweet request, "Come sit by me."

"I'm sorry for the intrusion," he said, rushing to her.

She patted the chair by her side. "Don't be silly. I'm glad for your cheer. Our Liege is so dreary. I didn't realize your ceremony was so soon, then I always have trouble accepting the fact you're grown."

"I turned eighteen in March!" His exuberance waned and he spoke with rampant worry, "Maura, when I last visited here, Rufus told me you'd returned to Dunheved! If I'd known you were still here, *starving*, I would have—"

"No, Marc." She rested her hand on his broad shoulder and sighed, "It's done." Silence reigned as Marc struggled to muzzle the multitude of questions rumbling inside him. Their tie was close, so close they'd always known each other's thoughts and feelings. Yet now it was as though he sat by a stranger. He'd never seen her this way—frail, wounded, and so full of woe. If only he could tell her of Simon's search for an end to this obscene betrothal, but the King had warned him not to encourage her hopes. He shifted uncomfortably in his chair and fumbled for happy words; Maura found them first. "Marc, please tell me, what's to happen at your ceremony?"

Marc flashed an exuberant smile. "I'm not quite certain. There's a formal affair where I swear homage and the King grants me knighthood. What excites me most is the melee! I'm to challenge several of the greatest knights from England and Normandy and—" He noticed her eyelids droop and said tenderly, "Maura, come, it's time for sleep." She didn't resist as he helped her to bed, blanketed her with thick pelts, and whispered, "You need rest."

"Marc?"

"Yes?"

"When I'm feeling stronger, I want to leave this room. Will you take me riding?"

"Nothing would please me more." He bent to kiss her brow, and she readily obeyed his gentle command, "Now, sleep."

*****

At last the day arrived for their jaunt on horseback. Maura, restive with anticipation, rose before dawn. Within a mere week, her strength and appetite had surged; she barely required any assistance whatsoever. Still, for some curious reason, she'd yet to venture outside her chamber. It was as if something odious lurked just beyond the door. This morning, though, she bravely decided to attempt a quest to the kitchens to fetch breakfast for herself and Rose. She dressed modestly in a woolen chemise, thick hose, and warm tunic, cursed at her brace for its constant interference in her daily rituals, and slipped on a pair of tall, fur-lined boots. Cracking the door to Rose's room, she listened and grinned at the soothing, gravelly snore, then donned her cloak to leave.

Maura started down the hall, then hesitated to the annoying blackness and muffled rustlings. She turned to go back for a candle, but was trapped by something huge and black lumbering about on the floor. Alarmed, Maura pounded on Rose's door. It swung wide, illuminating the hall with muted light. Rose stood bedraggled in the door frame, her head cocked quizzically, and eyes blinking in wonder. "Maura, what *are* you up to?"

"There's *something*," Maura gasped, "something out here, Rose. It's got hold of my foot!"

Rose glanced down, smiled knowingly, and waved away Maura's flurry. "It's only Alan."

"Alan!" Maura exclaimed and whirled round to see. "Who in God's blood is Al—"

The object of contention sluggishly unfolded his imposing figure from the floor, and brushed rushes from his mussed black hair. He scratched at his heavy beard, rubbed his vibrant blue eyes and, with a slight bow, greeted, "My Ladies..."

Maura snorted, shoved Rose inside her chamber, and slammed the door in Alan's bewildered face. "What goes on here, Rose?!" she hotly demanded.

"You really shouldn't curse in front of strangers, Maura," Rose countered.

"Don't distract me! Who is this Alan and what's he doing outside my door?"

"He's kindly agreed to watch over you, angel."

"At whose prompting?"

"The King's we believe."

"And is he here to keep me in or others out?"

"A bit of both I'm afraid," said Rose, and she haltingly added, "He's a member of the King's guard and—"

"Guard!" roared Maura. "Then he'll leave now. I won't have a guard watching over me!"

"You have no choice," Rose ended curtly.

Maura sat down hard on Rose's bed and spoke a bit less frantically, "Rose, am I being punished for attacking the guards? Tell me true, am I a prisoner?"

"No, no, angel," Rose assured as she settled beside Maura. "Few know of that episode. It's no secret, though, that you were savagely beaten. Alan is here only to protect you."

"May I still ride with Marc?"

"I'm not pleased with the idea, but yes, you may go. First, though, you'll accompany me to Mass."

"No, I don't think so," said Maura.

"You must offer thanks for your life!"

"Rose," Maura hotly returned, "if God allows this marriage to happen, He surely has deserted me!"

Rose gathered herself tall to caution, "Take care what you say, Maura!" and hurled a damning glare as her charge fumed back to her chamber.

Maura slammed the door separating the rooms, stormed to the shuttered window, and flung it wide. A brilliant orange sun peeked over the curtain wall and challenged the ire in her eyes. She rubbed them vigorously, then spotted Marc plodding through the snow toward the stable. Maura waved excitedly and shouted, "Marc!" He turned to her call and beamed a radiant smile; its brightness shamed the Sun's and instantly doused her anger. The tradesmen halted their work and gazed up at the window as she yelled, "May we go now?!"

Marc nodded and waved her down. She burst a delighted cry, and hurriedly closed and barred the window. A tiny mirror held close revealed her face still bruised, but the wave of her hair hid the wound on her brow, and a dab of face powder masked the countless other purple stains. She brushed smugly past Alan, and hummed a spritely tune as she flitted down the stairs to the stables. To Maura's chagrin, Alan followed determinedly, her fierce looks having absolutely no effect on his dull expression or brisk pace. Once inside the stable, she shoved between horses and grooms to Marc, and grumpily complained, "Does that horrid man have to follow me everywhere?"

"He's not *horrid*," Marc grunted, yanking a girth strap through a buckle. "And yes, those are his orders."

Maura arched a curious brow and wondered, "What are you doing?"

"What do you think, Sister? I'm saddling our horse."

"Oh no, not pillion." Maura frowned at the richly padded, double seated saddle, and firmly stated, "I'll not ride pillion!"

"Rose's instructions. You ride pillion or not at all."

"No, Marc! I'll have my own horse!"

"Then you'll ride sidesaddle," said he, removing the pillion, and swinging a woman's saddle upon the horse's back.

"No...I have only one good arm and need my legs to guide—" She paused to glimpse the horse's underside and finished, "...him."

"It shouldn't be a problem," Marc said calmly as he tugged the girth strap. "Besides, we'll only be walking."

"Traitor!" Maura sneered in jest and grabbed the reins. She refused the groom's aid and mounted on her own, grateful that Rufus had spared her favored arm. Once out of the stables, she drank in the crisp air, and marveled at the buff blue sky daubed with wisps of swirling clouds. A frigid wind teared her eyes and perked her mount's ears. She lifted her hood and, shifting with impatience, glanced about the bailey. Pearly peaks of snow cloaked the curtain wall and tradesmen's huts; glittering swords of ice embellished the overhangs. The scene was much subdued from the last time she'd visited the courtyard. Servants raised curious eyes to her mottled face as they slogged by, and she wondered what fantastic tale they'd been told of her episode with Rufus. The gelding pawed at the frozen earth. Maura turned in the awkward saddle, and carped, "What's keeping you, Marc? Hurry before Rose changes her mind!"

"I'm coming!" Marc yelled, urging his mare to Maura's side. Alan, cringing from the cold, staidly followed. As they sauntered through the main gates, Maura kept her gaze locked ahead lest a guard recognized her and, once across the drawbridge, she spurred her mount to a canter. Marc hurried after, chiding, "Maura, stop! I said we'll walk."

Maura's exuberance entered her gray steed, making him dance expectantly. "I'm terribly sorry Marc," Maura said, feigning ineptness and sporting a playful grin. "He definitely has a mind of his own. And how can I control him saddled like this? I only pray you catch us." With a sly wink, she sped away. Before Marc had a chance to react, Alan streaked by in pursuit. Marc grappled with his spooked mare, then charged after them. Galloping alongside Alan, Marc fretfully watched the distance lengthen between them and his wayward sister.

"I can't catch her!" shouted Alan.

"And you won't!" Marc returned. "Cut through the woods and meet her at the bend in the road! Stop her, Alan!"

Alan veered off the road. Marc reined his horse and mumbled, "And pray the gate's open." He cursed himself. What a damned foolish idea this had been! Even weakened, she was a formidable challenge, especially on horseback.

Maura flew recklessly down the lane, ecstatic as the wind threw back her hood and whipped her copper-orange hair. She laughed aloud and urged her mount faster. They'd never catch her, no one would, ever! Suddenly she came upon the bend gated by a sheer fence. There was no time to dodge the barrier! Maura lunged forward, gripped the horse's mane, squeezed shut her eyes, and prayed. She soared steeply through the air, landed with a jarring thud, and lost hold of the reins. The horse careened wildly down the road, rearing each time he trod the reins. Maura struggled vainly for control, all the while cursing him, her arm, Rufus, and the blasted saddle. She heard hoof beats, and the sight of Alan galloping to her rescue escalated the foulness of her speech. He rode to her side, swiped at and caught the tangled reins and, then dismounting, soothed the frenzied horse. Alan's furious glare enraged Maura, and she shouted, "Give me the blasted reins now!"

"No!" Alan yelled back. "God's teeth, woman! Enough lethal games. Like it or not, I'm to keep you alive!" He looked away, stilled his racing breath, and frostily announced, "We'll return to the castle where I can keep a keener eye on you."

Fury uglied her features as she dropped from the saddle and bolted for the trees. Alan raced after, easily caught her good arm, and jerked her around. Maura's boot assaulted his knee, slumping him to the ground in agony, and she promptly escaped into a dense thicket of pines.

Marc, having witnessed the entire spectacle, strolled to Alan's side and cleared his throat to stifle a chuckle. "Quite feisty, isn't she?"

Alan reached for assistance and howled, "I believe I'm crippled!"

"I doubt it," said Marc as he helped Alan up. "She's only bruised your pride a bit."

"Why didn't you warn me about her?" Alan grumbled, gingerly testing his leg.

"You're the King's guard and ought to be able to protect yourself against anyone. Yet then again, consider who she was raised with. Simon and I trained her well in the fighting arts."

"Yes, well it's a bit late to learn the *Lady's* military history. When we return, I aim to find a replacement for my post."

"Oh Alan, don't blubber so. Give her time, she really can be quite sweet."

Alan cursed beneath his breath, limped back to his horse, and turned to warn, "You'd best corral her before she flees the country!"

41

Laughing, Marc entered the forest and spotted Maura crouched by a trickling stream. His hovering shadow failed to break her intense concentration as she stabbed at the ice with a stick. He settled by her, and spoke low and firm, "You can't run away, Maura."

"I wasn't running away," she said bitterly. "I was enjoying myself, then *he* ruined everything!"

"No, *you* ruined everything. Come, it's time we returned or Rose will send soldiers to fetch us." When at last Maura looked up, Marc cringed at her battered face lit by the snow's brash glare. "Maura," he said gently, "you'll have to accept Alan."

"Perhaps, but—I won't—I can't accept Rufus. Marc, he'll murder me!"

The despair in her reply rattled him. He floundered for a reassuring word, only none came, so he rested a comforting arm round her shoulders. They sat awhile, watching the rushing water dance and swirl amidst jewel-like pebbles. She felt him chuckle and wondered, "What's funny?"

"Oh, seeing you wrangle with Alan. It's good to have the old Maura back, fiery and not a little stubborn. I feared she was lost forever."

"Marc, will you stay at Winchester and accompany me to Gloucester?"

"Those are my plans."

She snuggled closer. "I'll need your strength and your cheer."

"And we *will* enjoy ourselves," said he, "no matter what or who threatens our way. Now come, and mind the ice." They tread cautiously back to the road and discovered Alan gone. Marc noticed Maura's disquiet and smiled. "Well, you've managed to scare him off."

She didn't catch his humor and pledged, "When we get back, I must apologize."

Later that evening, while Maura shifted restlessly beneath her pelts and reflected on the past two lurid weeks, the most recent unwelcome surprise came to mind—Alan. She rose, wrapped her robe about her, and tiptoed to the door. Cracking it open, she beheld him sitting up against the stone wall, looking cramped and wretched, yet amazingly asleep. Maura crouched and shook him slightly. "Alan?"

He woke with a start, mumbled guardedly, "My...my Lady," and scrambled to stand.

Maura stopped him with a gesture, and a humble smile. "You look so uncomfortable. There's a thick mat inside my chamber. I'll fetch it for you." His protest was ignored as she left and returned quickly with the pallet. Together, they spread it flat, and she meekly offered as tokens of peace, a wool blanket and an apology. "I'm terribly sorry about today. You certainly didn't deserve my wrath. How fares your knee?"

"There's nary a mark, my Lady."

"Please, call me Maura. I promise not to cause you further bother."

"And I swore, Maura, to protect you in any circumstance, which I will strive to do without further upset."

Their bashful smiles eased the strain between them. "I'll leave you now," whispered Maura, "a bit cozier, I hope. Goodnight, Alan."

His relieved gaze and answer trailed her through the door, "Sleep well, my Lady Maura."

*****

Edith started awake to furious pounding and a hollered command, "Open for Lord Robert!" She sprang up from her pallet, threw on her tunic and, with a lurching heart, cracked opened the door. Three soldiers burst through, coarsely knocking her to the rushes. Brandishing torches, they scattered about the hut like startled rats. Edith gaped in shock as the intruders scrambled beneath her table, jabbed rumpled pelts with swords, and upturned her trunks, sacking and ripping the contents. They kicked bowls and baking pans from their neatly stacked piles. Garlic cloves and onions rolled over the rushes to be crushed underfoot. Sacks of flour and oats exploded to their slashing assaults, billowing clouds that set one sentry to sneezing.

Edith gathered the strength to stand, reached out long for mercy, and wailed, "No...no, *please*...stop!" One wickedly enthusiastic ravager scaled the crude, woven ladder to the storage loft where Edith kept hidden her special treasures. She screamed savage curses, clambered up after him, and yanked at his foot. Beneath his boot the rung tore, spilling them both to the ground. A box he'd stolen flew from his grasp, broke apart, and spewed the few precious remnants of her past in every direction. She gasped frantic breaths and groped madly among the rushes, retrieving a thin gold band, a christening gown, and a raveled hair ribbon.

As the room erupted in violence, she moaned softly and rescued a tiny quilt from the smoking coals—Simon's first blanket. The supple material soothed her wet, heated cheeks; she hugged it fast and rocked in anguish, her mournful cries deepening with the mounting bedlam.

Suddenly a baleful shadow blocked the torch's glare. Edith raised a tortured expression to Lord Robert's malicious one, and cowered as he barked, "Where is he?!"

The past four years she'd spoken nothing but English! She buried her face back in the cover's folds, and struggled for a French response; it came, muffled and broken, "He's... he's not here."

"Obviously. Where has he gone?"

"I...I don't know. He tells me little. Why do you want him?"

"Your saintly son has stolen a vital document of mine. He will be found and punished."

The blanket fell from her face. She defiantly met his dark glower, and her French flowed as easily as her rage. "He's your son as well, Robert! He was given that document freely by your seneschal, Avenal."

"Then he too shall be punished."

His stony expression and serene voice terrified her. He spoke as if the idea pleased him! This couldn't be the same man she'd loved for thirty years—so gruff, hard, and ruthless. She rose cautiously, searching for the familiar glint in his eye; she discovered only hate.

The soldiers flanked Robert, their expressions cruel, their torches dripping sparks. One smirked and tossed a swollen money pouch into the air, spouting, "The wench isn't as poor as she looks, my Lord. I've uncovered quite a stash of gold."

Robert seized the bag, cuffed the man's shoulder, then commanded, "Get out, the lot of you. Wait by the door for orders." Their swift exit plunged the room into sudden blackness. Edith fought to still her shaking and prayed for calm. Her tearing eyes refused to grow accustomed to the dark, but she still could sense his lording presence, hear his rasping breath, smell his anger. His nearness suffocated. She stepped back; he grabbed her arm and jerked her close. "Now you'll tell me," he growled. "Where is your cursed son?"

"On a mission for your dear brother, the King," she spat through clenched teeth. "At least one member of your despicable family knows and appreciates his worth." As suddenly as he'd restrained her, he set her free, and she wondered if it was only her brashness that unsettled him.

Robert retreated an inch and faintly demanded, "Fetch a candle." While she fumbled for a taper, he squeezed his palms together and strove to recapture his wavering command. He never should have set foot in this miserable hut, never spoken to her, never touched her! She set the lit candle upon the trestle table and slowly turned to face him. He gulped at her humble image...still the same lovely Edith, the woman he'd adored, yet who'd so viciously betrayed him! His fury blazed again and he stormed to the table, wielding a balled fist. "You'll tell me where he's gone or I'll sell you into slavery!"

"You wouldn't dare, Robert!" Her brazen reply shocked them both.

His fist rocked the table, his roar rattled the walls. "What makes you think you're any different from the rest of the scum who inhabit this putrid slum?! You chose to return here, to become *my* property. You will speak to me with respect, and I'll deal with you as I please!"

"I...I believed," she sputtered, "that you once cared for me."

"Never," he scowled. "You were nothing but a very willing servant."

She slumped to his insult, and dropped her voice and wounded gaze. "Then I was a fool, Robert."

He bristled to her repeated use of his Christian name. "No, woman, *I* was the fool to allow you into my home, my bed, to plot and scheme Odo's downfall! And now, what's your plan for *my* overthrow—murder? Or perhaps you'll incite your neighbors to rebel, or have Simon plant evidence again and concoct fantastic tales for the King, this time damning me. You want me ruined!"

"No...my Lord, I only want you gone."

Robert grasped her shoulders and winced to the silken sting of her hair on his arm. He reeled from her scent as a long suppressed passion stirred anew. Years of wretched loneliness had killed a vital part of him only she could revive. He held her face between his trembling hands, his panted breath clouding the small space that separated them. The thudding of his heart echoed in the deadly silence, and Edith's breath stopped as his hands pressed inward. "I could crush you so easily," he hissed, "then all my troubles would simply vanish..."

Edith's body sagged in his forceful hold, though she would not submit. Her hands covered his and she asked, "What stops you, Robert? You're so skilled at killing things—like our love. Few have known the closeness we shared. Maura and Simon did, but you destroyed their passion as well. And what has all this hate gotten you? A few extra hides of land, an empty manor home, a slave or two? Not your brother's freedom, not the crown. All you've succeeded in doing is shattering yourself, and driving off forever those who truly cared for you." Something in her stern tone, her moist eyes, and her steely expression doused his temper. His hands dropped dejectedly to his sides, and he wilted to the affection in her voice. "You once told me, that of all your children, you knew and loved Simon best. You took time to nurture and guide him." Her fingers lightly circled his arms as she brokenly continued, "You...you swore you'd annul your marriage to Matilda, marry me, legitimize Simon, only Odo advised against it. Why obey *him*? What has he ever done but cause you grief?"

Robert's face wrenched with torment, his fists clenched and unclenched. This damned woman and her devious wiles would have his soul! Hell, she owned it now, had stolen it four years past when he tossed her out—too late. He must get away before her charms bewitched him completely! He lurched from her side, but she caught his arm and wailed her demand, "Answer me! I give you the chance you never gave me. Tell me why you cast me out. *Why*, Robert? Tell me. I must know!" She clutched at his sleeve and ripped it. Bitter tears coursed down her face, wetting his fingers as she rubbed her cheek against his rough knuckles. At the tender gesture, Robert clasped her to his chest and, in the wavering glow of the taper, surrendered to his temptress.

Edith clung to his firm, sinewy body. Her mind whirled with desire and promise. Dare she hope he still loved her, would take her back, and make peace with Simon? His body screamed yes, yet would his lips agree? She sought them out, and crushed her mouth to his. It met only coldness. He stiffened and shoved her forcefully from his clench. She tumbled over the trunk stashed with coins, and landed with a sickening thud upon the tangled ladder. Too stunned to cry out, she whimpered and coiled herself in a tight ball.

Robert kicked through the rubble and knelt beside her, his vengeful words spitting and stabbing, "You filthy whore, I'll not be duped again! How could I have been so stupid to believe that walking pustule is my son! No son would treat his true father with such contempt. And your disgraceful show just now—" He reached into the trunk and extracted three pouches. "And I wondered how you came upon so much cash. Your body won't entice a thing from me, for to me you are dead, as your son will be if he dares challenge me!"

Edith pushed up from the floor and, finding her strength gone, whispered hoarsely, "Our son."

"He's not my son!" Robert hurled the pouches at her. Edith flinched as they struck, then she crawled to her mat; her consoling pelt muffled his abuse. "I must rethink my decision not to tax you," he blustered, pacing and flailing. "I won't have you living in luxury, not at my expense! And if there is another unfortunate incident, no matter how trivial, I'll personally torch this hovel with you and that brat of yours locked inside!" Robert strode to the door and paused an intense moment. "Heed my warning, woman! I will never back down and he *will* be found."

Edith emerged tentatively from beneath the cover, her words barely audible, "If...if you question his paternity, when next you see him, look deeply into his eyes. What you'll see is yourself—before you became a monster."

Robert groaned his rage and slammed his fists against the wood, flinging the door wide. Sharp commands and pounding hooves took him and his soldiers away. Edith's cat, hackles high and belly low, scurried from its hiding place and escaped over the halved door into the stable. Edith didn't move, couldn't move for the pain. She stared pleadingly at the dying embers, desperate for some comforting heat, a sympathetic touch, a kind word, but she was all alone. And try as she might, she failed to stave off the racking sobs that betrayed her sound defeat.

*****

CHAPTER FOUR - A TALENT FOR TRICKERY

In a vain attempt to thaw his numb legs, Simon stiffly circled the timbered hall's crackling fire while awaiting the arrival of Aubrey of Ryedale. He hated traveling in winter, particularly in the north. Not only was it savagely cold, it was too damned oppressive. Sixteen years had passed since his uncle had laid waste the whole north of England, razing all that hindered him: villages, forests, beasts, and men; little had sprouted to replace the scourge. The King's abhorrent tactics sickened Simon, though it was fruitless battling William with word or sword. Instead, guile and compromise seemed to reap the most prosperous rewards from his irascible uncle. Unfortunately, all that his uncle's vassals seemed to respond to were device and brutality.

Treacherous storms had delayed Simon's progress by a week, and only a fortnight remained till Christmas Court. Yet, with luck, his quest could be neatly resolved here—in this exceedingly paltry manor. Upon arriving, he'd been astounded by its meagerness. Simon knew well his father's greed, and easily deduced why Robert had shunned the Ryedale marriage contract in favor of Maura's union with Rufus, presumably the next King of England. The tiny wooden lodging consisted of a single hall furnished with few pieces of rugged furniture, centered by a hearth and sectioned with worn tapestries. A handful of rotted outbuildings and scrawny chickens and goats dotted the bailey, contained within a steep wooden fence that urgently needed patching. There were few servants about, though from one, Simon had learned that Hugh of Ryedale, Maura's betrothed according to Avenal's writ, was a widower and employed as a professional soldier for the King. Hugh's elderly father, Aubrey, tended the property during his long absences.

Simon snapped to alertness when a racket emanated from the opposite end of the hall. A tiny girl child skipped merrily across the room in his direction, a huge smile filling her comely face. She was chased by her nurse, a dowdy-looking woman, far past middle-aged, with a gruff voice and expression to match. Behind them, assisted by a cane, hobbled an old infirmed gentleman cloaked in long robes, with sparse hair and dangling yellowed skin.

Her golden-brown ringlets bounced as the little one tugged excitedly at Simon's tunic. He crouched to her level and she announced in a shrill perky voice, "I'm Emma. What's your name?"

He beamed at her exuberance and smiling doe eyes. "I'm Simon," he answered as he took her hand. "And I feel quite honored to meet you, my Lady Emma."

The excitement sparked by his ardent attention elicited a squeak of delight from Emma that set them both laughing. "I'm five years old!" she proudly exclaimed. "How old are you?"

"By last count, twenty-four," he answered. "Suppose we switch, just for the day. I'll be five—"

Suddenly, she was snatched away, and Simon stared up quizzically into the most malevolent glower. Emma instantly became sulky and whined in protest as she was dragged away by her grumbly nurse.

The elder gentleman approached, and excused with an appeasing smile, "I apologize for my granddaughter's curiosity. We don't see many strangers here." He kept his smile and offered his hand. "I'm Aubrey, Aubrey of Ryedale."

Simon rose from his crouch and accepted Aubrey's welcome. Despite his advanced age, Aubrey's handshake was warm and firm. Simon shook his head slightly. "No need to apologize. She is quite refreshing. I'm Simon."

"Simon FitzRobert?"

"Yes."

"Well I must say, I'm a bit muddled," said Aubrey. "When your father last called, he brought with him a young man whom Lord Robert claimed was his *only* son. If I remember correctly, the lad was dark."

"My father and I don't speak. Actually, I'm on a mission for my uncle, the King, not my father."

"The King?" Aubrey paled and his eyes widened as he stuttered, "My...my son—is there news of Hugh?"

Simon quickly assuaged, "No, nothing of that sort."

"Thank Heaven," sighed Aubrey and, with an outstretched hand, added, "Come, Simon, we'll sit. My legs tire easily."

Simon assisted Aubrey to a trestle table facing the hearth. Aubrey was pleasantly surprised by Simon's courtesy. "Thank you, lad. I am amazed that the King has taken time from his hectic life to concern himself with our menial affairs. What seems to be the problem?"

Claiming the seat by Aubrey, Simon waved away a servant's offer of wine, and began, "I won't mince words, Sir. I'm here concerning the marriage agreement drawn up between Lord Robert and your family. My father has either forgotten your agreement or purposely passed it over in favor of a betrothal with William Rufus, the King's second son."

"What!" exclaimed Aubrey, reddening.

"Breach of contract is a serious offense, Sir," continued Simon evenly. "According to the King, the bogus contract was signed at Sarum in August of this year, which makes your contract, dated a year past, the legitimate one."

"Has Lord Robert been confronted with his lapse of memory?"

"Not as yet. The matter will be addressed at Christmas Court, and there the King will acknowledge your contract's legality."

Aubrey sadly wagged his head. "I should have sensed trickery was in the offing. Last July we began receiving documents from Lord Robert's clerk making the most ludicrous excuses for terminating the contract. One letter claimed that while staying here, Lord Robert had been plied with undiluted port and coerced into signing the agreement. Another stated the document wasn't dated, the next that it wasn't scripted in Latin and contained misspelled words. I practically laughed when we received the latest note this past week, claiming that his ward, Maura was not a virgin and, on that technicality, the contract must be dismissed. What do we care of the woman's past? All I can hope for is that she will be kind to Emma, and perhaps give my boy sons. And I desperately need help maintaining this household. As you can see, it's fallen into a pitiful state." Aubrey winced as he shifted in his seat and rested his brow in his palm.

Simon picked at a knot in the wooden table and listened with a mixture of satisfaction and grief. He would have heartening news for the King and no doubt also for Maura. Yet Aubrey's speech failed to ease *his* discomfort over the prospect of Maura's marriage. He shrugged away his troubles, and declared, "Then, my Lord, the matter is settled. The marriage will be performed in accordance with your betrothal contract, the day following the Feast of the Resurrection. The King will address the situation with my father and, as penalty for his deception, Robert will most likely be ordered to increase the dower portion of the agreement. Is that satisfactory to you?"

Aubrey gratefully clasped Simon's hand. "Yes, my lad, quite satisfactory. And now, you'll sup with us?"

Nodding, Simon smiled. "I'd be honored, Sir."

Supper was a lonely affair, though, the offerings were lavish, well-seasoned, and of ample proportions. Attended by one servant, the two men sipped watered wine and engaged in trivial conversation. Slightly bored, Simon asked, "Where's Emma?"

"Her nurse insists she eat separately. I disagree, but if I question nurse's rules I'm harshly chastised. The child brings a bit of brightness into my dour life..."

By Aubrey's fading tone and distant gaze it was clear to Simon that he'd lost his thought. Simon resumed his meal, though grew uneasy at the elder's ceaseless stare. Finally, he set down his spoon, and questioned, "Is there something amiss, Sir?"

Aubrey shook from his trance. "I'm sorry, lad. I was only trying to recall...A number of months ago, we had word of a mediator of mixed Saxon/Norman blood, who proved quite useful in settling a dispute north of here. He was called Simon—Simon FitzRobert. Would you be that man?"

Simon nodded and answered, "It was in Richmond."

"Yes, indeed!" cried Aubrey. "Then, my Lord—"

"I'm not a lord, Sir."

"Well, you must be a knight."

"I'm not privileged with that title either."

Aubrey looked confused, then stated, "No matter, I'm still quite honored with your presence on two counts. You own a marvelous reputation in these parts."

Blushing slightly, Simon took a long draught of wine and sputtered, "I...I do what I can."

Aubrey sat up tall and his tone turned expectant. "A fellow vassal is having tremendous difficulties with his villeins. I fear revolt is in the wind. The sheriff is newly appointed and knows little English, I know none. Perhaps you could take time to translate gripes and offer solutions."

Simon protested, "I haven't the time. I'm late as it is—"

"With your expertise," Aubrey interjected, "it should take less than a day. There's been much suffering, so I hear. In Yorkshire we pride ourselves on Lord and villein living peacefully. Please Simon, make this an exception."

Every part of him screamed no, yet he heard himself easily succumb. "Where?"

"Pickering, a ways south of here. I'll send word immediately for a meeting to be assembled—"

"Tomorrow morning *early*."

"Yes." Aubrey beamed and lay his hand on Simon's shoulder. "And you'll sojourn with us this night. Now, I'm to bed. There's been far too much excitement this day for this very old man." Aubrey rose with difficulty, and Simon helped guide him toward a tapestry separating the far end of the hall from the rest of the chamber. "My servant will bring you a pallet, pelts, whatever else you may require."

"I thank you, Sir."

"No need, I'm grateful to you as will be my son and granddaughter." Aubrey drew back the tapestry to find Emma drawing with a piece of coal on the planked floor, the rushes stacked in a neat pile nearby.

Her face was smudged with black, and her intense expression relaxed to radiant as she boasted, "I've spelled my name, Grandfather."

"So you have, little one, so you have." Aubrey and Simon glanced at a chair flanking a bed and beheld Emma's nurse, limp and snoring. Aubrey whispered to Emma, "We'd best set the rushes right or your hands will sting from the rod."

The child's face pinched with disappointment while Simon knelt and began spreading the rushes over the letters. "What else can you spell?" he cheerily asked.

"Only my name. When Nursey's away, I draw behind my curtain."

"Yes, she's produced quite an expansive mural," noted Aubrey. "It's our secret."

"We don't mind Simon knowing, do we, Grandfather?"

"No, little one." Aubrey settled on the bed and added to Simon, "Nurse teaches the child Bible stories, the commandments, how to spin and embroider. Still, she allows few toys and less fun. I have too much to do to take on the task of finding someone more suitable. Do you know Lord Robert's ward, Simon?"

"Yes," answered Simon wistfully. "Quite well."

"Do you believe she'll make the child a good mother?"

Simon gazed into the child's sad eyes and, tenderly touching her cheek, assured, "I've no doubt."

"Good, another worry put to rest." Aubrey removed his outer robe and stretched out on his bed.

He was reaching for his pelt when Emma sprang up to protest, "No, Grandfather! No sleep yet, you've forgotten our story."

"Oh, child. I'm much too tired for stories this night. We'll have two tomorrow."

Again Emma's pout appeared, more intense, as she whined, "Just *one*, please."

The elder's eyes closed, and the child turned to Simon. Setting the last rush in place, he met her hopeful gaze and succumbed with a gentle grin, "I'd be happy to."

As he stood and swatted rushes off his leather braies, Emma gripped his hand and asked, "Do you have a daughter?"

"Unfortunately, no. I'm not married."

A comment came from the seemingly asleep Aubrey, "I have three maiden daughters who'd be delighted to discuss with you the prospect of marriage."

Simon snorted a laugh as Emma snatched up her ragged, soiled, faceless doll and ambled with him over to the hearth where a pallet stacked with pelts had been set out. He sat cross-legged and she plopped in his lap. Once comfortable, he asked, "What's it to be then—fairies, dragons, witches?"

Without hesitation Emma blurted, "Tell me a story of when you were little."

His smiling eyes settled on the fire and he remembered, "Yes, what a wondrous time that was." Emma snuggled in his arms as he began, "Once, way back, three young ones lived together in a grand timbered castle. The eldest, a boy, was a ruffian full of mischief. The middle child, a girl, was a whimsical creature who wavered between naughty and nice, and the youngest boy was a somber saint. Together they had many great adventures..."

And so, he chatted on and she joyously listened. His last tale flowed quickly to catch her drooping eyelids, "...And the villagers came upon a fair maid wading in a shallow forest stream. They were so overcome with her beauty, her flowing red hair, ivory skin and sapphire-like eyes, that they deemed her not of this earth and named her E'dain, which means fairy woman—"

Again, Emma was abruptly ripped from Simon's grasp, and he was issued a harsh reprimand from the nurse. "Sir, you mustn't encourage her whimsies! They bring idleness and disobedience."

Simon rose and sharply countered, "We were enjoying ourselves!"

Emma rebelled and thrashed against her nurse, setting up a grievous squawk that echoed through the hollow hall. Simon reached out, started to argue, yet held his tongue as the sneering nurse hauled the child away. He slumped back upon the pelts and, to the accompaniment of the Nurse's violent reprimand and Emma's piteous sobs, sadly watched the dimming firelight. The episode with the child deeply disturbed him. Emma desperately needed a kind, nurturing mother and he knew of few who would fill the role as perfectly as Maura. But wife to Hugh? That was a completely separate matter. Simon stripped off his leather tunic and braies and burrowed his way beneath the pelts. He curled to a tight ball and hugged his knees; the thought of her lying in any man's arms save his own engulfed him with the vilest jealousy and revulsion.

Too early came a serving woman carrying a wooden pail lined with leather, filled with cold water, and topped with soda and ash. Simon woke gradually, stretched and, with a shivering yawn, sat and rubbed his eyes. As she lay the fire, the servant furtively studied Simon from the corner of her eye. He ignored the intrusion, stood, and clad only in a linen shirt and long drawers, washed briskly all that was decent under the crowded conditions. He knelt over the pail, wet his face with a whipped lather, and began the arduous task of scraping off his stubble using Alan's too-sharp blade. Wincing to the dagger's assault, he listened to the dull moan of the wind and remembered painfully his frigid journey north. After he'd wiped his face and the blade, he rummaged through his saddlebag, extracting a woolen shirt and braies, two pairs of hose with garters, and a neck scarf. The servant left the sputtering fire and began readying the table for breakfast. Simon climbed into the woolen braies, tugged on both pairs of hose, gartered them, then wriggled into his leather braies. His top he layered in the same manner. After belting the ensemble, he stuck the dagger in his belt and, once cloaked and gloved, approached the servant, wondering, "Is Lord Aubrey awake?"

"Yes, my Lord, he's dressing. Will you eat with us?"

"I haven't time."

"Then I'll pack food for your journey."

"Thank you," said Simon, handing the woman his saddlebag. "Is the child up?"

As if she'd heard him, Emma came skipping from behind the tapestry and said with a firm hug, "I was afraid you'd be gone."

Simon lifted her in his arms and replied, "I'll bid you and your grandfather farewell, then I must leave."

Tears welled in her eyes as he set her down and took her hand. Aubrey appeared and, shuffling forward, stretched out his hand to wish, "Have a safe and successfully journey, lad. Will you attend the wedding at Pevensey?"

"I don't believe so." At a loss for his next word, Simon scratched his head and blurted, "Well I'm off to Pickering."

"The sheriff's name is Ralf, and he's expecting you." The three walked to the main doors, Aubrey continuing, "Not too happily I'm afraid."

"I've dealt with all kinds," said Simon with a wry smile. "Thank you for your hospitality and..." his eyes shifted to Emma as he exuberantly finished, "your splendid company!"

"May I come to the stable with you?" she asked.

Simon looked to Aubrey, who nodded, "It's fine. Nurse is not yet awake."

Wrapped tightly in her patched cloak, Emma jabbered incessantly along the way, speaking of her animals, dolls, imaginary playmates, and her father. From her obscure description of Hugh it was obvious that, to Emma, he was a stranger. Simon agreed to ride her once around the bailey. The third time round, he stopped at the main gates, kissed her, and set her on the frozen ground. Then promising that one day they'd meet again, he rode off for Pickering.

*****

Slumped over the dais, Sheriff Ralf, Tenant-in-Chief of Pickering's fortified manor home, sported a disfiguring scowl as he watched Simon stride the length of the hall. Simon stopped before the table, brushed snow from his shoulders and, with a slight bow, quickly took in his adversary. An unpleasant, gruff looking man, with greasy black hair and shifty gray eyes, Ralf didn't speak, he simply glared. Simon knew all the power games, and glared back—his piercing stare finally causing the sheriff to look away and shrink back in his chair. With no introduction, Simon removed his gloves and complained, "I experienced trouble entering your manor home. You don't want me here."

"We have no problems," grunted Ralf.

"I've heard news to the contrary." Simon swiftly checked the room—two guards, a few servants, too many dogs, and two other men, presumably butler and seneschal. From the great number of horses tethered in the bailey, he'd expected more of an audience. He returned his attention to Ralf and asked, "Where are the villeins?"

"They've been summoned," answered Ralf in a dull, aloof manner.

Simon poured himself a cup of wine and rested his slim backside on the table. He sipped, then demanded, "I'll hear the details now."

Ralf ruffled at Simon's audacity, yet obeyed and his snide words dripped disgust, "The loafing peasants working my fief haven't produced their quota in food stuffs this harvest, or provided sufficient services for the upkeep of my household. To punish them, I've supplemented my stores with their personal food allowance. From what I can determine from their gross mutterings, they are perturbed with my decision."

As Simon's eyes rolled in exasperation, the huge doors creaked open, and he turned to watch the peasants file into the hall, looking dreadfully sour. He'd grown so skillful at the art of observation that he could easily distinguish between the villeins, privileged peasants who allotted only a few days of their week to their Lord's service, and the bordars and cottars, who were subject to more onerous and servile duties. Ralf's serfs, no different than slaves, had no rights and wouldn't be allowed to attend this meeting. Simon felt an affinity for these conquered people; their blood was his blood, and he'd known too well the hunger and frustration that gnawed at their bellies.

A young, gaunt, bold-looking man stepped forward, ran his filthy fingers through his pale locks, and spoke, his voice rough from struggle. "My Lord." His bleary eyes lit briefly on Ralf, then darted to Simon as he stuttered, "We...we are glad for your presence."

Simon returned his nod and smiled. "I am not a lord. Please call me Simon. And you're called?"

"Edmund."

"Well, Edmund, why don't you tell me what's happened here."

While the peasant gathered his thoughts, Simon studied him and wondered if the smudge marks on his face were dirt or bruises. The man straightened and, inhaling deeply, began his woe, "Simon, we've had sad luck with the harvest. The storms blighted five fields worth including our portion. We have little to sell for cash and it's hard to work on an empty belly. We freely gave Sir Ralf what we could spare, kept only what we needed. He only quarters five knights—"

"What's he saying?" interrupted Ralf rudely in Norman French.

Just as harshly Simon returned, "Let him finish." Ralf glared at Simon, then with a snort, filled his wine cup. Simon turned back to Edmund and prompted, "Go on."

Edmund's round eyes betrayed fear as he stuttered, "Sheriff Ralf's guards came at night, with no warning, and stole our grain, vegetables, even took our salted meat! We have a few chickens, but no feed for them. Our cows are starving and give little milk. The snows came early this year. They can no longer graze."

Ralf responded to the villein's dramatic speech by standing and pounding the dais with his cup, cursing, "Damn you, what's the *bastard* saying?!"

Inflamed by Ralf's choice of words, Simon roared back, "I don't translate curses! You speak to me and to your villeins with respect or you won't speak at all."

Ralf shrank to Simon's retort and muttered, "What's he saying?"

"That you've stolen all their food!"

"Liars!" blared Ralf, wielding his fist. "Filthy, scheming vermin!"

In an eerily calm tone, Simon responded, "Is that all you have to say in your defense?"

With a great huff, Ralf stomped to the end of the table and conversed in hushed grunts with his seneschal. Simon turned back to the peasants and offered solace. "Please believe that your King does not wish to see you suffer. The trouble here seems simple enough to solve. Why don't you return to your cottages? It will take a few threats, yet I believe Sir Ralf will return your stores within the day."

The humble group gaped at Simon's words and, with awed whispers, shuffled from the room. Edmund alone stayed, and bravely approached the dais to grasp Simon's hand. "How can we ever thank you?" he asked.

Simon answered simply, "Never stop complaining."

Edmund chuckled along with Simon, then nodded sharply, and rushed to catch his friends.

"What was he laughing at?" Ralf barked to Simon.

"To know that, my gracious Lord, you'd best learn some English."

"I thought you came to help!"

"And that's exactly what I aim to do. I'll see your grain stores now."

Ralf glanced briefly at his seneschal, hesitated a moment, then answered confidently, "Yes, of course, follow me."

Simon trailed him down winding, wood stairs, under the earth, and emerged in the cold, moldy buttery. Ralf waved his hand over twenty or so neatly stacked burlap bags. The cold air burned Simon's throat, and he held his hands over his mouth as his doubting eyes scanned the room. Something was amiss. This meager amount of grain would barely serve Ralf's household three months. He decided to chance confrontation and commented with cool finality, "Yes, very nice. Now take me to your main storage compound."

Ralf heaved contempt and answered testily, "How dare you accuse me of hoarding!"

"I don't recall mentioning that word," simpered Simon. "However, while we're on the topic, if you don't show me your plunder—"

"What...what will you do?"

"I meet with the King in two weeks' time. When he hears of your treachery, he will gladly send a contingent of soldiers to redistribute your newly-found wealth and—"

"You wouldn't dare!"

"The King is my uncle, Sir. We're quite close and he rarely refuses me *anything*." Studying Ralf's confused and bitter expression, Simon remembered Aubrey's words, '...newly appointed sheriff'. Perhaps only a verbal lashing was needed here. "Ralf, why don't you sit a moment. I believe an explanation is in order." Ralf grudgingly plopped himself on a sack and, sporting a winning smirk, Simon went on, "It seems you're not fully acquainted with the rules of Norman society. Your villeins, bordars, cottars, and serfs provide you with food, services, and a small cash payment with which you feed and clothe your household and quartered knights. You in turn proffer your Lord, the King with taxes and military service. I believe you house only five knights."

"Seven!" corrected Ralf.

"Seven knights. Any break in the chain results in severe repercussions to all involved. In your specific case, your villeins will suffer illness, perhaps even starve from your greediness. Little food will be produced next year causing your knights to go hungry. They'll turn grumpy and most likely revolt, pillaging your home and the village, and leaving you with nothing. With no taxes received, the King will strip you of your fief and home and it's your turn to starve. Now let me see your other, and I'm sure, much larger storeroom."

Simon sifted his fingers through bag after bulging bag of oats, barley, and rye. The sacks, stacked ten high, filled every stall, and packed tight the loft of the stables. Now he knew why there were so many horses in the bailey. With a narrow glare, Simon instructed Ralf, "Tell whoever was planning to purchase these riches that you are no longer in the merchant business. One quarter of these supplies should serve your household well till next harvest, the rest will be redistributed to your villeins by day's end. Carry out this simple request and not a word of your indiscretions will reach King William's ears. Do you agree?"

Ralf sneered in response.

Simon chafed his hands together and the grain's dust powdered the air. He plucked his gloves from his belt and, donning them, said, "Then I'll take my leave. You'll be watched, so you'd best stay on good behavior or—"

"That's where you're wrong," Ralf growled, and in response to his sharp gesture, the guards closed and bolted the doors.

Cursing himself for not sensing this predictable reaction, Simon sprang into action, drew his dagger, grabbed the sheriff and, with Ralf's neck securely locked in the crux of his arm, grittingly warned, "I am expected at Christmas Court. If I don't show, there will be a search for me, and my trail ends here." Simon tautened his grip and shouted above the Sheriff's pitiful whine, "Command them to open the doors now!"

"Op...open," squeaked Ralf.

The doors flung wide and Simon took advantage of the temporarily blinding glare of sun and snow to bolt. He shoved Ralf into a pile of leaking grain and clumsily elbowed his way through the blinking guards. He sprinted across the slushy courtyard in E'dain's direction; trudging boots and screamed curses followed. Ralf's frantic voice grew closer, clearer, and Simon was pleasantly shocked to hear him ordering his men to halt. Simon leapt onto E'dain's back and turned to pant a final threat, "Behave yourself...and keep behaving yourself for you are now under surveillance. If caught again, your punishment will be confiscation of your title and property, and banishment. Return the food this night!"

E'dain carried Simon at a brisk gallop away from the perilous situation. As they flew under the gatehouse and thundered across the drawbridge, Simon let out a whoop of joy, and laughed crazily at his tenuous luck. The King didn't give a damn about the peasants' welfare. One day soon Simon's bluff would be called, and he'd end up stashed away with the grain, trussed in a burlap bag with a dagger stuck up his ribs. Simon rode down the lane, glanced east toward the village and noticed the villeins gathered around the well. His triumphant wave and brilliant smile told them the grand news, and by evening their food was once again in their worn hands.

*****

Simon made his way south, enduring pelting ice storms to arrive frozen and weary at the village of Berkhamstead. Berkhamstead Castle, a short distance northwest of London, was the site of England's surrender following its conquest by King William. Shortly after the affair, the castle was bequeathed to Lord Robert and now served as principal residence of his son, Will.

Will's invitation resounded in Simon's ears, 'Come visit...Father won't be there...We'll have fun!'. *Fun* Simon doubted, though there were a few truths to be uncovered here. With luck, Will would know of Maura's condition and of their father's imminent plans. The sun was fat on the horizon, cloaked in thick pastel clouds. A whipping gale stole his breath as Simon approached the torch-lit gatehouse with a pounding heart and, despite the frigid weather, sweat trickling from his temples. He strove to consider the situation rationally and thought, what was there to fear? He need only ask at the gate who was in residence and act accordingly. If Robert was visiting, Simon would ride straight to Gloucester. If not, he had heard that Will cherished luxurious living, and at present he could use at bit of luxury.

Simon's announcement that he carried an important message from the King to Lord Robert was answered swiftly by the guards. Lord Robert was away. Robert's son, William, would gladly receive the news. A winning smile graced his lips as Simon boldly surged ahead under the curtain wall. A groom led E'dain to the stables and Simon hurried across the bailey, over the second moat, up the outdoor stairs and into the stone keep. He easily found the great hall and, astounded by its opulence, stood a moment in the doorway to gawk. As he descended the short flight of steps, his amazed eyes shifted from the silver-threaded tapestries lining the walls to the walled hearth, a luxury he'd rarely seen. His fingers stroked the fine linen cloth that draped the dais, which was lavishly adorned with gold candlesticks and silver utensils for the evening meal. Woven mats blanketed the wooden floor, with no hound's droppings, old bones, scraps, or food stains visible on their smooth surfaces. Simon spun to a clattering interruption. A young fair-haired woman, shocked by his unexpected presence, had dropped a silver tray stacked with loaves of bread. He rushed to help, and was barraged with sharp questions, "Who are you and what do you want? How did you get by the guards? If Sir William hears you've trespassed, he'll—"

His hand raised for silence, Simon laughingly responded, "I'm not here to steal the candlesticks. I've come to see my brother, Sir William."

The servant dropped her jaw, closed it again, then firmly stated, "Sir William has no brother."

"Oh, indeed he has," answered Simon, his brow arched as he set the last loaf on the pile.

The girl stuttered as he helped her rise. "Sir...Sir William is expected to return soon. He's hunting. Will you be joining him for supper?"

"I do hope so," Simon replied with impish grin. The servant blushed terribly, set the tray upon the dais, and scurried away, turning before the door to perform a short bow.

Simon snatched up a loaf of bread and, smiling to himself, ambled over to the hearth. He glanced up the smoky flue, and ran his fingers across its marble mantle. As far as he knew, the only example of this recent invention was installed in the King's residence at the White Tower in London. How had Will managed to procure one? Munching the bread, he wondered at the drastic difference between his father's stinginess and his brother's self-indulgence. Why, at Dunheved, Simon hadn't been allowed a bed till he was twelve years old, and had been worked as hard as the few servants that inhabited the castle. On his journeys he sojourned with friends, mostly peasants. The only lavishness he'd ever known was when he visited the King. He felt out-of-sorts in such surroundings and, at the jolting sound of the doors bursting open, a quiver of nervousness crept his spine.

Will, looking quite regal, swept into the hall, yelping hounds at his heels, expectant squires tripping behind. He didn't immediately notice Simon, for he glared at the floor and grumbled to himself as he strode for the fireplace. Doffing his gloves, he let them fly; next soared his cloak, the clothing expertly caught by his boys. Simon, amused by this show of mastery, leant against the mantle, crossed his arms, and waited. Finally, Will took in Simon's scuffed boots and raised startled eyes to exclaim, "Simon! God's breath, where have you come from?!"

"Yorkshire, actually," Simon beamed and offered his hand.

A firm hand clasp brightened their smiles and Will slapped Simon's back as he guided him to the dais. "Why, when I last saw you, Father's guards were hauling you away. Am I housing an escaped prisoner?" Will asked with a sly grin.

"No, nothing that exciting. Uncle William changed their minds."

"Oh yes. I must admit I'm quite jealous of your cozy relationship with our dear Uncle William." They sat, and a clap of Will's hands produced servants from every entrance, carrying trays heaped with roasted venison doused with heavy sauces and plump onions, roasted pears dusted with cinnamon, and tankards overflowing with wine. "I'm famished," announced Will. "And you look a bit lean. You'll join me?"

"Yes, please," answered Simon, his eyes bulging at the succulent feast.

They dipped their hands in a communal washing bowl and began their meal. Between gulps, Will asked, "So, have you been spying?"

Simon almost choked at the question and mumbled, "No...no. I've been on a mission for the King." He leant close to his brother and eagerly searched Will's expression. "Would you happen to know, I mean have you heard how Maura—"

"Not to worry." Will lowered his eyes and smiled, "She has recovered completely. Marc said it had something to do with your expert medical advice. You are quite a mystery, Brother."

Simon didn't hear his last words, for a rush of relief surged through his veins, bringing on a light-headedness that sent his head reeling. Will noticed and, concerned, touched his shoulder, asking, "Are you well?"

His eyes opened slowly as Simon answered with a smiling nod.

"You do look pale," said Will. "It's the weather, I expect. Have more wine, Brother. There's no need to fret, Father is far away."

Simon silently obeyed, and Will watched him curiously as he downed his cup of wine. There was so much he yearned to know of this stranger beside him. Firstly, why was he here? Will shifted to face Simon and, finding his warm, trusting voice, questioned, "A mission, you said? What sort of mission?"

"Father's gotten himself into a bit of a muddle. It seems he's drawn up two marriage contracts for Maura, one to a poor soldier in Yorkshire and one to Rufus. The Yorkshire contract is dated first, so the Rufus document will have to be annulled."

"Oh, dear," said Will. "Does Father know you've been digging up all his dirty secrets?"

"Then you know he's done this on purpose?"

"I only suppose. I don't know a damned thing about this dismal mess. Of one thing, though, I *am* certain. When he hears this dreadful news, and that you played a part in destroying his grand design, you'd best hide yourself away. He's already furious with you, Simon, he doesn't need more fuel to feed the flames."

"I'm not concerned about myself. He's caused a great number of people much grief and will answer to the King for his crimes."

"Enough of this gloomy business," said Will. "Eat up. When you're done I'll arrange a bath to be poured and clean clothes to be set out. In two days you will accompany me to Gloucester and together we'll break the news to cousin Rufus. I'm to represent Father at the celebrations and, unfortunately, Rufus has been chosen to preside over Christmas court. The King is in Normandy battling again, and the holiday promises to be quite dreary. Perhaps your little announcement may spark a bit of excitement."

With a yielding grin, Simon's interest returned to his food. And while Will munched, a plan began to worm its way into his ever-scheming mind—one that, if successful, might rid him of this slimy rival to his inheritance forever. As his plot ripened, he decided to try out a whim, and see what reaction it elicited. "Simon," he said softly.

Simon, his mouth full of meat, looked up in anticipation.

"Marc also let slip that Maura called endlessly for you when she was at her worst."

The thick bolus of meat stuck in his throat, as Simon strained, "Sh...she...did?"

"Yes. Quite a touching demonstration, so I hear. There will be ample opportunities to meet with her at Gloucester, and become reacquainted as it were. However, I believe I should be the one to give her the news concerning her upcoming marriage to?"

"Hugh of Ryedale."

"Yes. Then her time will be yours." Simon looked about to drool, and Will puffed with satisfaction. This was the exact reaction he expected to his lie. This was going to be such great fun.

Through the remainder of dinner, Simon listened numbly as Will gloated about his rich life, his possessions, his hunting prowess, and his many women; all the while he screamed orders at his slavish servants. And Simon dreamed of Maura, the thought of being with her again allowing him to endure anything, including Will's incessant prattle.

*****

Supper done, Simon found the bath wondrously soothing and the clothes gaudy, though comfortable. He returned to the great hall, damp and eager to learn more about— Maura. He stopped short of the door when his ear caught giggling voices, one clearly

Will's, the other a deep, sultry woman's laugh. The doors were ajar so he peeked into the gaily lit hall, and beheld Will sitting before the fire with the mystery woman in his lap. She nuzzled his neck, her whispers enticing from him guffaws and squirms. Simon rested up against the door frame, crossed his arms, and loudly cleared his throat. The interruption caused both to jerk in his direction, and unseated the Lady. She self-consciously smoothed her rumpled clothes and mussed hair. Will stood to perform the same, then muttered, "Simon...My, you do sneak about, don't you? Come, I want you to meet my lovely visitor."

Before advancing, Simon regarded the woman a moment. She was tall, slender, and remarkably attractive, with glowing olive skin and dark umber hair that hung in a thick shawl about her shoulders. Her golden gown sparkled her black eyes, which narrowed to study him as well. A graceful finger tapped her lower lip as she murmured, "Yes, do come. I'm dying to know you, you immensely handsome creature."

Simon leapt the two stairs and bounded forward. Will eyed the Lady with contempt and dully proclaimed as Simon graciously took her hand to kiss, "I am pleased to present our new step-mother, the Lady Almodis."

Simon promptly dropped Almodis' hand and lifted his gaping expression to hers, as Will wryly continued, "And my Lady, this is my half-brother Simon..."

"What!" Almodis shouted, her face stark with confusion. "Step-mother to him! How can that be?!"

Dumbfounded, Simon continued to stare, wondering how this beautiful, provocative woman could possibly be married to his archaic father.

Will smirked at their joint astonishment and suggested, "Why don't we all sit, and I'll explain. It's a lengthy tale, yet a fascinating one. Would you two care to listen?"

Almodis and Simon shared uneasy glances, and then nodded to Will. Almodis draped herself languidly across the chair before the fire. Simon pulled up a chair for himself and, once seated, crossed his arms and his outstretched legs, anticipating an entertaining performance.

Deep in thought, Will paced, patted his black curls, and smoothed his slim mustache. His almost iridescent eyes twinkled as he enthusiastically began, "Well, let us see...Father married my mother, Matilda, Roger of Montgomery's daughter, in 1050, when he was barely twenty years old. The next year, he left her in Normandy very pregnant with me, and traveled with his brother, then Duke William, to England. They met with King Edward to secure William's succession to the English throne. And it was at Edward's court that Robert met Edith, Simon's mother. She was a Saxon serving maid and, I believe, only fourteen at the time. Is that correct, Simon?" Simon nodded, and Will burbled on, "Robert chose Edith as a gift for my mother, and returned with her to Normandy. Mother gave birth to me and gave me three sisters in quick succession. She was constantly ill, so Edith took on the task of raising us. During this time my parents started their heated arguments that often ended in physical battles. My father's priest threatened to annul their marriage if their fighting didn't end. Instead of risking an annulment, they began to ignore each other. This is when Edith replaced my mother in my father's bed. Not that I minded," Will shrugged. "I always felt as if she were my *real* mother. Edith was harshly shunned by Robert's companions in Normandy, especially his brother Odo, and when she discovered she was pregnant with Simon, Robert sent her back to England to seek safety and comfort from her family. But, alas, they cast her out."

Simon shifted uncomfortably to Will's story; the truth was not so entertaining after all. Almodis appeared uninterested, and fixed her gaze on a dazzling bauble gracing her hand.

"Is my tale boring you, my Lady?" Will asked snidely, noticing her indifference.

"No, not at all," Almodis answered without looking up. "It's quite fascinating. Go on, go on."

"Well...Robert managed a few visits and sent money to Edith through King Edward's court. Of course, Father returned to England in 1066, and after the hubbub of the invasion ebbed, Edith brought Simon to live with Robert at Dunheved. I was packed away to Roger of Montgomery's household, and my sisters were pawned off to wealthy barons. Robert and Edith lived together blissfully for quite a long while. I've asked my father about this time in his life, and he told me because of the ties he had with the Montgomery family, he couldn't risk annulling his marriage to my mother."

"He didn't have the decency to annul his marriage and marry my mother!" interjected Simon, sliding to the edge of his seat.

Almodis dropped her hand and stared aghast at Simon. "He speaks! I was beginning to wonder."

"Now Simon, calm yourself. She was a Saxon and—"

"Is a Saxon!" he flared, standing.

"You must see that Robert had much to gain from the Conquest. He couldn't risk losing what was due him simply because of his choice of a wife."

"That's a foul excuse!" said Simon. "The King was—is fond of my mother. He would gladly have granted them permission to wed."

"What an absolutely sweet story," interrupted Almodis sarcastically. "Now tell me, where is this Edith woman now?"

"I have no idea," answered Will. "Simon?"

"Not to worry, my Lady, she's no threat to you," Simon answered with a slight sneer. "She left Robert four years past and is living quite happily on her own in Dunheved."

"If I remember correctly, Robert threw her out," added Will bluntly. "But no matter, she truly was a sweet woman, and I do miss her terribly."

Simon grew sullen and slumped back into his chair. Almodis broke the tepid silence. "Enough about this Saxon woman. Will, you haven't answered my original question. How does Robert have a son about whom I know nothing?"

"I'll answer your question, my Lady," replied Simon. "Robert blames me for Odo's imprisonment and disowned me four years back."

"That's not the only reason he hates you, Simon," reminded Will.

"I realize that, but it's all she needs to hear right now."

Almodis tried to lift the plunging mood of the conversation and brightly stated, "I feel very fortunate to have such witty and handsome step-sons. Simon, will you accompany us to Gloucester?"

"Yes, I have business there with Rufus."

"Marvelous. Then I suggest we leave tomorrow, at dawn?"

"The sooner the better," agreed Simon.

"I was to hunt tomorrow," whined Will.

"You'll have countless opportunities to chase your precious deer at Gloucester," stated Almodis. "And with Rufus at the helm, one never knows what to expect. But now..." She stood to stretch and proudly toss her lush tresses. "I'm to bed. It was wonderful to meet you, Simon, and I pray we will talk further." Simon rose and watched askance as Will kissed Almodis' hand and cast her a dark, inviting look. She grinned in response and glided from the hall to linger outside the door.

Will finished his wine while pondering how to set his ingenious plan in motion. Simon, still a bit irked, nonchalantly scrutinized one of the tapestries covering the wall.

"Father chose well, didn't he?" noted Will, setting his cup down and wiping his mouth.

"For you or for himself?" Simon asked distantly.

Will chuckled. "You're much too frank, Brother. I apologize for upsetting you about your mother."

"No need. I should have known you'd take Robert's side."

"Simon, I must speak to you about Maura."

Instantly Simon's interest in the cloth evaporated and he hastened to Will's side, eagerly asking, "What about Maura?"

"I've been thinking quite a lot about this marriage problem. Since I will be representing Father at Gloucester, I feel I should take charge of the valid marriage writ and—"

"No."

Will gaped at Simon's obstinacy and felt a twinge of nervousness flutter his belly. "Now, now, Simon, surely it will be safe with me and..."

"I am grateful for your generosity, Will, yet I barely know you. The writ will stay on my person till this matter is fully settled."

Not often was Will at a loss for words. He poured himself another cup of wine and sat with a huff, his glare fixed on the shrinking flames.

Simon sat beside him and gingerly raised the forever-nagging question. "Will, after my battle with Father four years past, when I returned to Dunheved, you were there. Do you remember?"

Not breaking his trance, Will muttered, "Oh yes."

"You told me then that Maura had left for Normandy to marry. Why did you lie?"

"That's what I'd been told. She was to wed one of Roger's sons. I have no idea why the marriage never took place."

Simon shifted closer and his voice trembled as he probed further, "Was she punished...after I'd gone? Did Robert hurt her?"

"Punished? No, not really. She received a bit of a tongue lashing, that's all. I expect she'll happily relate all the details to you when we arrive at Gloucester." He raised his icy eyes to Simon's expectant gaze and, with a wink and a leer, said, "Should be quite a fiery reunion...So you must get your rest. You look dreadfully exhausted."

Simon nodded and mumbling, "I thank you, again," left the great hall. Once settled in his ornate, feathered bed, he slipped into a stirring slumber, replete with ecstatic fantasies of his beloved Maura.

Will stayed awhile in the hall contemplating his dilemma—how to rid himself of Simon without resorting to the messy business of murder. His hard-headed brother wouldn't yield to mere threats. Someone must convince Simon that it would be best for all if he took himself off somewhere and simply disappeared. Yet, who could perform such a delicate feat? Will reflected back four years to the glorious destruction of Robert and Simon's too-close bond. Simon had risked all to return for Maura, and clearly still was besotted with the comely bitch. At Winchester, Will had discovered much, most importantly, Maura's intense loathing of Simon. Of course, he realized with a jolt of insight—Maura! She and only she had the persuasive power to banish Simon forever. It could be so simple, so rewarding. All he need do was encourage Simon's expectation of a passionate reunion with Maura, while simultaneously feeding Maura's hate for Simon. Then he would arrange an explosive confrontation between the two at Gloucester which would surely result in Simon's humiliation and retreat. After the smoke cleared, he'd offer Maura solace and understanding, and secure her trust and affection. What wondrous Christmas presents—Simon finally out from under foot, and Maura tucked up beside him in bed, offering her gratitude again and again. And if, perchance, his crafty plan failed, well, then he'd simply have to persuade Robert to do away with his vexing bastard once and for all.

*****

Almodis snuggled her damp, pliant body against Will's, and murmured, "What is it, my love? You seem preoccupied with something, or could it be someone else?"

Will sat up in bed, and rested back against plumped pillows. "I don't trust Simon."

"He seems harmless enough to me."

"Yes, he acts the great innocent. I sense, though, that he's a bit of a rogue and I'm wary of his motives. I believed he was gone for good, and then he magically appears, quickly to become a nuisance."

She straddled him and, settling her thighs on his, asked, "Have you ever considered that the two of you could become allies?"

"Never," said Will, firmly. "There's far too much at stake."

"Concerning your inheritance?"

"What else?"

"Why would Robert bequeath anything to a bastard son?"

"A *bastard* son rules this land, my Lady," Will reminded pointedly.

"But you said yourself that Robert despises Simon. That alone should quell your worries." Her sensuous kiss brushed across his brow and came to rest upon his lips, lingering there as her naked body pressed to his and her fingertips scratched at his back. With an alluring sigh, she coaxed, "Right now, we have more important matters to attend to. It may be difficult finding time alone together at Gloucester and I'll need vivid memories to pleasure me when I'm alone in bed."

Will easily surrendered to his lover, yet as his hands squeezed her hips and jerked her closer, he fretted aloud, "I believe he's plotting an incident—an incident to disrupt Christmas Court..."

*****

The next evening a frosty mist hung low on the road to Gloucester, and ice crystals clung to Simon's hood and shoulders as he squinted ahead, desperate for a sign of shelter. A mournful howl resonated through the dark and swirling mist. The wolves were hungry; hungry enough to risk an attack on a guarded entourage. On more than one occasion he had done battle with the vicious beasts, and was not eager to tangle with them again.

They would have been quartered hours ago, but for Will's irritating insistence that they ride on a few miles to Bampton. And now the blinding fog threatened to scatter them from their intended route. The quiet was eerie, foreboding—and then came the screams. Disoriented, Simon spun E'dain around and charged back through the murky shroud. The entourage parted for him as he frantically sought the source of trouble. Will was nowhere in sight. Two of his guards broke from their ranks and joined Simon on his hunt. They reached the rear of the line of travelers and sharply reined their horses. Before them, circling wolves stalked the Lady Almodis and her two servants. Simon blurted orders to the guards, "Break the circle, distract them, use your swords—"

"Simon!" Almodis cried out, her eyes wide with terror. "Please—" The snarling dogs started to her squall and instantly launched their attack at her horse. Two rushed the gelding's hind legs, and sank their razor teeth into his fetlocks. Another sprang at his neck, slavering and wriggling as it clamped its muzzle to the horse's mane and ripped its muscular flesh. Almodis whimpered at the sight of Simon's horse prancing between the dogs. E'dain's expert kicks and dodges frustrated the beasts' assaults, though failed to close the distance between Simon and Almodis. Almodis' maids, assisted by the guards, galloped away to safety. In her panic, the Lady began to dismount.

Simon yelled "No!" too late. One wolf, gnashing on a hind quarter, left his lean meal and leapt for Almodis. He caught her boot in his jaws, tore the leather, and punctured her skin. She clutched madly at the pommel, thrashing her leg and groaning in agony. E'dain lurched forward. Simon kicked out and jabbed at the beast with his dagger, landing blows and gouges that stunned, yet failed to break its clamping hold. Then to their combined horror, Almodis' horse sank to the ground. Simon swiped out and caught Almodis' cloak. He yanked and the garment ripped away in his hands. He stretched out again, fervently groping as the haze swallowed up her desperate figure. For an instant, her shoulder reappeared. He grasped her sleeve and felt the silk rip, then grabbed again. This time, his fingers circled her upper arm and, mightily, he yanked. Her screaming face broke through the mist as she flew upward, moaning and flailing, clutching anything within reach. He hoisted her across E'dain's neck and they bolted away, the sound of the wolves' lusty mastication echoing in their ears.

A full mile up the road, they met Will, seemingly unaffected by the jolting events. Simon helped Almodis sit and, after her bulging eyes discovered they were free of danger, she lashed out at Will, screeching, "You bleeding coward! Where were you?! I could have been killed!"

"But you weren't, were you?" answered Will casually. "Why should I risk life and limb, when Simon seemed overly willing to perform the task for me?"

Almodis lunged for Will, wildly pummeling the air, and screaming a mixture of curses that made her ladies blush. Simon glimpsed blood on her gnawed boot, and restrained her arms, calmly suggesting, "My Lady, you have an injury that needs tending to. You can continue your squabble later. Now we must find shelter." He didn't wait for the others, cantered ahead, and resumed his search through the thinning fog.

The mention of her wound brought on its pain and Almodis grew silent and weak. She hugged Simon's arm and nestled back against his chest as her shock lured her into a disturbing sleep. She woke a bit woozy, swathed with a blanket, and propped in a chair. Religious icons adorned the surrounding walls. Her questioning gaze met Simon's comforting one and he said, "If you're able to walk, my Lady, I want you to come to my chamber. I need to dress your wound."

"I'm sorry?" she asked. "You wish to do what?"

"Tend your wound. My supplies are in my chamber."

"Yes...of course. If you help me up, I'm sure I can manage on my own." After two uncertain steps, Almodis boldly surged ahead and, with each long stride, her strength and guile returned. Simon held the door open for her, and she shot him a beguiling look as she swept past and planted herself on one of two stools crowding the tiny cubicle. He avoided her flirting eyes, and set straight to work. Kneeling, he poured her a cup of wine to soothe her nerves, then added the rest of the wine to a bowl of water. He dipped a cloth in the mixture and wrung out the material while Almodis removed her boot and hose. She placed her wounded foot on the other stool, hiked her skirt high above her knee, and smoothed back her mussed hair. Simon glanced up and received an alluring grin, as she asked, "Will this do?"

"Fine," he shrugged, "as long as you don't catch a chill."

A surprised giggle escaped her, and she watched curiously as he bathed her ankle. The skin on his hands was tanned and smooth; his fingers were long and moved with a transfixing grace. The quiet bothered her, and she praised in a whisper, "You own such a gentle touch. You obviously have been schooled in medicine. Where?"

Simon stayed focused on his work as he answered, "In a small village called Myddfai in Wales. Myddfai has been training physicians for centuries, and I—"

"Fascinating," Almodis cut in and her dark eyes fell on his intense expression. "Robert makes such pretty babies. You resemble your brother, yet also are so different." Simon dipped a finger in a small porcelain jar and daubed an aromatic ointment on her ankle; its sting made her flinch. "What is that?" she asked.

"Only a mixture of lard and wine. It will help stave off infection." He fashioned a bandage round her ankle, and ripped the material to tie a knot. "No stitches needed. Is there pain?"

"No...Do you mind if we talk further?"

"It depends on what you wish to talk about. I'm rather tired."

His answers were perplexing, and she foundered for a neutral topic. "I haven't thanked you...for my life."

"Don't mistake heroism for self-protection, my Lady. When the dogs were done with you, they would have come for the rest of us."

She removed her foot from the stool. He sat, and she at last caught his eye with an engaging smile. "And you are too modest. Will says your kindness is an act, and that in fact, you're a bit of a scoundrel."

"Will barely knows me," said he.

"Well then it's up to me to discover the truth." She reached out and stroked his jaw; her trembling finger caressed his bottom lip as she murmured, "And to do that I must know you...better."

His mild expression never altered as he covered her hand with his and placed it back in her lap. "*I'm* finished here."

"*I'm* not." She moved nearer, placed her hands on his knees and, studying his enchanting face, wondered what she could possibly say to capture this elusive creature. The direct approach seemed best. "I must offer you something for my life. Would you, kind Sir, accept my body?"

Not overly surprised by the proposition, Simon closed his eyes while his mind searched for a response that would dissuade, but not offend. He stood, slipped from her hold and, with a tender look, answered, "The thought is tempting my Lady, though I would prefer a vow of friendship."

"Fr...friendship?" Almodis jabbered her astonishment, "Friends with a man? What an interesting notion. I've never attempted such a thing and don't know—"

"My Lady, I'm sure my brother awaits you and I'd like to get some rest. You've had a great shock and need sleep yourself to recover." He motioned toward the door. "And now, if you don't mind."

Stunned, Almodis rose stiffly and stammered, "No...of course not...I...I don't mind. I didn't mean to bother—"

"You were no bother, and I pray you're not too uncomfortable tonight."

Her questioning look returned, and Simon clarified, "I'm referring to your foot."

"Oh...with your expert care, I'm confident I'll be fine. Well, then." She paused at the door, and accepting her boot and hose, blurted, "I do thank you...and will consider your request, Simon. Sleep well."

"Sweet dreams, my Lady."

As Simon's door opened, a door three chambers down clicked shut. Almodis hesitated in the hallway, unsure of how to react to Simon's sweet insult, for she couldn't remember ever being rejected. Shaking her head, she added the incident to the countless baffling situations that plagued her life. The terrible sound and sight of the wolves once again invaded her thoughts. Her fingers rubbed her brow as she fought to block the horror and it was replaced with Simon's unusual appeal for friendship. As she limped away, she thought—to be friends with her husband's enemy might prove quite intriguing.

Simon unfolded the worn woolen blanket gracing his pallet and stretched out beneath it, wondering about Robert and Almodis' curious marriage, Will's disturbing behavior, and Almodis' misguided gratitude. The haunting sight of the Lady slipping into the mist briefly vexed his mind. A broad smile forced the image away and replaced it with a glorious vision of Maura, ecstatically awaiting his arrival at Gloucester.

*****

CHAPTER FIVE - AN ASPIRING HERO

"Will we never get there?" complained Maura as she glanced eagerly down the crooked, potted road to Gloucester. She shifted restively in the straw-padded cart and, beneath a lush pelt, snuggled nearer to Rose.

"Patience, angel. Alan says it's not far and we should arrive by midday. Maybe if you ride it will help pass the time."

Maura rubbed her backside and shook her head. "No, the last race was the worst. I doubt I'll ever ride again."

Rose chuckled at her feigned discomfort. "It's by your own doing. If you'd let the men win once in awhile—"

"Now why would I want to do that?" interjected Maura. "They're pompous enough as it is. It's good for them to be humbled now and then."

"And it's wonderful to see you so cheery," Rose said with a wistful grin. She searched Maura's pallor and winced as she noted, "Your bruises have faded, your arm needs only a sling, yet you still look tired. You shared little of your thoughts at Winchester. Would it be too bold of me to ask—"

"I've thought of very little, and I prefer it that way," interrupted Maura. "I need to stay busy, to become so exhausted that when I sleep, I don't...dream."

"Thank God for Marc," said Rose. "He cheers you so."

"And Alan. He calms me."

"Yes, and Alan. The King was generous to allow us his protection." Rose turned deeply serious, and pressed, "Maura, you can't keep your cares from me. I've often heard you in the night, pacing, and once or twice weeping. You haven't been dwelling on Si—"

"No."

Maura's terse response and dull expression sent shivers through Rose, and she silently prayed, *Please Lord, you can't let her remember. The horrors of her past combined with her present woes will surely drive her mad. Please, no added misery, not now.*

"Rose, did you hear me?"

Rose left her pious musings to attend to Maura's excitement. "What is it, angel?"

"Marc's spotted the battlements. Soon we'll see Uncle William!"

With Alan at its fore and Marc at its rear, the cart squeaked across the drawbridge and under the gatehouse of Gloucester Palace, the customary site of Christmas Court. Maura knelt, her elation obvious as she took in her illustrious and exuberant surroundings. Magnificent furs and silks draped the privileged visitors mingling in the bailey. Hounds and children pranced through drifting snow and raced round towering bonfires. Servants, squires, and grooms, their faces pinched and rouged by the crisp air, darted anxiously about, tending to their charges. Marc dismounted and Maura leapt from the cart, shouting, "Marc, come! I must see the great hall!"

She whisked away before he could answer. With a sharp wave, Rose urged, "Go, catch her before she finds trouble. Alan and I will tend to the trunks."

Marc tore off after Maura, and shouldered his way through the bustling crowd, straining to keep sight of his sister's copper braids as they disappeared behind the keep's wood and iron door. He pried the door wide and had vaulted three steps when he heard her waggish words at his back, "Marc, you dawdle so. Hurry!" She laughed, grabbed his arm, and dragged him, whining, up the tightly-wound staircase.

"Maura, stop! Let me catch my breath."

"You talk like an old man," said she. "I want to see the great hall!"

"And what's so different about this one?"

"Marc," she answered in exasperation. "It's Christmas Eve!" At the top of the stairs, she let go his hand and skipped ahead, calling back, "I'll meet you there."

Marc paused a moment to pant. The hallway was deserted and his smile betrayed deep affection as he watched Maura gambol away, her cloak billowing out behind her, and her hummed tune echoing along the slim passage. To Maura, patience was no virtue, especially at Yule time. The holidays never failed to transform her into a merry, bubbling child, quick to laugh, and highly possessive of her happiness. Perhaps here she would receive the ultimate Christmas gift—word of her betrothal's dissolution. Marc's holiday wish was simple and selfless, *Please God, ease her troubles for these few precious days. Give her the freedom and opportunity to find fun.* A flash of silver disturbed his prayer and he spied movement at the opposite end of the hallway. Guards, three, maybe four, emerged from what appeared to be the entrance to the great hall. Marc's steps quickened with his thudding heart as he chased after his sister, yelling, "Maura! Stop...wait!"

She spun to his loping figure and asked peevishly, "What is it now?"

A grim, coarse voice addressed her back. "My Lady..."

She whirled round and gasped up into Rufus' choleric complexion. Marc reached her side and, as he bowed, he tugged at her arm, hoping she'd do the same. But she stood as if paralyzed, jaw slack, eyes wide, pale as snow.

"My Lady," Rufus repeated with a sardonic grin, "I'm pleased to see you well, and I wonder why you do not bow to me? Is it my appearance that offends you? My manner? Perhaps it's my odor? Your brother knows his duty well, then there *always* was a problem teaching you yours." His guise was garish and revolting; golden locks hung in oily tendrils to his shoulders, secured in an effeminate fashion by a jeweled circlet. Layered furs ballooned Rufus' already stout body, and his murky-gray eyes matched his foul mood.

Maura attempted to speak, but only a strangled squeak escaped her parched throat. Flashes of their last meeting swirled madly before her eyes, reviving her pain and panic. She wavered and Marc helped her stand, while struggling to explain, "My good Prince, Maura still has not fully regained her strength. Please excuse her odd behavior. We've only just arrived and she requires food and rest."

"Then see she gets it!" roared Rufus.

"I will, my Lord, I will," Marc said, tipping his head.

As he tugged on his gloves, Rufus sniped, "You both will join me this evening in the great hall. Tonight's feast begins the Christmas festivities, and Maura is to sit at my side. I've been picked to rule while Father is abroad, and I trust there will be no problems with his decision." He smirked at Maura's distress, and declared, "I expect complete submission and respect from you, my Lady."

Marc yanked Maura up against the wall as Rufus barged ahead. She shook her head to clear the chaos, and hung on her brother's arm for support. They warily watched Rufus stride the length of the hall and, as he disappeared, both exhaled loud sighs of relief. Maura at last found her voice, "I...I can't let him near me, Marc!"

"Surely," returned Marc, "if you stay with a crowd and never allow yourself to be alone with him, he can't hurt you again. You must have known he'd be here!"

"I'd hoped he'd be still battling." Maura's voice strained and her clutch tightened to her confession, "Oh, Marc, no one frightens me the way he does."

"And I understand why, Maura, it's just that your terror encourages his cruelty."

"I don't know how else to act when he's near. Marc, what am I to do?"

They both snapped to hollering behind them. Rose and Alan stormed down the hall in their direction, Rose's harsh demeanor aimed at Maura. "What's gone on here?!"

Marc countered passively, "Maura wanted to see the great hall. You told me to follow her and...we...we—"

"Met up with Rufus on your way. Will you never learn, child?!" flared Rose, waggling her finger in Maura's face. "We fight to keep you safe and you refuse to cooperate! Now come. We've found our rooms. There's unpacking to do, and you must eat and rest."

Maura hadn't the strength to argue and resignedly followed. Gloom cloaked her mind, crushing her hopes for deliverance and threatening to ravage the holidays. It produced no tears; she had none left to weep.

Rose and Maura stood frowning in the doorway of the tiny chamber they would share, and watched the servants set their ponderous trunk at the foot of the skinny bed. Left alone, they roamed the room. Maura sat down hard to test the depth and softness of the mattress, then slipped off her boots and cloak and unraveled her veil. Rose checked the rushes for mouse droppings, and the washing bowl for mold, and noted with disgust, "The water's ice." There was no hearth, and nothing to drape or hang clothes upon. Maura finally located the chamber pot. Though rusted, it appeared clean. No garderobe had been built into the dense stone walls. Rose chafed dust from her hands and attested, "We've been spoiled living in Adela's chambers. This room will suit us fine. All it needs is a bit more light, thicker pelts, and clean air." She hiked her skirts, clambered stiffly up onto the bed and, reaching long, managed to push open a small shuttered window near the ceiling. A slim band of light filtered through and they both smiled at its cheering effect. "Come," Rose said, "help me down, angel. I have something special to show you."

Piqued, Maura obeyed, then trailed Rose to the trunk. The lid creaked open to reveal a stack of silk gowns, tailored in the most vivid colors, and woven with intricate embroidery, jewels, and swatches of fur. Maura's eyes bulged. "Where, Rose? Where did you find them?"

"One day while straightening, I came upon a box stuck under the vanity in Adela's chamber. You can imagine my surprise when I uncovered these treasures." She removed the frocks, spread them over the bed, and carefully smoothed their creases. "I can't imagine why Adela left them behind."

"They were most likely her castoffs," guessed Maura.

"They'll fit you perfectly."

"And who am I to impress with these?" The silk slid from her fingertips and Maura's hopeful expression sank to glum. "Certainly not Rufus."

"Sit child, and listen well." Maura accepted Rose's offered hand, settled by her side and heard, "Christmas Court is for the young with its feasting, dancing, and yes, flirting. You must endure Rufus' presence, but you'll never be left alone with him, and I foresee many a handsome young man tripping over himself to spend one precious moment with you—the most fair and witty lady attending the celebrations."

"Oh, Rose," said Maura, gathering her in a quick smothering hug. "I love you for your optimism and appreciate your compliments, yet I don't see how—"

Rose interrupted Maura's doubt to remind, "We have no time for despair. I'll send for food, wine, and warm water. After washing, you'll rest. You must be fresh for tonight."

As Rose opened the door to leave, Maura called after, "Rose."

"Yes, angel?"

"Rufus announced that he rules while the King is abroad."

"William still battles the King of France," Rose confirmed.

"If Rufus rules, no one can deny him anything. Rose, he terrifies me!"

Rose's heart ached to Maura's wan expression, and she tenderly assured, "Not to worry, angel. Alan always guards your chamber. Neither he nor Marc will allow anyone to harm you." The door shut quietly and, as Maura wandered over to light four tapers set atop a towering candelabra, she considered Rose's comment. A comforting thought indeed, still, she wasn't entirely convinced of her safety.

*****

"Maura...Maura, wake up child. It's late."

Maura opened her eyes to Rose's dark visage and the odd surroundings. Fuddled, she sat upright. "Where are we, Rose?"

"At Gloucester. You must rise and dress. Marc will arrive shortly to escort us to the hall."

Maura hesitantly left the warmth of plush pelts and hugged herself against the frigid air.

"You must remove your chemise," said Rose.

Disbelief twisted Maura's expression; she fidgeted and shuddered. "I'll catch my death!"

"No, the hall will surely be toasty warm, and the chemise will show under the gown. We can't have that."

"Certainly *not*," Maura replied glibly through chattering teeth. "Rose, what's come over you? I don't remember you ever being this fretful over fashion."

"I insist that everything be perfect for this very special occasion."

Maura wriggled from her chemise and flung it to the rushes. Rose commented, "Your body has filled out nicely since your illness."

Maura cast her a leery look. "Rose, I do believe *you* are the ill one." She reached out a trembling hand. "Now, please...the gown."

"I've chosen the red one. A most fitting hue for Christmas Eve, don't you agree?"

"Yes, it's fine, fine. Hurry!" Maura snatched up the frock and hopped into its shimmery folds. Rose laced the back, cinching a bit too snugly and Maura squeaked, "Remember, I do need to breathe." She smoothed the sleeves, and glanced down the bodice plunging steeply between her breasts. "Pick another, Rose," demanded Maura as she whirled away and decided, "I won't wear this gown, not this night, not ever!"

"Oh yes you will!" Rose returned as adamantly. "It's quite lovely and flatters your curves—"

"Flatters! It does far more than that. I won't—"

"You will wear it and that's final."

"I'll feel naked!" Maura whined, tugging the bodice higher.

Rose slapped her hands away, and snapped, "Leave it! Now help me find your hose."

Maura mouthed retorts as she trailed Rose to the trunk, and began rooting furiously through mounds of garments. "Well," Maura conceded, "if I'm to wear this slip of a dress, you'll wear something other than that black shroud. There may be a lonely, stately looking, older gentleman present, desperate for female companionship, and you wouldn't want to miss *your* chance...would you, Rose?"

"Maura, you truly are horrible," huffed Rose as she hurried to answer a knock.

"No I'm not, I'm serious," countered Maura.

"Marc," greeted Rose. "Perhaps you can tame your sister."

"What's wrong?" asked Marc.

"She's being..." Rose whispered her final word, "*difficult*."

"I heard you, Rose." Maura spun toward the door, spilling a handful of clothes.

Her winsome vision dropped Marc's jaw; he sucked a breath and sputtered, "Ma...Maura...you look absolutely beautiful!"

The crimson frock clung like skin to her arms and bodice, flaring slightly at her hips; bands of ermine trimmed the neckline and cuffs, circled low round her waist, and dangled in a twisted cord to the floor. Maura self-consciously crumpled a handful of skirt, and blurted, "Why, thank you, Marc...Rose chose the dress. And you look wondrously handsome. Where did you find your splendid clothes?"

Rose rejoined the stocking hunt, and Marc sat upon the bed to watch and wait. He glanced up and divulged, "Will stopped me in the hallway, took me to his room, and gifted me with these and two other sets as well." Maura scrutinized him a long, wistful moment; his moss green tunic topped an ivory silk shirt, russet braies, and hose, the latter banded with black ribbons from ankle to knee. His expectant expression betrayed the innocence of a young boy, yet his height lorded over hers, and the width of his shoulders proved his maturity.

"That's rather curious," said Maura, breaking from her study. "Will's never shown interest in you before."

"Maura, move!" groused Rose. "You're making a terrible mess!"

"Gladly," she returned and settled by Marc.

"I think Will rather enjoys acting our Liege Lord," said Marc. "He said my Knighthood Ceremony will take place the fourth day of Christmas."

"Oh, Marc!" Maura gushed, clutching his hands. "Have I told you how immensely proud I am of you?"

"Too many times," he blushed. "Now we must go or we'll be late."

"I can't go barefoot—" Her slippers and linen hose suddenly flew into her lap. "Thank you, Rose," she blurted as she donned them quickly, then stood to follow her brother.

"Maura, wait!" Rose called out, "Your hair!" Wielding a wooden comb, she brusquely untangled Maura's tresses, sweeping the thick waves back so not to conceal her bodice. "There...you're as close to perfect as God will allow."

Maura worried, "My veil and my sling!"

"You'll wear no veil this night, my angel. Nothing will hide your charms." Rose gripped her hand and urged her from the room, falling in step behind Marc, and adding, "And the physician informed me that the sling comes off for Christmas. A day early should make no difference."

Maura and Marc paused awestruck in the doorway to the great hall. "Marc," she exclaimed, "isn't it magnificent?" Her bright eyes danced delightedly about the immense room, taking in the resplendent holiday decorations. Holly and ivy entwined the rafters and dangled from the dais and trestle tables, fat candles marking the hours till Christmas graced the dais, and an enormous yule log flamed in the central fire pit where it would blaze the full twelve days of Christmas. Maura's eyes lit upon the throne and clouded with dread; she grew silent and pensive.

"Maura, look!" Marc exclaimed, striving to distract. He pointed upward to a gallery crowded with chairs and instruments. "There's to be music!" Maura didn't seem to hear. After seating themselves at one corner of the dais, she continued to eye the throne warily and Marc decided, "You'll stay here by us till Rufus arrives."

"Where's Alan?" she vaguely asked.

"He didn't feel it was proper for him to attend."

"Not proper?" Maura replied, perplexed. "Now why would he feel something as silly as that? I must speak to him later."

"Maura," said Marc, "I've been considering your question."

"What question was that, Marc?"

"'What am I to do—about Rufus?'" he answered. Maura nodded to the memory, while Marc talked on, "And I've figured that if you act submissive to Rufus, and always agree with him, he'll have no cause to harm you."

"I suppose that depends on what I agree *to*."

"Maura," stressed Marc. "I mean what I say."

"I know you do. I don't believe he needs a cause to hurt me."

"He won't risk hurting you in a crowd," said Marc. "And you won't ever be left alone with him. I know it will be difficult, but if you're pleasant to him, you may survive Christmas court unscathed."

"What you suggest is far too simple, Marc, besides, how can anyone willingly be pleasant to Rufus?" Maura hushed to his frown, realizing with guilt how seriously he must have contemplated her dilemma. She smiled gently, and seized his hand, lauding, "What would I do without your brilliant mind to guide me? I will strive to do your bidding."

Marc beamed, and pressed her palm in return.

"Rose." Maura reached past Marc, tapped Rose's shoulder, and winked. "The feast is the ideal spot for Marc to choose his lady for the competitions! Don't you agree?"

"I do indeed!" Rose buoyantly agreed. They laughed at his flush of embarrassment and, teasing and chortling, the three launched into a jesting scrutiny of each arriving guest.

Will and Almodis, seated at the opposite end of the dais, hurled malignant glares at each other and grumbled discontent. "Who are you ogling now?" sneered Almodis, digging her knife in the linen cloth.

"Whom do you think?" replied Will.

She narrowly followed his stare and shifted irately as her search ended. "That red-headed bitch! She's only a child."

"Look again, my Lady," he commented with a lewd air. "Definitely not a child."

"Do you desire her?"

"Perhaps. And the haunting specter of wedded life with Rufus should make her overly ripe for my plucking."

Suddenly the woman's identity became apparent to Almodis. "She's Maura!"

"How astute you are, *Mother*. Do you suggest I begin my seduction now or later?"

Almodis' lips curled to a snarl. "If you lay one finger on that prissy little witch, I'll—"

Will spun and spat, "Silence, woman! What can you do to me?! Never forget that I see and hear all. Last evening, you shared a rather intimate moment with my brother in his chamber. Father would love to hear the torrid details of *that* encounter, don't you think? He can be quite nasty when angered. If you don't believe me, ask Maura. I'm sure she still bears the scars from when she displeased him." He stood and Almodis flinched slightly to his barely suppressed rage. "I will do as I please with whom I please and, at the moment, it does not please me to be with you!" With that, he left her seething.

Uneven wooden stairs hugged the wall of the great hall, led to the gallery, and climbed still higher to a dozen or so bedchambers which would house the less significant guests. Simon had claimed himself a cramped cubicle, deposited his saddlebag on its rock-hard bed, and ventured out to the balcony to spy on the jubilant crowd below. His keen eye swept the dais and quickly spotted Maura, Marc and—Rose, the ever-vigilant crow. The offensive notion of joining the festivities fluttered his belly. The majority of the folk present detested him, the food was notoriously poor, and he couldn't abide the drivel that passed for conversation. He wanted only to speak to Maura, and to do so he would have to leave the sanctuary of the balcony. As he haltingly descended the steps, Simon nervously fidgeted with the skirt of his bland tunic, then raked his fingers through his pale locks. The sincere and loving words he'd memorized evaporated and his heart throbbed painfully. He reached the gallery and what he glimpsed below made him pause. Splinters dug into his palms as he gripped taut the railing, and watched, with suspicion, Will stride with resolute grace across the room to Maura.

Rose, Marc and Maura respectfully stood to Will's advance. He donned a dashing smile as he first addressed Marc, "I've no doubt, Marc, that before this evening's done, you'll be pursued by a flock of ravishing maidens. The clothes suit you." His smooth gaze slipped to Rose. "Rose...Father and I are indebted to you for the sacrifices you have made, especially over the last month, to serve our family and protect and nurse...Maura." He stole Maura's hand, gently drew her closer, and murmured, "I've never seen you more beautiful." Their eyes met; the brown flecks that flawed the crystalline blue of his pupils disturbed Maura, and she turned away.

A peculiar response, thought Will, and he worried, "What is it, Maura? Are you not well?"

"I'm quite fine, my Lord."

"No, none of that formality tonight," said Will, weaving his fingers through hers. "After all, we are practically related. Please, you'll call me Will." He searched her vague expression for any hint of adversity. Spying none, he smiled and asked politely, "Would you care to sit by me at supper?"

"I'm to sit by Rufus."

"He won't be arriving for at least an hour. Please, share your delightful company till then. It's so lonely at my end of the dais."

"As you wish," she lightly replied as he led her away.

Marc and Rose stared stunned at one another, then broke into huge grins as Marc remarked, "That was quick!"

Simon watched, with rising distrust, Will guide Maura to a chair, scoot his seat too close, and boldly wind his arm round her shoulders. It seemed an awfully cozy way to disclose the contents of the Ryedale marriage writ. Intimidation spoiled his resolve, and he decided that when he met with Maura, it was best they met alone. Disheartened, he heaved a dejected sigh and trudged up the many stairs leading to his chamber.

To Will, Maura appeared apprehensive and distant. He tried to warm her with humor. "Maura," he said, turning her face to his, "Rufus has declared that he loathes his nickname. He claims it's juvenile and demeaning, and now demands to be called William. Such an unusual name, don't you think?" A faint smile stirred her lips. "That's far better," he praised, covering her hand with his. "I'm so pleased to see you well again. Father and I were quite worried."

The candlelight's reflection glittering on his burgundy tunic and his deep lilting voice mingled to ease her shyness, yet his eyes still disturbed her. Tongue-tied, she struggled for a polite response, and blurted, "I...I appreciate your concern...uhm...Will, there was a woman sitting with you at this table." Maura made a rapid scan of the hall, then pointed. "There she is, standing by the yule log, speaking to Lord Roger. Do you know her?"

"Her? Oh yes," he answered frostily. "Regrettably, I do know her. She is Father's new wife, the Lady Almodis. An unpleasant, disagreeable woman. Can't imagine why he married her."

"She's very beautiful," remarked Maura.

"Actually, their union had a great deal to do with land grants," said Will.

Maura jerked her attention back to the throne. Then she shifted to Will, her complexion a shade paler to ask, "Are you quite certain Rufus will be late?"

"I spoke to him a short while ago. He hunted too long, drank too much, and needed a nap. Trust me, Maura, it will be at least an hour before he arrives. You needn't fret." Will noticed blatant fright haunting her eyes. Though no one had ever confessed to the crime, Will reckoned Rufus had perpetrated Maura's battering at Winchester. He wondered if now might be the ideal moment to reveal the miraculous news of her betrothal's annulment. No, better to keep her tension high, for tension makes a woman so malleable. Yes, there was bound to be a better—The sight of a slumped figure ascending the stairs stalled his plotting. Simon! Why of course, now was the perfect time to issue his warning. "Maura, I feel I must caution you that Simon has arrived and—" Her drastic reaction made him pause. Her skin grew icy beneath his grasp, her hand clenched to a fist, and the expression she adopted was not one of fond remembrance. Will continued cautiously, "He sojourned at Berkhamstead on his journey here, and badgered me incessantly about you. He aims to confront you, Maura, and seems overly determined. I tried to put him off, but he won't be dissuaded."

Her pulse raced and tongue tripped, "I...I won't see him, I won't!"

"I can keep Simon from you," Will valiantly pledged.

Maura's warmth gradually returned, still she quizzed skeptically, "And how do you propose to do that?"

"Keeping Simon away will be simple," he gloated. "He won't risk a scene at a gathering such as this. There are too many visitors about who would love to see him hacked to pieces, including yourself, I dare say. And some are eager to perform the deed before an audience. I propose to keep you so busy, he won't get a single opportunity to harass you, and perhaps I can scheme a way to get him thrown from the castle. Rufus despises Simon. I can keep Rufus from you as well."

"Will," Maura scoffed, "don't promise miracles."

"I admit, Rufus is a slightly more difficult, though not an impossible challenge. Rufus and I have a special attachment—"

"I've heard of Rufus' *special attachments*," Maura remarked with a dubious eye.

Will burst a sharp guffaw. "Oh no, my Lady! Nothing as perverse as that. You may know, Rufus adores primping. I admit he looks the buffoon, though I do procure for him the finest cloth, leather for his pointy shoes, jewels, furs, perfumes. For my bother, he rewards me handsomely with gifts and hears my advice. All I need tell him is that while at Gloucester, I am to act your Liege Lord, and will dictate your actions at Christmas Court."

"Dictate my actions!" retorted Maura, snatching back her hand.

"It's a ruse...nothing more!" Will bristled at her unexpected gall and looked away, unsure his exhaustive efforts were worth the trouble. He turned back, softened his voice and expression, and added a wounded tone to his speech. "I sense you don't believe me. I don't have to help you, though, I've always craved the opportunity to be closer to you and if I can offer you assistance while we—"

"I didn't say I wouldn't accept your help," she cut in. "I'm wary of outrageous promises. My meetings with Rufus always end in disaster. It's difficult to imagine—" Maura glanced up and noticed a familiar face entering the hall. Beaming, she leapt up and waved furiously.

Will followed her happy gaze, rose as well, and asked, "Who is it?"

"Adela!" Maura exclaimed. "It's Adela!"

"Well, with the pampered countess' arrival, the excitement should increase three-fold. Shall we go greet her?" He matched Maura's dazzling smile, grasped her hand, and laughed as he trailed her tug across the hall.

At sight of Maura, Adela let go of her husband Stephen's arm, and squealed, "Maura! My dear Maura!" They rushed to embrace, and Adela broke their tight hug to gripe, "I was sick to hear of your betrothal, Maura. No one should be forced to stand within ten feet of that smelly fiend, let alone marry him! When I see Father, I will tell him exactly what I think of this atrocity—" To the shake of Will's head, Adela stopped her jabbering and atoned, "I'm terribly sorry. I won't speak of the beast again. Maura, you look simply stunning! There's no one else I'd rather have wear my gowns. Do you remember Stephen?"

"Yes, indeed. It's wonderful to see you again, Stephen."

"And you, my Lady," replied Stephen, executing a deep bow.

"And I'm sure you remember Will," said Maura.

"Dearest cousin Adela," greeted Will. He planted a kiss on both her cheeks, rested his hand atop her bulging belly, and winked. "And I see you've been up to mischief again."

"I'm so happy for you, Adela!" gushed Maura. "When's the babe due?"

"Sometime in March."

"And how's young William?"

"Growing far too quickly. Soon he'll be the height of his father."

Will drifted away to speak with Stephen, and Maura pleaded to Adela, "Won't you come sit with us?"

"I won't sit anywhere near Rufus," asserted Adela.

"No, by Will and me. Will assured me that Rufus won't arrive for awhile."

As Adela contemplated Maura's invitation, her fingers twisted the tip of her blond plait, her lips smirked and gray eyes twinkled. "And what goes on between you and Will?"

"Not a thing," dismissed Maura with a blush. "He's asked me to dine with him, and that's all. *Please* come."

"I'd love to, and I must get off these swollen feet." She glanced to the men and barked, "Stephen, Will come. We'll sit with Maura."

The men promptly obeyed and, as Will had predicted, within the hour Rufus lumbered in, drunk and disgusting. Will escorted an unsteady Maura to the center of the dais, and pulled out for her the chair flanking the Prince's. Before she sat, she recalled Marc's advice and bowed humbly to her betrothed, receiving in response a haughty grin.

"Rufus," said Will. "You wouldn't mind if I sit by Maura, would you?"

"I thought I told you to call me William," shot back Rufus.

"That's far too confusing. Would Cousin be acceptable?"

"I suppose," said Rufus. "*She* will call me William."

"I don't doubt she will," said Will.

Rufus dug his fingers into Maura's shoulder and squeezed; her nails bit the arms of her chair as the lurid sensation of squirming maggots tickled her skin.

"You'll stand with me, my Lady," Rufus commanded. Maura promptly obeyed and the congregation followed suit, with the lone exception of Adela. Instead of proffering her brother respect, she poured and loudly gulped a full cup of claret. Her resounding belch echoed throughout the hall. Rufus ignored her snub and spoke with a disruptive stammer, "Be...before we dine, I...I feel a prayer for Fa...Father's continued victory is fit...ting." A deafening moment of silence ensued. Maura glanced sideways at Rufus and saw sweat streaming down his temples; his breath was audible, his face ruddy, his hands quaking, whether from anger or embarrassment she couldn't fathom. She attended to her clenched hands, and offered a prayer not for the King, but for the strength to survive the meal and after.

Rufus rarely wasted time on prayer and, leaning close to Maura, grasped a handful of her hair to slur, "Af...after supper, you will join me in my chamber. There are matters that need discussing."

Maura wavered to his repugnant touch and stench. She gripped the table top and silently screamed her desperate entreaty, *Please Lord, spare me his anger*!

Will overheard Rufus' invitation and clearly saw Maura's revulsion. An excellent opportunity to appear the hero, he resolved and, once the prayer ended, he said, "Rufus, Maura will not join you anywhere—*alone*."

"What are you saying?!" Rufus exclaimed. "We are grown and she's no...no innocent. I...I rule while Father's away. If I say she'll come to my chamber, she will do so!"

Will hiked his reply a notch higher. "While at Gloucester, I am her Liege Lord. She won't be left alone with you and that is final! If you wish to meet with her, I will chaperone the event." Maura gaped at Will, astonished at his gall. She squeezed tight her eyes and anxiously awaited Rufus' retaliation. Instead a plate of noxious food was dropped before her. Rufus turned sullen and attacked his food with vulgar mastication. Her appetite promptly vanished, and Maura shifted a tentative gaze between her tormentor and rescuer. She sensed Will's scrutiny, and then felt his breath. "Drink the claret," he ordered in a tense whisper. She sipped and his hand covered hers, tipping the cup to dispense more. "No, the whole of it—quickly." With great difficulty, she gulped and gagged the contents of her cup, which Will immediately refilled. "Again—it will bolster your courage."

"No!" she protested, pushing the cup away. "It won't help! Nothing will! I must go before I do or say something to rile him."

"If you leave, you leave alone, and he will follow. I suggest you stay and attempt a resolution. Now, drink." Maura did as told, though, instead of making her bolder, the claret only intensified her alarm. The tenuous situation was deteriorating rapidly and Will intervened. "Maura, take my seat and let me speak awhile to Rufus. Perhaps I can encourage him to leave." After exchanging chairs, Maura's consternation instantly began to fade, and her hope for a pleasant evening surged anew.

"Cousin," said Will cordially, "it's been ages since we've chatted."

"Not that long," Rufus mumbled between slurps.

"We've yet to have a substantial discussion at Gloucester. Tell me, how was the slaughter?"

Rufus drooled a bit from his hung jaw, then wiped his lips on his sleeve and replied, "Do you mean Normandy?"

"Of course. And how many heads did you lop off?"

"None...It was all very boring. Except for one interesting incident..." Rufus paused and regarded Will with an indistinct leer.

"Well, don't torture me! Tell me what incident?"

"I was summoned to Uncle Odo's prison cell, which, by the way, is far grander than my apartments at Westminster."

"Odo doesn't care for suffering," said Will. "And what enlightening advice did he have for you?"

"No advice, a deal."

"A deal?" Will's eyes sparkled with anticipation; he wriggled forward in his chair and pressed eagerly, "What sort of deal?"

"My brother Curthose was with him." Rufus ripped a handful of bread and sopped it in his beef's blood. "They offered me a great deal of money to join their cause."

"To sabotage your father's battle plans in Normandy—" As Normandy dropped off his tongue, Will realized he'd spoken carelessly, and struggled to remedy his faux pas. "I...I meant to say, I've heard rumors that Curthose is plotting to harry your father."

Rufus puffed out more portly, and snidely demanded, "What else have you heard?"

"Not...not a lot..." Will fought to regain his composure, inhaled a calming breath, then continued steadily, "Father informs me of the news from Normandy. As you know, I rarely visit the continent."

"I know nothing about Curthose's harrying. I made inquiries while there and discovered my dear brother and uncle are reaching out to all the eldest sons of my father's staunchest barons. It seems some are impatient for their inheritances and are scheming a rebellion to speed matters along. You wouldn't be considering anything as foolish as that, would you, Cousin?"

"Rufus," Will sighed, wagging his head slowly and donning an expression of pristine innocence, "my allegiance is with King William, with my doting father, and with you. If I were planning to subvert, I'd never make the horrendous mistake of following such feckless idiots as Odo and Curthose. I swear they excel at failing."

"You'd best be telling me the truth, Cousin. And what naughtiness have you been up to while I was away battling? Sniffing around my intended's heels?"

"This is the first we've met since Martinmas. I'm to see to her safety and comfort here at Gloucester, and that is all. And why badger her? She's played her role well, showed you respect. There's absolutely no cause to hound her."

"I don't give a damn about her," harped Rufus. "I don't want to be here."

"Unless, of course," taunted Will, "*you* were wearing the crown." Rufus eyed Will with contempt, then dug into his meal once again while Will continued to tease dangerously. "Perhaps you should try it on. That should draw a rousing response from all present, though your sister may attempt murder."

"Enough, Will," growled Rufus.

"If you don't want to be here," Will emphasized with disgust, "go back to your chamber." He squirmed to Rufus' lack of manners, and quipped, "After your meal, that is." Then he tempted in an alluring whisper, "I've a present for you. A squire from my father's household, sixteen years old and very willing...to please. I'm certain you'd much prefer his company to this morbid group."

Rufus arched a piqued brow and said, "I'll finish here, make my excuses, then meet you in my chamber. Bring the boy."

"Agreed!" beamed Will. A huge sigh of satisfaction escaped him as he heartily launched into his meal.

Maura ignored the men's bantering and instead focused her attention on the merry crowd. She noticed Rose chattering with Adela's chambermaid; they had once been quite close. Marc was carousing with his fellow squires, and their table extolled frivolity and cheer. The abrupt sound of Rufus' throne scraping the planked floor broke her concentration, and again trepidation raced her veins. He stood and, in a majestic though wavering gesture, raised his arms high to proclaim carefully, "I'll take my leave now. I encourage everyone to stay, for there will be music, dancing, and of course, more claret. After Mass on the morrow, anyone who wishes to hunt may join my party. I wish all a good night, and God's grace." He stumbled from the throne, then straggled away to disappear behind the King's bedchamber door.

Maura turned an incredulous face on Will and sputtered, "How...why did he...what did you say to him?"

"I can't explain. I must leave for only a short while. Will you wait for me?"

"Yes," she smiled and quickly assured, "I swear I won't budge."

Will touched her cheek, then darted off. Rose appeared directly and asked, "What's happened, angel?"

"I don't exactly know. Somehow, Will got Rufus to leave."

"Did Will leave as well?"

"Yes, but he promised to return shortly."

"How wonderful! Now you can relax and truly enjoy yourself. I'm to bed."

"Don't go, Rose," pleaded Maura, suddenly feeling anxious.

"You don't need an old woman hovering near, not when coupled with such a handsome gentleman. Goodnight, angel. Wake me when you retire, I'll want to hear all." Rose squeezed Maura's hand, kissed her cheek, and then departed. Maura watched her pause beside Marc, and whisper something. Marc and Maura's glances mingled and he flashed her a brilliant smile. She waved back hesitantly, a knot of tension still paining her belly.

Will plopped himself into the throne and, beaming victoriously, patted the chair next to his. Maura readily deposited herself at his side and, for the first time that evening, grasped his hand. "Thank you," she burbled. "Oh, thank you, Will! I don't know how you managed to get him to leave so easily. Perhaps you'll share your secret with me?"

His hands gently cupped hers, and he answered in an impassioned murmur, "That's not the only secret I wish to share with you, my sweet Lady. What I desire, above all, is to enjoy a good bit of your company during Christmas court."

Her grateful gaze searched Will's face for sincerity; it betrayed no deceit. He'd proved himself well this night and had promised much. His looks were appealing, and if he could perform miracles and keep from her the two men she most despised, well then—her acceptance presently flowed from her lips, "I would love to spend Christmas Court with you, Will."

The evening sped by too swiftly and, along with the wine, Maura copiously drank in the mirth of her companions. She laughed hysterically at Adela's rude comments and

Stephen's bawdy anecdotes. And as she twirled, dipped and pranced with Will to the sprightly music, she felt a certain affection simmering for this seemingly flawless man with deeply disturbing eyes.

*****

Simon tossed in a light sleep. A loud knock on his chamber door woke him fully. He scrambled up from his bed, lit a candle, and cautiously cracked opened the door. What he beheld made him promptly shut it and press his body against the wood to hold it closed. The pounding intensified and was accompanied by a shrill whine, "Simon! Open the door! I've searched everywhere for you. *Please!*"

"No," Simon curtly replied.

"Open the door, or I'll tell Father. He's sent me to find you."

Simon's intuition to keep a safe distance from his unwanted guest wrestled with the worry that he mustn't refuse a message from the King. Worry won out, and he left the door, which immediately burst open to reveal the King's youngest, wildly carefree son, Henry. Perturbed, Simon sagged back onto the bed as Henry strutted up before him. Henry's tall slim stature, black fringed hair, and sculptured beard gave him an air of maturity which in truth he sorely lacked. His large brown reproving eyes glared as he scolded, "That was rude, Simon. I've come a long way with a Royal plea for help and you shut me out—"

"Henry," Simon interjected morosely, "why bother me?"

"Your language talents are needed."

"Pardon?" mumbled Simon, rubbing his sleepy eyes.

"There's to be a conciliatory meeting with the Prince of South Wales just west of here on the border. You do speak Welsh, don't you?"

"Yes...you know I do."

Henry continued his mocking interrogation, "And you do know the Prince personally, don't you?"

"Yes...we have met."

"Well then, we need you for translations."

"No," Simon firmly returned. "Find someone else."

"Simon, you're making me angry. There's no one else we trust."

Simon raised livid eyes and snarled, "I won't go on any mission with you, Henry, anywhere, or for any reason, for the remainder of my life."

"You can't still be mad about our last mission—"

"I am still *very* mad."

Henry perched uncertainly on the edge of the bed, and his sniveling intensified, "It wasn't entirely my fault. The Sheriff was grumpy to begin with, and how was I to know that his wife wouldn't appreciate my humor? Besides, we spent only one night in his prison."

"Henry please don't waste my time or yours with simpering excuses. I want you to go away."

"Simon..." Henry pulled himself erect, cocked his chin, and stated defiantly, "Father has issued me orders. I'm to render from Prince Rhys his lease payment and discuss ways of forging a lasting peace between our warring countries. He specifically said you were to accompany me and, as you well know, Father does not care for arguments."

Simon rose, scratched an irritating itch beneath the neck of his shirt, and muttered sourly, "I have something very important to see to here. When that's done, I'll consider joining you."

"What could be more important than Father's orders?"

"I need to speak to someone."

"Who?"

Simon hesitated answering, then mumbled under his breath, "Maura."

"Who?"

"Maura!" he shouted.

"Maura..." Henry's face pinched in deep thought as he struggled to recall the owner of the name. His face relaxed in a playful grin as he recalled, "Oh yes...Maura. A bit homely, skinny, far too tall, terrible freckle problem, and—" Henry cupped his hands at his chest and finished with a coarse laugh, "nothing of substance."

Simon flashed a scornful glare and pointed rigidly at the door.

"My, aren't we testy," commented Henry as he lounged on the bed. "I was only jesting, Simon. I'm dying to know...has she filled out at all?"

Simon couldn't help but grin at Henry's ridiculous expression.

"I take that to mean yes," said Henry, "and I'm certainly relieved, for if she does marry my brother, her nights are sure to be mighty lonely, and she'll be wanting a skilled companion to see to her nee—"

Simon's grin tensed to a grimace as he silenced the Prince with a sharp pinch to his ear. Henry howled and listened bug-eyed to Simon's hissed threat, "If you ever touch Maura, I swear I'll rip—"

"Simon, stop!" Henry squeaked, "I won't ever...I promise. Now let go!" Simon roughly shoved his cousin from the bed and received Henry's petulant comment, "You're taking the protective older brother act a bit far, aren't you?"

"I'm not her brother," Simon returned with a sneer.

"Well, Maura will just have to wait for your meeting. You're to accompany me. It will take only three days—one to get there, one to talk, and one to return."

"I want to see Marc's ceremony."

"That's no problem. I've asked and he's to be knighted the fourth day after Christmas. Maura's bound to attend and the three of you can have a grand family reunion." Henry was suddenly struck by a rare moment of solemnity. "Simon, jesting aside, I do need you."

Simon didn't want to agree, yet how could he ignore the King's orders? The young man before him was wise, impetuous, highly idealistic, and desperately in need of guidance, especially in regard to diplomatic matters. Henry looked upon Simon, six years his senior, not only as his cousin, but also as his closest confidant and mentor. Simon felt a somewhat misplaced obligation to watch over Henry and succumbed with a weary sigh, "I'll go."

Unable to contain his elation, Henry clasped Simon's shoulders and jabbered, "You...you won't regret this Simon! We'll have such fun, and—"

"That's where you're wrong, Henry," said Simon, squirming from his cousin's hold. "We won't have fun. We'll get the task done and return here. I must speak to Maura!"

"Yes, yes, of course you do. Now, I suppose we'll have to share this dreadful room. You don't mind the floor, do you?"

"No, I don't mind the floor, yet I do prefer the bed," Simon answered mundanely.

This time Henry's croak was joined by a surly pout. "I can't sleep on the floor! If you make me sleep on the floor, I'll tell Father and—"

"Then I'll just have to tell Uncle William what you whispered in the ear of the wife of the Sheriff of Richmond."

Henry looked aghast and blurted, "You wouldn't dare!"

Simon simpered in response and stretched out on the bed, warning, "You'd best get settled. I'm blowing out the candle."

"Wait a moment, Cousin. I don't even have a blanket!"

"Here." Simon tossed his coverlet over Henry's head. "Now hush!"

Henry shifted furiously in the stale rushes. His curses and disgruntled moans finally eased and he lay still. A few suspenseful moments passed, then a small, angelic voice emanated from the floor, "Goodnight, Simon."

Simon smiled a tight smile, shook his head in exasperation, and snuffed the candle.

*****

"You'd best leave me here." Maura stopped Will at the end of the hall leading to her chamber. "Alan, my guard, sleeps before my door, and I don't want to wake him. Again, I thank you, Will."

He lifted her hand and kissed her palm. His lips lingered and then he murmured, "It was entirely my pleasure, my sweetest Lady. And what adventures will we undertake on Christmas day?"

"I really don't know—"

"Riding!" spouted Will. "We'll go riding. I'll sneak away from Rufus' hunting party and return for you, say...mid-morning?"

"Oh yes," she heartily agreed, "that will be marvelous."

"Then it's settled," said Will. "I trust you'll sleep soundly and safely—"

Maura boldly touched her lips to his and pulled back to check his response. With a charmed nod and curious grin, Will left her. And as he ambled dreamily to his chamber, enticing thoughts tingled his senses and fed his conceit. There would be no challenge here. Very soon she'd invite him into her bed, and there she would continue to unveil her enchanting capricious moods, for in his women, he relished the element of surprise.

Maura stepped carefully over Alan, but nonetheless roused him with a stray nudge. "I'm sorry, Alan, I didn't mean—"

"No problem, Mau...ra," he yawned. "You shouldn't walk the halls alone."

"I wasn't alone." She crouched to his level, and asked with disappointment, "Why didn't you join us at the feast? I missed you."

"It is not fitting for me to mix with nobles. I was there, my Lady, you just didn't see me."

"Well then, I'll arrange for most of our meals to be served in our chamber, so you may share the joy of Christmas with us."

Alan smiled shyly. Maura rested her hand on his arm and said in earnest, "Alan, I have a favor to ask of you."

"Yes, my Lady."

"After the holidays, I'd like you to escort Rose to Dunheved. Sir William tells me that her sons have been quartered there. It's been ages since she's seen them."

"And what of *your* safety?" asked Alan. "Will you accompany her?"

"No. Sir William has invited me to stay at Berkhamstead till my wedding and I am considering it. I would need no extra protection there. Are you able to spare the time—"

He interrupted with a yielding gesture and assured, "I'll gladly escort her."

"I'm so grateful, Alan. Nothing would please her more. Are you comfortable here?"

"Yes, very."

"Then, I'll say goodnight."

"Goodnight, Maura."

The chamber was achingly cold. Maura slipped from her gown and into her woolen chemise, then crept between the pelts and settled quietly in a comfortable position. Rose shifted to face her and eagerly asked, "Was he sweet to you?"

"Very."

"Keep him close. He will help you forget Rufus."

"I'm sure he will try." Rose's stark features began to sharpen in the darkness, and Maura asked faintly, "Rose?"

"Yes, angel?"

"Did you love your husband when you wed?"

"Such a strange question. Love? Oh no, my child, I didn't even know him. In time, we came to love each other deeply. He was a brave and gentle man and I was fortunate to have been his wife."

"Was he killed fighting with the King's army at Hastings?"

"Oh no," said Rose. "Don't you remember, Maura? He died protecting your father."

"Protecting my father?" she echoed and pushed up on her elbow, her bewildered expression intensified by the shadows.

Rose shivered from the memory and somberly related, "When your family was attacked by the Welsh, Lord Robert rode with a battalion of soldiers to your rescue. He returned to Dunheved with the terrible news of the deaths of my husband and your father, and delivered two tiny orphans, you and Marc. He very wisely put me in charge of your care, which helped to ease my pain. You were a curious one, full of fury and spite. You didn't utter a word for an entire year, and then spoke only in broken French. And your horrific nightmares! I believe the same dreams haunt you still."

"I'm so sorry about your husband, Rose."

"Oh angel, there's no reason to feel sorrow for me. He died sixteen years ago. I do still miss him though."

Maura's fingers laced through Rose's, and she sputtered, "I wish I—"

"What...what is it you wish, Maura?"

"Being with Adela tonight, I suddenly realized that everything she owned is now mine, her clothes, her jewels, yet—why can't I have her happiness?" Maura exhaled a woeful sigh and despaired, "Rose, what horrible sin have I committed to deserve Rufus? I pray for guidance, but get no answers. It doesn't matter to me how I live, or where, or with whom. All I wish for is to marry a man who will be kind to me."

"Come to me, angel." Maura snuggled closer, rested her cheek on Rose's shoulder, and heard her soothing words. "We have survived much together and will survive Rufus as well. Now you must sleep and dream of Will...Christmas promises to be quite a festive day."

*****

CHAPTER SIX – THE GAMES BEGIN

The bleak gray of dawn peeked through arrow loopholes and windows as Simon and Henry nimbly descended the stairway to the great hall, and sidled between the snoring bodies of late revelers. Simon wrapped his scarf round his neck, shuddered at the thought of once again braving the bone chilling elements, and muttered, "Henry, on our journey and while meeting with the Prince, I expect you to try to speak English."

"Why ever for?" grumbled Henry. "I sound so low born when I speak that heathen tongue."

"For a number of reasons, actually. The Prince understands English and will appreciate your thoughtfulness, also you need the practice. It's a funny thing, but a King's subjects usually prefer their monarch to speak their language. It works wonders for his image."

"You really believe I'll be King one day?"

"Of course. After all, consider your competition."

With a winning smile, Henry nodded, tugged on his gloves, and pulled open the huge doors of the hall for Simon. Once in the passageway, Henry rewarded his cousin for his compliment with an exuberant pat on the face. Simon shoved him away, scolding, "Don't, that's irritating."

"I know it is," smirked Henry, and then he added, "I'm hungry."

"We'll stop for food along the way—"

"Simon! Simon, wait!" Henry and Simon paused to the strident command, and spun to see Will jogging in their direction. He reached them and panted, "Where? Where are you going?"

"And I'm pleased to see you too, Cousin Will," remarked Henry snidely.

"I've received the King's orders, Will," said Simon. "I'm needed for translations on the border."

"You must...must meet with Maura! She's expecting to see you today...and will be most disappointed if—"

"Did you discover all this last evening?" asked Simon, his voice thick with distrust.

Will stood quiet, looking rather dumb as he fumbled for a plausible lie.

"I do hope," Simon continued, "that during your cozy evening together you remembered to mention the Yorkshire writ."

"I...I intended to," gibbered Will, "then Adela arrived and well, she proceeded to steal Maura's company, and Adela doesn't take to interruptions kindly."

With a loud grunt of exasperation, Simon turned from his brother and trailed Henry toward the exit. Will scrambled to keep pace, and stammered, "Simon, I think it would be best if...if you leave the writ with me. To keep it safe."

Simon whirled, glowered fiercely, and spat, "I will turn over the writ only after I've heard from Maura that you've told her all!"

"Then when will you meet with her?!" flared Will at his uncooperative sibling.

"Your posturing last night makes me wonder why you're so eager for us to meet."

"Simon, stop dawdling," spouted Henry from the top of the staircase. "We must leave if we're to make your strict schedule."

Once again, Will donned a cloying look and spilled mock concern, "I know how close you two once were. This may be your last opportunity to meet alone before her wedding. I only mean to help."

"Simon!" Henry shouted as he started down the steps.

"I must go," Simon yelled hastily over his shoulder. "Tell Maura I'll meet with her directly after Marc's ceremony. Then and only then will you receive the writ."

Will smiled brightly after his brother and cousin and trumpeted, "Good luck and have a swift and safe journey!" Then as Simon's head disappeared down the stairs, his smile skewed to a snarl and he muttered, "You slimy bastards."

As they cantered across the scarcely awake bailey, Henry looked to Simon and asked, "What was all that nonsense about?"

Simon shrugged and slowed E'dain before Henry's long line of guards. "I really don't know, and the wondering is beginning to drive me mad."

*****

The frigid wind whipped back Will's hood, exposing his head and face to stinging, spitting snow. He watched sourly as Maura's steed vanished over the swell of the hill, and his ire flared. Chasing after Maura was rather like a hunt, though it lacked the excitement and delightful assurance of snaring his prey once the fun ended. He was cold, weary of her pranks, and grossly humiliated by her superior horsemanship. Yet this was all part of the game, wasn't it? Only Maura wasn't exactly playing fair. His thoughts wandered briefly to Almodis. There were no games with her. In matters of physical intimacy, Almodis was blissfully straightforward and accommodating. Then again, he was tiring of her possessiveness and jealousy, and age was making her body sag. It was definitely time to stalk out new meat and, as he licked the ice from his mustache, he desperately hoped a tumble with Maura would be worth all this wretched discomfort.

At Will's whining insistence, they returned to the castle at dusk. In the stable, he dismounted shakily while Maura stood by, offering assistance and sympathy. "I'm sorry, Will. I made you ride too long."

"No," winced Will. "It's only an old injury that flares up occasionally. When shall I collect you for the feast?"

"Will," Maura said softly as she wove her arm round his, "I'd like to sup in my chamber this evening. Would you come for me when the feast's done?"

"Why would you want to—"

"I want to spend some private time with Rose, Marc, and my guard."

"Your what?" Will asked with an astonished gape.

"My guard, Alan. We've become quite friendly and he seems lonely."

"Should I view this 'guard' as competition?"

"No. He's very kind and has no family near—"

"Say no more." Will interjected with affectionate sarcasm, "If you want to while away your precious time with some lug of a sentry, then I'll have to settle on a shorter evening, though one that promises to be just as pleasing as last night. Later, my sweet Lady." Will's kiss was brief, warm, stirring, and then he was gone.

Maura, all aglow, dashed back to her chamber and thrust open the door to Rose's radiant smile and enthusiastic deduction, "My, my, what that man does for you! I've never seen you this flushed!"

"It's not only Will, Rose. The wind pinked my cheeks and you know how I love to ride." Maura tossed away her cloak, veil and gloves, and yanked off her boots as she continued with a smirk, "And what mischief have you been up to? Scheming a scandalous rendezvous between me and Will?"

"A tempting idea, but no. I've been trying to decide between the rose, the blue, and the green gowns."

"For yourself or for me?"

"Maura...help me!"

Maura glanced at the frocks decorating the bed, and muttered, "The blue one is nice." Suddenly serious, she took Rose's hands and said, "Rose, I have something to tell you."

Anticipating dreadful news, Rose sank to the bed, and her voice trembled slightly as she asked, "Will this upset me?"

"Oh, no!" beamed Maura. "Quite the contrary, I hope. How would you like to visit your sons?"

"My sons!" Rose exclaimed as she sprang to her feet. "Are they here?"

"No, but they're not far away. Will told me of their return from Normandy. They are being quartered at Dunheved, and I've arranged for Alan to escort you there whenever you wish."

"Oh, angel!" cried Rose. She covered Maura's laughing face with huge sloppy kisses, and spun her furiously about the room. "This is the most wonderful gift I've ever received! I thank you and love you, my angel."

"And I love you."

"Will you come with me?" asked Rose.

Maura averted her eyes and mumbled uncertainly, "I'm considering staying at Berkhamstead till my wedding."

Rose's mouth dropped open. "With Will?"

Maura hesitated a moment, then nodded. "It seems he will also be there."

"This has happened so quickly," said Rose concernedly. "Are you certain that's what—"

"Rose," Maura interrupted and grasped her tighter, "at this moment, I'm certain of nothing."

"Promise me you won't make any rash decisions," begged Rose.

"I promise." A tender, quiet moment passed, then Maura sniffed and asked, "So when will you leave? Not soon, I hope."

"Not till I'm sure you're safely settled. Maura, I have something for you as well."

"What is it?!" she burbled, squirming with the expectation of a child. "Please show me."

Rose lifted a small box from the lid of the trunk, passed it to Maura, and watched amused as she ripped off its top. Maura stared at the contents for a long while, then said with a confused expression, "Rose, I don't understand." Two plain silver bands graced the box. She removed the smaller ring, slipped it on her finger, and held it up to glitter in the muted candlelight. "Isn't this your wedding band? And this," she said as she caressed the larger ring, "was your husband's."

"At Mass this morning, I asked of God a simple wish. That he allow you the opportunity to love again. And when that time comes, as surely it will, use these bands as a symbol of your love." Rose smiled sadly, "Besides, my knuckles are swollen. The ring no longer fits."

Maura wiped her tears with her sleeve, and tenderly kissed Rose's damp cheeks. "I will cherish them forever. And whomever I choose to wear this ring," she said, squeezing the man's band in her palm, "will truly be worthy of such an honor."

"Aren't we a pathetic sight, weeping on Christmas!" laughed Rose. "I'll fetch Marc and send for supper. You set out his new clothing, then cover them with pelts. I can't wait to see his face!"

"Nor can I," returned Maura excitedly. "I congratulate you, Rose. What a brilliant idea it was to have his ceremonial suit sewn all in silk. He'll make the most magnificent knight ever!"

"Yes, I'm certain he will. I'll send Alan in to help. It was very sweet of you to include him in our plans, angel."

Slightly embarrassed, Maura lowered her eyes, and muttered, "I feel he's part of our family."

"Now make haste! I'll return soon."

Alone, Maura examined the rings carefully, returned them neatly to the box, and plunged it deep within the trunk for safe keeping. As she closed the lid, she thought of Will, and a sense of foreboding crowded her mind.

*****

The meal done, Marc offered gracious thanks and rushed off to join his friends in a game of dice. Alan returned to his vigil outside the chamber door, and Maura hurriedly donned the dark blue gown, simply decorated with gold embroidery bordering its yoke and sleeves. She twirled once, allowing the skirt to billow high, then cling round her legs, and cheerily announced, "Oh, I do like this one! It has a sheen to it and I won't feel I'm popping out of the bodice."

"And it matches your eyes," noted Rose. "I believe it's the loveliest one of all." She fastened a sheer linen coif to Maura's head with a slim golden circlet. At the sound of a brusque knock, Maura began furiously preening her hair and fussing with her gown, while Rose just as excitedly hastened to the door. A quick gasp escaped her as she beheld Will, a vision in black, leaning casually against the door frame. His warm, inviting smile quivered her belly, and his silken words, "My sweet Madam, may I enter?" flustered her so that for a moment she couldn't speak.

Maura gently urged Rose from the door, and answered for her with a radiant smile, "Of course you may."

Will swaggered in and paused a moment to scrutinize Maura's striking appearance. His admiring gaze narrowed as he gestured for her to turn and, scratching his chin, he uttered a satisfied, "Perfect."

Rose broke their dreamy gawking with a clap of her hands. "You two must go, the evening's almost done."

"Oh no, Madam, it's only beginning," replied Will. "Yet before we leave I have a gift for Maura."

"You shouldn't—" Maura gulped her unconvincing words and gushed instead, "What, what is it?"

From a pocket inside his tunic, Will produced a gold necklace studded with sapphires, and remarked, "A small token from Father and me."

Maura and Rose joined in a chorus of aahhs; Rose approached to examine the jewels more closely, and breathed, "It's gorgeous—"

"And far too generous!" finished Maura.

"You, my Lady, deserve this and so much more," charmed Will. "Now, let me fasten it for you."

Maura spun and lifted her hair. Will deftly manipulated the latch, then with a playful grin, he let the gold slip from his grasp. The weighty necklace plunged down the front of Maura's gown and she slapped the bodice to halt its descent. Gently squeezing Maura's shoulders, Will murmured loudly enough for Rose to hear, "Will you fetch it or shall I?"

Rose covered her mouth and shook with silent laughter. Maura colored scarlet, swiftly retrieved the gift, and turned to Will, her voice calm and alluring, "Will you try again?"

Will's second attempt successful, the couple happily clasped hands and scampered away to the great hall. To Maura's added delight, Rufus had been injured while hunting and would not attend the festivities. As she sat at Will's side enjoying the servants' theatrical production of The Nativity, she felt her body warm and skin tingle with a curious contentment. Except for her one unsettling encounter with Rufus, Christmas Court was proving to be exceedingly glorious. There had been no sign of Simon, not a single nightmare, and she couldn't recall ever seeing Rose this bubbly. Maura delicately fingered the exquisite sapphires and sighed as Will's fingers sensually covered hers.

It was early morning when the two left the dispersing crowd in the great hall to return to Maura's chamber. They stumbled over snoring bodies and dodged roaming hounds. Upon reaching the entrance to Maura's hallway, Will abruptly stopped, plopped down into the rushes, and patted the space beside him. Maura cast him a befuddled look which he eased by answering, "It's quiet here. I want to talk."

"Will, we've talked the whole evening. If I don't return soon, Rose will worry."

"She'll worry if you arrive *too* soon." He reached up with a pleading look. "Come, sit by me?"

Maura bunched her skirts, settled by his side, and asked, "What shall we talk about?"

"You've yet to confess any of your past to me." Even in the shadowed darkness, he noticed her pale, and quickly clarified his request. "Tell me of your time at Winchester."

"I'm afraid that would be rather dull."

"Dull? On the contrary, my Lady. I remember attending a number of feasts at Winchester when Queen Matilda was alive. How old were you then? Eighteen? You had scores of pretty boys nipping at your heels. I wish my life were so dull. Did any of them catch you?"

"No," answered Maura, hugging her knees, "at least, not for long. Lord Robert's first priority has always been securing Odo's release from prison and, after depositing me at Winchester, he promptly forgot about me. Martinmas was the first occasion in three years where I'd seen the King and Lord Robert together. And that, as you know, was a disaster. Before then, I last remember seeing you at the Queen's funeral. And how have you filled your time over the years? You never married?"

"No." Will shifted closer to Maura and smiled contentedly; how he loved the sound of his own voice. "Father never bothered to arrange a match for me, and I'm too lazy to take on the task myself. I endured the grueling process of knighthood and must admit I excelled at the job. I trained under Grandfather Roger, as did Marc." He snorted a laugh and went on, "Then one day in the midst of a particularly gruesome battle, I asked myself, 'what am I doing here?' I toyed very briefly with the idea of joining in the ravaging of Wales, only—why bother soiling my hands? I'm much more suited to being Liege Lord, and I have countless spoils provided by Father which I oversee. I rule Berkhamstead and share a fair rapport with my peasants. As long as they pay taxes and provide me services, their free time is their own."

"What is Berkhamstead like?" asked Maura, warming to Will's enchanting face and voice.

"You've never visited?"

She shook her head, then rested her cheek on her knees.

"Oh yes, you were raised at that hell hole in Cornwall."

"Dunheved wasn't so terrible," argued Maura. "Lord Robert worked us hard and we received little in return. Though there were times that I thoroughly enjoyed living in that moldy mass of stones."

"It's grotesque, decrepit, and cold! Now I've personally seen to the decor at Berkhamstead. My palace is spacious, lavishly furnished, and replete with the newest comforts." He reached out, twirled a lock of her hair, and asked wishfully, "Have you decided whether to return there with me?"

His simpering and suave gesture flustered her. Awkwardly, she stood, swatted rushes from her skirt, and sputtered, "No...No, I haven't."

"Don't tarry long, my Lady," he said, scrambling to his feet. "At any time you may turn and I'll be gone."

"Will," Maura answered resolutely, "I won't agree to go till I'm fully comfortable with the idea."

"And how can I see to your full comfort?" he smoothly cajoled.

"You've been doing a marvelous job thus far, but I won't be pressured."

Will lifted his hands in surrender and assured, "Never will I be guilty of coercion. It's contrary to my nature." He took her hand and they meandered toward her door, halting a few feet from Alan's snoring hulk. "So," noted Will, "here lies your kind and valiant guard."

"It's very late, Will. I can't expect him to stay awake forever on my behalf. Besides, I hope I don't need protection from you—" Suddenly she was swept up in Will's taut clutch, his warm lips crushed to hers. She stiffened, then, softening, hungrily returned his kiss. Her arms wrapped his back, her fingers slipping between folds of silk groping for a firm hold. As swiftly as he'd seized her, he eased his grip and gracefully strode away, turning once to cast a beguiling smile and blow a tempting kiss.

*****

A shaft of wavering light filtered through the tiny opening above the bed, creating dancing shadows on the door. Muted voices sifted in from the bailey to disrupt Maura's frustrated attempt at sleep. She sat with an irate sigh and jerked the pelts close under her chin. Rose's gravely snore, always so soothing before, now maddened her as warring emotions rattled her weary, still alert mind. She despised confusion and loathed tricks, and her times with Will reeked of both. Still, his lure was indeed weakening her; his lips were sweet, his touch tempting, and his voice tantalizing. Peace—what she mostly needed in the little time left till her marriage was peace. And what peace would she possibly find locked in the arms of this vexing, though immensely appealing braggart?

An abrupt thud on the door jarred the shadows and startled Maura up to sitting. She clung to the bed curtains and listened beyond her hammering heart to rattling and gruff bickering voices.

The disturbance woke Rose. In a panicked stupor, she flailed through the blackness, crying out, "Maura! Maura, are you here? What's happened?"

"No, Rose, don't speak." Maura climbed across the bed and gently restrained her arms. "There's a scuffle outside our door. I will go—"

"No! You can't, it's dangerous—"

"I'll only listen at the door." Maura gingerly slipped off the bed, crept to the door, and tentatively rested her ear against its coarse wood.

"What do you hear?" demanded Rose.

Maura snatched up her robe draped across the trunk. Rose's trepidation swelled at Maura's actions and, shoving the pelts aside, she left the bed to insist, "No, you won't go out there! Let Alan deal—"

"Rose." Maura's steely, frigid fingers squeezed her shoulders as she argued, "It's Rufus. He demands to speak to me and won't leave till he gets his wish. I won't have Alan hurt. I *will* speak to Rufus."

"If you intend to risk death," Rose whispered angrily, yanking Maura back to the side of the bed, "then take this." Rose reached beneath her pillow, extracted something shiny, and slapped the cold handle of a dagger into Maura's palm.

Unaware of its existence, Maura stared aghast at the weapon, then swiftly lodged it up the tight sleeve of her robe. She broke from Rose's desperate hug with the hushed warning, "Don't leave this room," and flung wide the door. Alan's broad back blocked her view of the scuffle, though not its dialogue.

"You'll move from that door or I'll skewer you with your own sword!" threatened Rufus, his voice sliding between a whine and growl.

"The Lady is sleeping, my Lord," Alan stoically returned. "If you wish to speak with her, you may return in the morning."

"Alan," said Maura to his back, "I will speak to Rufus."

"Get back in your room!" Alan mumbled harshly.

"How dare you curse at me under your breath, you son of a dunghill!" flared Rufus.

Maura ducked under Alan's arm and boldly presented herself to her betrothed. His disheveled, sinister bearing terrified her, and once more her appeasing words stuck fast in her throat. Alan's hand clamped her shoulder and shook her from her frozen state. With great difficulty, she stammered, "I'm...I'm here, my...my gracious Lord. What is it you desire?"

"I hurt myself," Rufus blubbered, his face blotched, puffy, and pinched with distress, "and no one cares. Everyone has deserted me! It is *your* duty to nurse me." He staggered forward, grasped and tugged at her sleeve, sniveling, "Why do I constantly have to remind you of your duty to me? Why do you torment me so? Why?" One overly brusque tug dislodged the dagger and dropped it heavily into the rushes. Rufus' distress instantly vanished. His expression wrenched with rage as he lifted the dagger and shoved its razor edge beneath Maura's nose. "And who were you planning to stick this in?"

Alan pleaded to Rose at his back, "Rose, go fetch Will. Hurry!" She scurried from behind Alan and raced madly down the passageway.

The fleeting movement ruffled Rufus. "Where...where is she going?"

Maura cautiously eased the dagger from her face and answered, "I have no idea, my Lord."

"Tell me!" blared the Prince. "What plans did you have for this knife?!"

"I...I heard a scuffle and was frightened. I felt I needed protection—"

"Protection! You lying bitch. You knew it was me, you wanted to hurt me, perhaps even kill me!" He raised a knotted fist to strike. Alan lunged forward, knocked Maura to the floor, and unsheathed his sword. Rufus' powerful blow drubbed Alan's brow, stunning him long enough for Rufus to wield the dagger for a second strike.

Screaming, "No!" Maura flew up from the floor and threw herself between the men. She stretched high to halt Rufus' plunging arm, but instead her frantic grasp met the blade. A sharp cry escaped her as the knife neatly sliced her palm. Convinced her next move would determine their fates, she fell to her knees, grabbed Rufus' free hand, and rested her cheek upon his knuckles. Her breathless whisper begged, "Forgive me and my guard, my Lord. By your father's orders, he protects me. I knew nothing of your injury till your arrival here. And now I freely submit to you, my sweet Prince, and will return with you to your chamber to nurse your wounds. I beg you, my Lord, please, *please*, spare us your anger!"

A harrowing stillness followed Maura's plea, then Rufus stepped back, jerked his hand from her hold, and shook it once, sneering with disgust, "You're bleeding on me."

Alan reached for Maura, then the shout, "Rufus!" rang shrilly along the hallway, and startled them from their scare. Will sprinted to Maura's side and carefully eased her to her feet. As he guided her into Rose's comforting arms, he spotted the blood soaking her sleeve and yelled, "What have you done to her?!"

Rufus flinched to Will's fierce tirade and muttered brokenly, "I did...did nothing. She...she's hurt herself."

"You bumbling beast!" flashed Will. "I warned you to let her be. When Father hears of this, he'll—"

"You lied to me," countered Rufus. "You said you'd hunt and then you snuck away to be with her! I...I had good reason to be angry."

"That is our disagreement, Cousin, not hers! Now get yourself back to your chamber."

"Maura promised she'd return with me, to nurse me."

"I'll nurse you, you lumbering idiot!" Will sharply thumped Rufus' shoulder.

Maura watched with dizzy fascination Rufus cow to the attack and cry out a childish groan.

Will turned to her gape and asked tenderly, "Will you be all right?"

"Yes. It's nothing, just a scratch."

Will next looked to Alan, a deep red bruise already staining his brow, and shook his head in exasperation. "You both are foolishly brave. He could easily have murdered the two of you using no weapons whatsoever. Never challenge him again! You," he addressed Alan, "see to your bruise and the Lady's injury and guard her from the inside of her door for the remainder of the night. I'm grateful for your sacrifice." He bowed slightly, and spun back to Rufus, berating, "Why are you still here? Off with you!"

Rufus resisted and sputtered half-heartedly, "She said she'd come. I...I want her in my room!"

Will cuffed him forcefully down the hall and muttered, "And once there, what would you do with her? You'll have to settle for her company at the tournament tomorrow. I'm ashamed and disgusted with..."

Their figures and voices dwindled and Alan, though still bleary, hustled the women inside the chamber, mumbling his concern, "I'll see to your wound, Maura."

"It's nothing, Alan." Maura in turn examined his bruise. "This needs a cool cloth."

Before she could get away, he stilled her arm and spread her palm. "It's a bit deep, though clean. Rose, have you a linen cloth?"

"Yes, in the trunk."

"Binding should staunch the blood," said Alan.

"You seem quite adept at healing," noted Maura.

"When you guard this marauding family, a knowledge of quick patching is mandatory."

"I thank you for taking my blow."

"I admit, this is the first instance I've known Rufus' wrath. And I swear, as long as I am in your service, my Lady, it won't occur again."

"And I believe you," replied Maura, with sober respect.

"Would you have?" Rose asked abruptly while aiding Maura's bandaging.

"Would I have what?" Maura asked in return.

"Gone with Rufus?"

"If it would have discouraged further violence, then yes, I would have gone."

"Thank Heaven for Will, and, of course, you as well, Alan," Rose injected, and added with eerie finality, "Take care, angel, or you may not live to see your wedding day."

*****

Next morning when Mass was done, Will and Maura hastened through ankle deep snow across the bailey to the elevated platform especially constructed for the Royal Family to view the melee. A glaring sun threatened to transform the bailey into an enormous bog and the balmy weather freed them of their weighty cloaks, but not their concerns. Will looked with distaste at Maura's dull, unbleached tunic and said vehemently, "Swear...swear you will never agree to be alone with Rufus again!"

"Will," answered Maura with equal force, "I am to wed the man! Do you intend to lie between us in our bed?"

He hesitated a moment to admire the sway of her hips as she scaled the stairs, and considered confessing the details of the writ. No, a bit more tension, teasing, and molding were needed—and then she'd surely yield to his every demand.

Maura reached the top step and spun to ask, "Are you coming, or not?"

Rufus, slumped in an ornate chair centering the front row of seats, refused to acknowledge the couple. Instead, he wrinkled his face into a surly scowl and muttered curses to himself. Maura approached cautiously, slipped silently into the seat flanking his, and gripped the arm rail opposite. In response, Rufus shot forward in his chair and plopped his crossed arms on the railing, and his chin onto his scratchy, wool sleeve.

Adela's ebullient voice resounded from the top of the stairs, "Maura! Maura, don't soil yourself with his stench. Come, sit by me."

Maura turned to the invitation and shook her head. "I don't think that's wise, Adela."

Without a twitch, Rufus roared, "She stays by me!"

Adela strutted to Rufus' side. Her taut veil accentuated the puffiness of her features and gave her a comical air as she griped, "Oh Rufus, you are such a bore!"

"Don't call me that, you bloated bitch!"

"Call you what? 'Rufus' or 'bore'? I can think of quite a few choice slurs that suit you even better. Where shall I start?" she gritted, spittle glistening her lips.

"Adela, please, no scenes," pleaded Maura. "I will stay here. Would you sit behind me?"

"Don't interrupt, Maura. It's dreadfully rude." Adela resumed her verbal assault on Rufus, stomping her foot and furiously waggling her finger in his face. "You putrid swine! I own the same right as you to occupy that throne, no, more right! When I left Father, he was bemoaning your bullish pranks, yet he loves me and in fact sent me here to keep watch over you."

"If you don't shut your cavernous gob," Rufus hissed, "I'll have you and that spineless mate of yours tied to the mast of your ship!"

"How dare you slander my husband?!"

"I am regent here and I slander whom I please! You are nothing but a bothersome, gross sow and—"

At their screeching, Maura dug her fingers into her temples to ease the throbbing pain, yet it steeply intensified, making her yell, "Stop!" Her unexpected outburst hushed all on the platform. She kept her eyes downcast and gritted a despairing plea, "Adela, I want you to sit behind me. And can we pretend to be a happy family, if only to please the guests?"

Adela mulled over her request and glared back at Rufus, who had retreated to his sulky state. Flipping her plait indignantly, she stomped away, sat with a great huff, and grumbled, "I loathe that fiend!"

"You definitely are not alone in your sentiments, my Lady," replied Will, who was heartily enjoying the antics of his cousins. "Let us all attempt to make the best of a most difficult situation."

"Maura," wondered Adela, "you look exhausted. Is your quiet the result of some lusty wrestling last night?" She leered and roughly nudged Will, who grimaced at her crudeness and shifted away.

"No," replied Maura flatly, "I *am* tired, though it's not on his account. Tell me, where has Stephen gone?"

"He competes today and if victorious challenges your brother...what's his name."

"Marc. And if Marc is victorious will you still speak to us?"

"Don't be silly, Maura, of course I will. Only, Marc won't win," she added with a haughty smirk.

"Quiet!" Rufus' command shook the platform and its occupants, then he announced in a milder tone, "The games begin."

Maura hadn't attended a melee in ages and was eager to be entertained, especially by her skillful brother. The event opened as two knights bounded into the make-shift oval arena on their burly war horses, each man clad in full hauberk and helm, and equipped with a shield and a long, sharply pointed lance. They trotted to the fore of the platform and dutifully bowed their heads to the FitzRoy. Then each had a time on the field to flaunt his military prowess by executing tricky maneuvers on horseback. With great fervency, they galloped through the slush; leapt bulky obstacles; pierced bales of straw; and attacked a dummy fashioned of chainmail, fixed with a shield and set upon a tall post. Maura, though highly impressed by the display, knew if given the opportunity she could perform as expertly. However, she offered a polite comment to Adela, "Stephen rides well."

"Stephen does everything well," Adela readily boasted.

The moment at last arrived for the true duel, and the knights positioned themselves at opposite ends of the arena. At the brusque wave of a squire's arm, they thundered across the field, bodies steeled, lances aimed, shields braced. Maura hid her eyes from the explosive collision, and the brash clanging of metal jarred her from her seat. She stood and peeked through separated fingers, and was astounded to observe both men still astride their mounts. They rearranged their rumpled armor, trotted back to their starting positions, and replayed their rousing show. The fiercer second clash also failed to unseat either man. At Adela's insistent tug, Maura sat back down, hopeful a truce would now be called, but alas, they proceeded to charge each other again and again. With every deafening crash, she inched closer to Will. Her arm wrapped his, her brittle fingers crumpled his shirt, and his triumphant grin grew ever broader.

Maura's eyes flew open as a squealing Adela bolted from her seat. Maura cast a wary eye at the combatants and beheld Stephen still saddled, with his opponent writhing and groping through the mud in a desperate effort to gain his footing. Maura, relieved that the battle was done, and feeling rather ill, rose to leave. Again, Adela's screech demanded, "Maura, *do* sit down. I can't see!"

Maura obeyed, and to her deep dismay, discovered the battle was far from over. The men were presented with swords and commenced to wallop each other viciously, Stephen now owning a clear advantage. "Are the swords dull, Will?" Maura asked anxiously.

"Dull? Oh, no. That would make for a *dull* show, don't you think? Those swords could easily slice a hair."

Maura paled and winced as a loud thwack delivered by Stephen sent the grounded knight face down into the muck. She fretfully waited for him to rise; he didn't budge. Her crushing grip accompanied her gasp, "Is he...he dead?"

"I don't believe so, only stunned," said Will nonchalantly. "He'll rise in a moment."

"Someone must help him!" Maura cried out, and stood again.

Will jerked her back into her seat, his voice irritated, "Calm yourself. He's fine!"

"Maura!" yelled Adela. "How is Stephen supposed to find me with you constantly blocking his view?"

"I'm sorry, Adela," said Maura.

"There, see," noted Will, pointing, "his squire is helping him up."

The downed man rose painfully, removed his helm to spit up brown slush mixed with grass and, using his squire as a crutch, hobbled off the field. A booming cheer exploded from the crowd. They surged forward, making the fence bulge inward as they jeered and hurled mud missiles at the trounced knight.

"They shouldn't treat him so," protested Maura. "He performed bravely, and—"

"You wouldn't deny the peasants their fun, would you, Maura?" cut in Will.

"No, but I think he also should be congratulated."

"Heroine to the downtrodden, that's what you are." Will squeezed her hand and smiled tenderly. "And I applaud you for your concern. Here comes Stephen."

Stephen's stallion pranced splendidly to the podium and a beaming Adela waddled to the railing. Rufus grunted to the Count's bow, sagged back into his chair, and propped his thick legs upon the railing. A silken scarf impaled on the tip of Stephen's sword fluttered as it was thrust high in victory, then aimed in Adela's direction. She leant precariously over the railing and swiped madly at the air, finally capturing her precious gift. Kisses were blown and Stephen cantered off to the temporary stables for a brief respite. Adela haughtily waved the scarf in Rufus' face, taunting, "Spineless, did you say?"

Rufus batted at the material. Adela cackled and jerked the object beyond his reach, to which he snorted, "Get away from me, you...you...viper!"

"Pig!" she spat back.

Maura ignored them and asked Will, "Now is Marc to fight?"

"No. Stephen challenges the victor of the next bout and whoever wins that exchange battles Marc."

"Are you saying I must sit through two more—"

On her return to her seat, Adela caught Maura's whine and swiftly intervened, "Maura, come join me in my chamber. These chairs are horribly uncomfortable and I'm famished. We'll leave the men to their hideous games. Dearest brother," she called snidely, "surely you won't mind my borrowing your betrothed for a short while?"

Rufus turned and snapped, "Nothing would please me more. Women should be banned from tournaments. Your constant sniveling ruins the sport. Sod off, the lot of you! And don't return anytime soon."

"Will," ordered Adela, "send a squire to my chamber to announce Stephen and Marc's tilt. Maura, come."

They entered Adela's chamber, and as Maura's weary eyes roamed the room, she marveled at her cousin's talent for making any lodging luxurious. "Your chamber is lovely!"

"I always travel with my favorite comforts. It helps to make anywhere feel more like home. Sit Maura. Would you care for wine or food?"

"No, thank you," answered Maura, settling herself on the feathered mattress.

Adela instructed her servant, then sat heavily in a thickly padded chair, and rested her feet upon a stool topped with plump pillows. "Ah yes, that's much better." She unwound her veil, unraveled her plait, and combed pudgy fingers through her yellow locks. Comfortable at last, she asked, "How old is Marc?"

"Eighteen."

"A mere babe. He stands no chance against Stephen."

"You're so certain?" challenged Maura.

"There's no doubt. Stephen has been competing for years and to this day remains undefeated. I don't mean to dampen your spirit, Maura, Lord knows it's a bit soggy as is, but Stephen will prevail." Adela expected a retort to her bragging and, receiving none, turned sullen. "Maura, what's wrong?"

Without looking up, Maura tugged at her bandage and explained, "I didn't sleep well, the melee made my head hurt, and—"

"And...go on." Adela didn't take kindly to being put off, and demanded, "Tell me!"

There still was no answer; Maura shrank back on the bed and protectively hugged her body.

"Well, if you insist on being silent, I'll be blunt. You must find a way out of this marriage."

"There is no way out," said Maura listlessly.

"Nonsense. I will speak to Father on your behalf, that is, if I can locate him."

"And by the time you do, the wedding will have already taken place."

"Well then, you'll cloister yourself. Rufus can't touch you in a convent."

"I won't go to a convent," Maura answered sternly. "Somehow Rose and I will find a way to deal with—"

"It's your decision," intruded Adela. "I do hope you realize that given the opportunity, Rufus will murder you."

Maura's suppressed rage and frustration heaved to the frank portent, and her groaned response startled Adela, "*Why*?! What have I ever done to make him hate me so? I've seen him joking and cordial with friends and equals. I've seen weaker men intimidate him. But with me he's savage and ruthless. He's always despised me, always...always..." Her strained voice waned; she hung her head and focused despondently on her wrapped hand.

"Rufus was born cruel," answered Adela. "There's nothing complicated about the reason he mauls you. Rufus is not a complex man. It's simple jealousy that drives him."

"What?!" Maura asked aghast. "How can he feel jealousy towards me?"

"Jealousy...for Mother's love."

"What are you saying? Your mother's been dead and buried three years gone. Adela, you're raving—"

"I am not raving! I'm shocked at your ignorance, Maura."

Wounded, Maura rose to leave; Adela softened and begged, "Don't go. I'm sorry for the insult. Perhaps my explanation is difficult to believe, but it was always blatantly clear to me. Mother spoiled all her sons, even sent money to Curthose against Father's direct orders. That was the one time I saw them quarrel. When I was involved in my marriage preparations, and Henry was training at Odo's, Rufus enjoyed Mother's complete devotion. And then *you* arrived. Mother took to you instantly, and Rufus doesn't care for sharing. He started to bully you almost immediately, isn't that correct?" Maura nodded sadly. "And his attacks escalated and peaked after Mother's death?" Her nod deepened. "At her funeral," Adela continued soberly, "Rufus became furiously drunk and kept stammering about 'the bitch' causing her death. I took his slander to mean you."

"Causing her death!" Maura cried. "I nursed her, never left her side. I loved her! How could he think that, how?!"

"He wasn't at her side when she died...you were. She called for you...not him. He blames you, Maura, and punishes you to ease his grief. When you go, so will his pain."

Maura didn't reply at once; she sat pensively and focused again on her wounded hand. Adela's tragic words seeped through the mire that plagued her mind. Maura lifted a pained gaze to murmur, "I once believed my strength would always protect me, but when Rufus is near it fades completely away. In November, he came very close to killing me. My knees are worn thin from praying, yet the answer seems to elude even God. Adela," Maura left the bed to plead passionately, "can *you* help me? Can you tell me how, how am I to save myself?!"

Adela took her outstretched hands and answered, "If you won't take yourself to a convent, few options remain. However, you are my dearest friend and I will risk this offer...You will return with us to Blois on the guise of a visit. Once there, you will disappear."

"Disappear," echoed Maura, fuddled. "Robert's soldiers are everywhere, how can I disappear?"

"They are not in Blois. Yes, his daughters visit occasionally, but they won't recognize you. It will be comforting to have you near again." Maura turned away and, deep in thought, wandered to an open window as Adela warned on, "We all have our limits, Maura, and I sense you're close to reaching yours. An incident will no doubt occur, perhaps here at Gloucester, which will steal what little vigor you have left and leave you defenseless. Can you chance that happening?"

Maura spun to counter, "Will has sworn to help me!"

"He'll protect you till his own interests are threatened, then he will simply turn his back."

"I don't believe that—"

"Always believe it," Adela cut in sharply, "for it is true of all men!" They stared at each other; Maura shocked and saddened by Adela's dire opinion of the opposite sex, Adela appalled at Maura's naiveté. Then Adela reached out and gently added, "My sweet Maura, please consider my offer. We'll stay only another week at Gloucester, and during that time Will, Stephen, and I will keep you from Rufus."

"I can't answer now. I need time."

"That's fine, take your time and weigh your options carefully. This undoubtedly will be the most important decision of your life. One more thing, Maura—never confront Rufus with the knowledge I revealed to you just now. He doesn't like to be reminded of his infantile behavior. Now, from your pallor it's clear you need rest. You'll be comfortable here, and no one will know—"

Her speech was loudly interrupted by a knock which Maura answered. A pimply squire stood, rigid and nervous, in the doorway and sputtered, "My...my Lady, the last tilt is to begin shortly."

"Maura, help me rise," grunted Adela as she floundered up from her chair.

Maura aided her and asked the boy, "Who is to fight?"

"Stephen, Count of Blois, and Squire Marc of Dunheved."

"Thank you. We will follow."

"Maura, you need sleep!" insisted Adela.

"And I will get it later. I must be there for Marc."

Adela wrapped her veil and noted, "At times you are too giving for your own good."

As they slogged through the mucky bailey, Adela attempted to brighten the mood. "I saw my little brother Henry yesterday. But he's no longer little. I wish he were about. He's a bit of a rake, a good-natured one, and would delight in taking your mind from Rufus. He was with...I can never recall his name. Will's half-brother and Uncle Robert's mistake—"

At the mention of 'Will's half-brother', Maura broke away and hurriedly leapt the swollen puddles of slush. "Maura," Adela shouted impatiently, "wait, wait for me! I might slip. Wait!"

Maura paused, accepted Adela's arm with a dour sigh, and guided her the rest of their journey to the platform.

"What's come over you, Maura?" Adela chided. "You're so flighty, jittery, nothing at all like the calm, confident Maura I'm so fond of..."

The women settled in their seats and the tilt began. Maura's heart lurched to her throat as she watched Marc canter into the arena, his posture erect and lance held proudly. Stephen seemed no worse for wear, and met Marc in the center of the field. They exchanged a few words, clasped hands, and then separated to position themselves for their bout. Maura forced herself to watch their first clash and, though a fiery one, both men remained mounted. The mud rained through the air as they charged again and again, their furor sparking the crowd's frenzy. Will cringed at the strangling force of Maura's hold. She glanced briefly his way, then back to Adela and caught her astonished gape. Marc's expertise was clearly unexpected. All on the podium gasped and sprang up in unison. Maura jerked her head to the field, and saw to her ultimate horror, Marc groveling on the ground, frantically dodging his stallion's lethal prancing. Will's clutch tightened as he fought to curb her rising hysteria.

The squires appeared with swords. Marc struggled to his feet and took advantage of the distraction to launch a crazed attack. He rushed Stephen's horse, and grabbed and twisted the knight's boot. Stephen screamed in agony as he spilled backward from his saddle. The squires, not keen on joining the melee, dropped the swords and raced in a panic from the field. The crowd howled like a force from Hell.

Dumbfounded, Stephen stared up into Marc's forbidding silver mask. He rose cautiously, and inched his way toward a sword submerged in a puddle. Marc hauled up the weapon close to his feet and, wheezing dementedly, lunged at his opponent, ramming the side of Stephen's helm and pitching him back to the mud. Stephen's sword sliced through the air as he flew up from the ground, and landed blow after smashing blow to Marc's head and shoulders. Yet the arduous effort failed to weaken the squire. Marc returned his rage with groans and whacks, his treacherous assault finally driving Stephen to his knees. A sound swipe to the rear of the Count's head prematurely ended the gallant performance, and Stephen slumped forward to meet his defeat. The riotous horde crashed through the barriers and surged across the field, almost trampling Stephen in their frenzy. They hoisted Marc upon their shoulders and paraded him triumphantly round the field.

Adela dashed from the platform, trailed closely by Maura and Will. She fell to her knees at Stephen's side, heaving with distress and frustration as she tugged at his hauberk. Maura arrived and hollered back to Will, "Hurry, he needs help!" She restrained Adela's arms, warning, "He's too heavy. You mustn't strain. Think of the child."

Tears washed down Adela's puffy cheeks as she wailed, "Your brother has killed him. He's killed my Stephen!"

"No, Adela, he's only stunned. Will, hurry!"

Will shoved his way through the crowd, effortlessly flipped Stephen to his back, and yanked off his helm. Adela tore away her veil and, to its silken touch, Stephen stirred, choked, and gurgled. He opened one eye and cracked a defeated grin at his whimpering wife. She smothered his grimy face with kisses and sniffled, "Come, my love, you've had a grueling day. We'll rest together in our chamber."

On their sluggish walk to the keep, Will supported Stephen and Maura stayed close by Adela, who was straggling behind. As the Countess paused to catch a breath and mop mud from her face, Maura searched her drawn expression and wondered, "Adela, are you hurting?"

"No," she answered with a dismissing wave. "I'm exhausted and also amazed at your brother's skill. He'll make a fine soldier. You should be proud!"

"I am," beamed Maura.

"Then don't waste your time fretting over us. Go! Congratulate him."

"Are you sure you will be all right?"

"Of course I will, and so will Stephen. Now go and give him our praise as well."

They kissed and Maura darted off in search of Marc. There was no sign of him in the bailey or the great hall, so she vaulted the stairs leading up from the hall, hastened to the end of the passageway, and knocked softly on Marc's chamber door. "Marc," she called worriedly, "are you there?"

A faint "Come," answered and she pushed opened the flimsy door to see six ragged straw beds lining the walls of the cramped cubicle, a small table separating each. They were all deserted save the one nearest the far wall. Maura clambered over three beds and squeezed between the last two to reach her brother. He lay facing the wall, his body tightly coiled.

Maura sat and, with a tentative touch, asked, "What is it, Marc? I expected to find you ecstatic. You were so magnificent! Even Adela and Stephen send their praise. Marc, speak to me."

He shifted to his back and she discovered the cause of his quiet. The sheet, his neck, and collar were stained dark with blood streaming from a gash on his jaw. She struggled to hide her shock and pressed firmly against his hand that hid the wound, hoping to staunch the blood. "How?" she implored, her voice tensed. "How did this happen? I thought the armor prevented injuries!"

"It was my helmet that cut me," croaked Marc.

"Where else are you hurt?"

"Nowhere else."

"You must sit up, Marc. I'll fetch the doctor."

"No!" he demanded, gripping her arm. "I'll be fine. The blood's only oozing now."

"At least let me get you a clean cloth." Maura reached to the table flanking the bed and snatched up a linen towel. She switched the cloths and observed decisively, "If this is what victory brings, then you'll tilt no more."

"I will so!" asserted Marc as he sat, his eyes fierce. "I will fight on the day of my ceremony, and I'm to choose my opponent!"

Maura, wary of his abrupt manner, studied him intently. His light hair, darkened by sweat and mud, jutted up in coarse tufts; swirls of dirt smudged his pink skin and hands; and his eyes held a wild, spiteful gleam. She slowly removed the cloth from his jaw. To her relief the bleeding had ceased, though not his temper. "Marc," she questioned, swabbing the rest of his face, "are you upset—"

"Yes." He shoved her hand away, and revealed curtly, "I'm upset with you."

"Me! Whatever for?"

"You're keeping things from me!"

"No, I'm not—"

"Don't lie to me as well, Maura!" he flared. "Before Mass this morning, Will told me, he told me about last night and Rufus' visit, or have you forgotten?!"

"Marc, I didn't feel you needed to be invol—"

"I am involved!" he cut back, his distress spiraling. "He also informed me of your plans to stay with him at Berkhamstead."

"I haven't made that decision as yet, and if Will intimated I have, he's lying—"

"I don't care which of you is lying," he cried in anguish, "I only care about you!"

"I'm sorry I didn't tell you. No one was hurt and—"

He grabbed her injured hand and fiercely objected, "You were, and it might have been worse. You could have died! I won the tilt today because I pretended Stephen was Rufus. Maura..." His hands clamped her arms as he begged, "You must leave with Will now! Please get yourself away from Rufus. I have a bad feeling deep in my gut that you'll come to great harm here. And I...I..."

She panicked to his stammer and tortured eyes. "What, Marc? Tell me!"

"I leave the day following my ceremony...for Normandy."

"To Lord Roger's castle in Montgomery?"

"No...to war."

The dreaded words lingered heavily in the space between them. Maura stared numbly at her brother, not wanting to believe that he'd grown, would soon fight real battles, and might never return to her. Seized with emotion, they cleaved together in the gloaming. And Maura mustered the strength to rock him in her arms, her ragged voice whispering a lullaby, one she had lovingly sung to him so many years ago.

*****

A good while later Maura returned to her chamber to find a flustered Rose, pacing and fretting, "I was about to send for the guards! Where were you? You know better than to walk the halls alone."

"Oh, Rose," moaned Maura, "he's leaving. Marc's leaving!"

"Leaving? For where?"

"Normandy...to fight."

"Fight?" Rose regarded Maura vaguely, then lowered her eyes, and mumbled, "In two days, he will be a knight. It is his duty to fight."

Maura slumped, daunted, onto the bed. Rose attempted to ease her sorrow by offering, "I won't go to Dunheved. I will stay with you."

"No, Rose, you will leave with Alan as planned." Maura raised a wet, though tenacious, gaze. "I've decided what I need do to stay safe. For the remainder of our visit here, I want you to sleep elsewhere. There is an empty chamber two doors down. Rufus may return, and I won't have you in danger."

"I won't leave you!"

Maura stood, her expression austere. "You will move to another room!"

Rose cringed at the exclamation and retreated to a corner of the chamber; there was no disputing that command. She wrung her hands and spoke impulsively, "Will's called three, four times for you. He expects to escort you to the feast. I don't think it's wise for you to go. You need quiet and comfort, not more confusion."

"I'll help you move your things," said Maura, "then I'll dress for the feast."

As they gathered her few belongings, Rose looked sadly on Maura's miserable image, and blurted, "You need sleep!"

Rose's toiletries spilled from Maura's trembling hold, and she reached out and anguished, "I'm afraid to sleep. I'm afraid to dream!"

*****

Will was bored. He shifted in his seat, exhaled a disgruntled sigh, and pondered Maura. Her glazed vacant eyes roamed the hall, rarely settling on him. He resented her distraction, her silence, and sulked. "Maura, why did you agree to come here with me? It's obvious you'd prefer to be somewhere else, perhaps *with* someone else." She answered with a suspicious, uncertain look that only flared his disturbance. "Come, I'll take you to your room," he said. "Once we're at Berkhamstead, you'll be free of your worries—"

"I won't be going to Berkhamstead."

Her abrupt reply rocked his composure and he spouted carelessly, "How dare you tease me! You led me to believe you'd go. I've made plans—"

"Will," she interrupted softly, "I appreciate your invitation, but I need to get far away from England. I'll journey to Blois and stay with Adela and Stephen till Easter. That way I will be closer to Marc."

"Marc!" he exclaimed. "What in the bleeding name of Jesus does he have to do with all this?!"

Maura's voice stayed as bland as her expression. "It's settled, Will. I'll go to Blois at week's end. That leaves us four days of Christmas Court left to enjoy...together." She rose to go to her room and confidently took his hand. He blundered after and his mind raced to devise a ploy to break her hard-hearted decision. Damn her! How dare she have the audacity to refuse his generous offer! And what to do about Simon? What if he returned after she departed? Then there'd be no getting rid of him. Suddenly a flash of insight visited him. Why, she was planning to escape! Well, then he'd just have to shatter her delusions of freedom. No more games, it was far too late for games. He was certain she wanted him and tonight, she'd allow him into her room, her bed, and her body—tonight!

The pallet strewn before Maura's door was empty. Her grip on Will firmed and her anxious eyes darted along the passageway. "Alan...where, where is he?" she stammered. "He's never gone. I...I—"

"Perhaps he needed to relieve himself," offered Will lightly. "There's no need to fret, Maura. I won't leave till he returns." He marveled at his extraordinary luck! The oaf was at last out of the way. Yet Will's valiant guarantee of protection failed to smooth Maura's furrowed brow; clearly more drastic measures were needed. As was the custom in Rufus' household, few torches blazed along the expanse of the hall, allowing for much dalliance and mischief to happen amidst the semi-darkness. Before Maura could utter a protest, Will briskly drew her up against the door of her chamber, caught her in a firm embrace, and breathlessly muttered, "Where's your woman?"

Dreadfully fuddled, Maura sputtered, "I...I don't kno—" Then the answer came to her. "She sleeps elsewhere."

He sighed ecstatically and, fumbling behind her back for the door's handle, gushed forth, "What wondrous news! I won't let you slip away, not this night, not ever. Let me in your room, your bed! I can give you what no man has ever given you. I'll make you forget everyone and everything..."

To his ardent vows, Maura felt she was floating. She shut her eyes, shared eager kisses, and gasped to the excitement of his roaming touch. Forget...yes forget, for a few blissful moments she'd forget all the torment. She craved his lusty attention, the heat of his body, his—Something pointy and hard dug into her back, disrupting her pleasure and, looking about, she was amazed to find herself pressed up to the bedpost. Two candles flickered on a nearby table, shedding a muted, eerie light.

Will sensed her hesitation; he slowed his seduction and peered deeply into her eyes. "What, Maura? What is it? What's wrong?"

There...in his smiling gaze, she faced an intangible horror. Long buried, it surged its way into her waking mind, making her body convulse, her arms flail, her throat scream, "No! Get away! Get off me!"

Will shielded his head from her forceful blows, shouting back, "Stop! Maura, stop!" He stumbled from her tantrum, reached the door, and whirled round ready to explode with fury. Instead, he choked back his curses, knowing if he betrayed his anger, he'd lose her forever. Bent protectively, he hugged his balled fists and, not a little frightened, gingerly raised his eyes to her wild visage. Her deranged look had faded to the expression of a needy child. In need of what, he wondered as he inched forward and murmured, "Maura, I'm frightfully sorry. This has all happened so quickly, my feelings got the better of me. I should never have rushed you. It's only that..." His voice expertly quaked, "I'm so very fond of you. Can you ever forgive me?" He cocked his head in question while she continued her trance-like stare. An uncomfortable shiver crawled his spine. What was she seeing, remembering? Perhaps it was best to leave, but not before he'd determined her present opinion of him. "Maura," he said gently. She didn't respond, so he called louder, "Maura!" Her rigid glare softened to his yell, and she hung her head ashamedly. He strove to cheer, "We both desperately need a change of scenery. I'll call for you tomorrow and take you to town. Would you like that?" She answered with barely a nod. Relieved, he boldly came close and raised her chin. Never had he witnessed such raw misery. Yes, he deduced, the time was drawing near for the confrontation between the former lovers, and oh, what a glorious spectacle it promised to be! After all, it was Simon who deserved her blows, not he.

Maura stiffened to his light kiss, and numbly watched him slip out the door. Once alone, the tumult inside her began to boil and churn, pounding her mind, shattering her sanity. She let out an agonized groan, hurled herself across the bed, beat and clawed the pelts. What, she despaired, what had stopped her, made her strike out? What was it about him that repulsed her? Why couldn't she give to him, give to any man?! Ice filled her veins, only ice! The woman in her was dead and would never live again, never! She writhed on the bed, gagged on spiteful tears, and struggled to force her eyes open. They burned from weeping and exhaustion. Closing them for a few moments couldn't hurt. They needed soothing...only a moment to soothe...

Her fingers crawled the length of his wet, sinewy back, gripping his hips, urging him nearer. They melded together perfectly and their blended sweat, lips, and caresses jolted her body with wave after wave of ecstasy. She happily drank in his kisses and reeled to his sweet whisper, "Open your eyes, Maura. I'm here beside you. I'll never leave you. I love you wholly, desperately! Don't be afraid to see me...love me." Maura sighed as his pristine, pale eyes crystallized before her, wet and so full of passion, of hope. All her fears and doubts gone, she clung to him and buried her face in his warm neck. His fingers tangled and tugged her hair as he nuzzled even closer. The pulling hurt. Confused, she felt for his hand, but touched instead squirming fur…

Maura burst out a revulsive groan and bolted upright in bed. Pelts soared through the air as she frantically searched for him. He'd vanished, leaving in his place two skittering mice. Into the blackness she wailed, "Simon, don't leave me! Please don't go!" Stark silence answered and madness claimed her. She whimpered; raked at her hair, face, and tunic; chafed her arms to rid herself of his touch, his smell. "I'll stop him," she muttered viciously, staggering to the door. "I must stop him before..."

Alan woke too quickly and, helplessly, watched a mass of green silk billow away down the hall. He struggled to his feet, took off in pursuit, and caught Maura inches from the top of the sheer staircase. Her hair was disheveled, lips gray as her skin, eyes dark, swollen and vivid with fright. They shifted about, hunting for something or someone. "Maura," he worried, "Maura, what frightens you?"

"He's here," she gasped, "he's close!"

"No, my Lady," he answered knowingly, "Rufus is tucked up in his chamber and won't harm you."

"Not Rufus! Rufus tortures my body, he tortures my soul."

"Of whom do you speak? Who threatens you?"

"I can't say...I won't say! I will find him and stop him!"

"No, not this night." He cupped her elbow and cautiously steered her from the stairs. "This night, you will rest. All you suffer from are bad dreams. Now I'll take you back—"

"I won't go back!" Her shrill cry pained his ears. She strained against his hold and uttered crazily, "Not to that bed, not to that dream! I'll stay in the hall beside you."

"My Lady, no! You're chilled as it is—"

"Don't make me go back in that room. Alan, *please* don't make me!" Maura started and flinched from each attempted touch, mumbled coarsely to herself, shivered and fidgeted. He couldn't make out her words, but her tone was hateful.

With patient and calming assurances, Alan managed to coax her back to the door. He squatted by the door, and watched in wonder as she lay down on his pallet, bunched his cover into a tight ball and clutched it like a shield to her chest. He didn't understand her queer behavior, yet his heart ached to her suffering. In the short time they'd shared company, he'd grown quite fond of this curious lady, and his urge to protect her was great. Whom did she fear? Was it a phantom from her past, a devil from her dreams, or a living, breathing menace? Her vengeful words at last faded and her eyes closed shut. He waited awhile till her twitching ceased and, once sure of her slumber, settled her safe and snug in her own bed. The instant the door clicked shut, Maura's eyes flew open and remained wide till the break of dawn.

*****

CHAPTER SEVEN - COERCION

Maura dawdled her way down the hallway, Alan at her back, prodding. She paused at a chamber door, raised her hand to knock, then glanced back to Alan for courage. He nodded and said in his stoic way, "This is the right chamber. You'll feel better if you speak to him, and accept his offer of a visit to town. I'll be with you, always."

Maura tapped softly. The slightly ajar door swept open and she gazed at the curious scene before her. Will paced before a table seated with a balding, cloaked cleric. The cleric scribbled furiously as Will dictated, his voice dark and agitated. Maura turned to leave, but Alan shook his head and waved her on. She took a timid step forward and called, "Will?"

Will snapped to the intrusion, his face twisted in an ugly scowl which instantly mellowed to Maura's meek image. "Maura," he said, "I didn't hear your knock. Come in, come in. Only a few instructions needed and I'll be finished here." He mumbled rapidly to the cleric, who dusted, rolled, and tied the parchment. Maura caught Will's last order, "Make haste, man, and provide me a reply by this afternoon, no later." The cleric shuffled out the door, nodding to everyone present. Will closed the door and motioned her to sit, all the while exuding, "I'm pleased, yet also a bit astonished to see you so early. To be perfectly honest, I wondered if I'd ever see you again."

Maura stared down at her clenched hands and humbly began, "I've come to apologize. I don't know what came over me—"

"Maura," Will said earnestly, "there is absolutely no need for you to apologize. The incident was entirely my doing, and I won't tolerate another word on the sordid subject. We will continue on as if last evening never occurred." He approached her and crouched, his face even with hers. A brushing kiss blushed her cheek, and elicited from her a slight smile. "I pray you've come," he continued, "to escort me to town."

"Yes," she replied hesitantly, careful to avoid his eyes, "if you still wish to go."

Will studied Maura's elusive gaze and haggard appearance, accented by her tightly woven plait and bland tunic. He wondered if she'd slept at all. This escapade would undoubtedly require an inordinate amount of patience. Then again, if the brilliant scheme he'd concocted this morning succeeded, the effort would be truly worth the bother. He lifted her limp hand, drew her from the chair, and radiantly decided, "Then, we'll go." In the hall, Maura waved Alan along with a tense grin, then listened politely to Will's euphoric yammering on their seemingly endless journey to the stables.

*****

Black bulging clouds threatened a downpour as Simon spurred E'dain faster through the muddy streets of the borough of Gloucester. The Welsh meetings had concluded successfully and, to his joy, early. It was dusk on the eve of Marc's ceremony and Simon shivered with rampant expectation. Yet a bit of apprehension also lurked, causing a painful thudding of his heart. Dare he hope he'd see Maura, speak to her, perhaps even touch her this evening?

The raised drawbridge dropped and the main gates burst open to a rowdy contingent of soldiers. Simon cursed as he steered E'dain through their opposing tide. Then to his added dismay, he encountered in the bailey a horde of revelers, drunk and straggling, who further hindered his progress. Desperate for an opening, he restlessly scanned the bailey. A disturbing sight captured his eye. Atop the steps to the keep stood Will and Maura, apparently involved in a weighty conversation. No longer aware of the smothering wave of bodies, Simon urged E'dain forward to better his view. Will leant close to whisper and they kissed—not the kiss of mere acquaintants—the kiss of lovers! Rage boiled his belly as Simon sprang from the saddle, clumsily tethered his mare, and raced for the entrance. He forged his way across slicks of ice and through sticky bogs to arrive amazingly afoot at the base of the stairs. Vaulting the steps, he collided with a flood of exuberant gentry exiting the keep, and backwards he toppled, ending his fall with a spectacular splash in a pool of muck. Titters and guffaws exploded from his audience, but stopped abruptly to his thunderous string of curses. He stood, shook himself vigorously, and continued lamely up the now empty staircase. Inside the keep, he struggled up another winding flight of steps, and shoved his way down the main hall in his exhaustive search for the couple. Fingers bit into his arm, accompanied by a sultry voice, "Simon, wherever have you been? I've missed you terribly."

He spun to Almodis' coquettish grin and, disappointed, jerked from her clawing hold. "I had business on the border with Henry," he answered tersely.

"Now why in Heaven's name would you prefer that peevish baby's company to mine?" He didn't answer her pert remark and edged away, obviously stalking someone. "Simon," she said, following, "who are you looking for?"

"Maura," he mumbled as he tried to evade her interrogation.

"Maura..." Almodis repeated in a vexed voice. "I can't seem to escape that horrid name. Tell me, Simon, what is it about that girl that has every man in this castle totally captivated? Why do *you* need to find her?"

The crowd blocked his escape, so he turned and muttered, "I must speak to her."

"Well, I have no idea where she is at present. However, if you accompany me to the feast this evening, she surely will be there...with Rufus."

For an instant, Simon considered prodding Almodis for details concerning Maura and Will. It was his opinion, based on her catty disposition, that she most likely knew the secret intentions of all present. He quickly squelched his idea, though, as the aged, lumbering, hirsute figure of Roger of Montgomery appeared. The Earl eyed Simon with distaste, and grumbled to Almodis, "My Lady, since when do you wallow with swine?"

"How rude of you, Roger!" admonished Almodis. "I pride myself on being a loving stepmother to both my sons."

Simon took advantage of their bickering to steal away and cringed at Almodis' twittering cry, "Simon! You won't forget...about tonight?" He roamed the halls aimlessly, rubbed his aching backside, and began to entertain doubts that he'd *ever* speak to Maura. He was clearly the pawn in an elaborate ruse—for what purpose he didn't know. Too tired to think, he quit his search and returned to the bailey to stable E'dain properly. There, he discovered his saddlebag rifled. As he glumly led her to the stable, two bright thoughts remained—E'dain and the writ were still in his possession, the writ secretly pocketed in his cloak. His mud-drenched clothing stuck to him, itching and chilling his skin. Not exactly a suitable outfit for a Royal banquet yet, if need be, to speak to Maura he'd gladly attend the feast naked.

*****

Maura stretched languidly on her bed and reflected on her pleasant jaunt to town. How attentive Will had been, and so tolerant while she bungled about, tongue-tied and addle-brained. Her eyelids began to droop, then flew open to a knock. Grateful for the interference, she hurried to answer. Rose stood in the doorway, looking concerned and also muddled. "What is it, Rose?" Maura asked, stepping back for her to enter.

"You look absolutely dreadful! I should move back into your room to look after you, but no arguing now, Maura. Directly after you left this morning, Adela's servant delivered this note. She said it was quite important and—"

Maura snatched the parchment from Rose's hand, tore open the seal, and read the slightly smudged print.

"My dearest Maura, we frantically searched for you this morning, though no one knew quite where you'd gone. Owing to an unexpected invasion from Angevin troops, we must return immediately to Blois. And because of the danger, I believe it's unwise for you to visit at this time. Perhaps in a month or two the situation will have improved, and you can then risk the journey. I suggest that you indulge in Will's affection and reside at Berkhamstead till your wedding. As promised, I will attempt to speak to Father on your behalf and will strive to return before Easter. Meanwhile, try to enjoy yourself and congratulate your brother for us. Your loving Cousin, Adela."

Maura mouthed a curse, angrily crumpled the note, and hurled it to the rushes.

Rose, a bit daunted, asked fretfully, "What, what did it say? Answer me, Maura!"

"She's gone back to Blois."

"Is that all? Surely you'll see her again."

"You don't understand. I was to go with her and..."

"And what?" Rose arched a suspicious brow, and repeated loudly, "And *what*, Maura?"

"And disappear."

"Disappear! Are you mad, child?! I swear you own a death wish! And whose hare-brained scheme was this?"

"Adela suggested it and I—"

"Of course it was Adela! Never have I witnessed that woman having a single sane thought. I'm grateful she's gone and shocked that you'd ever consider joining in her nonsense!" Her harsh words struck deeply, and Rose, instantly remorseful, squeezed Maura's hands and continued gently, "Look at me and listen well. You must let go of this daft notion that someone will miraculously save you from this marriage. You will survive Rufus with strength, not foolishness. Now it's obvious you're not sleeping, so I will move my things back—"

"No Rose," interjected Maura, "not while we're at Gloucester. I would die if any harm came to you!"

"Oh, my sweet angel," Rose cried as they embraced, "I'd give my life if it meant you'd be free of that monster. What will you do now? Go with Will?"

"I haven't decided."

"After Marc's ceremony," suggested Rose with forced cheer, "if you're still undecided, you'll come with me to Dunheved."

"I don't believe I can ever return there."

"Not to stay at the castle. We'll sojourn at my son Richard's manor home. We shared such wondrous times there."

Maura strained a grin and patted Rose's hand. "I swear I'll make my decision by tomorrow evening. Rose," added Maura, "for the next few days, I need to be surrounded by those I love, you and Marc. Would you fetch him while I change?"

"Of course I will, and I can think of no better tonic to ease your troubles."

While Maura waited, she fingered a tiny porcelain jar topped with a gelled perfume. Inhaling the luscious gift quieted her riotous mind, and she again contemplated the dilemma named Will. It seemed such a simple decision to make. She truly was fond of him, felt relatively safe in his presence, and could easily overlook his foibles. And most importantly, at Berkhamstead, she'd be free of Rufus. Still, she knew a promise to stay at Berkhamstead was also a promise to bed Will. Maura supposed she was capable of playing at love and finding pleasure in fantasy, if only for a short while. Then with deep regret, she recalled the past few instances when she'd sought the passion she'd once known. Each dalliance had ended bitterly; she had hurt and been hurt. Perhaps with Will it could be different. Then why the terrible quandary, why?

*****

That evening, after shedding his drenched cloak in his chamber, Simon hung over the balcony and squinted at the merrymaking below. He easily spotted Rufus sprawled in King William's throne, and Will at his side, their raucous laughter echoing through the rafters. As far as he could surmise, they were the only royalty in attendance. Perhaps Maura was mingling in a corner out of view. His frustration swelled and, no longer fretful over the perfect line to deliver, he resolutely tramped down the stairs. At the bottom step, he paused at the sight of Almodis, smile brazen and black eyes aglow, barreling toward him. She swiped out and snagged his sleeve to foil his escape. Rather than chance tearing the only shirt he possessed, he surrendered and begged, "Almodis, please let go. I really don't belong here."

"What rubbish, of course you do. After all, I invited you, didn't I?" She picked a glob of mud off his tunic, wrinkled her nose, and commented, "You haven't changed."

"My clothes were stolen. I have nothing to change into."

"What an alluring thought." Her voice, lilting and airy, annoyed him, yet squabbling was useless. So constricting was her hold that it paled her knuckles. Simon swallowed, slumped, and allowed her to drag him to the dais, suffering her blather along the way. "Why didn't you inform me of your lack of clothing? I would have found you something decent to wear. But no matter," she added, fluttering her lashes, "the mud suits you and gives you a roguish air. Now," Almodis pronounced as she gently forced him into a chair, "you'll sit and eat with me."

"I'm not hungry," he countered, rising an inch from his seat.

"I sincerely doubt that," she answered with a harsh shove. "Have patience, my dear son. Maura should arrive at any moment."

In response to her hopeful words, Simon reluctantly stayed and glanced down at the bowl of congealing stew set before him. His belly lurched in protest and he swiftly downed a cup of claret.

Will snapped to movement at the end of the dais. Again, luck shone upon him. Simon had returned early! Donning a jubilant expression, he promptly abandoned Rufus and joined his stepmother and brother, exclaiming, "Simon! How marvelous to see you!" Simon's soiled appearance drew from him a slightly repulsed look. "Have you just arrived?" he wondered.

"His clothes were stolen," Almodis curtly explained.

"What a terrible shame," consoled Will. "I certainly can remedy the situation by loaning you an outfit or two—"

"I've already offered, Will," broke in Almodis with disdain. "Besides, your scrawny clothes would be far too small for him and..."

Simon's impatient eyes darted between his petty-minded relatives and his blood simmered. Finally he could bear no more of their prattle and bellowed with a thump of his fist, "Stop this nonsense! Where's Maura?"

"I haven't a clue," replied Will casually. "She's promised to attend."

"You've told her," Simon pressed, "about the writ?"

A cloying grin cracked Will's face; he squirmed in his seat and whispered his lie, "Well, I really haven't had the chance. It's Adela. She can be such a demanding pest. She's hoarded all of Maura's time since you've left. I haven't been able to steal her away even for an instant. But now that you've returned, her interest in her cousin should wane and..."

Only his eyes raged as Simon stood, straightened, and firmly announced, "Then I'll handle the matter myself. Pardon me," he begged to Almodis and she stepped from his path. His willful stride across the hall quickly turned stormy though, as he wrestled through the unyielding crowd.

Will sat a stunned moment then, realizing the catastrophe about to befall him, leapt from his chair. "Get out of my way!" he snarled to Almodis. She tenaciously held her stance and he thrust her to the rushes, squalling, "Simon, wait!" Alarm rapidly cleared the floor. Will reached Simon at the base of the steps leading to the main doors, grabbed the back of his tunic, and yanked, ripping as he shrilled, "You will not leave this hall!"

"You don't order me!" Simon roared. He whirled and struck out, easily breaking Will's grip.

"Now, now, little brother..." Will cowered to Simon's demonic look, pressed one hand to his brother's heaving chest, and urged with a nervous chuckle, "Calm yourself. Surely we can discuss this matter rationally."

Another explosive blow knocked away Will's hand and Simon blared, "Where is her chamber?!"

Demented laughter burst from Will. He stumbled in retreat and sputtered recklessly, "You really don't think I'd be foolish enough to tell *you* that."

"What have you been up to with Maura?!" raved Simon. He lunged forward, seized Will's collar and twisted, his chilling growl resounding throughout the hushed hall, "You'll tell me now or I'll wring the bleeding truth from you!"

Will strained and wriggled against Simon's choking hold; each frantic movement escalated his croaks and gags. A sharp gasp rose from the party as Rufus stood and strode purposefully toward the fracas. Simon, crazed with fury, saw no one but his rancid brother, and strengthened his hold.

"Release him!" Rufus' demand was cold, calculated, and final. Simon's taunting sneer defied his cousin's order, and he added a rough shake to his clench. Rufus puffed and snorted, "Do as I say or I'll separate that hand from your body." A snap of his fingers instantly produced four burly guards, eagerly brandishing swords. The glare of their blades broke Simon's trance, and he grudgingly eased his clutch. Will slumped heavily to the rushes, convulsing and hacking in dramatic agony. Rufus dug a stumpy finger into Simon's chest and grumbled, "Will warned me you'd cause a commotion. I believed you were too bright to attempt something so stupid. No one disrupts my court, especially scum like you. You're nothing here. Now, leave my castle before I chop you into tiny pieces and feed you to my hounds."

Simon swept a leery eye about the room. A wall of discounting, hateful looks challenged him, save one pitying gaze belonging to Almodis. He swallowed dryly, crept backward up the steps, and raced from the keep to the stables. He vaulted E'dain's bare back and galloped from the castle. Madness drove him on and on, down cramped village lanes, past the town's stone walls, and deep into the wilderness. Dense gnarled trees and E'dain's labored huffing finally tempered his pace and anger. He dismounted and absently led her for what seemed miles through the twisted forest. They stopped by a tumbling brook, where both hungrily gulped the crisp, rejuvenating liquid. Simon lifted his troubled face to an unwelcome spatter of rain, which quickly became a deluge. His mood turned as abysmal as the weather, and he shivered to the vile realization—to return to the castle an apology was in order—an apology to Rufus. He tugged at E'dain's mane; she raised her head and nuzzled his chest, a gesture he returned to her neck, using her mane to wipe the wet from his face. Never had he felt so cold, lost, and disheartened. Did Maura really want to see him or was that a lie as well? He mounted E'dain and started back, braced with the knowledge that very soon he'd discover the whole truth, however onerous it might be.

The late hour left few in the great hall, and those present lifted astounded faces to Simon, who stood in the doorway, his bold glare aimed at Rufus. A steely breath fortified Simon's resolve and he started across the floor, the gawkers shrinking from his stark, brooding guise. Rufus watched Simon's approach and, to each broad glide, his sardonic grin widened. Simon rounded the fire, dropped to one knee before the dais, and bowed his shaggy, damp head.

"I thought I ordered you to get out," mumbled Rufus, gnashing on a bone.

"Good Prince," Simon replied, "I would speak to you...alone."

"I don't like our little chats. Go away." Rufus hurled the stripped bone into the fire; the whizzing object narrowly missed Simon's ear.

Simon raised a humbled expression and clarified, "*This* talk, I swear, my gracious Lord, will be different."

"God's breath! It damned well better be!" warned Rufus, pushing up from his throne and clutching his goblet of wine. "We'll meet in my bedchamber. Guards! Stand outside my door. I don't trust this varlet!"

His fingers nervously drummed the arms of his chair as Simon sat meek and silent in the lavish bedchamber. He grew woozy watching Rufus' fervid pacing and endeavored to initiate the discussion. "My Lord, I have but a simple request."

"What?" barked Rufus.

"I beg your forgiveness for the commotion I caused, and I wish to return to the castle."

"No!" Rufus shuddered and demanded, "Why are you here?!"

"To attend Marc's knighthood ceremony."

"Liar! You're here either to snoop or to pester my intended, perhaps both."

"No, my Lord!" Simon rose in protest. Rufus' accusation betrayed his ignorance of the Ryedale betrothal. But Simon didn't relish being condemned for depriving the brute of his battering toy, and held his tongue.

"Then why risk death to sneak back here?" Rufus plopped down on the huge, ornate, curtained bed and fixed on Simon a relentless glower.

"I want to see the ceremony!" Simon flared.

"How terribly kind hearted of you," sneered Rufus.

"Will you let me back in or not?"

"No."

"Then I'll go." Simon shook with indignation, spun on his heels, and headed for the door.

"Wait!" Rufus yelled.

Simon snapped to the curious order and, tilting his head quizzically, waited.

"You...you could stay..." Rufus averted his eyes, fiddled with the tasseled bed curtains, and stammered on, "You could have any...anything you desire. A...All you need do is agree to become one of my household, and in return for your services, I...will grant you—"

"No!" was Simon's brash retort.

Rufus struck an affected pose and grinned garishly. "I disgust you, don't I?"

A sharp laugh escaped Simon as he waived all formality and sprawled back into the chair. "I'm sorry to disappoint you Rufus. Your doings with your willing *friends* neither shock nor disgust anyone, except perhaps the clergy. What sickens me is your cruelty."

"I'm not cruel," pouted Rufus.

"Of course you are, and you're a bully as well. Why deny that which brings you such joy?"

"And you're a pompous snot."

"Hurling insults wasn't my intent, Cousin," Simon said with a defeated grunt. "I'll take my leave."

"You'll leave when I dismiss you and not before!"

"Well, if you must have the last word—"

"Stop your drivel!" Rufus shouted, then softened, "There is a way you can regain my good graces. Are you familiar with my Father's survey of England?"

Piqued, Simon slid to the edge of his chair. "Are you referring to the Domesday Book?"

"The what?" asked Rufus, irritated.

"The peasants equated the census inquisition to the last judgment and dubbed the document, 'The Domesday Book'."

"How trite of them," replied Rufus mordantly. "My clerk reads me passages daily. I want to be intimately acquainted with the land and people I inherit." He abandoned the bed and paced again, his gestures intensifying with the volume of his voice. "And I'll own it all, Cousin! Every hide, hut, sheep, priest, baron, and slave will be mine, to do with as I please. Father is far too bending. In my reign, I plan to restore the death penalty he outlawed, and any vassal who dares challenge me will swing from the gallows, lose his limbs, have his eyes plucked out—"

Simon rolled his eyes and sighed, "I'm highly impressed with your love for your subjects."

"Would you lead a rebellion against me?" snapped Rufus, sensing Simon's offense.

"Once the rebels knew the identity of their commander," chuckled Simon, "they'd charge off in the opposite direction."

"How does it feel to be despised by so many?" snickered Rufus, drawing near.

"You should know," Simon snidely returned.

To the biting remark, Rufus looked away, then resumed his narrow glare, wiped spittle from his lip, and said, "You've distracted me. The other evening, I was shocked to hear my man read a passage from the survey stating you were granted the honor of Tenant-in-Chief of two rather large fiefs. One estate is in Cornwall, the other is in Sussex."

Simon gripped the arms of his chair, gaped, and blurted, "I'm a what?"

"A Tenant-in-Chief."

"There has to be some mistake!"

"No mistake. It seems Father is bestowing gifts without your knowledge, and his kindness seems quite upsetting to you, so I'll happily rid you of your distress. Turn the properties over to me and you can stay at Gloucester for the remainder of Christmas Court."

The startling news stumped Simon; he sat aghast and rigid, unable to conjure up a fitting reply.

"It's my final offer, Cousin, and I'm growing weary of our talk. Do you have an answer or not?"

"What?"

"Are you willing to part with your property for my absolution?"

"Part? Oh, yes!" Simon jumped from his seat and repeated vibrantly, "Oh yes, I'll gladly part with my land! It's yours, all yours. Enjoy it with my blessing! Now may I go?"

"Yes," Rufus answered. He waited till Simon reached the door and added, "There is one more thing."

Simon tried yet couldn't hide his annoyance, and asked flippantly, "What is it?"

"Your manners are lax, the proper reply is...*what is it, my Lord.*"

"What is it...*my Lord?*"

"If you so much as pull a face while here," responded Rufus, waggling his finger, "I'll lock you up till you can learn to respect your betters. If our little talk is a true example of your rudeness, then I imagine your lesson might take decades. So beware, little Cousin."

Simon beamed and bowed extravagantly, asserting, "I will strive to do your bidding, Your Grace."

"You know what your problem is, Cousin?" Rufus asked, peeved.

"What, my Lord?"

"You don't listen, therefore you don't learn."

"And do you know what your problem is, Cousin?" mimicked Simon.

Rufus couldn't help but smile. "What?"

"You're bored and your boredom is a huge problem for everyone. You hate these pumped-up ceremonies! Why don't you go find yourself a measly little war to direct? You're a soldier, not a diplomat."

The bristle left Rufus and he sulked. "I've tried. Father's ordered me here."

"I heard news that the Danes are planning an invasion of the east coast of England," noted Simon. "Surely the troops could use your expertise."

"The Danes changed their plans," Rufus said solemnly. "Father built castles on the coastline and burned everything else worth ravaging. There really was no point in invading."

"What a shame," Simon said as he faked a piteous expression. Rufus didn't notice. His longing stare and thoughts were directed instead at some imaginary battlefield. Simon's quick question rattled his fantasy, "Rufus, I mean, *my Lord*, where's Will gone to?"

"Why do you need to know?" asked Rufus in a faint, dreamy tone.

"I want to avoid him."

"That's understandable. Last time I saw Will, he was in a foul way, still coughing, and heading up to the floor above with a whining squire in tow."

"Well, I'm grateful for the information and your precious time and forgiveness. My Lord." Simon nodded and slipped from the room. The door supported his sagging weight as he exhaled a rumbling sigh and muttered, "Bleeding Jesus, how I loathe that man!"

Inside the chamber, Rufus mused over the meeting. There was no denying he enjoyed his cousin's spirited company and soggy, though becoming appearance, no matter how acid his tongue. Then again, an unsettling thought lingered. Rufus pondered how Simon had so expertly guessed his private desires and gaffes. In future, he'd take better care; to allow a conversation to stray to personal matters was dangerous. Never troubled for long, Rufus tossed back his goblet of wine, and shrugged off his worry.

The hall was void of living creatures and, staring down at the last smoldering coals, Simon knew it was far too late to seek out Maura. The confrontation with Rufus, albeit successful, had depressed him. His mediator skills were sorely wasted on his own nettling family. He could understand the violent emotions provoked by his father and Odo, yet why did the others enrage him so? Even Almodis, who seemed harmless, riled—He jerked to an unbidden touch and stiffened to Almodis' voice, "Simon...you were with Rufus a long while. Did your talk go well?"

The tone of her voice was somehow different, more sincere. He peered through the grayness and met the same caring look she'd shown at his banishment. His tenseness eased and, with a small grin, he answered, "Yes...as well as one can expect with Rufus."

She smiled knowingly and questioned, "What has Will done to anger you?"

"I don't really know," he readily returned. "It's what he hasn't done that's upset me, and I have a notion he's scheming something, something that involves me and Maura, and who knows how many others..." His ragged voice trailed off for fear of divulging too much.

"Will's forever scheming. I'm sorry I can't help you with your puzzle, Simon, though, I can provide you with a clean outfit for Marc's ceremony." She erased his suspicious look by assuring, "You needn't come to my chamber. I know where you're staying and will have the clothing left by your door. You once insisted I rest, now I return the order. Goodnight, Simon." A slight brush of her fingers across his hand took her away, but not the mystery. Why was she suddenly so kind and caring? What was her involvement in Will's charade? Would these vexing riddles never end?

*****

Rose started upright in her bed. A scream! She was sure she heard a scream! Another piercing cry thrust her from the safety of her pelts. She grabbed her robe, wriggled into the sleeves, and dashed from the chamber. A few feet from Maura's door, Rose paused and stared at the odd sight of Alan kneeling and speaking forcefully through the key hole. She inched closer and heard him implore, "Maura, come and unbolt the door! I can't help you till you unbolt the door. Please do as I ask—" Alan snapped to Rose's looming presence and they both jumped to another horrified shriek. He rattled the door and pleaded to Rose, "Why? Why won't she answer me? What's happening to her? There's no one in there with her, Rose, no one!"

"She's dreaming." Rose dropped to her knees by his side. "Maura," she called stringently, "open the door! Maura, wake up. Maura! Alan..." she said, low and trembling, "we must get to her before she harms herself. Can you force the bolt?"

"Force the bolt!" yelled Alan, his alarm rising. "I...I don't know. Rose, how will she hurt herself?"

"I can't answer that now! We have to get in that room. Break the bolt!"

"Stand back," ordered Alan. Rose wrinkled her face in anguish, tugged on her disheveled braid, and obeyed.

Grunting and heaving, Alan rammed his shoulder furiously against the door, each repeated effort failing. Then the most haunting wail of all sent his boot crashing into the wood. His next lunge flung wide the barrier. He rushed inside the chamber to find the rumpled bed empty, and twisted and turned in panic. "Where, Rose? Where has she gone?!"

Rose gestured for quiet and crept toward the corner of the room. As Alan's eyes adjusted to the dark, he beheld the peculiar image of Maura's coiled figure, huddled tight to the stone, her glazed eyes gorged with a terror that chilled his soul. He started round the bed, but Rose waved him back and whispered, "No, no one can get near her, only I." She crawled cautiously toward the corner, ever murmuring, "Maura, it's Rose, angel. You must wake up. It's the dream, only the dream. No one will harm you."

Maura cried a tormented cry, shielded her face, and pressed further into the recess. Rose lunged forward, seized Maura's wrists, and shook her violently. A horrible gasp escaped Maura as she wrestled the arms that bound her. Slowly Rose's loving gaze crystallized before her waking eyes and she slumped into her safe embrace. "He'll kill me, Rose!" Maura wailed. "Here at Gloucester, he'll murder me. He came so close this time. I saw it so clearly, the sword, the smoke, the man! It's Rufus and he'll kill me!"

"No, no, angel," Rose soothed and rocked, "it wasn't Rufus. This dream haunted you long before you knew him. I believe it's an omen, an omen of danger." Maura clung limply to Rose's chest; her sobs gradually lessened, yet her quivering increased.

Armed with the healing warmth of a candle and blanket, Alan joined them in the rushes. As he bundled Maura, her gaze shone heart-rending thanks, and she whispered, "I'm such a trouble to you."

"I only wish I could have done more to help," he replied.

"I'm sorry I was so harsh, Alan," said Rose. "If we hadn't reached Maura when we did, she would have run from the nightmare. She's hurt herself many times trying to escape."

"You spoke of an omen," said he. "I don't understand."

"And I have no explanation. All I can tell you is when Maura's exhausted or faced with danger, she dreams this horrendous nightmare. There seems to be no cure, but we can see that she sleeps undisturbed for the rest of this night, and the time has come for her to leave Gloucester. I will speak to Will in the morning. At the close of Marc's ceremony, she will journey to Berkhamstead."

Alan nodded and helped the women from the floor. Aided by Rose, Maura groggily climbed into her bed. The instant her head touched the pillow, she drifted off to a deep slumber. Rose stretched stiffly out at her side and Alan blanketed them both, watching awhile as Rose stroked Maura's hair and murmured endearments. He left the bed to examine the bolt and quickly deduced it was beyond repair. Tomorrow he would move Maura's things to Rose's chamber, and for the remainder of this eventful evening, he would guard from inside the door.

*****

Early next morning, Marc peeked through the crack in Maura's door and contemplated Rose's strange behavior. As far as his squinting could determine, she scuttled on hands and knees before the door, stopping every so often to dig through the rushes. "Rose," he called loudly, "what are you doing? Are you feeling well?"

She glanced up to Marc's familiar eye and answered, "The bolt splintered. I'm trying to find the sharpest pieces so no one will harm themselves."

His alarm ignited, he pressed inward, volleying questions, "What's happened?! Was it Rufus? Did he hurt Maura?!"

"Hush!" insisted Rose. She let him inside and issued a warning, "Don't you dare wake your sister! I was up the entire night seeing to her comfort, and I'm in no mood to deal with—"

"Rose," interrupted Maura weakly, pushing up from the bed, "he's caused no harm. I wasn't asleep."

Rose huffed distress and resumed her task. Marc hesitated just inside the door, and Maura answered his bemused expression with a faint grin and pat to the bed. He sat by her and she assured, "It wasn't Rufus, it was only my nightmare. Alan broke the bolt to help me."

Her too brief explanation somewhat quelled his worry, and he looked excitedly to Rose, then back to Maura. "Have...have you two heard the gossip?"

"Gossip? What gossip?" asked Rose. She stood unsteadily and massaged her aching hip as she shuffled to the bed. "Maura, you'd like to hear, wouldn't you?"

Maura nodded and Marc began, "Well, there was a scuffle at last night's feast."

Rose clicked her tongue. "Will Rufus never stop?"

"No Rose, it wasn't Rufus, at least not at the start."

"Then who—"

"Will and Simon."

Maura's mouth fell slack, and Rose scowled, "Simon! What is that yellow haired devil up to now?!"

"I don't know," returned Marc. "I heard their argument was over you, Maura."

"Was he hurt?" Maura blurted.

"Who?" asked Marc.

Rose swiftly answered for her, "Will, of course."

"Not badly. He did cough a bit, though."

"Simon tried to strangle him?!" gasped Rose. "There's no taming that fiend. He knows nothing but trouble! If he dares come near you, Maura, I swear I'll—"

"He won't come near her, Rose," Marc interjected in a somber tone. "Rufus banished him."

"Thank the Heavens!" Rose exhaled, her gaze and hands lifting upward. "My, I never thought I'd agree with anything that beast decided. Perhaps he does own a bit of sense after all. I'm pleased, aren't you Maura?"

Maura stared blankly; one hand gripped the end of her plait, the other the bed curtain. Then, wearing a staid expression, she pulled herself from the bed, walked to the trunk, and slipped into her tunic. Her light, queer speech confused them. "Marc, it's late and we must make you ready for your ceremony. I've so been looking forward to this day. Have I told you how proud I am of you?"

"Too many times," he mumbled.

"Maura, you must take time today to thank Will," said Rose. She bristled at Maura's disregard, and spoke crossly, "Did you hear, Maura?"

"Will you come help us, Rose? After his bath and dressing, Marc's to spend what's left of the morning in the chapel. I will accompany him."

"Maura," said Marc carefully, "Will has already offered his help, and I accepted. I hope you're not offended."

"No, not in the least," she replied, her tone still bland. "I'll await you in the chapel." She wrapped her cloak round her shoulders, stepped into her shoes, and left them dreadfully perplexed.

Rose started after, calling, "Maura, wait for me—"

Marc gently restrained her. "Let her be, Rose. She'll be safe with Alan. Perhaps now you'll tell me what Simon's done to upset you both?"

"Never!" raged Rose, breaking from his hold.

"Then I'll leave you as well." With a biting air, he strode away.

*****

Simon flapped his cloak vigorously, turned out its pockets, then lay it flat to examine its folds. Where? Where had it gone?! He clearly remembered touching the parchment last evening and fingering the bow that bound the scroll, but now the writ had vanished! He knelt and madly rummaged through his filthy clothing, tearing them further in his frantic search. He'd been so careful, so impeccably careful! Without the writ, what credence did he have here? Perhaps Rufus was correct, he was totally inept—a nothing. He had pulled the bed from the wall when a knock intruded. Cursing to himself, he pressed his back to the door and guardedly asked, "Who's there?"

"Henry."

Simon lifted the bolt and returned to the space between wall and bed, where he kicked at cobwebs and filthy rushes to no avail; the writ wasn't there. Henry burst into the room, sporting a too bright expression. At the sight of Simon's attire, he feigned shock, stumbled backward, and collided with the door. His hands clutched at his heart as he exclaimed, "God's teeth, Simon! At last, you've become one of us!"

Simon glanced up irritably and muttered, "You're back early."

"Yes, I wanted to take a look at Marc's ceremony. I do hope he gets severely trounced in the competitions. Now tell me, Simon, where did you get those ravishing clothes?"

"My stepmother loaned them to me." Simon wriggled awkwardly inside the vermilion silk shirt and tunic, and hiked up the droopy braies. "And I feel utterly ridiculous."

"But you look splendid! Did you say your *stepmother*?" Henry's doe-like eyes twinkled with mischief. "I've heard the most delectable tales concerning your stepmother. I question her taste, but could it be she fancies you?"

Simon tugged the sheet from the bed and answered, "I believe she acted out of kindness, nothing more."

"Yes, well, we'll see." Henry's brow knitted in a frown and he wondered, "Why are you destroying your room?"

"I've lost something, something quite important, and I needed it today."

"You'll have to search later. It's nearing mid-day and the crowd has already assembled in the great hall. Did you speak to Maura?"

"Not as yet. I will after the ceremony."

"Why is this meeting so vital, Simon?"

"It's not your concern, Henry."

"You worry me," commented Henry, lounging on the straw mattress. "The women attending the border meeting practically drooled when you walked in the door. And what do you do about it? The instant the formalities were done, you dashed away to meet with Maura. They, I might add, were dreadfully disappointed." Simon batted at Henry's feet. Henry swung them off the side of the bed to provide his favorite relative a seat.

"And I've no doubt you offered them condolence," Simon speculated in an amused voice.

"As best as I know how. They're quite a wild lot, the Welsh. And such a horrid language! Nothing but a rhythmic succession of retching burps. Would you teach me?"

"That wouldn't be an easy task, Henry," grunted Simon, yanking on his boots. "Besides, for the little you need to know, you should let your newly-found Welsh friends teach you."

Henry chafed his hands together in imagined delight. "You mean my newly-found Welsh women. Beds make such fertile ground for learning."

"Tell me, Henry." Simon snatched up his cloak and questioned, "How many bastards have you scattered across Normandy and England?"

"I've lost count," Henry dully returned.

"Well, you'd best take care. They may grow up to give you trouble. If you don't believe me, ask my father."

"I have far too many present cares to fret over the future. And, who knows, it may be an advantage to have my brood milling about the countryside. Come, or we'll be late." The cousins continued their lively bantering along the hallway. "Simon," Henry said, gesturing for emphasis, "you must agree, Welsh women are simply exquisite!"

"They're very nice, Henry."

"Except for one. That little snob of a princess. Wouldn't give me so much as a grunt."

Simon smirked. "Don't you mean a belch?"

"Very droll, Simon," simpered Henry, then he complained louder, "I first thought she knew no English."

"I've heard she can be difficult."

"Only to some, it seems," remarked Henry. "After you'd gone, she promptly found her English tongue and kept nagging me about you. When Marc's ceremony is done, I want you to return with me to Wales. You can have the princess and I'll take her buxom, dark-haired friend. We'll have the most marvelous time—"

"Henry—" Simon interrupted to stress, "You don't hear well, do you? I must stay and speak to Maura."

"W*hy*, Simon? Why do you fritter away your precious time on her, when women everywhere are yearning for you?"

"Henry, I believe you're a bit young to understand my intent."

Henry's face sagged to a sulk and Simon, much preferring his elated state, strove to sway his mood. "I must say, during the mediations, you handled yourself with great aplomb."

"I did *what*?!" asked Henry, deeply offended.

"You acted civilized," clarified Simon.

"Oh...Did I really?"

"Yes, I was quite proud of you."

"Simon," said Henry, askance, "I believe you're trying to improve my vocabulary again."

"I do what I can."

"And I applaud your effort. Well then," added Henry, while draping an arm round Simon's shoulders, "after the ceremony, we'll celebrate my civility and go to town! I'll take you to a tavern where the women are wild and the food is—" Simon stopped him forcibly at the foot of the steps, his stern expression softened by an affectionate smile. Before he could speak, Henry spouted in exasperation, "I know, I know, you must stay and speak to Maura!"

*****

Maura's knees ached from her lengthy devotions. She gazed tenderly at Marc kneeling by her side, and smiled. Clad in glowing white silk, with his eyes closed in prayer, and his auburn hair sparkling gold, he resembled an angel. And she knew of no one else who so perfectly fit the descriptions she had read in the Bible. Mid-day bells and a hovering, robed priest interrupted her prayer for her brother's protection. The priest presented Marc his ceremonial sword, jewel encrusted and blessed, then instructed in a raspy voice, "Go, my children. Your audience awaits you."

Their tranquil stroll to the great hall was marred by Marc's melancholy. "I feel we're walking to our doom."

Maura turned to him, circled his arms with her hands, and argued passionately, "No, Marc! You've trained your entire life for this honor. The hundreds gathered in the hall are there for you, to cheer the bravest knight in the Kingdom! And don't you believe for an instant that Rufus will destroy me. After all, when it comes to the fighting arts, I had the greatest teacher—you. We will both survive our fates, however grim they might seem."

They wandered on and Marc lamented, "You may think this childish, but I'd hoped Simon would attend my ceremony. He promised he'd come."

"You shouldn't have trusted him," she answered curtly. "He doesn't keep promises."

Wisely, Marc abandoned the volatile subject, and they continued on in silence. As they stood hand in hand in the huge framed doorway of the great hall, their quiet spread like contagion amongst the sprightly crowd. Will strode buoyantly to Marc's side and pointed to the dais. "I believe you'll be pleased to hear that Lord Roger, not Rufus, will preside over your ceremony." Marc peered expectantly across the room, past the fire pit to the Earl, and they exchanged radiant smiles. A firm clasp to Marc's shoulder accompanied Will's speech. "I wish you luck, and Father sends his praise. I know you're eager to get on with the formalities so we can proceed to the fun." He wove his arm through Maura's. "We'll leave you now."

She left Marc a tearful kiss and whispered, "I love you."

Will and Maura took their places by Rose at the far end of the dais. Almodis, acting as Lord Robert's representative, stood poised and proper at Roger's side, sensibly clad in a plain russet gown. Her tidy braids peeked from beneath her stark white whimple, and her neck, ears, and wrists were devoid of jewels.

Roger nodded to Marc, who began his long trek across the unnervingly still room. For courage, he locked his anxious gaze on Maura's gleaming expression. Then a familiar face snared his attention. Marc searched and, to his delight, he noticed Simon standing devotedly at the fore of the crowd, young Henry at his side. Simon's broad, bolstering smile gave Marc the strength he needed to still his quaking knees. He pulled himself erect, continued forward, and knelt before his Lord.

Almodis' buzzing family easily distracted her, and she stealthily inched her way in their direction to catch their secrets. Maura spied the object of Marc's diversion and glared lividly at her former lover. Yet when Simon's hopeful look left Marc to settle naturally on her, its intensity drained her anger and her strength. Rose tugged on Maura's arm and ordered in a terse whisper, "Look away! Don't let him steal your thoughts. Keep your mind on your brother. He is most important today!" Her outrage flared at Will. "How did he get back in the castle?!"

"I...I don't know." Will fingered his neck and insisted urgently, "Maura, you must speak to him, tell him you despise him, and order him to leave! Only then will he go."

"No!" she retorted. "I will not meet with him and that is final. Now hush!" She fixed her wide eyes on Marc, and quivered to the heat of Simon's stare.

Marc handed his sword to Lord Roger. The Earl held it upright as Marc leant forward and kissed its jeweled hilt. Next, Marc retrieved the weapon, straddled it across his knees, and braced himself for the accolade. Roger energetically delivered a sturdy blow to the nape of Marc's neck. Mark wavered, but held his stance and the crowd boomed a vivacious cheer. Roger quieted the audience, and his fateful words rang through the rafters, "Be a good knight and brave in battle! May God bless and protect you."

Marc lifted confident eyes to reply, "I will, my Lord."

"You may stand," beamed Roger, stout with pride. He assisted Marc into a polished hauberk, tucked a helm beneath his arm, and bestowed congratulatory kisses.

Maura hurried forward, gave her brother a brisk hug, and called out loudly as she spun to leave, "I must go. You were magnificent! Good luck at the tilt and please take care! I'll be watching and worrying." She was away before he could answer.

Marc whirled to Simon, who elbowed his way through the packed throng, his arms extended. Their fingers had barely touched when Will rudely whisked Marc from his friend, and dragged him, resisting all the way, to the stables. Once there, Marc jerked from Will's hold and railed, "I wanted to speak to Simon!"

"He's dangerous and a foul influence. It's best to avoid him." Will's voice suddenly rose in elation, "Wait till you see the destrier Father bought for you!"

As the coal-black stallion was backed from the stall, Marc promptly forgot his complaint and stared agog at the massive beast. He delicately stroked the horse's bulging neck and received an appreciative snort in response. "He's all mine?"

"Yes, and he'll serve you well."

"I don't know what to say...I'm so grateful. Will, thank you, thank you!" Marc gushed, continuing his admiration of his majestic gift.

"It's nothing you don't deserve." Will stilled the war horse while Marc mounted, and praised on, "We hear you're the most skilled soldier in Grandfather's garrison. You definitely proved your prowess in your tilt against Stephen. And who's the unfortunate bugger to be today?"

Marc gripped the reins and guided the expertly trained animal into the bailey. He glanced over his shoulder to utter, "All will know when I make my announcement."

Rose and Maura tightened their cloaks against a raggling wind and tramped through crisp mud to the platform. Rose struggled to keep pace and her voice strained unwelcomed comments. "Maura, I agree with Will. Confront Simon, confess your hate, and order him to leave! He'll listen only to you. At Winchester, even the threat of prison wouldn't budge him from your side."

Maura heard only the moaning gale. The platform's flapping canvas roof joined its sad song, then a new sound, harsh and ominous, drowned all the others. She raised a worried expression to find the owner of the vacillating bellow, and saw atop the platform Rufus striking a young page. The boy hurtled backward from the FitzRoy's brutal blow, crashed into the chairs, and hit the floor, wailing. Rufus resumed his vicious onslaught with his boot, pummeling the lad's belly and groin. Maura vaulted the ladder and threw herself between prince and page. She glared up into Rufus' ferocious face and screamed, "How vile can you be to beat a child?!"

"He spilt wine on me and will be punished! Move or the next kick is yours...my very foolish Lady."

She stood, postured, and challenged, "Then kick!"

Their heated space suddenly darkened as a flock of armed men circled and pressed inward. For a horrific instant, Maura believed Rufus would explode and kill her, no matter the consequences. Instead, his eyes shifted warily between her protectors—Lord Roger and Alan flanking Rufus' shoulders, and Roger's guard looming at his back. Rufus' bulk deflated and he cautioned in a snarl, "I'll have my revenge, my Lady, at a later, more convenient time. Ne...never forget my promise!"

Maura promptly turned to tend the child, while Roger berated, "God's breath, Rufus, stop your squawking! If you can't control yourself, leave, otherwise go sit in your chair and behave!"

"To Hell with the lot of you...you...you sniveling slime!" bellowed Rufus. He lurched to the fore of the podium and pitched into his exalted seat. It tottered steeply, then straightened as he forced his broad backside onto its cushiony folds.

"Rose," Maura called, cuddling the sobbing child. "Will you please take him to the keep and have the physician check his wounds? I believe he's more frightened than hurt."

"Of course I will," replied Rose.

With the boy wrapped in the crux of her arm, Rose passed by Will, standing aghast at the top of the stairs. He shook from his awe and reverently took Maura's hand, muttering as he guided her to the chair behind Rufus', "We'll let the baby sulk on his own." Her ambivalent expression baffled him, and he vehemently stated, "I'm astounded by your gall, Maura! Few can defy Rufus as you did and live to tell the tale."

"It wasn't gall, Will," she said quietly, squeezing his hand. "It was only exhaustion. I'm too tired to be afraid of him." She snapped her head to a flash of yellow hair in the crowd.

Will knew for whom she searched and coerced, "You must meet with Simon and demand that he bother you no more! Or do you enjoy the notion of spending forever peering over your shoulder?"

"I won't!" Her spread palms pushed tensely at the air as she harshly emphasized, "I won't be pressured by you or Rose or anyone! Now stop your nagging."

Rose joined them and whispered, "The lad will be fine." Then she noticed their discordant faces. "What's happened here?"

"She refuses to hear reason," answered Will.

"That's nothing new," commented Rose.

"Maura," stressed Will, "last evening I attempted, rather painfully, to stop Simon from barging to your chamber! If Rufus hadn't banished him, I cringe to think what might have occurred. Only *you* have the power to rid us of this vulgar pest!"

"I agree, Maura," said Rose, "and you needn't meet with him alone. I'll be there, armed, in case he oversteps his bounds."

Maura stared stridently ahead, dismissing their haggling with a tepid silence. The wind nipped at her cheeks and stung her eyes. She covered her face with her gloved hands, and breathed into her palms to create a little warmth. A sudden cheer gathered her scattered thoughts. Marc, resplendent upon his new steed, cantered into the arena, paused to nod at Rufus, then proceeded with his masterful show of horsemanship. Tears of admiration glistened Maura's cheeks as she watched him jab, chop, and dodge his spurious enemies. The contests of adults so closely matched the games of her youth. How she craved that time—a time laden with innocence, trust, joy and love.

Simon leant against the fat cord of twine that secured the tent serving as a makeshift stable, and watched his friend from a distance. It seemed so queer that Marc had made the brilliant transition from bumbling page to knight—the greatest knight in the kingdom, or so he'd been told. Seeing Marc this way made him feel ancient, and he missed their early times together, especially Marc's steadying influence, unbending loyalty, and strict virtue. Simon looked about the stables and noticed soldiers grooming their horses, loitering, and gaming. Soon, most would depart for battle, Marc among them, he supposed. And then a brief thought flickered—if matters had gone differently, Simon himself would have been a member of the troop, warring alongside these gruff strangers. He didn't miss the fighting, mock or real. His present vocations, though at times frustrating, were fulfilling and, for the most part, peaceful. Folding his arms across his chest, he cast a furtive glance at the podium. There Maura sat, straight and attentive, on the edge of her chair, her attention wholly focused on Marc. Watching Maura, Simon mused—there was nothing in this world his hungry heart missed more than her. He barely smiled and allowed himself a tad of hope, for at the ceremony her expression had betrayed little anger.

His demonstration done, Marc waited restively before the podium for the FitzRoy's cue; instead he was addressed by rumbling snores. Roger left his seat, shot a disgusted look Rufus' way, and declared, "Please excuse the Prince, Marc. It appears he is quite tired. We all are highly impressed with your show thus far, and are eager to know—who is your contender to be?"

Marc gulped uncertainly and hesitated. Everyone present would undoubtedly react severely to his choice, but there was no question in his mind as to the identity of his rival. "I challenge—" he shouted into the howling wind, "Simon FitzRobert!"

Stunned, Roger waited a moment, then replied hastily, "No, that would not be wise. Lord Robert will be displeased."

"I was led to believe it was *my* choice, my Lord."

"Yes...however..."

What joy, Will thought, as he leapt from his seat and rushed to the fore of the platform. Marc would perform the lethal deed and at last rid him of Simon! "Grandfather, wait!" he protested loudly, and reaching the Earl's side, whispered, "Why deny the lad his fun? And Father will be thrilled to hear of Simon's downfall."

The crowd buzzed with bewilderment which escalated when Simon's name blared from every corner of the bailey.

Simon, however, remained blissfully ensconced in his reverie. Maniacal guffaws at his back startled him aware, and his confusion surged to Henry's announcement, "And so you will finally be allowed the honor to play knight, Simon!"

"What are you babbling about?" Simon asked sternly, tugging against Henry's grip.

"Marc wants to fight you!" Henry exclaimed, a wily grin filling his face.

"Fight *me*!" Simon burst out a farcical laugh. "What nonsense. Let go!"

"It's true! Didn't you hear his pronouncement? Come, we must suit and arm you."

"Oh, no, I'll not be party to your outrageous schemes!" fumed Simon as Henry wrestled him toward the stacks of armor. Henry's laughter turned hysterical as Simon's struggling intensified. He nodded to two brawny soldiers nearby; each wrenched an arm and stilled Simon's flailing. Henry fought to stifle his glee, then sputtered between snickers, "Marc...Marc has challenged you. It is the code...of...of knighthood to accept his challenge."

"I'm not a knight!" Simon shrilly countered, yanking fiercely for freedom. "I haven't fought in years!"

"It wasn't that long ago, and if I remember correctly *you* were the best. Simon, you will disappoint Marc greatly if you refuse him. Do you really want to bruise his feelings on this very special day?"

"Oh Henry, why did you have to say it like that?" asked Simon with a perturbed sneer. His fury faded, and the soldiers stepped aside.

"Oh, what wondrous fun this will be!" extolled Henry, passing Simon a hauberk and helm.

A grunt was Simon's only response. Curses rumbled from his surly scowl as he obstinately donned the armor.

"God's blood, Simon, smile!" commanded Henry. "For the past week, your face has been longer than my hound's, and his company has been far more stimulating. What you need is something to set your blood atingling and, besides a warm woman, I can think of no better treatment than Marc, the invincible, bashing you about."

"I appreciate your concern, Henry," answered Simon cynically, "but I don't want to do this!"

"If you're a bit rusty, then it will be over fairly quickly. And not to worry, I'll be there to scrape up the pieces."

"What a marvelous friend you are," muttered Simon straightening his helmet. "I won't take my horse."

"Of course not! What would a Welsh pony know about the intricacies of a tilt? Take my Fulk. He knows the course intimately and will improve your jittery performance."

While Henry ran off to fetch Fulk, Simon paced fitfully, ruminating over his unfortunate talent for attracting trouble. And furthermore, why had Marc chosen him? He hadn't seemed at all hostile in the great hall. Perhaps Will had been feeding Marc defaming lies. Well, Simon thought, as Henry approached with his towering gray in tow, he'd soon discover Marc's motive, and would offer little resistance in return.

Panicked, Maura gripped Will's arm, and begged, "Stop this! You must stop this now!"

"Why would I want to do that?" asked Will dryly. "Opportunities such as these come far too infrequently to waste. I'll cherish seeing Simon pulverized, and I'm surprised the idea upsets you, Maura. Could it be you still harbor tender feelings for the rake?"

"No, you don't understand. It's Marc who will suffer! Please, Will, if you care for me, for Marc, please stop the tilt."

"You're acting silly. It is Marc's decision, Maura. You are his sister, not his mother. Now, sit still and behave yourself!"

Inflamed by Will's brashness, Maura left her seat and strained her entreaty on bended knee to Lord Roger. "My Lord, I beg you, please refuse Marc his wish. Don't allow Simon to fight!"

"Why ever not?" asked Roger. "Besides, Simon has already entered the ring, there's nothing I could do, even if I chose to. If the sight of blood disturbs you, Maura, take yourself to your chamber, otherwise take your seat."

Maura returned, bent and glum, to her chair. Rose strove to cheer, "Have more faith in your brother, Maura. Simon will be disgraced and I, for one, will be thrilled to see it happen."

"Listen to Rose, Maura, for she speaks the truth. And I apologize for my rudeness," added Will, his fingers weaving neatly through hers.

"You don't understand," emphasized Maura.

"Understand what, angel?" asked Rose.

Maura's hooded gaze shifted to the arena where Marc and Simon cantered to their meeting place. Her grim answer was but a whisper, "Simon will win."

The opponents' horses snorted and danced with exhilaration. Simon stared severely at Marc from beneath the brow of his helmet, and asked, "Why me?"

"I wanted the chance to beat you."

"And?"

"No other reason," answered Marc, too casually.

Simon looked skeptical. "I've never known you to lie," he said, offering his hand. "You'll get your chance quickly."

Marc grabbed hold, and warned with a wrenching grip, "Don't fake this match. I'll know if you do, and I swear, Simon, I will never speak to you again."

After a pensive moment, Simon nodded sharply and proclaimed, "Then let's begin."

Henry shoved gawkers aside and clambered up the fence for a finer view. His wiggling caused him to slip continually from the slats, and his frenetic mumbling alarmed bystanders. "I've waited too long to see this and what a superb competition it will be! I wonder how Simon will handle himself. It has been years, but no, he'll prevail, I know he'll win. He has to!"

The men trotted to opposite ends of the arena and squirmed with anticipation in their saddles. A brusque wave of a squire's arm sent them charging ahead at tremendous speed. The resultant crash catapulted Marc out of his saddle. He soared through the air, and landed with a sickening thud on his back in the frozen dirt. Simon fared no better. Jolted backwards, he somersaulted over the rump of Henry's horse, and hit the spiky ice face first. Neither moved. The crowd jeered displeasure. All on the podium sprang from their seats. Will firmed his grip on Maura to keep her from escaping to her brother, and exclaimed, "My, what a rousing start! I pray it's not over."

Maura strained against his hold, yet calmed as Simon and Marc stirred and rose to their knees. Shakily, they stood, took a moment to orient themselves, then accepted swords from the squires. The crowd hooted and howled their elation. Henry balanced on the fence, whooping himself hoarse.

The battlers trudged with their swords braced in an ever-tightening circle, till they were near enough to strike. Their feeble attempts at lunging and parrying frustrated the crowd, and shouts demanding blood soon shot from the ravenous horde.

"They want blood," Simon huffed, dodging a well-placed jab.

"Should we give them some?" asked Marc, a menacing grimace trembling his lips.

"It's entirely up to you."

"Then I say, yes!" Marc swung his sword to the sky, and savagely slammed its broad side across Simon's shoulder. The mighty blow drove Simon to his knees, then to his chest. Marc inhaled proudly, then let out a piercing cry as his feet flew out from beneath him.

Simon flung himself upon Marc and flattened him to the ground. Marc arched, thrashed, and kicked futilely as Simon's twisted face loomed near. "I sense you're angry with me!" he spat through bared teeth.

Marc writhed and groused, "Why would you think that?"

"Something in your eyes."

"Somehow you've hurt Maura," replied Marc in scornful gasps. "Rose says I'm too young to hear the truth, but I'm not too young for revenge!"

Simon eased his grip to Marc's curious words, and anger swiftly overtook his puzzlement. He'd been lured into a web of lies, robbed of his belongings and pride, mocked, and now he was to be humiliated! He swore inwardly that whoever devised this diabolical ploy would not triumph easily. He grabbed the jaw of Marc's helm and yanked it off. "Well then," he gritted, "let's stop our pretty dancing and make this a bit more interesting." Simon rolled to his feet. Marc scrambled away, and gaped in disbelief as Simon shed his hauberk and helm, clenched his sword's hilt, and postured for war. A shiver of dread crept up Marc's spine as he clumsily rose and stripped down to his ceremonial tunic.

Simon poked and prodded, provoking Marc to let fly a volley of fleeting strikes, which Simon expertly blocked. They raged on with perilous enthusiasm and the hushed crowd stood, bug-eyed and stiff.

Sporting a stupefied grin, Will spouted, "I've never witnessed such insanity. They'll kill each other! Isn't it marvelous?!"

Maura didn't answer his crass comments. She bit her lip, stared intently at her lap, and covered her ears with her gloved hands, hoping to drown the deafening carnage; it didn't work.

Expertly paired, the rivals whacked endlessly at each other with the flats of their swords. Time and time again, they dove to the ground, grappling and slithering in the freezing muck. Their ferocious blows extracted a toll not in wounds, but in exhaustion. The graceful fray at last turned ungainly. Grunting and wheezing, they slid and stumbled, delivering useless hits. Despite the cold, sweat poured from their heaving bodies, drenched their clothes, and clouded the air around them. Their only victory was in igniting the crowd's deafening impatience. Dung lifted from the stables rained down upon them. The pelting invigorated them, and their strikes intensified as they strove to end the grueling duel.

Marc swept his blade viciously at Simon's head, nicking his brow, and also knocking Marc off balance. He tripped in a hole and tumbled to the ground. Simon, blood trickling down his face, used his sword as a cane and hobbled close. Marc pushed up on his elbows to see gaping faces, scurrying squires, and Simon swirling madly before him.

"Please, get up," Maura mumbled, her hands clasped together as if in prayer. "Marc, you have to get up! I know you have the strength...*Please!*"

A turbulent silence accompanied the long delay. And then, Marc shut his eyes and collapsed. The audience's collective sigh swelled to a sonorous hurrah as they surged inward and bulged the reinforced fence. Simon knelt and extended a helping hand. Marc refused him. "No, Simon," he said faintly, his eyes shining with weary respect, "I'm really quite comfortable here. Thank you, it was a good fight, a fair fight."

"And it was a draw. You didn't lose, Marc, you merely slipped."

"Will you do me one final favor, Simon?"

"Anything."

Marc reached up his sleeve and produced a gaily colored scarf. "Take this. Give it to Maura. Perhaps it will help mend your troubles."

Simon gladly accepted the material, and fondly watched Marc sink back into the cushiony mire. He stood and wavered; a squire provided him a lance, and a hand-up as he mounted Fulk.

Maura's chest rose and fell in rampant grief, Rose's hands hid her anguish, and Will sat rigid and dumb. Rufus stood to Simon's approach, his hearty applause stirring the crowd to a frenzy. "Marvelous show, Cousin!" he bellowed. "I'm glad we made our little deal."

"Deal? What deal?" Rose asked, frantically tugging on Will's tunic. "Did you know about this, this deal?"

Will slapped away her hand and shrugged miserably.

Simon impaled the scarf on his lance and thrust it upward; its target—Maura.

Will's depression instantly lifted. This was it! The perfect moment at last had come! "Maura, do it now!" he gasped. "Tell him you hate him. Send him away. Do it now!"

"Yes, Maura," pressed Rose, "shame him as he did Marc. Curse him, spit on him! Make him go!"

A searing pain stabbed Maura's head. She cradled her brow, yet their deafening coercion spiraled and forced her to her feet. Will and Rose froze in suspense as they watched Maura walk steadily to the fore of the platform.

Simon sat slumped on the huge gray, his shirt tattered and stained, his skin encrusted with dirt, and a stream of blood trickling from his brow. Maura's face betrayed nothing as she stretched out and plucked the cloth from the tip of the lance. Will lunged forward to stop her, but Rose grabbed his cloak and jerked him forcefully back in his seat.

Maura vacantly met Simon's fawning gaze, then, deliberately, she dropped her eyes and the scarf. Caught by a breeze, the token of peace fluttered down, spooking Fulk. He reared; his hoof clipped the cloth, and plunged it deep into the murky earth. Maura turned her back on Simon and hurried from the podium.

Will laughed uproariously at Simon's defeat and Rufus avidly joined his hysterics. Will's mirth, though, promptly ceased when Simon dismounted and stormed toward the podium. Will squirmed in terror, yelping for protection. Simon ignored his ravings, and charged past the platform after Maura.

*****

CHAPTER EIGHT - THE BRINK

On the platform, Rose sprang from her chair. Will caught her arm and muttered wickedly, "I expect you're quite adept with one of these." He offered his dagger, whispering, "Use it with my blessing."

"I have my own," she growled. Her grimace unnerved him. He promptly released her and vowed never to make the dire mistake of crossing the Lady Rose.

Rufus scooted his chair close and the cousins exchanged winning grins, Rufus wondering, "Did you stage that glorious finale?"

"Oh no, I can't take all the credit. Maura's performance was enthralling, don't you think?"

"Yes...simply exquisite," laughed Rufus. "I've neglected to thank you for scaring Adela's party off so neatly."

"Thanks are fine, yet I prefer other compensation. The clerk cost me a whole mark!"

"Which nicely rationalized his sin, I'm sure."

"It was only a tiny lie," stressed Will. "The Angevins are always invading someone. I'd like the mark, and more, and I want it all by the close of Christmas Court."

"You'll get what's due you," sneered Rufus.

"Well, Cousin Rufus," sighed Will, rising and stretching. "Will you join me in the keep to witness what could prove to be the most thrilling competition of all?"

"I'd love to, Cousin Will! Care to risk a wager on the outcome?"

"No, I don't squander my money. There's little doubt who the victor will be. Come, or it will all be over by the time we arrive."

Arm in arm, they strolled good-naturedly across the bailey. Almodis, lurking beneath the platform, watched till the men disappeared behind the keep door, then followed surreptitiously in their path.

*****

Her heart hammering to burst, Maura flew up the dizzying staircase. She paused to gulp breaths and heard encroaching boot steps quickening, racing the stairs after her. Hounds bounded from her flurried figure as she dashed the length of the passageway and ducked into her chamber. She flung herself against the door, groped for the bolt, then realized with trembling exasperation—there was no bolt! Cursing, she frenziedly yanked at the trunk; it refused to budge. The door burst open. She spun and beheld Simon, his face a disfigured mess of pain and dirt.

"Simon, don't come any nearer!" pleaded Maura.

"I believed you wanted to see me!" he despaired while self-consciously wiping his palms on the skirt of his tunic. He searched her wretched expression, saw no anger, and stubbornly advanced.

Maura forced her eyes from his. It was dangerous to look at him, it was lethal! She wrung her hands, fought for control and stuttered, "You...you believed wrong." He inched closer; she begged louder, "Stop, Simon. I don't want you near!"

"I need to talk to you. You must hear me out!"

"There's nothing to say."

"You can't mean that!"

"I do. Now go."

"At Winchester you begged me to stay...why?"

"I was ill...frightened...I spoke nonsense."

"No! You knew it was me. You called out my name!"

She hugged her quaking body and retreated, yet the trunk blocked her escape. He chanced a bold step nearer, his reaching hand trembling, desperate to touch.

A strident command intervened, "Keep away from her, Simon! Get yourself from this chamber and castle! There's nothing but hate for you here." Rose loomed in the doorway, stern and rigid with her dagger poised to strike.

"No, Rose!" Maura shouted. "No more violence. He will leave peacefully. Put the dagger down!"

"I won't go!" countered Simon, never turning from Maura. "Not till you tell me—what happened after I left Dunheved?"

Rose surged forward, screeching, "Curse you, fiend! You won't torture her again!"

Simon whirled to her assault and sternly warned, "Stay away, Rose! I'm not here to battle you."

"You have no choice! You're as evil as Rufus and twice as ruthless. What deal did you make with him?"

He shunned her hysterics, turned back, and held tight Maura's shoulders. "Tell me, Maura, tell me what happened!"

His touch scorched. The room spun. She wouldn't remember—she'd go mad if she remembered! Maura grabbed the bed curtains for balance, and raked feebly at his biting grip. "Simon, don't, don't! You're hurting me...*Please* let go!"

Simon spun to Maura's gasp and easily blocked Rose's strike. The dagger dropped from her twisted wrist, making her howl and attack again. Her frenzied blows drove Simon up against the wall. He held back, afraid of hurting Rose; her fight intensified, and his sound shove sent her reeling backward into Maura's arms.

Rose never weakened, never hesitated. She clamped Maura's hand, and dragged her toward the door, ranting, "You'll come away with me! We'll leave the guards to deal with him."

Maura staggered along, then felt Simon squeeze her other hand and heard his sweetest voice, "Look at me, Maura...*please*, look at me." She gazed back into his damp eyes and listened. "I've searched years for you! I can't let you go. Stay with me awhile, talk to me."

"Release her or I swear I'll call for Rufus!" roared Rose.

Undaunted, Simon's hold tensed and his free hand tenderly skimmed Maura's cheek. Her tears welled to his loving gesture.

Rose's harsh yank and ultimatum sent Maura stumbling again for the door. "I will haul you from this room if you don't follow!" roared Rose. "Tear yourself away, he's a trickster, nothing more!"

Simon fiercely jerked Maura back. For a terrible instant, she felt her mind and body splitting apart and wailed, "Stop this madness! By God, let me go!" They released her. She stood a long torturous moment, heaving distress, her eyes squeezed shut...and then she looked to Simon. She accepted his outstretched hand. He drew her to the bed, and willingly she followed.

Panicked, Rose ran to the door and hollered, "Alan! Alan, where in Heaven's name are you?!" There was no sign of him so she heightened her squall, "Guards! Help us, please, guards!"

A loud commotion erupted in the hallway as heavy boot steps tramped from every direction. Yet Simon and Maura heard not a thing. They shared somber looks and let their fingers mingle, his stroking her palm, rekindling a spell that paralyzed. She could neither move nor break her gaze. A fever rose in her cheeks, her heart raced, and an aching shiver racked her body.

A scuffling at the door and the scraping of unsheathed swords jolted her aware. "Simon," she urgently warned, "you must go! Your enemies are everywhere."

"Are *you* my enemy, Maura?" His grip tensed. "Answer me! Are you?!"

"Go. They'll murder you!"

"My safety doesn't concern me."

"It concerned you once! If you won't go, I will."

"No! Stay with me. We'll leave together—"

She pried from his hold, covered her ears, and vigorously wagged her head. Her mind screamed—*don't listen, you can't listen, he speaks lies, killing lies, get away, run!* She snapped her head to the guards blocking the door, their swords brandished; then to Rose's condemning glare; and lastly to Simon, so close his breath warmed her cheek.

He ripped away her hands from her ears, and his cry, "You can't have forgotten our love!" at last ignited her ire.

"Our love!" she shrilled, her face contorted with hate. She lurched from the bed and raved, "Our love was an obscenity, as are you! You left me to be tortured for our sins. You let Robert take our—"

"He holds her against her will! Seize him!" Rose commanded the guards, drowning Maura's lament.

The guards pounced, wrenching Simon's arms to his back. He groaned and strained, choking on his misery, "Maura, you...you can't leave me! Don't...don't go. I never left you to be punished! I didn't know. You must believe, I never knew!"

She paused briefly in the doorway, her face awash with tears, and implored the guards, "Please...please don't hurt him."

Rose's fierce black eyes bore into Simon's, her spittle struck his cheek, and he cringed to her deafening portent, "Next time we meet, you will die!" Rose left him another gob of spit, and forced her charge from the door, but not before Maura graced Simon one last glance.

The devastation in her eyes fueled his vehemence. He tore loose of the guards and chased after them.

In the hall, Marc caught Maura's arm as she raced by. Her crazed look alarmed him. "Maura, what's wrong?! What happened?" She fought him; he shook her still and insisted, "Tell me!"

Whimpering, "No...no..." she struggled free and sprinted for the steps leading to the battlements.

Rose reached Marc and gasped, "I'll fetch Maura. You must stop Simon! Use any means, only stop him!"

Marc steeled himself and bodily blocked Simon's hurtling advance. "Let me by!" howled Simon, striking out furiously.

"No, Simon!" Marc winced at Simon's blows and crushing grip, yet answered with astounding calm. "Let her be, don't bother her more. She's suffered enough."

Their wrestling came to an abrupt halt as a pack of growling guards encircled them. Coarse snickering and laughter parted the testy group. Rufus eyed Simon with revulsion, then cracked a complacent grin. "Why am I not surprised to find you in the crux of all this upset? Not only are you impertinent, you have a terrible memory. The prisons are not very comfortable here at Gloucester. It's entirely your choice, Cousin. You either leave here now, or take a lengthy trip underground."

Light-headed from fatigue and disillusion, Simon wavered. Marc offered a bracing hand as Simon struggled inwardly to salvage a last bit of mettle, a daring retort; all he could find was hopelessness. "I'll...go," he mumbled. "Be...before I leave..." He paused and shot Will a murderous glare. "I would speak to my brother—alone."

"No!" Will strenuously protested, "I won't be alone with him!"

Rufus chortled at Will's terror. "Now, now, calm yourself, Will. Let's not show all how truly spineless you are. Do you actually think I'd let this puny turd harm my dearest companion?" Rufus crossed his arms and added with defiant glee, "Take one of my guards to Maura's chamber and hear Simon out!"

"I...I have nothing to say to the stinking traitor!"

Rufus' strident command, "Take my guard and go with him, now!" stifled any further argument. Will, bent and timorous, entered Maura's chamber with Simon following. Before Will could utter an objection, Simon slumped to the rushes before the door, pressed his back against the wood, and blocked the guard's entrance.

The soldier's pounding faded and was replaced by outrageous laughter from the group amassed outside. Will stood aghast, his face crimson and balled fists shaking. "Get away from the door and let the guard in at once!"

"You don't need the guard, Will," Simon said wearily. "I'm too exhausted to fight, and I humbly admit defeat. I have only one question to ask—Why? It's obvious you devised this entire farce. I simply want to know why."

Will sat back uneasily on the trunk, thought a moment, took a mustering breath, and began, "Your question betrays your stupidity, Brother. While you piddle your life away cowing to Uncle William, I impatiently await my inheritance. And the waiting can be extremely tedious. So I dream up ways to entertain myself—and the grandest game of all came to me at Winchester. When I saw Maura there, I was intrigued and her memory lingered with me. I wanted her body and I wanted you gone." Will braved a glance Simon's way—he sat hunched forward, staring down at the rushes, and didn't seem at all threatening. Will's courage and chest swelled as he squatted, swept up the fallen dagger, then flopped atop the bed's mussed pelts. He spun the blade's handle in is palm, and sent dots of reflected candlelight dancing across the walls. Smirking at his artistry, he gloated, "My plan was really quite simple, yet ingenious. I kept Maura's tension high and fed her hate for you, while feeding your hunger for her. Then I gambled on you doing something totally ridiculous to anger her—battling Marc, offering the scarf, and charging up here to harass her—how absolutely perfect! All of my players, especially Rufus, performed their roles flawlessly. And now, I will end my drama by announcing the news that will make Maura completely mine." He stood quickly, thrust the blade into the mattress, and swaggered over to his brother. "Were you wondering where this had gone to?" he asked, tugging a rolled parchment from his belt. A snort of triumph escaped him as he dangled the Yorkshire marriage writ over Simon's bowed head. Simon lifted his eyes and, with a long, ragged sigh, dropped them again. "Another foolish mistake, little brother. Never, *never* leave your possessions unattended." Will crouched and growled, "The sight of you sickens me! You're like a festering boil, always popping up and causing trouble. I'd love to see you dead. Unfortunately that's not within my power, at least not now. I can and will, though, encourage Father to punish you for your crimes against our family, and there are always...accidents." Will straightened and pointed rigidly at the door, "Now go—run away, far away, and hide yourself. And on your ride, think of Maura locked in my arms, writhing and moaning in ecstasy. It will happen, little brother, believe that it will!" Simon rose stiffly and let the door swing open on its own. Will stepped back and, with a snide grin, goaded, "What, no clever quip to end our conversation? Why Simon, you've lost your touch, in more ways than one, I dare say."

Simon fixed a blank stare on his brother, and spoke with scant emotion, "I do have a few words. You haven't won a damned thing, Will. I know Maura well. She will never succumb to you. And even though slight, there is always a chance of reconciliation between Father and myself." As he skulked out the door, his final words drifted back. "And if that should occur, *dearest* brother, what then becomes of your fortune?"

Simon's response torched Will's temper. He howled curses, ripped the bed curtains, and his final decree rattled the walls, "God's blood, I will see that bastard dead—and soon!"

All the hecklers had gone, leaving Almodis alone with Simon in the hall. Her expression dripped sympathy as she struggled to keep abreast of him, and asked, "You love Maura very deeply, don't you?" He stopped and stared, wrenching her heart with his mournful gaze. Her assuring words spilled easily, "She'll go with him to Berkhamstead tomorrow, yet not alone. I will follow and keep them apart and her safe." She nodded to the pressure of his fingers on her palm and, watching him stride away, brushed her palm across her cheek.

The chamber door burst wide and Henry started up from Simon's bed. "Simon," he exclaimed, "you were spectacular! A little slow at the finish, but that was to be ex—" He froze mid-word, as he beheld Simon's look—dark and piercing, it shouted caution. Henry knew better; still, he pressed, "I take it your talk with Maura went badly." Simon scowled, Henry shrank back, and gaped as his cousin stripped off his shredded tunic in a fitful frenzy. "Forget her, Simon! Forget them all!" Henry prodded dangerously. "You'll come with me. We'll go to Wales!" Simon snatched up his cloak. Henry panicked at his fierce silence, clutched his arm, and whined, "Where Simon? Where are you going?!"

Simon tried to shake him loose. Henry hung on tight, prompting Simon's retort, "Get off me!"

Henry obeyed and pestered from a distance, "I'll go with you, keep you company—"

"No!"

"Where will you go?"

"I don't know. Some place far from here."

"I may need you! How will I find you?"

"You won't, no one will!" Simon left. Henry sank limply to the bed, his disbelieving stare aimed at the swinging door as he prayed Simon would realize his fault and return. But he didn't come back. Henry cradled his brow, and silently cursed Maura. That hateful bitch—this tragedy was entirely her doing! If they should ever meet, he swore he'd make her life as wretched as she'd just made his.

Simon galloped from the castle. He kept his eyes forward, not daring to look back lest he weaken and subject himself again to his family's scorn. No, they were forever lost to him, and he was glad of it. He steered E'dain through the village gates and vowed not to tarry till he'd reached Dunheved.

*****

A soupy fog cloaked the battlements. Marc peered blindly through the smog, creeping forward, calling softly, "Maura, where are you? Please, answer me." A thick coat of ice clung to the stone, making his search treacherous. His nails chipped at the slick wall, groping for a hold; his boot tips dug into the gravel to steady his footing. A brisk wind briefly cleared the haze and what he saw made his heart lurch—Maura crouched precariously between the teeth of the battlements, her attention stuck on the bailey below. Any sharp word from him would surely send her over the brink. He spied the back of her belt. If he could get near enough without alarming her and grab hold, there might be a chance. His trembling fingers had barely touched the leather when she shifted from his reach, and he heard laughter, an eerie, giddy laughter. So, carefully, he tried again, this time managing to wedge his fingers under the belt. He firmed his grip, jerked backward, and yelled, "Maura!"

Her horrified gasp startled them both. She lurched forward, he back; his added weight yanked her off the wall, and they toppled to the roof. He searched through the mist for her face, expecting a tormented expression, only he discovered instead an elated, almost childlike visage. She scrambled to her feet, tugged on his arm, and twittered, "Marc, Marc! There are bonfires in the bailey! You *do* remember, don't you, how we used to build bonfires at Dunheved? Come with me. Take me to see them!"

He rose cautiously and answered, "Yes...yes, we'll go to the bailey. You must take care, Maura, the stone is slippery. Take my hand and I'll help you."

Marc breathed a heavy sigh of relief as she grasped his hand and dragged him down the stairs, her odd euphoria never ceasing. "We used to dance around the flames and when the fire calmed, we'd leap over it. You remember, Marc, don't you?"

"Yes, Maura, I remember, I remember," he replied, stumbling along.

In the bailey Marc's worry grew as, jostled by the crowd, he floundered to keep up with Maura's rapid pace. At last they broke free of the crammed bodies and paused before a bonfire. Maura stood entranced, her wide stare fixed deep within the depths of the flames. Marc's fascination turned troubled as he saw her eyes glaze over with a queer sort of rapture.

The fiery fingers of the pyre beckoned her to Dunheved, back to Simon and the garden where their loving had begun. Simon reached out to her, his radiance flushed her skin; ecstasy overtook her, luring her to his safe embrace. Touch his hand and all the hurt would vanish, just one touch and she'd have him back...back forever...

"Maura no!" Marc struck her hand from the flames, threw her to ground, and fell upon her blazing sleeve. She'd felt no pain till Marc's scream and now as the burning seared her skin and soul, she moaned in agony. Marc crushed her to his chest, anguishing, how could he leave for Normandy knowing her fragile state?! Yet he was powerless to help; the King had commanded and he must obey. As he rocked her in his arms, Winchester briefly stirred his mind. Rose's words, 'there's nothing left of her' came to him, and he realized their truth. *Who* was the culprit? Who possessed the incalculable strength to break her spirit? Rufus? Never. It would take more than brawn to defeat Maura. Simon? Marc recalled how inseparable they had been, and only one so close owned the power to hurt this viciously. But what?! What terrible deed had he done?

The shrouding mist descended, deepening Maura's sobs. Slowly the crowd thinned and, as the fires sputtered and shrank, Marc helped his sister up from the ground. His support gave her the strength to retreat to the keep, to Rose, to a chamber with a bolt, and to a bed that harbored no nightmares.

Before her chamber, Rose slowed her pacing as she noticed Alan's nonchalant approach. "Where were you?!" she raged.

"I...I didn't know I was needed," he mumbled in defense.

"Not needed! Maura was in danger, you are her guard. Your behavior was inexcusable—"

"Danger from what?! From whom?" he asked, his tone equally as sharp.

"Simon attacked her!"

"Simon?" he repeated, befuddled. "No, he would never! And I didn't know it was my duty to protect Maura from the person who asked me to guard her."

"What are you saying?!" Rose flared, hiking her arms high in exasperation. Their squabble halted to the wretched sight of Marc and Maura slowly making their way down the passage. "Maura!" called Rose, hurrying to her side and urging her from Marc's hold. "I'll take her now, Marc. Thank Heaven you were near!" she said, throwing a bitter look Alan's way. "What she needs most is quiet."

Alan sagged to the floor in a disgruntled heap, and Marc noted to Rose before leaving, "I'm due to depart late morning. If you have need of me before then, you know where—"

"Yes, yes, I promise to send for you."

With difficulty, Marc forced himself down the hall; he turned once to add, "Rose, she burned her hand."

"I'll see to it, Marc."

Rose waved him away, then felt Maura stiffen and faintly object, "Call him back, Rose. I need him."

"No, angel," she soothed, stroking her hair. "You need sleep, only sleep."

Tucked up in the feather bed, Maura dozed as Rose dressed her blistered hand. All the while, Rose's mind swam with tumult and guilt. Why had she been so foolish to suggest that Maura speak to Simon? Her heedless act was equal to handing Maura a dagger to carve out her own heart. Wrapping a bandage, she wept softly, wondering how Maura had come to burn herself and glanced up to see her awake and staring dully. "What is it, angel?" sniffed Rose. "What disturbed your rest? Is there pain?" Maura shook her head. "Then what? A nightmare?"

"No," Maura answered faintly, pushing up in the bed.

"You won't be getting up. I insist you stay in that bed till morning."

Maura hadn't the strength to argue. She gazed at Rose with such a dire look that Rose hastily climbed up beside her. Maura rested her head in Rose's lap and sighed to the comfort of Rose's fingers untangling her hair. "Will visited to say he will fetch you early morn," mentioned Rose. "You'll journey with him to Berkhamstead, and I will join you if you wish."

"Rose, you must go to Dunheved. Your sons."

"We'll see how you fare come morning. I'm amazed you've survived Christmas Court, Maura. No one should be forced to endure such torment, and for what purpose? So Lord Robert can acquire more land, more power. His greed is despicable and barbaric! There's never a thought for your welfare, you're nothing but disposable property... chattel." Rose's voice cracked with returning tears as she finished, "Then, aren't we all."

Maura shifted uncomfortably and sighed, "Rose."

"Yes, angel."

"How can I still care for Simon? I've tried to kill his memory, first by denial, then with hate. When I saw him at Winchester all that I'd locked away returned. He's always in my mind, Rose, always. I've never forgiven him, why can't I forget? Will this hurting I feel ever go?"

Rose's reply was cold and blunt, "The worst memories always last the longest. You'll never forget, Maura, and I don't believe we've seen the last of him."

"Would you kill him, Rose?"

"To protect you, most certainly. Now...you'll have no further bother this night, angel." Rose lifted Maura's head and helped her settle beneath the pelts. "Simon is far from here."

"And he'll never come back to me. I hurt him too badly."

Rose cringed at the yearning in Maura's confession. "You did not inflict the punishment he rightly deserves. Now, you must sleep, and dream of...Will. He will help you forget." Rose sat quietly, patting Maura's hand till she'd drifted off. Her tangled thoughts wandered back to Winchester. There, Maura had yielded to Simon's lies, and she had scarcely been able to tear them apart. The pattern had been repeated this night, and she thanked God that Maura's courage had prevailed. Yet there was little doubt—he *would* attempt another confrontation—he was that stubborn, that bullish. As she stood to begin packing, Rose pledged to use any means necessary to keep them apart, and prayed for God's intervention in her crusade.

*****

A slim band of sunlight peeked through the window and fell upon Maura's pillow. Its teasing roused her and she coaxed herself from under the consoling pelts. The basin's frigid water freshened her swollen eyes and flushed cheeks. She moved sluggishly to collect her clothes, dodging Rose's manic flitting. Her apparent cheer bemused Maura, and she commented, "I can never understand how you get such pleasure from drudging chores."

"Any task that keeps the mind and body busy is to be appreciated," returned Rose. "Hurry and dress. Will is due to arrive soon." Rose gestured to a tray of bread, dried fruit, and wine set atop the trunk. "And you must eat."

Maura was astonished to hear her belly rumble and, chewing on a withered apple, wondered aloud, "Why is he coming so early if we're to leave by mid-day?"

"I really have no—"

A loud knock intruded. Rose hurried to answer, and Maura wriggled swiftly into her tunic, downed the wine, and scoured the rushes for her slippers. Rose and Will mumbled quick greetings, and he hastened to Maura's side, asking fretfully, "How do you feel? I didn't realize meeting with that scoundrel would cause you such grief. If I'd known I would have never—"

Maura lifted her hand for quiet. "It's done, and he's gone. Both our prayers have been answered."

His dour expression switched to beaming delight. "You must come with me! I have the most glorious news to share."

Piqued, Rose drew nearer. "What news?"

"I'm sure Maura will tell all when she returns." He grasped her hand and urged, "Come, don't dally."

He forged his way down the hallway; she trotted behind and asked, "Where are we going?"

"Patience, patience! You'll soon find out."

Maura's enthusiasm began to dim as Will turned down the passageway leading to the great hall, and it was doused completely by the echo of Rufus' bellicose roar. Images of murder and mayhem swirled in her mind. She resisted his tug. "No Will, I can't. Not Rufus, not after last evening. Please don't make me—"

"Nonsense. There's nothing to fear. He won't attempt a thing while I'm present. Now come, my news concerns you both."

Warily, Maura followed Will into the empty hall. A great racket resounded from the bedchamber. Its door flew open and wooden bowls sailed weightlessly from inside. They crashed onto the opposite wall, their contents dribbling down the stones and collecting into gelled puddles. Hounds yelped and raced to the sight of the mishap, then proceeded to battle over their unexpected treats.

Will rubbed his palms together and commented with glee, "This should be marvelous fun. Rufus!" he hollered. "Come out to the dais! I must speak to you."

Maura hid at Will's back, her trepidation soaring as Rufus emerged from his chamber, his beard matted with gruel, his grimy hair askew, and grumbling something about poisoning. His woolly, protruding belly parted his robe; he scratched it proudly, and barked, "What is it?"

Will guided Maura's rigid body to a chair, and flamboyantly swept his arm toward the throne. "Dearest Cousin, do you wish to sit?"

"No! Get on with it."

"Yes...well then..." Will's face lit with smug triumph as he extracted from his belt a rolled parchment, delicately spread it upon the dais, and raised his twinkling eyes to Rufus' glower. "With due respect to you, my Prince, I will be brief. According to this flimsy piece of skin, Maura was betrothed to another, a full year before *your* betrothal was announced. What that means, Cousin, in simple terms, is that your union with Maura would not be legal."

"What?!" thundered Rufus, his fists rocking the table.

He swiped at the writ, but Will snatched it up, and laughed, "There's really no point in arguments or tantrums. She won't be marrying you and that's that."

Maura raised a muddled face and trembling hand to ask, "Will, may I...I see the document?"

"Why, of course."

Maura focused on the date—over a year ago, the King's signature and seal, Robert's mark—and her suspicions evaporated. Will spoke the truth! The parchment crinkled in her taut grip, as she burst a joyous squeak, and sprang from her seat directly into Will's arms.

Their ecstatic laughter enraged Rufus, and he stormed round the table, gnashing, "I'll have you arrested for treason, you son of a dunghill! I'll bury your whole cursed family!"

"And I'll see you flogged for Maura's beating," Will snarled back. Rufus' pomposity faltered and his glare dropped to his bare feet. "The crown rests uncertainly now, doesn't it, dear Cousin?" teased Will. "You try to be a good boy, and maybe you'll find some mindless slut willing to marry you. I seriously doubt it though. After all, this was the longest betrothal you've ever encountered."

Laughing hysterically, Will and Maura scuttled off to Rufus' booming expletives, and clung together in the darkened, deserted hallway. She sought the thrill of his lips, and sputtered, "Oh, Will...how...how did this happen and how can I...I ever thank you? It's not a trick, is it?! It's real, isn't it? Please say it's real!"

"It's real," he chuckled and, cupping her face in his hands, marveled at the profound change in her appearance. Her plain, unassuming beauty sparkled with a brilliance he'd not known before. He hungrily accepted another lolling kiss, then explained, "I felt uneasy when Father announced your betrothal to Rufus, as if I'd heard it all before. When I returned to Berkhamstead, I began to search for the source of my doubts, and late yesterday received the news I'd prayed for—an earlier marriage writ, conveniently forsaken."

"Who, who am I to marry?"

"Some poor sod of a soldier from Yorkshire." His hug tightened and he murmured, "I wish it were I, my sweet Lady. Now, will you come with me to Berkhamstead?"

"Oh, yes! Yes!" she gushed between kisses. "I must tell Rose! And Marc...Oh, my Lord, he's to leave soon!" She dashed off, stopped, then rushed back to his arms, "First, one more—"

He broke from her kiss, and laughed at her antics, "There will be plenty more of those later. Go tell Rose, make her smile again! Marc leaves within the hour. I'll meet you in the bailey mid-day, my love..." His gentle smile sent her sprinting away. After she disappeared, it turned priggish as he strutted back through the great hall to the Royal bedchamber. Rufus sat, bloated and gross, at the foot of the bed, and lifted his moping face to Will's greeting, "Don't look so glum, Cousin. You didn't really want to marry her."

"I thought you were my friend," Rufus sniveled. "You've betrayed me!"

"No, I've saved you...and I am your *only* friend. Never forget that! Besides, I only want her for awhile. She'll soon bore me, they all do. And when that happens, I'll send her back to you, so you can enjoy a few more delicious whacks before her wedding. The way I perceive matters, we both win." Will's gaze narrowed to a glare. "You still owe me money." Rufus stretched back, extracted a plump bag of coins from beneath his pillow, and hurled it at Will. Catching it, Will tested its weight and, satisfied, fastened it to his belt, asking, "Will you be staying at Westminster?" Rufus nodded. "Then I know where to send her. Well, I can honestly say that I don't recall ever attending a Christmas Court quite like this one, and I enjoyed myself immensely. Good-bye, Cousin and Godspeed." Will blew Rufus an exaggerated, mocking kiss, and added, "I will see you...whenever."

"One moment, Will."

Will turned in the doorway, and arched a brow in question.

"What of your brother?"

"My brother—the leech," chortled Will, unsteadily. "I feel he's been adequately humiliated and won't attempt another reunion. And to ensure his absence, I've sent someone to watch over him."

"It's a rotten shame," said Rufus. "I actually enjoy his company and would much prefer his loyalty to your flagrant boot licking."

Will's eyes blazed with ire. He stood huffing, unable to conjure up a stinging reply. Then, slamming the door, he barged away, spewing curses in the wake of Rufus' howled laughter.

Maura sped along the passageways and burst breathlessly into Rose's chamber, panting, "Rose! Rose!" Rose gasped and spun from the trunk; a stacked pile of clothing exploded from her grasp and cascaded through the air. Maura twirled a celebratory dance through the floating undergarments, grabbed Rose's waist, hoisted her high, and cried, "Rose, oh, Rose! I won't marry Rufus. That was Will's news. I won't marry him, I won't, I won't, I won't!"

Rose stammered her shock, "What...where...Wi—" Maura clutched her close and they dissolved into tears of joyous laughter. Rose swiftly regained her voice and flattened her palms to Maura's reddened cheeks. "You had faith, angel! I surrendered to gloom, neglected my prayers—"

"No, Rose, you were only trying to protect me." For a long comforting moment, Maura enjoyed Rose's hug, then suddenly pulled back. "Marc! If I've missed him, Rose, I'll never forgive myself. Where's my cloak?"

"You go, I'll find your cloak and follow."

Maura hurried to the bailey and was instantly swallowed up by the mass of departing soldiers. Her frantic search scanned the smoky courtyard, at last alighting on her brother. She grunted her way through the troops, clambered over heaps of armor, and nudged aside obstinate hogs, finally to arrive at his side. Her light touch startled him, which seemed odd, considering the surrounding din. "Marc," she sighed, "I was afraid I'd missed you." She wondered at his slight flinch. "When will you go?"

"As soon as I bridle my horse."

"I have the most marvelous news!" she said as she bent to fetch the bridle.

He yanked the girth strap taut and glanced her way, asking flatly, "What?"

"Will's found an impediment to my betrothal to Rufus—a previous writ promising me to a soldier from Yorkshire! I won't marry Rufus!" She waited but received no response, so she prompted, "Did you hear, Marc? Will's been searching since Martinmas for a cause to annul the—"

"It wasn't Will's doing, Maura."

His stark response irked her. "Of course it was Will! He told me not an hour ago, and I saw the writ. It has the King's seal and—"

"Simon found the impediment."

"You lie!" she railed. "How dare you defend him after he shamed you?"

"He never shamed me. He's my friend and will stay so till I decide otherwise!" His face and tone softened as he continued, "Maura, if you'd only listened to him, you'd know the truth. The King sent Simon to find a cause to stop the betrothal. That's why he left you at Winchester. I was warned not to tell you, in case his mission failed. If there's a liar about, it's Will, not Simon."

"No, I won't hear this, not now. I won't let you spoil my happiness!"

Marc huffed indignantly and swung into his saddle; his exit was blocked by Rose's imposing figure. "What madness is this? Fighting when you're to be separated for Heaven knows how long! You should be ashamed of yourselves. Marc, come down to me." He reluctantly obeyed and received from her a brusque hug and kiss. She handed Maura her cloak, and continued her farewell. "I will pray for your safety and quick return. Now, I'll leave you two to your farewells. Make them amiable!"

He waited till Rose was out of sight, gulped his anger, and agreed, "She's right you know, we shouldn't be arguing. Will you go with Will?"

"Yes."

"You'll be safe at Berkhamstead and that's all that truly matters." He helped her on with her cloak, and suggested with a wan smile, "Walk with me."

In troubled silence, they strolled to the main gate. Their farewell embrace was stiff and brief. Marc started to remount. Maura lifted her hand to his back and struggled to admit her grief, but no words would pass her quivering lips. His foot slipped from the stirrup and he whirled round to engulf her in a smothering hold. Their damp cheeks met, and Maura managed a cracked whisper, "If you can, write to me at Berkhamstead. You are always such a comfort to me. How will I manage without you?"

"As always, you'll manage just fine."

"I love you, Marc."

"And I you, Sister." They kissed cheeks and hands. He returned to his saddle and, with a forlorn wave, fell into the line of departing soldiers.

Maura's tears streamed as she stumbled forward, reaching out, desperate to say so much more. "Please, Marc," she anguished, "take care! When you return you'll come stay with me in Yorkshire...Marc!"

He was too distant to hear. She shuddered with a sudden chill and felt the solacing warmth of Rose's arms. "Come angel, we'll go inside where it's warm." On their journey across the bailey, Rose strove to cheer, "Your brother surely will prove himself a valiant soldier. Now, tell me, after Berkhamstead, where will you go? Back to Winchester and the marriage game?"

"Oh, Rose, there wasn't time to tell you. I'm to marry a soldier from Yorkshire and, of course, you'll move north with me and help run our household, won't you?"

"Yorkshire," Rose sighed in a contented way. "I've heard of its beauty and quiet. We could do with some quiet." Maura smiled in agreement as Rose pondered on, "And to atone for your turmoil, God will grant you a gentle husband. Our troubles seem to have come to a satisfactory conclusion."

Alan waited patiently in Rose's chamber. Upon their entry, he stood respectfully and asked, "Rose, are we to leave now?"

"Yes, Alan. I'll be taking only this bag."

He lifted the canvas satchel. "The cart awaits you at the base of the stairs. Maura...I've heard news that your betrothal to Rufus has been annulled. Is it true?"

"Yes, it's true."

"Then you'll no longer be needing my services."

She smiled tenderly and took hold of his free hand. "I will always have need of you, for you are my guardian angel."

Her praise prompted from him a severe blush, and she continued with deep emotion, "I'm grateful for your protection, and for my life. After Rose's visit to Dunheved, would you consider joining us at our new home in Yorkshire?"

"I would like nothing more, my Lady." His lips brushed her hand, and he ambled away.

Rose glanced at Maura's somber expression and insisted, "Now, no blubbering, angel. It will do us good to be apart, we've grown far too dependent on one another. I won't live forever." As she fought back tears, her gloved fingers grazed Maura's cheek and swept away a tear. "Relish your freedom, child, and enjoy all Will has to offer. We will be together again soon."

Alone in her chamber, Maura sat back upon the bed and listened. The raging calm unnerved her, and to break its din she mused...The past two months seemed such a blur, yet there were certain events that she recalled all too clearly—Rufus' beating, the herbs being forced down her throat, Alan's unexpected arrival, Marc's ceremony, and—Simon. Had he really found the Yorkshire betrothal writ? If so, why hadn't he told her? But then, she truly hadn't given him a chance to say much of anything. And now that he'd gone would she ever know the truth? Soon she'd discover if Will was indeed a liar and, no doubt, encounter even more surprises. Surprises, she prayed, she was capable of handling alone. What did it matter if she was disappointed with Will? At Berkhamstead, she would be rid of Rufus, and wasn't that what was most important? And what of this soldier who very soon would own her? Was he, as Rose predicted, a gentle man? She could only hope and pray...

Two servants arriving to remove her trunk stifled her pondering. She tugged on her gloves. The sight of her bandaged hand stirred again the memories of the horrors she suffered at Gloucester and evoked a woozy sadness. She gripped the door handle for balance, and decided she'd best seek out a priest's guidance before embarking on her nebulous trip to Berkhamstead.

*****

CHAPTER NINE - A RANCID CHARM

Will leant back on plumped pillows and, with an appreciative smirk, scrutinized his surroundings. Uncle Arnulf's castle—so raw, base, eccentric! Heads of beasts snarled from the timbered walls, and thick pelts stripped from every conceivable animal draped the trunks, crude tables, and bed. Torches, not candles, lit the tiny chamber, dripping hazardous sparks on the crisp rushes below. It was amazing the structure was still intact! Will laughed as he thought of his rather bizarre relatives. This had been his Grandmother Mabel's favorite residence, and she had no doubt been lured by its putrid ambiance. How she would have loved displaying her countless victims' heads on these rotted walls! He missed his devious times with her, especially when he had watched in awe as she mixed her lethal potions and rasped tales of murder and deceit. They had been of one mind and soul, never allowing anyone or thing to stand in the way of their ascendancy. She, unfortunately, had become clumsy, and been cut down in her prime; yet such a disaster would never befall someone as shrewd as he. As long as Simon stayed hidden and Almodis didn't miraculously become pregnant, everything his father now owned would one day be his—half of England, lands and estates in Normandy; enough power, wealth, and support to wage a rebellion, perhaps even seize the crown! His hopeful spirits shrank a bit as he thought of the waiting, and his envy raged. Why couldn't he have a bit of it now? Grandfather Roger had presented each of his sons with his own castle, and he had quite a few sons. Why had Will been cursed with such a damned miserly father, who selfishly showed little signs of aging?

Well, he thought, rising from his bed and donning his robe, there was no sense wasting precious time on self-pity when Maura lay in wait for his lustful attention. He gazed admiringly into a cracked mirror, smoothed his black curls and mustache. His body hardened at the thought of their imminent coupling. How adventurous would she be? How submissive? Please, he prayed, don't let her be difficult, he could abide difficult women anywhere but in bed. The bed was his domain, to command as he saw fit. A bit of his esteem faltered as he recalled their journey here. She'd seemed locked in a daze, consumed with secret thoughts, and had said little. At the evening feast, Maura had politely endured Arnulf's tales of carnage, but she'd barely returned any of Will's amorous glances. He laughed again, imagining how she would react to the news that once she'd been betrothed to Arnulf. At times her strangeness filled him with a certain apprehension. He scoffed at his weakness and reminded himself that she was merely a woman, and there wasn't a woman born he couldn't dominate.

With a determined tug on his robe's tie, he opened the door to leave. His jaw hung wide as Almodis appeared, seemingly out of nowhere, and asked with a suspicious sneer, "And where are you off to at this very late hour?" Before he could answer, she shoved him back inside the chamber, then shut and bolted the door.

"No...nowhere in particular," he stammered. "I felt a need to wander. And if you don't mind, I'll be on—"

"Oh, I *do* mind. I mind where your wandering might take you."

"Don't be bothersome, Almodis. Let me pass."

She stayed press to the door and taunted, "You once loved to be bothered, especially by me." A harsher push sent him sprawling onto the bed. She straddled his waist and continued confidently, "You're going nowhere, Will, at least not till I'm done with you."

"Tell me, Almodis," he asked with a nervous chuckle, "why are you here? At Gloucester, you insisted my presence nauseated you. You wouldn't give me so much as a pinch. And now, you're *so* possessive."

"You want a pinch, you'll have a pinch," she said as she squeezed the lobe of his ear and twisted.

He yowled in pain, yet didn't resist. She rolled away, crawled to the pillows, and sat cross-legged, her robe parting to reveal her lack of undergarments. Will obediently responded to the snap of her fingers, flipped to his belly, and crawled to her side; his hand slipped beneath her robe to explore.

"That's better," she sighed, tracing his lips with her finger. "And now, you'll keep your mouth closed and ears open, for I have a great deal to say." She quickly scanned the room. "Where's the wine?"

"I wasn't planning on staying."

"Yes, well, I can do without...for awhile. How long have we been together now?"

"It seems like forever."

"Ten years, Will."

"God's blood, that long?! No wonder you look so old."

"As old as you."

"You're a bit closer to forty, my dear."

She chose to ignore his last comment and went on, "During our years together we've overlooked minor indiscretions, at times even condoned them, though there is one indiscretion I won't overlook—Maura. Answer me this, Will, did she ever allow you liberties at Gloucester?"

"Liberties?"

"Yes, did you ever get more than a kiss or tickle from her?"

"No."

"I thought not, but you're still chasing her tail, totally absorbed and obsessed. Before long, you'll be making an ass of yourself, bringing her posies, and spouting poetry. The thought makes me want to vomit. I know her game. She'll keep you dreaming of an imagined coupling that will never happen, and in the end leave you broken. And I need you whole! As you so graciously reminded me, I'm nearing forty. My pickings get fewer every day. Maura is a dangerous woman, very dangerous."

"You speak rubbish."

"Do I? Will...I have never seen you do anything that remotely resembles a courageous act. Then, at Gloucester, you pushed me aside to attack your brother, who has more strength in his little finger than you have in your entire body. And why did you chance certain injury, or even death? To keep him from Maura! I won't lose you, Will, not to her, never!"

"You've never *had* me to lose. You're a plaything, nothing more. We use each other. Lately, you've begun to bore me. I need new, younger blood. The imagined coupling you mentioned will happen shortly, *Mother*. Would you care to watch? There are plenty of pelts for you to hide behind. The wild sow skin would suit you perfectly. Or better yet, you could join us."

She struck his face; her snide control crumbled and she gritted, "If you so much as wink at that little tease, I'll tell Robert everything!"

"Will you now?" winced Will, rubbing his cheek and removing his hand from her robe. "He's too busy to care."

"Not *that* busy. Would you care to know how he punished the knight who spoke rudely to me at our wedding feast?"

"If I fall from grace, Mother, you tumble with me," he said smugly, crossing his arms. "Robert will believe anything I tell him. I'll claim you raped me."

Will convulsed with laughter. "Me rape you! I believe the opposite is nearer the truth."

"Is she worth the risk, Will? Robert isn't that impressed with you now. He doesn't need much more damning evidence to cut you off completely. I have little to lose, a title, a bit of luxury, but you—all that wealth gone in an instant, disinherited for a snip of a bitch." From his pensive look, she knew she had sown a seed of doubt, and rushed to dig deeper. "Besides, there may be little cause for this argument. Maura seems to have lost interest in you. She's barely uttered a word to you since we left Gloucester. Perhaps your lurid romance was simply a figment of your imagination, or worse, she's discovered your lies. There are *so* many."

Will took a moment to study this provocative and vile creature beside him. The curve of her breasts peeked from beneath her robe, rising with each irate breath. Her long graceful thigh, still firm, brushed against his, and her loosened hair dangled wildly to her shoulders and beyond, swaying slightly to the tilt of her head. Wet were her lips; wet, red, and swollen in an irresistible pout. She was always willing, ready, and highly responsive to his carnal needs, even his more violent demands. And now, he'd frightened her, threatened her, and she was desperate. The possibilities seemed endless. Two luscious women vying for his attention! He could convince Almodis quite readily that he'd forsaken Maura, then when they reached Berkhamstead, the fun would truly begin! He moved closer; his fingers stroked her cheek, walked their way down her neck, and pinched the neckline of her robe, nudging it till it drifted from her shoulders. "And how do you intend to stop me from visiting Maura?"

She ignored his attempts at titillation and answered coolly, "As always, I will agree to all your wants, no one else would dare endure the pain. So, you see you can't leave me...ever. Starting tomorrow, you will begin revealing your truly rancid personality to Maura. It won't take much to put her off. Your brother is still foremost in her mind, and you can't begin to compete with him."

"You filthy whore!" He lunged for her throat; familiar with his assaults, she easily stopped his hand, and bit eagerly into his flesh. He sucked a breath, but didn't protest. She slowly released him and they rolled in a tight clutch off the pillows. Lust flamed her dark eyes as she swiftly stripped off his robe and crushed her lips to his. They wrestled; her hand groped between his legs, cupped his genitals and squeezed. He froze, his eyes bulging as he squeaked, "Almodis...what...what—"

"Before we proceed, I need to know—is it clear to you where we stand, or should I say, lie with each other?"

"Vividly clear. Now...now no more talk, and please, a little gentler."

"You *will* forget her?"

"Yes. I will send her to Westminster as soon as we reach Berkhamstead."

Almodis pondered his reply and, easing her grip, pushed up on her elbow. "Westminster? Isn't that where Rufus is residing?"

"Yes."

"Why in God's name do you want to kill the poor woman?" She lay back, spread herself lasciviously across the bed, and suggested with an impish grin, "No, let her stay at Berkhamstead. It will be such fun having a woman of equal rank to talk to. Don't worry, my son, I'll keep you so busy that you won't have a moment to drool over her. Perhaps she can advise me on the art of snaring a decent man. I do wonder why I keep ending up with hideous lumps like you in my bed."

"That's simple to understand. You *too* are hideous, my Lady. And when Father returns? What then?" he asked, looming over her pliant body.

"As long as I provide for his needs, which are few, he doesn't mind what I get up to. I can't imagine why, but I missed you, Will, and now you may pleasure me. Remember though, no visible bruises. It's so hard to explain them to Robert." She laughed a full-throated laugh. "He believes I'm *so* clumsy."

*****

Maura drew circles in the mist clinging to the green tinged window. A glass window—never had she stayed anywhere owning such a treasure. They had arrived at Berkhamstead late afternoon, in time for her to view the copper sun sink behind the curtain wall. She left the window and roamed the chamber, stopping to finger each rarity. There was a wooden tub padded with leather, a silver threaded tapestry adorning the wall, elaborately carved gold candelabras, and a garderobe. Heavy damask bed curtains shrouded an immense feather bed, topped with an embroidered quilt, and warmed by the fire pit set deep into the stone wall, stocked full of wood and crackling sweetly. Her trunk looked wretched by comparison. She opened its squeaky, broken lid and began removing her clothing. Two taut ropes strung behind the door would hold her frocks and, as she hung one tunic over the higher cord, she contemplated her present situation. Today, Will had seemed indifferent, which suited her fine. Ever since her illuminating talk with Marc, her mind had retraced every statement and expression of Will's, searching for a slip, a double-meaning, or an insincerity. He was a damned good liar. And then, last evening while supping in Arnulf's hall, Will, full of claret and himself, had confided that the Yorkshire writ had been served to him at Berkhamstead *before* he ventured to Christmas Court. So blatant a contradiction; too decisive to be a mistake. Why hadn't he told her immediately upon arrival at Gloucester? Why wait and subject her to such cruelty? To weaken her perhaps, hoping she'd come to rely entirely on him as her *Lord Protector*? She chastised herself for not recognizing the all too predictable ruse, and hoped he'd continue to ignore her, as that was her plan for him. But she also prayed for the opportunity to remain at Berkhamstead, for in these lush surroundings, she could live quite comfortably. She abandoned her task to answer a knock and, peeking warily into the hall, was amazed to see the Lady Almodis.

A broad smile and nod accompanied the Lady's request. "May I enter?"

"Of course, my Lady," Maura answered with a polite bow.

"No formalities, please," Almodis insisted as she glided into the chamber. "Please think of me as your equal, and call me Almodis. I felt the time was ripe for us to become better acquainted."

Maura quickly summed up Almodis—her raised chin, shifty eyes, clenched fingers, and stilted speech all betrayed her uneasiness. Eager to uncover the true intent of this meeting, Maura answered, "I was hoping you'd visit."

Almodis, not expecting such a glib response, sought a conversation piece and spotted the stacked clothes. "The servants will see to your clothes, Maura."

"I'd rather tend to them myself."

"As you wish. Where has your shadow gone to?"

"Pardon?"

"The older woman who trails you everywhere."

"Oh, Rose," said Maura. "She's visiting her sons at Dunheved."

"How nice for her," commented Almodis, too sweetly. She wandered to the bed and examined the gown at the top of the pile. Her fingers skimmed the silk. "You certainly have exquisite gowns. Do you keep a seamstress?"

"No, the gowns belong to Adela and were loaned to me."

"Then perhaps during your stay here, my seamstress can fashion you a few frocks of your own. You'll need a decent wardrobe when you become Lady of a household, wherever. And these," she noted as she extracted two dully colored tunics from the bottom of the pile, "these will have to go."

"Why ever for?" Maura asked, perturbed. "They are the most comfortable and the only warm clothing I own."

With an austere glance, Almodis stated, "Lord William rules here at Berkhamstead, and he forbids any of his women to wear clothing as drab as these."

Maura's annoyance flared. "And when did I become one of *his* women?"

"The moment you agreed to join him here at his glorious abode."

"I'll wear what I like!" snapped Maura, snatching the tunic from Almodis' grasp, and adding flippantly, "And are you also one of Will's women?"

"Watch your tongue, my bold Lady! I am your Lord's wife, and—"

"I thought you were my equal."

Almodis' rage threatened and, with tenuous calm and a garish grin, she replied, "Will you join us this evening in the great hall?"

"Perhaps."

"If so, I suggest you keep a good distance from Will. And the red gown you wore at Gloucester, never wear it again!"

"I wasn't planning to converse with him, or wear the gown."

"Fine. I want no trouble, and hope we can live here together amicably—"

"You lie as easily as he does."

"What?!"

"Worry not, my Lady. I won't take your precious Will from you, for you two make such a divine pair."

"So you are not as stupid or naive as I thought, though you are a fool for sending Simon away. How exceedingly cruel of you. Though I do believe you've come to realize what a drastic error you made." Almodis came up too close to Maura and tugged on a lock of her hair, commenting with distaste, "Your hair is so unusual—the color of red muck."

Maura swatted away her hand and fumed, "We've said all we need to say. I think you should go."

"Yes, I'll leave you to your work," said Almodis heading out of the room. "I did enjoy our little chat and pray we'll have many—"

Maura slammed the door on Almodis' last obnoxious word, and let out an exasperated groan. She stomped to the trunk and began hurling clothes in every direction till her wrath subsided. Will had spoken one truth at Gloucester, his reference to Almodis as 'an unpleasant woman'. She sank despondently onto the bed and held her hand up to the taper's light. The blisters had healed and the cut was barely visible. As she ran the coarse skin over her cheek, she wondered where Simon had gone.

Later that evening, after a soothing bath had restored her composure, Maura stood in the doorway of the great hall poised to face her nettlesome kin. As her eyes swept the room, she was not at all surprised to see an overabundance of garish decorations. Yet one oddity perplexed her—a deer carcass roasting over a walled grate. To lessen the risk of fire, cooking was usually undertaken in an outbuilding. She noticed Will and Almodis sitting side by side at the dais. The tables below them swarmed with boisterous soldiers, guards, and tradesmen. Will stood, and waved her forward, shouting, "Maura, please join us!" She strode across the room, cringing a bit as all eyes followed her. Sitting, she accepted Will's offered cup of claret. A delicious aroma lured her nose and eyes downward. There sat a silver plate stacked with venison and framed with plump cinnamon apples which set her mouth to watering. Will gestured with his spoon for her to begin, and mumbled between chews, "Maura, you look stunning. I see you've worn the necklace I gave you."

Almodis snorted in displeasure to his observation. Maura stroked the glimmering sapphires and purposely aimed her flaunting smile at Almodis. If provoked, she too could play shrewish games—yet the fun of irritating the pretentious Lady couldn't dismiss Will's deception.

Will leant close and noted invitingly, "I've arranged for musicians to entertain later. Do you remember our dances at Gloucester? It seems so long since I've held you in my arms." His pretty words took on an oily air, and Maura diverted her attention to the tables below. "Does your chamber suit you?" he probed further. "I long to hear your impression of my home. Well actually it's Father's, though I feel it's mine." He pointed proudly at the grate. "I slew that deer on our journey here. I love seeing my kill cooked." Her nagging silence irked him, and he hotly inquired, "Are your ears blocked, my Lady, or is your rudeness intentional?"

Over the din, Maura could hear Almodis' wicked tittering. Her family's antics soured her stomach and Maura rose to leave. Will's nails dug into her arm, forcing her back in her seat. His greasy fingers pinched her chin and jerked her face to his. "Your memory fades too quickly, Maura. I rescued you from Rufus and if you fail to show me proper respect, I can just as easily return you to him! You owe me much, and I aim to collect."

She squirmed against his grip, demanding, "Let go of me!"

"Never!" he asserted, holding fast.

Suddenly a knife plunged deep into the wood between them. Their wide eyes climbed Almodis' arm and stared aghast at her livid expression. "Do as she says, Will."

He hesitated. The knife rose and fell again, prompting him to release Maura, who bolted from the dais. The revelers hushed to catch Almodis' caustic farewell. "Maura, don't feel you must go on my account. You've barely touched your meal. Well, if you insist, I do pray you sleep well and—alone!" Then her curses lashed Will, "You damned fool! Maura has excellent reasons for ignoring you. Don't make the mistake of dismissing *my* threats. I love a dare. I suggest you tread carefully, my love, *very* carefully and leave the witch alone!"

Once in her chamber, Maura discovered to her chagrin that the door bolted only from the outside. She knew Will and Almodis to be disagreeable, but she had not, till now, considered them dangerous. The fire hadn't been stoked, so she swiftly shed her gown, left on her chemise, climbed between the closed bed curtains, and snuggled beneath the quilt. Trouble had accompanied her to Berkhamstead, and she longed for marriage to free her of her vexing family. Awaiting sleep, she offered a prayer for her well-being, and felt she received a warning in response—consider everyone treacherous unless convinced otherwise.

*****

Late into the second day of his journey, Simon's worst fears were realized. A harsh tempest had blown in from the sea, pounding the county of Cornwall with savage winds and blinding snow. The coarse wool of his cloak and his flimsy silk braies barely kept out the numbing cold. He hurried E'dain along, knowing they couldn't be more than twenty miles from Dunheved. A road sign bearded with ice confirmed his estimation, but the worsening storm filled him with rampant trepidation. If the storm continued its relentless course, he and E'dain could easily die on the last leg of their journey.

E'dain began to show signs of exhaustion. Simon dismounted and began the arduous task of pulling her through the drifts. The work warmed his body a bit, yet the glaring white of the snow blurred his vision and altered his sense of direction. The snow piled higher; the cold cut deeper. They stumbled along, his eyesight dimming as he squinted through the blanched sky for any signs of life. E'dain's balking increased and her reins slipped frequently from his frozen fingers. One hearty heave sent him sprawling, and he panicked at the numbness in his legs, and the harrowing feeling that somehow they had strayed from their path. Were they lost and facing certain death? Simon wouldn't lie in wait for the answer, so he struggled from the ground and continued on, talking loudly to himself to stave off his fatigue.

Before long, the outlines of thatched roofs broke through the solid whiteness. His strength surged at the saving sight and he floundered to the first cottage. All attempts to rouse the dwellers failed and he hobbled to the next hut, only to be refused again. He abandoned the homes, stumbled ahead, and prayed the village gates were near.

Huddled beneath pelts, Edith sat cross-legged by the fire, tacking the last few stitches in a worn tunic. The walls of her cottage groaned under the force of the howling wind, the shutters rattled, and the animals snorted and shifted restlessly in their stalls. As she sewed, her worries mounted. Would the storm outlast her wood supply? Would the snow cover her stove bracing the back of the cottage? If so, she couldn't bake her bread. And most importantly, was her cottage hardy enough to withstand the storm's assault? Her fretting peaked to a startling knock. She dropped her sewing and tugged the pelts tighter. There was no need to answer; whoever it was soon would leave. The hammering intensified. *Please*, she silently beseeched, *please go*! She cocked her ear to muffled cries, and recognized—Simon! Her cat yowled as Edith sprang from the ground, released the bolt, and flung wide the door. He stood, ashen and wavering, snow and ice coating his skin, his hand shaking terribly as he reached out and mumbled, "Come...come outside. I...I need your help...Hurry." He staggered away. She snatched up her cloak and slipped into her shoes to follow. The snow's eerie glow lit her way to E'dain, driven to her knees inches before the stable door. The gale drowned Simon's faint orders, yet Edith knew what help was needed. She ran back through the hut, opened the stable door, then grasped the reins firmly and waited. Simon positioned his back against E'dain's rump and yelled, "Pull!" Edith yanked with all her might as Simon shoved. E'dain rose a foot only to collapse again. Their next attempt hoisted her to her feet, and a combined push at her back propelled her into the stable.

Edith hurried to the main room to fetch ale and blankets. She returned to the stalls to find E'dain nibbling on straw, but no Simon. Outside the door, she fell to her knees beside his prone body, and spoke frantically, "Simon! Simon open your eyes!" His lashes fluttered and she waved her hand before them; his eyes did not respond. She chafed snow on his cheeks and slapped, imploring, "Simon, you must help me get you inside. You're frozen through!" With her strength to guide him, he struggled to his feet, and tripped past E'dain into the main room, where he collapsed on a pallet by the fire. Shuddering violently, he instantly lapsed into a fitful sleep. Edith topped a pot with water and set it to boil. She stripped off his clothing and covered his blue tinged body with pelts and blankets. "Simon," she begged, one hand tapping his face, the other holding a cup of ale, "Simon, please you must try to drink this."

Simon could hear her voice, but he couldn't see her, couldn't see anything but white. It hurt to move, his eyes burned; all he wanted to do was sleep...sleep.

"Simon! Wake up!" She lifted his head and forced the ale. He coughed, sputtered and flailed blindly at her hold. "Take a little more," she persisted, "it will help warm you." His resistance eased and he gulped the liquid freely. The empty cup dropped from her hand as he slipped back into slumber. Even in sleep, his body remained tense and his face careworn. Edith bathed his face with a warm cloth, and wondered what could have enticed him to tackle such a storm? If he were chased, he'd dare not come here for chance of endangering her. She glanced down at his silk braies and shirt. Never had he worn silk. Her strokes reached his arm; she cringed at the dark bruises staining his skin and spoke inwardly, *Oh, what a fantastic tale he'll tell come morning!*

Edith left Simon buried in pelts, briefly to visit E'dain, and found her standing, contentedly sharing a stall with Edith's cow. The mare's now warm hide quivered to Edith's tender touch and, as she returned to her son, she prayed he would recover as swiftly.

*****

The wind cracked a bolt and slammed a shutter against the wall, jolting Simon up from his pallet. His wide eyes stung from the brash light flooding the room. He flopped back down on the mat and hid beneath the pelts as footsteps crept past his head. The light dulled and he ventured a peek. Edith stacked wood on the fire, stoking it to a grand blaze, and hung a pot atop the flames. She wiped her hands on her skirt and, rising, caught his spying eye. "How do you feel?" she asked, cracking a small grin and crouching by his head. Her fingers smoothed his brow, and she sighed at its warmth. He offered no reply, and her concern heightened. "Simon, can you see me?" His bleary eyes brightened in response. "Good," she said. "When you feel able, I want you to eat. I'll fix you oats with hot milk and honey—"

"E'dain!" he gasped, pushing up on his elbows.

Her hand rested assuredly on his shoulder. "She seems quite content, and enjoyed the ale I served her this morning."

He sank back down, his head lolling from the exertion. Edith tucked the pelts about his neck and smiled. "Simon, it is wonderful to have you here again and so soon, but whatever made you brave this terrible storm?" He ignored her, and she repeated, "I'd *like* you to eat."

"I'm not hungry," he mumbled grumpily, staring at the ceiling. "How long have I slept?"

"You arrived early evening, it's now morn. The worst of the storm is done, only the wind's stayed."

He kept his harrowed gaze averted, embarrassed by his foolish act of leaving Gloucester without proper clothing or adequate provisions. If E'dain had died, he never could have forgiven himself.

Edith sat passively and watched his face strain and fingers crunch rushes as he tried to move his legs. They barely responded, and she encouraged, "Be patient, Simon. Give your body time to heal. Isn't that what you always tell me?" He continued to disregard her advice, till she voiced a curious question. "Did you fall from your horse?"

Their eyes met and he asked, "No, why?"

"The bruises on your body. I thought they might have been caused by a fall."

He exposed his arms and stared pensively at the damage inflicted by Marc. Shamed again, he hid his arms and muttered, "No, I didn't fall."

"Then can I assume you got them fighting?" she continued. Shifting to his side, he focused on the fire and her patience waned. "You know I won't stop asking till you start answering. Was it Robert? Did you fight your father?"

"No. I haven't seen him since Winchester. Do we have to speak of this now?"

"I suppose not, there's always this evening."

"I won't be staying. When I'm able, I'll go."

"Where?"

"I don't know."

"To Normandy?"

"I *said* I don't know."

"You'll tell me before you leave."

"Mother!"

Not easily dissuaded, she chattered on, "I'll fetch your oats."

"Don't bother."

"When did you last eat?"

"I don't remember!"

"Well," she huffed, rising in exasperation. "I'll leave you to your anger. When you're done with it, please let me know!" She replaced the milk pot with one filled with water and stressed sharply, "And you'll not be leaving this cottage till *I* deem you fit to go. Is that perfectly clear?"

His severe expression softened and, smiling weakly, he surmised, "Then I suppose I'll be staying forever."

She nodded in approval and returned his smile. "I would like that. I'm sorry for my prying..."

"I apologize for my mood, and appreciate your help." He struggled to sit and wiped his stinging eyes with the fur.

"The water's warming and I'll mix in soda and ash for your wash. But Simon, I don't believe your clothes are suitable for the weather."

"They're not mine."

"I wondered. Not to worry, I have some winter clothes of yours stashed in a trunk." She lifted the damp clothing and rubbed the delicate silk between her fingers. "Do you mind my asking, why silk?"

He snorted a quiet laugh. "Mine were ripped, those I borrowed."

Her doubtful look guaranteed the subject would rise again and, though he thought better of it, he nonetheless spilled the details. "I was at Gloucester for Christmas Court. My clothes were ruined and the Lady Almodis offered me a clean outfit."

"Almodis?" Her brows rose in a pleased arch. "Such a lovely name. And who exactly *is* this Almodis?"

"My new stepmother."

Edith's jaw plummeted along with the clothes, and she stammered, "But Ro...Robert's still married!"

Simon promptly explained, "His wife, Matilda, died in 1085, and he married Almodis sometime this year. I'm positive this marriage is strictly a political match. Almodis' hard to fathom, contrary one moment, pleasant the next. I'm amazed she had the gall to speak to me." His babbling had no visible effect on Edith's trauma, and he sighed, "I'm sorry I've upset you, Mother...You *did* ask."

"No, I'm not upset," Edith said, unconvincingly, as she strangled the cloth in her taut grip. "I'm...I'm grateful she was kind and surprised Robert hasn't soiled her mind with lies about you. He was here," she blurted impulsively.

"Here!" Simon almost stood to the shock, but his legs crumpled beneath him, and he gasped his worry, "When?"

"Almost a month back. He was searching for you."

"Did...did he hurt you?"

"No, but he was furious." She knelt and scooped milk into a cup. "He's convinced you stole the writ and swore to punish you."

"Do you think he'll return?"

"I don't believe so. That night...something occurred between us and he revealed more of himself than he'd intended. I feel he's afraid to come back."

"And now you've confused *me*," Simon said, yet he didn't delve further. He accepted the milk in one hand and clutched her shoulder with his other. "Perhaps it's best if you stayed with friends for awhile. Arthur...You can visit Arthur in Winchester—"

"I won't pester Arthur with my concerns."

"He welcomes your pestering! I missed him on my last visit, but on the one before, you were all he talked about. He misses you."

"Arthur's my dearest friend. I won't burden him, and that's final. Robert doesn't scare me, Simon. The week following his visit, I spotted a few suspicious faces lurking about, but now they've gone."

Simon hesitated with his next question; from her reflective look, though, he felt it was safe to ask, "Was it difficult...seeing him again?"

"Yes, it was a painful, enlightening visit. He's so different—cold and cruel. I hardly recognized him. And I hold his brothers totally responsible for his changing. Odo taught him treachery, William taught him greed, and he was an excellent student. Long ago, Simon, he was a sweet, honorable man. I'm sure you remember." Her somber smile cracked his heart. "You remind me of him, when he was young and vital...Simon, you must beware. Robert craves revenge against you."

"We must both be careful. I need to leave soon."

Her fingers touched his cheek as she nodded a whimpered plea, "I know, but please, not *too* soon." Rising, she emptied the warmed water into a small tub, and dusted and stirred the liquid with soda and ash. She presented him a linen towel and suggested, "No more troubling talk. You need to wash, and I need to find your clothes."

Simon stared at the ash floating on the water and wrung the cloth with his still stiff fingers. The intense anger he felt began to fade, only to be replaced by guilt and deep melancholy. His presence endangered his mother, yet only here did he feel wanted. Perhaps Henry spoke the truth; he should return to Wales. His doctoring skills were accepted and useful there, and the Welsh seemed more tolerant, less prejudiced than the Normans. Then what of his work for the King? What about Maura? He dunked his head into the tub, hoping to scrub away his confusion and distress. It helped, a little. With great difficulty, he completed his wash and donned the familiar clothes Edith provided. He tried standing; still his legs refused to cooperate.

Edith returned as he was brusquely massaging his feet. "Still no feeling?" she asked, setting a bowl of oats before him.

"They have feeling, but no strength."

"Then you're forced to stay...at least for awhile."

"There's no place I'd rather be held prisoner." He took her hand and added soberly, "I *can't* and *won't* put you in danger."

To dismiss his worry, she kissed his damp head and noted, "I sense we have a great deal to discuss, and now...you'll eat."

*****

Edith returned from the market to find Simon perched high upon a ladder, weaving thatch into spots of the roof thinned by the punishing wind. On this, the third day of his visit, the mild weather had warmed enough for him to work sans cloak or tunic. So deep was Simon's concentration that Edith was able to watch him for a time unnoticed. It was her opinion that his appearance had altered little over the years. Of course, he was taller, brawnier, his face more angular and mature. Yet his abundant pale hair, pristine sky-blue eyes, and pouting lips often betrayed a helpless innocence that readily reduced her to blubbering. Over the past two days, she had caught that brooding look too many times. It never lasted long, for when it appeared, he would immediately plunge into a new project, such as patching the daub on the outer and inner walls of the cottage, repairing furniture, and assisting her baking. He had spent an entire night boiling and mixing his medicinal herbal salves to restock his traveling supply. They'd continually shared a shallow sort of conversation, nothing of substance, and his fretful sleep told of a hidden misery. But his hesitancy to confess his troubles didn't overly concern Edith, for in good time he would reveal all—he always did.

"Simon!" she called. He answered with a broad smile. "Your legs must feel stronger, or you'd never risk death at the top of those wobbly sticks."

"I've replaced the rungs with thicker cord," he assured proudly.

She laughed and shook her head. "You'll spoil me. When you're done with that patch come inside. I have something for you." As she entered the cottage, a heavenly odor assailed her senses. During his stay in Wales, Simon had acquired the talent of concocting the most delicious stews—delicious as long as one didn't ask the contents. She'd done so once, and he'd rattled off an endless list of herbs and parts of animals she'd not considered edible. He'd promised the stew's safety and boasted of its medicinal properties, but she was convinced one spoonful meant certain death. Well, she still lived, and the potions he brewed did seem to give her added vigor. She was spreading out his gifts on the table when the touch of his hand on her shoulder made her jump. "Simon! Don't sneak about so."

"I wasn't," he said, sliding onto the bench. "What have you been up to?"

She swept her hand over a mass of tunics, shirts, braies and hose. "I can't offer you silk, though my gifts perhaps will last you longer..."

"I don't want you wasting money on me," he said, dubiously scanning the fine collection of garments.

"I didn't. They cost only a few loaves of bread. A fellow burgher no longer needed them. They were the proper size and, well, I couldn't ignore such a bargain."

"There must be something wrong with them." He twisted and turned the material looking for damage, yet the cloth seemed barely worn, well-tailored, and expensive.

"Perhaps the low cost has something to do with the circumstances—" Edith paused, unsure whether to continue.

"What circumstances?"

"They belonged to her son."

"And?"

"He died a week ago."

Simon rolled his eyes. "What a cheerful thought, wearing a dead man's clothes."

"Oh, Simon, he'd be pleased to know his shirts were keeping someone warm."

"What killed him?"

"Nothing contagious, the strangury."

"That's curable. How old was he?"

"What does it matter? I wanted to do something for you, you've done so much for me."

His morbid look strained her patience. She could wait no longer and blurted, "Was it Maura? Did she hurt you?"

"No, not intentionally."

Heartened by his response, she besieged, "Tell me what happened and I want to hear it all. It will do you good."

"It's complicated."

"I have the patience," she said, settling by his side, then prompting, "So you met with her?"

"Barely," he muttered, fiddling with a leather thong. "The old crone protects her too well."

"Crone? You're not speaking of Rose?"

"Yes."

"Simon," Edith chided, "she was your second mother!"

The thong snapped to his fury. "The witch attacked me with a dagger!"

"A dagger! Why in Heaven's name would she want to hurt you?"

"I don't know," he sighed, tossing the strings aside. "She hates me, they all hate me! Why do I spend my time serving a family that would sooner behead me than waste their sacred time talking? No one will tell me what crime I've committed! There was a moment when Maura came to me, willing to talk, to listen, then Rose brought in the guards. When I was last here, Avenal gave me a betrothal writ stating that Maura would marry a soldier from Yorkshire. It was dated a year before her betrothal writ to Rufus."

"Then Maura must at least have been grateful to you for ending her betrothal to Rufus."

"I never had the chance to tell her! Will's taken credit for rescuing her, and she's gone with him to Berkhamstead." His jealousy raged and his fists shook the table. "And the thought of them together is killing me!"

"Will?" Edith said, confused. "Robert's son? What role does he play in this travesty?"

"Every role—lover, hero, robber baron, murderer. He swore he'd see me dead."

"Will..." she hissed, her eyes stark with loathing. "It was at his insistence that Robert sent me back to England. He knew I was pregnant with you and, I'm sure, prayed I'd miscarry on the way. He's a wily one, full of the Devil. Why would Maura agree to go anywhere with him?"

"He's also quite charming." His temper erupted and Simon paced and railed, "He even had me fooled, for awhile. But he's no worse than the others. Their insides rot with hate! The wars flare again in Normandy. Marc's gone to fight."

"Young Marc's gone to war?" Edith's heart ached to the dire news, and she hoped, "Simon, perhaps you can help mediate a peace."

He laughed in disgust. "Peace? Peace bores the monsters. They itch to kill. Marc joined Roger of Montgomery's men, and they'll march with King William to Paris."

"Paris?"

"And when William dies, we'll have Rufus, who despises his brother, Curthose, and they'll happily carry on the slaughter till both England and Normandy are ripped to pieces. So much for my futile efforts."

"Simon, you've accomplished a great deal of good in your work for the King."

"When Rufus is crowned, all my efforts will have been for naught!"

"And if he *is* crowned, the need for your skills will be more critical. You can't quit, not now."

"Yes, I can and will! I've had more than my fill of hatred and deceit. I've decided to return to Wales and offer my skills as physician to Prince Rhys."

"Then you won't be back?" she asked with a trace of panic.

Gently, he replied, "Of course I'll come to see you. But I never want to see the rest of my family again! I'm held responsible for all their failures. Odo fell from the King's grace by his own doing, yet I was blamed. I discovered Robert's trickery concerning the writ and, if he finds me, I'll be punished. And why? Because I'm tainted with Saxon blood and have the guile to defy them—and that's something they'll never accept!" His hands flew up to cradle his throbbing head, and he roared a final curse, "To Hell, to Hell with them all!"

"Do you curse Maura as well?"

"No." His arms fell to his sides as he added limply, "She *too* sent me away. Soon she'll be married."

"You'll find someone to replace her in your heart."

"No, I won't and believe me I've tried! Why won't she speak to me? Why won't she tell me what I've done to hurt her?! I know she doesn't hate me—"

Her reply rivaled his despair, "Stop torturing yourself! You don't need her, we don't need any of them. And if she's to be married, you have no choice but to forget her."

"Have you forgotten your time with Robert?"

"Simon, you can't compare—"

"Answer me, Mother! Will you ever allow yourself to forget?"

"No." She rose and heaved an anguished sigh. "I'm sorry, Simon. I thought I could help you. I was mistaken."

He caught her hand and stressed, "You have helped me! You've allowed me the time and quiet I needed to make some sense of Gloucester and my future."

"Your future is my future and, from what I've heard, it sounds very tentative. If you must return to Wales, I will understand, as long as you swear to visit...occasionally. And you'll stay a few more days, not to do chores, but to talk together, like we've always done before."

He nodded to her humble request, and they hugged—a desperate hug huge with love, support, and uncertainty.

*****

Maura reveled in her new-found freedom. After her first unpleasant evening at Berkhamstead, she was practically ignored and allowed to entertain herself. She rose late, took her meals in her chamber and, depending on the weather, strove to ride every day. She developed an easy rapport with the servants, and spent a good deal of her time visiting them in their huts crowding the bailey. When away from the castle, her fluent English and common dress allowed her access to the villagers' private lives, and she relished mingling with the market crowds. Late at night, to keep her mind from troubling thoughts, she would compose detailed letters to Marc, and stash them away in her trunk, hoping soon to have the opportunity to present them in person. And by the end of her first week at Berkhamstead, images of Simon began to weave their way into her dreams. Gone were the nightmares; the dreams instead were steeped in passion and strangely comforting.

One late afternoon after a brief rain, she let her horse guide her through the forest while she marveled at the beauty of the surrounding countryside. The sun's gentle touch lured a thin mist from the ground, creating a veil of swirling crystals. A scarlet carpet of needles blanketed the ground; their color and the crisp air blushed her skin. She inhaled a robust breath and joyously realized that for the first time in years, she felt no need to escape. Were her problems at last behind her? The prospect of becoming Lady of a Yorkshire manor seemed promising and intriguing, and the idea of marrying a stranger didn't bother her in the least. On the contrary, it offered an opportunity to start a partnership anew, without the burden of a bruised past, or an abusive future.

Her horse's stumbling drew her gaze to the ground and she noticed a path of charred timber. She dismounted and bent to examine the sticks. Straightening, she froze agape, for before her lay the strewn remains of a recently razed village. Maura gathered up her skirts, hurried to the clearing, and crept gingerly through the still smoldering ruins. The oppressive quiet and ghostly images etched in the smoke unnerved her, still she staunchly kept up her search for survivors and clues. A scorched rag doll at her feet made her pause. She crouched and studied the doll a long anxious while, wondering why the devastation? The startling roar of thunderous hooves made her clutch the doll to her breast and dash for her horse, only to watch him canter away from the chaos. She twisted in panic as the steeds and their menacing riders, armed with bows and arrows, encircled her. Her alarm soared to the men's hoots and snickered comments, then she snapped to a familiar voice, "Maura! God's breath! What are *you* doing here?" The horses promptly parted and Will trotted forward, a bleeding buck strapped to his mount's rump. He slipped from his saddle, and roughly steered her away from his hunting party's ears. "You are not allowed here!" he scolded. "This forest is restricted to hunters. You could have been killed riding alone!" Wrenching the doll from her grasp, he added with disgust, "It's made your hands filthy!"

She jerked from his hold and countered, "From what I've discovered, I wouldn't be the first to perish from your games! What's happened here, Will?"

"One of my men will return you to the castle," he growled, waving sharply to a squire.

Maura stomped her foot and insisted, "Not till you tell me why this village was burned!"

"Damn your impudence!" he roared. "If you must know, the hovels were torched because, like *you*, my Lady, the peasants wouldn't leave here voluntarily. I needed the land to broaden my hunting preserve, and it is *my* land, to do with as I please! Does my answer satisfy your morbid curiosity?"

"And did you burn the dwellers as well?"

"Of course not," he scoffed. "They were given ample warning."

"Then where have they gone?"

"To Hell for all I care!" He gestured furiously to his squire, who approached timidly as Will continued his tirade. "I see by your expression that you condemn me. Curse me, Lady, and you curse the King, for I follow his example! Now, I won't have my hunting interrupted with any more of your insolent questions. Richard," he commanded, "return the *Lady* to the castle and see she's confined to her room for the rest of the evening. Perhaps then we'll have some peace!" He hurled the doll back to the rubble and stormed away, barking curses and orders. The hounds bayed in jubilant chorus and the hunting party departed.

Maura fought the squire's hold, but eased her struggle as she caught a spark of empathy in his eyes. "My Lady," he whispered secretly, "it's best you do as Lord William demands. I will see to your safe return."

Her eyes narrowed in question as she accepted the squire's hand up into the saddle. Was it her imagination or did he seem as scared as she'd been when first threatened? As they galloped through the now baleful forest, she fretted—just how ruthless could her host prove to be?

*****

A noise disrupted Maura's blissful dream. Her eyes wide, she lay still and silent, and watched the band of moonlight gracing her bed waver to the curtain's ripple. Yet there was no breeze! Gingerly, she stretched for her chemise and, in one brisk move, yanked it over her head, and bolted from the bed. The locked door barred her escape. She beat and kicked the barrier. Her frantic groans escalated, then stifled to the sound of a clearing throat. Maura spun and beheld—him. The silver moonlight haloed his figure, but the strike of a flint shattered the angelic image and revealed instead the devil Will. He moved with an arrogant guise about the room, lighting several candles from an oil lamp, parting the bed curtains, and murmuring, "I suggest you stop all that flailing about and make yourself comfortable. We won't be leaving here anytime soon."

Her hands trembled in their tight clench. She fought for control and yelled, "Why are you here?!"

"I'm amazed at your naiveté, Maura. Why do you think? I've come to collect what's due me."

She stayed stuck to the door, clawed the latch, and answered with amazing calm, "Leave here now. I won't let you hurt me."

"I don't intend you *harm*," he assured in a light, cheery tone. "Though, I must say, I'm quite disappointed with your ungracious behavior." He sat and lounged amongst the rumpled bedclothes, kicking off his boots, and chuckling a wicked chuckle. "Then again, you do have a history of spurning men who rescue you. Take as a pitiful example my brother, Simon. I realize he was dreadfully unsuccessful in his attempt, but he did try..."

Stunned by his confession, she blurted, "Then you admit he found the writ!"

"I admit nothing of the sort. I'm referring to an episode that occurred long, long ago and is no longer important. Now that I have you in my home, I find you impudent and prudish. You definitely need a lesson in manners." He patted the quilt at his side and grinned wickedly. "Come to bed, Maura."

"You can't force me."

"If you fight, you'll only excite me more." Peeved by her obstinacy, he gritted, "Come to me, now!"

Maura spun and strained against the door, pummeling, shrieking, "Someone, please, unbolt the door! Help me, I can't get out. Please, let me out!"

From beyond the barricade came muffled laughter. Her terror surged as she whirled to Will's sickening touch. "Don't waste our time trying to escape. Two guards stand watch to ensure our privacy. And have you ever considered that this might be fun?" His body flattened hers to the door and she winced to his repulsive caress. He stroked her hair, grabbed a handful, and yanked her head back, gritting, "Why did you come here? That last morning at Gloucester, you wanted me. I know you did! And now you ignore me, and I detest being ignored. This night you won't shun me!"

"I had to get away from Rufus!" she cried as he yanked harder.

Her squirming increased, his weight pressed harder. He pried her hands from the latch, and pinned them against the wood, warning, "Behave yourself and you won't see him again. Defy me and you'll be back by his side in an instant!"

Her spit dribbled down his cheek and Maura hissed, "I'll hurt you."

He roared a mocking laugh and tried to kiss her; she foiled his attempts by whipping her head from side to side. Her mind raced, frantically seeking a disabling tactic. She stopped resisting, accepted his kiss, and felt his power dwindle and grip ease. Her teeth sank into his lip, clamped tight, and ripped. She let go to his agonized howl, and soundly drubbed his ear, sending him reeling back through the bed curtains. The silver candlestick holder sitting on the bedside table caught her eye. She lunged for it as he leapt from the bed, jerked her back, and struck her jaw. Stars exploded before her eyes, the chamber spun, the light dimmed. Groaning, she groped blindly at the air and clenched hold of his tunic, shredding it as she sagged to her knees. The nudge of his boot toppled her to the floor and he dove upon her body. Her head cleared to his searing pinches. She arched and twisted violently, yet he held his mount, clamped her arms to her sides, and snickered, "I'm impressed, Maura. You're quite the lady warrior." Blood trickled from his lip onto her chemise; he licked a drop and taunted, "Rufus bragged of your romps. Your skills were wasted on him—"

"Rufus has strength!" she grunted, clubbing the floor with her legs. "You're a gutless liar!"

"I'll show you strength, my feisty Lady!" His knee wedged apart her legs, but her resultant thrashing almost knocked him to the floor. Her kicks rammed his swollen groin, making him moan and reevaluate his assault. There must be a simpler way to torture her for her impertinent ways. The guards outside! Yes, threaten her into submission with a vile memory. He slammed her arms against the now naked floor, and his face twisted in a wicked scowl. "Maura, if you don't stop this nonsense, I'll have my guards restrain you." His warning instantly stilled her struggle, and a raw horror dulled her eyes. Heady with power, he proceeded to batter her mind. "I'll tell you why guards frighten you. Four years ago, I watched from behind a tapestry, while my father's guards beat and raped you. A fitting punishment for your sins, don't you agree?" Her body convulsed, her head lolled; she groaned and whimpered to his scourge. "What I saw excited me. They were brutal, rough, ripped you, made you scream. I so wanted to join them. Father forbade it. And now...I'll at last have *my* fun."

The horrific memory flashed before her eyes. She searched beyond the guards, beyond the agony, and saw again *his* eyes—crystal blue, flecked with brown, peeking from behind the tapestry. She had cried to them for mercy, only each desperate scream brightened their ecstatic glow.

The sound of her chemise tearing jolted her back to the present. Fierce loathing stoked her strength and, finding one arm free, she attacked that part of him that sickened her the most. Her nails stabbed his eye. Shrieking, he hid his face and hurtled backward off her body. She flipped to her belly, scrambled to her knees, and swiped for the candle holder. His forceful kick drove her into the table, shattering its legs, and pitching its contents and her to the floor. A sharp pain piercing her side momentarily stole her breath, yet still her fingers continued their mad creep through the rushes, groping for the weapon.

"I've had quite enough, Maura," sniffed Will, swabbing his tears with his sleeve. "Now get up! I wasn't planning on killing you, but you've given me ample rea—" A muffled thud cut short his speech as the candle holder smashed against his skull. Will stood wavering for an interminable moment, his eyes bulging as he mouthed a curse, then he slumped to the floor in a crumpled heap.

Crazed, Maura dropped to her knees and raised her weapon to strike again, but he didn't move. The silver stick tumbled from her brittle hold. She hugged and rocked herself, her strangled whisper chanting, "I hate you, I hate you, I hate you...hate...you..."

*****

CHAPTER TEN - THE UGLY TRUTH

The night slipped away and Almodis' agitation swelled. Alone in her bed, she tossed in frustration and silently cursed her tardy lover. Damn him, where was he? Will had sworn he'd come to her this last night before Robert's arrival. She abhorred sleeping alone. Not that it mattered who lay beside her; the extra warmth provided a sense of comfort and security she craved yet rarely knew. Well then, she decided as she rose, threw on her robe, and barged from her chamber, *If he won't come to me, I'll just have to go to him.* At Will's door, she banged repeatedly, receiving only silence in response. A quick peek revealed an abandoned room, the bed not slept in. Blood coursed to her head, twisting her face to an evil scowl. She flew in a fury to Maura's chamber, and halted abruptly before two drowsy guards. Her roar, "Where is Sir William?!" startled them awake.

"He's inside, my Lady," answered one, "and does not wish to be disturbed."

"Disturbed!" she yelled, gesturing wildly. "Get out of my way!"

"We have our orders, my Lady," asserted the other.

"Move, or I swear you'll both be flogged when Lord Robert returns!"

No further coercion was needed, and the men obediently stepped aside. Almodis rested her ear against the door, heard nothing, and noiselessly slipped inside. She gawked in disbelief and stopped short at the violent scene before her. The side table lay in a shambles at her feet. Her foot nudged its pieces aside, and she crept round the clutter to examine the bedlam more closely. Will lay limply in the rushes, caked blood blotching his brow. Maura sat frozen by his side, her eyes vacant as a corpse's, hair disheveled, chemise torn and stained; she muttered gibberish. A curious calm gripped Almodis as she knelt and clasped Will's wrist. She prayed for a pulse and, receiving a slow strong beat in response, closed her eyes in profound relief.

A powerful shake to her shoulder made Maura shrink away, her arms shielding her head. "Maura!" Almodis shouted along with a second jostle. "Maura! What's happened here?!"

Maura's arms fell away and Almodis winced at her bruised jaw and bloodied lip. "Have you come to arrest me?" Maura asked in a chilling listless tone.

"A...arrest you?" Almodis babbled in bewilderment. "I don't understand. Why? What? Tell me what's happened!"

Maura peeled a matted strand of hair from her eye and aimed her bleak glare at Will. "He tried to rape me," her faint voice rasped, then cleared and strengthened to add, "I stopped him!"

"Indeed you did," said Almodis with awe. She racked her mind for a course of action and swiftly decided it was best to flee. "Help me get him to the bed," she ordered tersely.

"I won't touch him!" declared Maura, clamping her mouth in revulsion.

"I can't lift him myself! If he wakes on the floor with the bloody candlestick holder at his side, he'll remember all. If we tuck him up in bed and straighten the room, perhaps you've hit him hard enough so that he'll forget the entire incident. It could mean your life, my Lady! So I suggest you get up off that floor and help me!"

Maura did as told and rose, only to double over in pain.

"What is it?" asked Almodis, her irritation laced with concern.

"A pain...a pain in my side."

"Can you walk?" Almodis pressed. Maura barely nodded and straightened with difficulty. "Then take his feet," ordered Almodis. Together, they heaved Will upon the bed and rumpled the quilt to make it look slept in. While Almodis swabbed away the blood on his brow, Maura wiped the candlestick holder clean and set it on the undisturbed side table. She kicked the remains of the other table under the bed. At Almodis' touch, Will moaned, striking her panic. She swept up a blanket from the base of the bed, wrapped it about Maura's shoulders, and dragged her from the room.

Outside, they encountered the smirking guards. Almodis addressed them with forced cheer, "Sir William is fatigued and wishes to rest. I trust you will see to his privacy."

They bowed. She grabbed up Maura's hand, and tugged her along the shadowed passageway and across the great hall. Maura, still woozy, tripped behind and suddenly found herself in the Lord's bedchamber, its door miraculously equipped with an inside bolt. Almodis noticed her peculiar scrutiny of the iron latch and explained, "For the sake of convenience, Will quarters all his new acquisitions in the boltless chamber. Now come, we'll get you washed and tend your wounds."

Muddled, Maura regarded Almodis' flitting with suspicion. "Why are you helping me? You hate me."

"I don't *hate* you," replied Almodis as she pointed rigidly to the bed. Maura approached cautiously, sat, and continued her wary vigil as Almodis poured wine. From a richly embroidered case, she produced a mysterious vial, placed exactly three drops of solution into the goblet, and handed the mixture to Maura. "Drink this down, it will calm you."

"What is it?" Maura asked with distrust.

"Wine, of course."

"No, what did you add to it?"

"Oh, a few drops of lettuce oil. My physician prescribes it for sleeplessness. Wondrously effective." Resignedly, Maura sipped the potion while Almodis rummaged through a trunk and withdrew a clean chemise. "Put this on while I pour some water."

As Maura reached for the garment, she erupted in a fit of labored coughing, spitting and spewing wine across her lap and onto the quilt. The trunk's lid slammed shut as Almodis hurried to Maura's aid. She rescued the goblet from Maura's wobbly grip and questioned, "God's teeth, what did he do to you?!"

"The table," hacked Maura. "He kicked me into the table."

Almodis tore Maura's chemise, exposing her skinned and blackened rib cage. "Binding should help," she asserted and began to search for an appropriate bandage.

Maura slumped across the bed, clutched Almodis' quilt, and pulled it tight under her chin. The oil's effect was quick and telling; the contents of the room blurred, but the acute pain kept her alert.

"Well I can't do much with you bundled up like that," commented Almodis, a ripped sheet dangling from her hand. "For now the oil should ease your discomfort. We'll bind your ribs tomorrow."

Maura's qualms rose again and she asked faintly, "Why are you helping me?"

"For a number of reasons," answered Almodis as she sat beside Maura and sipped wine. "After I realized your infatuation with Will was done, I had little reason to dislike you. And well, I warned him to keep away from you, though, he does loves a dare. I just never suspected he'd—" The terrible bruise on Maura's face rekindled images from Almodis' grim past, and she requested, partly from curiosity, partly from concern, "Tell me all that happened."

The quilt, the wine, and Almodis' apparent sympathy all boosted Maura's trust in her curious hostess, and she readily spilled her tale, "This afternoon I was riding in the forest and came upon a burnt-out village and...Will. He bragged about his part in its destruction. I angered him by asking how he could have done such a horrid thing. And then, this night, I woke to find him in my room. I shouldn't have come here. He lied to me about the writ and so many other things."

"The writ?"

"The Yorkshire betrothal writ. He took credit for ending my betrothal to Rufus, and—"

"Wait!" Almodis raised her hand and paused a pensive moment. Finally, she related, "Simon came to Berkhamstead just before we left for Christmas Court. I overheard a conversation between him and Will about a writ and—"

Piqued, Maura pushed up on her elbows and prompted, "And?"

"They spoke of you. Will goaded Simon into believing you were desperate to meet with him."

"What?!"

"Yes, and Will tried to take charge of the writ. Simon refused to part with it."

Maura's heavy head dropped back upon a pillow and she sighed, "I wondered why Simon claimed I wanted to see him. How did Will get hold of the writ?"

"Stole it, most likely."

"How can you stand to be near him?"

"Time numbs the conscience," answered Almodis solemnly.

"I don't understand."

"I've been close to Will for ten years now. I overlook his weaknesses because I need a bit of fun in my life. Robert, as you may know, isn't exactly what one would call jocular."

"How long have you been married?"

"Only six months. I believed I was to marry Will. My Liege Lord, though, considered Robert the more profitable match."

"Does Robert know about your time with Will?" asked Maura.

"If he does, he doesn't say. We don't speak much and see each other less. Enough about me, please finish your story."

Maura's lashes fluttered, she forced them wide, then continued groggily, "He said he'd come to take what was due him, and I fought him, fought him hard. I stopped him, but I couldn't stop them, I couldn't..." Her voice slurred as her attention faltered.

"Them? Who—" Almodis leant close and strained to hear Maura's ragged whispers.

"Will said something queer...something about Simon trying to save me long ago. Was he speaking of Dunheved...Was he?"

"I don't know, Maura. I've never been to Dunheved and have only just met Simon. Why did you spurn him? Compared to the men I'm plagued with he seems quite remarkable. He won't admit it, but he saved my life."

"I don't hate Simon, I never did!" cried Maura unexpectedly. "When I'm near him, the horrors of our past return. I should have listened to him! I'll never know peace till I hear him out." Clenched in anguish, her fist struck the bed. "Why did I send him away, why?! He'll never come back, never—"

"Maura, let go of your pain and sleep. You needn't feel afraid here, the door's bolted and I won't leave you."

Yet Maura didn't seem to hear and continued her erratic lament, "I had to come here. I had to get away from Rufus! Will's eyes...his eyes are the Devil's eyes. They laughed at me, mocked me while I was tortured! I almost killed him, Almodis, I wanted to...I wanted to. Will I be arrested for what I've done? I had to stop him."

"I'll speak to Robert on your behalf, for I feel partially responsible for this travesty. No, I don't believe you'll be punished. Now hush and try to forget, if only for awhile."

Almodis tenderly tucked the blanket round Maura and snuffed the nearest candle. "Close your eyes, sleep. In the morning all will seem different."

Almodis, no longer stolid and harsh, exuded caring and remorse so convincingly that Maura willingly acquiesced. She shut her eyes and was instantly wrapped in a cocoon of warm and wonderful darkness. Almodis downed the last of Maura's wine and studied her daring guest. Why did she feel a sudden affinity for this odd woman, who but a day ago had been her enemy? Perhaps Maura's delirious jabbering had touched that tiny portion of her heart not yet rotted.

*****

Simon's mind flooded with glorious childhood memories as he galloped E'dain through the dense forest surrounding Dunheved Castle. Tumbling dark clouds cautioned him to return home and, as he turned E'dain back toward the castle, he yearned for a happier time, a time he'd ridden alongside Robert through these knotted trees—certain of his father's love. A week at his mother's cottage had drained his anger and confusion, allowing him to construct a vision of a more stable future. He would venture to Normandy to inform the King personally of his desire to return to Wales, and there he would continue his doctoring and peacekeeping efforts. And never would he attempt to see Maura again. Not a comforting thought, yet necessary for his sanity and no doubt hers as well.

Rose strode exuberantly up to Edith's door, and paused a moment before knocking. Four years had passed since their last meeting, and she felt a twinge of apprehension. She raised her fist confidently, then lowered it in doubt. Of course, she longed to speak to Edith, but the thought of what might occur when their conversation turned to Simon, which it surely would, soured her enthusiasm. Well, if anyone could make him see reason, it would be Edith. Before Rose could lift her hand again, Edith opened the door and gaped in joyous disbelief. "Rose! Is it really you?"

"Yes, oh yes, Edith, it's me!" Their smothering hug jarred Edith's bread loaves from her basket into the muddied snow and, treading on one, Rose gasped, "Oh my, your bread!"

"No matter," Edith laughed, "I'll make more! Please, come in, come in!" She ushered Rose inside; they again embraced, and Edith dribbled happy tears as she asked, "What brings you to Dunheved?"

"My sons," replied Rose, shedding her cloak. "While visiting them, I asked of you at the castle. The servants told me where to find your cottage." She grasped Edith's hands and gushed on, "I've missed you so!" A quick glance about the hut elicited her compliments, "I see you're well settled. And you look wonderful! How long have you lived here?"

"I returned to Dunheved two years ago. And how are your sons?" asked Edith, hanging their cloaks on pegs by the door.

"Richard is fine and has finally married! I may be a grandmother yet. Geoffrey was injured in battle, but is recovering nicely. They were a bit shocked to see me."

"As am I! Shocked but pleased. Sit and make yourself comfortable." Edith poured Rose a cup of ale, plucked up the one loaf left in her basket and, moving to the table, began slicing. "You'll stay for supper?"

"Oh no, I won't trouble you, Edith," Rose answered as she settled on a mat facing the table.

"It's no bother. The stew's made and only needs heating." Edith considered her next question carefully. If Simon was correct, she already knew the answer; nevertheless, she asked, "Are you traveling with Maura?"

"Oh no," Rose answered lightly. "It was she who arranged my trip here. She's gone on a visit to Berkhamstead. Edith..." Rose said tentatively, setting her cup on an adjoining mat, "I did come to reminisce, though, there is another purpose to my visit."

Edith's slicing turned more vigorous. "And would that reason be—my son?"

"Yes," Rose said firmly. She promptly forgot the joviality of their greeting, and brusquely demanded, "You must convince him to leave Maura be! He tortures her with lies of his love. She'll marry soon, and longs to be rid of her past."

Edith dropped the knife, whirled, and sternly countered, "My son is no liar, Rose! I have little control over whom he sees or what he chooses to say to them."

"Perhaps that's the problem!" Rose flared back. "You never did have any control over that ruffian. Maura's life would be free of bother if you had kept a keener eye on him!"

"My son is grown and does what he pleases! I don't believe your sons would appreciate you meddling in their affairs."

"My sons conduct their lives honorably." Rose paused, washed down her choler with ale, then softened. "Edith, we needn't argue. All I ask is that you plead with him to stay away. You, he might listen to."

"There's really no point. I've warned him many a time to avoid his family...especially Maura. So you see it makes no difference." Edith turned back to her bread and ripped fiercely at the dough. "Maura should speak to Simon, they could settle their dispute, and get on with their lives.

Rose stood to vow emphatically, "Never!"

Simon led E'dain into the stable and guided her to a stall stocked with fresh oats and water. He removed her saddle and, searching for a grooming brush, heard angry voices drifting from the main room. He cracked the door ajar, peered inside, and discovered to his dismay—Rose. Her back to him, she gestured angrily, and ranted incoherent prattle, not allowing Edith one word in defense. Simon noiselessly shut the door and wondered if she'd followed him from Gloucester. It didn't seem likely, so he cracked the door again, stuck his ear to the opening, and listened.

"I don't believe you've ever tried to reason with him! He is the most incorrigible, stubborn, heartless—"

"That will be quite enough, Rose! Simon *also* suffers. If anyone is heartless it is Maura. And I'm shocked at your callous behavior as well. How dare you threaten my son with a dagger!"

"I...I protect my charge from all dangers—" Suddenly perplexed, Rose stopped, and charged, "How do you know about the dagger?"

"I told her, Rose," interrupted Simon, striding brusquely into the room.

Rose spun to the sudden intrusion and paled to his heated glare. "I...I should have guessed...you...you'd run to your mother, tail tucked between your legs. You spineless fiend!"

"Get out! This is one place you have no say," yelled Simon. "Get out, Rose, before I toss you out!" He stormed past her to the main door, flung it wide, and searched outside. "Did you bring your guards with you? Mother, did you check her for weapons?"

"Simon, Rose, stop this madness!" pleaded Edith, positioning herself between the two foes.

Simon eased her away and his monstrous bellow, "Leave here now!" shook Rose to the core.

Clapping her hands snugly to her ears, she foolishly stood her ground. "I won't go till I've told Edith how you—"

Simon loomed larger, pried her hands away, and blared, "How I *what*, Rose?! How I've tortured Maura, badgered her, lied to her? My supposed sins can't compare to your stupidity! How could you send her off with Will?!"

"Will truly cares for her."

"Will loves only himself," Simon countered with a disgusted snort.

"He rescued her from marriage to Rufus, and saved her life!"

"I found the Yorkshire writ!"

"Liar!"

Edith stood tensely by, wringing her hands, and spouted, "He speaks the truth!"

Rose snapped to Edith, her glower darkening, "You lie as well!"

Simon threw up his hands in exasperation, left the women, and headed for his stack of belongings.

"Rose," stressed Edith. "Simon received the writ from Avenal not two months past, then rode to Gloucester to present the evidence to the King."

Rose sneered in Simon's direction, "So you found the writ. Nothing can excuse the torture you've inflicted!"

"What torture?!" Simon kicked away his saddlebag and resumed raving, "I helped cure her illness! I found a guard to protect her. I stopped her marriage to Rufus! And for these deeds, I'm to be stabbed. If not for you, she would have listened to me!"

"If you had resurrected her from the dead, I still would not let you near her!"

Simon's demented howl rattled the walls, "Bleeding Jesus, why?!"

"Enough!" Edith shouted. "I'll not have blasphemy in my home! We'll speak civilly, or not at all."

Simon slung his saddlebag over his shoulder and growled, "Fine. I'll go."

"No, Simon, not like this!" protested Edith.

"I don't trust myself around that wretch." He paused, cast a leery eye on Rose, and added, "Yet before I go, I'll just make certain..." His rigid grip on her arm barely restrained her pummeling, as his free hand swiftly circled her belt.

Edith rushed to Rose's aid. "Simon, stop! Don't hurt her!"

Simon eased his hold and, from the folds of her tunic, produced what he'd suspected—a dagger. He flourished the weapon in Rose's face and gnashed, "Was this meant for me or my mother?"

Edith's wide eyes swelled with tears at the gruesome discovery. "Rose...I don't understand. We were once like sisters. How, how could you hate me so?"

Rose slumped in defeat, staggered to the table's bench, and wept copiously into cupped palms.

As Edith started to comfort Rose, she spied Simon heading for the door. She reached the exit before him and barred his way, demanding, "I forbid you to leave! Why must you punish me for what's happened here?" His sleeves almost ripped from her taut grip. "If you go, you'll never know the truth about Maura. Once the matter is settled, you can do as you please, but now you'll stay and listen!"

For a few brittle moments, they stood posturing nose to nose, then Simon shrank a bit, blinked, and dropped his glare. He tossed his saddlebag aside, and churlishly plopped down by the fire.

Edith knelt by the bench and gently pried Rose's hands from her face. "Rose, please stop your crying and tell me what's happened to make us snarl at each other like mad dogs. And why the dagger?"

"Have him tell you! He knows all!" Rose sniffled, wielding her clenched fist at Simon.

"Had he known, he would have told me," said Edith. "We've both suffered these past years, longing for an explanation, but afraid to ask. Only *you* can ease our torment, and help Maura as well. Simon sensed that she too yearns for the truth."

Rose mopped her damp face with her skirt. "I carry the dagger only for protection."

"Protection from me?"

"No. Him."

"Why?"

Rose stared at her lap, twisted her wool skirt with her crooked fingers, and muttered, "He is a danger to me."

"Simon," called Edith, "come to the table and assure Rose you're no danger to anyone."

Simon yanked fiercely at strands of straw in his mat and answered curtly, "I'll stay here."

Edith aimed her weary huff in his direction, and spoke tenderly to Rose, "Then will *you* sit by the fire? Come, I'll help you. It will make you more comfortable."

"I want to go back to the castle," sulked Rose, not budging from her spot.

Edith stood, hands on hips, and surveyed the situation. If kindness wouldn't loosen their tongues, then she'd try gruffness. "You two can sulk and pout for all eternity, but neither of you leaves my home till this matter is wholly settled."

Simon rubbed at the back of his neck, and gazed up to the soot-stained ceiling; Rose continued to study her lap.

Edith returned to the table and, mightily stirring the stew, struggled for a way to break the deadlock. She spun to a rustling and beamed proudly at the sight of her son by Rose's side, entreating, "Rose, come sit by me and tell me what I've done." Simon offered his hand and helped her from the bench and down to his mat. His gentle touch magically doused the bile in her black eyes, brimming them instead with merciful tears.

"Why did you desert her, Simon?" she croaked.

"I never deserted her, Rose."

"Yes you did. You abandoned her...left her alone to face your father's wrath!"

Edith dropped her spoon to join them, then was gripped by a paralyzing fright. This long-awaited disclosure would surely uncover the elusive secret she feared more than death itself. But there was no stopping them now; the truth must be revealed, no matter the dire consequences.

"I left..." Distress cracked Simon's voice; he shifted uncomfortably, cleared his throat and, with painstaking care, began again, "I was told that if I stayed or took Maura with me, she would die. The only way to save her was to run."

"Who told you that?" asked Rose.

"I did, Rose," said Edith as she knelt on the mat across from theirs. "Robert planned to punish Simon for his role in the Odo affair. When he discovered Simon and Maura were lovers, Robert swore if they tried to escape, he'd kill them both. I warned Simon of his threat, yet he still wouldn't go, so I told him if he stayed, Maura would die."

"Edith assured me once I was hidden she'd bring Maura to me. I was only hours away from the castle when I realized how impossible that promise was. Then I returned."

"You did *what*?" asked Edith, astonished.

"I came back for Maura. Everyone but Will had gone. He treated me quite kindly, fed me, and lied to me about your whereabouts. According to him, *you*, Mother, had left to seek comfort with your family. I should have seen through that hoax. He also said that Robert had taken Maura to Normandy to wed Arnulf Montgomery, and I would never see her again. He gave me money, and cautioned me to stay away for Robert's men were out hunting for my hide. I stupidly believed him. I had no reason not to."

"Why would Will lie to you?" asked Rose.

"He speaks only lies, Rose," Simon affirmed.

Rose's body stiffened and her eyes bulged as she struggled to stand. "By God, what have I done? I've sent Maura off with a liar and—What else is he capable of, Simon?! What else?"

"I shudder to think," broke in Edith.

"Why didn't you warn us, Simon?" strained Rose.

"I had my suspicions," said Simon, "though, I wasn't fully aware of his treachery till that last afternoon at Gloucester. After the disaster with Maura, I met with Will. He bragged of his grand scheme, how he'd fooled everyone into believing he was the hero of Christmas Court. I would have told you my doubts, but you didn't give me a chance to say anything and, after my meeting with Will, Rufus banished me."

"At the time, I did what I thought was best to protect Maura." Rose reached out a desperate hand. "Please help me up! I must return to the castle, and send Alan to Berkhamstead to take her from—"

"Whether you leave tonight or in the morn makes little difference," noted Edith. "Maura will have to fend for herself awhile longer. Simon has told you his tale, now you'll tell us yours."

"No, Mother," said Simon. "*I* will go to Berkhamstead. I'll hear the truth from Maura, and no one else."

"But Simon, I don't believe she *can* tell you the truth," replied Rose. His pained gaze prompted her explanation, "The horrors she suffered at Dunheved are so deeply buried that I fear if she's forced to remember, she'll go mad. Till you appeared at Winchester, she'd never mentioned that horrid time. Then snatches of her memories began to creep into her conversation, with tragic results. Her resolve weakened, her nightmares returned. No, before you see her again, I must tell the whole truth, ugly as it is." She accepted a second cup of ale from Edith, settled herself for her lengthy account, and began, "I don't know exactly what occurred immediately after your parting, Simon. But I will tell you what I discovered upon my return to Dunheved..."

*****

"Maura, wake up! Wake up!" Maura woke sluggishly to Almodis' prodding, and her hectic tone forced Maura's eyes and ears open. "Robert's returned and is in a furious state! He's commanded your immediate presence in the great hall." Maura rose too quickly and dizziness dropped her back to the bed. Her hands supported her heavy head, which ached and pounded so that she heard each of Almodis' words as screams. "Maura, please! I've risked much for you, now you must cooperate," begged Almodis as she tossed an unadorned gown at Maura's side. "I can only guess what Will has told him of your adventure last evening. I've never known why, but Will's word seems to take precedence over all others. Now hurry, dress, and wet your face. Your mind must be clear for your interrogation."

"Interrogation?" asked Maura in sleepy shock. "I've done nothing wrong."

"I agree, however, convincing Robert of your innocence will be no simple task."

The pain in Maura's chest slowed her progress and, noticing her difficulty, Almodis intervened. "Quickly, off with your chemise. I'll wrap your ribs." The initial swaddling seemed to aggravate the hurt, then came a blessed numbing, allowing Maura to don the clean chemise and gown without further fuss. Frigid water from the washing bowl roused her fully. She whined in protest to Almodis' assault on her knotted hair and, tripping into borrowed slippers, followed Almodis from the chamber.

They paused respectfully at the rear of the dais as Robert stood and issued strident orders. "Almodis, you'll sit at my side. Maura, I want you before me—Now!" Almodis hastened to her seat. Maura rounded the dais, and stepped lightly before her Lord. She genuflected; the straw in the mat cut through her clothing, stinging her knees. It seemed forever, then at last, Robert grunted, "Rise." She stood, straightened and, after a sly glance Will's way, her stoic stare lit upon Robert.

Gray and miserable, Will sat hunched at Robert's side, his brow thickly bandaged. He mumbled behind his hand to his father; Robert nodded and, stone faced, leant forward to pronounce, "My son tells me you haven't been behaving yourself of late."

Maura replied, boldly and swiftly, "I disagree, my Lord. I've done nothing to displease you."

"Though, it seems you displease others. Will claims you caused his injury. Do you deny this?"

"No. I acted solely out of self-defense."

"And why did you need to defend yourself against my son?"

"He tried to rape me."

Will sprang from his seat and had to clutch the dais for balance. His injury paled his face and dulled his objection, "She...she lies, Father."

The creases between his brows widened as Robert eyed his pathetic offspring with disgust. "Sit down before you fall! You'll have your chance to speak later."

Will sat, yet whined on, "She enticed me, begged me to come to her, then refused me!"

"Enough! Maura, did you agree to accompany Will to Berkhamstead?"

With bowed head, she admitted, "Yes, I did."

"We will deal with this dismal mess later. Now, concerning a more important matter—Maura, when did you first hear of the end of your betrothal to Rufus?"

"The morning before we left Gloucester."

"That's a lie as well," spouted Will.

Almodis stood and demanded, "Let her speak!"

"I don't recall asking for *your* advice in this matter, Almodis," chided Robert. "Kindly hold your tongue."

"Your Lady Wife protected Maura after my attack!" complained Will. "I want her expelled from the hall."

Robert's resonant voice boomed, "One further word from either of you and you'll both be expelled from the hall. Now, quiet!" Robert tugged on the skirt of his tunic, regained his composure, and continued dryly, "Maura, who informed you of the Yorkshire writ?"

"Will did. He told me he'd been searching months for an impediment and had received the writ the night before. Then he contradicted himself on our journey here, saying instead he'd acquired the writ before coming to Gloucester."

"Father, there is no truth in what she says," said Will. "Simon left for Dunheved after Martinmas specifically to steal the writ and ruin your plans."

"Maura, did you conspire with Simon to end your betrothal to Rufus?"

"No!"

Will stood again in objection. "Then perhaps you'll tell Father why you felt the need to spend an afternoon alone with the traitorous dog!"

Robert's roar rumbled slowly from his gut, "You did what?!"

"Will pressed me to meet with him!" Maura gasped in protest. "Simon mentioned nothing about the writ. Will twists the truth, I fought with Simon, we—"

"Silence! Maura, it pains me to hear how little you've learned these past four years. I've decided to let Rufus watch over you till Easter. Prepare to leave for Westminster."

Maura dropped to one knee and groveled, her clenched hands raised as if in prayer, "No, *please*, my Lord, Rufus beats me!"

"Your behavior warrants a beating!"

"My gracious Lord," she implored, "*please* don't send me to Rufus! I beg forgiveness for my errors and will endure any punishment you deem fit. But please not Rufus' beatings, not *his* torture!"

Almodis rested her hand on Robert's arm and spoke lowly, "Robert, I would meet with you alone."

"Lady, I have cautioned you countless times not to call me by my Christian name in public."

"I heartily beg your pardon—my Lord, it is urgent that I speak with you in our bedchamber."

"Surely, it can wait."

"*It* may be able to—I cannot."

Robert yielded to Almodis' glib response and joined her in their bedchamber, leaving Maura and Will alone. Maura rose from the mat, and threatened Will with a malicious glower. "If you dare move from your chair, I'll scream to wake the dead."

Will patted his bandage and spat, "Don't fret, my Lady. I've learned my lesson and will never wrestle with *you* again. Though, I pray someday you'll learn your lesson as painfully."

"Tell me something, Will, has the truth ever mistakenly slipped off your viper's tongue?"

He sneered to her barb, and dropped his aching head onto his crossed arms.

Almodis sat at the foot of their bed, and snuggled up beside Robert. One of her hands smoothed his brow, the other kneaded his thigh. "You've forgotten to greet me properly," she cooed as her lips touched his. "I've missed you, Husband." She saw and felt his rigid countenance subside and, smiling seductively, urged him to his back. Her lips tickled his ear. "There's absolutely no reason to punish Maura. You can't blame her for accepting an invitation to escape Rufus."

"I can't abide the heathen," muttered Robert.

"I heard of several incidents at Gloucester where he blatantly tried to harm her. She spoke the truth, Robert. Maura met Simon only to send him away. She despises him. And her guardian was there the entire time they were closeted. Once Maura arrived here, she discovered Will's more lurid traits and spurned his advances." Her tongue traced the outer rim of his ear and she sensed a shiver on his skin. "If you must send her away, send her someplace safe, Winchester perhaps. You will need her alive come Easter, won't you?"

Enamored by his nymph of a wife, Robert wrapped his arms round her, and crushed his lips to hers. She pressed her hands to his chest and cajoled, "Later, my Lord. First, you'll inform Maura you're no longer angry with her, then I will happily see to all your wishes."

Almodis extracted herself from his hug, and Robert reluctantly rolled from the bed. She held open the door and added wryly, "And we'll also discuss why you conveniently neglected to tell me you sired another son. I hear his mother was your mistress for twenty-odd years, and still lives near Dunheved Castle. I'm dying to know if you felt the need to visit her on your last trip there."

Robert cast her a look of sublime submission, and wordlessly left the chamber. She tapped her pursed lips and, beaming triumphantly, trailed him to the dais.

Not bothering to sit, Robert again adjusted his tunic, and announced, "Maura, I will not send you to Rufus. You may stay till I can decide what to do with you, and if there is any further trouble between you and Will, I may reconsider my judgment. God's breath, I have enough problems without your petty squabbling! Now leave me!"

Almodis squeaked with joy and clapped as she hurried to Maura's side. Maura matched her ecstatic expression, they clasped hands, and scurried from the room. Will stayed in his seat, his scowl lifting as the women flitted through the door. "Father, may I have a word, please?"

"Why must you waste my time?" asked Robert as he splayed his fingers across his bald pate. "I have work to do. What is it?"

"I suggest you keep Maura here indefinitely."

"So you can maul her again?" snorted Robert. "Why can't you control yourself? What you need is a few months of battling in Normandy. That would give you something to think of besides women! And furthermore—"

Impervious to his father's ranting, Will interrupted, his voice teeming with suspense, "My spies have followed Simon to Dunheved. One has returned, and he believes Simon may try to meet with Maura again. He's made you *very* angry this time, hasn't he, Father? He's shattered your grandest dream, with delight, I'm sure. I know you crave revenge and I can help you achieve your desire."

Robert muttered, "Tell me more," his expression mingling with interest and mistrust.

"There are conditions."

Robert sat. "Such as?"

"What trifling pittance do you expect to receive from this Yorkshire contract?"

"Wasteland to the sea, and a manor in Helmsley."

"I thought you already owned Helmsley Castle and the rest of the village?"

"I do, but I don't own *that* manor! William gave that manor to Hugh of Ryedale for military service. I must have it! I must complete my land grants. I will own all of Yorkshire!"

If I disclose my spy's findings, and assist with Simon's capture, you will give me the Helmsley Manor. I'll not be an overseer. The fief will belong solely to me and be registered in my name. Is that acceptable to you?"

"I'll hear your plan first."

"It's relatively simple. We'll use Maura as bait. Simon will easily sniff out her trail and, being the brazen fool he is, march right up to our gate!"

"He's not stupid, Will," interjected Robert. "He won't come if I'm in residence."

"But you won't be. We'll pretend to go off somewhere, London perhaps, and leave Maura here alone. He'll make his dramatic move, we'll snare him, and lock him underground to suffer as he's made us suffer, for the remainder of his pitiful life!"

His voice animated but guarded, Robert shifted closer and said, "It might work. Where is your spy now?"

"Planted not far from Edith's cottage. Once Simon begins a move in this direction, my man's been ordered to return and relay to me the details, roads taken, speed of travel, whatever is pertinent."

"You've obviously been planning this for some time."

"For years, Father, years."

"Well, I pray it doesn't go the way of your countless other frivolous schemes."

"With your favor and soldiers, how can it fail?"

"Then make it happen," Robert announced with conviction.

As Robert rose to leave, Will blurted, "Father, one further thought. Your Lady Wife needn't know of our plans. Her tongue wags too freely, and she seems quite taken with your younger son."

"I didn't intend to tell her."

"Fine...I will keep you informed."

Maura and Almodis strolled down the hall, Maura burbling, "How can I thank you, Almodis? Whatever did you say to Robert to make him change his mind?"

"It's not so much *what* I say, it's *how* I say it. Robert is very open to the right sort of persuasion. He's thrilled to have found himself such a willing and experienced wife. I sense that before our marriage he did without women's attention for quite some time."

"I wouldn't know, but I'm deeply indebted to you."

"Nonsense. All I ask in return is that you share your company. Sometimes I feel quite lonely." Almodis, uncomfortable at having bared a weakness, paused, then found again her jovial spirit. "I believe it would be safe for you to return to your room. Will seems quite frightened of you," she laughed. "Maura, you possess the skill I most covet, the ability to fight back. Perhaps you can teach me a few maneuvers."

"Granted," said Maura, "if you share the art of your winning tongue."

"Oh, and how I love to win! Come, I'm famished. We'll rummage the kitchen."

Their peculiar friendship firmly cemented, they scuttled out of the keep and into the sun-kissed bailey."

*****

Rose, mute and reflective, sat a long while, gazing intently at the fire. To Simon her silence was excruciating; he nudged her to break her trance. "You *must* tell us, Rose."

"I'm not sure I'm able."

"*Please*, try."

"Did you truly return for her, Simon?"

"Yes."

"We must have already left for the convent."

"Convent?" Edith cut in, confused. "Why a convent?"

"I must go back to the beginning..." Simon's intense hovering, and Edith's anxious fidgeting unnerved Rose. She inched slightly away and, selecting a long brittle rush, poked at the fire. "I returned late morn. The instant I entered the keep I sensed something amiss. Perhaps it was the quiet, the keep was never quiet. I passed by the great hall where

I noticed Lord Robert eating, then on to my chamber to unpack. I missed Maura's greeting. She has the uncanny ability to know exactly when I arrive, and was always waiting in my chamber with a hug and kiss. Part way through my unpacking, I felt a need to check her room. If she were asleep, she'd want me to wake her. The sight of her in her bed eased my worries, but her room, her room had been ransacked. Pelts had been ripped and thrown from her bed, pieces of the washing bowl strewn across the floor. Then I saw blood on her sheets and on the bed curtains. I don't know how I found the strength to uncover her for I was convinced she'd been murdered. Yet she breathed, ever so lightly. I remember vomiting when I saw the bruises and gashes that scarred her body. There wasn't an inch of her that hadn't been beaten, save her face. It was queer, her face hadn't been touched. I covered her and ran screaming to the great hall. Lord Robert never skipped a bite as I described the horror. I now recall how he smirked while I pleaded on my knees for his help. Robert ordered me quiet, and told me he knew of her punishment, for he had commanded it, and was pleased his guards had performed their duty so well. I couldn't believe what I was hearing! I pinched myself again and again to wake, but stayed locked in the nightmare—and then Robert asked me the most terrible question of all—"

A thickness permeated the air, making Edith's breaths shallow. She knew the time had come and her suspicions would soon be confirmed. She rose and escaped to the table to await the imminent explosion.

Rose stopped to the sudden disruption, and took a moment to wipe tears that threatened her fragile control. She glimpsed the anguish in Simon's expression and realized, with great remorse, that she'd been dreadfully wrong. He'd known nothing and what she was about to confess would surely destroy him. His eyes begged her to continue. She gulped her ale to muster her strength and dampen her parched throat, then said haltingly, "He...he asked...if...if the baby was dead."

For a few moments nothing changed, no one moved or uttered a sound. Then Simon shook his head and asked, "He asked *what*?"

"If the baby was dead." Suddenly frightened, Rose watched Simon's body stiffen, his breath quicken, his face flush and crease in furious agony. He flailed balled fists at an invisible enemy, and howled, "No!" Then, as quickly as it arose, his ferocity faded, his body turned flaccid, and his voice cracked, "No, no she wasn't pregnant. She would have told me—"

"She was, Simon, at least five months gone."

He squeezed shut his eyes and cried, "Why wasn't I told! We kept no secrets. Someone must have known, someone—" A sickening thought jolted his grief. He stood shakily and, with uncertain steps, started for the table and his mother. "You knew..." His simmering accusation ripped through Edith's heart; tears streamed down her cheeks as she faced him and meekly met his glare. "You knew. All the while you ordered me to leave, swore she'd come to no harm, that you'd bring her to me. You knew and never told me." His groan, "Why, Mother, why didn't you tell me?!" ignited her panicked sobs.

Edith flung herself at him, clutched at his arms, and choked, "I...I couldn't tell you! You would have never left had I told you." Simon's arms hung limp at his sides; his eyes shone ice cold. "You are my only child!" she wailed. "I had to protect *you* and would have said anything, done anything to make you leave!" He jerked from her hold and she lunged for him, desperate and sobbing, "Don't pull from me, Simon! Please understand, you must understand! I had no choice! He would have killed you, killed you—" He shunned her frenzy, turned coldly away, and returned to Rose's side.

"There's more, Simon," said Rose gently, "even more wretched than the last. I don't know if you can—"

"I'll hear it all, now."

Simon took her hand for support and she began, her tone faint with struggle, "I returned to her room and bathed her. There was no sign of miscarriage, the blood between her legs was from the guards' assaults, more than one man had raped her. Robert came into the chamber and seemed unmoved by what he saw. His voice sounded distant as he told me that Edith had been banished, and you had run away. Again, he asked about the child. I wanted to lie, but couldn't. He ordered me to pack our things, for we would leave the castle shortly never to return." Rose's legs pained her. She squirmed for comfort as Edith refilled her cup. Her heart ached to Edith's lost look, and she reached up tenderly to touch her friend's cheek. Edith gratefully kissed her fingers and sank down beside her. "On our journey," she continued, "Maura woke in my arms. She could barely move, yet she didn't mention her pain. Instead she spoke sweetly of you, Simon. I had no clue of your tryst, and could make little of her rambling, but I let her talk on and on of how you'd dreamt of running away together, of living in bliss. I hadn't the heart to disturb her fantasy."

"Before long we arrived at a convent close to Dunheved. I remember looking up at the huge timbered building and being struck with a horrible sense of dread. I'd heard rumors that Robert had despoiled the house and claimed it as his personal property. The nuns were forced to do his bidding or else be rendered homeless. At first, Maura was hopeful that Robert would leave her there to bear her child in peace. I had my doubts. He left us and we were taken to a tiny chamber furnished only with a pallet and candle. I was allowed to remain awhile, and listened while she rattled on about how you'd soon come to take her away. I began to notice fear tremble her words, hunch her body, and cloud her eyes. She clung to me and her grip tightened as the hours wore on." Rose coughed and her unexpected announcement, "Simon, I'm cold," startled him from his turmoil.

He hurried to rise, and Edith insisted, "You stay. I'll fetch a blanket and stoke the fire."

Simon wrapped Rose in the coverlet; she swallowed more ale, swabbed more tears, and exhaled a long, doleful sigh. "A nun entered the room, bearing a cup of foul-smelling herbs. She said the time had come for me to leave Maura to contemplate her sins and pray for God's forgiveness. I yelled something, I believe it was, 'loving is no sin'. The Abbess entered next and stated quite harshly that Maura had committed the sin of fornication and must be punished. She then ordered me from the room. I refused and, while we argued, I overheard the other nun urging Maura to drink the herbs, claiming the potion would help her sleep and ease her pain. Maura refused. Lord Robert appeared at the door with his men to escort me out. I begged for one last moment alone with her and he reluctantly agreed. We said little, only held each other. I tried to comfort her by assuring I'd be just outside the door. Her haunted expression told me that she knew exactly what the herbs were truly meant for...and I'll...I'll never forget what she asked as I left." Tears tumbled again from her swollen eyes, tripping her speech, and quaking her body.

"Tell me, Rose, what did she ask?" Simon bent close to hear her raspy whisper.

"She...she asked, 'Simon won't come back for me, will he, Rose?'. I answered what I believed to be true—I said 'No'. I left her then, and stayed near to the door. A third nun, carrying more herbs, entered the chamber as Lord Robert and his men left. Maura called out to me, her voice a child's voice, full of terror. Time passed too slowly, and I heard commotion, sharp words, and gagging. When the nuns finally appeared, they looked quite harried. The Abbess was last to emerge. She locked the door, and said that under no circumstances would the chamber be opened till morn." Rose rested her hand gently upon Simon's damp cheek. "I see this is as painful for you to hear as it is for me to tell. If you need time—"

His hand covered hers as he insisted, "I need you to tell me all."

"Very well. I paced for hours, the horrible sounds of her agony cramped my belly, and pounded my head. I tried to break through the door and bruised myself in the attempt. Maura let out one lone scream, so long and deafening that I was positive it was her last. Then came a terrible silence." Rose's voice strained with despair, "When morning came, they forced me to clean the room! She was so far along, they almost had to kill her to kill the babe. Her child lay dead in her palm, cuddled tight to her breast. If she hadn't been unconscious, I could never have pried it from her grip. And her hands! In her pain she'd bitten through her skin, and she still bears the scars." Between sobs, Rose cried out, "Those women were not nuns, they were fiends from Hell! And Robert is the Devil himself!" The agony of remembering doubled her over. Simon's arms surrounded and comforted her, while she struggled through her final words, "I cleansed her but could do little else. When she woke, she cried only for the child. She was delirious, hysterical and kept demanding I tell her who had taken him, where he'd gone, why she couldn't see him, be with him. I couldn't tell her the truth, she'd have died if I told her, died! She was only a child herself!" A convulsing moan ended her tragic tale. Simon crushed her fast to his chest, rocking her as his tears bled down his cheeks and stained her veil.

Later, under a mournful barrage of rain, Simon escorted Rose to the castle. Both weary from their trauma, they mumbled disjointed thoughts and feelings. Rose lifted her face and squinted up into the deluge, whispering, "Even the Heavens weep for her."

"Rose," asked Simon, "why didn't the Montgomery marriage take place?"

"Somehow Lord Roger discovered the pregnancy and had the contract annulled. I heard a rumor that you had told him, and that is why, Simon, I've always suspected you knew the truth."

"But how could I have told him when—" He paused and shook with exasperation. "Was Will there?"

"I never saw him..." Her face turned paler and her breath quickened. "What if he was hiding? And, by God, I've sent her off with him! What have I done, Simon?! She'll never forgive me, she'll—"

"Will wants me blamed for every atrocity that visits our family. He must have been there, told Roger, and spread the tale accusing me. We should have run, run far away that summer before Robert's return. Why did I wait for him? How could I have been such a fool to believe he would hear me out, forgive me, and accept our love?!"

"No one thought Robert capable of such an abomination, Simon. There's no sense in dwelling on what might have been."

They stopped at the base of the hill leading to the castle. Simon took Rose's hands and assured, "I'll leave in the morning for Berkhamstead. I'd ask you to accompany me, Rose, but I fear for your safety."

"I agree. I'll send Alan to the cottage at dawn. He'll watch over you on your journey, and help you take Maura from Will. Bring her to Winchester. It's familiar and relatively safe. I'll script a letter explaining all that occurred this day, but letter or no, she will agree to see you. She still cares deeply for you, Simon. Please remember, you must take care when you speak to her. My greatest worry is that she has not yet accepted the death of your child. And heed my warning—make your peace, and then part! The Yorkshire writ cannot be broken. Now I'll bid you farewell and pray you have a safe journey. It was hard hating you and I'm glad it's finally done." She stretched up to kiss him, and paused to add, "Please, don't be harsh to Edith. She did only what was needed to protect you and loves you wholly. I'll stay with her through the week, then have my son Richard escort me to Winchester."

They hugged a strenuous, grateful hug, and Simon somberly watched Rose disappear over the crest of the hill. Not ready to confront Edith, he wandered aimlessly through the frigid rain, his mind a tangle of hellish images and portents. Part of him craved retribution, not only against Robert and Will, but against anyone who'd ever cast Maura a scornful glance, uttered a snide remark, or touched her rudely. The other part of him hungered for escape, to dig a hole, crawl inside, and hide from his vague and ominous future. Did the poison that rotted his kin taint his blood as well, waiting for the opportune moment to twist him into a monster? Once his father had been kind, caring, nurturing...

The streets where he and Maura had played as children and strolled as lovers, evoked memories too wrenching to bear, so grudgingly he returned to the cottage. He didn't immediately go inside but sat a ways from the door, and let the cold rain numb his mind and soothe his soul. The door creaked opened and shed a creeping light across the drenched ground. As it touched him, he glanced up at his mother leaning in the doorway, her expression miserable and needy. He softened her look by reaching out and beckoning, "Come."

Edith joined him and, oblivious to the rain, confessed, "I won't blame you if you can't forgive me. I only guessed she was pregnant and would have told you...but I was afraid."

"Afraid? Why afraid?"

"I was frightened of the power Maura has over you."

"She has no special power," returned Simon. "I simply love her."

"And that may be the most dangerous power of all," sighed Edith. "Even when you were children, whenever she'd call, you'd always follow."

Simon rested his arm round Edith's shoulders and drew her nearer. "It took great courage for you to sit by and allow Rose to tell her tale."

"No, it was the coward's way. The time was long past for you to know the truth. And I, not Rose, should have been the one to tell you."

"How can I blame you?" implored Simon. "You lost your whole world that morning."

"As did Maura, Rose...and you. Will you go to Berkhamstead?"

"Yes. I'll travel with Alan. Rose will spend the week with you."

"That's very kind of her." Edith's trembling fingers covered his and she quavered, "And your father? What if he is at Berkhamstead?"

"Perhaps it is time I spoke to my father." Edith's heart faltered to Simon's foreboding words, then raced with panic. He helped her up from the ground and, as they entered the muted light of the cottage, he caught stark dread cloaking her eyes...a dread not even a full night of comfort and encouragement could dispel.

******

CHAPTER ELEVEN - THE LURE

Maura watched, disturbed, as torrents of rain battered the window pane. Beyond the bleared screen, she squinted and saw that the moat had spilled its banks, transforming the bailey into a sea of mud. Tradesmen scuttled for shelter, strained to pull cartwheels from sucking muck, and frantically bailed out their huts. She shivered at their turmoil, chafed her arms, and shifted her attention to the soothing hearth. Almodis' insistent chanting cracked her fixation, "Maura! Maura! Did you hear me?"

Maura turned only her head. "I'm sorry, Almodis. What did you say?"

"Where is your mind?" Almodis lounged back upon Maura's bed and delicately plaited her umber tresses. "I said, Robert has at last decided to let you stay till your wedding. I'm pleased with his decision. Are you?"

"Oh yes, Almodis. Thank you for your help, and I have so enjoyed our time together," answered Maura with a tender look. "Where is Lord Robert now?"

"Hunting with Will."

"In *this* weather?"

"Nothing stops them from what they cherish most," said Almodis. "Frankly, I'm relieved they're out of the keep. There's been far too much whispering lately. At times I worry they're plotting *my* undoing."

"Oh Almodis, you talk nonsense," scoffed Maura. "Your skills are important to Robert, and he's obviously fond of you."

"Yes, he loves to parade me before his fellow vassals so he can gloat."

"And with good reason, though you also manage his fiefs as expertly as the King rules the country, and that makes you indispensable. Are you feeling well? You look a bit green."

"I'm fine, only nauseated. It will soon pass. And how are your ribs?"

"There's barely an ache."

"Good, come and sit," Almodis said as she tossed the silver comb aside and patted the quilt. "For the last two days, I've rattled off the secrets of my lurid past. I'm tired of my voice, now it's your turn to confess."

Maura hesitantly left the warmth of the grate and rested back against the bedpost. "Compared to your adventures, my life seems so dull. I'd only bore you."

"Then bore me!" Almodis leant forward and eagerly decided, "We'll begin with the men in your life. There must have been a few. You couldn't possibly have reached your ripe old age still intact."

"There weren't many and none worth wasting time reminiscing over—"

"I sincerely doubt that!" interrupted Almodis adamantly. "You can't escape that easily, Maura. Though I hate to sound pushy, I must insist—please tell the tale of you and Simon."

The quilt's richly colored embroidery stole Maura's concentration. She fingered the silken thread and grudgingly muttered, "Once, long ago, we were special to each other, but now it's done."

"I disagree. Simon admitted he still loves you."

Maura briefly raised her eyes. "When?"

"At Gloucester."

"Well, it matters not. I won't see him again."

"Don't be so morbid, Maura. He seemed immensely persistent to me. Now, you're dying to tell and I'm dying to know—was he a wonderful lover?"

"*Dying to tell?*" Maura crossed her arms with a huff. "That's rather presumptuous of you."

"Not at all," argued Almodis. "I'm only stating a fact."

"Can't we speak of something else?" begged Maura.

"No. You needn't be shy, I'm not easily shocked." As Maura reflected inward, her peeved look softened. Almodis flattened her palms together and excitedly discerned, "Oh, I see by your expression he was!"

"Was what?"

"A wonderful lover!"

"We taught each other well," mumbled Maura, blushing deeply.

Almodis flopped back upon the pillows and let loose a long, euphoric sigh. "Now I regret not finding out for myself."

"What?"

"Oh...nothing," Almodis replied with a furtive simper. "Were you together long?"

Maura stood and glided back to the window. The thought of divulging her most precious secrets etched a dubious crease between her brows, yet her tongue ignored her misgivings and she wistfully mused, "When I came to Dunheved I was five, and Simon was eight. We were raised together. He left at fifteen for Odo's castle in Kent to train for knighthood, and when he returned he was nineteen and so handsome."

"He still is," commented Almodis. "Fifteen is rather old, isn't it? I thought most boys begin training at eight."

"Simon showed promise as a scholar and was intended for the priesthood, so he was schooled by a cleric at Dunheved for seven years. I was able to learn from the cleric as well. Robert changed his mind about the priesthood when he realized Simon's military prowess. He sent him to Odo's where he would be well prepared no matter which path Robert chose for him. Five years back, the trouble started. Simon spent the mid-summer holiday with the King, and William tricked him into betraying information that placed Odo under the Crown's suspicion."

"Did this have to do with the Rome scandal?"

"Yes, but not the true story. Simon had been told that Odo was planning a pilgrimage to Rome."

"Will told *me* the true story," said Almodis, clicking her tongue. "Stealing the King's soldiers to attack Rome and take the Papacy! Odo's stupidity amazes me."

"Simon was banished from Kent," continued Maura glumly. "He arrived at Dunheved disgraced, hurt, and frightened. Robert and Odo have an intensely close bond. Robert worships him, and when Odo was imprisoned, Simon knew Robert would punish him for causing it. I tried to convince Simon of his innocence and urged him to leave, still he insisted on staying. He foolishly believed in his father's love, that Robert would listen to him, and forgive him."

Not expecting such a dour recital, Almodis rose from the bed and, with a slight nudge to Maura's shoulder, motioned to the thick pelts strewn before the grate. Maura, her expression pinched, readily accepted a consoling cup of wine, and settled beside Almodis on the floor. Her fingers tugged and stroked the fur as she rambled on, "I'd been so lonely since Marc left to train with the Montgomerys, that I found myself following Simon everywhere, constantly trying to cheer and distract him from his troubles. And my efforts helped, for as the months passed his anxiety seemed to lift. Then suddenly he began to act indifferently to me. It was so unlike him and terribly confusing." Her voice knotted with emotion, "I loved him, I'd always loved him, but my love had deepened in new and frightening ways. I wanted him to touch me and kiss me. I didn't know how to tell him, and each time I tried to get closer, he'd pull away." A gulp of wine steadied her quaking voice. "It was March...Edith and Rose left the castle for a lengthy visit to friends and family. I often wonder why they left us alone. There was a Shrove Tuesday festival in the village. We'd had the most marvelous time, played games, danced, and drank a bit too much mead. When we returned to the keep, we built a huge bonfire in the garden below our rooms. I don't know if it was the mead or the magic in the flames, but something gave me the courage to confess my love. And he instantly showed his passion for me was every bit as intense...We were foolish and reckless, and I remember being blind to everyone and everything around us." For the first time in her speech, Maura's somber gaze met Almodis' maudlin one. "I was so happy, Almodis, and I thought I made him happy. I must have been mistaken, for nine months after our first night together, Robert returned and Simon left me."

"You mean Robert banished him," corrected Almodis.

"No...Simon ran off without a word or a thought! I tried to escape with him, but he threw me against a wall. I fell into the rushes, and when I looked up he was gone."

"Surely, there must have been a reason for his peculiar behavior?" wondered Almodis.

"If there was, I never heard it. At Gloucester he tried to speak of that time. I've struggled to remember. It's all such a blur. I can make no sense of his words, only his actions. If he still feels for me, Almodis, why did he abandon me? I suppose now I'll never know."

"When did he leave you?" asked Almodis as she inched closer and traded her full wine cup for Maura's empty one.

"Four years past."

"And the other men...none could compete?"

"I used them to forget." Maura's buried strife gushed forth as she despaired, "But I can never forget! And since our meeting at Gloucester something within me has changed. I want him again and I'll gladly listen to anything he cares to say!" She paused, then finished brokenly, "But...I...I sent him away." Something in the flames caught her eye and coaxed from her a small grin, a whimsical voice, and secrets... "On hot summer nights we'd go down to the garden. The grass was cool on our bare skin, and we would—" As if slapped, she jerked and snapped at Almodis, "Why am I telling you this?"

"Because you want to."

"No I don't!"

"Oh, Maura, don't leave me in suspense! Tell me what you did on the grass in the garden."

"Talking with you, Almodis, has cast a strange spell over me. I tell you secrets I wouldn't tell Rose, and all I think or dream about is Simon!"

"And do the dreams bring you pleasure?"

"Yes, but..."

"Then why complain? You *ought* to be grateful." Almodis sat a moment in thought, then an enlightened spark glittered her eyes. She sprang from the floor and burst out, "I'll have my spies locate Simon, and then I'll arrange a secret rendezvous—"

"No you won't!" Maura soundly objected.

"You are entitled to a bit of peace and happiness before you're shackled to this hapless soldier."

"I can't let you risk the danger," pleaded Maura. "Not for my sake!"

"I wouldn't be doing this only for your sake," argued Almodis. "There are, of course, Simon's feelings to consider, and I intend to experience vicariously all the passion you two encounter. Besides, once my mind is decided no one can alter it. First, we must devise a plan. Where do you think he went to after that terrible afternoon at Gloucester?"

Maura returned to the window and her inner world as Almodis resumed her chanting, "Maura! Maura! Did you hear me?"

*****

On the second day of their journey, Simon and Alan arrived at an alehouse in Wallingford. The unbroken hours of riding had taken a harsh toll on their bodies and, stiff-legged, sore, parched and famished, they shouldered their way through the loitering crowd and into the common hostelry. They shunned the tables crammed with smelly, squabbling men, and chose instead a corner of the floor, cushioned with straw, and well beneath the dense cloud of hanging smoke. Simon massaged his aching legs as Alan waved for stew and ale; neither noticed a black-cloaked, hooded stranger huddled close by.

"This is where we part," said Alan, as the noxious stew was set before them. They quickly downed their ale, hoping to numb their tongues and noses to accept the putrid fare. "I'll ride northeast, you ride east, then north. I should arrive a day before you in time to discover who is in residence. Do you know Berkhamstead?"

"Slightly," Simon grunted as he removed one boot and wiggled his frozen toes.

"If you keep the pace we've managed since Dunheved, you should arrive mid-day on the Sabbath. Keep yourself hidden, then at dusk, come to the village well. If I'm *not* there, Robert is in residence and you will head directly for Winchester. Maura and I will meet you there. If I *am* at the well, you can assume it's safe to enter the castle."

A quarrel sent a bowl and a tankard crashing into the wall, narrowly missing Simon's head. He dropped his spoon into his stew and implored, "Is that all, Alan? I want to leave here."

"No, that's not all. I've enjoyed the tale you've entrusted to me on our journey and wish you a glorious reconciliation with Maura. But I know you too well, Simon. I'll warn you once and only once—don't do anything rash. I've lost count of the times I've had to drag you from your near-lethal mistakes."

"What could happen? I have the King's protection and you, a member of the King's guard, to watch over me."

"It's quite simple," replied Alan in his forthright way. "Robert will arrest you, lock you deep underground, and throw away the key. Most likely, you will have me for company. The King could be dead as we speak, and if he is still alive, he's too busy to rally to your defense. That leaves Rufus, who will happily sign your execution order. I'm now employed as your guard and am responsible for your life, yet you are also my good friend and I must insist you behave wisely. Should anything appear in the least bit suspicious—run!"

The clamor turned deafening and the dark man, content with this illuminating knowledge, skulked out the door, and rode in haste for Berkhamstead.

Simon and Alan broke through the tangled horde that blocked the doorway and gratefully drank in the clean, nippy air. Simon mounted E'dain and shivered beneath his cloak while listening to Alan's final instructions. "Now take care and don't rush! It's vital I arrive before you."

"Do you have the letter?" asked Simon, shifting restlessly in his saddle.

Alan smiled broadly. "Yes, it's safely tucked away and will be presented promptly to your Lady upon my arrival."

Simon clapped Alan's shoulder. "When next we meet, pray it's inside the castle." Sharp nods parted the two, and as Simon watched Alan canter away, his words 'your Lady' echoed in his mind, drawing from him a most radiant smile.

*****

Maura thrashed in her bed, desperate to escape her blazing nightmare...Flames leapt from the cottage's walls and danced a deadly dance across the rushes. Thick smoke gagged and blinded her. She swatted madly at her burning sleeve, then jerked to a new vision—Simon stood before her, his arms wide and beckoning. Maura clutched the sleeping boy in her lap and, reaching out to Simon, kicked at an unseen binding force. "I'm here, Maura..." came Simon's sweet lulling voice, "Come to me...I'm here." She gaped in horror as the flames jumped to his hose and braies, swiftly crawling upward, and devouring his body; he bubbled and blistered away to a pile of ash at her feet. The man—a black, malevolent shadow—towered above her, his gleaming weapon raised. The child's blanket muffled her screams as the sword sliced through the masking smoke...

Maura woke to her own horrified gasp and the bite of rushes on her knees. She clawed blindly through the blackness, groping for Simon and the child. Then gradually the dark paled and she knew her dream had come again. The bed promised sanctuary and, as she wrapped herself in the quilt's folds, she felt a deadening ache of loneliness. She fought back tears and began to question the prospect of remaining at Berkhamstead, for despite its many attributes, especially Almodis, it was proving to be a desolate, baneful place. She lay a long while, queer night noises stoking her upset. Finally, she succumbed to her malaise, rose, shrouded herself in a blanket and, uncertain of purpose or destination, left her chamber. Barefoot, she roamed the halls, sidling snoring bodies, sloshing through mud, and dodging nosy hounds.

The wind groaned through the arrow loopholes gracing the walls of the great hall, ruffling the tapestries and glowing the coals in the grate. Maura tugged her blanket taut beneath her chin, and peered beyond the dais where she could barely perceive the slumped figure of a guard propped against the Lord's bedchamber door. Any attempt to speak with Almodis would surely result in crossing Lord Robert, so Maura ambled dejectedly back to her room. On her way, she passed on tip-toe by Will's door. She noticed the door ajar and drifting whispers, and stole a peek inside. Will, Robert, and four others sat huddled about a table, perusing what appeared to be a map. A sudden breeze dragged the door across her bare toe; her gasp alerted the men and the door burst wide. Arms lunged out, captured her, and roughly hauled her into the chamber. Will thrust her at Robert, shouting, "I told you she conspires against you, Father! So now you're a spy, Maura. And pray tell us, who taught you this newest skill?!"

Robert's fumbling grip firmed as he demanded, "Why were you outside Will's door?"

"I...I couldn't sleep," she stammered, her frightened eyes darting about the room. "I thought a walk might help, then I heard voices. I was surprised to hear voices so late. Please, my Lord, I meant no harm—"

"Quiet!" yelled Robert. "Your empty excuses infuriate me! One of my guards will escort you back to your chamber and stand watch in case you feel the need to *wander* again."

"No, my Lord, please!" She wriggled from his hold, and spun to beseech, "Not your guard! I swear to return on my own, and won't leave my chamber till morn."

A bulky, sour-faced man clad in a hauberk emerged from a shadowed corner, his voice scratchy and dull, "You'll come with me, my Lady."

"You return with the guard, Maura, or with Will. It's your choice," Robert added snidely.

In a flash she was out the door. Robert's sharp gesture sent the guard hurrying after. On the race to her chamber, she vaulted the stragglers' bodies; mud splattered her arms, legs, and chemise; rushes cut at her feet. Inside the room, her half-empty trunk cooperated with her frantic tugs and scooted before the door. She hushed her panting, and pressed an ear to the coarse barrier. The guard's stark boot steps approached. Growing ever heavier, they halted before her door. She glanced fearfully down at the slim opening at the floor, beheld his lurking shadow, then heard him jiggle the latch, and felt his weight bend the wood inward. Her trembling lips sputtered prayers as she shrank away, and scrambled up onto the bed. With the bed curtains pulled wide, the flickering nub of a candle at her side, and the flimsy quilt her only armor, Maura forced herself to stay awake till dawn's rays glistened upon the window pane.

Loud knocking startled yet failed to lure Maura from her feathered sanctuary. An urgent feminine voice accompanied the next pounding, "My Lady, my Lady Maura, please come to the door!"

Maura recognized the youngest chambermaid's squall, and rushed to remove the trunk. Before opening the door, she asked warily, "Are you alone, Lily?"

"There's no one but me about, my Lady."

She cracked the door slightly. "Then hurry and come inside."

"No, my Lady, there isn't time. I've been sent with a message. Lord Robert requests your immediate presence in the great hall." The maid shoved a pail of warm soapy water into Maura's hand, executed a stiff curtsey, and scurried away down the hall. In a quandary, Maura washed and dressed hurriedly. Lily's nervousness suggested trouble was in the offing—another reprimand perhaps? She fretted as she deftly plaited her hair. Was her imprudent behavior last evening serious enough to compel Robert to send her to Westminster...and Rufus?

Robert's temperate tone met her as she entered the hall, "Come sit by my side, Maura." His mild expression calmed her anxiety as she eased herself into the chair flanking his. Will jerked forward in his seat and poisoned her calm with a venomous glare. Robert snapped his fingers, alerting a servant to refill his wine cup, and questioned flatly, "Maura, you'll tell me all you heard outside Will's door."

"Not a thing, my Lord."

"And again, why were you wandering?"

"I had a nightmare. The sounds in my room disturbed me. I couldn't sleep and thought a walk might tire me."

"The sounds were only mice. If you wish, I'll get you a cat."

Irked by Will's relentless glower, Maura mimicked his hateful look, and snapped, "It's not the mice that bother me, my Lord, it's the snake!"

Will slammed his fists on the table and shot up to counter, "Father, you can't allow her to slander me so!" Robert's indifference fed Will's fury; he wielded his knife above his head and hissed at Maura, "I swear I'll hack out that foul tongue of your—"

"God's breath!" hollered Robert. "Enough! I warn you two, speak civilly or you'll both be confined to your chambers!" With an exasperated sigh, he offered Maura a hunk of cheese. "Eat this. It should keep you quiet long enough for me to finish what truly needs to be said."

Before tasting the cheese, Maura worried aloud, "Where is the Lady Almodis, my Lord?"

"She feels poorly and lies abed," replied Robert. "After our talk, you may visit her. The Lady and I will depart mid-day to London and we will sojourn at the Tower. Will leaves before us for Westminster to visit Rufus. You'll remain here till our return, which should be no longer than a fortnight."

"Must I stay, my Lord?" asked Maura. "May I instead journey to Winchester? Or perhaps you'll allow me a visit to my betrothed in Yorkshire."

"No, you'll be safer here under my men's watch, and a bit of solitary time will give you the opportunity to reflect on your duties to me and to your betrothed. I suggest you seek our priest's counsel on this matter. Heed well his advice, Maura. Now, when you are done with your meal, you may go to Almodis."

Maura stuffed the cheese into her mouth, snatched up a stale bread roll, then rose and hastened the short distance to the Lord's bedchamber. In response to her knock, she heard a faint, "Come".

Entering, she found the bed curtains closed and the chamber stifling hot. The distinct stench of vomit struck her; she hesitated, then mumbled worriedly, "Almodis?"

Pale fingers parted the curtains and a small voice answered, "Oh, Maura, please come closer."

Maura hurried round the bed, yanked the curtains apart, and beheld a prone, ashen, and bedraggled Almodis, one hand resting upon her breast, the other draping her brow. Maura sat by her side. She dipped and wrung a cloth, carefully removed Almodis' limp hand, and mopped her brow. The kind deed elicited from Almodis a grateful sigh, "Bless you, Maura. That feels wonderful."

"You're very pale."

"I've been sick."

"Have you seen the physician?"

"There's no need, the sickness will soon pass. It always does." Almodis' evasive answer enhanced Maura's confusion and concern, and her next statement seemed displaced. "Maura, I'm terribly sorry but I can't seem to locate Simon."

Maura patted her hand and gently chided, "You should never have attempted such a thing. It's far too dangerous. Robert despises Simon, and..." she added through a gentle smile, "in a way, you *have* returned him to me. For that, Almodis, I'm truly thankful. Now, I'll fetch the physician. Robert expects you to leave here by mid-day—"

"There's really no need." Almodis firmed her grip and stressed, "I don't need the doctor to tell me I'm pregnant."

"Pregnant!" Maura gasped, letting the towel drop to the floor.

"Yes." Amused at Maura's reaction, Almodis let out a snorted laugh and suggested, "Close your mouth, Maura, you look rather dumb. Yes, I admit I was stunned as well. You'd think with four husbands and the countless men I've known, it would have happened sooner. But Maura, please keep your elation to yourself. You're the first I've told and it must remain our secret awhile longer."

"Why?"

"I've been told that early in pregnancy there's a risk of miscarriage and, because of my age and the sickness, I'm afraid—"

"The sickness is normal," blurted Maura.

Almodis eyes narrowed as she asked, askance, "And what makes *you* such an expert?"

A harrowed look lengthened Maura's face. She turned from Almodis' gaze, fidgeted, and fumbled, "I...I've heard things...from servants and I've known pregnant wo—" Too flustered to continue, she rose abruptly and paced, wringing her hands, and protesting too sharply, "Why must I answer to you?! Talking to you is like being in the confessional, tell all or be punished! I won't be pressured—not by you, not by anyone!"

Almodis pushed up in bed and wondered what she'd said to spark such an angry discourse. Then a closer inspection of her ward's distress gripped her with a vague horror. Suddenly, she realized the cause. "Maura," she called, reaching out tentatively, "what happened to your baby?"

Maura's eyes begged for solace and her blanched face matched Almodis'. She stopped pacing and, in a broken whisper, admitted, "I...I don't know."

"What are you saying?!" demanded Almodis, floundering up from the bed and seizing Maura's shoulders. "You must tell me, I have to know! What might my husband do to *my* child?" To Maura's anguished silence, Almodis shook her and cried, "You must answer me!"

Maura sagged in Almodis' grip, her grieved answer scarcely audible, "Robert took him away."

"Took him where?!"

"I don't know!"

Almodis sank weakly to the bed, crossed herself, and prayed in a piteous whisper, "God spare and protect me and my child from harm—" Despair interrupted her pious monologue, "Maura, will he take my child as well? Will he?!" Maura's visible torment shamed Almodis; she gulped away her callousness, and engulfed her friend in a comforting hug. "Oh Maura, forgive my prying. I shouldn't have forced you to confess, it was selfish of me. We'll speak of this no more."

"No..." Maura said, pulling slightly away. "It's time I told someone."

"You've never confided this to anyone, not even Rose?"

"No."

"But how could you keep something so horrible hidden away these many years? I can't believe you've never told Rose."

"Rose was there when they took him away. I've never mentioned it to her because she knows the truth, and I'm terrified of the truth. I can only pray he's safe...somewhere."

"Does Simon know?"

"I once thought he did, but now I wonder. None of that time is clear to me...Almodis, I angered Robert and he punished me. Why do you fear him? This *is* his child, isn't it?"

"Yes, of that I am certain. Will seems incapable of fathering a child. Robert and I were together at Pevensey three months past and I've only been with Will recently. I've missed my flow for three months. This is Robert's child."

"Then why do you fret? He will be thrilled."

"Will won't be...He'll let no one stand in the way of his inheritance."

"Surely he wouldn't, he couldn't—"

"Maura, you were a victim of Will's treachery. Yes, you saved yourself, yet don't believe for a moment that your battle is done. He'll seek revenge for his humiliation. When or how, you won't know."

"Robert will protect you and the child," asserted Maura.

"Robert could be dead before this baby is born!"

Almodis lapsed into hearty sobs. Maura hugged her tightly and comforted, "You need to stay close to Robert till the child is born. Then you'll come to Yorkshire. Rose and I will gladly watch over the two of you, and see your child comes to no harm. Almodis," Maura lifted her chin and asked, "have you ever considered you might deliver a girl?"

Almodis sniffed, "Yes...I pray for a girl, but I'm still frightened, Maura. Please, not a word to anyone. Will's spies are everywhere."

"I swear."

"And I will never, *never* divulge your secret." One particularly loud sniff preceded Almodis' confession, "I'm going to miss you. I wish Robert would let me stay."

"Remember what I just said, it will be safer if you accompany him to London."

"You won't be too lonely?"

"No," said Maura. "I'll visit with the servants, write letters to Marc, ride, and Robert's ordered me to meet with the priest."

Maura's last words slightly lifted Almodis' dole and she digressed, "Oh Maura, I swear, the priest is approaching ninety years and is a horrid old bull. I'm convinced he thinks me the Devil incarnate. Still, he *loves* hearing my confessions. He puffs so heavily that I fear one day my sins will give him a seizure."

The door creaked opened and in stepped Lord Robert, his scowl as dark as ever. His expression, however, lightened as he approached the women and noted with the slimmest of smiles, "Well, Maura, it appears you brought the cheer Almodis needed."

Maura stood respectfully. "I enjoy her company, my Lord."

"Fine. Almodis, I'll send your women in to assist with your packing. We'll leave shortly."

"May I stay with her till you go, my Lord?" asked Maura.

"If you wish," he conceded, then added pointedly, "While we're gone, Maura, you will be restricted to the keep and bailey."

"Can I at least ride within the castle grounds?"

"You will remain within the curtain wall."

In disappointment, she hung her head and muttered, "Yes, my Lord."

"Almodis, I expect no delay on our departure."

"Yes, Robert." His austere look quickly corrected her slip, "My pardon. Yes, *my Lord*."

A joint sigh of relief escaped the women as the door clicked shut. "Maura," said Almodis, cupping her hands, "I do feel better, more assured, and it's entirely your doing."

"Please, Almodis, try not to exaggerate your fears. I don't believe Robert would ever purposely harm you or your child, and the sooner he knows of your pregnancy, the safer you will be."

"We'll see. Perhaps I'll tell him on our trip. Maura...I'm...I'm so very sorry...about your baby."

"Talking about that time has helped to ease the hurt," said Maura, returning Almodis' taut grip.

*****

Maura's second night alone in the almost deserted castle passed far too slowly, allowing her more than ample time to think and reflect. The rain had at last ceased. As she circled the battlements, she marveled at the vividness of the sprouting stars and, while strolling, she pondered Almodis. Their curious attachment bemused her, their temperaments being so diverse, yet their lots so closely tied. Now that Maura's future seemed peaceably settled, she longed for Almodis' contentment as well. Her grumbling belly disrupted her musing, so she left the battlements and keep and squashed through ankle-deep mud to the kitchen hut. There she slipped off her caked shoes, stuck her head through the doorway, and made a brief study of the cramped hut. The only inhabitant, a plump, elderly, doughy-smelling woman named Agnes, sat hunched over a trestle table, intently absorbed in an embroidery square stuck up close under her nose. To Maura's light rapping, she set aside her sewing and rose from her stool, flashing a gap-toothed smile as she extended her hands and greeted, "My Lady Maura, what a surprise and pleasure! And what brings you here at this late hour? A rumbling belly, I suppose."

Maura stepped inside and sighed, "Yes, Agnes, and the keep's too quiet for sleep."

"It was cruel of Lord Robert to leave you here alone. How can I cheer you?" asked Agnes, placing a stool by hers. "Something sweet perhaps and, of course, gossip! There are a few honey cakes left from supper, and warm milk."

"That sounds wonderful."

"You sit and warm yourself by the oven, I'll fetch the treats."

An hour passed and, satiated to the point of discomfort, Maura dabbed her finger in the honeypot, dropped a blob of the luscious liquid into her milk, and grinned at the cook's animated storytelling. "You were talked about greatly the first week of your visit, and your battle with Sir William was the most exciting tale we'd heard in years! We are so proud of you, my Lady! A few of the younger servants haven't fared as well in their dealings with his Lordship. But this week, the Lady Almodis' adventures are on everyone's lips."

"What adventures?" Maura asked expectantly.

Agnes leant in close and spoke low as if in secret, "Her chambermaid tells us she's often sick and has missed her flow three months now. We believe she's with child and wonder who might the father be. Perhaps you could solve our little puzzle?"

"The Lady seems quite healthy to me," stated Maura firmly, "and has been very generous with her time and comfort. I won't hear her slandered."

"We mean no harm, my Lady," assured Agnes, "though she does treat us rather coldly."

"Have you ever spoken to her as you speak to me?"

"We wouldn't dare!"

"Why ever not? I believe she's terribly lonely and longs to do what we're doing now—snacking and gossiping."

"But her *temper*, my Lady," noted Agnes guardedly. "No one dares make the Lady angry."

"An invitation to share sweets and gossip would not make her angry. Securing her friendship would not only raise your status, but also her understanding of the servants' concerns."

"My!" exclaimed Agnes. "I never would have thought such a thing. It sounds so simple."

"That's because it is."

"Will you be staying with us after Lord Robert's return?"

Maura answered with a wry grin, "It depends on whether or not I behave myself."

"Well if you wish any one of us to accompany you to your new home, we would be honored to do so."

"I'm grateful for your offer and will consider—"

The youngest servant, Lily, her bright eyes bulging and golden hair askew, stumbled breathlessly into the kitchen, spouting, "Lady Maura! I thought I'd never find you. A man awaits you in the great hall!"

Maura sprang from the stool, tumbling it and her cup of milk in her zeal. Her urgent question, "What does he look like?" arched Agnes' brows.

"He's very nice, my Lady," noted Lily.

"No, his coloring...what color is his hair?"

"Black and a black beard as well."

"It's Alan!" All aglow, she hopped into her shoes, and paused briefly in the doorway to add, "Thank you, Agnes, for the treats and talk, but I must go."

After Maura had left, Agnes smiled knowingly at Lily and, patting her backside, surmised, "The Lady is lonely and magically receives a gentleman caller. The story gets ever so interesting. Go, little one, and see what you can see."

Maura struggled through the mud, scraped the soles of her slippers on the keep's top wooden stair, and hastened through the hall's immense doorway. She radiated joy as she called out, "Alan!"

He spun from the dwindling fire, his beaming expression mirroring hers. "Maura!"

She kissed his cheeks; he kissed her hand. Maura searched beyond his shoulder, to each side of him, then to her back. Worry dampened her cheer, she paled and implored, "Where's Rose?"

"There's no need to fret," assured Alan. "Rose is fine and has decided to stay the week with Edith. I've come to escort you to Winchester, and there she will join you. She sends her love and asked me to pass you this note." He offered the parchment and a nodded enticement, "It will tell you all you need to know." Maura smiled crookedly, and stuck the letter in her belt.

They both jumped to a loud inquiry, "Will you be wanting anything, my Lady?" Turning, they beheld Lily, hands clasped firmly before her, her body swaying, and a mischievous grin curling her lips.

Maura cast Alan a playful smirk, then announced to the servant, "Yes, Lily. Would you please prepare the chamber next to mine for the gentleman and," she glanced back at Alan, "are you hungry?"

"Famished."

"And have a meal prepared and brought to his room."

"Is that all, my Lady?"

Both Alan and Maura squirmed beneath Lily's acute scrutiny. "Yes, thank you and you may go," answered Maura. They waited, but Lily stayed put, prompting Maura to encourage with a dismissing gesture, "The gentleman is very hungry."

"Yes, my Lady, right away, my Lady," she spurted as she scampered away to their laughter.

"What was that all about?" asked Alan.

"I'm sure the cook sent her to find out all about you. Your mysterious arrival should keep them jabbering the night through. I'm so glad you're here, Alan. I've missed your snore outside my door."

"From you, my Lady, that is the sweetest compliment."

"Come," she said linking her arm in his, "we'll wait in my chamber for your meal."

When they arrived, Alan settled carefully on a plush chair; his smile widened at the depth of its pile and he marveled, "I don't believe the richness of Berkhamstead. It easily rivals that of Rouen."

"It's Will's doing," Maura scorned. "He insists on comfort."

Recalling Simon's commentary of Will's deceit, Alan asked cautiously, "Has he treated you kindly?"

Maura perched herself upon her trunk, her feet dangling, and replied with a snort of disgust. "No...but I knew of his lies before reaching Berkhamstead. We avoid each other, which suits me fine." Maura's vibrant question waved away the sour subject, "Did Rose visit her sons? Were they pleased?"

"Yes, it was quite a reunion. Her eldest, Richard, will bring her to Winchester."

"You mentioned she's staying with Edith?"

"Yes, they seem quite friendly."

"And how is Edith?" asked Maura, her smile awkward.

"We talked only a short while. She seemed happy, though a bit worried about her son."

Maura straightened, and asked with a hint of trepidation, "Has something happened to Simon?"

"I sincerely hope not. He's due to arrive here tomorrow."

The miraculous news thrust Maura from the trunk and she gasped, "Here?! Tomorrow? How?!"

Alan laughed gently at her fluster and pushed up from the chair. "My room and meal should be ready. I'll leave you alone to read your letter—in it Rose explains all. And when you've finished, knock. I'm eager to hear your comments."

Alone and dazed, she sat on her bed and yanked the parchment from her belt. Her fingers fumbled with the tie; she groaned, tugged at the obstinate knot, and finally raked it from the scroll. She spread the document close to the candle. The signature first drew her attention..."*All my love, Rose.*" Then she looked to the salutation,

"*My angel, I miss you and pray you are well. My advice may be late in coming, but I implore you to keep far from Will. He is a liar and a rogue. I am certain you have discovered this by now. I will try to be brief—on my visit to Edith's, I encountered Simon. I know this is hard to fathom, but we talked amicably. I will say simply that when he left you at Dunheved, he did so only to save you. He knew nothing of the child and, as you believed he would, returned for you within hours of his parting. I described as best I could the events of that tragic time and he shed tears for you and the child. His love for you is true and he is deeply wounded by grief and guilt. Simon and Alan will escort you to Winchester and away from Will! My encouraging your trip to Berkhamstead with Will was disgraceful and I hope you can find it in your heart to forgive me. It seems we weren't the first to be duped by Will's 'charms'. I count the days to our reunion, and I must warn you—make your peace with Simon and then you must part. My thoughts and prayers are forever with you. All my love, Rose.*"

Maura blinked tears of disbelief at the scrawled ink. She reread the letter, slowly, diligently. This was no hoax—these were Rose's words, delivered by Alan! Her eyes squeezed tight as a wash of ecstasy quivered her body, fluttered her heart, and quickened her breath. Upon standing, the lightness she felt weakened her knees. She would have the chance she prayed for—he would come, they would talk, and then...part? Was that possible? Wiping her eyes with the hand that clutched the parchment, she realized the havoc the innocuous words could wreak. She crumpled the note and tossed it into the grate, watching till it shriveled to ash.

Maura's rapid knock interrupted Alan's meal. Eager to share her mirth, he rose, opened the door, and slyly noted, "I see you've read the letter."

"Yes! Oh, Alan, I can't believe my luck. How brilliant I was to have sent Rose to Dunheved!" Her vivacious tone and hug dissolved them both to buoyant laughter.

A high pitched voice drowned their glee, "Will you be wanting for anything more, my Lord?" They quickly untangled their clutch and spun again to the highly inquisitive girl. Lily's cheeks were rouged from their unabashed show of affection, and she could scarcely contain her wiggling.

Alan's brusque answer curbed her fidgeting. "I'm *not* a Lord and have all I need, thank you!"

In her rush to flee, Lily neglected her curtsey, yet remembered her coy wish, "Sleep well, my Lord and Lady."

Their laughter erupted again. Alan sank into a chair, and chuckled, "She...she certainly performed her mission well."

Suddenly serious, Maura pressed, "When exactly will Simon arrive?"

Alan regained his poise and swiftly launched into a straightforward interrogation, "Well, there are a few details I must know before I can allow him to enter the castle. Firstly, who is in residence?"

"Only myself."

"And where are the others?"

"Lord Robert and his wife are at the Tower. Will has gone to visit Rufus."

"When did they leave?"

Maura thought a moment, then replied, "Two days past. They will be gone a fortnight."

"And did Lord Robert's soldiers accompany him?"

"Most did. He left only a few for my protection."

"Well then," Alan stated decisively, "there should be no problem. At dusk tomorrow, Simon will search for me at the village well. My presence will assure him it's safe to enter the castle."

Maura felt a bit like Lily as she struggled to contain her excitement. She clasped her jittery hands between her knees, and repeated dreamily, "Tomorrow, at dusk. How is he, Alan? Is he angry with me?"

"Why would he be angry?"

"The way we last parted. I heard he was furious when he left Gloucester."

"Never with you, my Lady."

Maura's damp eyes glimpsed Alan's food tray. "I'm sorry, Alan," she said, rising. "It's late and I've kept you from your meal."

"I've had quite enough, and I much prefer talking with you to eating. But I'm sure you'd rather be alone with your thoughts." He stood as well and nodded humbly, "Thank you, Maura, for providing me such luxury."

"It's what you rightly deserve. Alan, before I go there is one thing that troubles me. Lord Robert has restricted me to the castle. If I leave without his permission, he's bound to be furious."

"We'll concoct a crisis...something he can't possibly question, such as Rose has been stricken down with a serious illness."

"Yes, he's fond of Rose." Before leaving, she paused and lifted his hand. "Alan, how can I ever—"

"You needn't, Maura." His shy gaze fell to the floor.

Sighing, she released him and finished sincerely, "Thank you for returning Simon to me."

Alan's answer was a thin appeasing smile which, as she vanished, tightened to a grimace. His whisper told his persistent worry, "He's not here yet..."

*****

After a grueling night spent sharing E'dain's stall, Simon fought off an achy weariness as he rode the last leg of his journey to Berkhamstead. Wet snow plopped upon his nose and gnawing doubts vexed his mind. What if Will had succeeded in cajoling Maura and she—No, she was an excellent judge of character and not easily duped. But what if he tried violence to force her to submit? That wasn't likely, for she knew well how to defend herself. And then the most crippling concern surfaced—What if she shunned his explanation and sent him away *again*? The unease stirred by his anxieties spurred him faster along the road and sparked his impetuous spirit. He would not wait till dusk, he'd arrive early and discover for himself who was in residence.

E'dain slipped in the shallow slush and Simon wisely slowed her pace. His eyes tearing from the cold, he remembered the warmth he and Maura had shared and allowed himself a brief fantasy of a passionate reunion. Then suddenly with no prompting, E'dain stopped and pricked up her ears. Simon threw back his hood and, still as death, listened. Only his eyes moved, hunting the woods for any odd movement.

Naked tree limbs creaked to a gentle breeze, and a fleeting blur of silver decided Simon's course. He fiercely yanked E'dain round and tore away down the road. A dozen mail clad soldiers sprang from the forest and chased after him. A quick glance backward revealed his lead rapidly diminishing. His mind screamed—*scatter them*! He jerked E'dain, veered off the road, and sprang into the barely navigable wood. Three of the soldiers' horses slid attempting the turn, tossing their riders. The others easily kept up their pursuit.

Simon dropped the reins and hugged E'dain's neck, giving her lead to find the swiftest route out of the oppressive maze. Gnarled limbs swiped out, ripping his cloak, stabbing at his eyes, scratching his skin. He tore off the brooch securing his cloak. The cloth flapped into the face of an approaching horse and sent it crashing into a wall of oaks. More hooves thundered at his back, coming closer, faster.

The ground suddenly fell away. Simon arched and clutched the pommel as E'dain struggled down a steep embankment. Men and horses tumbled and rolled past him. E'dain leapt two shrieking soldiers and landed gracefully on flat ground. Simon risked another backward glance. Four had survived the descent and were almost upon him! It was useless trying to outrun them. He threw his leg over E'dain's neck and dove from the saddle. The ground greeted him with a harsh jolt. He rolled, frantically grasping at grass to slow his momentum. Rumbling hooves swiftly approached. Simon coiled his body, shielded his head, and wailed as horses trampled him, miraculously only grazing his back and legs. Before the riders could regroup, he scrambled to his feet and bolted back to the embankment. Crumbling soil frustrated his ascent, dirt and sweat blurred his vision, but a brief glimpse downward revealed three soldiers clambering behind. Grunting and heaving, he thrust his hands and boots into the dirt and forced his body upward. Finally, his clawing fingers gripped the ledge. He hoisted himself up the last few feet and, with downcast eyes and tremendous speed, bounded directly into the path of a galloping steed. The force of their impact sent Simon soaring through the air. His burning chest slammed against the ground. Horrible gasps convulsed him. He writhed in agony, and fought to regain his footing while frantically groping for his dagger's hilt. He flipped to his back and yowled as a mud-caked boot kicked his hand and dislodged the dagger.

The boot's owner straddled Simon, each foot planted securely on a wrist. Simon thrashed wildly, striving to unbalance the soldier, but the man's long sword descended and rested its cold blade on the side of Simon's neck. Each squirm and gasped breath sank the cutting edge deeper. A sticky wetness marred the weapon's shine and stilled Simon's resistance.

Encroaching soldiers, their weapons drawn, hovered over his prone body, sniggering and mocking his impotent state. Their leader sheathed his sword, released Simon's wrists, and grunted, "Get up!"

Simon rose stiffly, his body curled protectively and wary eyes darting from soldier to soldier, summing up their every twitch. Their panting and bent postures betrayed exhaustion. He wouldn't be beaten! He had to escape!

"Bind his hands," ordered the leader. "And take care, I hear he's slippery."

Three soldiers surrounded Simon; one yanked his arms to his back and proceeded to wind the biting cord. Simon's foot crept back between the soldier's feet. He jerked his knee and kicked the binder soundly in the groin. The squealing man doubled over. Simon spun and smashed his knee to his victim's nose. He shook off the cord and whirled, stabbing one soldier with his elbow, and striking another senseless. Arms and weapons shot out at him. He shrieked and flailed dementedly, twisted and dodged their piercing blows. An arm locked itself round his neck and tightened, choking his air and paralyzing his limbs. His eyes bulged at a rapidly advancing fist. There was an instant of ghastly pain, and then only blackness.

*****

CHAPTER TWELVE - A MUSTER OF ALLIES

A black pall descended on the miserable day, turning it to an equally dismal evening. In her chamber, Maura impatiently drummed her fingertips on the chess board, her eyes locked on the marble statuettes, her mind elsewhere. She spoke more out of politeness than curiosity, "Alan, tell me of Simon's work for the King."

Alan shifted his rook, stretched and sighed, "He's a mediator mainly in disputes between tenants-in-chief and their villeins. He keeps a keen eye on the more rebellious barons and sheriffs, and is an excellent Welsh translator. It's your move."

Absent-mindedly, she moved the first piece she touched. It was quickly taken, and disappeared in Alan's tight clutch. She huffed, then noted, "I've lived with the Royal Family for four years and have never heard Simon's name mentioned."

"His work was kept secret till this past November. The King didn't wish to appear conciliatory to his vassals till he felt sure Simon's efforts would boost his image as peacemaker."

"Do you know Simon well?"

"We met two years back when King William sent me to Wales to fetch him. I've accompanied him on several missions and must say he's rather good at his work."

"He was never very good at settling disputes between me and Marc." Restlessness forced her from her chair. From the window, she strained to see the main gates, but the dripping snow made the task nearly impossible.

"Maura, looking out that window is not going speed his arrival. Come back to the game, it will help pass the time."

"I can't concentrate, Alan. I'm no good at waiting. It is far past dusk, where *is* he?"

"I stood at the well from dusk to full dark. If he arrived today, he saw me. If not he'll find a safe place to spend the night and I'll return to the well tomorrow. He's most likely stabling his horse." Alan attempted to distract by lauding, "I must say you look quite lovely."

With a fleeting grin and a glance at her gown, Maura modestly excused, "It's one of Adela's castoffs." Her skittish fingers twisted an unfettered lock of hair. "Simon never could abide braids."

Alan smiled inwardly at her winsome, almost childlike visage, peering raptly out the window, and was ill-prepared for a pang of envy. He shrugged off his discomfort, attended to the board, and wondered, "Have you word from Marc?"

"No," answered Maura, firmly rooted at her watch. "I can only pray—"

A pregnant pause followed, its length prompting Alan to forsake the game and ask warily, "What is it?"

"Didn't you say you found few soldiers about?"

"Yes. I searched the castle this morning and—"

"A battalion just entered the bailey. The torches are burning." Maura's shoulders drooped as her nails shrilly scratched down the pane. "Lord Robert's returned."

"What?!" exclaimed Alan, jumping up and joining her vigil. Torches infested the bailey, glaring the troop's armor. His fists struck the glass, and his curse confirmed Maura's dread, "Damn! Robert's tricked us. I must warn Simon!"

Maura reached out for solace, yet grasped only air. The door slammed shut, leaving her at the mercy of bodeful thoughts. The blush drained from her cheeks, her body grew limp, and her arms hugged her cramping belly. It was too late for warnings or for rescues. The door burst open. Maura whirled and gasped as Almodis spilled into the room, panting, "Maura! God's breath, Maura!"

Maura rushed to her side and could scarcely mouth the words, "Is...is he...dead?"

"No." Almodis supported Maura's wavering body. "Robert's holding him in the buttery. He's been beaten and is barely conscious."

Maura lunged for the door handle. Almodis threw her body against the wood and yanked Maura's fingers from the latch. "No! You run to him now and you're both dead. Don't say a thing and listen, we have little time. A guard will soon arrive to escort you to Simon's interrogation. Somehow, Will has convinced Robert that you and Simon plotted his murder when you were at Gloucester, and Simon was headed to Berkhamstead to do the deed. It is *your* trial as well, Maura. Betray no emotion but hate, extreme hate for Simon. Deny any knowledge of his visit and keep your head no matter how they pressure him to confess. If you expose your true feelings, you affirm Will's conviction, and you'll both be locked away forever, or worse."

"But I can't!" wailed Maura. "He doesn't know I've forgiven him, and he'll believe everything I say. Almodis, I won't torture him again!"

"You won't be torturing him, you'll be saving him! I will be close by. If you falter, look to me. I know you have the strength to save him, I'm sure you have the love." To the guard's ominous pounding, Almodis pressed close to the wall behind the door, and strictly whispered, "I'll arrive before you through another entrance. Act as if you haven't seen or spoken to me. Go, and remember all I've said."

The guard's rough grip propelled Maura's diffident body along the passageways, down dank uneven stairs leading to the bowels of the castle. A harsh nudge thrust her through the buttery door ahead of the sentry. The permeating stench of spoiled wine, and Robert's thunderous call, "Maura, come into the light!" wrenched her belly. Her eyes and ears were drawn to an open, brilliantly lit corner of the room which lay beyond dozens of tightly packed wine casks. She squeezed her way between the barriers; splinters stung her palms, cobwebs veiled her face and clothes. Repulsed, she scoured her face rigorously with her slippery silk sleeve, then lowered her arm to Robert's order, "Maura, you'll stand by me."

Maura stared straight ahead as she approached her Liege, not daring to let her anguished gaze wander. If she should see Simon hurt and abused, she would surely crumble. Despite her heroic effort, the corner of her eye glimpsed his pitiful visage, slouched upon a bench, his bowed head almost touching his lap, and his hands trussed securely at his back. She clutched her skirt to still her shaking, and bit her lip to keep from crying out. Almodis stepped forward and extended a supporting hand, which Maura firmly accepted.

Sharp, biting shadows cut through the dark, intensifying the odious atmosphere. Will, eyes ablaze, lunged from behind Robert, yanked Maura from Almodis, and twisted her arm to her back. He spun her to face Simon and muttered wickedly, "This should keep you still!"

"It is not needed!" protested Robert.

"Remember my wounds, Father! I'll take no chances."

"She is not our prisoner!"

"Not yet..." Will jerked her arm higher. She threw back her head, moaning, as he goaded, "Look at him, Maura. He doesn't appear so valiant now, does he? I'd say he's rather pathetic, don't you agree?"

"Will, release her now!" Robert bellowed. "I conduct this interrogation, and if you cannot contain yourself, you will leave."

Will freed Maura with a harsh shove. She stumbled forward and dropped to her knees inches from Simon. Her fingers dug into the moldy ground, her head spun, bile rushed to her throat. She had lured him to Berkhamstead, and because of her he could die! Almodis' words pounded her ragged mind, 'I know you have the strength...'. She had no strength; she was weak, powerless to help!

"Turn to me, Maura," ordered Robert.

She stood, pulled herself erect and, with a vague expression, muttered, "My Lord."

"Were you aware of Simon's visit to Berkhamstead?"

"No, my Lord."

"Will has accused you and Simon of plotting my murder. This supposed scheme was planned at Gloucester. You have admitted meeting Simon there. Do you still lust for him?"

"No, my Lord."

Will paced impatiently before Simon. "Surely," he prodded, "you can say something more substantial than 'No, my Lord', Maura. Simon journeyed far to hear your words of love. How cruel of you to ignore him. Come nearer and tell him your *true* feelings." He shouted, "Wake him!" to the nearest guard. The guard cupped a handful of icy water from a pail at Simon's feet and splashed it in Simon's face with no effect. Will pushed the guard aside, grabbed Simon's hair, and wrenched back his neck. He struck him, screeching, "Wake up!" A dull groan gurgled from Simon's throat. "Damn you, open your eyes!" roared Will, foolishly slapping again. Simon's eyes flew open. He strained at his binding and, with an agonized howl, lurched forward. His head rammed Will's belly, reeling him backwards into Maura, and tumbling them both to the ground. Robert leapt from the chaos and gestured for the guards' intervention. They pounced upon Simon; boots pressed to his neck, arms, and legs stilled his revenge; cold dirt and throbbing pain kept him aware. He struggled to distinguish voices that drifted clearly, then faded with his faltering consciousness.

"Keep him still or I'll flog the lot of you!" Robert warned as he helped Maura to her feet. He directed his next spitting threat at Will. "One more outburst and I'll banish you from this castle!"

"Banish me?!" Will countered shrilly. "They plotted *your* murder! He defies *you*, delights in humiliating *you*, and you order *me* to contain myself? He's a rabid animal who must be caged!"

Their bickering allowed Maura one furtive glance at Simon. His suffering chipped away at her courage; she fought the weakness and declared loudly, "We never plotted against you, Lord Robert. Simon came here only to torment me."

That voice, her voice! Maura is here! Simon lifted his head slightly to hear more.

Will dragged her to Simon's side. "I'm afraid you spoke too faintly, he couldn't have heard you. Repeat what you said, Maura." He forced her to her knees and gritted, "Again, clearer, louder, tell him how he torments you! Tell him!"

She squeezed shut her eyes and quavered, "I...I despise you, Simon, ha...hate you... You will never come near me again."

A violent shudder passed through Simon's body. He'd heard wrong, she couldn't hate him! Her eyes—if only he could see her eyes he'd know the truth! He arched and thrashed; the ropes mangled his wrists, the boots pressed harder.

Will burst a maniacal cackle, "Louder, Maura! See how you torture him? What great fun! Tell him more!"

Maura's control snapped. She sprang up, spun, and thrust her screaming face into Will's. "Get away from me!"

Will seemed to consider doing as told, when Robert intruded, "Enough antics! I demand the truth, Maura."

Maura's rapid speech took on a tenacious edge that shocked even her. "Lord Robert, why would I have asked to be sent to Winchester or Yorkshire had I planned to meet with Simon?"

Robert thought a moment. "...To confuse me."

"Why would I plot with someone I loathe? Have I ever given you cause to believe I still care for Simon? His persistence is my worry, not yours, and I will deal with it in my own way."

"You're quite bold, Maura," said Robert, askance. "Suppose he came here not to see you but to kill me?"

"Kill you—the King's brother? He may be despicable, but he's not stupid."

"She sympathizes with him, Father!" Will parried fiercely. "See through her lies!"

"Quiet!" yelled Robert. "I'm tired of your ravings! Maura, Simon will be punished for his treason against my brother and myself. What sentence do you recommend? Surely you've dreamt of retribution for all the strife he caused you."

"Leave me alone with him, Father. It won't take long to coax a confession. I only need to aim for the perfect spot." Will's powerful kick cracked Simon's jaw and its force flung him to his back. Wild rancor consumed Will as his boot rabidly attacked Simon's shoulders, belly, groin, and legs. Simon convulsed to each kick, then finally lay limp. Will beamed with savage glee. "I agree with Father," he tittered to Maura. "You will be his judge. Shall he be whipped? Blistered with hot iron? Or perhaps you favor castration? It does seem fitting. I can perform the task here before you, or..." He extracted his dagger, presented it to her, and offered, "Would you prefer to take on the dirty deed yourself?"

A scream clawed at her throat, threatening to expose her deception. One hand accepted the dagger as the other clamped shut her mouth. She turned the weapon over and over in her palm, caressing its lethal power. It would be so easy. Will stood before her—deranged, unarmed, and vulnerable. Her fingers circled the hilt and tensed, and her breaths came in great gulps as she slowly raised her arm—

A curious thud stalled the mayhem. All whirled round to see Almodis lying in an unconscious heap on the ground. Robert sprinted to her side, roaring, "Fetch the physician, quickly!"

Will hesitated a moment, then with a perturbed sneer, snatched his weapon back, and joined his father's concern.

With all attention focused on Almodis, Maura dropped to Simon's side, and whispered close, "Simon, please hear me! I don't hate you. I could never hate you. I had to lie, to save..." She touched his bruised lips, stroked his bloodied cheek, and knew from his stillness that he couldn't hear. If he died before she saw him again, he'd die believing she hated him, and she would languish forever with that guilt. Bending low, she rested her cheek on his brow, and her tears mingled with his blood.

Huge, sturdy hands clasped Maura's shoulders, and lifted her weightlessly from Simon. She jerked away, twisted and gazed into the compassionate eyes of a stranger. His low, gritty voice cautioned, "Leave here now, my Lady, quickly before they return. I will watch over him." She didn't question his kindness, but frantically wove her way between the casks, not daring a glance back.

In the quiet of her chamber, Maura dropped to her knees, moaned a despairing moan, and beat at the rushes, gritting, "I can't let them torture him! I will stop them. I must stop them! He is innocent. Dear God," she pleaded to the ceiling, "you can't allow this to happen. He is innocent!" Her anger collapsed to hysterical sobbing.

A rustling at her side gagged her tears. Gasping, she recoiled against the door and squinted to see Alan! She crushed herself to his chest; they clung together a moment, then he pulled slightly away to ask, "Did the guard find you?"

"There was someone," she sniffed in a lost tone. "He promised to watch over Simon."

"Yes...We worked together long ago. He is Lord Robert's man now. I explained as well as I could the situation, and he's agreed to protect Simon till morning. He's heard Simon is to be taken to Westminster. If so, I will follow."

"Not alone. I'll come with you."

"No, Maura! It's far too dangerous."

"You can't stop me, Alan! If you don't agree, I'll go alone."

Her willful look convinced him it was useless to argue. All Alan could do was warn, "Then we must plan with care. If we act carelessly, we will *all* end up dead."

His bluntness struck deep. She shuddered and added with vehemence, "There's no time to waste. We have but a night to make our plans."

*****

In their bedchamber, Robert sat by Almodis' reposed body. In one hand he held a cup of wine, with the other he lightly tapped her cheek. "Almodis?" he called softly. "Almodis, please wake up."

Almodis woke slowly to his entreaty, struggled to sit, and asked groggily, "Why am I here? What's happened?"

"You had a fright and fainted. I never should have allowed you in the buttery."

Her sluggish voice turned frantic. "Where's Will?"

"Outside the door. He seems quite concerned about—"

"Never leave him alone with Simon!" Almodis seized Robert's tunic and yanked him close, direly pleading, "I beg of you, Robert, stop this madness!"

Quickly aloof, Robert pried her fingers from his tunic and his staid tone returned. "Simon will be punished for his crimes against—"

"Yes, yes, I know—your brother and yourself! But if Will has his way, Simon will be dead before your punishment is dealt."

His eyes large, Robert warned, "Take care what you say, my Lady."

"To save a life is not treason! At Gloucester, I heard Will blatantly threaten Simon. He warned of accidents..."

Robert wagged his head and scoffed, "You speak nonsense. Drink this wine, it will ease your delirium." She batted the cup from his hand, slumped back upon the pillows, and whipped her head from side to side, heightening Robert's alarm. "What ails you, Almodis?"

Her eyes fluttered open; she squeezed tight his hand, and frailly announced, "I carry your child."

Stunned, Robert sat mute awhile, then answered with a dubious voice, "No, no, surely something else troubles you."

"Robert, I know I am pregnant!"

He resolutely placed her hand at her side and spoke with chilling finality, "I have raised seven children, Almodis. I'm far too old and tired to take on another."

"Don't frighten me!" she raved as Maura's tragedy resounded in her mind. "I will bear and raise this child, Robert, with or without your assistance!"

As always, her brimming tears rattled Robert's command. His fingertips brushed a lock of hair from her furrowed brow and he soothed, "We will raise this child together, Almodis. And till he's born, you must take care."

She gratefully kissed his fingers and muttered anxiously, "And Simon? What's to become of Simon?"

"You needn't involve yourself in such vile matters. Why does his welfare concern you so?"

"I don't believe Will's claims of Simon's viciousness. He's been nothing but kind to me, and he once saved my life."

"He's more crafty than vicious," said Robert, disregarding her touting. "Simon flaunts the power King William entrusted to him. Though I'm loathe to say it, he *is* my son, and one day soon he will swear homage and call me 'Lord'. If need be, I'll beat him into submission."

Her husband's vengeful words sickened her. She swatted away his hand, pouted, and noted crossly, "I see nothing I say will change your mulish mind. Punish him if you must, yet *please*, Robert, keep him from Will! Grant this petty wish for me...for our child."

"God's blood, woman, you do exaggerate! If Will was involved in any chicanery, I would know of it. Tomorrow dawn, my troops will escort Simon to Westminster, where he will be imprisoned—indefinitely. You and I will sojourn at the White Tower. I can't abide staying with Rufus. Simon will have a short while to mull over his options, then we shall meet. Now, it draws late and you need rest."

"What of Maura?"

"I'm not fully convinced of her innocence."

"She is guilty of no offence, my Lord, and was ignorant of Simon's untimely visit. Let her return to Winchester till her wedding, and perhaps you'll allow me to join her there?"

"I will consider it. Now there's much to do in preparation for our journey." Robert's cold lips brushed Almodis' hand; he rose, smiled grimly, and departed. She rubbed his moist mark from her skin, and listened intently as his footsteps dwindled and then, with no sign of infirmity, she snatched up a blanket from the base of the bed. Her head and body shrouded, she crept to the door, peeked surreptitiously down both lengths of the hall, and snuck to Maura's chamber.

*****

Hunched up against the wall, Alan raked rigid fingers through his shock of black hair, and futilely insisted, "Maura, Robert's no fool. If you leave tomorrow, you'll surely arouse his suspicions."

"And if I wait, Simon could die before I reach him."

"He could be dead now!"

"No, Alan!" Maura argued passionately. "The guard, you said the guard would protect—"

"Will's a shrewd devil. He might've already arranged an accident—"

"He's not that shrewd!" cut in Maura hotly. "In the buttery, he offered me his dagger. If Almodis hadn't fainted, I would have killed him in an instant!"

A light tapping at the door preceded an urgent whisper, "Maura, are you there? It's Almodis. Please let me in. I have news."

They stood in unison and Alan asked, "Can she be trusted?"

"Completely," affirmed Maura.

Almodis slipped into the chamber. An engulfing hug told Maura's gratitude. "Almodis, you saved his life!"

"And by the look of things, Will's as well," Almodis added regretfully, breaking their embrace. "I must admit, I did time my collapse well, it was clear your strength was wearing thin and—" Almodis paused and cast a bemused glance Alan's way. "Who's this?"

"This is Alan—"

"No, wait..." She raised a hand, intensified her scrutiny, then her face relaxed in recognition. "At Gloucester...You were at Gloucester. Maura's guard?"

"Yes, my Lady."

"But I've seen you elsewhere."

"I serve the King, my Lady."

"My, my, the King does care for you, Maura. To allow you the use of one of his sentries is—"

"Almodis," Maura pressed urgently, "you said you had news. Please, is there word of Simon's fate?"

"Oh, yes. Robert will imprison Simon at Westminster, where Rufus is in residence. Robert's plans for Simon after imprisonment are as yet unclear, but I feel he's not capable of executing his own son. My worries lie with Will's intentions."

"I must see Simon, Almodis!" yelled Maura.

"That may be impossible."

"There has to be a way! Alan's brother resides in London. We plan to journey to his home tomorrow. Will and Robert cannot keep a constant watch on Simon. Once Alan discovers where his cell is, I'll bribe the guards to let me enter and—"

"Bribe them how?" asked Almodis.

"Pardon?"

"What will you offer them?"

"I have a little money, Adela's jewelry, and the sapphire necklace."

Almodis nodded in approval. "Let's pray they don't ask for more."

"Perhaps I can coerce Rufus into releasing Simon."

"Oh Maura, please come to your senses," sighed Almodis, rolling her eyes in exasperation.

"I have to try!" countered Maura.

Almodis' gaze slipped uneasily to Alan. "I'm impressed with your grand plans, and I'll work to rid you of your major obstacles, namely Will and Robert. Alan, come to the White Tower tomorrow at dusk. Don't enter the gates, a sentry will provide you a message and then you must act accordingly. Leave a map to your brother's home with the sentry. Maura, I will attempt a visit to Simon before I return to my chamber."

"One of Lord Robert's guards has vowed to protect him through the night, my Lady," spouted Alan. "He's called Godfrey."

"How gallant of him." She tugged a sparkling jewel from her finger. "I will reward his loyalty. By morning, Maura, I will have convinced Robert of your innocence. He seems content to send you to Winchester. If perchance you should speak to him, make clear your desire to return there, and carry all your riches with you to London. As you well know, Rufus is a greedy pig. Somehow," she said tenderly, touching Maura's shoulder, "we will secure Simon's freedom."

Maura's fingers closed around Almodis' and she blurted, "If he's awake, please tell him—"

"I know and I will. I must go. I wish you both luck."

"Bless you, Almodis, bless you," Maura gushed, pressing her cheek to her hand.

"My Lady," muttered Alan, with a reverent bow.

*****

By dawn the sky had vaguely brightened, yet thick snow continued its unrelenting fall. Maura sat rigid at the window, her attention riveted on the bailey. Alan kept his vigil before her door; his main concern—her running to Simon. They could plan no further till they arrived in London and received Almodis' message.

Maura's hands frantically crawled the window, lifting her from her seat as she spied a group of soldiers hauling Simon's limp body across the bailey. They tossed him carelessly into a straw-cushioned cart and left him alone, exposed and so still. Her panic erupted in a desperate squall, "Alan! Alan, come!"

He was beside her in an instant. "What's happened?!"

"It's Simon...there...he doesn't move." She hugged Alan's arm and cried, "He's dead! Will killed him in the night!"

"No..." Alan pointed and said with cautious optimism, "You see, Godfrey's with him. Why would he guard a dead man? Now, it's important we remain calm, for Simon's sake as well as our own—"

"And who might you be?!" Robert's bellow emanated from the hallway.

They whirled to his imposing presence, hands set firmly on his hips, his eyes narrow with misgiving. Maura touched Alan's hand to halt his speech, inhaled deeply, and explained with care, "Alan is my guard, my Lord, assigned to my service by King William. He's only just arrived with dreadful news of Rose's illness. I beg your Lordship's permission to journey immediately to Winchester to nurse her."

Robert's lips twisted in a scowl while he fumbled for a decision. Finally he blurted, "Yes, go. I can't think of what else to do with you. Yet take heed, Maura, it is crucial that you arrive at Pevensey a fortnight before Easter. Is that perfectly clear?"

"Yes, my Lord. I'm grateful, my Lord."

"When do you wish to leave?"

"As soon as we're able, my Lord."

"I'll send servants to remove your trunks." He turned to leave, then paused to ask, "Aren't you the least bit curious of my plans for Simon?"

"Why should I be?" she answered forcefully. "I wish to forget him, but no one will allow me to!"

Robert shifted his dark attention to Alan. "Watch her well."

"I shall, my Lord. And I pray you have a safe journey." Maura and Alan genuflected and kept their submissive postures till they were sure of his absence.

The tenseness left them and Maura managed a tiny grin. "Simon *is* alive."

"Of course he is. He won't allow Will to win. You of all people must know of his stubbornness." Maura answered with a meek nod, sat, and attended to Alan's directions. "We will leave immediately after Lord Robert's party. We'll travel south, then east. If we make decent time, we should arrive in London by dusk. Take only enough clothing to last you a week and, as Almodis so rightly said, bring all your riches with you."

*****

Curses punctuated Almodis' heated discourse as she slogged across the slushy bailey on her way to the fore of Robert's entourage. "Damn that Will and Robert!" she muttered under her breath, "I promised Maura I would visit Simon, then they lock the buttery door. If he's dead, I swear I will tear Will—" She stopped before a misplaced cart, and beamed at the sight of Simon's sprawled body. Snow blanketed his thin tunic and braies; brown and purple bruises stained his gaunt, ashen face; and his wrists bled freely from their hemp binding. A mournful sigh escaped her as she reached out to touch his leg.

Her horse's snort and the groom's high-pitched voice interrupted her wretchedness. "My Lady, your horse."

She turned, confused, then her sad eyes brightened as they fell upon the horse's blanket. "Remove the blanket," she ordered.

He passed her the woolen cloth. She hiked her skirts and clambered up into the cart, brushed the snow from Simon's clothes, and arranged the coverlet over him.

"A kind act, my Lady." She searched for the bearer of the compliment and noticed a tall, yet inconspicuous sentry, partially obscured by the cart's bars.

"Might you be Godfrey?" she asked.

"I am, my Lady."

"I had intended to speak with you last evening, but was rudely locked out of the buttery. I see you've performed your mission well." She slipped the ring from her finger and presented it with hushed instructions, "I sense I can rely on your loyalty and discretion. Take this as a token of mine. Continue to watch Simon. His greatest adversary is Lord William, as I'm sure you discovered last night. Together we shall see to his safety and quick release—"

"What are you up to, Almodis?" boomed Will as he guided his mount alongside the cart.

"I'm seeing to the comfort of our prisoner," she replied, her tone scornful.

"He'll have no comforts."

"You don't rule me! He will have a blanket." Will swiped at the cloth, but released it to her snarl, "Don't you dare!"

Will promptly stopped their squabble, and glaringly grumbled, "Father's shared with me some rather distressing news concerning...you. We must talk."

Seeing his invitation as an excellent way to divert him from Simon's cell, she readily answered, "Yes, we must. Come to the Tower, late evening. Robert will attend a meeting of the Curia Regis at Windsor and won't arrive till late morn. We'll have ample opportunity to talk and—"

Robert's sudden appearance stifled their plans. "Almodis, get out of that cart this instant! You'll make yourself filthy."

"Not till you agree that Simon keeps the blanket!"

"I don't care what he keeps! Stop your foolishness and mount your horse. We will leave now!"

Maura watched till the last squire of Robert's party sauntered through the gates. Alan returned from a trip to the stables, his voice thick with prudence, "Simon's horse has been caught and stabled. I had her saddled for you. With luck, Simon will ride her from London a free man. Is your packing done?"

"Yes. Alan, Almodis fought with Will over blanketing Simon and won."

"She seems quite strong willed. I'm relieved her sympathy lies with Simon."

"My trunks are on their way to Winchester."

"Good, then all is ready. On our trip to the stables, you need stop by the kitchen to bid farewell to the servants. Be direct about your plans to travel to Winchester to nurse Rose. If *they* believe your lie, all will."

*****

Seagulls soared over the battlements of Westminster Palace, diving and soaring amidst the banners whipping in the brisk wind. Ship masts sailing on the river Thames peeked over the curtain wall, and scaffolding dotted with stonecutters, clung tenuously to the sheer walls of the keep. Scores of tradesmen scuttled about the bailey, all busily involved in the renovations of Rufus' favored residence.

Almodis guided her horse behind Simon's cart as it creaked and rattled over dung, rejected stone and potholes, finally coming to a halt beneath the keep's staircase. She watched as Godfrey awkwardly hoisted Simon over his shoulder, paused a moment for balance, then trailed two of Rufus' guards under an arched entryway. Slipping from her saddle, she snatched up the blanket and forced her stiff legs to carry her after the sentries as they wove their way across the cramped buttery. Another arched doorway led them down a tightly wound staircase. They descended so deep that Almodis was convinced she'd soon confront the Devil himself. Their dizzying journey ended in a cave, pillared by spindly wooden beams and lit with torches jutting haphazardly from seeping clay walls. Two wobbly chairs, and a broad trestle table topped with ale jugs, crumbs of dried meat and bread, served as the only furniture. Almodis shielded her nose and mouth from the room's putrid odor, and reached out to touch the iridescent mold adorning the walls and low ceiling.

Two squinty guards, one squat, the other tall, abandoned their dice game and stood clumsily as Almodis threw back her hood and proudly straightened. Godfrey's belabored voice introduced, "This is the Lady Almodis, wife of Lord Robert, Count of Mortain, Duke of Cornwall and brother to our dear King. I suggest you show proper respect." Sober grins cracked their pasty faces as the sentries bowed. To Almodis they resembled moles, with twitchy noses, black bristly hair and beards, and beady eyes. The only difference between them was their height and the girth of their waists.

"I'll know your names," she said flatly.

"Thomas, my Lady," grunted the short, obese man.

"Roland," muttered the tall one, rather disrespectfully, as he snatched a key from its hook on the wall to unlock and open a tiny wooden door. He briefly glanced Godfrey's way and instructed, "Throw the bastard in here."

Almodis bristled to his crudeness, and watched helplessly as Godfrey staggered under Simon's flaccid weight across the room. He received no assistance as he knelt and crawled through the skinny opening, dragging Simon with him. Almodis boldly followed but was stopped by an insistent Roland, "No, my Lady, you wouldn't care to go in there."

"Take your filthy hands off me!" she snapped, shoving him away.

Godfrey's head poked from the hole and implored, "Please, my Lady. He speaks the truth. Simon is not yet awake. There is no reason for you to enter."

She grudgingly handed Godfrey the blanket, and stepped aside as Roland passed Godfrey a candle and directed, "Unbind his hands, bolt one wrist to the chain." Even with the faint taper, Godfrey strained to see through the blackness. Directly inside, the cell's ceiling rose high enough for one to kneel comfortably and dispense food or news. The roof then sloped steeply, allowing room for only one prisoner, lying flat or sitting doubled over. Godfrey groped about the sticky ground, found the wrist bolt, untrussed and bound Simon, then sheltered him with the worn, soaked blanket. It would offer little comfort from the dank cell, thought Godfrey, though, with luck and the Lady Almodis' staunch persistence, Simon would soon be freed.

Almodis confidently addressed the guards, "My husband's sentry Godfrey will guard this prisoner alone. No one visits without *his* permission." She untied a small pouch from her belt and tossed it on the table. "A young red-headed woman may arrive this night to see the prisoner. You will allow her entrance to the cell. Is that clear?"

The guards looked hungrily to the pouch, then to each other and replied jointly, "Yes, my Lady."

Godfrey emerged and cast Almodis a quick affirming nod. She lowered her eyes in response, tugged her cloak protectively about her, and ducked away through the entrance. Roland tested her pouch's weight, and muttered lowly to his portly partner, "Our job will be a simple one." He dropped a plumper pouch beside Almodis' and grinned greedily, "Orders from Lord William—keep the prisoner's food just beyond his reach. He won't last long."

Godfrey ignored their gross murmurings and settled uncomfortably before the dwarfed door, anticipating the most unusual and challenging task he'd ever encountered.

*****

It was near dusk and uncommonly dry when Alan and Maura arrived in London, but an ascending moon, candlelight reflecting from shop windows, and roadside torches bathed the town in a mock, tarnished daylight. Maura guided E'dain down crowded alleys, her attention constantly diverted by connected and crooked buildings perched precariously over swampy streets. Bizarre smells, both tantalizing and revolting, assailed her senses. Peddlers sang the wonders of their wares. Assorted meats and nuts sizzling over gutter side grills, barely cloaked the stench of sewage clotting the ditches. The smoky darkness swallowed up Alan; Maura anxiously kicked E'dain and hurried ahead. Raggedy dressed children sang and pranced round fires. The sight of well-dressed strangers ended their songs. They rushed Maura and pressed close to E'dain, thrusting out their hands for alms. Their sunken cheeks and eyes cried out to her, lurching her belly and aching her heart, yet if she surrendered to their protestations, she'd have nothing left for bargaining. Feeling captive, she cried out to Alan and the squealing children scattered. Drying laundry flapped in her face as she maneuvered down a particularly slim alleyway. She emerged from the damp maze to find Alan, dismounted and waiting beside a huge wooden wall. He stilled E'dain while Maura dismounted and removed Simon's and her own saddlebag, then he led the horses through a small hidden entryway in the wall. Maura followed wordlessly, clutching tight the satchels, exhausted and sore. Inside she discovered stables and an immense forge, its coals flaming. Totally bewildered, she asked, "Alan, what is this place?"

"My brother, Nicholas' home," he answered, settling the horses in stalls. "The hall is up these stairs. I'll introduce you, then head for the Tower."

They climbed a flight of creaking stairs to a wooden landing. Alan knocked twice and waited. The door was presently opened by a gentleman with a startling resemblance to Alan. He stretched wide his arms and beamed, "Alan! What a marvelous surprise!" He called jubilantly over his shoulder, "Judith, come quickly, it's Alan!" Alan guided Maura from behind his back and, hand in hand, they entered the cozy, simply embellished chamber. Two children, a boy and a girl, immersed in their supper, sat at a trestle table situated at the far end of the room. A fire set upon a tiled hearth centered the hall and tapestries served as dividing walls. Maura's belly grumbled in response to the luscious and peculiar odors wafting from a dangling cauldron. Awkward introductions followed. "Nicolas, Judith," began Alan cautiously, "this is Lady Maura, ward to Lord Robert, brother to the King. Please, may she stay with you while I ride to the Tower?"

"Is the King in residence?" asked Judith.

"No, he's in Normandy. I've stayed behind to protect this Lady. I know this may seem confusing, but please believe I will explain all when I return. She hasn't eaten since morn. Perhaps she can join your supper."

"I don't want to be a bother, Alan," said Maura meekly. "I'll wait by the fire."

Judith, a short, sturdy woman with straw-colored hair, forsook her uneasy expression and smiled warmly. "You'll be no bother, Maura. We welcome you. Come, I'll see to your comfort."

Maura listened to Alan and Nicolas banter in a queer, unintelligible tongue. Tensely, she sat at the table, her eyes lighting first on the two handsome children, still seemingly unaware of her presence, then on the lush bounty spread before her—dishes filled with fish, thin pastries, and stews she didn't recognize.

Alan left and the adults joined her at table, their conversation consisting mainly of stilted pleasantries and tight grins. While Maura tasted the fare, the scents and flavors swept her back to her youth. Friends in Dunheved frequently asked her, Simon, and Marc to sup with them, and they had offered her similar food. Finally, her puzzlement lifted—Alan's family was Jewish! She politely stopped her gawking, and finished her meal. Her full belly, the heat of the chamber, and Nicolas and Judith's droning talk encouraged slumber. She dozed in her chair, and Judith's soft suggestion startled her, "Maura, there is a mat beside the fire. You'll rest awhile."

Maura thankfully reclined on pelts by the fire and opened Simon's satchel, carefully extracting a woolen shirt. Her cheeks welcomed its soft, warm, musty scent. Impassioned memories struck her with a force that brought on hearty tears. Judith considered comforting her, then thought better of it, and left Maura to her private dirge.

When next Maura's eyes opened, Alan was at her side, encouraging with a gentle shake, "Maura, we must leave for Westminster. There you must make your appeal to Rufus. Take your jewels and money, but leave Simon's belongings here. With luck he'll soon be needing them. Come, there's little time."

The late hour had emptied the streets, and as they rode along the river to Westminster, Maura took advantage of the quiet to rehearse her petition to Rufus. Yet all the peculiar sights she had witnessed this night crowded her mind. She steered E'dain alongside Alan's horse and asked, "Why didn't you tell me you were Jewish?"

Stunned by her question, Alan took a moment then replied, "Would it have made a difference in our arrangement?"

"Arrangement?" repeated Maura, confused. "I consider our arrangement a dear friendship and, no, it would have made no difference. I feel a bit foolish, though, having badgered you to join in our Christmas celebrations."

Alan smiled, "Oh, Maura, I was grateful for the kind thought and company." His manner abruptly turned serious, "The mention of my religion can prove disastrous. My brother can rightly attest to that. His forge has been looted countless times."

"In Dunheved," said Maura, "there was a small Jewish settlement. Simon, Marc, and I were friendly with the children living in the district, and I remember many ugly incidents directed against—"

"Maura, see!" Alan stood in his saddle and pointed beyond the thatched roofs to the orange-lit skyline. "Yonder flies the banners of Westminster," he said, then quelled her enthusiasm with caution. "We'll approach slowly. You'll wait outside the gatehouse while I bluff the sentries."

Her heart pounding fit to burst, Maura watched Alan pacify his fellow guards. They waited impatiently as the iron grid portcullis screeched its way up into the gatehouse attic. Alan waved Maura forward as they trotted across the drawbridge and bailey, tethered their horses, and determinedly entered the keep. As the great hall drew nearer, Maura's footsteps and daring faltered. Alan's firm handhold and the wrenching memory of the horrible events of the previous evening mustered her courage. Very soon, she would see Simon, and with God's grace, hopefully speak to him!

The giant doors groaned wide to the peculiar sight of Rufus, alone and slouched over the dais, his palm supporting his jaw as he picked nonchalantly at his late meal. Maura and Alan stepped lightly down the steps, Maura carefully scrutinizing her nemesis. She cracked a winning grin, and leant close to Alan. "I will meet with him alone. He's sober."

"How can you tell?" asked Alan.

"He's alone, quiet, and not snoring," said Maura decisively.

Alan stepped back, released her, and watched guardedly as she glided up to the dais.

Maura stood before Rufus, waiting. The sound of his lusty mastication soured her belly, but he delighted in annoying her, and not till the last crumb of food had slipped down his throat did he grumble, "So it didn't take long for Will to tire of you."

"My visit has nothing to do with Will," she answered readily.

"You missed me," he said. His mocking leer revealed remnants of stew dangling from his stained and broken teeth.

"I have a simple request to make of you, my good Prince, nothing more."

His eyes bulging in disbelief, he shoved from the dais, and roared to the empty hall, "Check her for weapons!"

Sentries appeared from nowhere, and swiftly performed a rude search. Maura, not eager to ignite Rufus' ire, halted Alan with a gesture, and bravely endured the indignity. She sighed to the sentries' consensus, "She is unarmed, my Lord."

"Then, my Lady, you are welcome in my home. Come, we'll talk in my chamber... alone." He waited for an argument, but none came, so grabbing up his wine tankard and a cup, he shuffled to his chamber. He held the door open; she tentatively entered, and slid into the chair nearest the door. Rufus bolted the door and asked with shallow politeness, "Would you care for wine?"

"Ye...yes, please," she croaked in response.

His hard eyes brightened at her obvious discomfort. He passed the filled cup to her and asked haughtily, "I'm sure you are aware that special requests of my time are costly."

"I'm prepared to pay you well for your generosity, my Lord."

"What could you possibly desire from me?"

"Simon's release."

Rufus burst a chortle and flopped across his bed, spewing wine across the rumpled silk sheets. "Now why would I want to free that mongrel? I've waited years to rid our family of his slimy presence, and now he's exactly where I want him, tucked up and snug beneath my feet. Besides, I haven't the authority to release him."

"But you rule while your father battles in Normandy."

"Not in judicial matters. Father alone has the authority to sign his release document."

Maura's rising anger thrust her from her seat and she boldly approached Rufus, demanding, "What reason was given for Simon's confinement?"

"Uncle Robert mentioned something about Simon attacking him—"

"He lies! He's caged him for ending our betrothal, a mission Simon carried out under *your* father's orders. And how will King William react when he hears of your conspiracy with Robert? Simon is, after all, his favorite nephew."

"He won't hear about it. He's too busy battling, he's always battling, and one of these battles is bound to finish him. And then, everyone, including you, my bold Lady, will answer to me!"

"He'll know, by God, because," she cursed, flaring her fury, "I will tell him!" Maura stormed to the door and turned to add, "And while in Normandy, I'll reveal a great deal more...concerning your—"

"Wait!" Rufus yelled, pushing himself from his lolling position. She unbolted the door and paused, hoping her threat had struck the desired nerve. "Per...perhaps," Rufus stuttered, "we can come to a compromise?"

Her shoulders sagged in relief, and she taunted further, "No, your compromises are far too lopsided."

"I...I warn you, Maura." His broken answer betrayed his uncertainty. "You don't leave this chamber till I'm done with you."

She turned and rested back against the door, her victory smirk evident. "Well then, finish. I'm in a hurry."

Fantasies of punishment for her misbehavior at Gloucester had played on Rufus' mind for weeks. Now her penance came to him easily. "Maura," he said, too smoothly, "I will agree to Simon's freedom only after receiving from you a release document signed and sealed by my father. And there's more...I want a writ, my father's clerk can script it, attesting to the fact that you traveled to Normandy...alone. You will have no protection, and if I hear anything to the contrary, I myself will arrange an accident for Simon!"

A long, loud sigh of disgust left Maura; she wagged her head, and muttered, "Rufus, I've lived with you four long and hard years. I know you better than your priest does, and your doings aren't pretty. How you've kept your father blind to your ways is a mystery, but I swear I will pry wide his eyes if you so much as slap Simon." She took a calming breath and continued, "I agree to your terms, but you must consent not to betray our deal to Will or Lord Robert...You'll tell them nothing or I'll tell King William all and you will surely lose everything!"

"My God, woman, you're beginning to sound like that pompous turd of a bastard."

"Are you speaking of Simon?"

Rufus nodded.

"Why thank you, Rufus." Maura smiled confidently. "I believe that's the first and only compliment you've ever paid me."

A coarse grunt served as his answer, then he sneered, "Tell me, Maura, if you do betray my ways to my father and he believes you, which is doubtful, what bleak choices remain for the future King of England? My older brother, Curthose, who delights in clashing with Father, or myself, who loves and obeys him?"

"There's always Henry," spouted Maura.

"That baby-faced toad!" sniggered Rufus. "Oh Maura, I adore your humor."

"Don't laugh too hard, Rufus, you may rupture yourself...Now, about our deal, I'll leave for Normandy—"

"I want more payment than your foolish bravery and vow of silence," interjected Rufus.

Anticipating Rufus' request, Maura untied a pouch from her belt, stepped forward, and spilled a pile of silver coins before him. "Will this do?" she asked warily.

Rufus' eyes glittered as brightly as the coins; he smiled complacently and sighed, "A promising start, but not nearly enough."

"I have no more coins on my person, and won't offer—"

"I don't want your body." A distasteful scowl filled his ruddy face. "I want something far more pleasing—more money."

"I will render more when I return," Maura offered hesitantly, "and only if Simon still lives."

"*If* you return..." Rufus blurted, then struggled inwardly with his decision. Her ever-rising boldness baffled him, leaving him unsure of her motives. Yet he craved money, so what could he do but agree? He sat erect, then stood and stepped closer to intimidate. It always bothered him that she stood taller than he. She didn't flinch to his advance, but instead, cocked her chin assuredly.

Rufus averted his glare and thrust out his lower lip in a conceding pout. "You bring me Father's signed release, and a statement that you traveled alone, and I will release him, granted you add to this measly pile of coins. And betray nothing damning about me!"

Maura answered with a sharp nod and demand, "I will see Simon now!"

Rufus threw up his hands in exasperation and returned to his bed, mumbling, "Fine...stay forever if you wish. What a comforting thought, you and Simon spending eternity together in your cozy little cell." Her fingers clinched the liberating latch, but she froze to his final hissed threat, "I swear, Maura, if Father hears anything he shouldn't, Will and Robert will know of our meeting. I believe you realize the consequences of that grisly discovery. A boat sails at dawn for Barfleur. Be on it! Now get out of my sight!"

The door slammed behind her, and Rufus proceeded to play with his coins, stacking them and sifting them through his stubby fingers, a vacant but slightly pensive look clouding his face. Was he becoming feeble-minded? He'd just agreed to let her see Simon and asked for no remittance! He must stop this bothersome tendency to kindness before he sullied his ruthless reputation. First he would finish his wine, then he'd set his guards on her trail.

Maura leant back against the door and, while gulping deep steadying breaths, she caught an urgent whisper, "Maura, Maura...back here. Come." The voice was unfamiliar but tempting, and she found herself lured in its direction. A disembodied hand appeared in the vague light, captured her arm, and whisked her into the shadows. She struck at the hand's elusive owner. He expertly blocked her blow and stilled her fear with a lulling introduction, "Maura, it's Henry."

"Henry?" she echoed, unbelieving. She had known Henry as a young boy; this was no boy standing before her!

"What's happened?" he prompted eagerly. "Why are you here?"

She peered through the dark for recognizable features and muttered nervously, "I can't see you."

"Believe it's me! I know you wouldn't voluntarily visit Rufus. Tell me what's happened."

His emotional plea eased her doubt and she sputtered, "Si...Simon...Lord Robert has arrested him and he's imprisoned here at Westminster. I leave for Normandy at dawn to secure his release from your father."

"Who goes with you?"

"No one, I'll travel alone."

"You arranged this with Rufus?" he asked skeptically.

"What choice did I have?" She broke from his grip. "There's little time, Henry. I must go to Simon."

"I'll follow. Let no one know we've spoken. Go."

*****

Simon woke to searing pain. He lurched from the ground, slammed his head against the ceiling, and fell back to the mud. He groaned through clenched teeth, coiled his throbbing body, and yanked futilely at the chain. Three columns of light filtered through the bars in the door, cutting through the lurid darkness, and the horror of the past day flickered in his dulled mind—the soldier's gloved fist halting his escape, Will's frenzied tirade and attack, and Maura's confession of hate! The pulsing hurt returned, more violent than before. This was no nightmare, this was real! He had stumbled directly into his father's trap and now was his prisoner, awaiting what? And where was this place? His free hand gently rubbed his aching brow; his one good eye grew accustomed to the blackness, and the interior of the burrow began to lighten. Gripping the chain, he pulled himself up, then squinted toward the bands of light and saw to his joy and disbelief a tray stacked with bread and cheese. A tankard sat by the fare. Stiffly, he crawled toward the bounty, yet inches from his target he found himself stuck. Twisting and straining failed to get him closer. He started to call out but the resulting pain stifled his plea. So this was their game—he was to be starved. He heaved his body back into the depths of the foul cell and cradled his head in his hands, hoping for a swift end to his agony. Wiry fur brushed against the back of his hand, startling him from his anguish. He struck out blindly, his blow producing the rat's squeak and a muffled thud. Simon curled his body tighter, buried his head in his arms, and despaired—what other diabolical surprises lay in wait in this premature grave? Then forcibly quieting his worries, he silently waited to die.

*****

CHAPTER THIRTEEN - AT ROYAL ODDS

𝓕ear of recognition kept Alan out of sight as Maura flew down the stairs and burst breathlessly into the prison guards' chamber. Roland and Thomas, startled to their feet by her exuberance, clutched their sword hilts and steeled for attack. She struggled for breath, great gasps punctuating her command, "I...I...would see...see the prisoner now!" A heated silence followed as the guards studied her flustered appearance. Their beady eyes moved from her copper hair to Almodis' money pouch, then a common appeasing look set them in motion. Roland plucked the key from the wall, Godfrey stood in respect, and Thomas approached to check her for weapons. Maura didn't take kindly to this search, and squirmed as his grimy hands traveled her waist, patted her hips, then began a walk up her leg. She stabbed his chest with her knee, sprawling him to the floor, and snapped as she surged for the cell, "I keep no weapons there! The Lady Almodis has arranged my visit, and it would not be wise to cross her! Let me enter the cell now!"

The sound of squabbling voices drowned the rumbling of Simon's belly. He shifted attentively, straining to hear the cause of the trouble. Perhaps Will had sent his soldiers and it was time to die. The door creaked wide, illuminating half the cell with muted, patchy candlelight. He huddled in the dark recess, rubbed his good eye, and peered at the figure squatting in the doorway. The face was in shadow, then he heard a feminine voice, "There's no one in here."

A snicker answered her complaint, "Deeper, my Lady, stoop down and crawl deeper. You'll soon find him, or the rats."

Simon inched for the door, not daring to believe. Could it possibly be..."Maura?"

Maura jerked to his faint call and returned ardently, "Simon! Simon, where are you? I can't see you. Please, come into the light!"

A great ruckus exploded in the guard's chamber as two of Rufus' sentries stormed the room, proclaiming, "By the FitzRoy's orders, the Lady is to be removed immediately!"

Roland and Thomas' love of money overpowered their shaky allegiance to the Prince. An argument ensued as they attempted to stall Rufus' men. Their blustering boomed louder and closer, and Maura knew her time with Simon would soon end. Suddenly, he was before her, and she gasped in horror at his wretched appearance; half his face was battered black, his one eye swollen shut. She reached out to touch, but his hand caught hers and squeezed tight. "Why...why are you here?" his ragged voice implored.

Maura could barely hear for the tumult outside. Someone grabbed her shoulder and yanked. She broke from his pull, and her belly lurched at the thrill of Simon's lips on her palm. A second hand clamped her other shoulder, making her speak brokenly and too rapidly, "I've come to...to tell you—" She grunted and strained against the guard's hold. "Simon, you'll soon be free!"

"How?" he faintly pressed, strengthening his hold.

Rough voices rumbled at her back, "Get her from the cell!" Groping fingers found her belt.

Simon came closer, his one open eye begging. "Why did you come? You hate me!"

"I was forced to say—" Jerked backwards, she cried out, "No! Wait!"

Simon pulled her near, but he weakened. Her fingers slipped from his, and he helplessly watched her writhing body disappear through the opening. He dove for the slamming door and wailed, "No! Don't take her from me! By God, no!" Pain ripped through his body and he collapsed, straining at his shackle, moaning as the cuff tore open his wrist wounds.

Rufus' guard and Maura fought furiously. Her vicious kicks and sharp thrashing loosened his hold. She lunged for the cell door; he swiped at her hair, caught a handful, and yanked her back to the table. His hand slapped across her mouth, barely quieting her piercing scream.

"Enough!" commanded a new strident voice. A sudden hush descended as Henry strutted into the heart of the chaos and barked, "Release the Lady now!" The guard foolishly challenged the Prince and held tight his grip. A knotted fist accompanied Henry's hissed threat, "You'll obey me at once, or join the prisoner! Release her!"

The guard narrowed his glare and grudgingly complied. Maura bolted once more for the cell, but Henry lurched forward and barred her way. "Maura, leave this chamber."

"No!" she raved. "I must see him...Henry, *please* let me see him!"

Henry refused to soften. "Go now or I'll order my guard to haul you out!"

Maura frantically searched his eyes and expression, trying to discern his motives, but he appeared so controlled, so cold. And then he arched a brow, and whispered quickly, "Wait with your guard inside the main doors to the keep."

"Henry," she whispered in turn. "Don't betray my plans to Simon, but tell him—"

"Go!"

Maura sagged in defeat, left the chamber, and trudged the stairs. Her dour countenance told Alan all; he didn't pry, but solemnly followed her to the keep's entrance.

Once Maura was away, Henry continued to bark, "Open the door to the cell!" Thomas rushed to obey. Henry crouched low and had crawled in but a few feet when Simon seized the back of his collar and thrust his face into the mud. Henry flailed and blubbered under Simon's strangling grip. He twisted his face to the side, spat dirt and sputtered, "Simon, stop! Stop, it's Henry!"

Simon's hand leapt to the back of Henry's tunic, grabbed hold, and jerked him to his knees. "What have they done to her?!" he wailed.

Whipping his head, Henry spit more dirt, and choked, "No...nothing, she's unharmed. Rufus decided not to let her see you and sent his guard. She's a bit upset, that's all."

"Upset?!" Simon roared. "She screamed! What are you keeping from—" His pain intruded; he moaned and shielded his face protectively in his hands.

"Simon...Simon," Henry asked concernedly, "what have they done to you?"

Simon only groaned.

"No, don't talk," said Henry. "Try to calm yourself or you'll never heal."

"Do you actually think I'll be alive long enough to heal?" Simon returned. "What did she mean when she said I'll soon be free?"

Henry hesitated, knowing his answer would surely ignite another agonized outburst. But Simon sharply prodded, "You'll tell me, Henry!"

"I'm not certain, but I believe she mentioned something about traveling alone to Normandy to secure my father's signature for your release."

Simon's deflated figure swelled huge with anger. He wielded his cuffed fist and thundered, "Stop her, Henry!"

"I'll have nothing to do with her nonsense," Henry dismissed, flinching. "She's made her deal with Rufus."

"Rufus?! Get me out of here!" Simon's deafening response sent Henry reeling back against the door.

"I have no power, Simon."

"Rufus knows she'll die in Normandy. Stop her, Henry!"

"She seems quite determined."

"Then you'll go with her."

"She's agreed to go alone."

"What?"

"She's agreed to it, Simon."

"Then you'll follow her."

Henry shook his head. "No...and I mean what I say...I won't be involved in her foolishness."

Simon's rage crackled in the small space between them, prompting Henry to anticipate another pounce, and shrink even closer to the door. But none came, only the hissing of Simon's labored breath and his beleaguered plea, "Go with her, Henry. You owe me much."

His cousin's restraint scared Henry more than his outbursts, yet he continued to argue, "I don't know if I will."

Simon loomed closer, fury in his eye as he growled, "I've endured your foolishness countless times! You'll do as I say."

"She may not allow me to follow."

"Henry!" raved Simon.

"God's teeth, Simon!" Henry erupted. "I won't risk my life to follow some fool-hardy bitch who spits on you one moment, then plays your valiant rescuer the next! And how do I benefit from this debacle?"

Again came the silent ire. Henry sought a way out of their circular grappling, asking, "Why did Robert arrest you?"

"For many reasons...for no reason. You must protect her, Henry."

Something in Simon's voice, its hopelessness and futility, touched Henry's soul. Before him sat his closest companion, battered and shamed. He could offer little assistance on this side of the sea. If Maura failed in her quest—which was likely since the borders of Normandy were ablaze with war—Simon could easily fall prey to arranged accidents. Henry, however, could readily reach his father and secure the release. His words of surrender tumbled from his lips before he'd fully made his decision, "I'll...I'll do what I can. Do you have protection?"

"There is a guard outside the door. I know not his allegiance."

"He'll have one of my guards as company."

"I don't fear my father," said Simon, "it's Will that worries me."

The edge left Henry's voice and he answered with genuine affection, "Then he won't get near you. Someone's left you a blanket. Try to rest and keep warm...and don't speak."

"Henry?"

"What did I just say!" chided Henry.

"I need one more favor."

"I thought as much. What is it?"

"Please have your guard set my food within reach."

"So Will has already begun your execution." Henry sensed he was sitting in a puddle, and winced, "I seemed to have spilled your ale. I'll fetch more. Simon?"

Simon slipped to the ground with a miserable groan. Henry flung open the cell door and stuck out his head, yelling, "Fetch fresh food and ale at once!" When the pitcher, cup, and tray appeared by the door, Henry swiftly filled the cup and lifted Simon's head to drink. As Simon gulped, Henry continued to harp, "Your clothes are drenched. If your brother doesn't kill you, the cold will." Simon's head went limp in Henry's hand; he settled the prisoner gently in the mud, and tucked the blanket snugly around him.

Moving the tray close, Henry barely heard Simon's grim revelation, "There are rats in here, Henry."

"Then feed them and they'll let you be...but for God's sake don't bleed!"

Simon shivered under the coverlet and mumbled feverishly, "You needn't fuss over me. Go find Maura." Henry offered more ale, Simon pushed away the cup, and his fingers gripped Henry's wrist, tensing to his final entreaty, "Follow her, Henry, follow her and bring her back...to me."

The blurring lights stung Simon's eye as Henry left, and another figure entered and announced formally, "William FitzRoy wishes you to know that your freedom will be granted immediately."

At this stunning news, Simon found the strength to push up from the ground and ask dubiously, "What did you say?"

"Your freedom is to be granted."

"I can leave here?"

"There is a condition."

Simon's heart sank, but he asked nonetheless, "And that is?"

"Agree to become a member of Prince William's private household and he will gladly see to your release, comfort, safety—"

A well-aimed gob of spit ended the sentry's foul request, and Simon's demented scream, "Get out!" spirited him from the cell. He raged on to the shut door, his pitiful squalls fading with his consciousness.

Maura paced in Alan's shadow for what seemed an eternity. She barely knew Henry; how could she trust him? Accompanied by a majestic flurry of guards and hounds, Henry soon appeared, to be instantly barraged by Maura's questioning, "Did you see him? What did he say? You didn't betray my—"

"We've no time for silly questions," Henry cut in brusquely. He nodded to Alan, then turned to Maura, "When do you depart for Normandy?"

"Rufus said a ship leaves at dawn."

"Then we will leave within the hour."

"No, Henry! I'm to go alone!"

"Hush! We'll talk outside...Not so many ears about."

As they headed for the stables, Henry continued firmly, "Rufus suggested you leave on that ship for a reason. His spies will be aboard. If we leave tonight, we'll arrive before them and land at Boulogne, nearer to Father. There's no time to argue. Do you have supplies with you?"

"Yes, but—"

"Then wait here. I'll fetch the horses."

"But, Henry," she shouted to his back, "I will go..." Henry ignored her protest, and strode on to the stables, muttering rapidly to a tall, ginger-haired guard, who quickly loped back to the keep. Maura finished, "...alone," with a lame sigh, then begged, "Alan, what am I to do?"

"He's made an excellent point about Rufus and his spies."

"I agree, but if Rufus hears that Henry's with me, he'll kill Simon!"

"I don't believe Rufus is bright enough to see the connection, or that he'd intentionally harm Simon," said Alan. "Henry travels frequently to Normandy, and I'm certain he's provided protection for Simon. They are quite close. Rufus' spies will surely recognize me, so I must stay behind. "

Maura, not prepared for this sudden change of plans, felt a tremulous shiver wash over her. Alan passed Maura her satchel, reins were slapped into her palm, and a gloved hand hoisted her into the saddle of a strange bay mount. She fervently dug into her saddle bag, found, and tossed the sapphire necklace to Alan along with a dire plea, "Sell this. Rufus wants more money when I return!"

Desperately she reached out to take his hand, yet her horse bolted forward to join Henry's zealous party, and ripped their fingers apart. She heard Alan's faint cry, "Take care, Maura," as her gelding cantered across the drawbridge and down the lane to the docks. A foreboding premonition struck her as she looked to the fore of the pack. Perhaps her most potent danger sat haughtily upon a huge gray stallion—the self-proclaimed ruler of the rescue party—Henry FitzRoy.

*****

Deep inside the White Tower, Almodis lay naked beside a sleeping Will and reflected on their latest coupling. It seemed a bit perverse that despite the hatred brewing within her, she still felt pleasure when they came together. If he were ugly it would be easier to despise the vile creature he had become. Then again, he could be correct in his summation that she was every bit as vile as he. A fleeting vision of Maura's guard Alan passed before her closed eyes—mussed, rugged, large, and seemingly shy; an intriguing rare combination of attributes.

Will shifted to his side. A satisfied sigh hissed from his lips, and he draped his arm languidly about the curve of Almodis' hip. She twirled her fingers through a wispy black curl at his temple and thought further. He'd not mentioned the child she carried. If they loved again, it would tire him enough to sleep through the night. Robert would arrive early and—

Will's soft moan disturbed her plans. She nuzzled close and purred in his ear, "Again?"

A silly smile graced his lips as her fingers crept down his belly to tickle the soft curls between his legs. His hand tenderly guided hers, then suddenly stopped their play and strangled her wrist, making her gasp and start away. His grip held fast and his eyes flew open, their evil blatant. "Not yet," he snarled, "first, we'll talk."

"Later, my love. We'll talk later," smoothed Almodis. "I've missed you so. We have so few chances to be together. We must take advantage of each luscious moment." She mounted him, her abundant hair hung down and tickled his chest. "Let not a care plague your mind, lay back and let me pleasure you—"

In a flash she was on her back. Will loomed above her, his hands pinning her arms over her head. "I said...we'll talk."

Never had she felt this strength in Will; her pulse and breath surged as he smothered her body with his, and whispered lewdly, "Again, did you say? Oh yes, but first I'll know the father of this child." She tensed beneath him; he forced his weight, stilled her squirming and demanded, "You'll tell me now!"

She stared into his bitter-cold eyes, gulped, and felt her blood freeze to her unconvincing stutter, "Yo...yours...Of course it's yours."

"You lying whore! If this babe were mine, we'd have nine others by now!" Will drew back, struck her, and shoved a pillow over her face to muffle her scream. She thrashed and flailed. Her nails sliced at his face, eyes, neck, but he hovered just beyond her reach, chuckled at her turmoil, and swore, "When you're quiet, I'll remove the pillow. If you scream again, I'll kill you."

Her struggling abruptly ceased. Will tossed the pillow aside, and laughed louder as horrible gasps convulsed her. Her arms wrapped her body, hiding her nakedness, as she slipped from under him and shrank back against the headboard. "Don't hurt me, Will," she whimpered. "I'll tell you everything, only please, don't hurt me!"

He raised balled fists and his laughter rotted to a deranged cackle. "But I love to hurt you."

She coiled in a tense ball, hid her face, and silently awaited his assault. Yet his voice, not his fists, jolted her with its deafening charge, "It's Simon's baby!"

Panicked, she flung herself against his chest, clung to him and cried, "No! I've not been with Simon! You're mad!"

"Liar!" he screeched as he hurled her into the headboard.

Dangerously, she threw herself upon him again, rubbing her breasts to his damp skin, grinding her hips to his. "You're wrong," she wailed, "wrong! I visited him only to thank him. I'm three months gone, I've known him but a month! How...how could he—"

Will's powerful blow knocked her to the bed. He fell over her, his breath hot on her neck. Her mind raced. How could she escape his torture? The truth—he'd not believe the truth! She must seduce him, make him love her again! Her nails raked his back, her legs circled his waist. Almodis tried to tame the terror in her voice with stirring kisses and a sensual whisper, "I feel you want me. Your anger excites me. Let me hold you and take you inside. Please, Will, love me, *please*!"

He slipped to her side and slid his hand between her legs. His fingers dug their way inside her, fanning apart as they stretched and scratched. The scorching pain wrenched an agonized groan from her throat. She froze, fearful her cry would incite him further. A clutched pillow drowned her wails as his nails burrowed deeper and his voice, cool and deliberate, vowed, "If you lie and this is in fact Simon's baby, I'll reach higher and rip it out of you!" Her terror flamed his fury; he seethed and spat, "Not him, he'll have nothing that's mine, including you, my *love*. I swear I will kill you all!" He rolled back upon her and drove into her with a force that lifted her from the bed. Savagely, she beat at him, but her frenzy only heightened his cruelty, and lengthened his assault. As her pain intensified, her body and mind turned flaccid. The fight faded from her eyes, turning them dim, and lifeless. Finally, a shuddering groan took him and he collapsed across her limp body.

Almodis squeezed shut her eyes, not daring to speak or move, while Will's bloody fingers lovingly toyed with her hair, and he mimicked her sensuous voice, "Was that what you intended, my *love*?" He pulled from her and knelt, continuing his scorn, "Always know, your body is mine to do with as I please. And don't become accustomed to the title *mother*. There will be no child. Kill it, or I'll happily perform the task for you."

Once dressed, Will leant over her rigid body and murmured airy and sweet, "I'm thankful for your invitation, Almodis. I've enjoyed myself immensely." His frigid kiss drew from her repulsed groans which grew in length and volume as he paused at the door and finished, "Don't forget what I said...about the child."

The burning in her belly engulfed her entire body, radiating through her limbs, ripping through her skull. She writhed as nausea struck her; the fetid taste of vomit filled her mouth, dribbled from her lips and down her chin. Scream, she wanted to scream and never stop, but he would hear and return...return to murder her and the child! Maura... Maura would comfort and nurse her! The map to Alan's brother's home was hidden deep inside her trunk. She clutched the bed curtains and pulled from the bed, but her cramps strengthened.

On a side table sat a leather wine flagon, a present from Will. The wine would help ease the pain. Her fingers barely brushed the flagon's neck. It tipped onto the bed, and blood-red liquid surged obscenely across the silver-fox pelts. She rescued the gift, and gratefully brought it to her mouth. The acrid liquid stung her lips and she froze as the gulp burned her throat. She spat and gagged, and plunged a corner of the sheet deep down her throat to soak up—the poison! Will knew a great deal about poison. His grandmother Mabel had been the expert and taught him well. His threat wasn't a mere hoax, he thoroughly intended to kill them all! She must run, get help! With great difficulty, she rose. Almodis cried out as the fiercest spasm attacked, and dropped her heavily to the floor.

*****

Maura's mouth hung wide as she beheld the minuscule urine-soaked cubicle. "Not in there," she protested, retreating a step and shielding her nose and mouth from the stench.

Henry seemed amused by her response and smirked. "In there or up above where there lie thirty or so rough, burly, very lonely soldiers. They're not what I'd consider gentlemen. It's entirely your choice, Maura—you sleep with them or with me."

Maura regarded him suspiciously. "And are *you* a gentleman, Henry?"

"Well..." He folded his arms across his chest, cocked his head, and cajoled, "You'll soon find out, won't you?" A passed candle and an extravagant bow invited her inside. She entered gingerly, wincing at the stink, the lack of air, the filth. Two frayed straw mats, set too closely together, graced the floor; one ragged blanket served both beds. Henry strutted up behind her, tossed his saddlebag in the corner, and advised curtly, "You'd best get settled. We sail promptly."

She risked one final plea, "Henry, there must be somewhere else—"

"There isn't, Maura. Unless of course, you do everyone an enormous favor and stay in England where you belong!"

Everything about this babe in men's clothing annoyed her, especially his smug, derisive tone. She dropped her satchel at the foot of a mat, and simpered, "This will do just fine, Henry FitzRoy. I see traveling with you will bring me no benefits, only irritations."

"I certainly didn't want to agree to this blunder," shrugged Henry as he kicked at the dismal blanket.

"Then why did you?"

"Simon asked me to. Actually it was more of a royal command."

"What?" Maura flared. "You told him my plans! How could you? Now Rufus is sure to find out and he'll—"

"It made no difference!" cut in Henry. "Simon is concerned about your safety. Why, I'll never understand. I only pray I don't have to endure your whining for the entire journey!" He straightened his rumpled tunic and combed fingers through his dense, black hair. "I noticed wine barrels on deck. I intend to enjoy this crossing. Would you care to join me?"

Her look of disgust was accented by the surrounding squalor. "No...And you'd best have a clear head come dawn or I'm off without you!"

His dark eyes flashed disdain as he snorted under his breath, "I won't be lectured to by a woman!" and fled the cubicle.

Grateful for his absence, Maura allowed herself to relax a bit and scanned the room, striving to see it in a more flattering light. At least there was a blanket to stave off the chill. She pinched tentatively at the soiled cloth, and let out a sharp cry as dozens of insects dropped from its folds and scurried beneath the mats. The cloth soared through the air as she bolted from the room and started up the stairs. Then Henry's description of the deck crew came to mind. She slumped down on a step, closed her eyes, and saw again Simon's battered face. Why had he sent Henry with her? He'd offer no help, only harm. She felt so tired; she must rest if she were to ride the entire next day. Henry would not have the satisfaction of blaming her with delaying their journey. She rested her head upon a higher step and the boat's gentle rocking soon lulled her to sleep.

"Maura!" The toe of Henry's boot nudged her shoulder. "Maura! You mustn't block the stairway. You're liable to kill someone." He prodded harder. "Maura, get up!"

Sleepily, she mumbled, "There are bugs in the blanket and the mats. I'll stay here."

"They're harmless," said Henry. "Use your cloak as a cover."

Exhaustion carried his argument and she allowed him to help her up. On her mat, she tread in a circle, her eyes examining the straw for any dubious movement. Seeing none, she crouched in the corner and hugged close her knees. Henry lounged upon his mat, clearly enjoying her discomfort.

Maura shifted under his prying stare. She shot him a deadly glare. "Don't you dare move from that mat or I'll—"

"Or you'll what?" chuckled Henry. "You needn't worry, Maura. Why would I risk Simon's wrath just for the privilege of getting between your boney legs?"

Maura wouldn't grace his insult with a reply. She buried her head deep in her arms and prayed for sleep. The boat's rolling tipped her from her upright position. Henry watched, expecting her to rise and grumble more, but she didn't move. She looked awkward, and he carefully approached to remedy the situation. Maura didn't resist as he unfolded her crumpled body, removed her cloak and covered her. As he snuffed the candle and stretched out on his mat, a devilish smirk curled his lips. The revenge for her viciousness toward Simon came to him; he'd subject her to his well-practiced harassment tactics! And by midday tomorrow, she'd surely be begging to return to England.

*****

The boat pitched sharply to the tumultuous sea's churning, rocking Maura up against the wall and Henry onto Maura's mat. He groggily found himself snug against a warm, sumptuous female. With a lusty sigh, he wrapped her in a tight embrace and nuzzled his lips to her neck. She promptly woke and instinctively kicked out to break her captor's restraint. Henry howled as her booted feet drubbed his belly and groin, her fists smote his head. Maura screamed at the black convulsing lump at her side, "Let me go! Get away!" Her eyes gradually grew accustomed to the darkness, and she saw and remembered—Henry.

She kicked out again, but he seized her ankle, and screamed as shrilly, "Stop!"

"You're not here to help!" she cried. "You've come only to take advantage of a—"

"Shut your gob," he intruded, between groans. "It wasn't my fault. The boat rocked and I rolled..." The boat lurched as Henry continued haltingly, "off...of...my..." He closed his eyes and gripped the mat for balance. One violent sway sent one hand to his belly and the other to his mouth.

Queasy herself, Maura leapt up and attempted to drag him from the cubicle before he added to its unfavorable conditions. "Henry, no!" she pleaded. "If you must be sick, do so on deck!"

Henry agreed and ran crazily from the room, but he had scaled only four steps before his retching began. She covered her ears to his infectious heaving, and dropped back upon her mat, curses pounding her mind. This child would not hamper her mission! Tomorrow after docking she would escape him. A wiggly sensation inside her tunic made her shiver with revulsion. The bugs had settled on their new home—her body. She coiled her body, praying for sleep. *Harmless*, he'd called the bugs; as harmless as he, she warily wondered?

A jolting thud announced the ship's docking, and Maura woke alone. Heartened, she rose quickly, grabbed her satchel and cloak, and hurried onto the deck. Sea spray rose from the pilings. She paused a moment to enjoy its refreshing spatter and the brilliant sun. Then licking her salted lips, she elbowed her way off the boat. Horses crowded the wharf; she found hers readily from the long scar marring his neck. Seagulls rummaging the refuse from the ship waddled away from her horse's quick gait. There was no sign of Henry as she guided her mount toward what appeared to be a main thoroughfare. Once in the heart of the village, she would seek directions to Rouen.

And then, to her chagrin, *he* sauntered on horseback from behind a tree, still sporting his irksome smirk. His stallion blocked her horse as he asked snidely, "What's kept you?"

Muffled curses twisted her lips; she kicked her horse forward but he refused to budge. "We'll eat before we proceed," muttered Henry, "and you won't try to escape! I'm responsible for your well-being and I intend—"

"I'm responsible for myself!" Maura interjected fiercely.

With an indignant eye, he retorted, "This is not a pleasure jaunt through Normandy! From here on, it's war. And how many battles have you fought in, my gracious Lady?" Her incensed silence delighted him. He waved on his guards and rode ahead, sure that she'd follow.

Without prompting, her horse bounded forward and fell in line behind Henry's entourage. Her twisting and yanking at the reins had little effect on the hulking gelding. Irritation from bug bites flared on her skin; she wriggled in her saddle, reached to scratch an itch, and instead squashed one of the roaming creatures.

Henry's party alone filled the main room of the alehouse. Maura dourly endured the leering stares of his four guards, raked at her bites, and picked absently at the meat in her watery soup. She stole a secret glance at her Prince, and was astounded by his look of youthful innocence. Compared to his repellent elder brothers, Henry owned an attractive face. He favored his father in height, and his mother in fairness and color. What a shame such a pretty face hid such vile conceit.

He sensed her scrutiny, glared back, and said rudely, "We'll ride till dusk. Will that be a problem for you, my Lady?"

"Of course it won't," she replied as curtly.

"We should reach Father by dark tomorrow, that is, if the weather cooperates. I'm told he lays siege to a castle north of Rouen."

"Then we'll go," she said as she fastened her cloak and started from the room.

He rallied his guards and rushed after her, spouting, "Hold up, Maura. I lead this quest!"

His miffed tone didn't bother her. Perhaps she could anger him enough to desert her.

The weather stayed accommodating and, as they cantered over rolling hills, she had to admit he did know the safest and swiftest route to Rouen. Yet along the encroaching horizon, spiraling pillars of smoke smudged the cloudless sky. There was no denying war was near, too near.

Though Henry spoke not a word on their entire journey, Maura knew that her lack of complaints irked him. Through the smoky dusk, she noted a village marker stuck alongside the road—Abbeville. They stopped before what appeared to be a private residence. Henry dismounted; Maura followed suit, passed her reins to a guard, and asked, "What is this place?"

"A friend's cottage," mumbled Henry, yawning. "Ralph opens his home to traveling soldiers for pittance. We'll stay the night."

His second yawn prompted one from her and, too weary to argue, she trailed him to the door. As they entered Henry was instantly recognized, and an exalted cheer arose from a gang of boisterous soldiers. Maura quickly took in her surroundings—a long trestle table filled the hall, packed tight with soldiers; more men and hounds were strewn in corners and recesses; and three young women, sharing a familial resemblance, dispensed stew from a huge, bubbling cauldron. As they distributed the fare, they were subjected to a constant onslaught of pawing and pinching.

Maura had grown accustomed to quiet. The racket deafened her and pained her head. She tugged on Henry's tunic and interrupted his greeting to a jolly, wiry man she supposed was Ralph, "Henry, do you have a map? We must take time to plan our route." Without turning from his host, he removed a crumpled parchment from his belt and thrust it into her hand. The crowd cleared a path as Henry swaggered to the table, chairs were vacated, and stew and tankards set down for the honored guest. Maura removed her cloak, scratched at a few bites, then sat and ate voraciously. Once full, she spread the map out before her, and strained to distinguish the smudged lines. Her voice boomed above the din, "Henry...Henry! Which road do we take after crossing the Somme? Henry!"

But Henry didn't hear. She stared quizzically and noticed a euphoric spark gleaming his eyes. Following his gaze, she discovered its recipient to be one of the serving maids, buxom and black-haired. The maid returned his longing look, shoved her tray in her sister's hands and, beaming, dashed to Henry and jumped into his lap. They groped hungrily at each other, exchanged swooning, noisy kisses. Embarrassed, Maura looked away and busied herself with the map, but her curious gaze kept returning to their unabashed show of lust. Her eyes widened as Henry deftly unlaced the woman's bodice and slipped his hand inside to knead a breast. Her hands disappeared beneath his tunic to explore.

An unexpected twinge of jealousy struck Maura as she watched their fervor grow. She achingly remembered a time when she too had been overtaken by desire, locked in an embrace, ecstatically oblivious to the world around her. Sadly, she left the lovers and approached a maid to ask, "Where does the Prince sleep?"

The woman eyed Maura with a combination of shock and wonder. She pointed hesitantly across the room to a door leading from the hall. Coarse behavior normally didn't faze Maura, but as she struggled through the crowd, she slapped at the soldiers' nipping fingers and reddened to their lewd comments.

She entered the scantily furnished chamber and sank down upon the mat nearest the door. A larger mat lay opposite flanked only by a lit candle and a chamber pot. Maura crawled from her straw island, stole the candle, and positioned its base on the map's corner. She hovered close, but tears of exhaustion and defeat trickled onto the parchment, smearing the ink further. The memories refused to go and a wrenching emptiness filled her. How she craved Simon's strength, his smile, his touch! Would she ever know their passion again?! Tears continued to blur her vision. Maura discarded the map, stretched across the pallet, and tried to envision King William signing Simon's release. Before sleep claimed her, she vowed her love would prevail and set Simon free.

The lovers' loud and frenzied coupling awakened Maura. It pained her to listen, so she left the chamber, stumbled over piles of snoring soldiers, and finally settled in her horse's stall. In the wavering torch light, she ventured a peek at her bites. The sight of the rash seemed to spread the irritation, and she scratched on through the night.

"Henry, wake up! We must leave at once." Maura opened wide the shutters, hoping the dawning sun would stir him, but he grunted his displeasure and burrowed beneath his blanket. Maura watched his shrouded figure snuggle closer to his woman, who answered by pinning him in a smothering wrap.

"No! Not again!" yelled Maura, frantically searching for a weapon to cool their ardor. The chamber pot lay tipped on its side, its contents soaking the floor. She brightened to a half-filled tankard of ale sitting by the mat, snatched it up, ripped off their blanket, and doused their heads with chilly brew.

Frightful gasps strangled Henry; he sputtered ale and curses as he struggled to rise and confront his red-headed pest. Yet his lover's grip proved more persuasive. He surged back into her succoring embrace, unaware that his responsibility was furiously galloping away down the road to Rouen. Too slowly Henry realized the situation and lazily considered his choices. Should he stay buried in this woman's voluptuous, inviting body, or honor his pledge to chase the stupid, self-righteous bitch? Simon's words came to him, 'you owe me much'. Which was correct—Henry was heavily indebted to him. Sulkily, he left his lover's clutch and, ignoring her clawing protests, swiftly donned his clothes. Without a word of explanation or gratitude, he left her.

His guards moaned to his rousing kicks and shrill scolding, "You damn idiots! Get up. You've let her get away!" Henry's livid eyes swept the mass of snoring bodies and rested on Ralph, scraping congealed stew off the table. "Ralph," Henry shouted, tossing a coin in his direction. "For you, and..." he said, throwing another, "one for your daughter. When did my traveling companion leave?"

"It's been near an hour, my Lord," answered Ralph.

"An hour!" scowled Henry, sweeping his ale-dampened hair from his eyes. "Piss on all women! I'm done with the lot of them!" He thoughtlessly tramped over squirming bodies to the exit, grumbling, "Let me through, you stinking bastards!" Ralph listened a moment, heard more scurrilous curses, then the welcome sound of departing hooves.

Swathed only in a blanket, Henry's lover raced from the chamber, dodging rising soldiers and crying out, "Henry! Henry! Where've you gone?" Henry had seemingly vanished, and she desperately beseeched, "Father, where's he gone to?"

"He's off chasing that red-headed girl," said Ralph, digging harder at the stained table.

"What did he say? When will he return?"

"He didn't say, though he did announce he's done with women."

A great pout and heaving sobs sent her back to the chamber. Ralph, sporting a hopeful look, yelled after her, "Don't cry, my dear. You see," he said, holding up the coin, "he's kindly left you a whole mark!"

*****

Maura's hair and cloak billowed in the crisp breeze as she sped across the bridge spanning the Somme. Free of her tyrant, she laughed crazily at the unblemished sky, the open road, and the cheering sun. The hills grew steeper; she spurred her mount up the highest crest, and made a swift survey of the surrounding countryside. A short distance ahead, a walled village lay nestled between the gentle mounds, horrendous black clouds of smoke spewing from its torched buildings. One path, the road she traveled, led through the village, and beyond, dense forest hugged its walls. Striking through the forest would add too much time to her journey, time she couldn't afford to waste, not with Simon's life in jeopardy! Henry would surely be distracted with his woman for hours, thus giving her the time to study the map and decide another route to King William.

While contemplating her dilemma by a bubbling spring, she cooled her face, throat, and the rash that now blighted her entire body with numbing water, and decided that if she kept to the safety of the outside wall of the village, she would lose little time, yet if discovered—Clopping hooves and neighs intruded on her musing and startled her to her feet. Henry, a scarlet glower disfiguring his face, hurried along the path to the stream, brandishing a length of cord.

There was no escaping him! The stream was swollen and knotted with blocks of treacherous ice! She raised her arms in surrender, but before she could utter a word in defense, he grabbed her hands, slapped her palms together and wrapped her wrists with the hemp. Maura's humiliation exploded into rage; her bound fists rammed his belly and, shaking lose the rope, she bolted for her horse.

He clutched his waist, gasped a groan, and dropped to his knees, croaking, "Stop her, you bumbling fools! Stop her!" Maura scrambled onto her saddle. A brief glimpse backward revealed the four guards almost upon her. One lunged for the reins, but her horse lurched forward, knocking him to the ground. Henry appeared, wobbling and ranting. He leapt on his horse and took off in pursuit, his guards merrily joining his chase.

Maura galloped straight for the razed village. Somehow, she would get through! She had to get through and away from Henry! The smoke loomed nearer. A battalion of soldiers loitering about the village gate snapped to her advance and unsheathed their weapons. She instantly rethought her boldness and jerked her horse to the forest, but he balked and reared in protest. Thundering hooves pounded at her back. Panicked, she spurred her horse toward what she believed to be the least perilous option—the armed soldiers.

Henry gaped in disbelief at Maura's mad escape. If King Philip's men held this village, she would be cut down at the gate! He urged his horse faster. There was a slight chance he'd catch her, as he'd purposely put her on the oldest, slowest nag in his stables.

The soldiers' weapons glimmered forbiddingly in the blinding sunlight, prompting Maura to rein in her steed. Henry flew off his horse, unsheathed his sword from his saddle, then sprinted to her side, roaring, "You stupid bitch! You can kill yourself, but you won't take me and my men with you—" He froze and spun to the ominous sound of encroaching boot steps. Terror replaced his ire; his tone turned desperate, pleading, "Maura, *please* listen to reason and get off your horse..."

She caught his fear and slipped from her saddle, to be swiftly enclosed by Henry and his men. Henry's show of force didn't deter the village soldiers. They halted their advance feet from the curious circle and, with bowed heads, dropped to their knees before their Prince.

*****

CHAPTER FOURTEEN - HOMAGE

"Who razed this village?" demanded Henry, flaunting a prestigious air and gesturing the soldiers to rise.

"Your brother Robert FitzRoy, my Lord," answered the man closest to Henry.

Henry glanced at the carnage, then nodded, "Yes, I should have recognized his *benevolent* way. Is it safe to enter?"

"No, my Lord. The bodies have yet to be carted off and the buildings are collapsing."

"Is there a way round?"

"Yes, my Lord, through the forest."

Maura reached out to argue, "Not the forest, Henry. We can't risk a delay."

He shook from her protest and continued his interrogation, "Have King Philip's sympathizers been thoroughly defeated?"

"Some are not accounted for, my Lord."

Henry stood silent a pensive moment, then looked to Maura. He raised a quieting hand to her open mouth and his dark eyes cut deep. "Not here, we'll not argue here. Do you own a weapon?" She shook her head and was presently provided a sword by Henry's guard. "Hook it to your belt," instructed Henry. "Have you used one before?"

"Yes," replied Maura.

"I shouldn't wonder. Don't hesitate to wield it and don't concern yourself with riding over bodies. They're dead and won't mind. We must make haste. The enemy may still be in hiding and I would make a valuable hostage."

Attempting to exude a brazen stance, Maura nodded sharply, secured the sword to her belt, and mounted her horse. Henry guided his horse alongside hers and continued to counsel, "The smoke is deadly. Mask your face with your cloak and take shallow breaths. Stay near to me." His horse's prancing scattered the foot soldiers; Maura followed his canter and his guards trotted behind.

Maura's heart's frantic pounding almost jarred her from her saddle as they rapidly approached what appeared to be Hell on earth. A thick gust of black ash swallowed them as they entered the village. Her cloak offered little aid and, hacking, she kicked her horse faster. He stumbled. She glanced down and saw to her horror that Henry didn't exaggerate, scorched bodies and cleaved limbs lay scattered beneath her horse's hooves. The stubborn beast resisted her frantic kicks. She started to cry out for Henry when a blazing wooden wall not feet away crumbled in a thunderous roar. Flaming shards of wood exploded from the falling timbers, showering and stabbing her and her horse. He bucked, tossed her from the saddle, and soundly bolted. A distant voice—Henry's voice, cried her name. The swirling smoke briefly lifted and she found herself entrenched in carnage. She scrambled and slipped in the gore, her fingers clawing faces as she frenziedly groped in what she believed to be Henry's direction.

Something or someone halted her escape. Her body and blood froze at the thought that someone still alive was buried in the corpses, perhaps the enemy, aiming to drag her under—She risked a glance and saw her sword hilt tangled in gnarled fingers. The soldier's glazed eyes seemed to follow her as she madly fumbled to free her sword from his death grip. His face captured her morbid fascination; his eyes and mouth gaped wide with terror, blood streamed from his nostrils and lips, a scarlet grin severed his neck. She reached out tentatively and stroked his cold beardless chin. How old could he be, twelve, thirteen? Her gagging broke her fixation. She raked madly at the hilt, but his fingers refused to surrender her weapon. She attacked her belt's buckle; it held firmly. Desperately, she cried to the Almighty, "Please Lord, get me from this hell! Don't let me die here! Save me!" The boy's fingers at last yielded to her prayers and, lurching forward, she toppled onto a headless torso. Her scream split through the haze. A lone hand miraculously answered. She clenched hold and a brusque jerk landed her upon a saddle.

Henry felt Maura's face press into his back; her arms squeezed his waist. He glimpsed her blood-soaked hands and the massacre below, then his anxious eyes spied movement near a still-intact building. A quick wave mustered his guards and they continued their harrowing trek through the bodies. The instant his horse's hooves touched a clearing, Henry rammed his boots into its sides, and they raced wildly between shells of buildings, leapt smoldering timbers, and bounded over the village wall. They kept up their exhausting pace till they were miles from the threat. Henry guided his men into the forest for a needed respite and his strained voice tersely directed, "Maura, you can let go now, and get down."

Try as she might, Maura could not break her wrenching grip. If she lifted her head from his back, what further horrors would she be forced to endure? Fear shamed her. She had tried so valiantly to be strong, to prove she could survive this mission with no man's help. How miserably she'd failed.

A gentle hand and voice assured, "I'll help you, my Lady." The guard's warm smile calmed her and she allowed him to lift her from the saddle.

Maura balanced on quaking knees, and offered, "Thank you, Sir," while she dried her bloodied hands and face with the skirt of her tunic. Hearing Henry dismount, she turned to apologize for her cowardice. Stunned, she watched him sink to a senseless heap at her feet.

Late that evening, Maura lay alone in the dark. They had stopped to sojourn at another private residence with few soldiers and no daughters to distract her companion. She shifted on her mat, eager for sleep to deliver her from her waking nightmare, but the young soldier's face continued to haunt. She forced her thoughts to Henry, and saw again his listless body at her feet. He'd spoken not a word since being revived from his faint and, after a lackluster meal, she'd left him pouting by the fire.

A servant had kindly provided her water for washing and, owing to the rescue of her horse and saddlebag, she had been able to change her clothes. Yet the bathing failed to soothe the irritation that now engulfed her entire body. She paused in her scratching as the door creaked open and Henry's solemn face, lit by a candle, peeked into the room. "Maura," he loudly whispered, "Maura, are you awake?"

Maura, clad only in a chemise, wrapped her shoulders with a blanket and answered, "Yes...come."

He bent to retrieve something from the floor and crept with an uneasy gait into the chamber. The candle he set at the head of Maura's mat. He passed her a cup which she sniffed suspiciously, then he flopped upon the mat opposite, explaining, "I've brought you warm milk and honey to help you sleep."

Bewildered by his thoughtfulness, Maura sipped the milk and muttered staidly, "That's quite nice of you. How are you feeling?"

He pushed from the mat and sat up tall, replying, "I'm perfectly fine," with much bravado. Then he seemed to shrink before her, tugged at the straw beneath him, and averted his sheepish gaze.

"Henry," said Maura, feeling a brief pang of pity, "will we still reach your father by tomorrow dark?"

"Yes," he answered unsteadily, "unless we encounter further distractions. I'm eager to get this done."

"As am I."

He studied her keenly; she returned his glare, and noticed a glint of distress spark his eyes. With a blink, it disappeared. He rested his head back against his joined hands and haughtily asked, "Why are you doing this?"

"Doing what?"

"This foolish tramp across Normandy."

"To secure Simon's release. I thought you knew that."

"That's what I've been told." He yanked a strand of straw from his mat, chewed on it a long moment, then pointed it accusingly. "I don't believe that's the *true* reason."

"Henry," she said, "why else would I risk—"

"Maura," he interrupted, "I feel I must be honest with you—regarding Simon."

Piqued, she took a long draught of milk and prompted, "Go on."

"I know Simon quite well and he will appreciate all you've sacrificed for his freedom, but he won't stay with you."

"Henry, what are you talking about?"

Crossing his legs, he continued to wield his straw dagger. "Well, women absolutely adore Simon. I could never fathom why, but they swarm to him like flies to dead meat. I've never known him to be taken with any woman for long and, believe me, he's known some fine women. He cherishes his freedom dearly, Maura, and the work he does for my father sends him traveling constantly. He'll be sweet to you and may even lie with you awhile, but eventually he will leave you."

His transparent concern couldn't hide the true meaning of his commentary; he was jealous! Maura smiled tenderly. "I'm grateful for your interest, Henry, but you needn't worry. I won't take Simon from you. I feel responsible for his confinement and I seek his release simply because I love him."

"I really don't understand you, Maura," said Henry with a huff. "Most women are silly and predictable. You don't act at all as you should."

"May I take that as a compliment?"

"Take it as you like."

Maura examined the blood caught beneath her nails and ingrained in her knuckles. "I haven't thanked you for returning for me...in the village. The way I've acted, I'm surprised you didn't take the opportunity to bolt."

"Actually, I've wondered about your insolent conduct and have come to the conclusion that you are jealous."

"Jealous?" repeated Maura incredulously.

"Yes, of Sybil."

"And who may I ask is Sybil?"

"The inn-keeper Ralph's daughter, the black-haired girl."

"No, Henry, I'm not jealous of Sybil. I envy you. You obviously haven't a care in the world."

"You're wrong, Maura," he argued in earnest. "One day, I'll be King. That's a rather overwhelming care, don't you agree?"

"Yes it is. But I also believe if you learn to temper your conceit and control your impulsive behavior, you'll make an adequate King." She passed him the cup. "There's a bit left for you."

He downed the milk in one swig and smirked as she grimaced and clawed feverishly at her bites. "I apologize about the bugs," he said. "My father's physician ought to have an ointment to soothe the itch."

"And why didn't they bite you?" she asked, perturbed.

"They would never chew on someone as nasty as me. Also, I knew better than to stay the entire night in that horrid room."

"What!" she exclaimed. "You left me there knowing I'd be eaten!"

"You kicked me! I thought it fitting punishment."

His mischievous grin coaxed from her a slight smile and she sneered in jest, "Why, you rutting pig!"

"Rutting pig!" Henry laughed coarsely. "I've never been called *that* before. I rather like it. Maura, the sad truth is no one takes me seriously, so why should I?"

"Simon does."

"What?" he asked, surprised.

"Simon thinks very highly of you."

"And how would *you* know that?"

"He told me."

"When?"

"After his banishment from Odo's."

"But he returned to Dunheved," said Henry. "You were at Winchester."

"No, I came to Winchester later. Simon and I were together at Dunheved for over a year before we were forced apart."

Henry's eyes seemed to pop out of his head. Finally, a stammered question tumbled from his hung jaw. "To...together how?"

Maura blushed a bit. "*That*, I prefer to keep private."

"I never would have guessed—you and Simon! Well, I suppose stranger things have occurred. Tell me," he asked excitedly, "what did he say about me?"

"That you were brave, bright, and showed great promise."

Henry puffed with pride. "Did he truly?" His tone and expression took on a certain fervor as he continued, "When I was at Odo's everyone either seemed afraid of me or considered me incompetent. But not Simon...He took time to tutor me in my studies and military training. Not because he felt obligated to help a Royal cousin. I believe he genuinely liked me. Uncle Odo was civil to me but beastly to Simon. I'm glad Simon's slip of the tongue resulted in Odo's arrest." He paused a moment and his gaze fell to the floor; he seemed uncomfortable and fidgeted with the laces gartering his hose. "I missed Simon terribly when he left Odo's. Then I heard he'd run off, no one knew where. I constantly pestered Father to find him, argued that Simon's mixed blood and talents would make him an excellent emissary. Father finally agreed, more out of a desire to shut me up than any loyalty to Simon. Though, Father does care for Simon, sometimes, I think, more than he cares for his true sons." He raised damp eyes and confirmed with passion, "Maura, I love Simon as well! He's a brother and true friend to me and I'll do all I can to save him. If Uncle Robert dares hurt him, he'll answer to me and I'll make him pay for his—"

"Henry..." Maura gently restrained his gesturing and calmed, "If *we* cooperate, he *will* be released. Now we have a long ride ahead of us and must try to sleep." He nodded meekly and she smiled, "And please try to stay on your side of the room."

With two loud grunts, he yanked off his boots, and returned impishly, "I suppose I can't blame the boat this time. But Maura, if you feel a need for attention, don't hesitate to ask..."

Maura turned away, scratched, then bundled herself in her thick blanket. Henry stretched to snuff the candle and rested on his belly, his head on crossed arms. "Maura," he said frankly, "you must forget all that you saw this day or it will haunt you forever. Force your thoughts on finding Father and...freeing Simon."

She rolled over and spoke to the darkness. "Thank you, Henry."

"Whatever for?" he mumbled sleepily. "I've been nothing but trouble."

"For making me smile. I wondered if I'd ever smile again." She waited for an answer, but heard instead his breath deepen and lengthen in sleep. And contemplating the surprises that awaited them over the remainder of their nebulous journey, she soon joined him in slumber.

*****

That same evening in their White Tower bedchamber, Robert patted Almodis' limp hand and his severe gaze matched his speech, "You'll go to Winchester. A contingent of my soldiers will escort you there and there they will stay! You could have been killed! Has your rest eased your pain?"

Almodis' frown grew longer as she shrugged and raised mournful eyes to ask, "Where has Will gone?"

"That's the fourth time you've asked of him. I suppose he's hunting with Rufus."

Beneath his hand, hers clenched to a fist and she fiercely begged, "Robert, you must keep him from Simon! Send him to Normandy to do battle or back to Berkhamstead. Get him from Westminster!"

"Stop your nonsense, Almodis," returned Robert coldly.

"Have you seen Simon?" she rasped, tears tumbling down her cheeks.

"No...We will speak tomorrow."

"What's his punishment to be?"

"You're not to concern yourself with these matters. Has your bleeding stopped?"

"Yes."

"And the child?"

"The child's fine," she answered glumly.

"Then you ought to be happy." Wary of her volatile mood, Robert hesitated, then blurted, "I leave for Normandy—"

"No, Robert! Don't leave me, *please* don't leave me! I'm frightened."

"You know better than to interrupt. The situation in Normandy is far too precarious for you to accompany me. You will be safe at Winchester. My men will watch you constantly."

"Sometimes," she admitted in small voice, "I fear your guards."

"Did one of *my* men attack you?!"

"I didn't recognize him." A part of her wanted to scream the truth, but her penance for adultery would be far worse than Will's abuse, so she abandoned the sordid topic. "When do you leave?"

"In two days' time. You may depart for Winchester when you please."

She rested her hand on his thigh, her fingers kneaded sensuously, her voice turned alluring, "If your talk goes well...with Simon, would you consider releasing him?"

Robert removed her hand and answered stolidly, "It won't go well. He will remain incarcerated till after Easter. I can't allow him the opportunity to end the Ryedale betrothal. It is after all, my last chance to acquire more land." Her melancholy touched him; his fingers stroked the bruise staining her jaw, then cupped her chin and lifted her face to his. "I'll return to Pevensey a fortnight before Easter. You will join me there. Till that time take care and rest..." His caring words had little effect on her sour countenance and he asked, "What can I do to cheer you?"

"Pardon Simon," she answered flatly.

"You will stop this, Almodis!" His anger drove him to his feet.

"But Robert, your loyalty lies with the wrong son!"

She shrank from his furious glower and tirade. "Do not lecture me! I won't suffer your impudence. I'll go now!"

"No, Robert, don't go! Forgive me..." On her knees, she hugged his waist. "Forgive me, my Lord. I crave your comfort. Don't go!"

Her body quivered from the exertion; he softened to her closeness, and helped her back beneath the pelts. A kiss on her palm quelled her panic. "Very well," he said, "I'll stay the night, yet only if you swear never to mention Simon's name again!" She kissed his fingers in atonement and, using the stained skins, shamefully wiped her tears from his hand.

*****

The next morning, Almodis waited till Robert had departed for Westminster, then dug from her trunk the map to Alan's brother's home, plus a few baubles for bribery, and made herself ready for the short trip. Tightly enclosed by a contingent of soldiers, she rode north the length of London. The brightness of the day and the caress of the crisp breeze on her cheeks helped her forget momentarily her oppressive bedchamber. And the comforting thought of seeing Maura, sharing her grief, and receiving solace lifted her gloomy spirits.

Almodis reined her horse at the entrance to an alley that matched the drawing on the map. She couldn't risk endangering Alan's family, so she reached into a pouch tied to her girdle, and extracted a glittery ring. The guard at her side caught the jewel's sparkle. He gazed quizzically as she offered the gift with the instructions, "You, Sir, and your fellow sentries will wait here for me. I won't be long."

His nod ended a lengthy, tense pause. She left her horse and, as hurriedly as her aching body would allow, followed Alan's directions till she stopped in front of a stable. A tall, bare-chested man hammered a sword before a blazing forge. Briefly, she believed him to be Alan, but peering closer she realized there was a slight difference in their appearance. She approached timidly. Nicolas stopped hammering mid-stroke and gawked at his misplaced guest. Her crisp linen veil and ermine cloak proved she was not a needy neighbor.

"Pardon my intrusion," she said politely. "I wonder if you could assist me."

"I will try, my Lady," he replied, setting his hammer aside and squirming into his shirt.

"I'm searching for a young woman named Maura."

"Maura?" he echoed, confused. "Yes, she was—" Suddenly aware of the peril of divulging Maura's plans, he stopped. Yet studying the stranger closer, he concluded this lovely creature could not be the enemy. "She *was* here. My brother should know where to find her. Shall I fetch him?"

"No, I'll not disturb you further. Just point the direction."

Nicolas smiled slightly to her formal way. "He's just up the stairs. The door isn't latched."

"I appreciate your kindness," said Almodis. Nicolas nodded and resumed his work as Almodis stiffly climbed the few stairs to the landing. Her enthusiasm caused her to enter without knocking.

Alan, startled by her abrupt arrival, sprang up from his mat, patted his mussed hair, and bowed clumsily. "My...my Lady," he stammered. "I hadn't expected that you would come here."

Her tone and expression took on a defensive air. "Actually, I've come to see Maura. The man downstairs, your brother I expect, mentioned you would know her whereabouts. If it would be no trouble, I'd like to wait for her return." As she spoke, her eyes darted restively about, avoiding his unabashed stare. He sensed her unease and noticed several bruises mottling her bloodless face. "Do you mind if I wait?" she asked again.

Alan approached cautiously. "I fear yours will be a long wait, my Lady. Maura left two days past for Normandy."

"Normandy!" she wailed. "No, she can't have gone so far!" He lunged forward to stop her collapse and helped her to the table. She sat, thrust her head in her crossed arms, and wept.

Alan helplessly watched her anguish, wondering if she cried from pain or disappointment. Recalling her bruises, he supposed a bit of both. He reached out to give a consoling pet but, remembering her station, buried his hand in his lap. "My Lady, you needn't worry. Maura's in safe company. She's traveling with Henry FitzRoy. They're to meet with King William and secure Simon's release."

Her sobs ceased and her moist eyes met his. "Did you say Simon's release?"

Addled by her somber beauty, Alan gibbered, "Ye...yes...and...and if they manage good time they ought to return within the week."

"I'm so sorry, Alan," she sniffled, "I must seem such a baby to you."

"Not at all, my Lady. I only wish there was something I could do to ease your sorrow."

Her restlessness surged again; she stood and announced coolly, "I must return to the Tower."

"You're in no condition to go anywhere! Someone has hurt you!" he carelessly blurted, then quickly added, "my Lady."

"No, no one has hurt me...My Lord expects me at the Tower when he returns from Westminster. He meets with Simon as we speak. Have you seen Simon?"

"No, my Lady, I'd be recognized. I'm believed to be with Maura at Winchester. No one must know she's in Normandy."

She swabbed her swollen eyes. "I'll not mention a word. When she arrives, would you kindly tell her I've gone to Winchester?"

He nodded. "Maura's indebted to you for arranging her visit with Simon."

"I was wondering if she'd managed—" She paused, uncomfortable under his intense scrutiny. "I must go. My guards await me in the next lane."

He stood first and asked, "If you encounter Rose at Winchester, would you please say that Maura is visiting friends in London? Rose upsets easily." He extended a helping hand which she readily accepted, and wordlessly they strolled out to the alley. The calmness Almodis felt in this man's presence was unnerving and perplexing.

Alan disturbed their silence, "I'm sorry my news grieved you, my Lady."

"No, on the contrary," she said with a modest grin, "speaking with you has allayed my concerns. I will try to see Simon before I depart for Winchester. Have you a message for him?"

Still clutching her hand, Alan thought a moment. "Yes, tell him not to despair. I've no doubt Maura will succeed and return shortly with his signed release." He daringly kissed her palm; she hesitantly pulled from his grasp and walked away.

A ways down the alley, she turned and wasn't at all surprised to find him exactly where they'd parted, looking eager. Her hopeful words, "I pray we meet again," drew from him the most radiant smile, and shocked to feel a blush heat her cheeks, she hurried on. Alan continued his vigil till she'd slipped out of sight.

*****

Moisture from the cell's ceiling dripped on Simon's nose as he struggled with vexing questions. How long had he been in this stinking hole? If Henry had decided to cooperate and escort Maura, where were they? Were they safe? When would they return? Would they ever return? He could easily endure the rotten food, the filth, the vermin, and the gnawing cold, but loneliness and doubt were driving him mad. The clicking of the rat's teeth cleaning his tray accompanied his prayer for sleep, for only in sleep did he find escape, and Maura.

The cell suddenly brightened. Simon sat and strained to see his visitor. Into view came an unfamiliar, expressionless face with slate-blue eyes, covered with a peppered beard, and topped with shaggy brown hair. The stranger spoke with dry compassion. "We finally meet. I'm Godfrey and have promised the Lady Almodis to watch over you."

"Almodis?" Simon repeated, befuddled.

"Yes, she arranged your Lady's visit and provided you your blanket. But it's not your benefactress that visits now," Godfrey added, unlocking Simon's cuff, "it's your father. He would speak to you."

Simon had known this dreaded time would eventually arrive, and welcomed it. He forced his cramped body after Godfrey and, as they reached the door, spoke lowly, "I thank you, Godfrey."

"And I hope your talk goes well, my Lord."

Simon stood, swayed a moment in the blinding torch light, then brushed dirt from his braies and self-consciously wiped his grimy hands on his tunic's skirt. He squinted into his father's all too familiar glower, and gasped as Robert's guards plucked him from the ground and roughly deposited him in a chair.

"Leave us," ordered Robert, and the guards quickly dispersed. His father's behavior muddled Simon. Robert rarely risked confrontation unprotected. A cup of wine appeared under Simon's nose with the command, "Drink this."

He downed the bitter potion in two gulps and raised bleary eyes to his father's rigid expression. "I'm shocked, Father. No guards?"

"You're obviously in no condition to pose a serious threat to anyone. Why do you think I left you in that cell for three days before meeting with you? And I won't be alone...Will?"

Will skulked into the room, a sardonic grin splitting his face.

"Now I'm *truly* frightened," muttered Simon under his breath.

"What did you say?" demanded Robert.

Simon answered with an exasperated shake of his head. Will swaggered to the table, rested forward on his palms, and sneered, "You should take better care of your appearance, little brother, though I *am* amazed you look so well-nourished."

"Do either of you have anything important to say," asked Simon peevishly, "or are we to spend our entire time together trading insults?"

"Will, control your tongue or leave," sighed Robert. "I won't tolerate a repeat performance of your drama at Berkhamstead. Now Simon, you will answer my questions—"

"Do you actually expect him to tell the truth?" interjected Will, ignoring his father's threat. "Why bother with all this formality? Punish him and have done with it."

"I'll warn no more, Will!" A bracing breath restored Robert's command and he asked, "Simon, you stand accused of pilfering documents from Dunheved Castle, interfering in matters that are solely my concern, harassing and lusting after my ward, plotting my and my brother's ruin—"

"And mine as well, Father!" cut in Will.

Robert's strict glare shut Will's mouth, and he finished, "And various other indiscretions. What say you in your defense?"

"Believe me, Father, I regret our reunion at least as much as you," said Simon wearily. "Maura's marriage document I took under the King's orders. No, not took, it was given freely."

"Yes, and Avenal has been duly punished for his betrayal."

"What!" Simon rose and viciously returned, "He did nothing wrong! How dare you hurt him because of our troubles? You're the one who deserves punishment!"

"You willfully defied me!"

"I never defied you! I only stopped a disaster. Rufus would have killed Maura, or perhaps that's what you intended all along. Hasn't she suffered enough abuse?"

"Any abuse Maura suffered was meant for you." Robert paced, fidgeted with the hem of his tunic, and fought to steady the wavering in his voice. "If you had stayed at Dunheved and accepted the sentence due you—"

"And if I'd stayed," Simon added with irony, "I suppose you would have let us marry and allowed us our child."

"So you knew about the child and still deserted her," chuckled Will. "How gallant of you. No wonder she despises you."

"You lying, stinking bastard!" burst Simon. "You were there when I returned for her! You knew where she'd been taken—"

"No...no...no." Will waggled his finger in Simon's face, and chided with a smirk, "You're terribly wrong, little brother. *You* are the bastard, *I* am the legitimate heir. I praised the day Father finally heeded my advice and threw Edith out, that Saxon whore!" Simon rose slowly from his chair, his fists clenched and reddened face glaring through a mask of dirt, yet Will recklessly scorned on, "And Father, it *was* Simon who betrayed

Maura's pregnancy to Grandfather Roger and ruined the Montgomery marriage, as he ruined the Rufus betrothal, Uncle Odo, and who's his next victim to be? Don't be a fool, old man, destroy him now, before he destroys you!"

Simon stormed round the table, startling Will from his seat. Robert barred his advance and shouted, "Sit down!"

"Get him from here," gritted Simon, "before I strangle his scrawny—"

"I said sit!"

"Father," said Will, "I suggest we bring at least one guard back, preferably the largest one. Your boy seems rather testy."

Simon glared at Will, postured a moment, then realized there was no use playing this spineless lump's violent games. He slumped back into his seat and hid his torment behind splayed fingers. But what use was talk? To his father, he would eternally be guilty, and as long as Will was near not an intelligible word would be spoken.

"Simon," said Robert, "it seems you've conveniently forgotten that I am your Liege Lord. I'm owed your absolute respect and—"

"I owe you nothing!" Simon tried to rise, but Robert clamped his shoulder, and shoved him back in the chair, making Simon rage louder, "You were quick enough to forget I was your son when Odo fell from grace!"

"And because of your treason he was unjustly imprisoned!"

"My treason? He stole the King's legions with the intent to kill the Pope! I consider *that* more than a just reason for imprisonment. And you know as well as I that he's never known the inside of a prison cell. He lives more comfortably than Will."

"Odo spent precious time training and educating you. He deserved your obedience!"

"The same blind obedience you pay him? I was told he planned to meet with the Pope to seek instruction and guidance, and that's all I told Uncle William. How could I have betrayed him when I was ignorant of his true motives? Father..." Simon's voice tensed with emotion. "Would you have trailed him to Rome and joined in his crime? You taught me never to ignore my conscience. Would you have shunned yours?" Robert remained rigid, unyielding, and Simon raved on, "Or was it a joint conspiracy?! Odo would seize total power as Pope, depose William, and you'd become his puppet king."

Robert's tenuous control almost snapped; he raised his arm to strike, but something stopped him and sent him pacing instead. His words rumbled with fury, "How dare you speak to me this way? I am your Lord!"

Simon's fist rocked the table. "How dare you treat your son like a common criminal? Uncle William believes in me, loves me, but then we share a common shame—bastardy."

"If William loves you so, why does he waste your skills? You ought to be in Normandy, battling for him, for me!"

"Your legitimate son doesn't feel the need to soil his hands for anyone. I fight battles, Father, with words, not swords. I didn't inherit your delight in killing."

"Father, I've heard enough of his impertinence," sniped Will. "Beat him now!"

"I agree," said Simon. "I've nothing more to say."

Robert surged for Simon's throat, seized his collar, and jerked him from the chair. Nose to nose, he groaned his frustration, "You were the best I had, the perfect warrior, a scholar! I was so proud of you. Under my guidance, you would have achieved excellence and been afforded anything you desired. And how did you repay me? You destroyed everything sacred we shared, trust, hope, love—"

"Love! What would you know of love?" Simon spat in disgust. "You're rotted with hate! All I wanted was Maura, yet without her to bargain with you'd lose your precious property. How much more suffering is needed to feed your greed?" He ripped from Robert's hold, squeezed his hands together to keep from striking out, and choked back tears, "Why didn't you hear me out? You condemned me without a trial. I never defied you, I worshipped you! I would have done anything you asked, fought your wars, died for you, anything! But you never let me explain..."

Simon's confession wounded Robert. He turned away, but Simon forced him back around and thrust his face close. "You will hear me now! That last night at Dunheved, you would have killed us all without a thought. Why did you banish my mother? She loved you and was blameless. How could you torture Maura and murder your own grandchild?! You are the guilty one, Father, and someday soon you and your *saintly* brother Odo will stew in Hell!"

A fleeting glint of compassion lit Robert's eyes; his fingers circled Simon's arms in a desperate grip, strain and urgency strangled his voice, "It's not too late! Kneel before me, son. Kneel to me, call me 'Lord' and all will be forgiven. Swear homage and you walk from here a free man. Do as I say, do it now!"

"Never!" sneered Simon.

Will stared aghast at his father. Robert's furrowed brow gleamed with sweat, his bent body shuddered, and his anguished wail rattled the room. Simon was winning, breaking Robert's spirit. A multitude of portents convulsed Will's mind. If they made peace, Simon, as second son, would inherit Robert's property in England, a substantially greater take than his piddling hold in Normandy. No, he couldn't let him win, he'd kill him first, kill him! Reaching for his dagger, Will crept toward the table and slyly muttered his appeal, "Don't let him torture you, Father. He's nothing. I'm the one who truly loves you. Uncle William has given him power over you. Rid yourself of this Saxon cur while William's away. No one need know."

"Silence!" hollered Robert. His head whirled, sharp pains stabbed his chest, the walls pressed closer. He had to get out of this chamber and escape this insanity!

Robert staggered for the stairs, but Simon's dire warning blared through the stagnant air and slowed his retreat. "If Odo is freed, Father, he'll fall again and, this time, take you down with him." Robert yelled for his guards and there followed a rush of tromping boots.

Simon spun to Will's stealthy advance, freezing his attack with a threat, "Challenge me and you die! Drop the knife and disappear!"

Without hesitation, Will tossed his dagger, shouldered crazily through the returning guards, and crouched in a darkened area under the stairs.

Simon turned to the cell door and saw his barrow in a new, beneficial light—a sanctuary from his deranged family. Yet before he reached the door, Robert's guards grabbed him. They dragged him to a pillar, wrapped his arms round its knotty girth, and bound his wrists. "Wha...what now?" he stammered, his tone thick with dread.

Robert's grave voice loomed near, "I've decided to offer you one final chance."

Simon twisted to see his father but a burly guard blocked his view. Huge hands seized both his shirt and tunic and effortlessly tore them from his back. The chilled air and fear raised bumps on his skin and Robert's bodiless voice continued to haunt, "You won't escape punishment, but it's your decision how severe your sentence is to be. You will be flogged. After ten lashes you can stop the guard simply by agreeing to swear fealty to me. If you cannot bring yourself to make the correct decision, you will be beaten till unconscious. And don't consider faking your collapse. That folly will only lengthen your punishment."

Robert stepped before Simon—so cold, formal, exact. The son searched the father's eyes for the glint of affection he had betrayed earlier, but found nothing, no hate, no despair...nothing. Simon wavered on wobbly knees, and embraced the pillar for support.

"Your answer, Simon, what's it to be?" Simon hung his shaking head. With a loud snort, Robert nodded to the brawny guard, but Will strolling back into the chamber distracted him. "Leave here now!" he shouted, pointing rigidly at the stairs.

"Oh, Father, I've waited years for this. Don't spoil my fun."

"You ghoul! If you're so eager to see people suffer, then you'll accompany me to Normandy. Go and ready yourself for the journey. We depart at dawn."

"No, you decrepit old sod! I stay in England!"

"There are two pillars here, Will," retorted Robert. "Would you care to hug one as well?"

Will heaved embarrassment and rage as he caught Simon's triumphant smirk. For a brief moment, he considered tearing the whip from the guard's hand and having at Simon himself. The alarming sight of two guards coming for him cooled his temerity, and he scurried away.

As the lashes stripped the skin off his back, Simon allowed himself only one expression of pain, his nails gouging deep cuts in the bark. He forced his mind to Maura's suffering, and the thought that at last he shared her torture kept him quiet and standing.

Robert remained in the chamber till Simon sank unconscious to the base of the pole. It had taken so long, too long. Each lashing only empowered his son's pride, his stubbornness, his spirit. Robert crouched to check his breath. He'd seen men die when subjected to a lesser scourge, but still his son breathed, and he was shocked to hear himself whisper, "Thank God." His purpose wasn't to kill Simon, only to teach him respect—something he'd lost in himself years past. He too had felt each biting lash, hoping to ease the heavy guilt that endlessly plagued him, but still it lingered. His fingers brushed the gash on Simon's cheek. As Simon fell, the guard had struck one last time, whipping his face. For an instant, Robert considered killing the guard, only—the blame was no one's but his own. Sadly, he recalled a time long ago when Simon had been knocked senseless from a fall. Robert had held him through the night, praying for his recovery. If only they could return to that gentler time!

Roland's question broke his fleeting reverie, "What's to be done with him, my Lord?"

"What?" Robert mumbled.

"What's to be done with the prisoner, my Lord?"

Pensively, Robert stayed beside Simon, then shook his head and faintly replied, "I don't know..."

"We can't leave him there, my Lord."

Robert stiffened and stood, his stoic mask firmly set. He cleared his mind of cumbersome emotions and muttered, "He'll stay in his cell till a fortnight past Easter." Hurrying from the chamber, he rested against the wall at the foot of the stairs, wiped his damp face and eyes with his sleeve, and agonized. Simon and Edith were forever lost to him. And what was left? Will? What a pretty monster he'd created there. Hope lit his dripping eyes as he thought of the child not yet born. Yes...the child would replace Simon in his hardened heart!

Roland and Thomas tossed Simon into the cell, not bothering to manacle him. Once the door shut the rats thrust their noses in the air. The stench of blood stirred them to a frenzy; they swarmed over Simon and plunged their teeth into his seeping flesh.

Godfrey and Guy, Henry's guard, returned to the chamber, Godfrey asking, "Do we still have a prisoner to guard?"

"Yes, he got spanked a bit, that's all," sniggered Roland.

Confusion turned to panic, as Godfrey spied a trail of blood running from the pillar's base to the cell door. "Fetch the key!" he shouted. The guards stood stupefied, and he hotly explained, "The rats, you fools! Once they smell his blood, they'll rip him apart. Pass the candle!"

Godfrey flung open the door and crawled inside. The flickering taper scattered most of the vermin, he beat off the stragglers. Roland tried to close the door, but Godfrey's boot stopped him. "Leave it," he said, "he won't be going anywhere and we need the light." He set the candle by Simon's side and, in a vain attempt to staunch the bleeding, wrapped the blanket taut around his chest. Then letting out a deep desolate sigh, he settled back against the cell's weeping wall, where he would hold his watch all through the long night.

*****

CHAPTER FIFTEEN - EXCEPTIONAL FAVORS

"Damn this blasted rain! I'm soaked to the bone," cried Henry, desperate for warmth, as he stamped in a circle in the King's tent north of Rouen. "And because of your hare-brained romantic scheme, I'll surely catch my death!" Henry downed a long swig from a flagon of wine, swabbed his mouth with his sleeve, and let out a flagrant belch. "Lord, this is vile stuff, but it's all there is. Would you care for a swig, my Lady?"

"Perhaps it will warm me a bit," replied Maura, shrouded in a blanket. She sipped, shuddered, and frowned. "It *is* horrible."

"Ah, but there comes a point where the taste becomes irrelevant." He swiped the flagon from her and guzzled more. "I'm sorry, Maura," he said after another belch, "I thought Father would be here."

"How could you know he'd still be at Rouen? Besides, Lord Roger said he's to arrive tomorrow mid-day."

"Yes, well...I need to fetch provisions—food, blankets, better wine, and...are you still itching?"

"Terribly."

"Ointment, I mustn't forget the ointment. And I forbid you to leave this tent while I'm away."

She regarded him curiously. He was fidgety and restless, and not only from the cold. "I'll not budge," she said, "I swear."

"Then I'll return shortly. Try to make yourself as comfortable as possible considering..." His eyes swept the slick ground; mud oozed between rushes, and buckets were scattered haphazardly to catch the leaking rain, some near to overflowing. "And I'll dump these," he said, snatching up a few pails. Yet he hesitated and, instead, stood gawking at Maura.

"What is it, Henry?"

"Pardon?" he asked dreamily.

"Is there a problem?"

"No..."

"Then go."

"Yes...I'll go."

Maura smiled affectionately as Henry slipped away under the tent's flap. Since they had made peace it had been quite pleasant to be with him. He reminded her of a playful puppy, a bit ornery, too eager to please, and craving constant stimulation. Maura tugged the blanket closer, chafed her arms for heat, and ambled casually about the tent, scrutinizing its contents. The heavy downpour battered the roof and a brusque wind rippled and strained the tent's walls. Two chairs flanked a trestle table used as a desk, with parchments strewn across its top; a thickly padded cot, piled with skins, sat close to a wall; various pieces of armor and weapons were piled high up against another wall; and a short awning entryway jutted from the circular room.

There wasn't much to interest her, so Maura ducked under the flap and peered out over the crown-shaped roofs of dozens of tents crowding the mouth of a blackened curtain wall. Dense gray clouds hovering low veiled the keep, and at Maura's feet rushed a stream swelled by the deluge and sewage. She listened but heard no sounds of war, only the wail of the tempest. An eerie peace prevailed. Two young bedraggled soldiers strolled by the King's tent. They paused at the startling sight of Maura, women being forbidden from the siege site, and grinned lewdly. Uneasiness gripped her and she returned to the safety of the inner room. Bored, she listlessly thumbed through the stack of documents gracing the King's desk, but found nothing intriguing, only maps and drawings of the bailey and interior of the keep. Blank sheets of parchment lay in a neat pile, a quill and ink well nearby. A notion struck her; instead of waiting for the King's clerk to draw up Simon's release documents, they could perform the task themselves, and leave for England immediately following the King's arrival! She rubbed her hands together over a hooded candle and joyously imagined Simon's deliverance, wondering, would they be allowed time together alone—time to forgive and remember?

Henry stumbled into the room, drenched, his arms bulging with bread loaves, cheese, two flagons of wine, and a porcelain jar exuding an offensive odor. He spilled these riches across the table and flashed her a winning smile.

"Henry, this truly is a feast!" flattered Maura. She plucked the porcelain jar from the pile, sniffed, and recoiled from its stench. "I hope you don't expect me to *eat* this!"

"Don't be silly, Maura, it's the ointment. It is guaranteed to kill any living creature that dares nibble your luscious body." He playfully chomped at her hand. "*Tiny* creatures, that is."

He retreated in feigned horror as she teasingly waved the jar under his nose. Another whiff made her question, "But will I be able to live with myself?"

"Well, one thing's certain," he chuckled, "on your return trip you'll sleep soundly on the ship's deck with no distractions."

She smiled slyly and arched a brow. "Then I'll take care to apply it liberally this night."

Simpering, Henry sliced his dagger through the cheese and ripped apart the bread. Maura settled herself cross-legged on the cot, accepted her share, and said intently, "Henry, explain something to me."

"Mmmmhhh?" he mumbled through a mouthful of bread.

"I expected a war, but the armies seem to be having a friendly visit. It's so quiet."

"Yes, too damned quiet," he said, emptying the first flagon.

"What's happening here?"

Henry sighed gruffly, sat in his father's chair, and plopped his feet upon the table. "Laying siege doesn't necessarily mean hand-to-hand combat, Maura. Actually the armies prefer a siege like this one, there are fewer casualties. If what's happening here is following the usual pattern, my father's men first attempted to starve King Philip's men out of the castle by blocking grain deliveries and setting fire to nearby fields and storage buildings within the bailey. If unsuccessful, they next try poisoning the water supply and ramming the main doors. Lastly, they'll collapse the curtain wall."

"How?"

"Sappers dig mines under the base of the stone and slip supporting beams along the expanse. Once they're assured of downing a substantial chunk of wall, they burn the supporting beams and the wall comes tumbling down, just like Jericho. I saw Marc," he added nonchalantly. "He's digging a tunnel."

Maura dropped her jaw, bread, and cheese; leapt from the cot, and rushed for the exit, gasping, "I must see him!"

"No, Maura!" shouted Henry, launching from his seat and grabbing her arm. "You can't enter the mines. It's far too dangerous."

"For him as well?"

"It's his duty to accept the dangers. I mentioned you were here. He'll visit when his work is done. Wine!" Henry spouted brightly. "You need more wine."

"No, I don't think so."

"You're *so* dull, Maura. Don't you believe in enjoying yourself?" he asked a tad too giddily.

"Of course I do, when the time is right, but it's *not* the right time, Henry." She glanced to the door and grudgingly abandoned her flight to Marc, suggesting instead, "While we're stuck here, I feel we should script Simon's release document."

"Fine, do what you like. You needn't write anything impressive. Father doesn't read well."

"Must I write it in Latin?"

"He wouldn't care if it was in Greek."

"Good. My Latin is poor."

"You write Greek?!" exclaimed Henry, agape.

Maura rolled her eyes and supplanted him in the King's chair. She removed the stopper from the ink well and, dipping the quill, encouraged, "Help me, Henry. Simon mentioned you excelled at composition and I've noticed you have an impressive vocabulary."

"That's Simon's doing. He teaches me a new word each time we meet. I admit I do speak well, but writing..." He paused to a flush of embarrassment.

"But Simon told me your teachers believed you'd become an excellent clerk."

Slightly wounded, he attested, "Maura, over the past four years my aspirations have risen high above *clerk*." He grabbed a map and studied it distractedly.

In regret, she muttered, "Oh, I see...Well then, what if we make this a joint task? You dictate and I'll play scribe."

Henry dropped the map and beamed waggishly, "Yes! Let's fuddle them all and script it in English. Do you know English?"

"Yes, but I think it should be in French. Do you know English?"

"Enough to get by." He draped his thigh on the corner of the table, and continued his sprightly interrogation. "Did Simon teach you English?"

Maura tested the ink on the parchment. "No, Edith taught me to speak and write English. She learned to write while a servant to King Edward's wife. Simon and I spoke English when we were together, except...well, at times we spoke French."

"And Marc, what language does he prefer?"

"He speaks both English and French, but curses in English. He says it sounds more vulgar than French."

Henry laughed. "It's difficult imagining Marc cursing. Your household must have been quite confusing."

"No, it seemed completely natural. I lived a truly marvelous life...before I left Dunheved. Now, how should this read?"

Intrigued, Henry probed further, "So you write in English, French, and Latin?"

"Yes. What is the date?"

"It's the third week of January. I don't know the exact day. Do you *read* Latin?"

"Yes, I need to be able to read it to write it...Why?"

"I'm stunned. I thought girls spent their childhood studying embroidery, music, theology, dance..."

"Rose and Edith insisted we all have a thorough education. At first we resisted, yet as we grew we came to realize the value of learning. And Henry, your mother was a very learned woman, as are your sisters."

"Yes, and I dare say far more intelligent than my brothers. Adela would make a formidable queen, don't you think?"

Maura smiled in agreement and launched her own interrogation, "Are you friendly with your brother Robert Curthose?"

"Not overly. We *were* close, but when I was ten Rufus enlisted my help in dousing Robert with water from an upstairs window while Robert strolled in the bailey. Our relationship hasn't been quite the same since. I've discovered it's best to play Rufus and Robert off against each other. They both believe they have my full allegiance. That way, whoever wins—I win."

"That makes perfect sense, I suppose."

"Maura, when I become King, you could prove every bit as useful as Simon. And I must say you're a hell of lot prettier than he is. As you know, I'll need advisors, mediators, translators, and clerks. A female clerk..." he pondered with a mischievous smirk. "A novel idea that would certainly shock the clergy, which is such great fun."

"And when do you expect to become King?"

Henry's pained gaze slipped to his lap, and when it rose again, it was as if the question had never been raised. "Let's get this done," he said resolutely.

While he gulped the last of the second flagon and casually dictated the writ, he scrutinized her intent expression and careful scripting. So this was the sort of woman that attracted Simon. He'd always wondered, and now seeing her this way, it wasn't so surprising. Simon didn't share Henry's preference for simple, clawing women. He seemed much more at ease with women who could converse as intelligently as he. And she *was* attractive in an awkward sort of way. She owned far too many freckles of course, was a bit too thin, and her height was intimidating. He preferred to look down at a woman, it seemed fitting that way. But her hair—he wouldn't mind catching his fingers in its lush waves; her skin glowed pink, and he was sure its touch was feather soft. If only he had an opportunity to—He hiccupped and clumsily set the flagon on the table, praying he wouldn't be required to make any critical decisions this night.

Maura dusted the ink and proudly passed the parchment to him. "Will this do?"

He blinked at what he beheld as a mess of mere scribbles, widened his drooping lids, then squinted. "It's fine...fine."

"Somewhere, I must add a sentence that I traveled here on my own."

"Don't bother, let Father's clerk do that...Maura?"

"Yes?" she asked attentively.

"No...nothing. I'll leave you with the ointment and keep guard outside." Glancing at the ceiling, he cocked his head and listened. "The rain seems to have let up and the air will do me good." He rose carefully, swayed, and had to grip the arms of the chair for balance.

Maura stood to help. "What is it?"

"I suppose I'm tired."

"I'll hurry then."

"No, take all the time you need." Henry snatched up the flagon and wobbled out through the entry. The stench of fear permeated the damp night air and, leaning against the hemp that secured the tent, he whispered an anxious prayer, "Please God, let us secure Father's signature and leave here before this siege erupts into total war." The cook who had provided him food had told of late raids by King Philip's men. He must tell Maura; expecting trouble would make her better prepared to defend herself. Again, he found the flagon pressed to his lips. It was vital he keep a clear head, but he couldn't seem to stop himself. The deadly potion failed to warm his blood, so he shivered and hugged himself in the bodeful quiet.

Henry craved Maura's solacing company and peeked under the flap, only to be astounded by what he beheld. Clad only in her chemise, Maura stood with her back to the entry. The table's candles silhouetted her body, allowing him to view her shape vividly beneath the lucid garment. His leering stare traveled from her feet upward. She was long, willowy, and slim-hipped; his hands could easily encircle her tiny waist. She set one foot on the cot, lifted the chemise to her thigh, and smoothed on the ointment using long graceful strokes. Wisps of hair had escaped her braid and glistened like tiny flames in the taper's light. She slipped her chemise off one shoulder to tend her upper arm, and he grasped the flap as the tent's furnishings whirled before his bleary eyes. No longer able to contain himself, Henry took a bolstering swig of wine, gulped it, and crept up behind her. His hand covered hers.

Maura's violent gasp whirled her round; the jar flew to the ground, spilling a portion of its noxious contents. "Henry," she cried, "you scared me!"

She bent to retrieve the jar and he crouched beside her, his large eyes reeking innocence. "I...I'm sorry," he stumbled. "I was cold and...and thought you might need help with your back."

"How long have you been watching me?" she demanded, suddenly feeling naked.

"Not long," he said unconvincingly.

Maura hid herself in her blanket and stole the flagon from him. "I think you've had quite enough of this."

"I apologize, really I do," sniveled Henry. "But you're not done and we can't have you scratching yourself raw. Please let me help, Maura."

He cast her a look so sincere, she felt her anger melting, and muttered, "It's true, I can't reach my back."

Henry hid his foxy smile and motioned to the cot. Maura haltingly handed him the ointment, perched herself on the edge of the bed, and unveiled her back. A look of rakish triumph spoiled his innocence as he rubbed his palms together and proceeded to loosen her braid. Her hands flew to her head to stop him, but he slapped them away, insisting, "I'll check your scalp for bugs." His fingers worked magic, parting strands with easing, circular movements, then walking down her neck, kneading knots of tension on their journey.

Maura's eyes closed and breath deepened as her shoulders welcomed his soothing touch. Slowly, she realized he wasn't applying the ointment. She turned slightly and chided, "Henry, the ointment, use the ointment." This brief distraction was all he needed. His hands slipped from her shoulders to her breasts, only she was quicker and stopped his exploration by clamping hold his wrists. "No!" she yelled. "You apply the ointment or stand in the rain till I'm done!"

Highly miffed, he scooped a glob of ointment, slapped it on her back, and rubbed it roughly into her skin all the while whining, "You never let me have any fun. It wasn't my fault. My hands happen to do as they please."

"So I've noticed. Will you never quit?"

"Maura," he answered decisively, "the day I quit, they'll be hammering nails in my coffin."

As he spoke, his fingers roamed lower and lower, prompting her to remind, "My back doesn't go down that far!"

He huffed frustration and wiped his hands on his braies. "Well, then I suppose I'm done. Now explain something to me, Maura. Why do you hide your exquisite body under layers of shapeless wool?"

"It's not exquisite and I wear wool for the simple reason that it would be ridiculous to travel battlegrounds in silk. Now," she added, wrapped again in her blanket, "I'm tired and wish to sleep on *this* cot. There's a mat underneath for you." As he reluctantly unrolled the mat, she noticed his pout and asked, "What is it now, Henry? Are you sulking because I spurned you?" He shrugged and she probed further, "Hasn't any woman lingered in your mind for more than a few ecstatic moments?"

He thought a long, groggy while, then answered, "No."

"Well...that makes you a very lonely man."

"Not necessarily," he claimed. "And who lingers in your mind? Simon?"

Maura sank her head into the King's pillow and responded with a slim smirk.

"Lucky devil," he muttered. "He certainly seems smitten with you."

"Someday, Henry, there will be someone."

"Perhaps...My advice, Maura, is for you and Simon to bed down soon...You're awfully tense."

"I thank you for your concern," she said warmly.

"It's available...anytime." He stretched out on the mat and shifted to face her. "Maura," he said soberly, "there have been raids at night. Don't sleep soundly and keep close the dagger I gave you."

"I will. Goodnight, Henry."

"Goodnight, my Lady."

As her breathing slowed, Maura's hair, now free, cascaded down the side of the cot. He wiggled closer and combed his fingers through its silkiness. The tender act roused his body. Though terribly difficult, he would have to accustom himself to the fact that he could not have her. He shifted away, and realized that since their congenial night together, she had been forever on his mind. He sought to remedy the unfortunate situation by sniffing the spilt ointment, listening to the dripping rain, and finally drifting off to sleep.

They woke to a tremendous crash and the quaking ground jogged them from their beds. "The wall!" Henry cried, scrambling from his mat. "It's down!"

Maura studied him intently. He stood, his anxious gaze aimed at the ground, and his head cocked alertly. She wriggled into her tunic and listened with him. At first there was nothing, then came sharp commands, flurried steps, the clanging of armor and weapons, and finally...shrieks. "Henry, what's happened?!" she implored, joining him in the center of the tent.

He spoke with rampant worry, "Philip's men may charge the tents and this is the one they'll come for first. Get your dagger. We must flee now!" Maura acted as swiftly as his speech; she belted her tunic and secured the dagger to her waist. Henry hooked his sword to his belt and reached out to her, blurting, "Come, hurry!"

They burst through the entryway, but were stopped at the fore of the tent as dozens of frenzied soldiers blocked their escape. Henry grabbed a sprinting sentry and yelled, "What's happened?"

"The enemy's sappers attacked the mines," he panted, "and the fighting jarred the supporting beams and brought down the wall. Philip's army scaled the stones! They're on their way—" He wrenched from the Prince and bolted away.

"Marc!" cried Maura. "We must find Marc!"

"There isn't time!"

"I will go to Marc!" She resisted mightily as he struggled to drag her with him. They wrestled and stumbled through the mud, then from above a curiously chilling sound stilled their fight. Scores of flaming arrows rained down from the heavens. Screeching soldiers dropped from the darts' assault.

Henry's shrill command, "Do not fight me!" jostled Maura's resistance, and she followed.

They ran and quickly became entangled in a small contingent of men. She lost Henry's hand as another flurry of arrows cut through the heavy clouds, randomly impaling the soldiers. A man fell at Maura's feet, the weapon jutting from his eye. The deadly buzz sounded again. Someone flung her to the ground and dropped over her. She strained under her protector, gasping for breath, and trying to cry out, but the wails of wounded soldiers drowned her pleas. As arrows stabbed the ground by her head, the body above her jerked once then seemed to wilt. Her frantic wriggling finally freed her from its weight. Henry lay on his belly before her, unconscious, an arrow stuck in his shoulder. She knelt and yanked him to his side. "Henry!" she cried, "Henry, wake up!" Rubbing and slapping his face were of no help, and she knew the next firing would soon come. She could see the King's tent through the chaos; it was so near, yet seemed a kingdom away. Another whirring sent her diving across Henry's body. Miraculously, they were spared the deadly pricks. She muttered a fleeting prayer of thanks and scrambled to her feet.

Clutching his hands, she groaned as she tugged him on his belly, sliding him through the muck and over bodies to the tent's entryway. With a resounding grunt and a great heave, she propelled them under the flap just as another barrage of arrows hit. One punctured the tent and its flame began an insidious creep up the wall.

Maura paused for breath. Suddenly the flap lifted and Marc, his face blackened and bleeding, rushed inside. She dropped Henry's arms and almost trod on him striving to reach her brother. "Marc! Oh, Marc," she wailed, catching him in a desperate hug. "I thought you dead! Help me. Please, help me get Henry inside. He's been hit!"

"Philip's men are advancing this way," he warned. "You can't stay!"

"I won't leave him!"

Marc's bellow, "Help's needed! The King's tent!" instantly rallied a troop contingent. The wall now blazed brightly. While Maura drenched the flames with buckets of rain, Marc beat at the wall with blankets and volleyed orders. "Get the Prince under the table! Arm yourselves, quickly! Maura," he shouted, stealing the pail from her, "you join Henry."

"But, Marc—"

"Now!" he demanded. Vicious rumblings encroached and Marc's intense expression sent her scuttling under the table. "Hide them with the blankets," he instructed the soldiers. The table was swiftly draped; the cloth hung an inch from the ground, allowing only a view of boots. The men donned the armor, unsheathed their swords, and braced for attack. It came quickly. With a great combined howl, Philip's men stormed the tent, swinging maces and brandishing swords. Maura winced and tensed to the fierce screech of clashing metal. How could they survive such savagery? She clung to Henry and pressed her head to his chest. Relief engulfed her as she heard his heart's strong steady beat. His skin was cool, yet dripped sweat; he shivered violently. She sat and covered him with her tunic's skirt. Boots intruded on their cramped refuge, perilously rocking their table. She glanced up between the separations in the blankets and saw Marc, his face distorted with rage, teeth bared, and foam spewing from his taut lips. His rival's boot tread on her hand. Swiftly, she gripped her dagger and plunged it deeply into the soft leather. A sword instantly answered her assault, sweeping downward and slicing her forearm. She recoiled from the strike and screamed as a body rammed the table, scattering the blankets. Frantically gathering up the cloth, she cloaked herself and Henry, and stared up into the face of Marc's victim, dangling upside down from the edge of the table. Blood spurted from his nose and gaping mouth, spattering their cover. At the gruesome sight, Maura grew woozy, and her dizziness surged as she realized the blood that soaked the wool came not from the dead soldier but from herself. The light, already faint, faded to black as Maura slumped heavily over Henry's still figure.

Maura woke to hauberk-clad strangers lowering her onto a mat. The towering beams above told her she was in a great hall. She whipped her head from side to side, straining to find Marc and Henry. Had she been captured, had they? She struggled to sit but was gently restrained and blanketed. "No, my Lady, stay," said a young, pale-haired soldier. "Your brother will be with you shortly."

Her voice and body shook, "Hen...Henry...where?"

"Beside you, my Lady."

Attending soldiers blocked her view of his face; his chest was bare, his skin gray. She saw a candle, the flash of a dagger, a cloth dyed red with blood. As she stretched out to touch his arm, the blond soldier intervened. "You wouldn't want to see, my Lady." But she did want to see! Everything about him that had annoyed her before, she now craved!

"Maura!" Marc's face appeared before her, lined with dirt and worry. "Have you pain?"

She hadn't thought of her wound. "Henry...is he dead?"

"No," said Marc, carefully lifting the blanket and easing up the sleeve of her tunic, "his wound is superficial. Why are you here, and why with Henry?"

His harsh tone confused her. She tried to answer, only her lips refused to cooperate. He continued to talk, his voice dwindling, then encountering her wound, he blared to no one in particular, "I need wine, bandages. Hurry! There's a lot of blood."

The blood, she remembered the blood, but why was there no pain? Marc tugged at her arm and she heard him rip her chemise's sleeve. The sounds of the hall blended to a discordant drone. The ceiling whirled. She shut her eyes and felt herself floating upward. Marc held her fast in his arms, his voice sounded distant, "You must stay very still, Maura, and if need be, bite into my shoulder."

Bite his shoulder? Why would she want to bite his shoulder? She buried her face in his shirt and hid from the moans and misery, but a nearby groan made her shove from Marc's hold. "Henry!" she cried, looking to the spot where he had lain.

"No, Maura!" Marc returned as desperately. There was no Henry, only the sight of red liquid being poured over her jagged gash, liquid that scalded and split the cut wider. A shrill scream masked all the other sounds of agony; it was her own scream, and then came silence.

*****

"Henry!" The bellicose voice roused Henry from his light sleep. He struggled to rise, but the brace that held his arm hindered his balance.

"Fa...Father," he stuttered, growing quite pale.

"What's this I hear about you bringing a woman to my tent?!"

"Not a woman, Father, Maura. I escorted Maura to your tent. She was determined to see you. I ensured her safety, nothing more." Exhausted and pained, Henry slumped back upon his mat.

William's dark scowl lightened; he lumbered closer, knelt, and tenderly touched his youngest son's cheek. "Let me see what you've suffered."

"It's nothing...a scratch."

"Scratches are not braced. I'll have you sent to Rouen, where my physician can have a look at you."

"Let me stay, Father. I can help hold the castle."

"No, I have sufficient forces here, you're not needed."

"But I want to help. You knighted me this past summer for precisely that reason."

"I have other plans in mind for you. I believe I ordered you to stay in England and watch over Rufus."

"Why do you allow rule to someone who has to be *watched over*?"

"Henry..." said William impatiently.

Henry paused and sulked. There really was no point arguing the matter. To his father, he would always be a child with no true purpose.

"And what's all this?" William asked, motioning to a mass of rumpled parchment strewn alongside Henry's mat.

"Oh," said Henry with a twinge of anxiety, "I was...writing." He shifted and extracted one intact sheet, thoroughly scripted, and passed it to the King.

William took a long look, and remarked brightly, "I'm highly impressed, Henry! You've done very well. I only wish I had taken the time to acquire such a talent. Now tell me, what does it say?"

Henry braced for the eruption and answered swiftly, "That you insist upon Simon's release and if your order isn't instantly carried out, all involved will be severely punished."

The skin slipped from the King's fingers, and his austere look struck terror in Henry's already thudding heart. "Simon's release from where?"

"Uh...prison."

"And *who* is responsible for his incarceration?"

"I can't say."

"You will say," fumed William.

"No, Father," said Henry, pleadingly, "It will only cause him more harm."

"This is unacceptable, Henry! You will betray the scoundrels to me. Was it Rufus?"

"No."

"My brother Robert?" asked William firmly.

Henry grew rigid and dropped his timorous gaze to his lap.

"Damn him!" flared William. "Robert knows I'm too busy wrangling with Philip to stop his treachery. What are his plans for Simon?"

"I don't know, my Lord," Henry feebly answered.

"And Rufus...What has he done to halt this debacle?"

"Not a thing."

"That lazy, inept fool! Why I'll—"

"Simon was taken secretly!" cut in Henry. "I heard of the episode from Maura. He's being held at Westminster, and Rufus will release him only if he receives your signed statement demanding his freedom."

"He doesn't need my signature!" William's arms beat at the air as he paced and kicked away scorched pieces of wood that once had been a bed. "I swear my cursed family delights in tormenting me!"

"You can't presently return to England, but Maura can. Please, Father, sign the writ and deal with Robert and Rufus later. Simon needs your loyalty."

William's fingers massaged his aching head. The thought of Simon holed up in the squalid cells of Westminster set his blood boiling. But he was powerless to help. His army south, in Maine, was encountering fierce resistance and begged his presence, and he had overstayed his visit here. Henry's wan, deprived look infected him with a heavy dose of remorse. He knelt and reached for a quill.

"Bless you, Father, bless you!" gushed Henry, grasping his hand.

"My clerk will attach my seal," said William decisively. "Marc can see his sister safely to the coast. You will recover at Rouen and, once the enemy in the south have been vanquished, I'll return and we'll spend some needed time together." The King planted two swift kisses on Henry's cheeks and rose to leave, muttering, "Keep yourself safe and out of mischief, lad."

Henry's eyes pooled with tears of gratitude as he choked, "I...I'll try. Father, wait!"

William paused in the door. "What is it?"

"After my wounding, Maura dragged me to your tent..." He hesitated and, with difficulty, admitted, "I suppose she saved my life."

The King replied with deep indulgence, "Then we are forever in her debt."

"Hurry back," rasped Henry as his father's great bulk disappeared out the door.

*****

When next Maura woke all had changed. The hall was gone, as were the soldiers, Marc, and Henry. She lay alone upon a thin mat set on a planked floor in an empty chamber. Sunlight filtered through an arrow loophole behind her, casting a radiant cross on the facing wall. It must be dawn, Maura thought, as she strained to lift her head. The effort caused blurring eyesight, and a heavy sadness weighted her body. She whispered to the ajar door, "Marc," then forced her ragged voice louder, "Marc, are you there?" He answered briskly and, before he could ask how she fared, she blurted, "Has the King arrived? It's crucial that I speak to him." She tensed to his distraught expression, and asked urgently, "What's wrong?"

"The King," answered Marc carefully, "the King's come and gone. He asked to see you, but you were asleep."

Maura flew up from the mat and fiercely gripped his shoulders. "No, he can't have gone!" She struggled to rise, yet dizziness kept her on her knees. "He was to come midday, it's only dawn!"

"But Maura," he said gently, easing her back to the mat. "You've slept a full day and night since the raid."

She wailed with panic, "No! I don't believe you!"

"Why would I lie? You mustn't exert yourself, you've lost a fair amount of blood." But Maura didn't hear his caution. She tried to rise again, and he forcibly held her prone. "No, Maura! What's come over you? Why did you come here with Henry? He's not to be trusted. It was a foolish, dangerous act!" He stopped his lecture to search her anguished expression.

She futilely fought his hold, her faint moan echoing in the vacant chamber. "Bring him back, Marc, bring him, bring—" Her sobbed plea abruptly faded as she lapsed once more into unconsciousness.

He laid her back down and lovingly stroked her cheek. "Rest, sister. Only rest will give you back your strength." Through his kind touch, her weakness infected him. He buried his face in his hands and languished; he loathed this place, there was nothing but horror here. How he longed to return with her and Simon to their idyllic Dunheved, where he'd be free of the terror and despair that forever plagued him!

*****

Almodis appeared quite unexpectedly before Roland and Thomas and interrupted their dice game. "I would see the prisoner," she said, the guile in her voice gone. She looked to the cell door and saw it was open. Confused, she strode across the room and warily wondered, "Where's Godfrey?"

A tall, slim, red-haired young man stood and answered, "He guards the prisoner from inside, my Lady."

"And who might you be?"

"Guy, my Lady. I serve Henry FitzRoy. He's ordered me here."

Her bewilderment grew and she repeated, "I would see the prisoner."

"I don't believe that's wise, my Lady."

"I don't care what you believe! I will see him."

Godfrey woke to her familiar voice, and stuck his head out the door. "My Lady?"

"Godfrey," she said with a relieved smile. "Please allow me a moment with Simon."

"As you wish, my Lady. The door must stay open, the light keeps the rats away."

She winced at his announcement, inhaled deeply and, hiking her skirts, boldly crawled into the cell.

Simon lay on his belly, a candle by his face, and she called out lightly, "Simon?"

"Maura!" he gasped faintly, struggling to raise his head.

"No, it's Almodis." Bending closer, she noticed a darkened spot on his cheek. The wound was new, still moist, and caked with mud. "Was he bitten?" she asked Godfrey.

"Not on his face, my Lady."

"Fetch water, Godfrey. I will cleanse his face." Godfrey left to fill the pitcher with water, and Almodis spoke delicately, "Simon, after our visit I leave for Winchester. Maura should return within the week. According to Alan, Henry is with her. Please believe that she loves you, and don't despair." There was no response to her hopeful speech; he lay deathly still, his unseeing stare reflecting a distant agony, his fingers scratching the dirt.

Godfrey, sloshing water, squeezed in beside Almodis, and produced a clean linen towel. Tenderly, Almodis smoothed the soaked towel over Simon's face and bathed the gash. "Godfrey," she gently chided, "you must try to keep the cut clean, or a terrible infection could result.

"I'll do my best, my Lady."

"And the blanket I gave you," she added, "It's to cover him, not to—"

"No, my Lady." He stopped her hand from touching the make-shift bandage. "You will hurt him."

An uneasiness crept her spine and she trepidly asked, "*How* did Robert punish him?"

Godfrey lifted the candle and held it near as he peeled back a corner of the blanket to expose Simon's scourged back. There was no skin visible beneath the congealed blood.

The towel fell from Almodis' hands as they muffled her startled moan. She recoiled against the door, and gasped, "Why?!"

Wagging his head, Godfrey rewrapped Simon's back, and lowered the candle. "We must get him from here!"

"How, my Lady?"

"I don't know...I don't—" Almodis paused to the sound of a rough demanding voice resounding through the open door.

She leant toward the light and heard the new voice ask, "Is this cell full?"

"It holds one man and can house three more," answered Roland.

"A wagon in the bailey holds fifteen poachers. William FitzRoy demands their imprisonment. Who occupies this cell?"

"Lord Robert's son."

There was a pause in the terse discourse, then the stranger asked tentatively, "Lord William?"

"No, Robert's bastard."

"And what's his crime?"

"Treason"

"Of what sort?"

"That we don't know."

Almodis pieced the scanty clues together. There were prisoners awaiting incarceration under Rufus' orders and too few cells. A scheme flashed in her mind—a scheme that, if performed expertly, could result in Simon's freedom. And there was no one more expert at performance than she. "Godfrey," she said eagerly, "Follow the Prince's sentry. If he suggests to Rufus that Simon be freed to make room for the poachers, insist upon Lord Robert's order that he stay imprisoned till a fortnight after Easter. Keep repeating Robert's wish."

"What good will that serve, my Lady?"

"There's no time to explain, just do as I say, then return here and continue your vigil. If Simon is released..." She paused, dug into a pouch tied to her wrist, and removed Alan's map. "Take him here, to Alan's brother's home. I must leave for Winchester. Your loyalty has inspired my trust. After Simon is safely away, I want you to join me at Winchester to serve as my personal guard."

"I will be honored to serve you, my Lady."

"Bless you, Godfrey, and pray Rufus acts quickly. Now go!"

Almodis reached down and smoothed Simon's matted hair from his brow. Her heart ached at his silent torment and she mourned, "I'm sorry for your father's cruelty. I did try to stop him but he can be so bullish. It may help to know that he was quite shaken from your meeting." Her hand rested on his. "I must go."

His hand tensed. She could barely hear his plea, "No...*please* stay."

"I must go and speak to Rufus. With luck, I may be able to convince him to release you...with luck. Simon?" His eyes shut and hand relaxed and she knew he could no longer hear. Shedding her cloak, she covered him with the dense fur, and rambled on with deep emotion, "Keep still and warm, Simon. When next we meet, you and Maura will be reunited, and I will do all I can to keep you together...forever." She emerged from the cell pale and shaken, and beckoned to Guy.

"Yes, my Lady."

"Guy, keep watch over the prisoner and see to his comfort. Godfrey will soon return."

"I will, my Lady."

"I have one last request. I seem to have misplaced my cloak. May I have use of yours?"

"Of course, my Lady." He grinned knowingly, snatched his mantle from a peg on the wall, and offered it to her with a compliment, "It was kind of you, my Lady...to visit Simon."

"Yes, I'm fond of my stepson." She smiled plaintively at the young man's politeness as he draped the cloak around her shoulders. "I'll take my leave and I thank you, Guy."

"My pleasure, my Lady."

Almodis waited a fretful hour before requesting to meet with Rufus. The doors to the great hall at last groaned opened for her and she entered to Rufus' boomed greeting, "Well, if it isn't the great whore!"

"And I'm thrilled to see you as well, dear Prince," she simpered back.

His guise was as gross as ever, his skin spotted with sores, eyes reddened and lids puffy from drink, his hair tangled and beard smeared with his most recent meal. "What do you want?" he grumbled. "I've no time for petty complaints."

"And what *do* you have time for?"

"Hunting."

"Oh yes, how thoughtless of me for deterring you from your one true passion. Are you to go alone?"

"Of course not. Will's to accompany me."

"I fear not, Rufus. Will is at this moment on a ship bearing for Normandy."

"What?!" he roared, heaving from his throne. "He...he promised he'd join me!"

"Now, Rufus, you mustn't blame Will. You see, his quick trip to Mortain is punishment for offending his father."

"Are you sa...saying that Uncle Robert's responsible for his departure?"

"I am."

Rufus slurred his sneer, "That rancid old goat. When he returns to England, I'll throw him in Simon's cell and leave them to rot together."

"Oh, Rufus, you can do better than spout idle threats. Be creative with your revenge."

"How?"

"You tell me," she encouraged. He sat for a long while, staring vaguely, brow furrowed, lips protruding, and she grew impatient. "Rufus, I don't have forever."

"Wait. I'll think of something brutal."

"Don't strain yourself. I can suggest an act of vengeance that requires no confrontation whatsoever."

"What?"

"Free Simon."

"No!"

"But Rufus, is it wise for you to cooperate with Robert's folly? After all, I hear Simon is your father's favorite nephew, and when he discovers you did nothing to prevent his imprisonment, he will be very displeased."

"And why do you slander your husband, Almodis?"

"Robert angered me." She pulled on her gloves, smoothing each finger sensuously. "Don't you worry, Rufus, I'll keep your kind deed a secret if, in turn, you keep mine. We'll say Simon escaped."

They stood posturing for a long moment; Rufus was first to drop his glare. "I might consider your request..."

Might wasn't good enough and she taunted, "I hear the poachers have rid your forest of deer. Without sufficient prison space, the thieving peasants will just have to go free."

To his howled, "Never!" his knotted fists quaked the dais and, it seemed, also the hall.

"I wholeheartedly agree," remarked Almodis with distinct calm. "And now I'll leave you to your decision. Make it fast, Rufus."

"And where are you off to?"

"That's my secret," she answered with allure as she gracefully glided away. "Goodbye, dearest nephew."

Almodis felt hopeful as she reined her horse where the drawbridge met the main road. Turning east would take her and her guards into the heart of London, and a strong impulse to gallop to Nicolas' home engulfed her. Yet the danger of such a gamble was too severe, not only for her, but for all those she had come to care for of late. So instead, she led her sentries west toward Winchester, and mused how refreshing it was to consider someone else's welfare above her own.

*****

Maura woke beneath the shadow of a stranger. With great effort, she pushed up on her elbows and examined him apprehensively. Wisps of thinning gray hair haloed his head; his gaunt leathery face sported a stubby peppered beard and a kind mouth. His armor was well used, the hauberk's links rusted and in spots forced apart; a dented helm was tucked beneath his arm. Cool gray eyes studied her as intensely and, with a reverent bow, he addressed her in a warm resonant voice, "My Lady."

She forced herself to sit, and apprehension was evident in her faint request, "Where is Marc?"

"Your brother was needed in the bailey. The archers need direction, and they perform best under Marc's mild demeanor. He agreed to allow me to watch over you." Her suspicious look prompted his assurance. "You needn't be afraid."

Maura *wasn't* frightened, she just didn't care for being watched over. Then again, her stiff body needed exercise, and her mind needed rousing. The smell of smoke and death hanging in the air nauseated her. "I'd like to walk," she said abruptly, floundering to rise.

"Then I will escort you," he answered with an offered hand. The sight of crusted blood staining her tunic instantly dizzied her. His palm cupped her elbow, supporting her uncertain steps as they left the chamber. "It's safest on the battlements," he advised. "We'll take the stairs slowly."

Maura side-stepped the kneeling archers positioned at the crenellations in the battlements, her sentry following close at her heels. She stopped and her somber gaze swept past the bailey to the tumbled wall. Flaming arrows intended for Philip's stragglers leapt the strewn stones and dove into the tents' skeletal remains. Voluminous clouds of smoke spewed from the blackened mess, dusting an already gray sky.

Her interest returned to the bailey, lingered its way over the charred out-buildings, and came to rest upon a darkened corner. She inched nearer to the ledge, squinted through the veiled smoke, and strained to behold a man in cleric's robes standing at the side of a wide hole. His hand drew a cross over each limp body as they were tossed into their crowded grave. Maura squeezed close her stinging eyes, hung her head, and swallowed the bile that crept up her throat. "I've seen quite enough," she said with a solemn sigh. "Please help me inside."

As they wandered along passageways, Maura tried to dismiss the surrounding horrors with trivial talk and questioned, "Are you a guard?"

"No, my Lady. I am a constant soldier."

After all she had witnessed, his answer sickened her, and she quipped with disgust, "And do you *enjoy* your work?"

Taken aback by her disparaging tone, he staidly returned, "My Lady, it is what God created me to be, and what I've trained for all my life. It is all I know, and all I do."

"Is there a family pining for you...somewhere?"

"Yes. I've been away a full three years. My daughter is five years old. I've been away for over half her life. I miss her and my father, sisters, and wife terribly. My wife died in childbirth."

Instantly regretting her callousness, Maura stammered, "For...forgive me my rudeness."

"I understand your confusion, my Lady. You needn't apologize."

His ready kindness disturbed her and she switched thoughts. "Could you take me to Marc?"

"No, my Lady. He's policing the downed wall. Your brother is highly respected, and he has earned the soldiers' complete trust."

"He offered little of his feelings, but I believe he's miserable here."

"Marc owns a heavy conscience and finds it hard to kill. Some consider that cowardice. I, however, believe it admirable. Bravery seems to abound in your family. The tale of you saving Prince Henry has filtered through the ranks. We are highly impressed, my Lady Maura. You should be proud to have shed blood for your King."

"What I did had nothing to do with fealty. Henry saved me, not I him."

They paused in the doorway to the great hall. Maura rested her hand on his arm and spoke lowly, "I'd like to stay awhile with the wounded. You needn't follow."

"Would you be bothered if I *did* follow?" he asked. "Perhaps together we can lift their spirits."

His acute gaze unnerved her and she attempted to discourage. "Surely you are needed elsewhere."

"I'm to watch over *you*, my Lady. Come." He clasped her hand and guided her into the mass of moaning soldiers. Feeling her resistance, he turned and assured, "Your presence and beauty will do wonders for their morale."

Maura stared askance. Beauty? Was he blind? She fingered her scraggly braid, scraped dirt from her neck, and lowered her shamed gaze to her torn and stained tunic.

He cupped her chin and lifted her dour face to his bright one. "The ale bucket is on the dais. They are thirsty and scared, many will die. Anything you can say to soothe their souls will be appreciated."

They roamed the floor together and, bending to each man, they offered ale, soft words, and a tender touch. It was late evening when they returned to her chamber. He stopped before the door and again took her hand. "I can see you're exhausted. I'll take my leave so you can rest. Marc will return presently. It has been a great privilege to walk with you, my Lady, and...I look forward to seeing you again in the near future."

He kissed her hand and, as he turned to leave, Maura called out, "Wait! I thank you for keeping me company, and being so kind. I don't even know your name."

"It is Hugh, my Lady. I am Hugh of Ryedale." And with that, he left her dreadfully bewildered.

*****

CHAPTER SIXTEEN - A CURING LOVE

Roland exuberantly hurled the dice upon the table; one tumbled from the edge, rolled across the ground, and stopped abruptly against the toe of a boot. Roland and Thomas' wide eyes climbed from the shoe, up over stout legs, and landed with great shock upon Rufus' scowl. They heaved from the table and fell to their knees beside an already kneeling Guy, Roland blubbering, "My...my Lord, we...we didn't hear you enter."

"Yes, and what if I'd been a scoundrel intent on rescuing the prisoner? You'd both be dead on account of your silly games." Rufus' anger switched to puzzlement as he spied two plump coin pouches gracing the table. He sensed theft and lumbered forward to examine the curious scene more closely. The two guards shared guilty looks and cringed at the thought of Rufus' retribution for their sin of bribery. "What's this, then?" he asked in a light, though perturbed tone as he stole up both bags in one fat hand. "I give you only enough money for your own up-keep. Who has provided the extra? I don't need a reason to flog you, so you had best be truthful."

Thomas, his head sagging low, concocted a swift lie. "Sir William offered us a few coins to ensure the prisoner's comfort."

"Comfort!" Rufus' sardonic bellow struck terror in the guards' souls. They groveled, their pitiful show throwing Rufus into cackling fits. Finally regaining his gruff composure, Rufus tied the pouches to his belt and announced, "Since I'm ridding you of your prisoner, it seems fitting I also rid you of your present."

Roland foolishly raised his head in protest. "But, my Lord, Lord Robert has ordered him restrained till a fortnight past Easter."

"Piss on Lord Robert," spat Rufus. "Get up, you sniveling vermin, and bring me my cousin. I would talk to him."

"Which cousin, Sire?" asked Thomas rather dumbly.

"The one in the cell, you dolt!"

"But my Lord, that's not so easily done," said Guy.

"Enough of your impudence! Fetch him quickly."

"But..."

"Now!"

Guy crouched by the open door and prodded a sleeping Godfrey. "Godfrey, the Prince wishes to see Simon."

Godfrey scrambled from his slumped position and asked, "Why? Is he to be punished further?"

"No, it seems he's to be moved."

"Too late, I fear."

"I pray not, for all our sakes," said Guy. "Come, take his hand. I'll help you."

Together they dragged Simon on his belly through the cell door. He lay senseless, hidden in the harsh shadow of the table.

Peeking into a pouch at his newly acquired wealth, Rufus started to the shuffling ruckus and, expecting to see Simon's pretty face, flashed scarlet at the timorous guards. "You putrid slime! If you insist on dawdling, I swear I'll—"

"My Lord," Godfrey interjected boldly, gesturing at his feet, "the prisoner is here."

Rufus despised confusion and abhorred disobedience. He stormed round the table but stopped short. A ragged gasp shuddered his portly figure as he gaped down at Simon and wheezed, "Is...is he dead?"

Roland replied calmly, "My Lord, if dead, he would have been removed from the cell and buried."

Rufus sneered at the guard and squatted by Simon's shoulder. He shook him, received no response, and asked in a bothered voice, "Whose fault is this? Will's?"

"No, Sire," answered Guy. "Lord Robert had Simon flogged."

"Why?"

"We know not, my Lord."

Rufus spat curses and rose; visibly shaken, he turned his troubled gaze on Godfrey. "Are...are you Robert's guard?"

"Yes, my Lord." Godfrey curiously regarded the Prince. Rufus' guise was unsettled, his voice almost caring. Never had Godfrey seen the Prince this way, and he decided to risk sharing the truth. "I serve Lord Robert but was requested to guard Simon's welfare."

"By whom?"

"I can't say, Sire."

Rufus examined the sentries' guarded expressions. He recognized Guy, and slowly became aware of one of Simon's benefactors—Henry. He silently thanked his brother, wondering enviously how the whelp was always afforded Simon's loyalty. "Is there a place you can remove the prisoner to...A safe place?" he asked unsteadily.

"Yes, Sire," answered Godfrey.

"Then do so at once!"

"Simon will appreciate your graciousness, my Lord."

"That I sincerely doubt," muttered Rufus as he turned to leave. Yet he paused, and approached Godfrey to whisper, "I'll arrange for a cart. It will await you at the buttery door. Send me word on his condition."

"I will, my Lord," Godfrey answered with disbelieving look.

Rufus slipped one last glance at Simon, and mumbled as he strode away, "And they call *me* a beast."

*****

The cart plodded its way through stubborn crowds, Godfrey at the reins, Guy at his side, and Simon, blanketed with Almodis' cloak, sprawled across cushioning straw in the rear. Curious passers-by slowed their pace to sneak a glimpse of Simon's wretched figure and hurried on, fearing contagion. Godfrey held little hope for this expedition. Simon had not stirred since the Lady Almodis' visit two days past. It was a miracle the Prince had granted Simon freedom, but it may have been granted too late.

Thick snow dulled the guards' view as Godfrey struggled to avoid colliding with pedestrians, and Guy searched the crowds for Robert's spies. At last they arrived before Nicolas' stables. There was no one about, so, leaving Guy to keep watch, Godfrey rushed up the stairs to the hall. At his rapid knock the door swung wide, but before he could utter a word, Nicolas tersely instructed, "Lead your horse into a stall. I'll attend you shortly."

Godfrey's boot kept the shutting door ajar and he urgently blurted, "Wait. Sir, wait! I mean to speak to Alan. Is he about?"

"No..." answered Nicolas, suddenly wary. "What is your purpose here?"

"I was given your address by the Lady Almodis."

"You'd best enter and explain yourself."

"I've left an injured friend outside in the snow."

"Then bring—"

"What is it, Nick?" Judith's inquiring face appeared in the doorway.

"This man has asked to see Alan."

"Alan is away at the moment," she said pleasantly to Godfrey. "May we be of some help?"

"Do you know...Simon?" asked Godfrey.

"Simon? Why, yes!" Judith's face beamed with hope. "Have you news of him?"

"Yes, he's waiting in the alley and needs immediate—"

"He's here!" Judith exclaimed joyously as she brushed past the two men and sped down the steps. She rushed to the alley, ignored Guy and the cart, and swept her befuddled gaze down both lengths of the road. "But where?" she called to the dusky wet sky.

Guy answered, "If you seek Simon, Madam, he's here in the cart."

"The cart?" Judith uttered anxiously. She approached the vehicle and gingerly tugged the cloak from Simon's limp form. "Oh, my Lord!" she cried. "Nicolas, come quickly!"

At once, Godfrey and Nicolas appeared. "Get him inside!" Judith rashly ordered.

"No, Judith!" Nicolas retorted, his eyes shifting uneasily. "This insanity must end!"

She glared in disbelief, nudged him aside, and chastised in a hissed whisper, "How dare you refuse Simon? Look about you, dear husband. Simon's appeal to the King enabled you to ply your trade. He helped build these stables! Have you forgotten the time he doctored our youngest? If it wasn't for his compassion, we surely would have lost her. How can you deny him the safety of our home?"

Nicolas wagged his head in shame. "No, I haven't forgotten all he's given us. But, Judith, his presence is bound to endanger our family and livelihood."

"We will deal with those problems if they come. Now help these kind men carry Simon upstairs. I'll fetch the leech."

Hours later, Alan somberly trudged up Nicholas' steps. Once again, his constant vigil at the docks had been for naught. Where was Maura? She ought to have returned by now, unless she'd met with treachery in Normandy. He shook his head to dismiss the horrid thought and entered the hall. Expecting all to be asleep, he paused and sniffed thoughtfully at a peculiar odor. A bright light added to his confusion. He advanced further into the room, noticed the fire stoked and flaming high, and he froze at the queer scene before him. Over a limp body reposing by the fire hovered a gnarled white-haired woman, shrouded in woolen rags. Judith knelt opposite her and, to the old one's muttered requests, passed bowls topped with gels of various hues. Alan glimpsed the children tucked up on their mats, and squinted toward a darkened niche, his eyes widening at the startling sight of Godfrey. He suddenly realized the prostrate figure must be Simon and briskly crossed the room to ask Godfrey, "What's happened?"

"William FitzRoy freed Simon."

"Rufus!" exclaimed Alan in shock. "What has he done to Simon?"

"The Prince is not responsible for his present condition. That fault lies solely with Simon's father. He ordered him whipped."

"You've done well to bring him here, Godfrey."

"The Lady Almodis helped win Simon's freedom and provided the map to your brother's home. Now that you're here, I must go. The Lady requests my immediate presence at Winchester."

"But how did the Lady—"

"I have no idea," interrupted Godfrey. "She seems a remarkable woman."

Alan nodded slightly and clasped Godfrey's shoulder, entreating with passion, "You must thank her...for Simon. Hopefully, he'll soon show his gratitude in person."

"I pray he's able, Alan. Is there word of his Lady?"

"Maura? No."

"She'd best return quickly. He may not survive his wounds."

"Yes...well, he'll know of your sacrifice when he wakes, which I've no doubt he will. We thank you, Godfrey. I'll see you out."

After Godfrey left, Alan knelt beside Judith and rested a fretful gaze on Simon's back. He watched the old woman deftly dab a thick smelly concoction over the shredded skin. "Who is she?" he whispered.

"A healer, with a fine reputation," answered Judith. "She first bathed his back and is now applying an herb poultice to encourage healing."

"Has he wakened at all?"

"No, and I don't expect him to for some time. There's still no sign of Maura?"

Alan wagged his head despondently.

"Will there be danger for us, Alan? Danger on account of Simon being in our home? We couldn't turn him away."

"I recognized a contingent of Lord Robert's milling about Westminster. You needn't worry," he assured patting her hand. "I'll keep a close watch on them."

"Simon will stay till he's well."

"That may not be possible, Judith."

The healer's distressful words interrupted, "His wounds are festering. You've called me too late. There's nothing further I can do for him here, but I will leave you a few remedies. I doubt they'll help, but they won't hurt." She handed Judith a pouch packed with herbs and advised, "Keep the room hot and him warm. Burn these herbs and have him inhale the smoke—it may ease his pain." A second pouch was offered. "These herbs make the poultice. Blend them with lard and apply the mixture to his wounds three or four times each day. Get him to drink ale, wine, milk, whatever he can manage. He'll most likely refuse food, if he wakes at all."

"We thank you for your generous help," said Judith, then she directed to Alan, "Please fetch the coins Nicolas received for Maura's necklace." Alan left and returned promptly with a jingling leather bag. Judith poured out a few coins and pressed them to the healer's palm. "Again, we thank you, Simon thanks you."

"I've been little help," rasped the woman as she accepted Alan's helping hand, rose stiffly, and shuffled out the door.

*****

Her mind weary and empty, Maura sat upon her lonely mat and stared vaguely at the loophole's reflection, the light now dull and quivering with rain. A soft tapping preceded Marc's entry. Her solemn mood worried him, and he asked, "How do you feel?"

She fixed her blank gaze upon him. "I'm fine. It seems quieter this morning."

"The last of Philip's army has been routed and it's time for us to start for the coast. But first I'll change your bandage."

Maura offered her arm; he gently removed the soiled cloth and examined her wound. "It's healing nicely," he observed as brightly as the dour situation would allow.

"Before I leave, I will see Henry," she said adamantly.

Securing the new bandage with a knot, he hesitantly concurred, "I'll take you to him. Make your visit short. We must be on our way before more trouble looms. And on our journey, I insist you tell me everything that's happened—*everything*."

With a woeful sigh, she allowed him to help her from the floor. While he procured a blanket to serve as her cloak, she waited for her mind to clear, then clutching hands, they ambled down the passageway. Marc strove to cheer by asking, "And what did you think of Hugh?"

"He seemed pleasant," said Maura, "though a bit severe."

"He's a fine gentleman and an excellent soldier. You should be grateful."

"It was kind of him to walk with me."

"Not only for his company," corrected Marc.

"What else?"

"Maura, you don't know?"

"Don't toy with me, Marc. Know what?"

"He's to be your husband.

She stood stunned and gaping. "I'm to marry *him*?"

"Yes. After I arrived here, he sought me out. Understandably, he wanted to know all about you. Didn't Will tell you his name?"

"No. He said I was to marry a poor soldier from Yorkshire. His name didn't seem important at the time. I imagined a young man. Hugh's...older..."

"You did like him?"

"Yes, but—"

"Maura," Marc replied frankly as they continued down the hall, "accept that he will be your husband and consider yourself lucky. You *almost* wed Rufus. Here's Henry's chamber. I'll wander close by. Don't dally."

Maura rested against the wall and pondered this newest, most surprising revelation. Marry Hugh? How ludicrous to wed a man she would never see. Yet for a privileged woman, her choices were few—a life of matronly solitude in Yorkshire, or cloistered forever in a convent. At least in Yorkshire she'd be with Rose and Alan, and Marc could join them when the wars were done, if that miracle ever came to pass. Hugh did seem kind, and wasn't that her simple wish? But then, what did it matter whom she wed, or why? The prospect of marrying for love was rare in her elite society. Marriage was reserved to form alliances, to acquire property and status, to obtain a lasting peace between warring countries, or to establish a dynasty. And what of *her* love? She'd failed in her mission and would likely never see Simon again. Perhaps it was for the best. Already too many had been placed in peril because of her hare-brained romantic scheme—as Henry had so aptly stated. Hugh had mentioned he had a young daughter. Was she suited to be a step-mother? Would their marriage be blessed with more children? Tears clouded her eyes as she rubbed the moon-shaped scars marring her hands and resolved, if this union was God's will, then God's will she must accept.

Maura wiped away her turmoil with her filthy skirt. She would not appear upset before Henry. After his ordeal, what he needed most was cheering. She knocked, forced a smile, and entered to his faint command, "Come."

He struggled to sit, but Maura's halting gesture stilled him. "No Henry, please don't. There's no need." She settled beside his mat and asked warmly, "Is there much pain?"

"None that compares to yours," he replied, waving his braced arm easily. "According to my father's physician, I should be strutting about by week's end." He turned suddenly grave. "I woke under the table. You were slumped over me...bleeding. I was scared."

"Henry," she murmured as she reached for his free hand. "I'm perfectly fine. Very soon, I will leave here. Marc's to escort me to the coast."

"I'm sorry it can't be me, Maura. I did promise Simon I'd watch over you, yet our roles seem to have been reversed. However, I will have my guards travel with you as far as Westminster." He firmed his grip. "I'll miss you."

"But Henry," she said with a tender smirk, "didn't you say you never think of any woman for more than a few ecstatic moments?"

His large sad eyes seemed to melt as he confessed, "I've always believed my sister Adela to be the strongest woman I know...but you...you own a quieter, gentler strength. At Gloucester, I questioned Simon's obsession with you and he claimed I was too young to know his feelings. At the time, I took his remark as an insult. Now I know precisely what he meant."

His stark honesty moved her and she felt her tears return. "Simon would never intentionally insult you." An awkward silence followed her response, which Maura ended with a burst of feigned gaiety. "I've met the man I'm to marry!"

"Yes, I heard," he replied glumly. "Hugh's a good man."

"And he seems kind."

Henry pulled her close, his voice tense and urgent, "Maura, feel free to ignore this advice. I know you think of me as an immoral, erratic pup, most do. But when you return to England, spend every moment till your wedding with Simon and if there's a way to continue your trysts after the ceremony, do so. Hugh may be kind, but he's an old man. After your marriage, he'll stay long enough to make you pregnant, and return briefly nine months later to do the deed again. He'll then proceed to get himself killed and Uncle Robert will find you another old man to marry. And the tragedy will be repeated time and time again, till you drop dead from birthing too many children. It's vital you see to your own happiness! You're young, vibrant...lovely. Don't deny yourself the pleasure you've known and rightly deserve, for you'll never find another finer than Simon, never! Believe what I say, for it is indeed the truth."

She wiped a tear and sputtered, "There...there really is no point in discussing my reunion with Simon. He won't be freed, nor will I see him again."

"Why ever not?"

"I was sleeping when your father visited."

"But *I* wasn't," spouted Henry proudly. He slipped his good hand under his blanket, produced the rolled and beribboned parchment, and passed it to Maura, beaming, "It really was quite amazing how swiftly I remembered my letters."

"Oh, Henry!" she gushed as her face lit with joy.

"It's all there, the demanded release, the statement that you journeyed here on your own, and Father's signature and seal. Rufus can't challenge it."

Her jittery fingers unrolled the skin and her smile broadened. "Henry, what magnificent scripting!" She winked and teased, "I'm convinced you'll make a marvelous clerk. How can I ever thank you?"

"Let me visit you in Yorkshire. I promise to behave myself."

She brushed her fingers lightly across his cheek. "I'll welcome you anytime."

Henry caught her escaping hand, his impish guise returned, and a bubbling excitement overtook him. "One more favor—I'll have a kiss."

He wiggled so, Maura imagined his tail must be wagging. "I suppose it would be fine, considering you're practically an invalid."

She offered her cheek, but he pinched her chin and jerked her lips to his. Expecting his ruse, she let their lips mingle a sweet moment. "Well that was certainly regrettable," he mourned as she gently pulled away.

"Why?" she asked, slightly insulted.

"Now I'll feel even lonelier."

"You can always return to Abbeville and...Sybil."

"But she doesn't speak to me like you do. Actually, we don't talk much at all. Please don't tell Simon about...about...the ointment. He wouldn't understand, and at times he lacks a sense of humor."

"All he'll know is I wouldn't have survived our mission without your help. He's bound to be tremendously proud of you, and thankful, as am I. We owe you so much." Marc appeared in the doorway and Maura started to rise.

"No Maura, wait," Henry beseeched, clenching her hand. "Father is indebted to you for saving my life. Always remember that, and never forget—me."

"Forget you? How could I possibly forget you?" she said brokenly, engulfing him in an intense, grateful hug. "It's time for me to go."

"May I attend your wedding?" he blurted.

"Of course you may."

"Please take care and be happy."

"I'll try." As she stood, her mood sank to his dismal look and she heartened, "Don't be sad, Henry. Easter is only two and a half months away. I'll expect you then, at Pevensey."

She stuck the parchment in her belt, cracked one last hopeful smile, and slipped away, leaving him brooding on his mat.

*****

The sun, an ebullient red, lifted over the eastern horizon, bathing Marc and Maura in a rouged glow as they sat on the docks at Boulougne. Their faces drooped long as they absently tossed pebbles into the bubbling foam hugging the pilings. Maura sighed deeply. "Being with you these last two days has been so comforting, Marc. I don't want it ever to end."

"Thank you for sharing your past," said Marc sadly.

"Not knowing must have been so confusing for you," said she.

He nodded uneasily.

"I didn't keep quiet on purpose, Marc. I couldn't remember all that had happened, then I saw Simon at Winchester and—" She hesitated to his rising upset. "Marc," Maura continued carefully, "you seemed upset when I told you Simon and I had been lovers. Are you angry with us?"

"No. How you suffered because of your love is what sickens me. I can't agree with Henry, Maura. See to Simon's release, say what's needed, then run from him." His tone turned threatening, "If he endangers you again, I'll—"

"It won't be only Simon's doing," retorted Maura. "Will you punish me as well?"

"Forget him! He'll only cause you more grief."

"How can you speak of Simon like this? I thought you loved him. He loves you!" They paused a heated moment, then Maura begged, "Let's not argue, not now. I think we fight purposely, to ease the hurt when we part. It eases nothing. Tell me, Marc what truly bothers you?"

Lifting his eyes to the sea, he thought a long doleful moment, then rapidly spilled, "I don't want to return to Rouen. When I first arrived in Normandy, I believed myself a good soldier, now I feel a coward."

Maura grasped his shoulders and forced his face to hers. "How can you say such a thing? The soldiers respect you and rely on you!"

"But I'm forever dreaming of ways to escape!" he despaired. "Too many lives have been wasted, and for what? Sick games staged by grown men."

She cupped his hands in hers and soothed, "Marc, come stay with me in Yorkshire. No one will know."

"Deserting would prove I'm a coward. I swore homage. I must return!"

"Come with me," she begged. "Rose and I will care for you."

"No. They hang deserters!" His shoulders slumped in defeat and his voice softened to that of a young boy's. "Maybe the wars will soon end, then I'll visit, and forget what I said about Simon. Listen only to your heart and his."

"You'll come to my wedding?"

"I don't think I'll be able."

Henry's guard approached. "You may board now, my Lady."

They stood and, overcome with sorrow, hugged desperately. "Heed your own advice, Marc," murmured Maura, loosening their embrace. "If your heart needs to return to England, I'll be waiting in Yorkshire. I love you."

"And I you," he sniffed and waved limply as she turned to follow the sentry.

*****

Maura remained on deck the entire crossing with no distractions. The boat's gentle rocking and the solacing noise of slapping waves quieted her discontent. Her mind ached with the weight of her relatives' contrary though well-meaning advice. Of only one thing was she certain—compared to the soldiers' misery, her suffering was trivial.

The weather worsened as the ship neared Westminster. At the dull thud of docking, she hurried down the plank and searched through snowy darkness for her mount. Once upon his back, she impatiently fingered the parchment, shuddered beneath her blanket, then rode the short distance to Westminster Palace. She tethered her horse at the base of the keep's stairs and, with anxiety churning her belly, hastened to the great hall. "The FitzRoy is expecting me," she proclaimed to the grim guard manning the hall's doors.

"He's supping and will not be disturbed."

"He will see me!" she flared.

The guard ruffled at her gall, then eyed her soiled and pitiful figure with distaste. "And who might *you* be?"

"Tell him Maura has returned...from Normandy."

The guard grudgingly vanished behind the doors and quickly reappeared, grunting, "The Prince does not wish to see you."

Maura shoved by him into the hall, and surged past the roaring fire to the dais. Snickered laughter greeted her. Rufus was not alone. The Prince dined with his catamites; their girlish coifs, painted faces, and garish clothes rocked Maura's mettle. Rufus, intently involved in flirting with one young lad, had yet to notice her.

She straightened and called, "Rufus!"

"Wh...what!" he stammered, snapping to her shout. He grew ashen at the sight of her and haltingly rose.

"We made a deal and I've come to refresh your memory."

"We made no deal," he sneered.

She yanked the crinkled parchment from her belt and thrust it under his nose. "I would obtain this and you would free Simon."

"You speak rubbish."

She stiffened, gestured, and fumed, "I gave you money!"

"Stop your squawking!"

"Read the writ! Your father demands Simon's immediate release."

"You never saw my father, you lying bitch!" he cursed, unrolling the parchment. His darkened eyes fell upon the King's seal and grew round with shock.

"The truth is before you, unless you've grown blind with drink."

"Damn your impudence!" roared Rufus as he swatted away the writ. "You promised me more money!" His boys cowed to his growing rage, but Maura held firm her stance as he thundered on, "And if it's on you I'll find it!" His stubby fingers shot out, seized the front of her tunic, and yanked her onto the table. Platters of spongy bread and meat hurtled from the dais to be instantly set upon by yelping hounds. She shared the dogs' vehemence by rabidly sinking her nails and teeth into Rufus' arm.

Rufus yowled, flailing wildly to break her bite; one fierce swipe flung her backward off the table and over a bench. She landed in a twisted heap dangerously near the fire. While Maura rolled from the flames, one frenzied hound forsook his scraps and clamped his muzzle on her exposed leg. The uproar drew charging guards, their swords brandished as they rushed Maura's thrashing, wailing figure. Rufus' bellow, "Stop!" stilled their advance. His shrill whistle scattered the dogs and, to his men, he commanded, "Help her up."

Maura stood alone, hissing wrath and spitting skin.

"You attack me again, I'll have you disemboweled and feed your innards to my hounds!" Rufus hollered, then sneered, "They seem to enjoy your taste. Now leave the money and get out!"

"You'll get it only when Simon is freed!"

"Then I'll have it, for he's no longer a prisoner."

"What?!" Her eyes bulged to the astounding news, and she sputtered, "But...but you said, you told me, it wasn't in your power to release him."

"I lied." His uproarious laughter flushed the birds from the rafters. His boys joined in his mirth, their throaty guffaws aping his.

"Where's he gone to?" Maura demanded.

"Not far, I suspect," Rufus casually replied. "When last I saw him he was near to death."

Her body numbed, her face paled; the guards, the pretty boys, and the diving birds faded, then crystallized to her wail, "Death!" She stormed the dais, and thrust her clenched fist at Rufus' glower. "What have you done to him?!"

Confidently, he cloaked her puny weapon with his huge hand, slammed her arm to the table, and gloated, "*I* freed him."

Maura wrenched from his hold, snatched up the writ, and raced from the hall. She had to find him, speak to him, confess her love before—

The guards loped in chase, but Rufus stopped them. "Halt...Let her be. I'm weary of her hysterics."

"She owes you more money, my Lord," reminded one particularly handsome lad.

"You needn't waste your precious time fretting over my finances. In good time, I'll get what's due me...I always do. Now come and sit upon my lap."

Maura stumbled down the steps to the bailey and floundered through biting wind and blinding snow. Her mind swam with dread. Where was Simon? Was he at Nicolas'? She couldn't travel there alone, she'd lose her way! Each soldier she encountered, she stopped and peered intently into his bemused expression, hoping to recognize a familiar face. But she encountered only strangers. Her fingers grew stiff from the cold, and a deadening numbness spread from her limbs to her trunk. She must seek shelter! Not here, it would be suicidal to stay here. Amazingly, she found her way back to the keep's stairs, only to discover her horse gone. In her madness, a daunting thought flickered—Rufus had stolen him and aimed to take her prisoner! A despairing moan rumbled from her gut as she whirled and twisted, searching frantically for a place to hide from Rufus, Robert, Will, the corpses, the arrows, the flames...

The ravaging storm had all but emptied the bailey. On horseback, Alan squinted through the stinging snow, kicking and urging his balking steed along. A soldier manning the docks had mentioned seeing a woman disembark the last arriving ship. Panicked, Alan fretted—why hadn't Maura waited for him? He prayed she hadn't attempted to confront Rufus on her own. If she *had* made that deadly decision, he would steal her from Rufus' clutch. He dismounted at the base of the keep's stairs, tethered his horse, and gripped tightly the hilt of his sword. As he climbed, a shivering movement beneath the open staircase stole his attention. He peered between the wooden slats and spied a hunched figure. "Who's there?" he shouted feebly against the roaring wind.

Maura attempted to curl her brittle body in a tighter ball, then realized she knew the voice. "Alan!" she cried.

"Maura!" he burst out as they met in a strangling hug. She frantically searched his pinched expression; her lips trembled but refused to speak the dreaded question, and he promptly eased her struggle. "He's alive." She sagged in relief and swayed as the full force of her exhaustion and the storm attacked. "God's breath!" he exclaimed worriedly, "You're frozen to the bone!" He swiftly shed his mantle and bundled her tightly, blurting, "Come, Simon needs you."

As they rode, Maura rested back upon his chest. Her silence concerned him and he wondered if she were asleep. Yet a quick glance revealed her eyes wide with fear and so much more. It seemed forever, but at last they climbed the stairs to his brother's house. She paused before the door and asked in a childlike tone, "Is he hurt badly?"

To ease the shock sure to come, he rested his hands on her shoulders and hoped, "The sight of you will surely ease his pain."

Maura saw through his forced optimism and, passing him his cloak and the parchment, entered. She tread quickly to the fire. Simon lay on his belly, his ripped back smeared with a leafy ointment, his lower body draped with thick pelts. The oppressive heat, his horrible lesions, and his blanched, bruised face dizzied Maura. She swallowed her distress as a heavy calm engulfed her, a calm that sent her to her knees and told her clearly—this was where she belonged, where she was truly needed and loved. Her fingers caressed his stubbly cheek as she whispered close, "Simon...it's Maura. I've come back." He stirred slightly to her touch, but his eyes remained shut and his skin burned hot beneath her stroke. She stretched out by his side, pressed her lips lightly to his, and lay her cool cheek upon his brow.

Alan realized he was intruding on an intensely intimate moment, so, careful not to wake the others, he crept to his mat and unrolled the parchment. He gaped at the sloppy script topping the King's mark, and admitted with guilt and shame that even *he* had doubted Maura would succeed in her mission.

Judith woke promptly at midnight—Simon's worst time—to stoke the fire and offer him comfort. But listening, she heard no moans, only crackling flames and a misplaced whispery voice. Fretfully, she raised up on her mat and searched beyond the fire. What she beheld drew from her a quick gasp. Haloed by the faint glow of the fire, Maura sat cross-legged on the mat, Simon's head resting in her lap. Maura's murmuring never ceased as she bathed his brow with a damp cloth. Judith could not make out her curing speech, though knew this night her own nursing would not be needed.

Thick snowflakes swirled through the roof's vent, drifting down to sputter on dying coals. Maura sat slumped over Simon; her back pained her, and sweat dripped from her brow and trickled upon Simon's thick, downy hair, shining silver in the dim light. In sleep his misery was well masked, he appeared peaceful and content. Holding him in her arms stirred images in her tired mind, visions of their wondrous history as enemies, comrades...lovers. He'd not moved since her first touch. Could he sense her nearness, her caring, her love? No longer able to sit, she lifted his head and sank wearily down beside him.

Simon woke with a gasping jolt. Maura fought to still his flailing, yet panicked as he rocked to his back. A demonic force overtook him; he howled in agony and clamped hold her arms. His eyes, crazed with fever, bore through her, veins bulged from his brow and neck. She strained against his grip, crying out, "Alan! Help...help me, Alan!"

The unexpected eruption jostled all from their beds. Nicolas and Alan rushed to Maura's aid. They pried Simon's fingers from her arms; her wound gushed fresh blood, and Alan yelled above Simon's wailing, "Maura, get away!"

Maura grudgingly retreated. Alan and Nicolas battled Simon's frenzy and, with great difficulty, managed to wrestle him to his side. But he still refused to weaken and his continued thrashing only heightening his anguish.

Maura threw herself into the mayhem, and yanked futilely at Nicolas' and Alan's hold, shrilling, "Let him be! You're hurting him. Let go and leave him to me!"

The men looked doubtingly to one another and haltingly obeyed.

Maura squeezed Simon's hands, forced them still, and begged loudly, "Simon! Simon, hear me! Fighting will only worsen your pain. Simon, *please* do what I say...lie still!"

Simon heard a faint 'lie still'. How could he lie still?! He had to fight, his father was murdering him! But this new touch was strong, tender and so familiar. The silken words loomed closer, clearer, "You're safe here. There's nothing to fear. It's Maura. I won't ever leave you." Her sweet face gradually crystallized, but her touch scorched and the burning gutted his body, sapping his strength. His fight weakened; he twitched and muttered gibberish.

Maura urged him to his belly and swiftly directed, "Hurry! Fetch blankets and feed the fire. Make it blaze!"

Nicolas tended the fire, while Judith sprinkled herbs upon the leaping flames. Alan gathered up pelts and blankets, and Maura carefully piled them upon Simon's back. As he watched her, Alan noticed blood seeping through Maura's sleeve. "Maura," he said, reaching out to stop her. "Your arm!"

"Not now," she answered, flinching from his concern. "We must break his fever."

"You're bleeding!"

"It's no matter!" she retorted. "Help me save Simon!"

Not often did Alan feel useless, and he pleaded, "What else can I do?"

"Keep the fire high." She reached out and took his hand, encouraging, "And stay close. He needs to know his friends are near."

Maura resumed her cross-legged position, took Simon's head again in her lap, and continued her stroking and cooing. The smoking herbs choked her and teared her eyes, still her resolve held firm.

Judith appeared, carrying a roll of cloth. "Maura, let me tend your wound. You can pet him with your other hand."

"Not now, Judith."

"Do you want to lose your arm?" Judith asked sharply. "Here, it will take only a moment to freshen the bandage." She swiftly unraveled the soaked cloth and, before Maura could utter a protest, spread a dab of herb poultice across the gash.

Maura jerked away, gasping, "It stings!"

"And that's a good sign," assured Judith as she wrapped the linen snugly.

"Judith," Maura despaired, "I feel so helpless. Do you think he knows I'm here?"

"I believe he thinks he's still in the cell. If only he could speak, he'd tell us how to treat his condition."

Maura looked up quizzically. "I don't understand."

"Don't you know?"

"Know what?"

"Simon is a revered physician."

"Physician?" wondered Maura.

"Yes...In the past, he shared his medical knowledge with my family, enabling us to keep quite fit. It grieves me that there's little we can do for him in return. Maura, your presence could be the force that saves him. These last few days, when he's called out, he's called for you."

Laboriously, the night wore on with no change. At dawn, Judith, Nicolas and the children left the stifling chamber to Alan, Maura, and Simon. The quiet was so intense, Maura could hear the chattering of Simon's teeth. She wondered how much longer God would allow his torment, and briefly recalled her illness at Winchester. It must have been Simon who'd prescribed the herbs that diluted the poison and doused her fever. Why hadn't Rose told her? But then, at the time Rose never would have acknowledged Simon's help. A physician? Of course, it made perfect sense. He'd always owned a penchant for healing. Her pride for him swelled her heart, and she murmured with passion, "Simon, I know you have a little strength left. I love you so, *please* don't leave me now." He seemed to hear her endearment, for suddenly his trembling strengthened, and his breath became labored gasps. A tense moan and shudder took him; he stiffened for a timeless instant, then went limp in her arms. Sweat streamed from his body, drenching her tunic and the mat below them. Maura's strength sputtered away as she buried her face in the pelt's fur and sobbed her thanks to God.

*****

Judith loomed over Maura, her arms folded across her chest and her expression stern. "Now that he's resting peacefully, you'll eat, wash, dress, and sleep."

Maura nodded meekly, and Alan called from the table, "Don't let her frighten you, Maura, she's all bluff. Join us. I long to hear of your adventures in Normandy."

She glanced at Simon's pristine expression. It had taken so long to recover her rightful place by his side, she wasn't eager to move even the few feet to the table. "Later, Alan. I'd like to stay here."

"Maura, he's not about to go anywhere," said Judith. "When did you last eat?"

"I don't recall. Please Judith, I want...need to stay by him."

"Oh, very well." Judith returned to the table, ladled a fish and vegetable stew into a bowl, poured ale, and brought the meal to Maura. At the stew's luscious odor, Maura's appetite struck with a vengeance and she gobbled her fare. Afterwards, with a pail of warm, sudsy water, Judith lured her from Simon's side, and behind a cloaking tapestry. Maura quickly stripped and, as she scrubbed the layered grime from her body, she noticed the bug bites had scabbed over, and reflected fondly on her first night on the ship with Henry. She offered a quick prayer for his well-being, hurried to finish her wash, and then resumed her vigil by Simon's side. While watching her soiled tunic fuel the flames, a deep sigh of satisfaction left her. Maura reveled in the suppleness of Judith's linen chemise and blanched wool tunic. And as her fingers brushed over her chafed, rouged cheeks and shiny skin, she thought, how glorious to be clean! Her musing was disrupted by the horrific sight of Simon's back. Who had done this brutal deed? Will, she suspected, and cringed to the memory that she'd once confided in and trusted him, and had come too close to sharing his bed.

Bowl in hand, Judith knelt across from Maura and asked, "Would you care to apply the poultice?"

"Yes, please," eagerly answered Maura, as she crawled round Simon's body and accepted the bowl. It bothered her that she could no longer watch his beautiful face as she delicately spread the paste on his shredded skin. With each application, he tensed. "I don't want to hurt him," Maura said, pausing the treatment.

"It helps more than hurts," assured Judith.

Maura took a steadying breath and continued with a feather touch.

Simon's fingernails scratched at the wood floor. His eyelids opened to slits, then fluttered wider to the astounding sight of flames. This couldn't be Hell, he thought vaguely; Hell would never smell this appetizing. He could neither muster strength to push from the floor, nor find a voice to ask his whereabouts. He listened, heard a woman's voice, and felt a stinging, burning hurt. The touch, so soft and stirring, had come before.

A fleeting movement caught Maura's eye. She leant over his body and saw his fingers clawing the floor. The bowl of paste dropped from her grasp as she scuttled on her knees into his sight, crying out, "Simon...Simon!"

It was Maura! Her hair hung before his eyes, yet he couldn't see her face! In vain, Simon twisted and struggled to push from the floor; he strained to speak, but could make no sound.

Maura's heart lurched at the sight of his opened eyes. She bent closer and stilled his fluster with a whisper, "Simon, don't try to rise. I'll come down to you. Let me help you to your side."

She lay facing him and shuddered to his tortured gaze, awash with need and longing. He reached a trembling hand. Their fingers mingled and, letting go a strangled cry, she surged into his smothering clutch.

*****

CHAPTER SEVENTEEN - A QUANDARY AT WINCHESTER

In the days that followed, Simon's impatience with his infirmity waned as his strength stubbornly returned. He no longer required the fire's intense heat, and so was moved to a corner of the hall that afforded, with the help of a dividing tapestry, a bit of privacy. To his chagrin, his voice remained elusive, cracked and whispery. Yet what his lips refused to say, his expression sincerely conveyed.

Maura basked in his adoring gaze. She tended to his every need. Exuberantly, she shared tales of Henry's heroism and the very few lighthearted moments of their journey to Normandy. And revelations of the loyalty of Simon's friends, relatives, and, most perplexing of all, Rufus, helped to repair his sense of isolation.

The tempest's onslaught continued and drove most of the town's populace indoors. However, it failed to stall Robert's soldiers' hunt for Simon. Each blustery day, Alan ventured out to check on their steady progress. He purposely shunned the subject while at home, not wanting to disrupt Simon's healing with worry. But how long could he keep the encroaching peril a secret? On his lonely rides, he reflected on how deeply he'd come to care for certain members of Lord Robert's peculiar family. He resolved to see them well and safe, then return to Rouen to seek the King's permission to join Maura's new household in Yorkshire. The future gleamed promising, yet he was forever haunted by the memory of Almodis' last distraught glance. He swiftly swept the image away. To think of such things was foolish—foolish and lethal.

On the fourth day of his recovery, Simon woke first. Maura slept facing him, cuddled close and serene. His fingers skimmed her brow, smoothing her hair from her face, then moved to caress her cheek, brush across her lips, and came to rest on her swan-like neck. Try as he might, he'd yet to convince himself that she was real and not some fever-bred phantom. She fed him, bathed him, encouraged and soothed him—yet only two weeks past she had freely confessed her loathing for him. Confusion and uncertainty tangled his mind, and neither could he communicate.

Maura shifted on her mat, snuggled nearer, and woke to soft kisses. A gentle warmth washed over her as she returned a kiss and caught her fingers in his tousled hair. She longed to hear his voice and reluctantly loosened their embrace to murmur, "What a sweet way to wake. You must feel better."

To Simon's astonishment, his voice emerged full and clear. "Yes, I do feel stronger."

Elation filled her as she pushed up from the mat and burbled, "Simon! Your voice! It's come back. Now you can tell me, how can I make you more comfortable?"

"There's nothing more you need do."

Her exuberance wilted as she touched his scarred cheek. "How can Robert hate you so?"

"I'm not what he wants me to be," he answered and pressed her palm to his face. "I can't believe you're here."

She sank back by his side and purred, "Believe this," as their lips met once more.

"You won't leave?" he worried.

"Never…" she sighed, kissing away his fear. When next she eased away, his dubious look again appeared. There was no denying his feelings; every touch, word, and gaze reaffirmed his intense love for her. How could she ease his suspicions and prove *her* love still true? She cupped his hands between hers, steadied her voice, and confessed, "I know you're unsure of my love. God knows, when you left me at Dunheved, I wanted to despise you and spent the next four years convincing myself you deserved my hate. I buried most of what happened between us, the good and the horrible. I had to...to survive. But then, I saw you at Winchester and our past began to creep back—"

"I left only to save—" he blurted.

"No Simon, let me finish," she insisted, her grip firming. "After I sent you from Gloucester, something within *me* changed. I cursed myself for not hearing you and believed you were gone forever."

"Then why did you say you hated me?"

"I feared if I'd told the truth, Robert would have killed you. Now I see it would have made little difference. I'm glad for your stubbornness but also sorry for it. If you had forsaken me, you'd never have suffered—" She paused, her heavy guilt quavering her voice. "I need you to believe I still adore you! And I need your help. Here in your arms there's no question of what's right—I belong with you. But we can't stay here forever. The Yorkshire betrothal cannot be broken and Easter is but two months away! What are we to do? You almost died, Simon! If we're caught again, Robert won't bother with mere punishment, he'll simply order our executions. Rose says we must make our peace and then part. Help me, my love...Is that possible?"

Her ponderous question exhausted him. His frustration and pain flared, and his long dark sigh told all, "No."

*****

After Simon's long rejuvenating nap, they temporarily abandoned their troubles, and their conversation turned sprightly and reminiscent. Maura found the contents of his saddle bag fascinating and, as she spread Simon's own salve on his wounds, said with distaste, "This is as rancid as the ointment Henry used to cure my bug bites. What's in it?"

"Eryngo, red alder, parsley, broom flowers, and stinking iris," said Simon, grimacing at each dab.

"I much prefer the lotion that cleanses your back."

"Yes," he agreed, "honeysuckle, wild roses, and camphor are easier on the nose. But the salve heals quite nicely. Thank you again, Maura, for rescuing E'dain."

"It's Alan who deserves your thanks, he recognized her. Simon, tell me all about your doctoring."

"That would be a lengthy task. I'd much rather talk of—"

He was interrupted by Alan returning from his watch. He looked cold and afflicted as he hastened to their corner and blotted their mirth with a terse message, "Robert's men are near."

Simon wincingly pushed to his side. "How near?"

"I spotted two at the entrance to the alley. Simon, you can hide in Nicolas' storage room. Maura, it's time for you to leave for Winchester."

"No!" she moaned.

"Maura, you of all people should know—Lord Robert is not known for leniency. If they discover you here, everyone in this house will be arrested and tortured. Except of course, the two of you—you'll only be murdered. I'll have no argument! Simon, speak to her, make her see reason while I fetch the horses."

Alan darted away. Simon sat, removed the earthen jar from Maura's grip, and took her hands in his. "Look at me, Maura."

She refused to lift her head.

"Maura, please..."

Slowly raising woeful eyes, she beseeched, "Don't send me away, *please* don't send me away!"

"We can't risk these good peoples' lives! I'll come to you as soon as I'm able. Somehow, we'll find a way to be together." He wiped her tears and one of his own and forced a wistful smile. "Dreaming of lying with you is the perfect remedy to speed my healing. Rose is at Winchester, and I know how terribly you miss her." His fingers bit into her shoulders. "Maura, I *will* come to you...very soon."

"But, Simon," she argued, "Robert's men guard Almodis at Winchester! Surely, they will recognize—"

He hushed her fretting with a vow. "They won't stop me. Nothing can keep me from you!"

Alan reappeared too quickly. "Nicolas' apprentice holds the horses where the tunnel ends. Maura, come!"

"You'll give us a moment...alone," insisted Maura.

With an uncertain nod, Alan obliged, and moved swiftly to his mat. Lifting it, he found the latch to a trapdoor; he tugged it open and slipped away under the floor.

Maura's voice and body quaked with sadness and fear. "Simon, you must take care. Please don't take any rash chances or—"

"I won't, my love," he assured, brushing the back of her hand along his jaw.

"I'll be waiting...Adela's room."

"I remember."

"Please thank Nicholas, Judith and the children for me," she strained, her voice barely containing its misery. "Insist they keep the money from the necklace."

"I will." He kissed her fingers, her mouth, then he stiffened and jerked back. "If I hold you, I won't let go. Take Almodis' cloak. Go quickly!"

She scrambled from his side, grabbed the cloak from its peg, and paused at the trapdoor. Their woeful gazes mingled a last time; Simon nodded, and she vanished. Maura clambered over burlap sacks to Alan. They scrambled along a dank tunnel and emerged into snowy light. Mounting their awaiting steeds, they bounded away, kicking up white clouds in their wake.

Simon had scant time to mourn, for the instant Maura disappeared, Nicolas raced into the chamber, panting, "Simon, the soldiers are in the alley! I'll get you to the storage room." Simon struggled to stand and Nicolas snatched up a blanket to wrap his nakedness. "You may have to hide awhile and will catch your death if not covered. Hold my arm and give me your weight." With his friend's support, Simon hobbled to the trap door, sat in its opening, and snapped a frantic face to Nicolas. "Drop forward," Nicholas rapidly directed. "The sacks will cushion your fall." Simon hit the sacks with an agonized groan. Nicolas jumped down beside him, swiftly rearranged the sacks to make a burrow, and helped Simon curl into the hole. As Nicolas stacked bag after bag upon Simon, pain and the horror of being buried alive made Simon cry out, but he cut his protest short at the sound of coarse bellows from above. Heavy boot steps joined the commotion. Simon heard the squeak of the trap door and felt the added crunch of soldiers leaping onto his hiding place. He bit into his hand to keep from moaning and tasted blood.

Sharp orders were volleyed, "Search the tunnel! Rip the sacks!" Daggers snagging at the dense weave jostled Simon and swelled his fear. His breath stopped and eyes bulged as a frigid blade scraped the tip of his nose.

"Please..." entreated Nicolas, "spare my supplies! I keep only feed for the horses here."

"Why do you need a tunnel?"

"Our home has suffered raids. We need an escape route. Who...who or what are you searching for?"

The blade retreated and Simon breathed again.

"Simon FitzRobert, son of our Liege Lord, Robert of Mortain. And why do you suffer raids?"

Nicolas' mind scurried about, trying to discern a believable answer. "Fifteen years ago, King William asked our family to travel from Rouen and settle here. I make armor and weapons for the King's armies. We are Jewish, and a few of our neighbors are offended by our presence."

The sentry who appeared to command the others, stared dumbly at Nicolas for a long while, then huffed, "Do we need to inform you of the consequences of hiding a prisoner of the crown?"

"My brother is a member of the King's guard," explained Nicolas defensively. "He told us of Simon's release and that his freedom was ordered by William FitzRoy."

"We follow Lord Robert's orders!" boomed the soldier as he stabbed a sack and was attacked by a burst of oats. He cursed, swatted at his hair and cloak, and gruffly rallied his men. "We'll leave you," he glared at Nicolas, "with the warning—if your lie is discovered your family will suffer more than raids!"

*****

Late that evening, Simon sat hunched before Judith, his back to her as she spread the salve and noted, "A few scabs have reopened, but amazingly, very little damage was done."

His splayed fingers kneaded his furrowed brow. She felt his tension and sensed his guilt. "You mustn't blame yourself, Simon. Nothing came of the search. Nicolas was able to salvage the spilt feed, yet he and I are agreed. We can allow you only two days more. The soldiers may return."

"I'll go sooner," he offered, his voice rough with strain.

"No...Two days to gather your strength, then you'll go."

Simon passed most of those two days with Judith and the children, sharing games and tales, and when he could bear a shirt on his back, he ventured down to the stables. His attempts to assist Nicolas were short-lived; he tired easily and would soon slump on a bale of hay where he brooded, morose and distracted.

His last night in London, Simon dreamt of Maura. She lay pressed fast against him, swathed only in a vaporous cloak. His fingers attacked the veil, groping, ripping, desperate for her touch. His need for her hurt as he found her warm lips and gripped her silken flesh. Wrapping to her, he rolled to his back. The pain and his own cry startled him awake.

Judith instantly answered his distress. "You're safe Simon, you've had a nightmare, that's all."

"Not a nightmare," he whispered.

Her hand rested on his damp brow and she fretted, "If you're feverish, you'll stay longer."

Simon removed her hand and, with a gentle squeeze, assured, "I'm fine, Judith. It's time I left."

She nodded and murmured a plaintive, "We'll sorely miss you."

"There's so much I need to say to you and Nicolas," said he.

"You'll say it when your troubles are done and you next come to visit. And I insist you bring Maura." And what she'd long prayed to see—Simon's smile, fleetingly appeared.

*****

Her pinched face framed by the open window, Maura searched Winchester Castle's bailey, praying that this was the day Simon would come. Five long days had passed since her arrival, allowing ample time for her morbid imagination to take full flight. She was convinced he'd been recaptured and, if not killed, buried so deeply, that no one would ever discover his cell. Time had also dredged up nightmares and portents that made her question their imminent meeting. Rose knew of Maura's adventures in Normandy, yet not eager for Rose's scowling disapproval, Maura had confided only to Almodis her planned tryst with Simon.

She paced the path she'd worn through the rushes. As her wishful gaze swept the bailey, Maura spied Almodis striding toward the main gates, her troop of guards marching behind. Almodis stopped, whirled, and with furious gestures and curses to match, sent the men scattering; Godfrey alone remained. Maura's chuckling prompted Rose to ask, "What's so amusing?"

"Oh, Rose…it's Almodis. She's insulted her entire collection of guards."

Rose joined her at the window and, clicking her tongue, remarked, "The gossip that woman breeds is outrageous."

"She is my friend," said Maura defiantly. "I won't have her slandered."

"Well," Rose answered as she deposited a pile of fresh tunics on the bed, "if what's said is true, she's an evil influence on you."

Maura rolled her eyes in exasperation. "Rose, please don't start."

"I won't...for now, but only because you need to leave this chamber. You've closeted yourself long enough. It's not healthy to deny yourself fresh air."

"But it's comfortable here, and didn't you say I deserved a bit a comfort? Besides, I ride with Almodis every day."

"*That* in itself is unhealthy," quipped Rose.

"Rose," she said gently, "I need time by myself to resolve what's happened over the past few weeks."

"I know it hurts you to have left Simon," said Rose decisively, "In time, you'll come to see it was for the best. Don't wallow in the gloom of your past, think of the future and your betrothed. You mentioned he's handsome, brave, and kind. Be content with that, Maura."

Sadness dulled Maura's eyes. "I appreciate your advice, but I'd still like to be alone awhile."

"You're alone far too often," grumbled Rose as she turned to leave. "I'll return to fetch you for supper."

As the door clicked shut, Maura returned to her steadfast vigil at the window.

*****

His long journey done, Simon dismounted and guided E'dain through the dense crowd flocking Winchester's market square. Sleet whipped by a savage wind bit at his cheeks as he glanced up into the forever gray sky. He limped along, wincing at jarring bodies and the stench of dangling pig, sheep, and calf carcasses, long past fresh. He paused to invigorate his senses at the baker's stall, his mouth watering as he inhaled the sumptuous offerings. A stolen fingertip of honey cost him a swat across the back of his hand. He yowled in surprise, then turned the baker's glower to a beam with a shining coin. As he munched a bun, his eyes darted from stall to stall, finally alighting upon his target. He smiled and hurried toward a stall hung with vibrantly colored silks, bleached crisp linens, and intricate lace. There was no one about, so Simon leant over the counter and called, "Arthur! Arthur, are you there?"

From behind damask curtains poked a chubby, blotchy face, decorated with a peppered beard and topped with silver, shoulder-length hair. "Yes? What? Simon!" Arthur's emerald eyes glittered with glee as he swung round the counter and caught Simon in an effusive hug. "My God, lad, it's wonderful to see you! Come behind the stall where it's warm. My old bones gripe in this nasty air. We'll share ale and talk."

Simon raised a hand in protest. "No Arthur, I'm disturbing your work. I'll return later."

A dismissing wave eased Simon's concern. "My assistant will mind the stall. He needs the practice and I need a rest." The dense damask hid a tiny storage area, stacked with bolts of material, roofed with skins, and centered by a fire. Simon sat cross-legged by the flames, removed his gloves, and spread his palms to soak in the warmth. Glancing up, he quickly took in his friend's jolly appearance. Arthur's playful expression and sparkling eyes never failed to coax a smile, and his thick paunch jiggled as he chuckled warmly down at Simon. "How long has it been, lad?"

"Six months, a year?" guessed Simon. "Far too long."

"I agree," returned Arthur as he plopped his lumbering figure down opposite Simon. He shifted his full-length tunic for comfort, and poured and passed a cup of ale. "And how is your sweet mother?"

"Quite well. She sends her love."

"I wish she'd deliver it in person."

"She's been busy."

"Tell me, what brings you to Winchester?"

"I really can't say."

Suspense gripped Arthur's voice. "Are you engaged in another secret mission?"

"I suppose it could be called 'secret'," replied Simon with a furtive smirk.

"Has the King returned?"

"No, he still battles in Normandy." Simon shrewdly switched topics. "Arthur, I need a favor."

"Of course. What is it?"

"I need a place to stay."

"I'm surprised you felt the need to ask. My home is yours. How long can you visit?"

"Six weeks."

"Six weeks?" Arthur arched a brow and paused a pensive moment. "I'll be leaving in a week's time for the continent to procure more supplies. If you don't mind being on your own, you could mind the cottage for me."

"Are you certain I'll be no trouble?"

"You'll be doing me a favor. And while I'm still here, I'll relish your company." Arthur scratched his head in wonder. "Six weeks...I don't believe I've ever heard of you staying anywhere for that long. This *must* be important. Come, Simon, I can't bear the intrigue, open up to me."

"I truly can't."

"Hmmm...If it's not the King's business then perhaps it's personal. A bit of a rendezvous, eh? Not a village girl, there would be no secret there. And besides, each time I've tried to introduce you to a woman, you're far too busy. If she's taken you from your hectic schedule, she must be quite special."

Simon placed a log on the fire and suppressed a grin, answering, "Arthur, don't keep on. I won't tell you and that's final."

"Oh yes you will. I always manage to squeeze the truth from you...eventually." Arthur slapped his knee. "Why, of course! So you've set your sights high...she's royalty!"

Simon flushed scarlet and rose to leave. Arthur stretched out, caught his leg, and begged, "No, lad. Don't go, stay. You tease too easily. Humor an old man. What harm can there be in guessing?" Simon surrendered and sat again, his expression uneasy as Arthur babbled on. "Here at the market I'm witness to every bit of gossip seeping from the castle. Let's see, at present there is one royal lady and her ward in residence." Arthur's eyes twinkled as he sighed, "The Lady Almodis...I've heard tell all high-born men in the country dream of sharing her bed, and most have. But she's your step-mother. No...you're not foolish enough to—"

"Almodis is a sweet lady and a fine friend," cut in Simon, eyeing Arthur with amusement, "and that is all."

"I see her often at the market. She's a beauty with an acid tongue and a delightful sense of humor. We get along marvelously! If only I were high-born," Arthur sighed. "The Lady's ward has just arrived, but already tongues wag about her recent exploits."

Piqued, Simon drew nearer and pressed, "Who? Who do they wag about?"

"For the past week she has accompanied the Lady Almodis on her trips to the market. Lovely thing she is. Quiet...There's an air of sadness about her. She speaks beautiful English."

"What gossip, Arthur? What's said about her?"

"You've never been interested in gossip," said Arthur, casting a leery eye. Then he cracked a knowing grin. "Ahhhh...your eyes tell all your secrets, my boy. It seems the Lady has just returned from Normandy, where she joined in battle to save the youngest FitzRoy and was wounded in the process."

"Wounded?!" choked Simon, agape.

"That *is* what's whispered."

Simon leapt up, knocked over his cup of ale, and blurted, "I must go!"

"Wait, Simon!" cried Arthur in pursuit. "Go where?"

"To the castle!" Simon shouted back.

Arthur's question, "Do you think that's wise?" fell on deaf ears, as Simon was swallowed up by the squirming mob.

Arthur spoke to E'dain, who chewed contentedly on a swatch of wool. "Well, I suppose he'll have to return to fetch you, and I did get my answer." Embarrassed by gawking shoppers, he stopped his conversation, shoved E'dain's nose away, and took on an accommodating expression as a customer approached his stall.

Godfrey struggled to keep pace with Almodis as she stomped across the drawbridge and down the village lane. She stopped, hands on hips, and sniped, "Are you coming or not?"

"Yes, my Lady," he puffed.

"Godfrey, you must try harder to keep those horrid men from under my feet!"

"I'll try harder, my Lady."

A gust of wind whipped back her hood, disheveling her neatly woven braids, and sleet pelted her face, further inciting her ire. "Blast!" she cursed, shrouding her head, "I'm sick to death of this stinking weather!"

"There's nothing I can do to remedy that, my Lady," he noted simply.

Surprised at his answer, Almodis glanced at his wry grin and smiled. "You do cheer me, and for that I'm grateful." A loping figure approaching stole her attention; his hood had blown back and there was no mistaking that unruly golden mane. "My word, Godfrey," said a stunned Almodis, "it's Simon!"

Simon grumbled to his feet, "Why didn't she tell me? Why am I always the last to know?"

As he strode past, Almodis swiped at his wrist. He whirled, instinctively wielding a balled fist, then froze to her demand, "And where are you off to in such a flurry?"

Hand still raised, Simon flashed a shocked smile. "Almodis!" he cried, spreading his arms to hug. But his hearty welcome was disrupted by a gathering crowd.

"Don't stop," she muttered. "Hug me. It's expected." As they warmly embraced, she whispered in his ear, "I do hope you weren't planning on bursting through the main gates. If so, yours would have been a very short visit."

"Robert's men believe I'm headed here?" he whispered back.

"Yes indeed," she concurred through a tight smile. "And all the guards have been alerted. I may be able to cajole the men policing the main gates to let you in, but we must be sly." Still clutching his hands, she stepped back and swept an admiring gaze from his head to his toes. "My, my," she said appreciatively, "you do heal nicely, don't you."

Simon tensed their grip, "Almodis, I must thank—"

"Not now," she cautioned and, as he turned to speak to Godfrey, she blurted, "No, Simon. Don't acknowledge him. And lift your hood. We'll say you are a messenger newly arrived from Mortain, relaying an important message from Lord Robert. Keep your distance and don't utter a word. Now come." Simon did as told and followed a safe distance behind. He watched curiously her performance with the guards. At first they appeared cautious, then as she explained coquettishly why she had returned so swiftly, they seemed to melt in her giggly presence. They nodded and clumsily stepped from her path. She motioned sharply to Godfrey, and Simon, bent and shrouded, trailed them through the gatehouse.

Once inside the bailey, Simon trotted to her side and muttered in awe, "You are brilliant!"

"I know. We'll go to my chamber first. There are things that must be said."

"But your guards—" reminded Simon.

"Not to worry. They're at the alehouse in the village drinking themselves into a stupor."

As they entered the security of Almodis' chamber, Simon clutched her hand and spoke with deep emotion, "I thank you, my Lady, for...my life. Confronting Rufus took great courage—"

"No, Simon," she interjected, "bravery played no role in my doings with Rufus. I toyed a bit with his mind, such as it is. The true heroes of this adventure are Maura, Alan, and his family, and we mustn't forget Godfrey."

"Godfrey," said Simon, "I don't know how to—"

"No need to thank me, Simon," said Godfrey mildly. "I'm happy to see you looking so well."

Almodis cast an affectionate gaze Godfrey's way. "He understates things so masterfully, doesn't he, Simon?" Godfrey blushed scarlet as she continued to tease, "And you do enjoy your new position as my personal guard, don't you, Godfrey?"

"I certainly do, my Lady."

"Simon, have we upset you in some way?" she wondered, noticing his frown.

"No one will accept my thanks!"

Her smile turned to a smirk. "Oh, I know someone who will gladly accept *anything* you care to offer." Suddenly she took on a serious tone, "But before I take you to her, I must warn, you have little time. My guards may return shortly. Make quick plans to meet later this evening, somewhere less obvious. And more importantly, Maura is deeply scarred by your past. Be patient with her, Simon, she needs time to adjust to your over-enthused presence. If I find that you've pressured or hurt her in any way, I swear I'll—"

"Stop, Almodis," Simon returned sternly. "Don't waste what little time we *do* have. I would never hurt her...believe that."

Impressed by his boldness, Almodis took his hand and decided, "Then we'll go."

They moved swiftly yet cautiously along dim corridors to Maura's chamber and as they walked, Simon asked Almodis, "Is Maura well?"

"At times she's a bit morose, but physically she seems fine. Didn't you just see her?"

"Yes, but I heard some bewildering news that makes me think she's keeping things from me."

"I haven't a clue what 'things' you suspect. Here we are."

Eagerly, Simon reached for the latch. Almodis' hand covered his as she insisted, "No, let me. I'll soften the shock."

A splash of frosty water from her washing bowl helped stave off Maura's sleepiness. She removed her tunic to continue washing for supper and paused to a light rapping. Rose couldn't have returned so quickly, she thought, and wouldn't bother to knock. She had just witnessed Almodis' departure from the castle, so who could be her visitor? Uneasiness filled her; she clutched a tunic to hide her flimsy chemise and called out guardedly, "Who's there?"

The door cracked open and Almodis' beaming face popped inside. With a tight chuckle, she announced, "Maura, there's someone here who wishes to speak with you."

She swung the door wide and Simon stepped into the room, transforming Maura's tentative expression to one of exquisite joy. The tunic fell from her slippery grasp as she gawked in wonder. This was not the same man she had left only five days past; his color was high, his eyes clear, his smile warm and brimming with hope.

Simon took a giant step forward, but her amazed expression made him hesitate. Her happiness failed to mask the doubt sparking her eyes, and his heart and smile sank at the terrible thought of being spurned yet again. His sudden lost look startled Maura from her trance. She tripped on the tunic, and he laughed nervously as she rushed into his eager arms.

Almodis let go a dreamy sigh as she watched their impassioned embrace, then shook to alertness and cautioned, "There's no time for that now." They ignored her and she stressed louder, "Simon, Maura stop!" As if doused with ice, they parted and turned to hear, "Hurry! You have plans to make, unless, of course, you enjoy battling Rose."

Godfrey poked his head in the door, confirming, "The Lady Rose is presently on the stairs."

They shared anxious glances, Simon urging, "Where? Where can we meet?"

Maura searched her mind and promptly found the perfect solution. "Go to the old Minster's ruins on the west side of the keep. Opposite the crumbling wall, you'll find a small bedchamber. You can enter from the bailey."

"When?"

"Rose retires shortly after supper. As soon as her eyes shut, I'll come to you."

"Simon, go quickly," said Almodis strictly.

Still unsure, he refused to let Maura go.

Maura reached to caress his cheek, vowing, "Simon, believe that I will come." A fervid kiss sealed her pledge.

"I'll escort you out," proclaimed Godfrey tersely, as he broke their clutch and hustled Simon through the door.

At the click of the latch, Maura's euphoria withered. Almodis came close and offered a sympathetic hand. "Maura, how can you look so glum? He's come, just as he swore he would."

"But Almodis," she worried, "he sensed my doubts."

"Then we will rid you of those meddlesome doubts. Tell Rose I've invited you to my chamber after supper for a chat and not to bother waiting up. She won't suspect a thing, and it will be such great fun to prepare you for your night of—"

"Maura!" The women snapped to Rose's fractious greeting and imposing figure, hands on hips, and chin cocked skeptically. "What's gone on here?" she demanded.

Maura gingerly side-stepped Almodis and, her voice heaped with innocence, cajoled, "Oh, Rose, I'm so pleased you've returned. We were only visiting. Would you care to join us?"

Rose, her black eyes accusing, strode rigidly by them. She slowly opened the door joining their chambers, turned to hurl one last venomous glare, and punctuated her displeasure by slamming the door after her.

*****

While Maura soaked in Almodis' luxurious wooden tub and contemplated her shriveled toes, Almodis draped her entire wardrobe across her bed. She tapped her chin, twisted her mouth, and shook her head. "I can't decide. You'll have to choose, though it wouldn't matter if you greeted him in a sack. He'll have it off you quickly enough. Maura? Did you hear me?" Almodis glanced up petulantly. "Stop thinking so hard," she chided. "You'll permanently crease your brow."

Maura started to protest, "I'm not—"

"Don't lie to me," Almodis piped in. "For days you've been dreaming of Simon between your legs—admit it."

"I should introduce you to Henry," sighed Maura in exasperation. "You two are *so* alike."

Almodis rested her forearms on the wall of the tub. "The *baby* Prince?" she asked pointedly. "No thank you! I don't want a fumbling adolescent. I desire a grown man with the patience to teach and learn—" Maura disappeared beneath the water's bubbly surface. "Maura?" called Almodis, poking at the water. "Where have you gone?"

Maura gasped and sputtered as she resurfaced. "Al...Almodis, please pass me my robe."

"I will if you tell me what's happened to your guard."

"Alan?" Maura asked. She stepped from the tub, slipped on the robe, and hurried to the fire.

"Yes...Alan. He's been conspicuously absent." Almodis handed Maura a jewel-embossed hairbrush, and wandered over to her vanity where she sampled several vials of perfume, dabbing the scent on various body parts.

"He's gone to Normandy to speak to the King," said Maura.

"About what?"

"Joining my household in Yorkshire."

"Aren't you the lucky one," taunted Almodis, "surrounded by all the pretty boys."

"Don't talk nonsense, Almodis."

"When is he due to return?"

"Soon."

"What will he do till your wedding?"

"I have no idea. What are you plotting, Almodis?" asked Maura leerily.

"You know how intensely I despise my guards, except of course Godfrey. It would be pleasant to own a guard who's gallant, selfless, and easy on the eyes."

"Own?"

"Borrow then."

"He's not my property to lend, Almodis. You need to discuss the matter with Alan."

"Could you be a dear and ask for me?"

"Since when are you shy around men?"

"The last time I spoke to him, I was a bit...awkward. Here, let me," Almodis offered, snatching the brush from Maura.

Maura winced to Almodis' assault on her damp hair and remarked, "*You* awkward? I find that terribly hard to imagine." She strolled to the bed and began perusing the many gowns strewn before her. Almodis, caught in a tangle, followed. Maura's inquiring touch hesitated over a modest sea-green frock. "This one's quite nice," she commented. Swiftly shedding the robe, she wriggled into the gown, and smoothed its fit.

"Well? Would you?" pressed Almodis.

"Would I what?" Maura teased.

"Ask him for me?"

"I suppose."

"Oh, Maura bless you!" gushed Almodis. "Turn. I'll lace it for you, and I do believe you've picked the most flattering one of all." Maura yanked the bodice higher and Almodis questioned, "Why are you ashamed? You fill the bodice beautifully." Almodis glanced down her front and remarked enviously, "It's only now that I have breasts worth viewing." Her hands caressed her swollen belly. "In a few months' time, I expect you to be swelled up with Simon's babe."

"No!" Maura replied adamantly.

"Why ever not? You'll be wed to Hugh from wherever in less than two months. No one will ever know or care."

"I won't wish for something that may never happen. When they forced my baby from me, they hurt me inside. My body has never fully recovered."

Not expecting such a frank reply, Almodis averted her gaze and turned starkly silent. The lines returned to Maura's brow, deeper than before, as she sat before Almodis' vanity and allowed her to finish combing out her hair. Almodis grew worried at Maura's listless mood and wondered, "Where's your enthusiasm, Maura? Why do you fret so? Is it those doubts you spoke of before?"

"Yes..." sighed Maura, sinking her chin into her palm.

"Simon obviously has no doubts," noted Almodis.

"He's not well, Almodis."

"He seems in rare form to me. Why is it so difficult for you?"

Maura caught Almodis' brushing hand, turned to face her, and motioned for her to sit. Almodis did so, listening attentively as Maura explained, "When I'm with Simon it's not difficult, but in the week we've been apart everything's become quite muddled. I do know that if I lie with him tonight I'll think of nothing else and ignore all the risks and dangers. Almodis," she added, squeezing her friend's hand, "if we're caught this time there will be no—"

"Maura," argued Almodis, "you're both older now, less frivolous. You've suffered the dangers and know to be more careful. I'll do all I possibly can to protect you. My guards are bumbling fools. They won't suspect a thing, and besides Simon is expert at becoming invisible...sometimes." With a seriousness Almodis rarely exhibited, she rose, paced before the fire, and continued, "You *do* realize that if you had decided to take any other man to your bed, there would be little problem. Even if that man were Will, Robert would simply look away. Simon torments Robert. He wakes from nightmares crying out for him and for...Edith. He hates Simon's gentleness and confuses his own softness with weakness. Yet in Simon it's a great strength, a strength that Robert refuses to accept. Simply put, he's jealous of Simon and that's why he wants him out of sight."

"I've never been close to Robert," said Maura wistfully. "Once long ago, he was gentle and loving, especially with Simon."

"His feelings for Simon are far more intense than his loyalty to Will," added Almodis. "Will, however, possesses a curious power over Robert, the power to have his every lie believed."

"Do you and Will still...speak?"

"No." As Almodis stared into the flames, she paled and fretted, "He terrifies me."

Maura tensed. "Why?" She pressed. "What's he done?"

"I won't spoil this night with tales of a monster. But I advise you to stay well away from him. He can be quite treacherous. Maura, may I be blunt?"

"Please..."

Almodis settled by her ward and lamented, "We are Robert's chattel, to be used and disposed of as he sees fit. He's made your past a hell, and your future can't be altered. So you must take pleasure when and where you can find it. I know we haven't known each other long, but I feel an affinity for you. At Berkhamstead, when I confessed my past, I bragged and purposely left out the more lurid bits. Perhaps if I share those with you, you'll realize how truly honored you are to own Simon's love." Taking up a mirror, Almodis fingered wisps of hair crowning her brow and spoke to her reflection with scant emotion. "I was wed at twelve to an older baron who took great delight in raping and battering me. He lived ten long years after our marriage. The only joy I found in our union is that he perished while attacking me. A month later, I was shackled to another old, impotent man, who amused himself by watching his friends abuse me. That farce lasted four years. My third husband was younger, but alas, he preferred to populate his bed with young boys, and shunned me altogether. It was then that I discovered any attention was better than none, so I began inviting strangers into my bed. During that desperate time, I met Will." She shifted uncomfortably and, for a slight moment, betrayed a hidden vulnerability. "I know it's hard for you to fathom, but our first years together were fairly pleasant. At times, he was gentle and seemed to appreciate my company out of bed as well. As the years wore on he hardened, trying to compete with the devils he calls friends. And then came Robert, and he *truly* is a mystery. I'm aware of the horrors he's committed, but I believe he feels genuine affection for me. He's capable of kindness and, as you can see," she said, sweeping the mirror over the contents of her vanity, "he's extremely generous...to me." A misplaced smile interrupted her grave speech. "I think he pretends I'm Edith and is somehow trying to buy back her love. I feel little for him, except perhaps gratitude for giving me this child." She turned abruptly to Maura, her gaze and voice keen, "I may seem quite experienced to you, but I excel only at the techniques of love, I've never felt the emotions. Maura, I would kill to have what you will know this night! It's a rare gift, so don't you dare let it slip away! If you do, *I* will never forgive you, and I doubt *you* will ever be able to forgive yourself." Embarrassed by her fervor, Almodis quickly swiped away an escaping tear. She tipped a vial of perfume, dotted the place between Maura's breasts, and began babbling and fidgeting. "There...you look absolutely radiant. You'll need blankets, and I've made up some sweet mead, my own potent recipe, and I stole you honey cakes, for you will surely have a hearty appetite after..."

Tears stung Maura's eyes as she stopped Almodis' flitting with a gentle hand. "Why didn't you tell me this before?"

"It depresses me and I so want you to be happy. Are you still confused?" Maura lowered her moist gaze and nodded. Almodis lifted her chin and spoke softly, "I can't decide for you. You promised to meet with him. Go, talk to Simon, confess your doubts. And when the time comes and he touches you—then, and only then, will you have your answer."

*****

Simon leant up against the door frame and watched his foot tap at the charred remains of a fire. He huffed, raked his hand through his hair, and aimlessly wandered the dreary chamber. A nervous itch crawled up his back. Struggling to reach it, his arm became tangled in a dangling spider web. As he swatted at the sticky veil, he jumped to a flock of mice scuttling from their nest of moldy rushes, and pitched upon the rock hard bed. *No wonder no one ever comes here,* he thought, shivering from the many drafts that swirled about the chamber. Impatience flared his discomfort; he rose and paced a tight circle. Arthur had suggested he mingle with the peasants returning to the bailey from the fields, which was excellent advice, but the toilsome wait was driving him mad! Sitting again, he purposely caught his fingers in the holes of a worn blanket, and shared his frustration with the oppressive silence, chanting, "She will come, she will come..."

Maura snuck out of the keep, stopping sporadically to retrieve her tumbling presents. She mouthed a curse as the blanket slipped from her fumbling grasp and tripped her. The cakes spilled to the ground. Squatting, she dusted them against her skirt, rose with a deep bracing breath, and stealthily continued across the moon lit bailey. She neared the door to the old minster, and her quandary intensified as she spied a pacing figure shadowed on the crumbled wall. Inches from the door, she hesitated and set the blankets on the ground, and the mead and cakes on the blanket. Primping her hair and gown failed to calm her, so pressing her palms tightly together, she inhaled deeply and ducked through the entrance.

Simon halted his pacing and gaped in wonder at her striking visage. He instantly sensed her reserve and wrestled his impulse to grab her. Her hands still clamped together, she sat stiffly on Rose's old bed and meekly met his penetrating stare. Anxiety stabbed her belly and the frigid air fed her restlessness. She struggled to sit still; if he guessed she was cold, he would want to warm her, and she didn't want his touch, not yet. Swallowing dryly, she asked, "Have you been waiting long?"

"No, not long," Simon answered skittishly. He sat on the opposite bed, and plunged his fingers deep into the mattress' brittle straw.

"You haven't said where you're staying," she said, her expression vague.

"In the village with Arthur. He's an old friend of mine and my mother's."

"And how is...Edith?" Her uneasy gaze slipped to the floor, and her knuckles paled from their taut clutch.

"She's fine...Maura, we needn't make small talk. Arthur said you were wounded in Normandy. Is that true?"

"It was nothing, a scratch."

"Why did you hide it from me?"

"There were more important things to say."

"Did Henry help at all?"

"Of course he did. There was a raid. Henry caught an arrow in his shoulder. We hid under a table and I tried to help Marc, but..." She paused to the shuddering memory.

"You saw Marc?" Simon anxiously asked. "How is he?"

"Miserable..." She eased her hands apart and absently picked at cake crumbs on her skirt.

"You shouldn't have gone to Normandy," he berated.

"Simon, don't start." She raised her eyes and stressed, "You were imprisoned because of me! I had to try to help."

"Let me see your wound."

"No!" she insisted. Her mind screamed leave, but her body refused to budge.

Her stark expression betrayed grave misgivings and Simon's panic surged. He struggled for the perfect words to keep her near. "Maura, why did you choose this place for our meeting?" he tenderly asked.

"For the past two years, this was home for me and Rose."

"I don't understand. You chose to live here?"

"No, we were forced."

"By whom? Robert?"

"No, Rufus wanted us out of his way." Her rising discomfort caused her to babble, "It...it wasn't till last November that the King discovered Rufus' cruelty and allowed us Adela's chamber, but we learned much from our suffering, how to garden, scavenge, steal—"

Exasperated, Simon stood and demanded, "Stop, Maura! What has happened since London to change your mind about us? Was it Rose, did you tell her—"

"No, Simon, it wasn't Rose. It was time, time to remember and—"

"And?"

"Dream...I know if we come back together, it will all happen again! We need to forgive each other and carry on with our lives—separately."

"No!" He lunged forward, his alarm and voice spiraling, "You can't mean that!"

"But I do," she said staidly, raising a halting hand.

His restraint died and he raged, "In London, your kisses, caresses, sweet words, were they all lies?! Why are you torturing me?!"

"I'm not torturing you, I didn't lie!" she cried, burying her anguish in her hands.

"Look at me, Maura!" He dropped to one knee and frantically clutched at her fingers. "The memories aren't all nightmares! I'll help you remember the joy, make up to you the hurt. I need to be close to you, touch you...*Please*, look at me!"

She refused his plea. He rose, jerked away, and clamped his mouth to stifle his moan; he wouldn't allow her his agony, she'd only pity him! Tears threatened as he spoke with a tremulous calm, "If you're not convinced that staying with me is right, if loving me means running away then...go. But Maura," he despaired, "I'll always—" he spun to a shuffling noise and found himself alone and whispering to the groaning wind, "—love you."

*****

CHAPTER EIGHTEEN - TENUOUS BLISS

"God's blood!" Simon cursed aloud, ramming his fist into his cupped hand. What had he done?! He'd sworn to be patient, not to pressure her. And it had taken only a few terrible moments to drive her from the room and perhaps his life! He could hear himself railing at her, not believing his words, yet helpless to stop. Almodis' warning came to him, 'She's deeply scarred by her past'. Rose's tragic tale flashed in his mind, and Maura's confessed fear, '...if we come back together...it will all happen again!'. The nightmares she suffered were of the beatings, the raping, their dead child! He'd run off and left her to be tortured! Of course her memories blotted all joy they might have shared. It was a miracle she hadn't spat at him! Guilt over his selfishness sickened him; he inhaled deeply to quell his nausea, and slumped on to the bed. Then, beyond his grinding teeth and pounding heart, he heard weeping. He rushed to the door and found Maura sprawled amongst the blanket, cakes, and mead, her face hidden in her arms, heart-rending sobs quaking her shoulders. How could he save her from this misery? Her tears drove him to his knees and he lay a tentative hand on her shoulder. "Maura, Maura, don't cry. I'm sorry. I never meant to—" He paused as the memory of their last night at Dunheved tainted his thoughts. He'd failed to soothe her then; this night had to be different, and he heard himself murmur, "I'm here to help you, *please* let me help you."

Maura felt his touch and, lifting swollen eyes, searched his shamed expression. Her fingers tightened to his. Simon reacted swiftly to her needy gesture; he swept her and the blanket up, and carried them to her old bed. His succoring embrace surrounded and gently rocked her. "Talk to me, Maura. I need to help you."

"Oh, Simon," she sniffed, "I'm so frightened."

"Of me?"

"No, never you...I fear we'll be found out." A violent tremble took her and she clung closer. "Hold me! *Please* hold me!"

He bundled her in the blanket and clutched her fast to his chest; his cheek he rested on her hair. "We're safe here. Robert and Will are far away and..." A fat mouse scurrying through the rushes snared their attention, and confirmed his next comment, "...no one would ever willingly visit this hovel!" Her slim smile revived his hope and shattered the gloom.

"I'm so sorry, Simon," she said, wiping her eyes on his offered sleeve. "I didn't intend to hurt you, but my fears made me cruel. Everyone has been so free with advice—contrary advice that clashed with my nightmares."

"Whose advice?"

"Rose, Almodis, Henry, Marc...All are convinced they know what's best for me. I love them for their concern, but..."

"Maura, you've always known your own mind. How could you let them confuse you?"

"I had to listen!" she pressed, gripping his shoulders. "You almost died! I can't risk our lives, not again."

"You won't. You had nothing to do with my capture. I foolishly rode straight into Robert's trap, and learned my lesson rather...harshly. How can I ease the pain I've caused you?"

"I need—" She hesitated to a queer sight. A squat, banded candle scored with numerals sat on the table.

He answered before she asked, "I must leave at dawn when the peasants depart for the fields. We have but eight hours left together. What do you need from me, my love?"

"I need to know why you left me at Dunheved!" she returned, her eyes narrow and voice tense. "Rose said you ran to save my life, but that makes no sense to me."

"I pray it will after I explain. It's a long tale and before I start you must tell me how you warmed this pit. Where did you find wood?"

"We stole it and stacked it against the far wall. I noticed there were a few pieces left."

"Then I'll make us a fire."

Maura felt his reluctance to release her. "You needn't worry, Simon," she softly assured. "I'll not run off again." She rested back against the stone wall and watched enthralled as he shed his cloak and tossed it on the other bed. He wore no tunic, only a bulky, unbleached shirt, carelessly tucked into black braies. She hugged her knees and wistfully remembered him always looking mussed and scruffy, yet always beautiful.

He left the chamber and returned swiftly, one arm stocked with wood, the other brimming with Almodis' treats. Setting the cakes and mead on the rickety table that parted the beds, he turned and scanned the room. "Where did you make the fire?"

"Just outside the door. The chamber gets a bit of heat, while the bailey draws most of the smoke."

He nodded and crouched to stack the kindling.

She felt a certain comfort in the fact that his appearance had changed little in the years they'd been apart. His silky hair was longer, hanging low on his neck, and paler. How she had loved catching her fingers in its lush locks. His skin was bronzed, she supposed from much travel. In summer, she had been so jealous when he'd turned a golden brown while she freckled and burned apple red. And now his beautiful brooding face was creased with deep thought and she knew he was rehearsing his speech. Maura ached inside as she watched him glide gracefully across the room, and catch up and shred an old blanket to top the kindling. She wanted so much to touch...

Simon struck a flint and caught the spark to the cloth. The tiny flame quickly flourished and danced nimbly among the aged wood. A breeze moaned through a loophole in the wall; its frosty fingers tickled the back of Maura's neck. She shivered and pulled her shroud tighter.

As he spread his cloak before the fire, Simon noticed her discomfort, so, with a cautious smile and outstretched hand, he murmured, "Now come, and I'll tell you all."

At his touch, the chill left her body. They settled together on the cushiony wool. She nestled back against his chest and he wrapped the blanket round his shoulders and his arms round her. "Look, Maura," he said brightly, motioning to the door, "we're not alone."

Past the fire and beyond the broken stones, a bulging moon sat upon the curtain wall, shedding its luminous glow across the virgin snow. The fire and his body spread a contenting warmth through her limbs. She relaxed and cuddled closer.

There was a keenness to Simon's voice as his grim tale commenced, as if every word, every inflection had to be flawless for her to believe. "When I left you to go reason with Edith, I discovered Robert knew we were lovers. He blamed Edith and was hurting her..." His wrenching confession often tripped his words, but Maura's bolstering touch enabled him to continue. And as she listened, the heavy doubt cloaking her mind gradually began to lift. Nearing the story's end, grief cracked Simon's voice and bent his back; his moist cheek nuzzled her shoulder. "When I came back to Dunheved, everyone and everything was gone—you, I was told, had left for Normandy to wed. A cathedral in Wales took me in, sheltered and cared for me. Alan came to fetch me two years later. Between then and Martinmas, I never stopped searching for you. At Winchester, I couldn't believe I'd finally found you, but the hate in your eyes told me you'd not been told the truth. Do you remember battling the guards?"

"Yes," she whispered with remorse, her fingers skimming the length of his forearm. "I cut you...I didn't know it was you."

"I know that...now. Afterwards, when I took you to your chamber, you clung to me and begged me to stay. You gave me hope that in your heart a bit of our love still lived."

A brittle silence descended as Maura struggled to piece together his puzzling tale. She could easily accept *his* actions for he truly believed he was saving her life. Still one stabbing doubt remained, making her stiffen and ease from his hold. "Simon, why did Edith lie to you when she knew I'd be punished?"

"She believed what she told me."

Her arms shielded her body while she vigorously wagged her head and sputtered with panic, "But...but she left me alone...locked away with the guards!"

"She couldn't have saved you. Robert had her banished."

"Edith deliberately left me to be punished!" Her frantic eyes darted from Simon to the door, then fixed glaringly upon the flames. She started to crawl toward the door. "Edith...she hated me, hated me because you loved me!"

"Oh no, Maura." He crept after her, striving to soothe, "She loves you, she has always loved you! That time still haunts—" His arms dropped loosely to his sides as he watched her terror turn inward, her eyes gorge with fear. And he knew she had returned to Dunheved, to her chamber, and to the guards...

Brutal images battered Maura, the sentries' huge, rough hands pinning her to the bed, beating her, chain mail tearing her skin as they forced her to submit. She heard again her endless screams, and her mind screamed louder—escape! The fire barred her way! Her nails dug her scalp, her palms pressed her eyes as she wailed in torment, "Simon, save me! Make the guards go away. *Please*, make them go!"

Softly and swiftly came his rescue. "Maura, I can't fight the guards in your mind. Only you can." He cupped her face in his hands and his tenderness cut through the savage visions. "I can only help you forget."

"How?" she cried, "I still see and feel it all!"

"Stay with me." His pale eyes caught and held hers. "We'll turn the nightmares to sweet dreams. Tonight you tried, but couldn't leave me." He inched nearer; his hands swept back her hair, his lips brushed across her brow. "Believe and trust in me. Let me hold you...I'll comfort you."

Maura buried her face in his shirt and rubbed her heated cheeks against its coarse weave. Snug in the safety of his arms, she was free for a blissful moment from the horrors of their past. Her heart thudded with his and her breathy words warmed and tickled his lips, "You came back for me. I always knew you...you would come back."

His head spun to her murmurs, her nearness, her scent. He sank to his side and lay silent and still...waiting, as her fingers searched temptingly beneath his shirt, skimming his taut muscles, feeding his impatience. Her mouth lingered over his, then broke away to plead, "Make me forget, my love! Give me back our joy."

Their lips crushed together, and when at last they parted for air, Simon stripped off his shirt.

Maura glimpsed his wounds and winced, "Oh Simon, how can we—"

"No, Maura," he ardently insisted, "I've healed, there's no pain. Please don't stop! Turn. Let me see you!"

She presented her back, fretting, "But I may hurt you if—"

"At this very moment, my sweet..." he swore as his fingers fumbled and twisted with the gown's laces, "...hurting me is impossible."

His last liberating tug on the stubborn strings drew from them both a long euphoric sigh. She stretched before him, her breath quickening as he eagerly peeled the frock from her shoulders, freeing her breasts, and tugged it down over her hips, and beyond her knees. She eased one leg loose and kicked the dress away.

Simon froze awestruck over the long winsome length of her body, till a yank on his waist cord broke his trance. Maura knelt before him, her radiance and sweet purring instantly banishing the creases from his brow. "Simon, you look every bit as frightened as when we first loved. What worries you?" He could give no answer and kept his wary look. She caressed the stiffness from his neck and shoulders, and charmed away any doubts with swooning kisses and coos, "I want you so...I never stopped wanting you, needing you..."

Her fingers and lips ventured lowered, evoking from him a delirious sigh, and soft whisper, "But do you forgive me?"

"There is nothing *to* forgive. Let me hold and touch you, *make* you believe I love you, and nothing else will matter. Perhaps with my help, you'll find a way to forgive yourself."

Desire blushed away his guilt. He struggled from his braies and hose, and surged into her sumptuous embrace. They sank, sighing, to their sides and slowly, so not to break the spell, sent their lips and fingers exploring...

Simon's touch grew strenuous, compelling. "I know I'll wake from this dream and find you gone!" he moaned. "It's happened too many times before, Maura. I wake in agony!"

"Feel that I'm real." She drew his hand to her breast. His lips zealously followed, stirring within her a fever that coaxed her confession, "I've dreamt of this moment too, and wake burning for you." She pressed his hand to the damp curls between her legs, begging, "Simon, touch me, love me now!" Her thighs wrapped and hugged his hips as she guided him, stroking and enticing, inside. She wriggled to the heat of his flesh, sending him deeper and sparking an eruption of bliss that quivered them closer. Smiles radiant, they lay still a rapturous moment, quietly savoring their reunion.

The fire sputtered to coals, but their passion blazed hotter as they glided together evenly, sensuously. Careful not to touch his back, Maura's fingers tangled and tugged his hair, feathered his arms and chest; his fingers scratched lightly at her back, then crawled lower to knead and grip her hips. The joy of moving inside her wasn't enough—he craved the whole of her! He gathered her in a crushing grip, and buried his face in her neck, his choked plea desperate, "I...I can't let you go! Stay with me forever. I'll take you far away. We'll run—no one will find us!"

Maura felt her bones would break, and gasped her warning, "Simon you mustn't dream. We can't hope! We have but a short time together. All we can do is—"

"No!" he groaned. His fierce kisses smothered her protests as he spread her back upon the cloak and rose up on his knees to vow, "I will make this night last forever, and give you all the love, all the pleasure you deserve and so...so much more."

Her senses reeled to the miracles he worked over her body—nibbles, strokes, licks, all rocking her with immense jolts of bliss. Her cry of ecstasy raised her up; she flung herself against his chest, her frenzied fervor tumbling them back to the ground.

Their fingers gripped and arms stretched high as Simon covered and filled Maura. They strained to an ever soaring passion, melding skin, mingling sweat, mounting groans. A raging need overwhelmed and exhausted him; with her luscious body urging, undulating beneath his and the taste of her hungry kisses, he realized he could not fight it forever. He pressed her hands into the rushes, his mouth to hers, and surrendered to a long suffering moan.

Afraid to let go, they stayed limp and entangled for a long while. Their tears and dampness blended and froze to the sweep of a frigid breeze, making Simon reluctantly break their hold to grope for the blanket. And cuddled beneath its warmth, they drank in more joyful kisses, and whispered sweetly of their love.

*****

Almodis started and flew up from her bed, her eyes vivid with fright. "Godfrey!" she screamed. Instantly her door opened and boot steps trotted to her bedside.

Godfrey parted the curtains and asked urgently, "What is it, my Lady?"

She cocked her head, listened, and trembled her answer, "There's someone..."

"Where?"

"Here! In my chamber!"

"No, my Lady," said Godfrey. "I've not moved from my pallet. You've had a bad dream, that's all. Shall I fetch your servant?"

"Are you certain...there's no one?"

The fear clouding her eyes and blanching her skin unsettled him and he asked, "Would you like me to search your chamber?"

"*Please*," she begged.

With only strips of moonlight to guide him, Godfrey clunked about the room, knocking into chairs and trunks. The noise woke Almodis' mind further and she realized—Will couldn't be here, he was in Mortain with Robert. Yet as her belly grew, so did her fright. She had no doubt Will would carry out his vow to murder her child. When would it happen and where?! Her stomach churned to the sickening thought of Robert's bumbling guards. Of course, there *was* the ever-faithful Godfrey, but she had a need for someone else, someone calm, strong, and gentle, who could perhaps come to care for her in other ways. A tender vision of Alan's face came to her, jealousy tarnishing it as she thought of her ward. Maura loved and was loved. Why couldn't God grant her the same blessing? But then, she and God had never been on congenial terms.

Godfrey made a final sweep of his arm beneath the bed and, satisfied, rose to say, "There's no one, my Lady."

Almodis visibly relaxed, and managed a bleak smile. "It must have been a nightmare. You needn't worry further."

"If you'd like, my Lady, I'll sit inside the door."

"That's a sweet thought, but no, you may return to your mat." She called after his departing figure, "Godfrey..."

"Yes, my Lady?"

"I thank you for your perseverance and kindness."

"My Lady..." He nodded, bowed, and disappeared behind the door. As Almodis drew close the thick curtains and stretched for the extra pelts piled at the bed's foot, she froze and gasped at a fluttering low in her belly. Surely it was an upset caused by supper. Then the tickling came again! Almodis started to call out for Godfrey, but instead found herself giggling to the queer movement. Her hands caressed her belly and a brilliant smile graced her fuddled expression. The child seemed to respond to her loving touch, making her tingle with delight. She must tell Maura! As she settled carefully beneath the pelts, she imagined what a marvelous time they'd have on the morrow, sharing secret desires and joys. And in the dark, she warmed with a curious peace, and crooned to her child a lullaby.

*****

Simon rhythmically combed fingers through Maura's tangled locks as he asked, "Do you feel tired?"

"No..." she sighed, "content, ecstatic, loved...not tired."

She felt him tense to his confession, "Maura, I was afraid you'd leave me again. I don't know what I would've done if you'd gone."

"Simon, you needn't fret so," she soothed, stroking his cheek. "I'm here and you were correct, I've always known my own mind, it just got buried beneath all *my* worries." She paused and pushed up on her elbow, her expression slightly pinched. "You don't believe we'll be found out?"

"Not if we're careful, especially me...I've this tendency to act rather impulsively."

"Do you really?" she answered with a chuckle. "*I've* never noticed."

Her warm laughter drew from him a dazzling smile and his arms hugged her back. His roaming touch discovered tiny bumps on her skin. "You're chilled. I'll fix the fire."

"No." Her grip squeezed. "Stay by me."

Vigorously, he chafed her back and arms. "Does this help?"

"Oh yes, please never stop!"

The candle's flame danced to a whistling breeze, and Simon's gaze shifted briefly to the open door. "The moonlight's gone, and another storm's brewing." He sniffed the smoky air. "I predict snow. We'd best get off this floor or we'll be stiff by morning."

"I pray you'll be," she tittered as they scrambled up and dove onto her old bed. But their raucous laughter shortened to gasps, and vapored breaths clouded the tiny space between them.

They traded strong, brusque caresses to stave off the frigid air, and Simon complained, his teeth chattering, "Bleeding Jesus! How could you live here?"

"We had no choice. The servants stole us blankets and saved us leftovers. But Rose barely survived our second winter, and certainly wouldn't have lasted this one."

"You two are still close?"

"Closer."

"Yet you haven't told her...about us?"

"No. I anticipate an ugly explosion."

"She'll soon grow accustomed to the idea."

"I'm *not* certain of that, Simon...Are you hungry?" she asked, stretching for the treats. "Almodis gave me these tarts and mead."

"I'm famished. A cake please, but no mead." He glimpsed the shrinking candle. "We've only five hours left, and I don't wish to spend them sleeping."

"Nor do I." She presented him a cake, bit one herself, and remarked with a wrinkled nose, "A bit stale...but they'll do."

Simon gulped his down and focused greedily on the remaining tart. "There's only one left. You don't want it, do you...my sweet...my love...my angel?" He planted wet sloppy kisses over her face, deliciously distracting, as his fingers crept toward the table. Only she was quicker and, snatching up the cake, hid it beneath the blanket.

Mischief glittered Maura's eyes as she lured, "You can have it, if you can find it." Simon exuberantly vanished. She squealed and swatted the lump under the blanket. "Simon! It's not there!" Yet her resistance ebbed as his tongue sought out every crumb.

"They've gone everywhere!" he laughed, his caution muffled. "If I don't eat these, the mice surely will."

"We couldn't have that!" Maura gasped again, then dissolved into squirming hysterics.

"It might take awhile," he confirmed.

"Oh, Simon!" She paused her laughter to sigh a plea, "please, don't feel you need to hurry." A tremor of bliss coursed through her and she reached beneath the blanket to tug at his hair. Her finger found and dipped inside his mouth; she yelped and jerked from his bite. He caught her wrist, his coarse cackling thrilling as playful nips climbed her arm. Then abruptly he stopped. "Simon?" she called, baffled. His severe face popped out from under the blanket. "Why did you stop?" she wondered with a frown.

He extended her arm to examine her gash. "*This* was nothing?" he questioned worriedly. "Why wasn't it stitched?"

"There wasn't time, so many had been wounded..." She sat to his censuring look and defended, "Simon, I *had* to go to Normandy. I—"

"My God, woman," he softly interjected as his arms cradled her, and lips lightly brushed her wound, "I've missed you so."

"You also missed some crumbs," she said with a beguiling grin.

"Where? I was certain I got them all."

"Try here..." Maura's finger tapped her lips, and eagerly Simon pressed her back on the bed, his mouth searching, sampling her delights; his body covering and filling her completely.

They remembered well how to make their loving last. Time and again as their fervor neared its peak, they would pause their passion awhile to whisper secrets and soft moans, share kisses and caresses, then cleave back together.

Simon braced himself on his arms and hovered near. "We'll meet here every night till you leave."

"Oh, yes..." she breathed, arching to kiss the hollow of his neck.

"Then I'll follow you to Yorkshire."

"Don't speak of Yorkshire...speak only of us."

Simon paled; his arms quaked and he collapsed by her side.

"Simon, what is it?" Maura fretted. Her alarm thrust her up, but the weight of his hand splayed across her belly kept her prone. His fingers crept her thigh, urging her to her side and, cupped together, they loved again. Maura molded his hands to her breasts. He buried his damp face in her hair, crying out her name as he shuddered violently against her back, his grip so sharp that for an instant, pain and pleasure blended. She waited till his tension eased, then turned to find his ardent hug. Their eyes shone rapture as she murmured, "Sleep, my love. I won't leave you." He strained a meek smile and, curled in the crook of her arm, promptly obeyed.

She tucked the blanket close under his chin and shifted nearer to pet his pale locks. His breath warmed and tickled her skin as she studied his angelic expression and wondered how they had survived their separation. Each was an intricate part of the other; alone she had been so lost, so broken. And now, at long last, cradling him in her arms, she felt whole again. The fear of waking alone made her fight sleep, but his closeness kindled within her a lulling calm, and she drifted away to his promised—sweet dreams.

*****

Caught in a light sleep, Maura shifted contentedly; beneath the blanket her fingers sought out Simon, but grasped only straw. She bolted up, almost tumbling from the bed, her frantic cry echoing, "Simon! Simon, where—"

"I'm here!" He rose fully dressed from the far corner of the room and rushed to her side. Clutching her fast, he felt her heart beating to burst.

"Why didn't you wake me?" she asked.

"You looked so peaceful, I couldn't."

She eased away and twisted toward the table. A thick puddle of tallow lined the base of the candle holder and a gray pall thinned the darkness. She heaved a bitter sigh and mumbled, "It's dawn."

"Very soon, I must go." He grasped a handful of her hair and let the silken strands sift slowly through his fingers.

She warmed his palm with her cheek, and whimpered, "*Please* don't go."

"But I must...It's too dangerous." He grudgingly tugged on his boots and lay with her awhile longer, their somber expressions and desperate kisses lengthening with the encroaching light.

"My gown..." said Maura as she forced herself up. "Where's it gone? I won't stay here—not alone." He found it in a corner, and as it veiled her willowy form, Simon's upset soared and he winced to her quavered request, "Would you lace it for me?"

Valiantly he tried but failed and, flustered, hurled a curse and the laces to the floor. He enfolded her in the blanket, muttering, "This will have to do." He sank solemnly back on the bed, swiped at a wayward tear and, avoiding her damp gaze, strove to cheer. "What will you do today?"

She stood, drawn and woeful, in the center of the chamber and answered lamely, "Eat, attend Mass, ride with Almodis, argue with Rose...dream of you. What will you do?"

"Keep busy," he gulped. "I...I'll help Arthur with chores. He's been so generous. I'd like to repay—"

Maura let the blanket fall and dropped to her knees at his feet. Her arms clenched his waist as her tear-choked voice swore, "Simon, I love you! Say you believe me!"

"I haven't a doubt," he murmured, lifting her to his lap. "But why are we so sad? It can't stay light forever. When the peasants return from the fields, I'll return to you." He rose and gently set her on her feet. Neither wanted to be the first to let go their embrace. Simon finally broke their fervid kiss to gasp, "Maura I must—"

"Go quickly!" she finished. He forced himself from her arms, snatched up his cloak, and darted out the door.

For a long while Maura gazed hopefully at the door, waiting and praying he'd risk returning to her. A scampering mouse reawakened her caution. She crouched to retrieve the blanket, burrowed her face deep within its folds and, breathing in its musty scent, quivered to the memory of his magical touch and heard again his impassioned words. Cake crumbs stuck to the cloth. Tasting one, she smiled to the delicious memory, then wrapped tightly, began her long and sad journey back to her chamber.

Noiselessly, Simon latched Arthur's door, hung his cloak, and removed his muddied boots. His toes nudged aside clutter as he tip-toed to his mat, separated from Arthur's by a pile of glowing coals. Stripping off his shirt, he wiggled for comfort beneath a warmed wool coverlet and sighed with lush contentment. It wasn't as if he'd *truly* left her; his day would be rich with thoughts of her sparkling laugh, the thrill of her tempting touch, and the lingering taste of her sweet lips.

*****

Rose entered Maura's chamber, set a tray of bread and wine on the vanity, and a pail of sudsy water by the garderobe. She opened wide the shutters, her scowl intensifying to a blast of frigid air. Turning to leave, she swept a quick glance at the bed and paused to the puzzling scene. Maura was seemingly asleep, still fully dressed, and a blanket stuck with rushes draped her shoulders. Rose ventured a closer look and sniffed a curious smell. Was it perfume? Maura rarely wore scent, and her cheeks and mouth were rouged as if fevered. Recalling that Maura had spent the evening with Almodis, Rose bristled and wondered what mischief they got up to during their suspicious meetings. Something was terribly amiss. Almodis, most likely, was dragging Maura down a steep path to degradation. And what disturbed Rose most was that Maura seemed to be skipping merrily behind the Lady. Well, whatever the allure, this nonsense would only last six weeks more, then Maura would at last be rightly settled with a husband and family. "Maura!" Rose prodded her shoulder and called louder, "Maura! Wake up. You've slept past Mass."

Maura moaned and stretched, rubbed her eyes and yawned a plea, "Just a little while longer."

"No. Almodis will soon be by to take you riding and I insist you eat before you go."

Maura left the blanket behind, staggered groggily to the washing basin, and froze to Rose's exclamation, "You're unlaced!"

"What?" Maura asked as surprised. She whirled to face Rose, her hands guarding her back.

"I *said* you're unlaced."

"I tried to remove the gown myself."

"And did a fine job of it. Where are the laces?"

"They're...they're here somewhere," stuttered Maura, her toe parting the rushes, pretending to search. "I was so exhausted I fell asleep before I could get the gown off."

Rose's expression soured as she sneered, "You've never looked guiltier," and, waggling her finger, chided, "If I find you're lying to me, I'll—" A loud knock interrupted her scourge, and stomping toward her chamber, she barked, "I'll leave you to the *Lady*. And I expect this food to be gone when I return." Her haranguing trailed Maura to the door, "And you'd best put on something warmer!"

"Yes, Rose," Maura replied flippantly, "whatever you say, Rose. I must get the door."

One door slammed as the other opened. Almodis spilled in, bursting, "Maura, tell me all!"

Yet before Maura could utter one secret, Rose reappeared, her forced smile almost a grimace. "I've decided to stay while you dress and eat."

"Rose, I'm not a child!"

"Your actions of late clearly dispute that claim," retorted Rose, striking a formal pose.

Almodis' excitement dribbled away as she said with a snide humph, "Hurry, Maura. The weather's rapidly turning nasty and we must stop by the market."

Maura slipped off her gown. She ashamedly turned from the women's piercing scrutiny to hide her blush, hurried into a thick woolen chemise and russet tunic, belted the ensemble, and rolled on her hose. "Why?" she asked, turning back a skewed smile.

"Why what?" asked Almodis.

"Why are we stopping at the market?"

"Oh, to purchase cloth for your wedding dress."

Maura's smile drooped as Almodis clarified, "The market will close for Lent and Arthur has the finest cloth I've ever encountered."

"Arthur?" Maura repeated, piqued.

"Yes," answered Almodis irritably. "Did you forget to clean your ears this morning? Arthur, the Saxon cloth merchant. You've met him."

"But I never knew his name."

"Maura," cut in Rose, swatting rushes from the blanket. "Did you fall from your bed last night?"

"I must have," she answered absently.

"That's mine, Rose." Almodis yanked the blanket from Rose and heaved it to the corner of the room. To Maura, she gestured sharply and hissed, "Aren't you ready yet?"

"No," she answered with a teasing smirk and disappeared into the garderobe, calling back, "I need to wash...my ears. I won't be long."

While waiting, Rose and Almodis exchanged sneers and shared the same blustery postures—dark glowers, crossed arms, toes impatiently tapping the rushes. Maura returned, donned her cloak and began plaiting her hair as she dryly commented on their bitter guises, "This promises to be a cheery day."

Almodis grabbed Maura's hand and dragged her out the door, Maura protesting, "But my hair!"

"On the way," Almodis returned, "do it on the way!"

Maura pulled the latch to shut the door, but it was pulled back. Rose, cloak in hand, strode smugly into the hall.

"Rose," Maura asked, "where are you going?"

"With you," Rose answered with too broad a smile. "I pray there will be no objections."

Almodis flashed scarlet as her lips mouthed silent curses.

"But Rose," said Maura, "you loathe riding."

"Perhaps I was too quick to judge and should try again." Rose tugged on her gloves and simpered at Almodis. "I may even find it fun. We shouldn't dally," she added with mock gaiety, "the weather's rapidly turning nasty."

Rumbling a groan, Almodis stormed away down the hall.

"Almodis, wait!" cried Maura, then spun to Rose. "Why today, Rose?" Rose didn't answer and, continuing to sport her offensive grin, swept by Maura. Maura lifted a harried gaze toward Heaven and moaned, "Please Lord, spare me this insanity!"

Maura sprinted past Rose and met up with Almodis in the stables. The unfortunate groom saddling Almodis' horse was receiving the brunt of her petulance. "God's breath!" she yelled, flourishing her crop. "What *is* your problem? If you don't show some speed, I'll have you—"

"Almodis! Stop!" shouted Maura as she hauled a saddle into a stall. "He's not to blame." Searching about, she asked mildly, "Where's Godfrey?"

"Waiting in the bailey. It seems we make him nervous." Almodis watched curiously as Maura placed a woman's saddle astride her mount, and blurted, "Maura, what—"

"I...I thought I'd ride sidesaddle today," she blushingly interrupted as she began to thread the girth strap.

"Oh, Maura!" Almodis' hands flew to her mouth and, through smothered giggles, she gushed, "How splendid for you!"

Rose, annoyed by their antics, strode between them, demanding, "Why is it splendid?"

"Because Rose, it seems..." spouted Almodis, "our Maura has at last become a *true* Lady!"

"'A true Lady'?" Rose grunted her displeasure, "I've never heard grown women speak such insipid nonsense. Ever since Maura was five years old, I've insisted she ride sidesaddle. But did she listen? No. No one ever listens to me!"

Maura rested her brow on the saddle and her shoulders shook with muted laughter.

The friends took advantage of Rose's difficulties with mounting to hurry ahead to the bailey. Swirling snow kissed Maura's cheeks; she blissfully inhaled the moist air and sighed, "He was right."

"What did you say?" asked Almodis.

"Nothing."

Almodis squirmed with discomfort and shot a bothered glance over her shoulder. "Maura, order Rose to return to the keep!"

"No," answered Maura with an amazed laugh, then nodded a smile as Godfrey guided his steed into step behind them. "Good morning, Godfrey."

He returned her smile and mumbled, "My Ladies."

As they sauntered through the gatehouse, Almodis snapped, "Rose will ruin the day!"

Maura reined her gelding alongside Almodis'. "She's too busy grumbling to herself to hear us." She twisted in her saddle to check on Rose's progress and added concernedly, "I can't recall the last time I saw Rose on a horse."

"She's a meddling witch!"

"Almodis!" Maura crossly exclaimed. "If you keep on, *I* return to the castle. Rose is a dear and I couldn't manage without her."

"Of course you could."

"But I choose not to."

"She suspects something, that's why she's spying on us. Why don't you tell her about Simon?"

"It's not that simple, Almodis."

"Then I'll tell her."

"Don't you dare! I will tell her when the time is right."

"And you know as well as I there will never be a right time. Enough of that dismal old hag!"

They arrived at the road's fork and Maura asked, "And which way shall we go today?"

"The lane that will take us far from old women and guards, except Godfrey of course," said Almodis. They guided their mounts onto the lane curling into a dense wood. Almodis beckoned Maura closer and burbled, "Maura, I can wait no longer. I'll hear now what occurred last evening, in the middle of the night, and this morn."

With a sly grin, Maura replied, "I won't tell all. It's private. But I will say that Simon and I came to an understanding and have agreed—"

"That's an interesting way to phrase it," cut in Almodis. "And just how many *understandings* did you come to? I take it more than one or else you'd be straddling that horse."

"Almodis..."

"And was your agreement as ecstatic as before?"

"No," blurted Maura as she ducked a dangling branch.

"No!" Almodis echoed, her jubilation plummeting. "Was he too ill to perform? Did you fight? You couldn't have changed your mind!"

"If you recall, I hadn't quite made up my mind before—Almodis!"

Almodis started to Maura's cry, and grabbed the pommel as her horse danced among a flock of hissing, snapping geese. Her murmur and touch quickly tamed the beast's upset and she continued to pry. "Don't toy with me, Maura. I order you to confess!"

Maura stared straight ahead and appeased, "It wasn't as ecstatic before, because..." She paused to lengthen the suspense, then turned a beaming face to Almodis. "It was a great deal better!"

"'A *great* deal better?'" said Almodis with a disappointed frown. "Surely you can do better than that, Maura. You're as bad as Godfrey. I want details!"

"You'll get none, Almodis."

Realizing her prodding would unleash not one confidence, Almodis mellowed and remarked, "Well, I commend your choice of a location for a romantic interlude. Was it dreadful?"

"Yes. But there were times I hardly noticed. Luckily when we left in November, Rose remembered to latch the door, so the pigs stayed out."

"I still don't think you would have noticed," said Almodis, chortling at the mental image. "Splendor among the sows...But jesting aside Maura, guests are expected shortly and I've been preparing the castle for their arrival. If you want for anything, bedding, fresh rushes, pelts, candles, you need only ask."

Maura stretched out to squeeze Almodis' hand. "I'm grateful to you Almodis. I almost left him, but then I remembered your advice and..."

"I understand," answered Almodis with deep affection. "Before Rose catches us, I must confess an amusing secret."

"What's that?"

Almodis shiftily began, "I first met Simon at Berkhamstead, and on our journey to Gloucester, he helped me through a difficult moment. I meet few gracious men and felt I couldn't allow such a precious gem to slip from my grasp. So to repay his courtesy, I offered him...my body."

"You did *what*?!" asked Maura, appalled.

"Before you attack, Maura, hear me out. Simon politely rebuffed me and asked instead for my friendship. I was shocked! Yet the more I considered his odd behavior, the more respect I gained for him. He'd let no one, not even me, ruffle his thoughts of you."

With a wagging head and tender look, Maura announced, "You, Almodis, are simply the most amazing woman I've ever known."

"And you Maura, are the luckiest." Almodis reined her horse and sprightly suggested, "Let's wait for the old crone to catch up." Then she turned to yell, "Rose! What's keeping you? We'll be all day!"

*****

Simon's morning had proved disastrous. He'd managed somehow to irritate Arthur's cow and she'd kicked over a full pail of milk. Cutting wood for a promised cupboard had begun well, till he discovered he'd sawed all the pieces crookedly. And hammering—he prayed he hadn't permanently damaged his thumb. Disgruntled, he left the cottage with the slim hope that perhaps he could be of better use to Arthur at the market.

Rearranging bolts of cloth behind his stall, Arthur jerked to Simon's unexpected offer, "Arthur, allow me."

"What are you doing here?" asked Arthur suspiciously. "Have you finished my shelves and cupboard?"

"Not exactly," muttered Simon, taking over the stacking. "I've encountered a few problems..."

"That's not surprising," said Arthur, arching a brow. "And might these problems have anything to do with thoughts of silken thighs?"

Simon reddened and whined, "Arthur...stop."

"Why, when it's such a lark to tease you?" Arthur chuckled and ruffled Simon's hair. "I always get such a divine reaction. Simon, I want the matching colors together. When did you return to the cottage?"

"At dawn."

"A successful evening, I trust," said Arthur, smirking.

"Quite enjoyable, thank you," said Simon, simpering back.

"Simon, orange and green do not match. Maybe you should go back to the cottage. I'll have my apprentice—"

"No. Arthur, I want to help."

"As you wish, but go slowly. And when you're done, you'll tell me what happened to your back."

Simon stiffened. "My back?"

"When I left this morning, you weren't completely hidden by the blanket and I saw the damage. Now I must see to my customers. Call if you need me and try to keep your mind on your task." His hand clasped Simon's shoulder and, with an affectionate grin, he added, "I *do* understand your difficulty, lad, after all, I'm not that ancient and remember clearly how hard the waiting can be." Simon smiled wanly after Arthur, then launched avidly into his work.

Arthur hummed a blithe tune as he arranged his goods along the stall's counter. He did so enjoy Simon's company, and to think he might have been his stepfather! For a brief moment he allowed himself a euphoric thought of the lovely Edith. It seemed only yesterday that the Norman soldiers had arrived to take her and Simon away to Dunheved and shattered his heart. With a somber sigh, he surveyed the massing crowd. Only three market days remained till Ash Wednesday. The townsfolk flurried about in their rush to purchase supplies to last the six weeks of Lent. Arthur was hopeful he would peddle a good portion of his merchandise by the close of the market, then spend his earnings on fun and new fabrics in Normandy and France. However, a creeping worry had begun to disturb his well-laid plans—and that worry's name was Simon. Arthur guessed Simon's father to be the perpetrator of his injury, and shuddered at the odious thought that he had lost Edith to such a fiend. A crash behind the curtains interrupted his musing. He muttered, "God's teeth, what now?" then shouted, "Simon! Simon, are you all right?"

"Yes, I'm fine," Simon yelled back and added with scant conviction, "There's no problem."

"Perhaps you'd better come out here where I can keep my eye on you."

Simon slipped sheepishly around the curtain. "I'm sorry Arthur."

"You're hopeless!" flailed Arthur. "Please stop trying to help me."

Simon sulked and turned away. A stab of remorse softened Arthur and he offered a reprieve. "Wait Simon, I have an idea." He pointed to the spot at his side. "Stand right here, don't move or touch anything, and try to appear pleasant. Perhaps your pretty face will lure the ladies to my stall."

While Arthur busied himself with his merchandise, Simon rested his elbows on the counter, his face in his hands, and smiled a silly smile. He rather enjoyed his new job and, attending to the bustling mob, wondered, was it his imagination or did everyone seem happier?

"Oh dear..." Arthur said, straightening. "I spy trouble headed this way."

"What?" asked Simon, twisting to see.

"A burly warrior, and three ladies—The Lady Almodis, the Lady with the silken thighs, and an older woman, crow-like and perturbed."

Simon whispered a sigh, "Maura..."

Arthur stared wide-eyed at Simon and repeated, "Maura?"

"And Rose!" Simon quickly ducked under the counter.

"Simon, what are you doing?"

"Almodis knows I'm here. Rose doesn't and she's as fierce as a wild boar!"

"Are you saying the crow won't be pleased when she discovers you are dallying with the Lady with the silken thighs?"

"Exactly."

"Well, they are looking this way."

Almodis whispered excitedly in Maura's ear, "I believe I just saw Simon disappear behind Arthur's counter. Could that be possible?"

"Very...He's staying with Arthur."

"He's seen us! Come, before he escapes. Oh, what great fun!" Almodis dragged Maura briskly through the crowd, with Rose, sore from her ride, limping behind, and Godfrey cautiously trailing. "Arthur!" Almodis trumpeted as she approached, "It's marvelous to see your smiling face this dreary morn."

With a happy bow, Arthur returned her lavish greeting, "My Lady...pardon...my Ladies! You've never looked lovelier." He winked at Maura, and spoke to her in English, "If you come up very close to the counter, I'll show you my special collection."

Simon's eyes darted from boot to boot, frantically wondering which to choose. All six were practically identical! It would be just his luck to pick Rose's.

"Tunic, gown, chemise—what's it to be then?" enticed Arthur.

Almodis rubbed a piece of red silk between her fingers and grumbled, "A wedding gown."

"Wedding?" asked Arthur, intrigued.

"Yes. For my ward, Maura. She's to marry some poor sod from Yorkshire. Do you like this, Rose?"

"Red?" scowled Rose. "Never!"

Arthur cleared his throat. "Then I suppose congratulations are in order."

"Not really," Almodis answered mundanely, briefly raising her eyes.

But Maura hadn't heard a word. Carefully, her foot searched beneath the curtains. To Simon's delight, a boot nudged his arm. He waited for its second nudge and quickly slipped off the shoe. His warm fingers massaged her chilled toes, then climbed her leg to her garter. Maura bit her lip and tugged sharply on Almodis' cloak.

Arthur and Almodis traded sly grins, Almodis barely containing her chuckle as she asked, "What is it, Maura?"

In a clenched whisper, Maura begged, "Distract Rose...for a few moments...*please*." She squeezed shut her eyes and gripped the counter as Simon unrolled her hose and planted kisses behind her knee. "Please, Almodis, hurry."

"Rose!" boomed Almodis. "There's an exquisite necklace you must see a few stalls down. We'll leave Maura a few moments...to decide." Almodis didn't wait for Rose's protest, but cupped her elbow and steered her away.

The instant they were out of sight, Maura dropped down, crawled beneath the curtains, and lunged into Simon's arms. Their fervor rocked the stall and Arthur kicked Simon's leg. "In the back with you two. I'll not have my counter destroyed!"

Simon and Maura dashed round the back of the stall. Their furious fondling and kissing tripped them over bolts of strewn material and toppled them to a sprawled heap. They ecstatically rolled in slippery silk, tangled themselves in crisp linen, chafed against coarse wool. Their lusty laughter rang through the thick curtains, infecting Arthur, then his chuckling abruptly halted at the sight of Rose barreling her way back to the stall. He tensely warned, "Maura, choose something quickly. The crow returns!"

Simon scrambled madly from the ground and yanked Maura to her feet. With great fluster, they searched for her boot and exchanged relieved looks as it sailed in from the front counter. Maura hopped about, tugging it on, then reached to straighten her mussed braid. Simon's fussing only worsened the mess. They snapped to a horrified gasp and beheld—Arthur, agape, as his fierce eyes swept the chaos. "What have you done?!" he growled. Their suffering innocence tempered his wrath. "Hurry, say your farewells. I'll keep her occupied."

Between exuberant kisses, they managed a few words. "Simon, I must go."

"It would help tremendously if you would tell Rose about us!"

"I promise," she sputtered, "...I will...tomorrow."

"And please don't keep me waiting. It's such agony!"

"I won't...I won't." Her lips locked to his, Maura groped about and snatched up a bolt of material. They parted to bitter sighs. She smoothed her rumpled tunic and strolled sedately through the opening in the curtains. "Rose, I've found something," Maura announced, her voice slightly quavering as she presented the cloth for Rose's inspection. Rose answered with a snort of disgust.

Arthur scratched his head and stifled a guffaw as he took away the bolt of black wool. "That may be your opinion of the ceremony, my Lady, but it really isn't fitting. May I suggest this—" He passed her a measure of pale blue damask, and continued coyly in English, "Perhaps it will remind you of someone's eyes."

"Thank you, Arthur," beamed Maura. "It's absolutely perfect."

Rose clicked her tongue and chided, "Maura, what's happened to your mind?" Peering closer, she added, "And your hair?"

Maura glanced longingly at the opening in the curtains and felt heat rise in her cheeks. "I suppose I caught it on a bolt of cloth," she answered distantly and, as if to mask her ardor, donned her hood.

Rose's dubious look changed to one of concern as she lay her hand on Maura's brow. "You're feverish. When we get back to the keep, I insist you rest." Rose pressed a coin to Arthur's palm. "Thank you Sir, for your time and patience."

"I thoroughly enjoyed your visit. Please come again soon." He grinned after them, then poked his head through the curtains and watched Simon stumble about, trance-like, collecting and rewrapping wrinkled cloth. Arthur's chuckle returned as he examined the mess and commented, "You two certainly are enthusiastic."

Simon started to his message and fumbled the bolt he was wrapping. "What did you say?"

"Nothing important. When you've finished here, I suggest you take a leisurely ride out of town. It's painfully clear that nowhere is safe—" Arthur paused to bat his eyelashes and finish, "when Simon's in love."

*****

CHAPTER NINETEEN - THE CROW

Simon restlessly watched a drop of tallow make its languid journey down the side of the candle. Four hours' worth of molten fat lay in the candle holder. Where was she? A recurring haunt came to mind—Maura chained to the post of her bed, with Rose, fiercely vigilant, standing guard. Why was it so hard for Maura to tell Rose of their meetings? What frightened her? He shoved from the bed, took up the flagon filled with wine, and strolled past the stoked fire into the bailey. As he spilled the burgundy colored liquid into the snow and packed the flask with snow, he briefly considered going to her chamber and discovering for himself the cause of her delay. Wisely, he returned to the room, set the flagon back on the table, and marveled at the chamber's cheerier ambiance. At least ten candles banished the gloom, scented rushes carpeted the ground, fragrant sheets covered the now enjoined beds, and a blanket sewn with thick pelts topped the sheets. The stench of mold had vanished. An excellent setting for a tryst—a tryst not meant for one. He turned to leave. Approaching footsteps, light and rapid, stalled his reckless plan. Maura swept breathlessly into the chamber; her scarlet gown matched the glow of her cheeks, and her sapphire eyes danced at his beaming presence.

Simon delightedly scooped her in his arms and tossed her on the beds. He leapt over her and growled with feigned fury, "Where have you been? You drive me mad!" His fingers caught and twisted her gown's laces, tickling.

Maura's hysterical laughter spilled out the chamber and echoed out into the bailey, halting Rose's stealthy advance. Feet from the chamber's door, she glared aghast at their wrestling shadows, and the color drained from her face. Simon! Her fists balled with rage and her blood boiled as she fought the urge to confront them. How dare he endanger her again! Their laughter faded to murmurs; she pressed fast to the wall, bated her breath, and listened...

"Rose wouldn't sleep! She kept fidgeting. Simon, stop tickling me! I'll die laughing."

"I want in!" he grunted, his fingers hopelessly tangled in the laces. "Who dressed you in this blasted armor?"

"Almodis. She thought the gown that laced up the front would highlight my—"

"Maura, I'm the last person in the world you need to entice! That woman definitely has a sadistic sense of humor," he gritted, and bit at the strings.

"No, Simon, don't rip it! It's Almodis' gown."

"Serves her right."

"Here...take my hand." She guided his touch along her leg to her inner thigh and beyond. "See...nothing blocks your way."

"Ummm," sighed Simon, "he was right, it does feel like silk."

"He who?" Maura tried to sit, but Simon's tickling set her to squealing again.

Embarrassment made the blood flood back to Rose's face. She raged back to her chamber, swearing, she'd soon force an end to this calamity!

Simon rested back on his heels to undress, and Maura knelt facing him, kissing every bit of exposed skin. His eyes and voice sparked with excitement. "Maura, I've been practicing something!"

She cocked her head quizzically. "With whom?"

"Don't be silly. Take my hand, I need your help."

"With what?" she asked. Their fingers laced neatly together, and her eyes widened and breath tightened as she watched him sink carefully to the bed—on his back. Happy tears brimmed her eyes. "Simon, it must hurt."

"No, not really," he strained with an anxious grin.

"We must take care."

"I promise to tell you immediately," he said, rigidly removing his braies, "...if there's any pain."

As she took in his aroused body, Maura's breath strained her breasts against the taut laces. Her mouth hungrily tasted him, her lips and tongue lingering, tempting, drawing a path up his belly to his neck, his ear, his mouth. She mounted him; he squeezed shut his eyes as the sensation of floating engulfed him and he gripped her hips to keep from falling. Her fiery hair hung free and long and whisked across his chest, rousing him further. His hands skimmed her curves, tugged the laces, and rounded her back as his hips rose to meet hers. Too suddenly Simon's stabbing cry doused their passion.

Maura jerked away, but he held tight her waist. She twisted in protest. "No, Simon. It's too soon. I'm hurting you!"

"No, I'm fine." Even with her aid, he rose with difficulty, begging, "Stay with me. You could never hurt me."

Together they sat with their arms and legs entwined. Her heart ached to his upset and she sadly suggested, "We must try to be patient."

He pouted and wrinkled a handful of gown. "I hate this shroud!"

"Then remove it," she simply said. Simon grasped each side of the bodice and, with scant effort, popped every lace. Freedom and comfort made her sigh as he lifted it over her head and heaved it to the ground. His admiring gaze prompted her to ask, "Have I changed?"

He took a few moments to scrutinize every bit of her, then confidently he answered, "You've only grown more beautiful. And rounder, in places."

"Show me."

"Here." His hand closed over one breast, his other hand covered the other. "And here...Have I changed?"

"You are as magnificent as ever!"

Simon kissed his thanks and glanced about the chamber. "Did you do this?"

"Yes, it took me most of the afternoon."

"It brings to mind my chamber at Dunheved."

"That's exactly what I intended," said she. "We loved on pelts."

"I recall every kiss, every caress." Simon's cheek cooled her brow. "No one could know what we've known."

"Or have what we have."

"It's a rare gift."

"Too rare," Maura said wistfully as her fingertips played across his chest. "I daydream about us."

"Tell me."

"We escape Robert's clutches and run to the mountains of Wales, where we live...and love."

"Funny," he added with a somber smile, "...I dream the same dream." His smile faded, leaving only sadness and his lament, "Why did I wait for Father to return to Dunheved? We could have escaped the madness, the cruelty—"

"Don't dwell on the bad, Simon. We haven't time."

"We'll have more than enough time to dwell on only the good when I follow you to Yorkshire."

Maura abruptly stopped his dream. "Almodis said Robert's sending troops to guard me in my new home."

As if slapped, he pulled from her hold. "Soldiers!"

"Yes. I'm to be a prisoner. Robert knows your persistence too well."

"He can't stop me!" he cried, cheeks blazing red.

"He can and will! Simon, don't fight your father, not here!" With a troubled sigh, she sank across the beds, her arms beckoning him again into her safe embrace. "Speak no more of the future, only of the present and...the past. Take me back, Simon, make me remember..."

His gaze softened and mind drifted as he searched for a stirring memory. When it came, he shifted to his side, lay his head on her shoulder, and draped his arm across her breasts. He lightly stroked her arm and began, "It was late July. The keep was stifling and the night brought no relief. We left my chamber and—"

"Ran to the river..." Maura's mind immediately woke to the memory and her eyes, ablaze, locked to his.

"As we swam a storm broke..." Simon snuggled nearer, seeing again the shearing bolts of lightning, hearing the deafening peels of thunder. "We snatched up our clothes and raced naked through the forest."

"Then we found the—stable," she added excitedly as his shadow covered her.

"The horses had wild eyes...like yours now," he whispered, his knee parting hers, his fingers stroking. "An empty stall awaited us padded with fresh straw."

"We were dripping, gasping!"

"With each streak of light, I could see mist rising from your skin." His words and breath quickened. "The thunder drove the horses mad and us to a frenzy."

"Will we ever know that frenzy again?" Her fingers traced his lips, her body moistened to his touch.

"It's growing...now." Guiding her hand lower, he urged, "Feel what you do to me."

She eagerly spread beneath him and, as he surged into her, a greater frenzy empowered them. They strained as one, gripping, scratching, their lips crushing together, drowning their cries of love. Never had they felt this passion—it coursed through their veins and rocked their very souls. Yet as their bodies writhed in ecstasy, their eyes shared the same terrible dread—how could they survive being torn apart—again?

*****

Maura lay naked and serene on her belly, her cheek resting on crossed hands. Simon straddled her back. A soft moan escaped her and her body lengthened to his healing assault on her tired muscles. His hands pressed and kneaded her neck and shoulders, the smooth motion rippling the lean muscles of his arms and thighs. "Simon," she sighed, "how long do we have?"

"Three hours."

"Share your time in Wales with me. We've been there together only in our dreams. Where was the cathedral?"

"In a small coastal village called Menevia. I'm surprised I made it there alive. You remember it was a harsh winter. I was promptly robbed of the money Will had given me and was forced to steal to survive. I arrived at Menevia half-starved and frozen. Luckily, the cathedral contained an infirmary. I woke feverish, surrounded by hymns and votive candles. I thought I had died and gone to heaven." His fingertips tickled over the breadth of her back as he went on, "They reckoned me to be a poor waif newly escaped from a Norman stronghold. I'll never forget their shock when I told them my true identity." He bent to kiss the nape of her neck, then collapsed to his side and gathered her in his arms. "Shall I go on?"

"Yes, please," she implored, nuzzling his cheek.

"I knew no Welsh." Simon peeled a strand of hair from her brow and returned it to its rightful place. "They spoke no French or English. So we conversed in Latin, which was awkward. Shortly after I arrived, the Bishop of St. Davids Cathedral—that's the Cathedral in Menevia—a man called Sulien, who spoke fluent French, returned from a peace mission. I also met a Saxon woman from the village. And together, they taught me Welsh."

"A woman?" she asked hesitantly.

"Yes, Gael, wife of the village pennaeth—which is the equivalent of a chieftain or baron. I became quite close to her husband Rhodri as well. The villagers allowed me to stay and work in the infirmary. Sulien decided I had a talent for healing and sent me to Myddfai, a mountain village northeast of Menevia, to learn medicine from a kindred of physicians living there. In a year's time, I learned all they could teach me and I returned to Menevia to ply my trade. I lived with Rhodri, Gael, and their young son Gruffydd for near a year, then Alan came to fetch me."

"And what exactly did you do in the infirmary?"

"Practiced mostly herbal medicine. I also performed some surgery, a great deal of stitching, set bones, and helped in difficult births. I was content, poor but free, and the commote gave me a strong sense of belonging."

"Then why did you leave?"

The air had cooled. He stretched to fetch the pelts and tucked them close about her. "Well, as you know, Alan can be quite persuasive. He told me the King had grown weary of internal disputes. A great number of the robber barons had never bothered to learn English. If they couldn't understand the peasant's complaints, then their problems didn't exist. Alan convinced me that William wanted the conquerors and the conquered to talk, and I had been chosen to be their go-between." Simon shifted to a disturbing thought. "I'm constantly haunted by my last night at Dunheved, my father ranting that the Saxon in me had betrayed him, that I spoke the Devil's tongue and he would never hear me again. I felt what all the English must feel—invisible. The monks assured me I could always return to Menevia, and they were eager for me to try to forge a lasting peace between the Saxons, Normans, and Welsh. So, I came back to England and, under the King's protection, began my rather frustrating work as mediator." He slipped beneath the pelts to share her warmth. "I believed you to be in Normandy, and journeyed there whenever I could manage, praying I might see you, just a glimpse...somewhere."

"Rose calls you a 'spy'."

Simon snorted a laugh. "That's how I'm viewed by the Norman baronage. I admit to sharing rumors of plotted rebellions with the King. In each case, the end result would have been far more damaging than William's rule."

Maura's clutch tightened as did her voice, "Your missions must be terribly exciting and...dangerous."

His flat expression dismissed her drama, yet his words admitted, "I've been imprisoned and driven from countless villages, and earned too many scars grappling with tempers. But I believe more good than bad has come from my efforts. It's comforting to know there are some, though few, who are willing to talk and listen."

"And you've continued to practice your medicine?"

"Constantly. At Martinmas I was glad of the chance to help you. And since you're here beside me, I assume Marc and Rose heeded my advice."

"According to Marc it took some fighting, but yes they did." Maura puffed with pride. "I knew you were destined for greatness."

"Greatness?" With a blush, Simon shrugged. "No...I do what I can."

She took his humble face in her hands and kissed him, long and full, then answered his questioning gaze. "I haven't thanked you for uncovering Robert's trickery, and helping me after Rufus' attack at Martinmas—"

"How did you survive that monster for four years?"

"Painfully..." Maura sat up, moistened her constricted throat straight from the flagon, then held the flask out for Simon. He waved away her offer. A ragged breath began her reflection. "I remember little of when I first arrived at Winchester. It took some time for my body to heal. Queen Matilda personally nursed me. I knew she suspected something horrible had happened, but she never spoke her suspicions. Adela had returned for the birth of her first child and, together with Matilda and Rose, helped me recover. As soon as I was up and walking, Rufus began his harassment. It started with snide remarks and shoves, and quickly escalated to screaming and cuffs. Then Matilda died and the full force of his anger erupted. Adela says he blames me for his mother's death and he won't be appeased till I'm dead as well. I hid from him and tried to fight back, but all that you and Marc taught me seemed useless—"

"No one can beat Rufus, Maura."

"I see now that banishing us to this chamber was a blessing of sorts. But then I made the error of complaining to Uncle William about Rufus and well, you know what happened next." She rested her hand on his cheek. "Robert said it was you who found me at the base of the stairs."

"Yes, I did." His hand closed over hers. "Leaving you then was every bit as difficult as leaving you at Dunheved. And..." He hesitated a moment, considering, then asked, "What about Will?"

"He charmed me." She shifted to her back and focused on the mold decorating the ceiling's rotted wooden planks. "I had to escape from Rufus and from you. He offered the opportunity."

"He's quite convincing—had *me* fooled as well."

"Marc roused my suspicions about him before I left for Berkhamstead, and Will continued to feed them on our trip and after we'd arrived. Berkhamstead was so comfortable, I wanted to stay, and tried to keep my distance, but—"

"What did he do?!" Simon asked with alarm.

She shrank in his hold. "I don't want to tell you."

"Did he hurt you?"

"...Yes, but I hurt him worse."

"Good."

"I believe he might have hurt Almodis as well."

Simon's eyes narrowed, his jaw clenching as he gritted, "He's far more dangerous than Rufus. Rufus is a stupid, brutal pig, but Will...he's a cunning coward, pretty, with a silver tongue. Keep away from him."

"You must as well," emphasized Maura. "Please Simon, don't seek revenge for what he's done. Keep yourself safe. Was he there when Robert beat you?"

"He tried to be, but Robert sent him away. Maura, my suffering can't compare to the torture you were forced to endure." Again he hesitated, recalling Rose's worry concerning the child, but he had to know why she hadn't told him. He took her hand, touched then kissed an arc of tiny silver scars reflected in the candlelight. "Why...why didn't you tell me?"

A shudder passed through her, quaking her voice, "I didn't know I was pregnant till Edith returned. Not that I was ignorant. I was so blind to anything but us, I didn't think of it. A servant finally told me why I was so sick. By that time, we'd been forced apart and were arguing...I feared you'd be angry with me."

"Angry?" he stressed. "How could I be angry—"

"Simon..." In protest, her hand splayed across his chest. "Much of our past haunts me, yet that time is the most horrific nightmare of all. Someday I will tell you, but not now—I...I can't."

Gently, he took her face in his hands and to his soft murmur, "I'm so lucky to love you," her tears dampened his fingers. "In a month's time," he whispered, "I'll need to share your strength. Hold me."

They clung together, Maura promising, "Tomorrow, I'll come to you at dusk."

And with deep melancholy, Simon sighed, "There will never be enough time, my love, never."

*****

They never slept, but filled the final hours of their night with more talk and more love. In the pale light of dawn, Maura staggered into her chamber and flopped across her bed. She closed her eyes and drifted off to a mumbled prayer that Rose not wake her too soon. When next she opened her eyes, a brighter light peeked through the shutter's frame, warming the chilled air. She sleepily shuffled to the wash basin and broke the ice that had formed. A touch of its frigid contents woke her fully, and sent a foreboding sense washing through her veins. There was no fire, no tray of food set on the vanity, no sudsy water by the door to the garderobe. She flung wide the shutters and squinted into the dazzling sun, burning directly overhead. Tentatively, Maura tapped at Rose's door and called her name, but got no answer; the latch refused to yield to her push. Her confusion rising, she hurried to the chamber's main door, and found it also locked. She flew back to Rose's door, her pounding and kicking rivaling her railing, "Rose! Rose, open this door. Let me out! Talk to me."

"Why?" interrupted Rose's harsh and scratchy voice from the opposite side of the door. "You haven't talked to me."

"If...if you let me out, Rose," Maura stammered carefully, struggling to contain her alarm. "I swear to...to tell you everything."

"No, Maura, I no longer believe or trust you. What I'm about to do will save you from yourself. I'll release you only after I've cast Simon from your life and this town!"

Maura panicked to the slam of Rose's door; her shriek, "Rose, come back!" blared throughout the Keep, disrupting Almodis' war with a servant three chambers away.

Almodis charged to Maura's room with Godfrey in tow, and called through the door, "Maura! Maura, what's happened?"

"Almodis!" cried Maura, rushing toward the liberating voice. She pressed fast to the wood and frantic was her plea, "Open the door, Almodis. Rose locked me in! I must catch her!"

In vain, Almodis fiddled with the latch and stepped away, motioning for Godfrey to have a try.

"If she's taken the key, my Lady, there's really no point," argued Godfrey.

"Where's she gone?" Almodis asked Maura.

"After Simon. Please hurry!"

"Maura, didn't you hear? She's taken the key."

"Then break it down!" yelled Maura.

"I will not do that, my Lady," replied Godfrey. "I'll return shortly with some tools."

"Calm yourself, Maura. I'm certain Godfrey will—"

"Calm! You've not witnessed Rose in full fury!"

"Surely Simon can hold his own against her," scoffed Almodis. "Did she take a weapon?"

"She *is* a weapon!"

An eternity of waiting passed till Godfrey's return. A few clanks, twists, and hammers swung the door wide. Maura burst out; Almodis grabbed her arm, almost yanking it from its socket, as she reproached, "No Maura! You race by the guards manning the front gates and they'll race right after you! If you'd followed my counsel and told her days ago, none of this mess would have occurred."

"Send Godfrey after her!"

"Maura," muttered Almodis, exasperated, "He's sworn he doesn't know Simon's whereabouts. If Robert's men discover he lied—"

"Rose threatened to kill Simon!"

"Nonsense. You told me they'd reconciled. Come...We'll wait on the battlements for her return." Maura hesitated to Almodis' tug and strict suggestion, "You must trust in Simon's persuasive powers and...bull-headedness. Now come." Maura grudgingly complied. The women continued their wrangling all along the way, Maura whining and wringing her hands to Almodis' wild gesturing. Godfrey trailed a safe distance behind, wagging his head.

Arthur snapped to alertness as Rose's flapping figure stormed up to his stall. "My Lady," he greeted with caution, "it's a pleasure to see you again so—"

"Where is he?" she barked.

Arthur scanned the crowd in innocence. "Where's who?"

"Simon."

"I...I don't know of whom you...you speak—" he gibbered.

"You'll confess or I'll have every sentry stationed at the castle scour the entire village till he's found and imprisoned! And I'll have them throw *you* in with him."

Her feral countenance and savage snarl warned this was no bluff, and Arthur strove to calm. "My sweet Lady, surely there's no need for such blus—"

Her slamming fist rocked the counter and shut his mouth. "Tell me where he is!"

Before swaying to her temper, he asked warily, "Why ask me?"

"It took a whole night of pondering, but at last I remembered—Arthur—Edith and Simon's dear friend whom they visited each and every year."

"And if I tell, what will you do?"

"Talk to him."

"That I doubt. First, you'll answer for me a few questions. Is this Maura Lord Robert's ward?"

"Yes."

"The same Maura whose liaison with Simon led to the great debacle?" Her austere nod forced his disclosure, "He's asleep in my cottage." Rigidly, he pointed the way. "The end of the market lane, left down the alley. A bench sits out front."

Rose whirled and stomped away, her cloak whipped by a brisk gale. Arthur watched anxiously after and called over his shoulder to his apprentice, "Come out to the counter. I've something important to attend to and won't be long." Then he followed her... surreptitiously.

Simon stirred to Rose's boot's nudge but didn't wake. She kicked again and yelled, "Get up!"

He shook the sleep and fuddle from his head and, once focused, sprang from the ground, gasping, "Ro...Rose!"

"You will leave this town alone...and immediately," she ordered, barely suppressing her ferocity, "or I will have you arrested."

"Now, Rose..." he rasped.

"Don't speak, just go."

He rubbed his thigh, throbbing from her kick, and inched forward, his arms outstretched, his grimace submissive. "Rose, hear me out..."

"Don't touch me!" She jerked back and wailed, "Are you mad?! You've been locked up, beaten! What will it take to keep you from her? I warned you to stay away! I warned Maura!"

Simon straightened and coldly stated, "And we chose to ignore you."

Her forceful blow hurled him against the wall. Stunned, he slid to the ground and hid his head from her second strike. She yanked him up by his hair and shrieked, "Leave here now, or I'll—"

"Stop!" he howled and ripped her hand, full of hair, from his skull. They thrashed about till his fury reigned and he shook her—hard. Fear instantly replaced her wrath, as he shoved her away and gritted, "You'll sit! And for once in your wretched life, listen!" She wilted to his lethal glare, sat quickly, and flinched to his spat vehemence, "I will stay here till Maura leaves for Pevensey. We will share every night and I will join her in Yorkshire. And there is nothing you or anyone can do to stop us!"

"You'll kill her!" she spat back.

"We are careful!"

"I discovered your secret."

"You were looking for it."

"And so are Robert's guards. Almodis knows of your meetings. She's not to be trusted. She'll betray you to Robert."

"Her loyalty lies with Maura. She's freely offered her help and blessing."

Rose stuttered her whine, "I...I don't understand you. Why can't you accept what will be and leave Maura to start anew? Why must you selfishly risk all, including her life for...for—"

"Love?"

His simple answer rattled Rose; she heaved away and buried her face in her palms. He knelt before her and removed her hands to plead, "Look at me." His hand cupped her chin; his penetrating stare drew her eyes to his. "Rose," he said in an impassioned whisper, "your family is my family, your sons are my brothers, and you are my second mother. Your husband—I remember how special he was—no, how special he still is to you. If Robert had commanded the two of you to part forever, what would you have done?"

"There's no comparison, Simon. We were married..."

"All we've ever wanted is to be married. Answer me, Rose what would you have done?"

Remorse stabbed him as he watched her expression wrench with grief. Her gaze turned distant, her breath labored. Tears streamed down her cheeks as she spoke, so faintly he had to lean close to hear. "I would have done anything to stay with him. I loved him dearly and miss him still."

"I know you do and Rose, you've answered your own question. Give us our time, please don't deny us this tiny bit of happiness. Maura was afraid to tell you—with good reason. She loves you completely and frets for your safety."

Rose stood and struggled to mask her defeat with a firm look and comment, "It's clear there is nothing I can do to stop your recklessness, I never could. I must get back."

Simon rose wearily and offered, "I'll walk you."

"No. My abrupt departure surely alarmed the guards. You'd best stay hidden." Her fierce look briefly reappeared to caution, "Simon, I'll be watching closely and *always*. The instant you become careless, you will hear from me!"

"I'll expect it and will welcome the discipline," he said with the faintest grin.

Rose looked away for a long moment and then left. Arthur ducked unseen into the stable adjoining his cottage and waited till her dark figure disappeared down the lane. Entering, he found Simon, head in hand, stooped by the fire. Simon jerked to Arthur's touch and enthused comment, "I laud your way with women, lad. The crow flutters to my cottage fit to kill and leaves with her wings clipped." Simon wordlessly shook from his hold and Arthur noticed the red welt staining his cheek. "What's happened, lad?" he worriedly asked.

Simon wagged his head slowly and lowered his gaze back to the fire. Arthur rambled to break the glum silence, "I came by to check on you and now I must return. My apprentice has probably made a shambles of the stall. We'll talk of this episode later. If you have need of me—Simon?"

"I'm fine Arthur...please, just go."

With a helpless nod, Arthur obeyed.

On the battlements, the women leant precariously over the ledge, searching. Almodis' squint widened and she boomed, "I see her!"

"Where?" cried Maura.

"She's near the main gates."

"How does she look?"

"It's too far to tell. Come, we'll wait in your chamber for her return."

They descended the stairs and, upon reaching Maura's chamber, Almodis commented, "You give that woman far too much power. If Robert can't get Simon to forsake you, how can Rose?" Maura was too flustered to answer. They entered and Almodis turned sympathetic. "Do you wish me to stay?"

"Please," croaked Maura.

They steeled to the menacing sound of the key turning in the lock to Rose's chamber. She strode into Maura's room, nodded rigidly in Almodis' direction, and muttered, "I would speak to Maura alone, my Lady."

Rose's relentless glare ruffled Almodis and she knew that Rose did indeed have unusual power. "Maura," Almodis said uneasily, "if you need me, I'll be in the kitchen, cursing the cook." The stifling tension drove Almodis from the chamber, but she lingered behind the door to listen.

Maura flinched to Rose's berating, "Why didn't you tell me?!"

"I knew how upset you'd be and—"

"What did you expect?!" Rose ranted as she paced. "That I'd simply sit back and give you my blessing while you risked your life?"

"We *are* careful."

"Not careful enough!" Rose sat heavily on the bed, heaved an exasperated sigh, and continued steadily, "I've had word from my son, Richard. He and his wife are expecting a child. He's asked for my assistance and I've been considering—"

"No!" Maura cried, gripping her hands. "Rose, don't leave me!"

"You don't need me, Maura. You have Simon, Almodis, your betrothed. I'm in the way."

"No, you're wrong!" Maura argued strenuously. "It's not only my need for you, we need each other. I love you and would be lost without your nagging comfort. I so wanted to tell you about Simon, for only you know how desperately I love him."

Rose squeezed Maura's hands; her eyes grew moist and her gaze distant as she mused, "On that terrible day at Dunheved when I rocked your battered body in my arms...I'll not forget your expression when you spoke of Simon. It held no pain, only a reverent glow. If I hadn't followed you last evening, your expression would have betrayed you—that glow has returned." She pulled Maura into a tight clutch. "I will die if you come to any harm!"

"Nothing will happen!" assured Maura. "Simon and I need time to remember, and to make new and glorious memories to lock away inside."

Raising Maura's chin, Rose winced at the dark smudges shadowing her eyes. "You are exhausted, angel."

"He gives me such joy, I don't need sleep."

"And you'll make yourself ill or, worse yet, become more careless. I expect you don't plan to sleep this night." Maura blushed slightly and Rose patted her hand. "Then I must insist you rest now, and when you wake, we'll walk and talk...only the two of us."

With an immense hug and kiss, Maura sighed in easy surrender, "I would love that."

*****

"Maura? Maura!" Maura grudgingly opened her eyes to Almodis' wily grin. "You must have had quite a vigorous night. You've slept away most of the day!" Still caught in an intoxicating dream, Maura grunted her answer and shifted away, but she couldn't escape Almodis' prattle. "So you and Simon have defeated the mighty Rose! I was concerned when I didn't see you last evening. I thought perhaps she'd murdered you both. Then when I came to fetch you this morning, she politely ordered me away, saying you were up all the night and needed to rest. You've rested enough! Maura," she prodded, "get up. I need someone to share my excitement. I visited Arthur and he has invited us to the Shrove Tuesday festivities tonight in the village."

Maura rolled over and mumbled drowsily, "I know, Simon told me."

"I'm shocked," said Almodis. "You actually speak to each other?"

"We spent the entire night speaking...and touching..."

"Touching..." Almodis echoed dreamily and coming closer, pried, "Touched how?" Maura's silence drew a huffed response from Almodis, "How am I ever to know the intricacies of *true* love if you don't tell me?"

"I've no doubt that one day, Almodis, you'll discover those intricacies for yourself."

Maura was amazed at Almodis' flush of embarrassment, which she hid with a quick question, "Have you been to these festivities before?"

"Many times." Maura stretched and struggled to rise.

"Arthur said we're to wear masks!"

"Yes, I know."

"Isn't it intriguing?!" beamed Almodis. "And if you allow me to borrow one of your peasant dresses I can mingle with the crowd and no one will—"

"Peasant dresses?" asked Maura, a bit insulted.

"Yes, those hideous tunics you wear." As if God was punishing her barb, Almodis gasped in sudden pain and hugged her belly.

"Almodis!" called Maura, rushing to her friend's side. "What is it?"

Her dark eyes lit with glee and she stifled a giggle. "It's the baby."

In wonder, Maura stared at Almodis' rounded belly and, with a tentative reach, asked, "May I?" Almodis grasped her hand and excitedly guided it to the site of the kick, but their bated anticipation wilted to frowns as Maura sadly sighed, "There's nothing."

Maura reluctantly removed her hand and Almodis noticed a queerness in her expression, a lost look tinged with envy. She gestured for Maura to sit and comforted, "I know you too will be blessed with children. How could God deny that miracle to someone as virtuous as you?" Almodis sat as well and wiggled for comfort. "Maura, I've a favor to ask."

"Yes."

"If possible, will you be with me when my child comes? I think of that time often and feel afraid."

"You know I will." A reassuring moment passed, that Maura reluctantly broke by suggesting, "There are plenty of *peasant* dresses in my trunk. Why don't you rummage?"

Rose, looking slightly pleasant, entered from her chamber toting a cloth bag. Immediately she chided, "Maura, you'll catch your death parading about in only a chemise."

Maura ignored her, hurried to her side, and grasped up her hands. "Rose, will you come to the festivities? Say you'll come!"

"I'm far too ancient for such nonsense."

Almodis interrupted from the depths of the trunk, "Maura, do these tunics come in any color besides dingy gray?"

"Keep digging," said Maura. "I know there's a russet one."

Rose gently pushed Almodis from the trunk, grumbling, "Must you make such a mess?" She shoved the bag into Almodis' hands. "Godfrey asked me to give you this."

Almodis peeked inside and let out a squeak. "The masks! Maura, come look!" She removed one embellished with peacock feathers, rested it on her nose, and struck a noble pose.

"How grand you look!" complimented Maura, clapping her hands. "The mask will surely betray your station, *my Lady*. How will you mingle?" She snatched the mask from Almodis and snuck up behind Rose, who was busily ransacking the trunk. To a tap on her shoulder, Rose whirled around and peered through eye holes at Almodis' pout. "How perfect!" exclaimed Maura. "Rose must be the peacock!"

With a swat to the feathers, Rose muttered, "Don't be ridiculous, Maura."

Almodis extracted a mask of fearsome-looking feathers, replete with spiky beak and said, begrudgingly, "Then I suppose I'll have to settle for the hawk."

"Suits you," Rose mumbled as she turned back to the trunk. Yet her taunt did not elude Almodis, who promptly pulled a face and stuck out her tongue.

The last mask emerged, a mass of white, enmeshed with silver. "And of course," announced Almodis, presenting Maura the lush work, "for Maura—the dove."

Rose crossed the room and thrust the russet tunic at Almodis, who swiftly shed her gown and awkwardly wriggled through the tunic's neck hole. Belting it too tightly with one of Maura's braided girdles, Almodis frowned with distaste and whined, "Maura, I'll be no hawk in this sack, I'll be a cow!"

"Don't belt it," said Maura, unwinding the cord and arranging the skirt to flatter Almodis blossoming figure.

"Yes!" beamed Almodis with a billowing twirl. "It is rather comfortable."

Maura began an enthused search through the trunk. "Rose, off with your black. You'll wear my green tunic and the chemise with matching embroidery."

"I won't and that's final," grunted Rose.

Maura turned her most entreating look on Rose. "We only want you to enjoy yourself."

"I won't go!"

"Oh yes you will," sniped Almodis, spinning by.

"Rose, I remember the fun you had when you took us to the Shrove Tuesday fair at Dunheved."

"That was ages ago."

"What exactly goes on at these celebrations?" asked Almodis dizzily.

"Theater, dancing, singing...and, of course—" Maura smirked and smoothly added, "...romance."

"Well," said Almodis grumpily, "that excludes me. I abhor theater, sing like a drowning cat, and no sane man would look twice at—"

"Don't speak so quickly, Almodis," interjected Maura with an air of mystery.

Rose stood pensively at the window. Elated voices from the bailey below drifted upward; their joy entered Rose, brightening her scowl. Her gnarled fingers tapped the plush, moss-colored wool as she lightly remarked, "I wouldn't mind seeing some theater."

"Then it's settled!" spouted Maura. She slipped into a bleached white tunic, girdled it with a silver plaited sash, and attacked her hair with a jeweled brush. "We'll leave immediately after supper. I don't want to miss a thing!"

*****

Somber and thoughtful, Simon and Arthur sat on their mats, separated by the fire topped with a sputtering pot of stew. Simon's palm supported his chin, while his other hand jabbed a rush at the flames.

Arthur stirred the concoction and stated soberly, "I'll leave tomorrow after I've boxed up my remaining merchandise. Take proper care of the cottage for me."

"I will," said Simon, his tone flat and hinting of sadness. "I'll also help you with the boxing and finish the cupboard while you're away."

"Don't tire yourself, lad. She's coming tonight?"

"Yes."

"If you feel the need, you two can slink back here for awhile. I'm sure to find something in the square to keep me occupied."

"Thank you, Arthur for—"

"And if there's a way, she could stay with you here till—" Fascinated, Arthur paused and watched a spark catch Simon's stick and creep threateningly upward. He winced as it met Simon's finger, then continued guardedly, "Perhaps she'll pretty the place up a bit."

"Perhaps," Simon mumbled vacantly, sucking on his thumb.

"Simon, there's something that needs saying."

Simon raised weary eyes. "I've been waiting."

"I'm worried about you and with good reason. You don't look well, haven't been eating properly, and your moods shift far too drastically. Yesterday, you were all smiles, till the crow came calling that is, and since then your brow's so furrowed, you could plant corn on it!" Arthur chuckled, but stopped when he saw his joke was lost on Simon. "I'd like to help. Talk to me."

"This is my problem, Arthur. I won't burden you."

Arthur rose stiffly and, while he paced, his voice quavered with frustration, "Simon, you are without a doubt the bravest and most foolhardy man I know. You've always owned the uncanny ability to plunge headlong into trouble and emerge victorious. And most times it has proved to be an admirable trait. Other times it's simply been foolish." He stopped abruptly and glanced down at the top of Simon's head. "This time—is it foolish?"

Without looking up, Simon cracked the scorched stick and answered in a rapt whisper, "I love her...completely."

Arthur scratched his bearded jaw and spoke to the bubbling cauldron. "Well then, there's nothing left to be said about the matter. If I had been a bit bolder twenty years past, my life would have been a great deal happier. I envy you, lad, but I'm also sad for you. It will kill you to leave her."

At last Simon raised his head and jolted Arthur with his innocent response, "But I won't leave her."

"Do you know the danger of your words, lad?" warned Arthur, crouching by his side.

To which Simon answered with a chilling calm, "I will marry her, Arthur."

*****

CHAPTER TWENTY - A CURIOUS PORTENT

The coming of March had ushered in erratic weather, frigid and snow blown one day, clear and balmy the next. The latter showed itself on the much anticipated eve before the start of Lent, Shrove Tuesday.

Melting snow coursed down roofs, collecting in huge puddles and transforming the market square to a sticky bog. Thick batches of straw were hastily lain and helped somewhat to staunch the muck. The square hosted a makeshift stage; opposite, the bakers' stalls served refreshments, and the common boasted a roaring bonfire. Merriment abounded throughout the raucous crowd. Muddy-faced children scampered about, caught in games and gleeful chases, and too closely teasing the fire's flames. Dark places squirmed with courting couples. The burghers, delighted with their holiday, gathered to share drink and song and tales. Jugglers bickered with Passion Play characters for a piece of the stage. And settled on bales of straw before the stage were musicians tapping drums, strumming lap harps, and testing pipes, flutes, and whistles.

Maura entered the square and was instantly swept back to her youth. Awestruck, she wandered in a dream—a curious dream teeming with beasts, birds, ogres, and fairies. A gusting wind jarred the dense throng; it yanked at torch flames, snapped canvas that draped closed stalls, and blew back Maura's hood. She freed her unfettered hair from her cloak and, all atingle, raised up on tiptoe to scan the masks, wondering, *Where is he*?

She started to Almodis' touch at her elbow. "I hate to disappoint you, Maura, but it's only me. This wind has parched my throat. Come, we'll have some mead." Almodis' brusque tug jerked Maura through the spirited crowd, past the musicians and twirling, stomping dancers to a group of ale-swigging burghers.

"Almodis," said Maura as they claimed a bale for themselves, "you haven't purposely lost Rose, have you?"

"I'm shocked you'd accuse me of such a thing," smirked Almodis. "She's to meet us at the stalls. I'll fetch the mead, while you wait here. Rose can spot you easily," she said, and added with a sly wink, "...as can others." Making her way toward the stalls, Almodis reveled in the appreciative nods she received from every male she passed. It was simply marvelous, she thought, not to be recognized.

Maura inhaled deeply the wafting aroma of cinnamon and roasted chestnuts. A shiver of anticipation chilled her skin. She wrapped her cloak tighter and smiled at the sight of Almodis returning with two steaming cups of mead. Her eager reach was ignored as Almodis peered intently beyond Maura, her eyes twinkling with her murmur, "How absolutely perfect."

To the thrill of warm, moist lips on her neck, Maura's befuddled look melted to a rapturous beam. A strong grip clenched her waist, hoisted her high, and set her feet on the bale. She spun and beheld—her lion. His growl, low and seductive, "Would you dare join me, my dove?" sparked her fervor, and squeaking joy, she leapt into his waiting arms.

The heat of Rose's glare disrupted their hearty kiss, but their amazed smiles directed at her spectacular plumage coaxed from her a slim grin, and she promptly forgot her complaint. She stepped aside and sternly urged, "Off with you," and called after, "Maura, you're to return with me, and I won't be staying late!"

Almodis' envious gaze trailed the couple; she offered Rose Maura's mead and dreamily commented, "They *are* beautiful together."

Rose stiffly accepted the drink, sat, and sighed, "Yes, that they are."

Almodis turned on Rose an astonished stare. "Rose, we finally agree!"

"How shocking!" exclaimed Rose. Almodis plopped down beside Rose and, together, they continued their fond watch, Almodis swaying and clapping to the driving beat of the drum. Rose switched her study to Almodis, her childlike visage so enthused, innocent, and infectious. She leant close and gently warned, "Soon the riding must stop. You must take care..."

"But Rose," Almodis whined, "I do so cherish my rides with Maura."

"The weather's warming. You'll enjoy a walk with her equally well."

"I will stop only if you promise..." Almodis took Rose's hand and continued brokenly, "to...to join us."

Rose lowered her eyes, and squeezed Almodis' fingers in assent. A clearing throat garnered their attention and in unison they chuckled up at Arthur's pig snout. He swept an inviting arm Rose's way. "Would you care for a whirl, my Lady?"

"I didn't know pigs danced," said Rose in a twitter.

"On the contrary, my Lady. Pigs are highly intelligent creatures, and know well how to amuse themselves."

"I couldn't," blushed Rose.

"And why not?" countered Almodis. "Peacocks love to make a spectacle of themselves."

"But Almodis, I shan't leave you alone with this rowdy bunch."

"Nonsense," replied Almodis with a dismissing wave. "I'll be fine. Now go and, though I know it's difficult for you, try to enjoy yourself."

Maura and Simon needed no words as they hugged, swung, and dipped to the music. The ardor brightening their eyes told all. Both believed this moment a dream, for never in real life could they be this happy. He grabbed her waist and spun her high in the air and, easing his grip, let her slide back into his embrace. His lips brushed hers, then slipped the length of her neck to linger upon the swell of her breast. Tickled by his fur, she dissolved with lusty laughter and firmed her clutch.

In a blur of gold Simon bounded from her side. Maura steadied herself and twisted and turned every which way to find him. Beyond the flurry of skirts, she spotted him, his eyes inviting a chase. She shouldered her way through the crowd and spied a glimpse of yellow dart away down an alley. Maura tore down the street, struggling to keep afoot in the slush. Both her hunt and the alley ended at a towering wall of stones. Gasping, she darted about, calling, "Simon...where've you gone to?" The heavy quiet and cutting shadows unnerved her; she crept backward, her gloved fingers groping the damp rock. The pounding in her chest hurt, then faltered as a growling Simon pounced from nowhere. She shrieked and dashed back down the alley, he charging crazily behind. They slid round a corner. Simon swiped at her cloak but missed and landed soundly on his backside. He sprang back to his feet, his mad cackling rousing several hounds who joined their chase with yelps and nips. They raced to the crest of a hill. Maura's heaving chest stung and Simon's puffing breath burned the nape of her neck. With a last desperate lunge, he tackled her, and they rolled crazily down the hill, stopping abruptly on the bank of a rushing stream.

"And now that I've caught you, my sweet dove," Simon panted, "I'll just have to eat you up!"

Maura squirmed beneath him and whimpered a desperate, "Oh yes! Please do!"

*****

In Arthur's cottage, Maura balanced logs on the smoldering fire while Simon draped their drenched cloaks upon a trestle table and drew it nearer the flames. She briefly scanned the room and commented lightly, "Arthur's cottage is very cozy."

"A bit too cozy," said he. "I'm building Arthur storage to clear the floor."

Maura rose to study a large, rough looking cupboard bracing the broadest wall of the room. "Is this your work?"

"Yes," he answered uncertainly.

"Why, you've done an excellent job," she said, proudly stroking the smoothed wood.

"And you're an excellent liar."

"I would never lie to you. You're chock-full of surprises. When did you learn carpentry?"

"On my travels, my friends teach me useful skills and I try to teach them something in return."

"And what can you teach me, my love?" she lured.

"Not a thing." With a woeful sigh, Simon knelt by the fire and reached out long, asking faintly, "Come here by me?" She eagerly obliged, and as he picked ice crystals from her hair, he confessed, "I've tried to help Arthur but everything I touch turns to disaster."

"I don't believe that!" she firmly countered and, resting her hands on his thighs, asked, "What have you done for him today?"

He thought a moment, then recalled, "I hammered, thought of you, and joined the wrong pieces. I smoothed the grain on the wood, thought of you, and made the piece too thin. I milked the cow, thought of you, and well, made her angry...She kicked me."

"Oh, Simon...no!" Maura threw back her head and spilled a warm laugh, but his fingers sliding down her neck, halted her cheer.

With a wounded look, he suddenly uttered, "Maura, I—"

"What is it, Simon?" she fretted.

"Most times I...I feel useless."

"You must never feel that." Maura hugged his neck and tenderly assured, "For here in my arms, you can do no wrong." She touched her lips to his and, searching his face, was shocked to see how pale and gaunt he'd become; dark circles shadowing his eyes intensified his brooding countenance, and she concluded, "It's your weariness that makes you sad. Rose insists I sleep. Doesn't Arthur encourage you to rest?"

"We don't talk much, and tomorrow he leaves for Normandy."

"Then I suppose I'll have to care for you. Swear to me you'll sleep this night."

He broke her hold and squeezed her hands between his, stressing, "But I want to sleep with you!"

"Simon, if I don't return with Rose to the castle, Robert's guards will come after me and find you." He sagged in her arms; she laced her fingers through his hair, and said softly, "You'll rest here awhile by me."

They settled on their sides. A feather plucked from her mask smoothed his brow as she gazed lovingly into his reddened eyes. Her adoration surrounded him with a rich sense of warmth and safety, and he whispered, "The way you look at me makes me feel so...special."

Maura kissed his brow, the tip of his nose, and her sweet reply tickled his lips. "That's because you are."

*****

Almodis tapped her foot to the vibrant music and chuckled at Rose and Arthur's high stepping. Then from the corner of her eye she caught a figure approaching. She focused only on his boots, stained and worn thin. They came to an abrupt halt before her. Her wide eyes climbed the length of his long form and came to rest on his forbidding mask. Silver and black fur framed his eyes and glistened his cheeks, and a long, pointy snout highlighted the formidable effect. As Almodis peered curiously at the wolf, a knowing smile graced her lips. She cocked her chin invitingly and said, "And so you've come back." The familiar magic in his gaze lured her from the bale; she happily accepted his paw and followed him into the crowd.

Heavy rain spattered their cloaks as Rose and Arthur bustled to his cottage. Giddily, Rose proclaimed, "Oh I feel quite dizzy! I haven't danced in years. I'm grateful to you, Arthur."

"The pleasure was entirely mine, my Lady. And I appreciate your advice concerning Edith. I intend to travel to Dunheved to visit her as soon as I've purchased my supplies from the continent. I'm thrilled to hear she still speaks of me."

"Quite fondly. She appears to be comfortable, though lonely. She still suffers harassment from a few villagers on account of her time with Lord Robert, and she constantly frets over Simon. You must give her something pleasant to ponder."

"I'll try my best. Here we are…We'd best knock."

Maura and Simon woke to loud rapping and Arthur's muffled cry, "It's Arthur…and Rose. May we enter?"

"Of course," croaked Simon, rising shakily and helping Maura to her feet.

Rose's happiness soured at sight of their rumpled appearance. She swiftly crossed the room, her arm sternly extended, her tone strident, "Maura, fetch your cloak. It's time we returned."

"No," said Maura, weaving her arm round Simon's. "We've been here only a short while."

"Your mind obviously wasn't on the time. Simon, convince her! She won't listen to me."

Simon draped Maura's cloak round her shoulders and offered, "I'll walk you to the square."

"No!" retorted Rose. "I don't think that wise, Simon."

"I *will* walk with her, Rose," returned Simon in kind.

"Oh, as you wish. But you'll come now!" Rose spun on her heels and hurried from the cottage.

Arthur caught up with her flurried pace, and Simon and Maura strolled a ways behind, dawdling. Wrapped to him, Maura pressed her head to his shoulder. "Will you dream of me?"

"I always do," he sighed.

A spattering of hail had dampened the merriment and scattered the crowd. Almodis and Alan braved the elements to bask, hand in hand and eyes locked, in the steaming heat of the sputtering bonfire. She dropped his hand to the ominous sight of Rose's rabid approach and flinched to her tirade, "Thank God we didn't have to go searching for you as well!"

Almodis didn't bother to counter; her sad eyes silently thanked Alan and she slogged back to the Castle.

"Come, angel," Rose said with a tug to Maura's hand.

Maura tugged back and spouted, "No!"

Rose's ire swelled her already formidable figure. "I'll have no argument," she said with forced calm. "Simon, reason with her. Make her see the danger." Her sharp attention darted to Alan. "Alan, I would speak to you a moment."

In the worsening storm, Simon raised Maura's hood. "Though I'm loathe to admit it, she speaks the truth—you must go." Her hand slipped dejectedly from his, but he stole it back, pulled her close, and fiercely kissed her farewell. He at last broke away to whisper, "This has been the most glorious night of our lives and we'll know many, many more. You won't be alone tonight or ever. I'm always with you…always." But his ardent words failed to cheer and his heart sank to the sight of her quivering lip.

Rose shoved Simon away, fuming, "Let her go! You're no help. Maura, come with me now!"

Maura listlessly tripped after Rose and, with each forced step, her anger and frustration surged. Why were they constantly pulled apart, their happiness dashed, their passion stifled? She glanced over her shoulder and beheld him standing before the bonfire; flames quivered the air surrounding him, haloing his head and cloaking his body. She stopped and struggled with an overpowering urge to break away and race back to his arms. They would run, escape, be together always!

"Don't dally, Maura," muttered Rose, firming her already rigid grip. "We must hurry and get you into dry clothes. I wouldn't be at all surprised if you've made yourself ill."

As the cavernous mouth of the gatehouse swallowed up Almodis, Alan, Rose, and Maura, a sudden deluge of rain snuffed the bonfire, torches, all the laughter, the joy...and Simon.

In Maura's room, Rose helped strip her of her wet clothes, her incessant nagging chipping at Maura's brittle nerves. "I demand you wear this wool chemise. This night you'll need the extra warmth. It was foolish of you to leave the market square. I warned Simon that if I caught him being careless I would..."

Maura swatted Rose's hands away and shouted angrily, "Why is Alan outside my door?"

"I feel safe when he's near."

"Then have him sleep before your door!"

"Stop this nonsense and calm yourself!" chided Rose, stepping back from her volatile charge.

"You said you don't trust me," Maura accused, "and now I'm your prisoner!"

Rose ignored her ranting and stated mildly, "I will leave you to sleep."

"Are you going to lock me in?" blared Maura.

"Should I?" returned Rose, head cocked and brow arched. Then her posture and voice softened, "Dry your hair before you get in bed, angel."

Maura clutched at her cramping belly; dread blanched her face as she reached a desperate hand toward Rose's clicking door and whispered too late, "Rose, *please*...don't go."

*****

Simon shifted restlessly on the crunching straw, prompting from Arthur a deep concerned sigh. "Simon, please try to settle down."

"If I'm disturbing you, Arthur, I'll go outside."

"Don't be ridiculous. It's horrendous outside and I don't trust you. You're liable to wander straight into trouble. Share your problem, lad."

"I'm worried..."

"About Maura," cued Arthur.

"Hmmm. On her way back to the Castle, she turned and gave me a look—a lost look I remember from long ago."

"She's most likely sleeping sweetly, as you should be." Arthur sat and poked a stick to ruffle the fire. "Now, what is it, truly?"

Simon sat cross-legged opposite Arthur and shuddered beneath his blanket. "Alan's returned and—"

"The brawny sentry who borrowed my wolf mask?"

"Yes. He says the King requests my presence at Rouen...in three weeks' time."

"For what reason?"

"*That,* he doesn't know." Simon chafed vigorously at his arms. "Why is it so cold in here?"

"It isn't. And what happens if you don't go?"

"I don't know," Simon shrugged. "I've not challenged my uncle before."

"And does Maura know?"

"No, I can't tell her—yet." His fingers raked through his mussed, damp hair. "Alan believes I can delay my leaving by a week, or possibly two, by telling William that he had trouble finding me."

"That sounds promising." Arthur stretched out on his mat and rested his head on crossed hands.

"But I've not lied to William either."

"Why is it a lie? Surely Alan did have trouble finding you here. I swear, Simon, at times you delight in worry. What you mostly need is rest. Now lie down." Simon did so and as he noisily wriggled for comfort, Arthur heard his shivering and remarked with affection, "You're accustomed to a hot body warming you. It'll be a long, hard night. Would you care to hear one of my boring tales of the past, guaranteed to lull you asleep?"

Simon answered with an affirming grunt.

"Fine. Which one will it be then?"

"My favorite," mumbled Simon, "when you first met my mother."

"Why what a surprise," chuckled Arthur. "My favorite as well."

"And when you're done, Arthur, tell me again why you didn't marry her."

"Yes, well..." Arthur paused, shifted toward Simon then wistfully began, "Many, many years ago in the market square, a lovely young maiden with flowing chestnut hair and doe-like eyes wandered up to my father's stall and..."

Arthur's gentle drone soothed. Simon shut his eyes and tried without success to imagine a gentle way to tell Maura of the King's request. Only his worries instead drifted to her curious look—the look that always preceded her terrible dream.

*****

Maura tossed fitfully in her bed, knowing full well what would befall her if she allowed herself to sleep. Exhaustion weakened her resolve and drooped her eyelids, so she forced her vision on the gauze curtains glittered by the flame of the bedside candle. A pang of loneliness stabbed her and she hugged a pillow fast to her chest, pretending it was Simon. The comforting thought allowed her momentarily to forget her fear, and she risked closing her eyes.

The instant she drifted off, the nightmare struck...She clutched at the sleeping child curled in her lap as a rampaging fire danced about her, licking at her skirts, singeing the child's blanket. Paralyzed by an unseen force, she watched a man and woman thrash about the room in brutal combat. The smoke briefly parted, exposing a new and more ghastly clue. The man's sword cleaved the woman's head from her body. It tumbled and rolled to Maura's feet. The face, still agape and twitching, too closely mirrored her own. She raised horrified eyes to see Simon—flames haloing his head, cloaking his body, his outstretched arms beckoning. She sensed dampness and felt for the child; he'd vanished and in his place lay the tiny, coiled body of her crying infant. Blood soaked her skirt, dripped from her hands, and she cried out, "Simon! Simon, save us. The man will kill us all! Save us!" From behind Simon, the man loomed, tall and ominous, his sword wielded high, his face a mask of black smoke. Maura struggled to find her scream, but the deadly glint of the plummeting sword shocked her to silence. She wrestled in vain her invisible binding and watched helplessly as Simon arched in horrible agony and collapsed across her lap. Together they toppled into the pyre...

Maura's piercing scream jolted Rose from her bed and Alan from his mat. Rose stood frozen in the doorway that joined their rooms, and stared aghast as Maura bolted from her bed. She ran headlong into the hallway door and staggered from the blow. The door flung wide and she collided with Alan. Thrashing viciously, she acted out her dream—her balled fists pummeled his face and chest, her deafening wails shrilled and pained his ears. Their wrestling only made her ferocity spiral. Alan floundered to gain a firm grip and duck her wild strikes, but his caution failed miserably and, to end the insanity, he drew back and struck her jaw. He instantly regretted his violence, fell to his knees, and gently supported her crumpled figure. His plea cracked with remorse, "Maura, wake up...*please*, speak to me..."

Slack-jawed and wide-eyed, Rose, haltingly approached. "What *have* you done?" she bade accusingly.

"What could I do, Rose?" he wailed in defense. "I shook her, called to her, but she wouldn't wake! I had to—"

Almodis' panted arrival intruded. "What's happened?! I heard screams! Where's Maura?" No one moved or spoke. Almodis squeezed between Alan and Rose, knelt by Maura, and asked, "Has she fainted?" Alarmed by the dark swelling on Maura's chin, Almodis' insistence sharpened. She bristled at Alan's guilty expression and Rose's sobs. "Someone tell me what's happened here!"

Alan wiped blood from his lips and stammered, "Maura was having a...a nightmare. She tried to escape and...and I had to stop her before she hurt herself."

"It appears you stopped her too well!"

He wagged his head in shame. "I couldn't have hurt her badly."

Almodis swiftly examined the bruise. "You're obviously not familiar with your own strength..." Her thumb caught a scarlet drip escaping his mouth and she added, "Or hers." She rested a consoling hand on his shoulder and lauded, "You are quite a gentleman, Sir. Don't fret so, you did what was needed. Now please carry her to the bed." She rose and stringently volleyed orders. "Godfrey, on my vanity there is an embroidered box. Please fetch it, and bring wine, strong wine. Make haste. Rose, your tears are heart-rending, but hinder rather than help. If Maura wakes to your sobs, she'll surely believe her death is near."

Rose, impressed by Almodis' masterful stance, sniffed and swiftly dabbed her face with the cuff of her chemise. She joined Alan by the bed and tucked the pelts snugly about Maura's still limp form. Godfrey reappeared with basket and bottle of wine in hand. Almodis extracted a small vial from the box and confidently approached the bed, nudging all aside. The vial's foul stench permeated the air as she leant over Maura and waved the bottle under her nose. Maura groaned and jerked her head away, but her eyes remained shut. Almodis tried again and her attempt produced more than the desired effect. Maura flew up from the pillows, striking out and squalling misery. The vial soared through the air; the liquid splattered the pelts and spoiled the rushes.

Alan forcefully removed Almodis from the bed, bent over Maura, and pinned her flailing arms to the bed. He stared into her clouded eyes, but saw no recognition, only terror. His hold weakened to her despairing cries. "Help me wake her, Rose," he begged, firming the pressure on her arms. "She still dreams! Talk to her, soothe her. I won't hit her again!"

Rose stroked Maura's brow and cooed, "It's Rose, angel. You needn't fear. We want to help you, let us help you."

Maura's fight eased slightly and Alan encouraged, "Keep talking."

Instead Rose listened to Maura's faint cry. "He's dead."

"Who, angel? Who is dead?"

"Simon...he's dead. The man struck him down!"

"No, child. He's safe with Arthur."

"I'll go to him..." she grunted, straining to rise. "Let me go to him!"

"No, Maura, I'll go," blurted Alan. "But before I leave, you must swear to lie still."

Finally he caught her anguished gaze and, receiving a nod, ever so carefully released her wrists. He left the bed and headed for the door, but Almodis blocked his way, asking, "And where are you off to?"

"Arthur's."

Her expression challenged his sanity as she turned him to the window. Streaks of light filtered through the closed shutters and peals of thunder rumbled the floor's planks. A blustery wind battered hail against the shutters and strained their fragile latch.

"A trip to Arthur's would prove as perilous as Maura's dream," she said. "And once Simon hears she's delirious, you'll have to restrain him as well. *That* task, I believe, would be a bit more difficult." Almodis led him a distance from the bed and spoke secretly, "You've witnessed this odd behavior before?"

He nodded. "At Gloucester, but there Rose calmed her quickly. The dream was worse this time."

"Do you know its cause?"

"From what Rose told me, when Maura's anxious, exhausted, or threatened, her dream returns. She can hurt herself trying to escape it."

Almodis stared past Alan to the bed and muttered under her breath, "It's because they've been forced apart."

"Pardon?"

"Nothing. Alan, you've done well here. Continue your watch before her door."

"Yes, my Lady."

"And..." she reached out and touched his shoulder, but couldn't quite meet his gaze. "I'm grateful for your company...in the square."

Awkwardly, he removed her hand and returned it to her side. Only he could hear his reply, "I wish—"

"Alan, please come," interrupted Rose.

He turned away and Almodis followed a step, wondering aloud, "What did you say?" She got no answer and returned to her box and Godfrey.

Maura, still woozy, sat up with Alan's aide, mumbling, "I hurt you."

"No. You *did* scare me, though." He narrowly studied her jaw.

"Alan, I'd rather have a bruise on my jaw than a broken neck from tumbling down the stairs," she said to ease his distress. "I thank you...again."

"And I know Simon's alive and well. But to be sure, I'll check on him tomorrow."

"I apologize for my selfishness. I've yet to greet you properly."

"You've been slightly distracted," said he. "I'm glad I was close by. Rose knows you well."

"Too well."

"I'll take my leave. If you have further need of me, you know where—"

"To look," finished Maura with deep affection.

Alan rose, and with a slight bow bade them all, "Goodnight."

Godfrey passed Almodis a cup of wine; she added a few drops from another mysterious vial and presented the oily concoction to Maura with the directions, "Gulp this down."

"What is it?"

"The same potion I gave you following your nasty encounter with Will. You'll sleep soundly with no dreams to vex you."

Maura downed the liquid and sank her pounding head deep into the pillows.

Noticing Rose's afflicted look, Almodis asked her, "Would you care for a cup?"

"No, I'll stay by Maura the rest of the evening, so I must keep alert."

An explosive gust of wind ripped the shutters' latch, slamming them against the wall, and rousing from the group a startled gasp. Godfrey stepped forward and placidly suggested to Almodis, "We should leave Maura to rest, my Lady. And you'll feel safer in your own chamber."

Almodis took a cautious stride toward the bed. "Maura...I—"

Rose stopped her with a gesture. "Your drink is potent. I don't think she hears. Thank you, Almodis, for Maura and myself."

The door closed behind Godfrey and, after tending to the shutters, Rose settled in a chair for her night long vigil. She gazed lovingly on Maura's wan face, angelic in sleep, and sighed in dismay. Grudgingly, she had come to accept the fact that Maura was indeed a grown woman capable of making her own decisions and committing her own mistakes. Nevertheless, Rose's need to nurture and protect was great. This damnable dream was lethal, not only for its contents, but also for its devastating effect on Maura's health. Rose probed her soul for a way to rid her of this havoc without denying her happiness, yet found no solution. Of only one thing was she certain—if Maura started to crumble now, there would be nothing left of her come Easter.

*****

Next evening, Simon cursed and kicked his way through grumbling hogs and loped across the bailey to the minster. He stopped short at the sight of a cloaked stranger lingering by the broken wall. He ventured another look and peered intently through the muted torch light. The figure pushed back her mantle's hood. It was Almodis! Chilling dread raced through his veins and, in an instant, he was in her face, demanding, "Where is she? What's happened?!"

She shook from his pinching hold. Never had she seen him this agitated and intense and, with a daunted look, she strove to calm, "Maura's well and will be with you soon enough."

His eyes glared doubt. "Then why are *you* here?"

Almodis chose her words carefully; she dared not rile him or her delicate scheme could be dashed before it was even attempted. "I won't lie, Simon, she's had a terrible night. Something to do with a nightmare. Rose is distracting her while we meet. I need to ask you a few questions."

His dubious gaze narrowed. "What questions?"

"Have you had dealings with Sir Roger Bigod, Sheriff of Norfolk?"

"I know of him, but we've not met."

"Are you certain?"

"Yes. What's this to do with Maura?"

"Patience, my son. Would his guards recognize you?"

"No."

"Good. I have all the answers I need. Enjoy your evening."

She turned to leave, but he urged her back and gruffly insisted, "You'll not go till you tell me your game!"

"I can't, there isn't time." She pried his fingers from her arm and rattled on, "Meet me here after Maura leaves at dawn. I swear to explain all to you then. She needn't know of our meeting."

"Almodis, you *must* tell me—"

"No. Tomorrow at dawn...be here." She skulked away into the night leaving him frightfully bewildered.

He sat on the bed, pensively rubbing the back of his neck. What could Almodis possibly be up to? Her outlandish behavior threatened his trust in her, but then again, she had proven her loyalty many times. Maura's rapid footsteps broke his musing. She paused in the doorway, swathed tight in a blanket, her careworn expression stark with dread. His radiant smile dulled her fears and she rushed to his arms. "Oh, Simon," she cried, "I was afraid!"

"Of what?" He sat back and held her on his lap; her bruised jaw immediately caught his eye. "Maura," he fretted, "what—"

Her fingers on his mouth hushed his worry. "Last night I had a dream, the same dream I suffered as a child. Do you remember?"

"Oh, yes."

"My new fears mingle with the old. In this dream the man with the sword struck *you* down. I didn't wake, yet ran from my bed to save you. Alan had no choice but to use his fist to stop me."

"So I see." He shifted her face toward the candle and examined more closely the bruise. "Does it hurt?"

"No...I'm convinced the dream is an omen of your death! Alan searched for you today but he couldn't find you."

"I rode with Arthur out of town, then returned by way of the high road. Maura, it's only a dream. You can't let it bother you, we have enough troubles as it is. Perhaps if you share it with me—"

"No I won't burden you." She rose abruptly and hurried to stack the wood. Her voice took on an odd, cheery lilt. "I'd best build the fire or the room will never warm—"

"Maura, come back. What if Alan's not there to wake you the next time the dream comes? You could kill yourself! Tell me your new fears and your old—"

"No, Simon!" Her upset tumbled the neat stack of kindling and her hands flew to her temples. "Don't keep on with this..."

The terrible thought of driving her away ended his persistence. He wisely stayed on the bed and asked with great caution, "Then tell me what you want of me."

She came back to him, her eyes wet with regret, and cupped his hands in hers. "I need to know you're safe...always."

"How can that be?"

"It's quite simple." Her fingers stroked his as she explained, "I wake beside you each morning, we share every moment of the day, and, at nightfall, we lie, love, and sleep...together."

"And that will take a miracle."

"A miracle I constantly pray for, but now, my love, what I need is you." Her kissed plea was desperate. "Don't let me sleep! Please, love me..." She stood and let her blanket fall, revealing only her clinging chemise. He nudged the silk straps from her shoulders and watched in awe it drift liquidly to the floor. His arms wrapped her back, his cheek pressed her belly. How he longed to gather her up, hide her away, and protect her forever! But now she needed something else and he would gladly give her anything. Her fingers sensuously massaged his scalp, and he sighed with bliss as his hands spread over the low curve of her back, cupped her hip's firm flesh, and lifted her weightlessly to the bed.

As he slid along her body, her senses reeled to the alluring scent and texture of his leather tunic. He covered her against the chill and rose up on his knees to disrobe. The vision of his taut body thrilled and dizzied her. She pushed up to feel, but he urged her to her back and enticed, "Lie back, my sweet. Lie back and enjoy what little I can offer." His lips nibbled at her toes, then crept her leg. Each moan that escaped her, roused him further, yet he tempered his passion. He would give all before taking any for himself.

Seeing him before her, with candlelight shimmering his hair, the nightmare briefly jarred her mind. And then a solacing memory cast it away—when they were lovers at Dunheved, the dream had magically evaporated. During that wondrous time, they had shared every secret, fear, and delight. How could she deny him anything? Suddenly, her passion peaked and burst beneath his generous touch; she cried out and clutched him close, gasping her vow, "I swear to tell you all! It's the only way to find peace, at least for a short while."

"When you're ready," he whispered back, "...only when you're ready." Simon moaned as her limbs encircled and clasped him tighter. Swelled up with love, he rubbed into her heated flesh, rolled to his back, and took her over him.

*****

Dawn came too soon. With each rendezvous, they chanced a bit longer together. At last they peeled apart, forced themselves from the beds, and feebly pulled on their clothing. Welling tears blurred her vision as Maura knelt to search for her slippers and, standing, she found herself again in his hug. His words had a strange, almost airy ring, "Maura, I feel that today promises to be—"

A drip spattered her cheek. "What?"

"Different...Perhaps even happy." He kissed her lightly and sighed, "I must go. I love you."

"And I love you...so very much."

Simon hid against the outside wall till her footsteps had faded, then returned to the chamber to await Almodis.

She glided into the room, looking remarkably fresh for the hour, and noted, "Maura seems especially grave this morning."

"It gets more difficult...to leave."

"Perhaps I can fix that."

"How?" Again his leery look appeared.

Almodis wandered the room, her fingertips lightly skimming its contents, and spoke in a lecturing tone, "Most of the workers have left for the fields, we have little time to spare. Listen and remember well. At midday you will come to the gatehouse."

"The gatehouse! You're mad!"

"The gatehouse. You will play along with everything I say and do. Is that clear?"

"I don't understand. How—"

"You needn't understand, just do as I say. With luck and your complete cooperation, my ingenious plan will succeed. Now, hurry along and meet me...midday."

Her sly manner irked him; he trembled with exasperation and sprinted away. Almodis called after, "Simon! Make yourself look a bit scruffier and remember—play along!"

As he trailed a group of workers through the gatehouse, he wagged his head in worried wonder. His stepmother seemed to delight in sowing confusion. Then again what choice did he have but to 'play along'? For aside from her irritating ways, Almodis did seem to possess the remarkable ability to unleash magic.

*****

TWENTY-ONE - ALMODIS' GRACIOUS GIFT

Simon sat slouched on the bench in front of Arthur's cottage, absently smoothing his thumb over a piece of wood and intently following the ascent of the sun. The unsettling stillness bothered him and riddled him with immense guilt. His neighbors were off toiling the fields, a chore in which he would be obliged to participate should he expect to stay in Winchester the whole of Lent. Yet first his curiosity concerning Almodis' antics had to be satisfied. Through a thin veil of clouds, the warmth of the peeking sun at last touched the top of his head. He tossed the wood aside and, stirred by anticipation and not a little dread, began his trek to the gatehouse. On his hurried journey, he remembered Almodis' instructions to make himself a bit scruffier, and dutifully mussed his hair, loosened his shirt, and squatted for a finger full of mud to smear on his face. As the keep and gatehouse loomed nearer, his consternation grew and he wondered what new mayhem awaited him across the drawbridge.

Almodis stood erect and regal before the main gates, arms crossed, a tumultuous scowl disfiguring her face. Even before he'd reached the bridge, Simon sensed her fury; he stopped and cocked his head in question, but she kept her choleric posture. A playful impulse to join her game tickled him and he swaggered onto the bridge. She waited till he was just within reach—then attacked. Her hand shot out and grabbed hold of his ear. She dragged him across the bridge, Simon yowling and swinging wildly at her arm. Before a contingent of guards she shrieked, "You impudent bastard! You're late again!"

Astounded and more than a little daunted, the guards withdrew from the mounting scuffle. Almodis released Simon's ear and expertly faked a kick to his knee. He dropped to the ground with an agonized groan. Almodis spun to the guards and extravagantly complained, "Sirs, what you see before you is a shining example of cowardice, moral decadence, and ineptitude. May I introduce my dear cousin, Simon. And I do so only on account of my sweet, innocent, and lovely ward, Maura, whom you met this morning."

Simon stood, brushed himself off, and braced for her next atrocity. Almodis knew the guards couldn't comprehend a single word of her speech, but she cherished her performance, and grabbed a fistful of Simon's hair as she continued dramatically, "This despicable rogue's only talents lie in escaping bad debts and sullying unsuspecting maidens. If it were my prerogative, I'd lock him deep under the earth to rot, and toss the key in the river. However, alas, he's managed somehow to worm his way into my dear ward's delicate heart." She shoved him back to the dirt and pressed her foot to his chest. "Now, kind Sirs, as I mentioned to you before, my ward is soon to be shackled to a loveless, strictly political marriage. And though it riles me, if this snake can bestow on her a bit of pleasure till that time, my only option is to turn away—which I order the lot of you to do as well—and let him have at her. I might add that he thrives on attention, so I highly suggest you ignore his pranks, as I constantly strive to."

A feigned kick by Almodis to his backside prompted a well-timed moan and arch by Simon. "Get up, you scum!" she commanded. He did so lazily and, seized by his shirt's collar, found himself nose to nose with his crazed *cousin*. Her hissed muttering sprinkled his face with spittle. "Dearest Cousin, listen closely. I depart for Pevensey in but a few hours and all, I repeat *all* of Lord Robert's guards and soldiers leave with me. Sir Roger Bigod will take over residence and at my overly gracious request, will allow you the freedom of the castle. He's been duly warned of your depraved behavior and you'd best shun him!" Simon reddened to her tightening grip. "If I receive word you've caused anyone harm—particularly sweet Maura—I'll personally geld you! Now, get your loathsome self from my sight, and if ever again you take advantage of my position as a member of the Royal Family to procure your women, I'll—"

"You'll what?" Simon snarled, batting her hand from his neck. "You pumped up hag! Don't you ever shut that sewer you call a mouth? You dare degrade me?! How many beds have you heated climbing to your exalted station in life?" She swung her arm high to strike, but he grabbed it, threatening, "If you touch me again, I'll yank every strand of that rat's nest from your empty head!"

One guard strode forward, his fingers circling his sword's hilt. "Your vile words dishonor the Lady, Sir! I suggest you hold your tongue or see it cut out!" Simon spun to the unfamiliar guard, puffing and glowering to his challenge. At once, two other guards joined Almodis' protector, their swords brandished.

Almodis' heart leapt to her throat. Her scheme was indeed working—all too well! She swept between the factions and tittered, "I deeply appreciate your concern for my honor, Sirs, nevertheless, I want no bloodshed. So, I beg you, sheath your swords and allow me a word with this toad...alone."

One sentry spat at Simon's feet, the others repeated his insult and together they retreated into the gatehouse.

Once they were out of sight, Simon grasped her waist, spun her in the air and, with a jubilant kiss, exclaimed, "Almodis, I love you!"

"Yes, I know, I know. Now put me down." She calmed her fluster by straightening her hair, cloak, and gown. "It was the best I could manage under the circumstances."

"I've never witnessed such an eloquent performance!" praised Simon.

"Over the years, I've learned the art of sounding impressive while actually saying nothing at all."

"How can I—I mean *we* thank you?"

"I need no thanks from Maura. She's given the gift of enriching my rather bleak life. All I ask from you is that you treat her well. I care deeply for her." Almodis led him from the bridge and spoke critically, "Simon, in four weeks' time, Maura must leave on her own for Pevensey. This is Robert's order and it will be obeyed, or all of us will suffer. I'll send Godfrey to escort her."

He seemed not to hear her last words and swore, "I could never hurt Maura. Please stay shy of Will, and take care of yourself and my brother or sister to be..."

"So you've heard?" beamed Almodis.

Simon nodded and, suddenly severe, squeezed her hand in warning, "Keep Godfrey near...always."

"I will. Simon," she said, squeezing back, "I hope..."

He knew her simple wish and assured, "We'll meet again. And when we do, you'll teach me your expertise for conjuring such elaborate schemes."

"It's quite simple when you have an overabundance of time. I didn't inflict any damage, did I?"

"No," chuckled Simon.

"At times, I tend to overplay my role. I could have ordered the guards simply to let you in, but that would have been boring. And now, they're so confused, they'll make a point of avoiding you. I'll tell Maura the news before I leave. Wait a few hours, then come back to the keep and surprise her in her chamber. And don't you squander one ecstatic moment." She kissed him lightly on the mouth, and plaintively bade him, "Good-bye, Simon."

As somberly, he watched her stroll to the gates. He turned away, then spun back to her urgent call, "Simon—wait! Please remind Maura about Alan. I'll surely require more than one competent guard at Pevensey."

He didn't wholly understand, yet nodded to the hopeful glimmer in her eyes, and called, "He'll soon join you."

Villagers halted in their tracks and gawked after Simon's racing figure. He had but a very short time to straighten the enormous mess cluttering the cottage. Dare he hope Maura would consider spending their last precious weeks together in Arthur's humble abode?

*****

In her bed, Maura struggled to sit, stretched, and sighed an achy moan. To her distress, Rose paused mid-stitch and set her sewing aside. Rose shifted in her chair before the fire and, with a hooded glare, clicked her tongue. "What mischief do you two get up to in bed?"

Maura burst a sharp laugh. "Do you *truly* want to know?"

"No!" retorted Rose.

"I hate to disappoint you, Rose, but my arms ache from wrestling with Alan, not Simon."

"Then perhaps a hot bath will soothe your muscles."

"Oh Rose, I would love that!"

Rose sat pensively by Maura's side, took her hand, and pressed gently. "I heard you crying this morning. Was it something Simon—"

"Oh, no. I know it's silly, but I miss him."

Rose's gaze turned wistful as she muttered, "No, angel, it's not silly. Almodis requests your presence in her chamber. Go, and when you return, your bath and meal will be waiting."

*****

Almodis' vibrant command, "You'll come with me to the stables!" greeted Maura and, before she could open her mouth to respond, a wave of servants, guards, and pages swept her down the passageway.

Puzzled, Maura stuttered, "I...I thought you weren't to ride."

"Nonsense...I'm perfectly fine." Almodis turned to bellow orders at her flitting entourage, then grabbed Maura's hand and hastened to the stables.

Maura found her horse saddled and bridled. She swiftly mounted and escaped into the bailey. Chaotic with blustery tradesmen, carts, horses, hounds, and trunks, the courtyard only escalated her confusion. She twisted to see Almodis, magnificent in her fox fur cloak, astride a pristine white mare. "Almodis," Maura called in question, "what goes on here? I know Sir Roger's household is moving in but—" Almodis held to her mystery, trotted by, and waved her on. They arrived at the main gates and, while awaiting their opening, Maura glanced back and was astounded to see the unruly crowd forming itself into an orderly train. "Almodis," she asked again, "why—"

"I'm leaving," Almodis cut in abruptly.

"No!" Maura cried, "You can't!"

"Yes, I must." Almodis leant closer to whisper, "I'm the cause of your troubles. Robert's guards and soldiers are no longer here for you, they are here solely for me. When I go, they will follow. Ride with me to the fork in the road and when you return to your chamber, you'll find a very special gift."

Conversing softly, at times with chuckles, the women led the parade down the rutted road. At the fork they stopped to embrace, Maura's voice faltering as she assured, "It will be simple to convince Alan to join you at Pevensey. I'll miss you terribly."

"We'll be together again—soon enough. In four weeks' time, I'll send Godfrey to collect you. Maura, I know you'll be tempted, but please don't try to escape. You cannot hide from Robert. If you weaken, see and touch the scars on Simon's back."

"Beware of Will," cautioned Maura.

"He's a persistent haunt, yet I will have Godfrey and, with luck, Alan to protect me. Now get yourself back to your chamber and relish that gift!"

Rain mingled with her grateful tears as Maura sharply reined her steed, turned him around, and galloped madly back to the castle. Sprinting grooms met her brash return. She flew off her horse, left his tending to the boys and, hiking her skirts, dashed to the keep.

Her back to the door, Rose hummed while arranging fresh clothes on the trunk at the foot of Maura's bed. She heard the door latch and, without turning, asked, "Well, what was the Lady's grand surprise?" She froze to a deep resonant reply.

"Rose, how wonderfully considerate of you!"

She whirled and was stunned to gibbering by Simon's dazzling smile. "Si...wha..."

"A bath for me?" Simon cocked his head toward the tub and, in a gushing gesture, splayed his fingers across his chest. "You shouldn't have."

Rose's gape widened as he began to disrobe. His cloak and tunic flew to the bed; then, as he wriggled from his shirt, she finally managed to burst, "Simon, stop! You've... you've gone mad!" Rigidly, she thrust her pointed finger at the door. "I insist you leave here immediately!"

He smoothed his hair, smirked a bawdy smile, and winked. "Admit it, Rose! All these many years you've hidden your true feelings for me. Shall we?"

"Oh, dear Lord!" Rose wailed on her rush to the door and hollered, "Guards!" down the passageway. Then hearing no boot steps, her railing wilted to a meek, "...Guards?"

Simon's explosive guffaw drowned her feeble call. He snuck up behind her, tickled her waist, and spun her to face him. His eyes teared with delight. "There's no one left to save you!"

Rose struck at his hands, flinched, and stammered, "What...what are you saying? Doing? You'll get us all killed!"

"No, not this time, Rose. They've gone!"

"Who's gone?"

"The guards! Robert's guards have all flown after that wonderful, scheming, genius of a hawk—the Lady Almodis."

Her bulging black eyes traveled his smooth, sinewy, naked chest. "I...I don't understand."

"We needn't hide anymore!" He paused in eager anticipation, awaiting her jolly reply, still her grouchy look remained. His hands fell dejectedly from her shoulders. "I swear, Rose," he griped, "you must find great pleasure in misery. Can't you at least pretend to be happy, if not for me, then for Maura?" She stayed dull and aloof, so he decided to shock a response from her and untied his waist cord.

His ploy worked beautifully. Rose stiffened and masked her crumbling composure by bellowing, "Simon! Stop this shameless behavior immediately! If you dare remove another piece of clothing in my—"

The door flew wide and, with an exclamation of sheer exaltation, Maura burst into the chamber. She hurtled herself into Simon's outstretched arms and tackled him to the bed.

To their voracious hugs and kisses, Rose snorted her disgust, "Don't you two ever tire of pawing at each other?"

"You ought to try it yourself, Rose," Simon blurted between noisy kisses. "It just might melt your perpetual scowl."

She hurled a pillow in his direction, slammed the lid of the trunk, and stridently announced, "I'll leave you two to...whatever. And when I return in a few hours' time, I do not expect to be embarrassed by what I discover—"

"She does go on, doesn't she?" Simon tossed the pillow back and it bounced off the top of Rose's head. Maura, sure of the explosion to come, dove beneath the pelts.

"You devil!" Rose fumed, storming round the bed. "You lecherous devil!" Simon leapt up and they stood huffing nose to nose. He growled and stomped forward; Rose gasped in retreat. She waggled a furious finger in his face, repeating, "A few hours only! And don't you dare embarrass me!"

He snapped at her finger and she lurched for the door. Once there she spun back, arm and lips poised to rant, however, a squeak was all she could manage as he chased her out the door. He latched it, turned, and cracked a devious smile. "Oh, how I love to make her crazy!"

Rose, listening against the coarse wood, heard his bragging, and let loose her seldom seen smile, revealing almost all her stained and crooked teeth.

The pelts parted and Maura's beaming face popped through, laughing. "You always did and though she'll never admit it, she loves it too." She scrambled from the bed and peeled off her tunic. "Hurry, Simon, or the water will go cold."

A long elated sigh rose as they sank into the steaming bath. "This is heavenly," said Maura, hugging Simon's neck, "and such a tight fit. It seems each wish we make comes true."

As Simon kissed her lustrous smile and rouged cheeks, her radiance filled him with a certain conviction and he ventured, "Dare we wish for more?"

*****

Grief stooped Alan as he dodged puddles on the battlements and watched Almodis' party fade from view. He cursed himself for foolishly believing the Lady might require his services. The King didn't need him, and had refused his request to join Maura's household in Yorkshire. William had suggested instead that he guard Rufus. He'd just as well guard a boar! Maura had fleetingly mentioned something about Almodis' desire for another guard and that she'd specifically asked for him. Then why was she gone and he still here? It was ridiculous to pretend he was still Maura's guard, yet he dare not follow the Lady. Perhaps Simon and Maura could help cure his quandary. How odd—in a quandary over a woman! When had it begun—at Nicolas', in the market square, in Maura's chamber? And why now? Had it all been a product of his needy imagination or did her furtive expression betray—No, he was a fool. She had left to join her husband, and he must forget her.

A bitter blast of sleet stifled his musing, and deepened the morbid pall that cloaked his mind. Never in his forty years had he felt this torn, this vulnerable. And his tumult mirrored that of the Royal Family. They were splintering, lying in wait for the King's death. Who would pounce first? He held no loyalty, only revulsion for the two elder sons, one a feckless fool, the other a mindless beast. Henry FitzRoy, the youngest, showed slight promise as a potential ruler, though seemed to possess the maturity of a five-year-old.

As Alan descended the uneven stairs he cursed his King for not allowing a neat solution to his dilemma—to journey to Yorkshire with Maura and Rose, and serve their household as guard, soldier, steward—hell, he'd settle for groom. And he cursed his family, with the exception of his brother Nicolas, for deserting him simply because of his decision to serve William, a King who had consistently preserved the interests of their Jewish community. He couldn't intrude on Nicolas' family and add another mouth to their struggle. Perhaps he'd travel with Simon, though he doubted Simon's skills as mediator would be exploited if Rufus won the throne. And the likelihood of that debacle occurring grew greater each day the King spent battling.

Yes, he decided as he trudged to the kitchen to secure his eating place at the communal table, he'd discuss his muddle with Simon...and Maura. How exceedingly grateful he was for her friendship. From her, he had discovered much about women; then again, there was still so much to learn...

*****

Naked, Maura lolled on the bed, laughing, as Simon tickled away her dampness with a sheet. "You're making it all up," she snickered in response to his animated tale.

"No. Every word is true. Henry would sit in the Welsh and English meetings and whisper lewd suggestions in French to any woman present—old, young—he's not overly choosy. I tried to stop him. His legs are dented from all the kicks I planted on them."

"What happened?"

"If luck was with us and no one knew the language, the women ignored him or giggled. However, we weren't always so fortunate. Often as not, there was a father or husband present who could translate a few basic ideas, and we were taken into custody. Then there were the odd times when the women not only understood, but wholeheartedly agreed to his temptings. Either way the discussions broke apart."

"If he was such trouble, why did you take him with you?"

"His father insisted he learn my trade, and once I designed a method to keep Henry's mind on the mission, he began to show a bit of promise."

"And your method was..."

"I'd not allow any women or female beasts within a mile of the meeting place."

Maura wagged her head in doubt. "Simon..."

"I swear, Maura, it's all true. And you haven't told me how you two fared in Normandy."

She stiffened to his question and paused briefly to compose a harmless rendition of their adventure. "Well...our first night and day together were a bit rumbly, though soon we made peace and when we parted, he was actually quite sweet."

"Sweet!" exclaimed Simon. "I've known Henry to be many things—highly conceited, crafty, ruthless, and oft times even generous. Never '*sweet*'! You, my dear, must have cast a heavy spell on him." Simon sat up, distanced himself up against the bedpost, and arching an uncertain brow, asked, "How sweet?"

Maura busied herself with plumping pillows and replied flatly, "I wouldn't have survived Normandy without his help."

"He told you to say that."

"I mean what I say, Simon..."

"How else did he *help*?" he probed.

"If I tell you, you'll only get angry."

"I'll get angrier if you don't tell me."

"Well...before we became friends, he tried to sour my opinion of you by discussing your '*many*' women."

"My many what?!" shouted Simon, almost toppling from the bed.

"Yes, he mentioned something about bees swarming to honey—you being the honey, of course. Those weren't his exact words."

Rage flushed his cheeks and he balled his fists as he lashed out, "That lying vermin!"

"I told you you'd get mad. I'm sure he exaggerates, but Simon, I'm not blind. I notice how the ladies' eyes rest on you awhile longer than they do on other men. And I'd be shocked if over the past four years one of those bees hadn't—."

"Maura..." His face stayed red, but his tone softened. "I..."

"You needn't confess anything to me," she said uneasily, averting her gaze.

"No, I need you to know. I did try to find you in a few other women—very few—and was always disappointed. Then I dreamt a dream, as vivid as an omen, that I'd soon discover your whereabouts and we'd be joined again. I had combed every inch of Normandy, France, and England when I received William's message to ride to Winchester, and...there you were."

Entranced by his eloquence, Maura crawled near, hugged him close and rested her cheek upon his chest. "I yearned for the passion we had known, and I hurt—a very few men, trying to forget you. I too was disappointed, and glad now that I was. At Berkhamstead, I finally came to accept the simple truth—I could love no one but you."

His arms wrapped her shoulders and he murmured, "No woman alive can compare to you."

"Henry didn't always lie," she said as her hug tightened. "Before I left him, he told me, 'you'll never find another finer than Simon,' and I wholly agree."

He puffed with pride, then smirked. "And I take it, he spouted this praise after his attempt at seduction."

Without thinking, Maura blurted, "Yes, before I—"

"Ah ha!" Maura shrank from Simon's flailed tirade, "That stinking rake! I'll kill him, I will. I'll go to Normandy and wring his spindly neck!"

"Oh, Simon." Maura flopped back on the bed, placed her foot on his heaving chest, and laughed. "You'd be amazed if he hadn't tried. And in truth, it was quite funny."

"Make me laugh," he sneered.

Her toe traced his collarbone as she explained with caution, "Henry was near to drunk, and under the ruse of rubbing ointment on my back, tried to..."

"What?"

"Touch my breasts."

"I am not amused. He will die...slowly and painfully!" He kissed the sole of her foot and stretched out beside her, his voice tense with irritation, "Henry truly believes every woman was set on this earth solely to service him. He'd best take care! There's already an army of little Henrys roaming the countryside, and when they grow big and strong and decide they don't much care for *Papa*, that's when the real trouble begins."

"You care for Henry," said Maura.

"I shouldn't."

"Have you told him what you just told me?"

"No...He wouldn't listen."

"To *you* he would..." Maura wound a wisp of his golden hair round her finger and added, "For you are his hero." She rose and tugged him from the bed. "We'll talk more of Henry later. Rose will arrive soon and, she'll die if she finds us...dare I say it...naked. And we have work to do."

"Such as?" he asked, absently stepping into his braies.

"After we've replaced the soaked rushes—"

"You splashed me first," he countered.

"We must convince Alan to travel to Almo—I mean Pevensey. Simon?"

"Yes?"

"I hope this is not overly bold of me. If you believe Arthur wouldn't take offense, I'd like to stay with you in his cottage, till..." She paused to roll on her hose and turned on him a hopeful look.

"But Maura," he answered in a questioning tone, knotting the cord to his braies and glancing about, "the cottage smells as if the animals sleep in the main room, because frequently they do. It's so cluttered one can barely move about. It has no bath, toiletries, garderobe—"

"It has you..." she sweetly interrupted.

Simon flashed a blinding smile. "I'm sure Arthur wouldn't mind a bit. We'll invite Alan and Rose this night for supper." His enthusiasm obvious, he sat to tug on his boots, and blurted, "However, first..." He waited for her head to emerge from her tunic's neck hole, then patted the pelt by his side. "Come to me."

"Simon, there isn't time...Rose..."

"Just one kiss," he whined, "you can't deny me one kiss."

"If you insist," she readily conceded, straddling his knees.

They sank back on the bed and froze mid-kiss as Rose's icy comment chilled them. "I see you two have made little progress."

*****

Late that evening, contented by a warm meal filling their bellies, Simon and Alan sat hunched over Arthur's table, sipping ale. Simon's finger traced the rim of his cup as he asked, "So, have we convinced you?"

Alan's hand covered his mouth, then supported his chin. "I really don't know what to do, Simon."

"If I had to choose between Almodis and Rufus, *I'd* know what to do."

"It does sound simple, doesn't it?"

"I'm sorry, Alan." Simon refilled Alan's cup. "I know from my own problem, finding that simple answer can seem nearly impossible."

"Will you go to the King?" asked Alan, uncomfortable with the present topic.

"No, I'll wait as you suggested. Now, back to Almodis. Forget the bad you've heard about her. It isn't true. Go to her, talk to her, and then decide. We both believe she cares for you."

"Talk to her?" Alan took a long draught of ale and wiped dampness from his brow. "For me, that's not an easy task. Now you...you're always so at ease around women. They tongue-tie me, especially the Lady. Share your secret."

Simon chuckled. "There's no secret. For the first fifteen years of my life, I was surrounded by women, three of them extremely strong-willed. And I learned quite quickly that if not for the women tending the land while the men play war, there would be no country left for the King to rule."

"And I was raised with seven brothers and no mother," said Alan. "I've been page, squire, and guard only to men. No, I did escort the Lady Adela to Blois for her marriage—the most harrowing three months of my life."

"That's sad, Alan. I don't know what more to say. Almodis has Will after her. Presumably, he's trying to rid her of the child."

"Child!" Alan choked on his ale. "What child?"

"Robert's child. According to Maura, Almodis' near to five months along. Will wants no competitors for his inheritance. Heaven knows, Godfrey's competent, but if Will decides to strike at Pevensey, he's sure to bring soldiers. And I don't believe Almodis will confide her fears to Robert."

"Say no more, Simon," said Alan with a resolute bang of his cup. "Come morning, I leave for Pevensey."

Across the fire from the two men, Maura and Rose lounged on mats munching bread. Maura swatted away an escaped lock of hair and cast an anxious glance at the table. "If anyone can convince Alan to go to her, Simon can."

"I'm not altogether comfortable with your scheme," said Rose, brushing crumbs from her skirt. "Alan is such a gentle soul, Almodis will eat him alive!"

"They'll make a sweet couple."

"And in your fanciful mind, you believe everyone should be happily coupled."

"Why is that so bad? We could all do with a bit more love." Maura chafed a handful of rushes into the flames to watch them sparkle and die. She held a second handful out to Rose, and suggested, "Smell."

Rose's wrinkled nose relaxed to the pleasing scent. "Lilac?"

"Yes, Arthur dries the flowers himself. Speaking of Arthur, Almodis told me of your romping time with him on Shrove Tuesday."

"I must admit, I thoroughly enjoyed Arthur's company. He is a true gentleman." Rose's censuring gaze swept the jumbled room. "So you believe you'll be content *here*?" Maura's rapt expression prompted her comment, "I suppose that was a foolish question. Simon may be a devil, but he's a handsome, amusing devil."

"Rose!" Maura exclaimed with a gentle laugh. "What's come over you?"

"Your happiness, my angel." Appreciatively, Rose's fingers stroked a bolt of black and mauve brocade. "Oh, I do like this. Where does Arthur come upon such exquisite cloth?"

"The village weavers provide some, the rest he purchases from Normandy, France and Spain. And Simon claims he receives bolts from as far away as the Holy Land! Rose... you'll come visit, won't you?"

"Of course, and I will spend my remaining time worrying about you. Will you have enough to eat?"

"Arthur has a good supply of salted meat, grains, beans and dried fruit. He owns a cow, a goat, two hogs and chickens. We'll share labor to get whatever else we may need."

"Labor?" asked Rose.

"Yes, Rose...work." Maura ladled her a cup of warm honeyed milk from a simmering pot hanging atop the flames. "You're no stranger to work. Have you forgotten our time at Dunheved and on our own?"

"Forgotten? How could I possibly forget that squalid time! Why do you choose to relive that wretchedness? Don't expect the peasants to accept you. They know your station and will resent your presence. And then there is the ugliness of your sinful life to consider—"

"Rose, look about you—this isn't squalor. My life at Dunheved was bliss before Simon left. Simon has known the people on this lane his entire life and has their respect. And as for our *'sinful life'*, if we could marry, we would. I know we have God's forgiveness, so what others think, including you, doesn't bother me." After a swig of milk, Maura wiped her mouth and went on, "Besides, Simon told me that in most villages, marriages usually don't occur till the bride is pregnant. So we are definitely not the first couple to live sinfully."

"Well that sounds all well and good, though I'll still worry about you."

"You needn't. For once, I can truly say I'm fine, and wholly happy."

"You will attend Mass?" asked Rose.

"If the priest allows sinners in his chapel, we will go." Maura's arms wrapped her knees and her tone mellowed, "It was kind of you, letting Alan use your room."

"And I will feel very privileged sleeping in Adela's grand feather bed. I'd best not grow used to it, though. There will be no feather beds in Yorkshire."

Maura squeezed Rose's hand. "You won't be too lonely?"

"No, angel. While you were bathing, I met Sir Roger's wife, Eleanor. We've planned another visit for tomorrow, and she requests my presence in the hall for meals. Well—" Rose paused to yawn, and stood with a stiff stretch, "it's very late. My old bones ache, and I must be getting back." Her fingers skimmed and patted Maura's cheek. "Please, angel, promise me you will eat and sleep." Maura agreed with an endearing nod. The men stood respectfully as Rose approached the table. "Alan, unlike some in this room, I need my rest. We'll go now."

Alan draped Rose's cloak round her shoulders and with a hint of shyness sputtered, "Maura...Simon, I'm grateful for your time and encouragement." His lips brushed Maura's hand. "We'll be reunited soon. And Simon..."

"This is not good-bye," finished Simon. He clapped Alan's shoulder and offered, "I wish you luck."

Rose brusquely cut in, "Simon, when distracted Maura forgets to eat, so I expect you—"

"I'll stuff food down her gullet, Rose."

"Fine. Alan, come. Goodnight, my angel, I'll visit tomorrow...Simon."

Simon latched the door after them and turned to complain, "Tomorrow?" Maura looked on her clasped hands with a vague sadness and didn't seem to hear. His smile wilted and his arms circled her waist. "What troubles you, my love?"

"I hope, we've done the right thing, about Alan and Almodis. I don't want to endanger anyone."

"All we've done is relay Almodis' wishes. Alan decided on his own."

"What finally convinced him?"

"I told him of the child."

"I pray each night..." She hesitated, rubbed her cheek against his palm, and then spread his hand over her belly. "That I'm pregnant."

"As do I," he whispered.

They stayed wound together a solemn moment, then Simon motioned with his finger for her to stay. He disappeared to a shadowed corner of the room and returned laden with a bulky blanket. He passed it to her and, in the light of the fire, she knelt and carefully unfolded the quilt across the now joined mats. Drawing a sharp breath, she exclaimed, "Oh, Simon, it's the most magnificent piece of embroidery I've ever seen!" Her eyes and fingers danced over the interwoven circles. Sewn in lavender, smoky blue, and vibrant red threads, the design exuded warmth and, from the obvious toil involved in its making, deep love.

"The women of the village made it for Arthur," said Simon. "Obviously, they hold him in high regard. He's given it to us."

"Oh, Simon, he mustn't." Maura gathered up the quilt and hugged it close.

"Why ever not?" he wondered, kneeling at her side. "He has ten more."

"He must be a very special man. Perhaps one day, I'll know him better."

"He is, and you will. This room is also very special—to me."

"I remember you used to visit him here," said Maura.

"Not only that, this is the place I was born."

Maura's expression lit with wonder. "In this room?"

"Yes. When my mother returned from Normandy, pregnant and alone, her family refused her. Arthur's family took her in."

"Tell me more," she mumbled through a yawn.

"I will, but now we must obey Rose's orders—to sleep."

"You're not angry about her visiting?"

"Of course not. You know how I love that old crow."

"And she loves you." They stretched across the quilt, Maura curled in the crook of his arm, her head resting on his shoulder. "Everyone's been so gracious, including Rose. When I first told her I planned to stay here, she didn't spout one argument."

"As much as she grumbles, Maura, your happiness is most important to her, especially now. And are you happy?"

"Blissfully!"

"Then perhaps you could show me..." He kissed her wrist, the bend of her arm, her neck, her lips, then murmured, "...in the morning."

"Now..." she slurred.

Simon smiled at her drooping eyelids. "I'd love to, my sweet, though I prefer you awake." He helped her sit to undress, and, snuggling beneath the quilt, gathered her in his arms to vow, "I will find a way to keep us together—forever."

And to his wonderment, Maura didn't protest; she nestled against him and sighed, "I know you will."

*****

Wakening to a rooster's crow, Simon gladly assigned Maura her first task as a villager—milking Maude the cow.

The following weeks proved ecstatically busy for the lovers, and they reveled in their return to a more arduous and simple life. As they settled easily into daily rituals, they drew on strengths they'd gained from their rustic upbringing and recent past. Maura's expertise shone in the fields, and she instructed Simon how to clear and break the hardened ground and scatter only seeds best equipped to survive a late frost. As she had at Dunheved, she lorded over the beasts. Too frequently she found herself tangled in muck with Arthur's swine and seemed to be endlessly chasing his he-goat through the village. And with an eerie quickness, she learned from Simon the art of reweaving the cottage's wattle and patching the daub cracked and pitted by March's volatile weather. Simon proved to be the superior cook and mender; his skill at stitching skin transferred readily to cloth. With his main distraction now close by, he at last was able to complete Arthur's shelves and cupboard while Maura stacked and organized strewn bolts of cloth. And together, as Arthur had hoped, they 'prettied the place up a bit'.

Mornings were spent in the fields or shepherding beasts on the common. Then following the main meal, late afternoons and evenings were reserved for play—strolling and riding for miles, gathering with friends for drink and talk, reading Arthur's poems and prose aloud, and composing detailed letters to Marc.

Rose visited regularly, bringing gossip from the castle, extra food, and cheer. She marveled at Simon and Maura's transformation, and their effusive bliss came to infect her. Simon's teasing dissolved her to fits of ecstatic tears and, exuberantly, she joined in their fun, jabbering tales and secrets she'd not shared before.

Maura watched with rapt fascination how Simon fared with their fellow villagers. With his closest friends, he shared an easy manner and they often sought his advice as if he were a village elder. Others blatantly loathed his mixed heritage and connection to the Crown, and harassed him at every opportunity. He claimed their crudeness didn't bother him, yet at times she'd catch a wounded or ruffled look, and wonder if this were indeed true.

After their morning toil in the fields, Simon suffered twinges of guilt as he mended Maura's blistered, bleeding hands, though she complained little. His pride in her swelled when he watched how bravely she endured the rude comments spouted by a small number of priggish neighbors. And he learned much from such incidents, especially tolerance, patience, and calm. Mostly, he envied her special gift of finding joy in the simplest of pleasures.

The village healer, named Alta, called frequently and Simon encouraged Maura to attend their meetings. A gnarled, white-haired woman, with piercing slate eyes and yellow saggy skin, the leech neither smiled nor strayed from her interests. For long hours, Alta and Simon would trade secrets of their profession, bruise and boil herbs, and concoct odoriferous, mystifying potions. On a number of occasions, the healer bestowed her ultimate compliment and requested Simon's presence and opinion regarding a baffling malady. Maura would tag along, Simon always finding a way to include her in the sometimes discomfiting procedures.

As their time together whisked by, they rarely mentioned what was to come; instead they immersed themselves in their engrossing life. Happiness spilled from them in the lilt of a song, a tender look, a brisk kiss, or a soft touch. They struggled endlessly to capture the elusive answer that would keep them forever together. And to give each other strength, they held tight to their love and each other.

*****

A fortnight had passed since Almodis' departure. The afternoon dripped with a heavy, relentless rain. Inside the cottage, Simon was attempting futilely to practice defense tactics with Maura. "Maura," he pleaded impatiently, "I don't know who or what you'll encounter at Pevensey. You must and will be prepared to defend yourself. Now come and fight me!"

"No, not there...here." Maura stretched seductively on the mats and purred, "We'll wrestle here."

Simon snorted a laugh and dropped to her side. "You're hopeless, absolutely hopeless."

They started to a loud and urgent rapping and scrambled to their feet as Rose barged into the cottage, exclaiming, "Maura, come quickly! Adela's returned and is in the foulest mood. She calls for you and only you."

"I'll follow," Maura replied and pleaded to Simon, "You'll come?"

"Adela doesn't care for me, Maura."

"I need you."

"Then I'll come."
Snatching up their cloaks, Maura shouted at Rose's back, "Did she bring the baby?" They chased after her fretful reply, "It's still inside her, I fear not for long!"

*****

CHAPTER TWENTY-TWO - A DOMESDAY PROPOSAL

"My dear Maura!" Huge with child, Adela flashed a swollen smile and waddled open armed across the floor of her chamber. "I can't tell you how overjoyed I was to hear you wouldn't wed my brother—the beast!" The friends embraced as closely as was possible, and Adela retreated to arch a suspicious brow. "My, my...let's have a look at you. A bit rumpled, but nonetheless radiant. What *have* you been up to?"

Maura frowned with concern. "Adela...why are you here?"

"You're not happy to see me?"

"Of course I am. But you will have that child at any moment! Come and sit." Maura guided Adela to the bed, helped prop her back with pillows, and worried on, "Why risk danger to yourself and the baby by coming to Winchester now? Where's Stephen?"

"I don't know, nor do I care," Adela humphed with folded arms. "Would you pour me wine?"

Maura sat and emptied wine from a silver flask gracing the side table. She passed the elaborate matching cup to Adela and questioned, "You've quarreled?"

"I'm afraid it's gone a bit farther than that. I've left him."

"You've what?!" Maura exclaimed, her shock forcing her to her feet.

"Left him! He's a stinking coward and doesn't deserve me!" As fast as it erupted, Adela's agitation quelled, and she turned practically giddy. "Now, tell me, it's not your betrothed who's put that color in your cheeks. And from comments I've heard, it couldn't be Will. Why did Rose have to fetch you from the village? Don't tell me you're dallying with a peasant!"

"Adela, stop this nonsense. Why is Stephen a coward?"

A soulful sigh left her and she gazed upward as if offering God a confession. "He rode off to join Father's army in Maine, looking so gallant. Then as fast as he'd gone, he returned, sour and withdrawn. And of course I learned the truth not from Stephen, but from a fellow knight, a rival of sorts. It seems that as the battle began, Stephen wilted, snuck out the postern door, and scurried back to Blois." Blazing red, she gritted, "I've never been so humiliated! How could he do this to me?"

"To you!" Maura grabbed the sloshing cup from Adela and snapped indignantly, "Have you any idea the torment soldiers are forced to endure?! If you did, you'd be cheering his actions! You should thank God he's alive to see and father this baby. You're behaving like a spoiled child!"

"Maura, that hurts!"

"It was meant to!" To Adela's escaping tears, Maura softened and atoned, "I'm sorry for the insult."

"I had hoped returning here and confiding in you would help heal my wounds. Now you stab me as well!"

"I said I was sorry."

"Well then...enough about my gutless husband. I didn't think to ask, are you using my chamber?"

"No."

"Good. Then I needn't ask you to leave." Adela recovered rapidly from her gloom, and her garrulous mood returned. "Well, supper should soon be ready. You will join me in the great hall. We have much gossip to catch up on, and you'll tell me who this mystery man is, and—"

"Adela, I won't be supping with you." Maura offered a hand, tugged Adela's floundering figure up from the bed, and cautiously added, "I'm...staying elsewhere."

"Elsewhere?" Adela asked.

"I'm staying in the village with...a friend."

"A friend? I see. Will you desert me as well?" sneered Adela.

"Desert you?" Exasperated, Maura flung up her arms and cried, "Who has deserted you? You called for me and I came!"

"I need you by me, Maura!" Adela gripped Maura's hand with crushing force. "The child's due any moment and I'm afraid."

"You've had one child. Surely you know what to expect..."

"Oh, yes, I remember vividly. Definitely one of life's more appalling experiences. I swore never to have another."

"You can't mean that!"

"Yes...no, I don't know! All I know is I'm frightened and I need you."

"You have your servants, your physician. How can I help? I know nothing of childbirth."

"I despise my physician and left him in Blois. My women hate me." Adela's ungainly figure paced the room, her fidgety fingers pinching her dense yellow hair into a fat braid.

Maura's determined gaze followed her and she spoke firmly, "Adela, I will remain with my friend. When your time comes, send Rose to fetch me."

Adela stretched her thin lips to a grimace. "Confess Maura! Who is this vagabond who tears you from your family? If you don't tell me, I'll share with Uncle Robert your secret of playing peasant!" Her cold blue eyes narrowed to fierce slits. "I have the power to order you back!"

Simon, listening from the hall, decided he'd heard quite enough and strolled into the room, his palms spread in a peaceful gesture. "Here is her vagabond, Adela."

Adela plopped down hard on the bed; her dropped jaw finally closed to exclaim, "God's teeth! And what slime have you crawled from Cousin...I can never remember your name. I always think of you as Uncle Robert's horrendous mistake. And from what I hear of late, he wholly agrees with me." She aimed her scowl at Maura. "How can you sully yourself with this...this...common bastard?"

"Stop, Adela!" Maura shouted in defense.

Simon wove his arm through Maura's and calmly assured, "She doesn't bother me, though it's obvious she delights in upsetting you. If you ignore her, she'll soon stop. I think we should go."

"Yes, perhaps we should," agreed Maura as she followed Simon's lead to the door.

"Maura!" Adela rose clumsily and hugged the bedpost to plead, "You can't leave me!"

Maura turned a staunch expression and reminded, "When your time comes, send Rose for me."

Adela's fists beat at the bed and her wails resounded through the closing door, "Maura! I'll not forgive you...and I *will* tell Uncle Robert. Don't desert me for that varlet! Maura, come back!"

Maura tensed to Adela's tantrum; Simon urged her on, talking idly, "So Stephen reconsidered his alliance to William. He's wiser than I thought. Why didn't Adela volunteer her martial expertise? She'd make a fearsome opponent."

"Next time we meet, I'll suggest it. Simon, I won't have her speak to you that way."

"The whole blasted family speaks to me that way!"

Maura pouted. "She's supposed to be my friend."

"And your friend is scared." His arm draped her shoulders. "I shouldn't have to remind *you* to be patient. She'll apologize when she truly needs you."

A week passed with no word, atoning or otherwise, from Adela. Maura and Simon were toiling the King's demesne field, Simon wrestling the plow, Maura scattering corn and dusting them with a fine soil. The sun's early harshness stung their eyes and blushed their skin. Simon stopped the oxen a moment to catch a breath, wriggled from his tunic, and swabbed his eyes and brow. Admiring Maura's lithe figure as she bent to pat the ground, he chuckled and shared his thought, "What do you think Uncle William would say if he happened on us at this very moment?"

Maura straightened and muttered, "Most likely, you're doing a splendid job, keep at it."

Simon spied a black dot scuttling up the hill. It grew larger and he recognized Rose. "Maura," he said, "I believe Adela's time has arrived at last."

Maura cast a fretful glance Rose's way and shakily passed Simon the bag of seeds. "I promised to go to her."

"Calm yourself," he suggested with affection. "Babies take their time coming into the world."

"But I don't know how to help her!"

"Rose will be near."

"Simon," she pleaded, "...*please* come!"

"Go. I'll finish here, then follow. But I'll wait in Rose's chamber—safely out of sight."

She kissed her thanks and leapt over planted rows down the hill to Rose.

"I'm filthy, Rose, I must wash," said Maura on her hurry to Adela.

"Then we'll stop first in my chamber," said Rose.

They slipped into the cramped room. Maura doffed her cloak, bunched up her sleeves, and poured water into the washing bowl. "Are her women with her?" she asked anxiously, wringing her hands in the cold water.

"Yes, but her screams are for you. The pains have been with her the entire night. She's exhausted."

"Simon will soon follow and stay close in case he's needed. Please watch for him, Rose." Maura wiped her hands and face on a passed towel. She struck a steely posture, gulped a bracing breath, and entered Adela's chamber. Panic instantly seized her as she realized she was alone with the lolling, moaning Countess. In two broad steps, she was at her friend's side, soothing, "I've come, Adela."

Adela's groping hands and fevered eyes sought Maura. In a small voice, she croaked, "My servants have all left me...to die. You must save me, Maura!"

Maura's hand cooled Adela's brow as she tenderly lied, "They've not left you. I sent them off to rest and eat." In a loud whisper, she called over her shoulder, "Rose, come quickly," then her sympathy returned to Adela. "The pain will soon go and your child will be in your arms."

Rose rested a hand on Maura's shoulder, and Maura muttered low and urgent, "Please find where her women have gone and why." Suddenly, Adela grabbed Maura's hand with a crush so rigorous Maura feared her bones would snap. Agony glazed Adela's eyes and arched her body. The pain finally eased, though she failed to recover from its intensity and continued to writhe and gibber.

Maura mouthed prayers for Rose's quick return, and sighed heavily as Rose whispered in her ear, "She speaks the truth. They've left her and I can't say I blame them. She screamed the most vile curses at them all through the night and refused their suggestions to speed her labor. She hurled the water pitcher at Sir Roger's physician, so he won't be returning. The babe should have arrived by now. I don't believe she has the strength or desire to see this child born."

"No! There has to be a way to help her. Is there sign of Simon?"

"No."

"Then go find him and drag him here!"

"What good can he be?" asked Rose. "She won't have him near."

Adela's howl rattled the bed, and Maura's plea turned desperate, "Please, Rose, hurry! Fetch Simon."

Rose hadn't far to go. She met him loping down the hall, hustled him into her chamber, and swiftly proposed, "I'll stay with Adela and send Maura to you. There are problems..."

Rose left and soon Maura entered. She stood close by the door, nervously fiddling its latch, and explained, "She's suffered constant pains since last evening and has no strength left."

"Is the bed damp?" ask Simon.

"Soaked."

"Is there blood?"

"A little."

"Does she want to help push the baby out?"

"No, she only moans. What can you do?"

Simon sagged to the bed, his fingers splayed and dug into his scalp. "I don't know, let me think."

"There isn't time to think!"

Suddenly, he lifted his face and a notion lit his eyes. "We could make her pains harder!"

"Harder!" cried Maura. "Simon, they're killing her now."

"The ones she's having obviously aren't effective. If they were stronger, they might force the child from her body."

"How is it done?"

"I'll need help and a little time. Make her comfortable and keep her calm. Maura, don't let her give up hope."

Simon spun to leave; Maura swiped out and caught his arm. "Where are you going?"

"To the leech."

Her grip weakened as she implored, "Please, Simon, hurry back...*Please*!"

In the tarnished light of a tiny cottage, Alta and Simon launched a frantic search through her extensive stock of herbs. He sniffed and examined stalks and crispy leaves bundled in the many baskets stocking the room. She eyed the batches of dried flowers that hung the rafters and shook her head in doubt. "I don't use blighted rye often and only to bring on a missed flow. I use savory only for cooking. Have you done this before?"

"No, I've only witnessed it."

"Why both herbs?"

"I don't believe one alone would be severe enough to speed her labor, and I'm afraid to try anything stronger."

"Ah, here is the savory. The black blight powder will be stored in the basket near the door. And did it work?"

"Did what work?" Simon blurted as he nicked a hole with his dagger in a linen sack scrawled with a ragged 'R'.

"Using the herbs."

Simon paused a pensive moment. "No...but we have no other choice. I'll bruise the plant to get its juice. Could you measure a dram of powder? We'll add each to the water and steep a broth."

Using her scales, Alta weighed the powder and whisked it into her bubbling cauldron. Simon stirred in the juice and cringed with impatience. He rubbed at the tension strangling the back of his neck. "*Please*," he beseeched, "come back with me."

"Oh, no," Alta decided. "If I treat the Countess and she dies, the King will raze the entire village. You have your woman's comforting way to aide you. Pray the potion doesn't prove too strong..."

Simon found Maura standing round-eyed and ashen in the doorway joining the bedchambers. With a trembling reach, she accepted the steaming cup from him, and listened warily to his instruction, "You must convince her to drink every bit."

The mixture's rank odor repulsed her and she offered it back. "No...I can't."

"This juice will help, not hurt!" His fingers bit her shoulders and he strictly pressed, "Maura, if she doesn't drink it, she and the child will surely die."

"Simon, I—"

"Tell her anything—that the drink will make her pains go—anything!"

Wordlessly, she left him. He latched the door, paced, and filled his waiting with prayers. Laboriously, the time dragged on and a leaden black cloaked the sky. Simon smelled snow coming as he leant out of the shuttered hole carved in Rose's chamber wall. The bailey seemed curiously empty; few torches burned and fewer persons roamed the usually bustling courtyard. All was too quiet, he thought, inside and out. The potion should have had its effect by now. Still, he dare not enter Adela's chamber, for his hated presence would surely impede any progress being made. And he knew all too well that soon, for better or worse, Adela's torment would be over.

All dozed in Adela's chamber, Rose in a chair, and Maura up against a bedpost. Suddenly, Adela's eyes flew open. She heaved her upper body from the bed and let out a deafening, anguished groan. Rose and Maura floundered awake and launched a valiant effort to wrestle Adela back to the bed. A constant searing pain attacked the Countess' body and heightened her shrieks. Maura cried out for Simon's help.

Adela glimpsed Simon's entrance and was instantly consumed by crazed loathing. The bed curtains ripped in her grasp as she lurched to the edge of the bed and wildly swung her arms, screeching, "You murdering fiend! You've poisoned me. I'm dying! My baby's dying!" Simon caught her toppling figure and wrestled her back to the bed, his head and shoulders battered by her rock-hard fists.

Rose and Maura joined in his struggle and together they managed to restrain her. With an interminable slowness, the shrillness left her screams and the fight drained from her convulsing body. Maura tenderly covered her and the three retreated. In view of the bed, Simon crouched against the wall and, head in hands, anguished—did Adela speak the truth? Was he murdering her and her child? He had been so careful with the dosage, and the risk had been warranted, hadn't it?

Before sputtering coals, Rose slumped in the chair and quietly sobbed into cupped hands. Maura stayed by Adela and lightly stroked her limp arm. Her mind weary and dull, she droned an incessant plea, "Adela, help us. I know you have the strength to birth this child. He longs to see you...love you. Please help us."

Adela's unexpected grunt, "God's blood! I want to sit," startled Maura aware. The Countess' fury focused once again on Simon. "And tell *him* to get out!" Simon raised an astonished face to the conversation. Adela's bile surged and she hollered, "I want you out!"

Rose hastened to assist Maura and, as Simon stood to leave, he grinned at his cousin's grimace and suggested, "When she strains, get her to curse Stephen and me. That should speed matters up a bit. I'll send her servants in to tend her."

His last task complete, Simon returned to Rose's chamber and collapsed across the bed. He heartened to the sound of Adela's grunting and yearned for the child's squall, yet only dissonant memories jostled his worn mind. The first birth he'd been called upon to assist, he had arrived too late. He twisted on the bed recalling again the horrors he had discovered—the mother alone, dead, mutilated. Someone had tried to rip the child from her and pieces of its tiny body lay strewn over the blood-spattered bed. The sparse contents of his belly burned his throat as another, even sadder event intruded on the grisly scene. He saw himself, much younger, cowering outside his parents' bedchamber, terrorized by his mother's wails. He longed for the child's cry; instead came a deadly hush and the terrible image of Rose clutching the tiny, still bundle from the room. How many times had he waited for the cry? Six, seven? And what of his own child? Maura had shared her nightmare, her ordeal with Rufus, her adventure in Normandy, her visit with her betrothed, but the tale of her forced abortion had yet to pass her lips. Would it ever?

"Simon? Simon..." Maura's sweet voice ended his torment. He opened his wet eyes and gradually focused on the surprising vision before him. A contented smile graced Maura's lips as she rocked the squirming babe in her arms.

"I didn't hear a cry," he spouted, rolling from the bed.

"He didn't cry. He babbled." She tucked the blanket away from the child's face so Simon could see. "Isn't he handsome?"

"No. He resembles a piece of withered fruit."

"Simon..."

"How is Adela?"

"She's sleeping. She worked very hard at the end and seemed to enjoy the cursing." Wonder filled Maura's eyes. "He dropped from her body into my hands. Would you like to hold him?"

"I don't know," he questioned nervously, as she placed the boy in his rigid arms.

"This is your one and only opportunity. If Adela knew you were touching Theobald, she'd kill us all."

"Theobald!" He gazed lovingly into the baby's puckered face and cooed, "How could she burden you with such a horrendous title?"

"It is awful, isn't it?" commented Maura. "I suppose she named him for some Pope. But I will call him—Bald. After all, that's what he is."

Simon gazed up into Maura's beaming face and laughed; she joined his mirth and they kept on till tears streamed down their cheeks.

*****

A spark from a flint split the blackness of Arthur's cottage. A second strike met the wick of an oil lamp and illuminated a path to the table. Exhaling a long, audible breath, Simon sank onto a bench and poured two cups of ale from an earthen pitcher. Maura slipped onto the bench opposite, and used the lamp's flame to light the table's candle. Her palm supported her chin as she forced a grin Simon's way. She had shared little on their walk home, and now a distant and queasy gaze marred the happiness she'd shown moments before. Simon studied her upset and wondered what grim reminders this episode must have dredged up. He leant across the table and traced her jaw with his thumb, praising, "I'm so proud of you. After all had given up hope, you kept faith. Tell me what you feel."

"I feel numb," mumbled Maura.

"You must be exhausted."

"I suppose. I'm too jittery for sleep."

Simon hauled himself to his feet. "And I'm far too tired for anything else."

Her hand covered his and patted. "Then go lie down. I'll join you shortly."

"What will you do?"

"Write a note to Marc. Soon...you may see him."

"Don't be long," said he as he placed a lingering kiss on her palm.

Maura lifted a sheet of parchment from a nearby stack, dipped a worn quill in a bowl of ink and wrote, *Marc...*, and then the quill took on a life of its own. It scribbled over the skin, flourishing circles, flowers, leaves, and the numerals XXVI, XXVII, XXVIII... XXXI. Godfrey would arrive on the thirty-first of March, only six days away! Her moist eyes fell upon Simon, already asleep by the fire, and despair welled up inside her. Where had their time gone?! How could she possibly find the strength to walk away from his warmth, his comfort, his love?! He lay on his belly, his cheek resting on the back of his hand and their quilt draping his waist. Her gaze shifted to his back where thick ruby welts had replaced the scabs, and she recalled Almodis' caution, 'You can't hide from Robert'. Stinging tears blurred her sight and dribbled down upon the parchment, smearing the ink. She abandoned the quill, squeezed shut her heavy eyelids, and nuzzled her face deep into her crossed arms...

When next Maura opened her eyes, the table was gone; the parchment, ink, benches, cupboard—everything had disappeared. She tried to rise, but a gnawing, elusive pain paralyzed her now prone body. Her fingers searched beneath her and scratched at a straw mat set upon cold stone tiles. Flickering at her side sat a lone candle; its malevolent shadows cut across the walls and ceilings—tall ceilings with black yawning corners. A crucifix adorned the wall opposite, the Savior's face obscured.

Maura tugged away the stiff sheet that shrouded her and found herself clad only in a flimsy chemise. She lifted the frock to find the cause of her pain and discovered her breasts marked with odd cuts and scrapes and her belly tender and distended. With a tremulous touch her fingers skimmed her wounds and the queer bruises blotching her thighs, then traveled lower to graze the crusted blood matting the hair between her legs. The biting cold worsened the pain and she whimpered in terror.

Faceless hooded creatures crowded about her and muttered in unison, "Fornicator... sinner...must be punished...drink the herbs, every drop. They will make you sleep...make the pains go." A cup filled with a vile, clotted liquid smothered and gagged her. She batted it away. Bindings chafed her wrists, burning. Frigid metal scraped her teeth, and she retched to a thrusting spoon and harsh demand, "Drink them, swallow them!"

Alone again, Maura cried to the baleful shadows, "Rose, save me! Simon's gone, left me. There's no one...no one!" She heard only the echo of her pounding heart. Maura struggled up from the mat and lurched to the door; she beat and kicked, and heard muffled sobbing just beyond the thick barrier. "Rose!" she screamed, "They've poisoned me! Poisoned—" A stabbing low in her belly stole her breath and buckled her knees. Her cheek slammed the stone floor and her hand jammed between her teeth. She bit hard till she tasted blood.

To the headless crucifix, she wailed, "What have I done wrong?! I've only loved. It's not a sin to love!" Her fingers wove together and clenched tight. "*Please*, Lord, make the pain go, make it go! I swear never to sin again." Yet she would have no mercy. The hurting struck again, sharper this time, convulsing and wrenching from her a constant and terrible scream. Her belly seemed to rip apart as she strained the baby from her body. For a long while, she lay very still, then carefully felt beneath her soaked skirt and gathered him up. He fit so perfectly in the palm of her hand, and as she gazed into his too tranquil expression, she murmured, "You're so tiny, so quiet." Her soft kiss failed to stir him. "Open your eyes and see me, love me...You needn't be afraid—" Another stabbing pain shattered their moment. Maura clutched him close, scrambled under the sheet, and cowered. "I won't let them take you away! Simon will come back. He'll rock you in his arms and he'll not leave us again...ever—"

Suddenly plunged into blackness, Maura coiled her body tighter and brought her cupped hand to her lips. A sticky wet spilled over her mouth as she kissed her empty palm. "No!" she cried as her fingers groped feverishly through the bloodied sheets. "My baby! Where's my baby gone?!" She flung away the sheets and stumbled for the door; it swung open easily and she ran, sobbing to no one, "They've taken him...stolen him! Give him back! Bring him back...Give me back my baby!" Grief and agony racked her body and tripped her to the ground, where she retched violently into the snow.

Strong arms surrounded her; a hand cooled her brow, and she heard his soothing words, "I'm here, my love. Your belly aches from emptiness and excitement. Come inside."

Between gasping sobs, Maura cried, "The baby—Simon, the baby!"

"Theobald's fine."

"No...*our* baby—our baby is—dead. Robert killed our baby!"

Simon crushed her fast to his chest and whispered, "Yes, my love, I know, I know." With great care, he helped her stand, his eyes widening to her stained mouth, hands, and tunic. He sniffed her hand and dropped his shoulders in profound relief. "It's only ink, you've spilt the ink. Come, take my hand, you'll feel safer inside."

Tucked up clean and warm in Simon's loving clutch, Maura spoke her anguish in a dull, broken whisper, "I...I...only could remember pieces of that time, the rest I refused to believe. Now it's all come back and I want...no, I *have* to tell you...After the guards, they took me to a convent..."

When her horrid tale was done, she slipped into a peaceful slumber. Simon cradled her in his arms and tears dripped from his clenched jaw. He stared at nothing, though saw so clearly every gruesome facet of her story. How could God allow such an abomination, and in His own house? A vicious shudder took him as revulsion and rage crushed his soul, and he plotted vengeance against his father and brother—schemes that, if carried out, would turn him as monstrous as they.

A glimpse of Maura's now serene face dampened his ire and he bent to kiss her brow. Panic gripped him most often in the early hours of dawn. Only six days remained before Godfrey would come to take her away! Arthur's words echoed in his ragged mind, 'It will kill you to leave her'. Again an aching shiver struck. He gathered her closer and offered a bleak prayer for Almodis' magic to endure and grant them their wish—to wed and escape to Wales. But a faint and creeping light intruded on his simple prayer and stole away the safety of the dark.

*****

Maura endured the following three days with an eerily calm and cheerful bearing. Now that the most tragic element of her dark past finally had been put to rest, she vowed to fill every moment of their last days together with abundant joy. On the fourth day, Rose appeared at the cottage late afternoon, intent on grumbling, "Adela ordered me to assist with her packing. I refused, and I now need a place to hide."

Simon interrupted his meal and stood with a chuckle. "You can always find sanctuary here. Please, Rose, join us."

"I'm grateful, Simon, but no, I've eaten. Adela aims to leave in the morning, and I couldn't be happier. My, how she frazzles me!"

"Should she go, Simon?" asked Maura, picking idly at her food. "Isn't it too soon?"

"If she's well and strong, there's no reason why she can't travel."

"Even if there was a reason, no one could stop her." Rose sampled Maura's stew and remarked, "Not bad. You're improving."

"Well, Rose, one sure way to speed her leaving is to help with the packing," said Maura. "I'll return with you. Perhaps it won't seem so awkward if we work together."

"Oh, bless you, Maura. Only you can coax a smile from the mighty Countess."

"And I can move a trunk or two," offered Simon.

"Yes, Simon, she'll welcome your help, now that she's going. I'm furious! She's not uttered a single word of gratitude."

"You two go." Maura scraped the leftovers into a pail and headed for the halved door leading to the stable. "The hogs are awaiting their treat. I'll soon follow."

Simon and Rose ambled down the lane, their arms circling each other's waists. "Rose," said Simon humbly, "I do appreciate you speaking in my defense to Adela, though it makes no difference—she will always hate me."

"I don't understand her. She has a fine husband, two beautiful children, riches, power, her health, and she does nothing but gripe. She's a...a..."

"Bitch?" finished Simon.

"I never thought I'd ever hear myself utter such an offence. Yes, I wholeheartedly agree—she is indeed a bitch!" Rose flashed a crooked smile, and added, "I rather enjoyed that." Her hold on him firmed. "I'll miss you so. How is Maura coping?"

"Better than I."

Panting, Maura rushed up behind them and caught hold of Rose's free arm. Bolstering smiles spread across their faces as they marched boldly onward to their nemesis.

After an abrupt visit Maura flew from Adela's chamber. "I really can't take any more of her abuse!" she raged, slamming the door behind her.

Simon grinned at her glower. "What was it this time?"

"She continues to harp about how you're sullying me, and how before she goes she must fix my addled mind!" Maura's arms wrapped round his neck and she let out a dismal sigh. "She's changed somehow, hardened."

"Most likely, she had no choice," commented Simon. A glint of mischief gleamed his eyes as he pressed her to the door. One hand cinched her waist, his other hiked her skirt and, burying his face in her neck, he growled lewdly, "And she's right, I love sullying you—every bit of your luscious body, especially your addled mind."

Maura glanced about nervously and let out a quiet laugh. "Simon, not here."

"And why not? Everyone in the castle is convinced I'm a slimy, lecherous devil and I must strive to earn my reputation, mustn't I?"

"And what of my reputation?"

"I'm afraid it fares no better. By some you're called..." He nibbled her earlobe and breathed secretly, "a lusty wench."

"By whom?" she demanded, feigning shock.

"A number of Sir Roger's soldiers, Sir Roger himself, and, undoubtedly—Henry."

"Well then," she muttered coarsely, and wriggled against his hips. "We mustn't disappoint them. I'd be honored to have you service me...but Simon, could we find somewhere softer?"

He fondled a breast and tickled her lips with a lusty sigh, "Everything feels deliciously soft to me."

Their lips crushed together and Maura's head thudded against the door, provoking from Adela an irritated, "Who's there?"

They quaked with laughter while their lips stayed tightly clasped. Maura tensed and sputtered, "Simon, stop! I'm getting splinters in my head!"

He paused, stepped back, looked one way, then the other, and shrugged. "Why bother? There's no one watching." Smirking a wink, he spun on his heels, and casually strolled away.

"Come back here!" Maura lunged for him, caught hold of his tunic's skirt and pinched his backside. With a yelp, he sprinted away along the hallway. She started after him, rubbing her head and calling, "Where are you off to?"

He turned an impish look. "Somewhere softer."

"Then wait for me!"

Simon raced down the stairs, Maura chasing close behind. He didn't leave the keep, but instead darted down a slim passageway just inside the main door.

Maura twittered her warning, "Simon, you're headed for the chapel!"

Simon ducked through the first door he encountered, spun to catch her, and stepped backwards off a top step. He tumbled down the remaining four, and landed with a tremendous crash upon a trestle table. Amid an explosion of parchments, the table, and Simon tipped to the ground.

Maura stood stupefied in the doorway, her chin dropping ever lower as her eyes darted after a flock of fluttering pages. She nimbly leapt the stairs and the table and offered a helping hand. "Simon," she worried, "what *have* you done?"

"I tripped down the blasted stairs!" he cursed, swatting at a floating parchment.

"Are you hurt?"

He grabbed her hand and pushed up from the floor. "No, I don't believe so."

Maura stifled a guffaw and asked, "What is this place?" Two trestle tables remained upright, each stacked with three tall piles of parchment. Two of the piles contained clean, crisp, newly scripted pages; the third held stained and ragged skins, their printing smudged.

"I've a notion I've been here before," mused Simon as they lifted the table top and balanced it upon its still erect legs. Simon raised a sheet of parchment, his eyebrows merging as his lips silently mouthed its words. Then, setting it aside, his expression relaxed in recognition. "It's the census."

"The census the clerks have been compiling the entire year?!" gasped Maura. "Simon, you've strewn at least a volume of it!"

"God's blood!" he cursed, as the enormity of the disaster jolted him. "Maura, help me!"

"Help you how?"

"Stack it again!" She watched with sly amusement as he flitted about the room, frantically scooping pages and sputtering panic, "It's organized by counties. Please say you remember Latin!"

"Perhaps. And what do I get for helping you with your little mishap?"

He reached out and pledged passionately, "Anything! I swear...I'll give you anything! Hurry, the scribes may return."

"Yes, they may...at any moment." As she stooped to gather the strewn text, she smiled to herself. It was the Sabbath and the scribes most certainly wouldn't be returning, though he needn't know. She squinted at the scratchy print and struggled with the Latin. "Worcestershire—I think. I do believe the clerks must have imbibed a great deal of wine while scripting this. Simon, what *does* this say?"

Simon widened, then narrowed his eyes and stammered, "*Abbot Walter proved... his...his right to these five hides at Bengeworth in four shires in the presence...of Odo, the Bishop of Bayeux and other...barons of the King.* Why can't I ever escape dear Uncle Odo?"

"Will this census include all of England?" asked Maura.

"Most of it, and bits of Wales as well."

"Why did Uncle William commission such a grand task?"

"He never told me," said Simon. "Most likely to determine how the country's divided, who owns what, leases what, rules what, perhaps for nothing more than tax purposes. I suspect Father's name appears quite often on these pages."

"Just how wealthy is he?"

"He owns roughly 800 castles and manors scattered throughout every shire and is, after the King, the wealthiest landowner in England. He also owns the county of Mortain in Normandy, and whatever else he's accumulated from my three sisters' marriages."

"How can he manage all those properties?"

"He portions out land to loyal knights, fellow vassals, and family. He owns it, they manage it. Odo, William, and Robert's holdings amount to more than half of England."

"I had no idea." Maura peeled a crumpled page from the sole of her boot and questioned on, "How was the information gathered?"

Simon inserted the sheets she passed in their proper places while briskly explaining, "From statements in county courts, interviews with landholders, county geld accounts, and word of mouth. After the initial survey, the inquisitors discovered countless lies and omissions. The next band of commissioners sent out weren't so polite and threatened severe penalties for deception. Villagers equated the inquest with Judgment Day and dubbed the census 'The Domesday Book'."

"And how do you know all this?"

"I served as translator for a number of commissioners."

Maura peered severely at a tattered piece of parchment and wagged her head in frustration. "Well that is all quite fascinating, though if no one can decipher it, what good will it be?"

"Have you located Yorkshire?" wondered Simon.

"No...Why?"

"I want to know what Robert aims to gain from your marriage to this Hugh of Ryedale." Scanning the stacks, he discovered the Yorkshire pile unscathed. He thumbed briskly through the stack, at long last tugged a sheet from the pile, and studied it intently. "Hugh and his father, Aubrey, own a vast amount of waste land, one manor house in Ryedale, and, ahhh, this may well be the treasure—a fortified manor house in Helmsley, strategically placed and flanked on all sides by waste land. An excellent site from which to extend Robert's power east to the sea and west to York. He already owns a great deal of Yorkshire and Helmsley, including Helmsley Castle. This manor will complete his command of the north."

"Only *one* manor!" noted Maura. "And the manor may not be included in the contract. Either way, Robert gains little property from the union."

"The property itself is not as important as the principle," Simon argued. "When I ended the Rufus betrothal, Father lost face and power. The Yorkshire contract, meager as it is, is perhaps his final opportunity to regain his esteem."

Maura plopped forlornly in a chair, her bottom lip thrust out in a pout. "Let's finish here and go."

As Simon snatched up the final pages from the rushes, he noted, "I'm listed in the census—someplace."

"Of course you'd be, as Robert's son."

"No, he refused to acknowledge me. I'm recorded as Tenant-in-Chief."

"No..."

"It's true. Two manors, one in Sussex and one in—I forget. I didn't know of the holdings till Rufus told me—"

"Rufus?" she interrupted, her suspicion rising.

"Yes, he informed me of my wealth at Christmas Court."

"Why would he bother to tell you anything pleasant?"

"As a bribe."

Simon replaced the last sheet, and they visited each pile to even the edges. "Simon," probed Maura, "you're confusing me. What bribe?"

"While at Gloucester, I wanted to talk with you. Instead, I managed to get myself banned from the castle. To get back in, I made a deal with Rufus—my two manors for a few precious moments of your time."

"So that's the mysterious deal Rufus spoke of at the competitions. Simon, I'm flattered! What a hardhearted bitch I was—for your sacrifice, you received nothing in return. And how did you come to own two manor homes?"

"Uncle William granted them to me—in secret. He's constantly trying to give me presents, land, money, titles, a knighthood. Swear to me you won't mention this to anyone..."

"What?" she asked, piqued.

"Once he spoke of arranging a profitable marriage for me with a widowed countess who was also being considered for another member of my family."

Maura's eyes bulged in disbelief. "Was it Almodis?"

"No names were mentioned. I thought the family member had to be Will, and at Berkhamstead, he was with Almodis. When she was introduced as Father's bride, I was, as you can well imagine, struck dumb."

"What a spirited union you two would have shared!" remarked Maura.

"I declined Uncle's offer, and he never mentioned the matter again. I suspect he realized the disaster that would have erupted had Father known we were vying for the same woman. I don't believe Almodis knows any details of the matter, and she needn't know any now."

"I agree."

"Uncle gets frustrated when I refuse his favors," continued Simon. "So lately, he's been bestowing gifts without my—"

"Without your what?"

"...Knowledge." Simon turned introspective and his voice took on a fanciful quality, "I've never asked William for a thing. Though if I did, I don't believe he'd refuse me..." Caught in deep thought, his attention again drifted.

"Well, I don't think he'd make you King," prompted Maura.

The parchment beneath his fingers crumpled to his enlightened expression and urgent announcement, "I must speak to Adela!"

"She won't speak to you."

"This time, she just might. Wait here for me!"

In a flash, he was gone. Maura spread the wrinkled page on the table and, pressing it flat, imagined the cousins' undoubtedly animated meeting and smiled. Replacing the sheet, she found herself staring at the title "Sussex" and hastily shuffled through the parchments. Her roaming eye caught his name, *Simon FitzRobert*, and she read on, *holds in demesne one manor in...* Amazing, she thought, as she carried his holdings with her to the fire pit. She had always known the King and Simon shared a deep affection for one another, but she'd never realized the extent of their bond.

The chamber held a damp chill, and the pit was neatly stacked with wood for the morning fire; all that was needed was a flame. A flint provided the spark, and as Maura rested back on her heels to await the mounting warmth, her mind wandered back over the past few glorious weeks. Their incessant struggle to devise a plan to stay together had resulted in nothing that seemed feasible or safe. Looking about her, she wondered what in this mass of titles, names, and numbers had ignited a new notion in his genius and impetuous mind. She knelt before the fire for what seemed a long while, then heard a rustling, and glanced up to see Simon, sporting a self-satisfied smirk and leaning crossed-armed in the doorway. She mimicked his smirk and remarked, "You look pleased with yourself."

"I am," he said, latching the door.

"I take it she didn't curse you, hurl anything at you, or hit you?"

"She wasn't exactly kind, though she did agree to my request fairly quickly."

"And what request was that?"

"I'll tell you in a moment. First..." Maura started to rise; Simon stopped her with a gesture. "No, stay. I'll come down to you. There's something I need to ask." Simon knelt facing her and squeezed her hands between his. He paused an excruciatingly long moment to clear his throat and wet his lips, then ever so carefully began, "In the midst of all the turmoil surrounding us, we've forgotten the one person who truly loves us, and who also owns the power to grant us whatever we may want—Uncle William."

Maura nodded and questioned, "Simon, I don't—"

"Please let me finish." His hands slid up her arms and rested a gentle grip on her shoulders. "The King has asked for me. When I see him, I will suggest that Robert be punished for his crimes against us."

"Punished how?"

"I will ask William to annul the Yorkshire betrothal contract, and, then, I'll ask for...you. If he agrees, and I can return before your wedding day, will you—" He stopped again and swallowed dryly, but the effort failed to ease his scratchy throat and his pause lengthened.

She gazed into his twitchy, bemused face and felt her mind and body flood with elation, then shudder with dread. He'd die in Normandy! Uncle William would never punish Robert for Simon's sake, and how could he possibly get back to her before Easter, only three weeks away? She searched closer; her questioning gaze met his hopeful one, and its intensity blew her qualms away, as he haltingly continued, "...and I ask you this in the presence of most of the inhabitants of England and bits of Wales—will you—"

Her finger tips brushed his lips as she ardently interrupted, "I'm astonished you felt the need to ask. Of course, I'll marry you."

He let go a blissful sigh and grasped up her hand to kiss; instead his lips touched parchment. "And what do you have here?" he asked, holding the sheet toward the light.

"The page listing your manor."

He balled the sheet in his fist and tossed it into the flames. His lips skimmed her neck and thrilled her with a murmur, "Your future husband has nothing...and everything."

A gentle laugh rippled from them as they melted together and sank into the rushes. Maura pushed up on her arms and hovered over him, her voice a trill of excitement, "How shall we celebrate our betrothal?" He didn't answer immediately, and stared pensively beyond her. Slipping to his side, she attempted to retrieve his attention by patting the rushes. "I believe we've found our 'softer place'. Did you bolt the door?"

"Yes," he answered absently, shifting to face her. His expression brimmed uncertainty, while his fingers deftly loosened her braid. "Is it possible? Do you truly believe it will work?"

"Well, it's worked every time before," Maura said with a seductive snicker, as she searched under his tunic and tugged the cord that secured his braies.

"No, Maura." He stopped her hand and became even more serious. "I mean our plan."

"Please, Simon," she fervidly begged, "no doubts, no worries...not now! We have at last found our answer and will defeat Robert, using as our only weapon a sheet of parchment marked by the King! We *will* be victorious!"

"And if violence proves necessary?"

"I'll risk anything to stay with you..." she vehemently stressed, "anything!"

"Then I suppose," he stated, "the matter's settled."

She urged him to his back with frenzied kisses, straddled his waist, and yanked the cord from his braies. He strained to sit and muttered uneasily, "Here? What if the scribes return?"

"You've forgotten, it's the Sabbath. *Here* is absolutely perfect." Her arms buoyantly swept the air in company with her observation, "Thousands of vassals, peasants and beasts can witness our celebration. And if we happen to jar a few sheets loose in our fervor, only we will know why parts of the Domesday Book are askew."

"You are indeed a lusty wench!" he commented with glee.

"And you are every bit a lecherous devil," she replied in kind.

"This must be true love," Simon chortled, tickling her chin with a handful of rushes.

"Why is that?"

"Why else would we chance being nipped by these?" He crunched the rushes and sent their chaff soaring. "We'll be scratching for days."

"And I..." murmured Maura as her mouth and body caressed his, "...will welcome the itch."

*****

The door to Adela's chamber creaked open and Maura warily peeked inside. Encumbered beneath pelts, Adela lay sprawled across her bed, her mouth gaping wide. The bed curtains quivered to her rattling snore. Noiselessly, Maura crept to her trunk, discarded in a darkened corner. Wincing to the lid's squeak, Maura felt a despairing twinge as she carefully packed the clothes she had taken to the cottage. Bidding farewell to her new-found village friends had been difficult enough. How could she possibly repeat the same doleful words to—She dropped a stocking and as she bent to fetch it, the lid slammed shut. Adela started awake, sputtering, "Who's...who's there?"

"It's only me, Adela."

"Maura..." Adela stretched back upon her pillows, focused a damning glare and snipe, "So, the bastard's gotten his fill and is abandoning you. Serves you right. You have no sense when it comes to men. You're far too gullible."

Maura whirled round to rage, "And what sense has taken you hundreds of miles from *your* man? Will he be there when you return? Perhaps not, for I'm sure, like myself, he's gotten his fill of you!"

"Maura, I'm shocked! What has this scoundrel done to ruin my sweet friend?"

"He's encouraged me to confess my true feelings and, at the moment, what I feel for you, my *dear* friend, is pure disgust."

Rose strolled in from her chamber, beaming proudly. "Bravo, Maura. I wondered how much longer you could contain the truth." Then she turned her scorn on the Countess. "Adela, you should be groveling on your knees, giving thanks to God for Maura and Simon. Without their selfless aid, you'd surely be returning to Blois tacked up in a coffin."

Adela spat curses, flung aside the bedclothes and, throwing on her robe, stormed from the chamber.

The trunk creaked louder as Maura reopened it and rested her brow on the lid. "I shouldn't have angered her. Now, she'll most likely refuse Simon's request to travel with her party."

Rose brushed back Maura's hair to search her drawn expression. "He'll leave at dawn?"

"Yes..." Maura sniffed and added, "He feels the safest passage will be with Adela."

"Don't feel you need be strong around me, angel." Rose's hand patted her shoulder. "I love him too, and will miss him sorely."

"Rose, come with me to our old chamber. Simon's waiting there and we have something to tell you."

Rose stopped Maura from closing the trunk's lid. "Before we go..." Rose said as she plunged her arm into the bowels of the trunk and rummaged. Her eyes brightened as she found the object of desire, and her fingers emerged holding a tiny box. "Remember, angel?" asked Rose, placing the gift in Maura's palm. The tender memory welled Maura's eyes with glittering tears, and grief shook Rose's voice as she closed Maura's fingers over the box. "There is no one more deserving of my husband's ring than Simon."

*****

Rose sat rigidly on her old bed, her head cocked and expression intent as she listened to Simon's version of the plan. "...So you see, Rose, Maura must go to Pevensey alone. We can't have you involved for I may have to take her by force from Robert. It's far too dangerous."

"I've spoken to Sir Roger," broke in Maura. "He's kindly agreed to have two of his soldiers escort you to your son Richard's manor. And when I arrive at Pevensey, I will tell Lord Robert we've quarreled and I no longer want you near. I don't believe he'll suspect a thing."

Tensely, they awaited her reply. She stayed too still, only her eyes shifting, then she stood and resolutely stated, "Then I must pack."

Astounded to their feet by her swift surrender, Simon and Maura stared at each other, and Maura addressed Rose, "Did you hear us correctly, Rose?"

"Of course. I may be old but my hearing is excellent."

"Where's your fight, your argument?"

"Don't be ridiculous Maura, why would I waste precious time fighting over what is clearly meant to be? Now, I'm sure you two want to be alone." Rose took Maura's hands and, with a loving gesture, brushed a wisp of hair from her brow, kissed her cheek, and murmured, "When he's gone, come to me. We'll both need comforting."

Simon trailed Rose from the chamber. They mumbled shy, strained good-byes, and then Rose clenched tight his hands and said with deep affection, "Simon, I'll pray for your safe journey and quick return. And if you two fail to visit me at Dunheved on your journey to Wales, I will never ever forgive you!"

"Rose," he answered with plaintive smile, "I would never risk losing your loyalty."

She pecked both his cheeks and patted his hand in assurance. "I'll tell all to Edith, using great discretion."

When Simon returned, Maura was waiting beneath their quilt; he undressed and crawled between her wide and welcoming arms. They clung together and shared a bittersweet love, each touching something wondrous in the other they'd not known before. They whispered idyllic dreams of their life in Wales and made new and glorious memories to savor while apart. Though as the time slipped away, a sneaking light intruded and brought with it a dread that chipped and splintered at their fragile plan. But neither dared betray their silent anguish—that these could well be their last moments together.

Simon grudgingly left Maura's embrace to dress; she sat and solemnly scrutinized each graceful detail of his every movement. He stretched back beside her, kissing away her tears while struggling to contain his own. "Believe in my love and believe I'll return," he choked, crushing her to his chest, "for nothing...nothing can keep me from you."

"I love you so," she quavered. "I will always love you."

The room grew ever lighter. Maura sluggishly tugged on her chemise and tunic while Simon frantically searched the contents of his saddlebag. He took her hand, urged her from the bed, and slipped over her head a woven cord, hung with a tiny silver vial containing a mysterious powder. Quizzically, Maura turned the vial over and over in her hand, and finally asked, "Simon, what—"

"Vervain...it will ward off any nightmare..."

"Have you found someone to watch over Arthur's cottage?"

"Yes."

Her fingers touched his damp cheek and her voice was ragged with sadness, "You...you must go or Adela will leave you behind. I'll walk you to the stables."

"No!" He squeezed a fistful of her hair and pleaded, "You must stay here. I couldn't leave if you—"

She pressed her cheek to his palm, then kissed the silver band that circled his finger. "When you return, we'll never say good-bye again." Stepping back, she cried, "Go!"

He raced to the stable, patted E'dain's neck, then leapt on Maura's saddled horse and galloped away, barely squeezing between the closing main gates.

Maura ran, her mind crazed and screaming, *Simon, don't leave me! Come back. We needn't have the King's permission. We'll run, escape, Robert won't find us! Don't go!* But instead of in the bailey, she found herself high up on the battlements, driven to her knees by a heavy emptiness. She clutched her blanket tighter and peered through a descending mist to watch his charging figure grow smaller, and finally disappear behind a wall of trees.

Rose arrived on the battlements, her heart aching as she gazed tearfully down at Maura. She bent and took her charge's limp hand, softly urging, "Come, angel, we'll go inside where it's warm."

Simon reached the tail end of Adela's party. Reining Maura's gasping steed, he snapped to a movement and twisted back, expecting to see her. Only a veil of fog and despair followed him. He turned and, nudging his mount's girth with his heels, vanished into the mist.

*****

CHAPTER TWENTY-THREE - MORTAL CONCESSIONS

With a disgusted shudder, Simon burrowed deeper into the hay and bundled tighter in his cloak. He glanced up through a weak light at the massive creature towering above him. He and Maura's steed had shared a relatively pleasant journey thus far, however, if he was forced to share the beast's stall for one more night he'd go mad!

Adela's party had arrived at Rouen the previous evening to find the King absent, presumably detained in battle. Since joining Adela's entourage four days past, Simon had been consistently refused any comforts except for food, and he had decided quite readily, that comforts weren't worth wrestling her burly guards over. And he also had surrendered to the reality, as he scraped furiously at the filth coating his skin, that if Uncle William didn't arrive by the morning, he'd have no choice but risk the dire prospect of washing in the scum-encrusted communal tub.

Soldiers' snores rumbled from every stall, making sleep impossible, and Simon pondered how to remedy the situation. He could always escape in his mind back to Winchester...and Maura. Her winsome image came easily to him—galloping down the lane, the sun's brilliance sparking her windswept hair; laughing, her skirt hiked high as they rolled together in the tall grass by the river; and tangled to him on their quilt by the fire, her nakedness gleaming with flickered light and sweat, and her sweet lips tasting...Instead of sleep, his reverie only produced more discomfort. Besides Maura, fresh air was what he mostly craved so, snatching up his saddlebag, he left the stable to wander.

A few hounds, most likely lured by his stench, joined him for his traipse through the bailey. He gulped in the clear, crisp night air and looked up into a sky garnished with glittering stars. He rounded the keep and paused by the kitchen hut to sample the aroma of baking bread, but doing so only reminded him of the scraps he'd been forced to accept on his journey thus far, and hunger worried his belly. Just beyond the kitchen sat the huge wooden tub. Usually crammed with grimy, wrangling soldiers, it now stood empty, a thin coat of ice skimming its surface. Determinedly, Simon approached and leant out over its wall to crack the ice. To his amazement, his palm cupped clean water! He hunted for onlookers; there were none. As he swiftly shed his clothes, he reckoned the frigid water would surely kill every bug that dared crawl his blackened skin, and was exactly what was needed to calm a certain part of his anatomy. He snatched a chunk of soap from a woven basket set at the tub's base, borrowed a coarse towel from a rope line nearby, dipped the towel in the water, and vigorously scrubbed himself. His limpid blue eyes peered out from white foam as Simon dove into the numbing water; sputtering and gasping, he ducked under again and again till he was totally free of soap and filth. He whipped drops from his hair, then vaulted the wall, and stole another towel to scour himself dry. The kitchen wall provided a soothing warmth as he donned the last remaining fresh clothes from his saddlebag. Swathed in his cloak, he gazed dreamily up at the sliver of moon dangling just above the curtain wall and mused—Maura was now at

Pevensey. His next tremulous thought set his chafed body to quivering—Who was there with her?

Simon found a skinny spot on the kitchen floor to sleep, and it seemed that as soon as his eyes closed, a broom swatted him awake and shooed him and the countless other men up from the kitchen floor. "Get out!" bellowed the rotund, tempestuous cook. "The King's approaching. How can I work with you disgusting louts under foot? Out, now!" The men tumbled out the doorway, then scattered like startled mice across the bailey. Pages, guards, and Adela's soldiers jostled Simon in their rush to prepare for the King's arrival. Tradesmen paused in their morning crafts to join the gathering crowd. Simon collected his wits, slung his saddlebag over his shoulder, and strode toward the main gates with a resolute bearing.

The gates groaned wide and in pranced the knights' horses. The soldiers' posture—arms thrust high in a sign of victory—elicited hoots and cheers from the squirming on-lookers. Their squires followed on foot, dragging their masters' ravaged armor and bloodied weapons. Simon made a rapid search for Marc and grew worried at his absence. Then his attention was diverted by a sudden spiral in the jubilation. In sauntered the King, a tight circle of guards surrounding his horse. Simon stared aghast at his uncle's gross appearance. He'd grown huge! His belly bulged over his saddle's pommel, his haggard face was deeply creased with age and worry, and dark sagging blotches shadowed his bleary eyes. Though once inside the gates, his subjects' shrill adulation drew from him a beaming expression and straightened his bent figure, creating a dazzling illusion of regality. Simon elbowed his way through the horde only to be knocked to the ground by an overzealous guard, feet from the King's stallion. William's eyes glared accusingly down at the stupidly bold reveler, then sparked with affection as they came to rest on Simon. "Help him up!" he roared at his sentry. Stiffly dismounting, William met his nephew with an ample hug and effusive greeting, "It's marvelous to see you, my boy!"

"I was worried, Uncle," said Simon as they ambled, arm in arm, to the keep, "that you'd come to some harm."

"I'm fine. Philip's harassment tactics lasted a bit longer than expected, and you've arrived sooner than requested."

"Actually a bit later," clarified Simon. "Is Marc with your battalion?"

"He's riding with Roger's knights. They are routing out the last of the French stragglers and will arrive shortly. I'm filthy, parched, and ravenous. What chamber are you using?"

"None as yet."

William's voice rasped with bother, "And why not?"

Simon averted his gaze as he floundered for a neutral reply.

"Answer me, lad! Who has kept you out?" William bristled at Simon's irksome silence, then ordered, "Fetch your belongings and follow me."

"I have my belongings," mumbled Simon as he hurried after and fretted inwardly, how much of the last few days could he safely betray to his uncle? He couldn't chance maddening anyone, particularly Adela. She had great sway over her father and one wag of her viperous tongue could swiftly dash his delicate plans.

He continued to trail William across the great hall and into the Royal bedchamber where, with great ado, servants flitted about, briskly removing their sire's cloak and boots, stoking the fire, and turning down the pelts draping his ornate bed. A wooden tub was rolled into the room; buckets of boiling water followed closely behind. In strode the cook, laden with a silver tray steeped with a most sumptuous feast. Wine was poured and the King's chair plumped with pillows. Simon viewed the flurry with uneasy astonishment. He retreated from the commotion to wait outside the door. The King's gruff voice ordered him back. "Simon! Where have you gone? Stand before me, now!"

The servants stepped away, and Simon returned and stood before his King, now seated with his thick legs propped, and munching on a leg of quail. William pointed rigidly to the foot of the bed and mumbled, "Sit," then looked to the door and called, "Aggy?"

A rosy cheeked, plump matron instantly appeared at the door; with a cloying grin and profound bow, she replied, "Yes, my Lord?"

"Who is in residence?"

"Why, your daughter, Adela, my Lord."

"Well that explains a great deal. Send her to me at once!"

"Yes, my Lord," Aggy answered as she straightened, then darted away.

"You needn't be afraid of Adela, my boy," said William with a wag of his head.

Simon snorted a laugh. "Believe me, Uncle, I'm not. I don't think it would be wise to anger anyone—just now."

"I agree, Adela can throw quite a fit when riled. She often frightens me." A hint of suspicion clouded William's eye as he handed Simon a cup of wine and began his interrogation, "Henry tells me you've been in prison. Is this true?"

"Yes..." Simon answered with extreme caution. "I...I was released over a month ago."

"And did I hear him correctly when he blamed your father?" William awaited Simon's response; again he received only silence. "Why protect Robert?" The King argued. "What fatherly act has he bestowed on you these past four years? My spies say he's in Mortain, wisely out of my reach. When I see him again, and eventually I will, he'll pay for his treachery by—"

William's vengeful scheme was cut short by Adela. Babe in arms, she lit the room with a garish glee. "Oh Father, I'm so pleased to see you!" she gushed. Then she spotted Simon—Her smile twisted to a grimace, her twittering to a growl, "God's teeth! What are *you* doing here? How dare you set foot inside this—"

"That's enough, Adela," demanded William as he and Simon stood in respect.

"Father! If you only knew how this fiend tortured me, you'd insist he be flogged and cast from—"

"I said stop!" William's glower softened to a silly grin. "I'll see my grandchild. And what have you christened him?"

Adela's glee returned as she proudly passed her son to her father and spouted, "Theobald!"

Simon's hand hid his smile as William commented, "A fine name to match a fine boy!" The King squeezed her hand and pulled her close to kiss her cheeks. "I'm so proud of you, little one." Adela gathered the babe back in her arms, and William sat with a curt sigh. "Now...you'll tell me what war goes on between you two. Simon, speak first."

Simon cleared his throat, glanced briefly at Adela, then proceeded, "At Winchester, Adela's birthing pains were proving useless. Her women and the physician in residence deserted her. I mixed an herbal tonic to strengthen her labor—"

"You tortured me!"

"I admit your pains did increase," appeased Simon. "If they hadn't..." He paused, uncertain how to phrase his next statement, then shrugged and bluntly finished, "You and Theobald would be dead."

"Liar!" she screamed. "You vile putrid lying snake of a bastard! Father, I demand you heave this fiend from the battlements. How dare you take credit for the birth of my son?! My fortitude and only my fortitude brought Theobald into this world and no outlandish tale you spew will alter the fact that—"

"Adela, stop your fussing!" William blared. "You'll drop the child! Now, I don't comprehend a bit of this mess, though I do insist you attempt to reconcile your differences. After all, families ought not quarrel."

"I'm willing," said Simon as he sat on the bed, drew his leg up and rested his chin on his knee.

Adela stomped one foot, then the other, squalling, "Never! And if you grant him the freedom of the keep, I return to Blois. His stench sickens me, so I'll take my leave!" Her chin cocked haughtily, she spun on her heels, and stomped away, whining so all could hear, "No one understands or listens to me, only you, Theobald."

Simon again clamped shut his mouth, till he noticed William's shoulders quaking with muted laughter. William stopped his chuckle to caution, "Oh, my boy, you've really ruffled her wings this time. I strongly suggest in the future, that you make a concerted effort to avoid her."

"Will she leave?" Simon asked hopefully.

"I'm afraid not. She constantly threatens to go, and at times I wish she'd make good on her offer, but she's my little one, and I love having her near. You will have the chamber at the top of the rear steps. And as a reward for his bravery, I'll allow Marc to share the quarters with you."

"Thank you, Uncle."

William stretched long to pat Simon's hand. "And I am beholden to you for my daughter's and grandson's lives. Now leave me, for I must wash and rest. Join me for a late supper in the great hall. There I will announce my plans for you." With Simon's aid, William rose shakily, and muttered, "Go...and get yourself settled."

Genuflecting, Simon bowed his head, felt the gentle brush of the King's hand on his shoulder, and did as told.

*****

After depositing his belongings in his chamber, Simon locked the door and began a meticulous search for Marc through the crowded halls of Rouen Castle. A blustery commotion erupted at his back. He spun around, braced for trouble, and warily witnessed a bedchamber door burst wide, allowing Henry to hurtle backward at great speed from the room. He slammed against the wall opposite and slid down the stones with a whiney shriek, "Bitch! Horrid bitch. I'll tell Father!" Henry continued to mumble curses as he crawled to his feet. He straightened his clothes, palmed back his hair and, sensing intense scrutiny, raised a snarling face to growl, "What are you gawking at...Simon!" Henry's eyes lit with merriment and disbelief as he enveloped his cousin in a rough embrace. "Where've you come from? Are you here to see me?"

Simon did not return Henry's lavish salutation; instead he jerked from his hold and raised a quieting hand. He nodded toward the chamber and asked curtly, "What have you done?"

"Nothing...I...I was only visiting my new nephew. You look quite fit, Simon, though a bit severe. Is there something wrong?"

"I'm looking for Marc," answered Simon. His austere glare ended their meeting and he resumed his search down the hall.

"May I join you?" Henry asked, fidgeting and tagging at his heels. Simon's grunt prompted Henry's pout, "Simon, what bothers you? You don't seem pleased to see me...Simon?" Simon stopped abruptly, and Henry collided with his back. "I'm sorry, Simon...I didn't mean—"

Henry found himself atoning to an accusing finger. He swallowed with difficulty, then raised fearful eyes to Simon's scowl. "We will talk," stated Simon bitterly, "after I've found Marc."

His cow eyes round with innocence, Henry shrank in Simon's shadow, and his small voice pouted, "It wasn't my fault."

Simon retorted with a bristled, "What wasn't your fault?"

"Whatever it is that you need to speak to me about."

"God's blood, Henry!" railed Simon, flinging his arms in exasperation. "I'm sick to death of your sniveling nonsense and I don't want you near. Leave me. I must find Marc!"

Henry continued to pester. "He's not yet arrived." Then, he asked with hesitation, "I suppose you've seen Maura?"

"Yes, I've seen her," Simon gritted.

"May I further suppose you two spoke?"

"We do speak, yes."

Henry's genteel words swiftly turned vulgar. "Then I can only presume she broke our confidence. That tramp swore she wouldn't—"

Suddenly slammed against the wall, Henry whimpered to Simon's lethal grip and savage tirade, "I'm already furious. Don't give me another reason to kill you!"

"Simon!" Henry squeaked in terror, "I...I didn't mean—Don't kill me! Let me go! Simon, I can't breathe. Please, let go!"

Simon opened his hand and Henry again slumped to the rushes, this time coughing. Simon strode a few feet away then turned a murderous glare to warn, "Stay away from me! I'll come to you if and when I'm ready to forgive, which may very well be never."

Henry scrambled up and in a fit of temper, kicked the wall and cursed in pain, "God's breath! Why does my damn tongue always get me in a tangle?" Melancholy curbed his anger and, dusting his clothes, he mumbled, "Perhaps at supper I can make things right again."

*****

Unable to find Marc, Simon decided there would be no better time than the present to confess Robert's crimes and his own humble desires to the King. He returned to the Royal bedchamber and asked a young squire crouched by the door, "Is Lord William asleep?"

"No, my Lord. Do you wish to speak to him?"

"Yes."

"Your name, my Lord?"

"Simon."

The squire vanished into the chamber and reappeared to request, "Please enter."

Simon rubbed sweaty palms together as he walked to the King's bed. William pulled himself erect and snapped his fingers in the direction of the wine flask. The squire promptly poured two cups, presented one to the King, one to Simon, then left the room to a dismissing wave. William's fond smile instantly cured Simon's nervousness. As he had done countless times before, Simon crawled upon the bed and sat cross-legged and attentive at his Uncle's feet. After a wide yawn, William muttered, "So now you wish to talk. Proceed."

"Father did imprison me."

Simon's alarming revelation woke William fully and he demanded, "For what reason?"

"He claimed I plotted his murder. Now I know the true reason for his anger was my ending of the betrothal between Rufus and Maura."

"And I'm immensely proud of you for carrying out my request so brilliantly. A brother's trickery is the worst of crimes." William finished his wine with a gulp and continued pointedly, "At Rouen, Henry had me sign a writ commanding your instant release. Did Robert honor the document?"

"Rufus released me before the document arrived at Westminster."

"Rufus? That's indeed puzzling," said William. "I didn't realize Rufus cared for you."

"It's all a bit complicated."

"And was your imprisonment Robert's lone crime? I expect the truth, Simon, nothing less."

"He had me flogged as well," admitted Simon.

"Turn and show me."

Obediently Simon exposed his scarred back and flinched to William's rage. "He had you beaten for performing your duty to me?!"

"And he harassed my mother as to my whereabouts."

"That despicable worm! He'll soon know the burn of a whip himself!" William's ferocity melted to sympathy. "How fare you now, my boy?"

Simon smoothed his clothes and replied, "I'm fine, thanks to family and friends, especially...Maura."

"Maura?" The King's dark eyes brightened to her name. "Yes, she would have been grateful to you for ending the betrothal. If she is wanting for anything, she need only ask."

"Actually, Uncle, she does want for something." Simon paused a long moment for calm, considered the oil swirling on the surface of his wine, then raised a tenacious expression to declare, "She...no, *we* want to choose Robert's punishment."

"And what punishment do you suggest?"

"That the Yorkshire marriage contract be annulled."

Bewildered, William sat up taller in his bed. "Surely the punishment does not fit the crime. Nothing more?"

Simon swallowed a sip of wine and blurted, "That you also agree to *our* marriage."

"You and...Maura?"

"Yes...we...we love each other."

William's tongue tripped on his reply, "Lo...Love did you say?" He scratched thoughtfully at his sparse gray beard. "You're quite correct, this *is* a bit complicated. Robert will be incensed."

"We are aware of that."

"I can't protect you forever," stressed William.

"We realize that as well."

"And if I agree, where will you live, what will you do?"

"Ideally, I'd like to take Maura to Wales and continue my doctoring."

"And what of the work you do for me?"

"I'll do what I can—in secret."

"Yes, unfortunately it would have to be that way...again." William struggled up from his bed, stretched and, rubbing his backside, griped, "Riding is vicious on my old bones."

"Have your tanner put extra cushion in your saddle," suggested Simon.

William smiled and nodded, "Thank you, my boy, I'll do just that. I'll miss having you near, to cheer me and think for me."

"I won't be far away."

Sniffling, William sneezed, swabbed his nose with a cuffed rag, then wandered to the fire and sat with a rumbling sigh. "Why didn't Maura accompany you?" he wondered aloud. "She's not one to shy away from danger. The tale of the orange-haired beauty who dragged my youngest to safety is still a favorite amongst the troops."

Simon untangled his legs and dangled them off the side of the lofty bed. "She's journeyed to Pevensey. We decided to curb Father's suspicions by pretending her marriage to Hugh will proceed as arranged."

"An excellent notion. Well, I'll require a few moments alone to ponder your plea. Await my decision in the great hall."

*****

Simon sat an interminable length of time at the dais, seemingly entranced by fissures in the wood. His dagger stabbed at the cracks, skewering crusted pieces of meat and moldy bread, while his nails dug his furrowed brow and drummed the table top. He abandoned the dais to roam restlessly about the immense room, kicking coals, fingering tapestries, and picking wax drippings from fat candles set upon tall iron posts. As he meandered, he hoped—of course the King would agree. After all, they were such simple requests. And it would make their decision much less of an ordeal if only—

"My Lord?" The squire's impish face suddenly appeared before him.

Simon managed a tentative grin and followed the boy to the bedchamber. William remained seated, his robes now hiked above his puffy white knees, and his swollen feet entrenched in a steaming pail of water. He sneezed again into his damp rag and, pinching at his rosy nose, mumbled, "Come into the light, Simon."

Clenching the hem of his tunic, Simon stepped forward and gulped. "Are you ill, my Lord?"

"It's nothing serious. I lingered too long in the rain. Might you brew me a tonic to ease my aches?"

"Of course."

"Fine. I have considered your requests—"

"And?" Simon interjected eagerly.

"Patience, my boy. I have decided to grant you your wishes..." Simon released his hem. He squeezed his eyes shut and palms together, and his loud sigh of relief drowned all but the last of the King's words, "...concessions."

With wide eyes, Simon gulped again. "Concessions?"

"Yes. Nothing too demanding—for you." William wove his fingers together, cracked his knuckles, and concisely began, "My eldest, Curthose, occupies a castle twenty miles or so down the Seine at Les Andelys. I need you to go sniff out his plans."

"Spy on my cousin?"

"Precisely."

Simon hung on the bedpost to protest, "You *know* his schemes. He's in league with Philip and plots to sabotage your battle plans or accidentally skirmish with your troops. Whichever, he aims to give you trouble."

"I need strategies, dates, locations. Victory in our next battle is vital if we are to hold our advantage over Philip. And by the glory of God we'll soon march to Paris!" William's balled fists thudded the arms of his chair. "Time is of the essence. I will not suffer any trouble!"

"Paris?" Simon's face soured with confusion. "I thought your only intent was to keep Normandy intact."

"Yes...that is my primary intent. If more property is seized in the process, who does it hurt?"

"Only a thousand or so soldiers and innocent villagers," returned Simon mordantly, then he wagged his head in disgust. "When does it end, Uncle?"

"Never! I intend to be battling in Heaven."

The insult tumbled recklessly off Simon's tongue, "If Heaven will have you."

"God wouldn't dare refuse me!" roared William, rising inches from his seat. He eased his cumbersome form back into the cushions, yet his glower stayed savage.

"Why waste time playing lethal games?" asked Simon, skirting the subject. "If your eldest is a nuisance, confine him."

"I refuse to behave like *your* father, Simon. I respect and encourage my children's vindictiveness. It will prove useful to their survival after my death. I love my children and fear them, and that's how it should be."

Simon mellowed and whined, "There's so little time, Uncle. If I'm to stop the marriage, I must return to Pevensey before Easter."

"It will take you two days at most to gather the information I need, and you will have assistance."

"From whom?" asked Simon, askance.

"I plan to assign Marc to the mission and also...Henry."

"No, Uncle!" argued Simon adamantly. "Not Henry."

"Yes, Henry. He's recently taken an interest in espionage, and this is an excellent opportunity for him to hone his skills. He remains friendly with both his brothers and can easily sneak you into the castle."

Simon slumped his shoulders and pouted.

"Don't give me that face!" hurled William. "Do you want to marry this woman or not?"

"Yes!" Simon parried.

"Then you'll do as I say. I have one further request to make of you. You will accompany my troops into battle—"

"Not as a soldier!" Simon stood tall in defiance. "I swore an oath as doctor, and we made a solemn pact when I returned from Wales! I won't—"

"I've not forgotten our pact. Now calm yourself and hear me out. Two of my physicians have...have recently left my service. Their replacements have not yet arrived. Would you deny treatment to my wounded?"

"No," said Simon ruefully.

"Then it's settled. Tomorrow dawn you will depart for Andelys to visit my eldest, and upon your return, ride immediately into battle as my chief physician. Then I will release you from your obligations, and you may return to Pevensey to marry your beloved. Are these terms agreeable to you?"

"Do I have a choice?" remarked Simon.

"No, and don't look so damned morbid! If I have to row you there myself, I'll get you to Pevensey in time. I can always extend Hugh of Ryedale's, Maura's intended, term of service by a week or two. He's one of my most competent soldiers. Do you wish to meet him?"

"I'd rather not. And he needn't know our plans."

"I agree, though it grieves me to think that he'll suffer from this debacle."

"He won't mourn long," said Simon with a touch of disdain.

An oppressive quiet lingered, then a playful grin cracked William's glower. "I don't suppose you had to wrestle with Maura to convince her to agree to your proposal."

Simon smirked. "I suppose it depends on what sort of wrestling you're alluding to. Why do you ask?"

"I had to tackle my sweet Matilda to the ground before she would consent to be my bride. She never regretted her decision though and, as promised, I did make her Queen." Suddenly earnest, William's eyes clouded with woe, and his hushed wavering voice advised, "Heed my words, lad. Praise God each and every day that your wife adores you. Cherish that love and be always faithful to her, for then and only then will you both be truly content."

"I will, Uncle," Simon returned as soberly.

William removed his swollen feet from the pail, rubbed his soles brusquely with the hem of his robe, and begged with a gruff whine, "And don't you dare christen your firstborn son after me! There are far too many Williams. It's downright confusing." The King stood with difficulty, clasped Simon's hands between his broad palms, and said, "I am certain you will, as always, perform your tasks honorably, and I swear to reciprocate in kind. I will instruct my clerks to begin scripting the documents you will need. Go now and prepare for supper. The soldiers will be performing an amusing skit this night, and it should prove quite entertaining."

Simon genuflected before William and whispered meekly, "I am grateful to you, my Lord, as will be Maura."

The King's hand settled upon Simon's bowed head and he replied with great affection, "For all your trials, you and your lady deserve a bit of peace and happiness. Rise, my boy, and go."

*****

In the physicians' quarters, Simon pounded four cloves of garlic. He added half to a pot of boiling wine, and set aside the remainder to serve as a poultice for the King's aching limbs. As he stirred the blood red tonic, he wondered why William's physicians had left his service, then lost the thought as he recalled the silliness of supper. He chuckled, remembering Henry's submissive grins and Adela's poisonous glares. For the entire evening, William's babies had squabbled amongst themselves, volleying food and the basest insults. The soldiers' outrageous skit, his children's antics, and copious amounts of wine had tickled the King to hysterics.

Simon's musing struck an ancient memory, and his mind ventured back to the supper where he and Maura had suffered their first intimate moment. The scene appeared to him with vivid clarity...

His father sat erect in the Lord's chair, presiding over his family and the band of servants, soldiers, and villagers occupying the tables below the salt. Rose stood stiff as a statue at the far end of the dais, her shifty black eyes darting after Maura, who had refused, with a tempestuous grunt, to sit at the dais. She had chosen instead the company of dogs. Marc's white curls haloed his smudged, pudgy face as he blubbered distress and toddled across the rush strewn floor after Maura's frisky figure. And Edith hovered lovingly over Robert, chattering while administering to his every whim.

How proud Simon felt! At eight years of age, he was at last allowed the seat beside his father. Yet an annoying twinge of jealousy stabbed him as well. Six months before, two elfin creatures had invaded his domain and robbed the attention that belonged rightly to him and him alone! He watched with loathing as Maura frolicked between the tables with *his* hound. Suddenly, as if she sensed his scrutiny, she halted her game and turned her glare on him; fiery, copper hair framed her stormy face and livid sapphire eyes pierced his soul. Feeling uneasy and not a little afraid, he dropped his eyes to his meal. She returned to her play, and Simon, now entranced, continued to cast furtive glances her way. From a lower table, she stole a bowl of honey cakes and, gathering Marc on her lap, offered one to the fussy boy. Simon listened in wonder to her peculiar cooing. Ever since Robert had delivered the waifs, Maura had spoken to no one save Marc, speaking only a queer gibberish. And the unearthly looks that passed between the siblings disturbed Simon deeply.

The hour was late and Edith interrupted Marc's dessert to carry him off to bed. As she attempted to pry him from Maura's protective clutch, she was savagely attacked. Maura raked wildly at Edith's face and drubbed her arms and belly, her grievous squalls paralyzing the gaiety of the hall. Simon scrambled frantically to his mother's defense. Maura gripped tight her bowl and swung crazily at his racing figure. The cakes soared through the air as the bowl smashed his jaw and knocked him senseless to the rushes.

Hours later Simon woke to Maura's tiny hand smoothing his throbbing chin. After that memorable evening, she was never far from sight and, to his amazement and delight, he found he preferred it that way...

The brew boiling over the side of the pot scattered his reverie. He dropped a dollop of honey into the mixture and, licking a dab off his ring, bit his knuckle and cringed. Lord, how he missed her!

Simon delivered the draught and the poultice to the King's squire, receiving in return a detailed map of Les Andelys. He trudged wearily to his chamber and was perturbed to discover Henry there, busily arranging a mat between the two slim beds. "What *are* you doing?" Simon asked irritably.

Henry raised a beaming face to answer, "Father suggested I stay with you tonight, to ensure I rise at dawn."

"I'll allow you here only if you swear to keep still and sleep. I won't be kept up by your ramblings."

"I'll sleep, Simon. I promise."

Simon tripped over Henry's squirming feet and pitched onto the bed. He shot his cousin an irate look then angrily plumped his pillows to create a comfortable seat. The map he spread across the pelts and, without looking up, duly suggested, "You can take the other bed. The rain delayed Roger's men and they've set up camp across the Seine."

As Henry transferred his belongings to the bed, he wondered a bit too sprightly, "What do you have there, Simon?"

"A map of Andelys."

"I'm pleased you asked for my assistance."

"Who told you that?" Simon briefly raised narrow eyes then returned them to the map.

"No one, I just supposed—"

"You supposed wrong, Henry."

"Simon, why do you hate me so?"

"I don't hate you. You...you annoy me."

"I'm sorry for my comment...about Maura." Henry stripped down to his braies and hose and, shivering, crawled beneath the pelts. "I spoke before thinking."

"You never think, Henry, at least not with your head."

"Simon...about my time with Maura, nothing undue occurred and I did help her...to help you."

"I know you did. She told me as much."

"And so we're friends again?"

"I suppose. Now hush." Simon's finger prodded the parchment. "I need to study this map."

"Goodnight, Simon."

"Uhmmm."

A belly full of wine quickened Henry's slumber. His dreams, odd and unsettling, woke him with a start. Only a single candle, set on a table between the beds, remained alight. Henry studied Simon—he lay on his bed, blanketed by the map, his eyes focused vacantly, not on the parchment, on the wall opposite. In a concerned voice, Henry asked, "Simon? Can't you sleep?"

Never breaking his trance, Simon answered faintly, "Don't want to."

"Why not?"

"I'm not tired."

Henry rolled to the edge of his bed and examined more closely Simon's vexed expression. "You look tired to me," said Henry, "tired and worried...about Maura?"

"Yes," mumbled Simon.

"Did she heed my advice?"

"And what advice was that?"

"To spend every moment till her wedding day with you."

Simon twisted his head to meet Henry's mawkish gaze and, through a strained smile, complimented, "Yours was excellent advice, Henry, and yes, she did indeed heed it."

"Simon, please don't take offense to this question..."

Simon shifted to his side, bother in his voice, "What, Henry?"

"Well, ever since Maura left me..." Henry sat up and idly rearranged pelts as he stumbled through his awkward query, "...not every night, mind you, but on a few occasions, I've dreamt of her and I was wondering if, well—" With a tense swallow, he quickly finished, "if she's as skilled a lover as she is in my dreams?"

"Skilled?" Simon snorted a laugh and quipped, "Imagining the nature of your dreams, I'd have to propose she's not only skilled, she's an expert. Now, go to sleep!"

"Expert?" Henry replied with dreamy sigh. "You must miss her."

Simon breathed, "Painfully," in the direction of the candle and snuffed the light.

Still Henry's voice continued to ring merrily through the blackness, "I do too. Mind you, not always, only occasionally—"

"Henry..."

"I'm sleeping, Simon, I'm sleeping..."

*****

The campfire's smoke clung heavily to the morning mist. Marc rubbed his tearing eyes and peered for the hundredth time down the long, puddled road. He had received the bewildering news upon rising—two of the King's men would collect him late morning and he was to accompany them on an espionage mission for the King. Exhilaration pulsed through his veins as he craned his neck to see further down the road, and his heartbeat faltered to the sound of approaching hoof beats. At the sight of two horses trotting in his direction, he stood tall in the stirrups and pondered again why he had been chosen for such an endeavor. He tapped his steed's rump with a crop and the beast lumbered forward to meet his fellow spies. The riders loped nearer and Marc's belly soured as he recognized Henry, then lurch with exaltation. "Simon!" he whispered in awe. Eagerly, his heels urged his mount to a trot. "How can it be you?!" exclaimed Marc as he clasped Simon's extended hand and matched his exuberant smile.

"Marc! You look—" Simon paused, remembering Maura's fretful and insightful description, 'He looks so old'. Marc's hair, straw-like and matted with grime, stuck out in odd tufts, dirt lined worry creases in his face, and his once innocent eyes now seemed tainted and listless. Fumbling for a neutral comment, Simon blurted, "—well."

"I can imagine how I look, Simon," said Marc, "and *well* doesn't describe it." He nodded stiffly and greeted, "Henry..."

"Marc..." Henry snidely returned.

Marc turned his attention eagerly back to Simon, "What is this all about?"

"We're to visit Henry's brother, Curthose, at his castle in Andelys, and pry from him the mischief he intends on his father. Do you have supplies to last you two days?"

"I carry all I own."

"Then let's get this done!" shouted Simon and, with a wave of his hand, Henry and Marc bounded after his mount's canter.

They alternated between a rapid walk and slow canter, and kept to the path hugging the Seine. Simon and Marc's horses almost touched as their riders engaged in spirited banter. Henry, feeling shunned, slumped in a sulking posture and lagged a length behind. Marc's eyes livened again as he gazed admiringly at Simon, and a contented warmth enveloped him. When just a boy, the same secure feeling had always accompanied Simon's presence, and he recalled his childhood prayer, *Please, Lord, someday may I be exactly like him.*

Simon cocked his head Marc's way and patted his saddlebag. "I have a stack of letters for you."

"Letters?" asked Marc.

"Yes, from Maura. She's been quite diligent about writing you a passage each night."

Marc pondered Simon's curious statement. When last he'd seen Maura, he had warned her to keep from Simon, that he would only cause her more pain. Clearly, all she'd kept herself from was good judgment. Simon had enjoyed her company 'each night'. Then why was he here? And where was she? Had he abandoned her yet again? Marc heaved with contempt and sharply reined his horse. Henry's mount reared in surprise, and Simon's halted to the abrupt commotion.

Marc shot Simon a look stark with revulsion as he spat, "You...you've left her... again!" His brandished fist clenched the reins too tightly and his horse danced in confusion. "I warned her to stay away...that you'd only—"

"Marc! Marc, listen," pleaded Simon. "I've not left—"

Henry barked his interruption, "Bleeding Jesus, Marc! You could've broken my neck!"

"Quiet, Henry!" Simon shouted. His hand cloaked Marc's fist and he stressed carefully, "I've not left Maura, I'm here because of her. Have patience and I will tell you all...later. The sooner our mission is done, the sooner I return to England and her."

While Marc considered Simon's defense, Simon shot a perturbed glare Henry's way, and in response received a flailed retort, "Why are you angry with me? Why am I always at fault? Marc carries on like a damned fool, and I get blamed!"

Simon shook with exasperation and shouted, "I apologize, now let's stop this ridiculous sparring!"

By midday, the castle's timbered keep jutted high above the treetops. The scouts warily approached the castle and were astonished to see the main gates opened wide, with soldiers and townsfolk entering and leaving at their leisure. Nevertheless, they could tempt no risks and slunk through the gatehouse with donned hoods. Henry ordered a groom to tend their horses, and together they slogged through slush to a make-shift fence corralling a tournament field. Henry and Marc stood to attention as Simon rattled off terse instructions, "Prick up your ears and mingle. Listen for Philip or William's names mentioned in tandem with battle plans. Take a good hour and meet me on the left side of the field beneath the Royal enclosure. Above all...take care."

Marc nodded in assent and dutifully vanished into the crowd. Unfortunately, his excitement at having been selected for such a quest blotted out any secrets he might have heard. How odd, he rejoiced, to be assigned to prevent a battle, how odd and simply glorious!

Henry, delighted at not being recognized, listened surreptitiously to a word or two, then promptly forgot his purpose and began ogling the women. As the hour neared its end, Henry convinced himself he'd heard nothing significant, and hurried to the enclosure to enjoy the tilts.

On the contrary, Simon uncovered fascinating revelations and fine details of Curthose's present plans to sabotage William's next battle. He tucked the salient information safely away in his mind and wove his way to the enclosure. There he met Henry and Marc and the three hung on fence posts, chatting quietly as Simon keenly scanned the raised platform.

Robert Curthose, a squat and ugly man, stood with hands on his hips at the platform's fore. He swept his fierce countenance over the boisterous crowd, and they presently hushed to his scowling bellow, "Bring on the knights!"

Simon clicked his tongue in jest. "Tilting during Lent. How sacrilegious! It's always amazed me how these pompous vermin slink to Mass each morn then, with little thought, slaughter hundreds in the afternoon."

Scorn dripped from Marc's reply, "Oh, but Simon, these men think themselves far more important than God. Why else would they demand to be called *my Lord?*"

"Excellent point, Marc," commented Simon. "Henry, you look bored."

"I am."

"Then help me determine who's present."

Hoots and jeers erupted from the throng as additional members of the Royal Family gathered up their finery and clambered the ladder to the pedestal.

Simon scaled the fence and squinted keenly to distinguish faces. "Tell me who they are, Henry."

"Cousins, I think..." guessed Henry as he scrambled up by Simon's side. He shaded his eyes and deduced, "Yes, cousins from my mother's family, and the fat one is Robert's latest conquest—she's as trollish as he. I believe Roger of Montgomery's son, Robert of Belleme is there—he's an inhuman beast." Henry's eyes shifted appreciatively to the far side of the podium where there sat an attractive, raven-haired woman wearing an all too familiar smug expression. "Simon..." Henry motioned in her direction and asked, "Isn't that your half-sister Denise?"

Simon followed his point and replied with a pinched expression, "I don't really know."

"Simon!" Henry berated, aghast. "How can you not recognize your own sister? Shame!"

"The one time I met the Lady Denise, she greeted me with a gob of spit. Since that time, her lovely visage has not remained—" Simon's exclamation boomed, "I don't believe it!"

Henry and Marc spurted, "What?" in unison as they twisted to locate Simon's astounding discovery.

"Will! It's Will!" Simon hissed, "Rufus' clinging playmate is entertaining his archenemy—Curthose."

"Oh what great fun!" burbled Henry.

Joining them on the fence, Marc wondered aloud, "Who is his Lady?"

"She's no matter," muttered Simon.

"She *is* lovely," sighed Henry.

"Pull in your tongue, Henry," snapped Simon. "Don't you dare consider—"

"Simon," Marc cut in, "is there a chance Will's involved in any of Curthose's plans?"

Simon returned his scrutiny to the platform and muttered, "That is my prayer."

The gang of knights bounded upon the field and romped through their ritual feats of horsemanship. Henry's elation rocked the fence and his shrill cheers strained all ears near. In contrast, Simon's lethal glare never left Will; his insides churned with rage as he studied his brother's every move, and strove to read his lips and thoughts. Marc, in turn, eyed Simon's clenched jaw and white knuckles, drawn taut from his firm grip on the post.

"Simon," asked Marc, tugging on his cloak, "tell me, what's to happen after the melee? Simon?"

Never moving his eyes from the object of his hate, Simon flatly answered, "Join Curthose at the feast, ply him with liquor, hear his plans, and then confront him."

"Confront him? Confront him how?" asked Marc. His question failed to distract Simon, and Marc reluctantly turned his focus on the knights.

The knights cantered from the field and the competitions began. Mud balls, jeers, and insults pelted the combatants. Simon suddenly whirled round and caught Henry's hand, armed with a sloshing missile, and forcefully demanded, "Give me all your money!"

The mud slopped to the ground as Henry cried, "What?!"

"Any money you have, I need it—now!"

"Simon, let go." Henry shook from his grip and sniveled, "You've gone mad again!"

"No, Henry, I swear I've not. Quickly, I'll repay you double, I promise. Hurry!"

"Oh...very well..." Henry thrust muddied fingers inside a jingly pouch secured to his belt. He carefully selected a few coins and returned them to the pouch, the rest he grudgingly passed to Simon.

"I love you, Henry!" Simon exclaimed with great flair, as he whipped off his cloak and tossed it to Marc. "You two wait here. I won't be long."

Fuddled, Marc started after Simon, calling, "Simon, what—"

"You'll know soon enough. Keep a sharp eye on Henry. Never let him wander!" Simon sprinted away, and moments later ducked beneath the canvas wall of the makeshift stables. He sought the next competitor, yet, strangely, there was no one about. Then from the opening to the bailey came a wisp of a boy, guiding an enormous stallion, and dragging what appeared to be a padded shirt. Simon's flurried approach scared the boy and he flinched to Simon's panted query, "Who fights Lord William?"

"Why, I do, my Lord."

Simon's bulging eyes traveled the boy's lanky body, and he burst out laughing, "You?! What's your age?"

"Fourteen, my Lord."

"Who paid you for this farce?"

"I swore not to say."

"You *will* say for this." Simon spread his palm.

The boy's eyes glittered with greed as he placed a tentative touch on the tarnished coins and readily divulged, "Lord William and the Duke's son paid me."

"Why am I not surprised?" beamed Simon. "You won't fight today. Take this gift and betray our meeting to no one."

The boy gushed, "Bless you, my Lord, bless you!" as he skipped backward to the entrance, then tore off into the bailey.

Simon securely fashioned a hauberk plucked from a mountain of armor; he then hurriedly fumbled through scads of helmets and donned one that masked him fully. After he'd tucked every last strand of hair beneath the neck guard, he hooked a ponderous sword to the hauberk's belt, mounted the stallion and—waited.

Will strutted in from the bailey, his slavish squires flitting behind. He paced before Simon, closely inspecting him and the horse, and nodded his approval. "The shirt works well. I assume you've been well rehearsed as to your performance."

Simon bowed his head.

"You're taller than I recall."

Simon slouched.

Will spied the sword and tested its edge. He sucked blood from his finger and muttered, "A nice touch. Our goal after all is authenticity." He peered curiously into the helm's eye holes and shrank from the intensity of the boy's pale glare. "Can't you speak?" he questioned, then assured, "You needn't fear me. Perform as you've been instructed and you should survive the tilt—intact."

Simon mumbled incoherently. Will sniggered at his response and confidently directed, "You may jab a bit, yet I will always keep command of the duel. Wait to be called and if I do, by chance, kill you, your family will be amply compensated." Simon's ire flared to Will's waggling finger, "Your sole task is to make me appear brilliant. My Lady will not be disappointed..."

Simon's armor vibrated to his thudding heart, and rancor boiled his blood as he watched Will glide from the stable. His brittle fingers circled and strangled the sword's hilt as he rasped, "Scare him, don't kill him. I need only scare him, scare him, scare—"

Will's squire raised a beckoning hand. Simon kicked the stallion forward and emerged into mist-blown light. He accepted a passed shield and lance, and shifted impatiently.

Henry crouched low, scooped and molded a plump ball of mud between his palms, then jumped to Marc's shrill cry, "Henry, come! Is it Simon?"

"Where?" he asked, leaping on a rung of the fence.

"There, at the entrance to the stable?"

"I can't tell. Who's to fight?"

They both shifted their rapt attention to the knight positioned at the far end of the field. Helm tucked beneath his arm, Will roused the expectant crowd with a valiant smile and exuberant wave.

Marc straddled the top rung and shouted, "God's teeth! It's Will!"

"So you *do* curse," noted Henry with sneering satisfaction. He clapped Marc's shoulder and boomed, "How absolutely marvelous!" Henry fondled his oozing mud ball and muttered wickedly, "I'll discover the identity of our mystery knight." He balanced precariously atop the fence and heaved his wad of mud. It smacked the nape of Will's neck, pitching him forward onto the saddle's pommel. His horse's spooked charge came close to unseating the gallant hero. He wrestled the reins to regain control, spat curses, and madly searched the crowd for the culprit.

Henry cast an eager look the mystery knight's way and waited for a sign of approval. Simon slightly lifted his lance and Henry let out a jubilant whoop, the force of which tipped him backwards into the source of his ammunition—the puddle. Stumbling, he slipped again and again till, at last, Marc yanked him up by his collar. Wildly, Henry danced and squawked, "It's Simon! It's Simon!" He dangled over the fence and hugged himself, proclaiming to all, "Oh, how I'm going to love this!"

In sharp contrast, Marc's glower darkened with fright. "But Henry...Simon will kill him."

Will flung mud from his fingers and snarled, "I'll find that blasted ruffian, chop him to pieces, and feed him to the hogs!" He donned his helmet and cringed to the guffaws that chased him to his former position. A quick glimpse at his opponent caused an unexpected flutter in his belly and he clenched taut his reins.

The massive war horse pawed the dirt in anticipation, and Simon, his every muscle steeled, locked livid eyes on the squire's dangling scarf. The boy glanced Will's way, then Simon's. He purposely waited an endless moment to swell the suspense, and plunged his arm downward.

*****

CHAPTER TWENTY-FOUR - THE SAINT

Simon's mount thundered across the field, spewing clods of mud in his wake. Will's horse balked, reared, then bolted forward to the bite of spurs.

As his rival loomed nearer, panic wrenched Will's gut. All was not as it should be! The boy's posture was overly intimidating, his aim too exact, his speed too great! At once, the tip of the lance was upon him! He dropped his pole, shielded his face, and howled in terror.

Marc squeezed shut his eyes to the scathing clash of metal. Henry pried his wide and saw Will soar weightlessly through the air and crash to the ground with a sickening crunch.

Will's eyelids fluttered open to the dizzying sight of wispy clouds whirling furiously above him. He blinked to clear his vision, and pondered—perhaps if he lay deathly still, the boy would simply go away.

Simon sharply reined his horse, thrust his lance to the ground, and dismounted. He glanced briefly at his pathetic brother, then to Henry and Marc. Their vivacious praise drew from him a smug grin and a thought—had Will learned his humility lesson, or was there a need for more instruction?

The privileged folk stood dumbfounded, and Curthose heaved with contempt. The impudent runt had made fools of them all! Why, he'd have him arrested and flogged for his insolence. He lumbered to the edge of the podium and roared, "You! Approach the platform."

Simon paid him no heed, turned his back on the stage, and strode briskly toward the stable. Henry and Marc froze their jubilant antics as the triumphant scene began to unravel. Curthose's furious gesture produced a gang of guards charging from the stables. Will took advantage of the uproar to scramble to his feet and charge Simon's back with his brandished sword.

"Your back! At your back!" screamed Henry.

Marc blared, "The guards!" and threw one leg over the fence.

Henry vaulted the barrier first and raced crazily to Simon's defense. Simon braced for the guards' attack then heard the swish of Will's weapon. He spun too late and caught the plummeting blade between his helm and hauberk's collar. The cold metal sliced through tunic, shirt, and skin, and forced him to his knees. A guard swung his sword high to finish Simon. Henry dove into the turbulence and hollered, "Stop!"

His outburst halted all movement. Curthose rubbed his eyes and squinted curiously at the peculiar drama. "Henry?" he called out in wonder. "What are you doing here?"

Henry stood with a nonchalant air, dusted his clothes, and noted calmly, "I've come for a visit, though I must say, Brother, I'm deeply distraught by what I've witnessed here." He gestured with distaste at Will. "Why protect this buffoon? Call off your guards and let him fight his own battle."

Simon focused maliciously on Will's quaking knees, and hissed heaving breaths to Henry's life-saving appeal. He needed only a few moments to recoup his stamina and then—revenge!

"Let the tilt resume!" shouted Henry. "I guarantee an exquisite match."

"Do you know this spindly scoundrel?" asked Curthose.

"No, but regrettably I know this one all too well," Henry returned, nodding to Will. "And I suspect you'll be delighted to hear how intimate he's been lately with Rufus."

"What are you implying?!" raged Curthose.

"Only that they share more than the same grandmother. Now, won't you relish seeing him spanked?"

"Henry, come join me!" Curthose beckoned excitedly. "Guards, retreat. Continue the tilt!"

Madness claimed Simon. His steeled arm swept at Will's ankles, tripping him. But Will regained his balance and aimed a fumbly blow at Simon's head. With one nimble move, Simon leapt to his feet, swung his sword, and blocked Will's strike. A quick twist of Simon's wrist plunged Will's sword deep into the mud, and a savage kick broke Will's grip on the hilt. Simon slammed his heel to Will's chest, knocking him on his backside; the toe of his boot nicked his chin and sprawled him in the mud.

Will slithered backwards, gasping frantic breaths, and whimpering for mercy, "Whoever you are, please let me live...I'll give you money, land, anything, but please don't kill me!"

Simon crouched, ripped off Will's helmet, and smeared a handful of mud and manure over his cringing face. On his knees, he straddled his wily brother's legs, poised his weapon high above his head and, with ferocious speed and true aim, drove the blade into the earth. Will screeched as cold metal scraped his loins and Simon warned in a disguised snarl, "Don't dare return to England anytime soon. If I find you there, this sword will fall again, only next time it won't miss its mark! Then, my gracious Lord, what will you have left to wave in your Ladies' faces—your curly little tail perhaps?"

In vile humiliation, Will hid his face and convulsed with sobs. Simon thrust the sword deeper, stood, and casually strolled away.

The crazed, jeering crowd surged the fence, straining it inward. Curthose nodded appreciatively to Henry and commented, "A bit rude. Still, he has potential. Perhaps I can find a use for him."

"I'll fetch him for you," Henry called as he leapt off the podium and sprinted after Simon. He caught up to him in the main stable by their horse's stalls and helped him wriggle from his hauberk.

"I'm in debt to you, Henry," said Simon with a bit of a quaver. "It was a foolish thing I did."

"Not at all, Simon. You were utterly magnificent!"

"Where's Marc?" asked Simon, wincing as he stripped off his tunic and shirt.

"I'm sure he follows—" Henry gasped and paled at the stream of blood winding its way down Simon's chest. "Simon, what? I didn't realize he'd—"

"It's but a scratch. In my saddlebag you'll find a jar of ointment. Please fetch it for me."

Henry swiftly obeyed and rifled madly through the crowded satchel. At last he extracted a corked jar. "Is this it, Simon?" he asked. Simon nodded, and Henry guardedly watched him pry open the jar, scoop a fingertip of salve and dab it gingerly on the gash. The resultant sting caused Simon to fumble and drop the jar to the hay.

"Let me," offered Henry, bending to retrieve it.

"I came too near to killing him," gritted Simon as Henry's gelled fingers tenderly touched his wound.

"What's he done to make you hate him so?"

"He's a whey-face bully—" Simon's blustering ended prematurely in a grunt of pain. A hug to the stall's post steadied him and he continued, "He attacked Maura and Almodis."

"Attacked Maura? Well then, in my estimation, he deserves execution! What induced you to spare—" Again Henry faltered as he saw for the first time Simon's scarred back. "God's blood, Simon!" he exclaimed aghast, and gibbered, "Who? What?!"

Simon sagged wearily down to the hay. "Will also watched with great joy as Father whipped me."

"Did Will recognize you on the field?" Henry joined him in the hay. "What did you say to him?"

"I warned him to stay out of England. I don't believe he recognized me." Simon pressed his stained shirt firmly to his wound and went on brokenly, "I...I couldn't risk that occurring. He'd head straight to Pevensey and—" His head hung lower as his fingers clawed at his hair. "God's blood, how I loathe my brother."

Blood continued to ooze from Simon's shoulder, and worry laced Henry's comment, "Simon, this is not only a scratch. You're too pale. Rest here awhile. I'll fetch wine."

"No!" wheezed Simon as he floundered to rise. "It must be only a scratch! I've wasted enough of our precious time with my petty games."

"Wasted?" Marc's staid voice drifted over the horse's backs; he appeared at the stall's opening and lauded, "Oh no, Simon. Your petty game quite likely bought Maura a week or two of safety. I consider that an excellent use of our time. And Henry's correct, you need a short rest."

Simon's tone took on a tenacious ring. "I'll rest after we've accomplished our task." He ripped his shirt and used a long, thin piece of material to fashion a bandage. Marc helped Simon wind the fabric under his armpit, over his wound, and around his neck to secure it. Simon gingerly wriggled back into his tunic, and instructed, "Henry, the success of our mission rests with you. At supper, you will sit by Curthose, ply him with wine to loosen his tongue, and milk him of his conspiracies. *Never*—and I repeat, never—actually agree to assist him in his treason. Marc and I will be listening at the table below with the tradesmen. Coax your brother to his bedchamber, keep him rambling till the hall clears, then make your excuses and leave. Fool his guards into following you outside. Marc will stand watch at the hall's doors while I induce Curthose to alter his plans. Meanwhile, you lead our horses just beyond the main gates, and use the remainder of your coins to bribe the guards. Convince them to let only us out, then bolt the doors. I predict Curthose won't bid us a fond farewell. Are you clear to your roles?"

The two young men nodded—Marc with swift exactness, Henry with wavered uncertainty.

"Fine, then let's get this done."

Henry led his cohorts to the stable door, then turned on them an uneasy expression and stark warning, "Don't allow Curthose to catch you. He is *not* a kind man."

*****

While Curthose grandly touted his misdeeds, Henry encouraged his brother to down his third cup of wine. Curthose daintily chewed his sauce-laden pheasant, washed the bolus down with a fourth cup, and nursed his fifth cup as he spewed intricate plans of sabotage from his greasy lips. "Father is so predic...dicta...dull. Always, his archers strike first, then his foot soldiers, then his mounted knights. My o...only sin is slippiping Philip scant clues as to lo-location, number of troops, da...ates...which may or may-may not give him a slight ad...advantage. It, how...ever, gi...gives me a gr...great advantage!"

"You are too sly, Brother. I envy you. To Father, I will eternally be a baby," complained Henry. "He saw fit to dub me a knight last summer, yet never allows me my rightful place in his army. So I need to look to others for instruction. And you, Brother, own the brawn and genius to mold me to your valiant image. I'm eager to learn more.

How are Philip's troops faring, and what is your advantage if they succeed in shattering Normandy? Father has already promised you the Duchy, what more do you seek?"

"You a...are too naive, Henry. Why...why, the kingdoms of France and, I...can't think, of course—England—of course! And if...if you felt the urge to off...offer your ex...expert assistance in my en...en—plan, I...I would in...inturn be ob...liged to offer you an ex...exalted po-position in my court. Which, which would you prefer-fer—heir or chan...chancellor?"

Henry snickered, "I would stay a baby awhile longer."

"Philip figures to...gra...gradually chip away at Father's hold on Nor...Normandy with light skir...mishes over the spring, then then make a bold de...ci...sive strike in summer-mer," stumbled Curthose.

"If I'm to aide your mission," tempted Henry, "I need know where the next skirmish will be—that is, if you're privy to that information."

"Of course I am!" boasted Curthose. "Philip plans a rear ass-assault ju...just east of Rouen on the next Sab...bath-bath. He intends to...to catch Father on...his knees!" Curthose threw back his head and laughed alone at his lame joke, while Henry hid his smirk and chuckled inwardly at his feckless sibling.

Marc gulped down boiled meat and Simon picked idly at his meal, all the while listening with growing respect to his cousin's verbal maneuvers. Occasionally, Simon felt immense pride for Henry, and this was indeed one of those occasions. There was no denying he possessed a shrewd mind, when he chose to use it, and was a born diplomat. Perhaps one day he would aspire to greatness. Simon cocked his head to the brothers' clucking and heard a spot of gossip that made him chuckle.

Curthose plopped his boots on the dais, spattering muck on his meal, and threw back more wine. "Henry," he sputtered, "what's...what's become of...of our mys...mys...mystery knight?"

"Gone," Henry mumbled, munching on a roasted apple. "And what's become of our gallant cousin Will?"

Curthose spit wine as he spewed, "It...it seems he got his braies imp...imp—stuck on the sword and was toooo rattled to pu...ll loose. The crowd th...th...rew all sorts of nasssty thinings at him. Last I...I saw of him, he-he was limping to the stable-ble with a gap...ping hole in his seat. What a spec...spec...specta...cu...lar perfor-orma-ma, hell, show! I...I'm grateful to...to you, Henry. I ha...haven't en...enjoyed any...thing so-so much in years. We can be-be ass-assured Will wonot be showing his pret-ety face a...a...around here any...anytime sooon." Curthose rose woozily, stretched, belched, and yawned. "I...I think I...'ve im...im...drunk too much wine. I'm we-weary, Brother. Join me-me in my chamber-ber? We'll talk...talk further."

Laboriously, the hours wore on and the great hall cleared, leaving a few hounds nosing for scraps, two or three revelers too drunk to rise, and Simon and Marc watching stealthily from a shadowed corner. At long last, Henry emerged from the bedchamber, exuding triumph as he bellowed over his shoulder, "I'm gratified you felt comfortable confiding in me, Brother. Your secrets are forever safe with me..." He nudged a dozing guard with his boot, and whispered, "My excuses, kind Sir, would you mind terribly accompanying me outside for a few moments? I've, alas, imbibed too much wine and need to piss, and all this day, I've had the oddest sense I'm being followed." The guard slowly rose and wordlessly trailed Henry out of the hall.

"Keep your dagger braced, Marc," muttered Simon, "and stand watch by the main doors. Yell at the first sign or sound of trouble." They parted company. Marc skirted the tables and, with mincing steps, snuck to the doors; Simon skulked to the chamber, cracked the door a tad, and peeked inside. Curthose lay sprawled upon his bed, his bloated belly rising and falling with each grating snore. "Perfect," whispered Simon, and he slipped through the opening, tiptoed to the bed and, ever so cautiously, nudged Curthose's dagger from his belt. He poked his cousin's ribs with the blade's hilt, prodding, "Robert...wake up." Curthose snorted his displeasure then resumed snoring, louder than before. Simon poked again, harder. "Wake up! Robert!"

With a gasping, sputtered start, Curthose pushed up on his elbows and coughed, "Wha...what's happened?" He focused terrified eyes upon Simon. "Henry? Where? Who...who are you?!" His pudgy fingers fumbled along his belt, then amongst sheets and pelts for his dagger; his muttering heightened with his alarm, "Gu-gu-guards...guards... guards!"

"No guards, Robert," noted Simon with deliberate calm. "They've wandered off, and look what I've found." Simon stuck Curthose's dagger in his own belt. "I see you don't recognize me. Perhaps you are still dreaming and I'm your conscience—and your conscience has for you some timely advice." He dragged a chair near, straddled it, and scorned, "You damned fool! Wherever did you get the notion that wrangling with your father will make you King, when in truth each fray drops you farther down the line of succession? You needn't bother with your newest scheme—William won't be duped. You boast too loudly, and now there's no time to devise a new ploy." Simon stood to roam the chamber, his fingers brushing the many gilded treasures adorning the vanity and walls. "Why don't you wile away your time doing what you do best—stuffing your gut, swilling your rank wine, and playing silly games? And I highly advise you to confine your decadence to within the walls of this castle. Your father may be ancient, but he can still defeat you—easily." Simon downed the last of the wine in Curthose's cup and announced, "I'll take my leave..." as he bowed and ambled out the door.

Curthose shook from his disbelieving trance and surged up from the bed, bawling, "Guards! Guards!"

Simon poked his head back in the door and added with a sly wink, "Oh, I've forgotten to thank you for supper—Cousin."

Curthose's next thunderous roar rocked the keep and, at last, was answered by tramping boot steps.

Marc spied the advancing horde and charged across the hall, yelling, "They're coming! They're coming!" Simon joined his fleeting retreat out the postern door. They raced down the stairs and sped across the bailey, the soldiers' heated breath at their necks. The main gates groaned open the width of a slim man, and as Simon struggled to keep afoot in the mud, he puffed his gratitude, "Bless you, Henry. Bless you!"

They squeezed between the gates, sprang upon their steeds, and were away in a flash. Curthose's soldiers hollered futile curses as the gatehouse guards shut the mammoth doors and bolted the soldiers inside.

A mile or so down the lane, the spies slowed their frantic pace in a grove of towering oaks. Their panted breath and panicked laughter produced an enshrouding cloud of vapor which shimmered in the moonlit night. Henry slid from his saddle and collapsed in the dewy grass, giggling and baying, "We were magnificent!"

Simon slipped to his feet and laughed as heartily, "That we were!"

"And I was brilliant. Wasn't I, Simon?"

"Yes, Henry, you were indeed brilliant."

Marc dismounted slowly and asked with a disagreeable sneer, "Why do you waste time encouraging him, Simon?"

"Because it's precisely what he needs most."

Marc grunted and tugged at the girth on his saddle.

Henry rolled to his feet and strutted over to Marc. "What are you griping about now? You are so damned morose!" Unwisely, Henry jabbed at Marc's mouth. "What will it take to twist that scowl to a grin? Tell me, Marc," he pestered, "what will it take?"

"I really wouldn't, Henry," cautioned Simon.

Marc caught Henry's hand and forced him to his knees with a fierce clamping tug.

"Ow!" yelped Henry. "Let go! I was only teasing. Let go!"

Marc released him and, snorting disgust, returned his attention to his saddle.

Henry glowered and grumbled, "I'd hate to be around when you *fail* at something." An agreeable thought lit his mind and eyes, and he cheerfully suggested, "I've a splendid idea! There's an alehouse not far from here that has the most exquisite—"

"Food?" piped up Simon. "I'm famished!"

"Yes, I forgot. You're a boring old man who's pining for his love. The food is quite scrumptious, as are the serving wenches. I'm not sure about you, Marc, only my interest lies not with the food...Shall we?"

Simon looked to Marc for approval and received a wary nod. The men mounted their steeds and Simon exuberantly waved them on. "Lead us, Henry!"

A little over an hour later, the inn's flickering torches peered through dark and leafless tree limbs. Henry wiggled in anticipation, pointing and shouting, "There! Less than a half mile, straight ahead."

"Henry, you have an amazing sense of direction," praised Simon.

"No, Simon, what's amazing is my sense of smell. How fares your shoulder?"

"It's mighty sore."

"Then we'll tend it with ale. Marc, don't dawdle so."

Marc answered with a grunt.

The three shouldered their way through a pack of soldiers loitering in the doorway. Once inside, Marc and Simon stood on tiptoe to search through dense smoke and crammed bodies for a space to sit. Henry hopped onto a table; he scanned the bustling room and seemed a bit perturbed at not being immediately recognized. Then he noisily discovered, "I see three seats!" He gestured to a far corner and, leaping down, ordered, "Follow me!"

Marc grimaced and coughed as he swung at the hovering cloud and reluctantly trailed behind Henry. With much squeezing, jostling, and shoving, they at last claimed the table. Marc cast Henry an indignant look and corrected, "Only two seats, Henry."

A weary soul snored in the third, the top half of his body sprawled across the table and his face resting in a puddle of ale. "Don't worry, Marc," sniped Henry, "I won't make you stand." He tipped the chair and chuckled as the man slumped to the filthy rushes.

"Henry!" Simon scolded, amazed and a bit amused.

"He's perfectly fine," dismissed Henry. "He didn't even wake."

Simon and Marc sagged into their chairs; Henry stood on his and announced with glee, "Now to get the ladies' attention."

"I'm afraid to watch," mumbled Marc, shielding his eyes.

Henry waved his arms furiously in the direction of a great cauldron bubbling with a nondescript stew. The innkeeper, a plump man with sparse hair and rosy cheeks, beamed and waved back. Henry in turn raised three fingers and rubbed his belly. The keeper nodded and, to two rather harsh-looking young women, directed, "It's the youngest FitzRoy and two others. Stew and ale, and aim to make the Prince happy." The serving maids huffed in protest, snatched up bowls and tankards, and sulked over to the corner.

Henry saw them approaching, rubbed his palms together, and said with rakish grin, "Ah...here comes—"

"The food?" hoped Marc.

"No, you dolt, the women!"

One maid swiftly plopped a tankard and bowl down by Henry, only she wasn't quite fast enough to escape his groping. His arm circled and clinched her waist, his head rested on her hip, and he murmured, "Nell..."

A quick thrust of her hip knocked his head away, and she jerked from his hold, complaining, "No, Henry, not now. I've work to do."

Not discouraged, Henry stretched across the table and swiped for the other maid's hand, pleading, "Mary..."

She slapped his insistent fingers and griped, "Are you blind? We're busy, Henry!"

Henry shoved back in his chair with a gruff snort.

"Well, Henry." Simon took a long draught of ale and smirked. "It appears you've lost your charm."

"Just you wait!" flared Henry. "When their work calms a bit, they'll return—begging for me!"

A nearby scuffle stole Simon's attention. He turned to see Nell grinding an overly affectionate soldier's fingers under a wooden bowl, while Mary screamed curses in his ear. Simon twisted back, chuckling. "They don't appear very amorous to me."

"They can get fairly frisky," noted Henry, with wry grin. "And I prefer that quality in *my* women. Oh, to have a woman again," he sighed dramatically, then emptied the contents of his tankard in two quick gulps. "It's been so long, I've quite forgotten how..." He paused to let out a lusty belch.

"And how long is so long?" teased Simon.

"Almost a fortnight!"

Simon wagged his head with feigned pity. "You poor soul."

"Yes, Simon, you can make fun!" retorted Henry in a wounded voice. He snatched up Simon's cup and stole the remainder of his drink. "I suppose Maura lets you prod her when...whenever you please!"

Simon's eyes shifted uneasily to Marc, whose jaw clenched tighter to each crudity that passed Henry's flapping lips. "Tread lightly, Henry," cautioned Simon.

"That leads me to wonder." Henry turned his blather on Marc. "What say you to Simon's scurrilous doings, Marc? Bedding your fine sister without benefit of matrimony! You must have some opinion. Say something, Marc!"

"I don't like you, Henry," returned Marc.

Henry downed Marc's ale and simpered wickedly. "I'm not exactly sweet on you either. Yet your handsome sister likes me—enormously! So I can't be all that terrible." As Mary swept past, Henry grabbed a handful of skirt and yanked her back. His rude act sloshed ale down the front of her tunic. "You agree, don't you Mary?"

"God's breath, Henry!" yelled Mary. "Look what you've done."

"I want more ale! The most potent you have!" he shouted back, then batting his lashes, his tone turned severely maudlin, "And also a little...understanding." He winked lewdly at Marc and Simon and boasted, "They love mothering me."

Mary topped the tankards, jerked her skirt away, and muttered, "Strange sort of mothering, Henry."

Henry's rapidly blurring attention returned to Marc, and he wagged his finger in time with his stuttered lecture, "The trouble with you, Marc, is you...you've been battling fa...far too long. You've forgotten," he mumbled quietly, "that is, if you've ever known," then continued exuberantly, "how to enjoy yourself and are desperately in need of some robust loving! Now, who...who's it to be, Mary or Nell? Or perhaps, both!"

"And what makes you so confident they'll do *your* bidding?" asked Simon.

Again Henry's ale vanished. His sleeve wiped foam from his bearded chin, as he spluttered, "Even...tu...ally, they all do. How long have you been deprived, Marc? Must have been awhile, Father doesn't allow women near his soldiers." He whispered as in secret, "I have to sneak away to get my fill," then boomed, "How long? Come Marc, confess! You needn't be embarr..." he hiccupped and finished, "...assed. A month? Two? A ye—" At Marc's averted gaze and scarlet cheeks, Henry's pickled mind groggily concluded, "Bleeding Jesus!" He waved wildly in the air and banged his tankard on the tabletop. "Nell, hurry and fill my cup. I...I've just discovered the most shocking news! I can't believe—you...you've never—How...how old are you, Marc? Ten?"

Simon wielded his spoon in Henry's direction. "I'll warn you only once more. Don't push him!"

However, Henry was too inebriated for reason, and pressed on, "Now I know why you...you're so st...sti...stiff!"

Marc tried ignoring Henry, except that each stabbing jest cut through his resolve and knotted his insides. His cheeks burned with shame. It would be wrong to fight Henry in his condition, only—Marc's fingers strangled his tankard's handle—if Henry didn't hush, he'd have no other choice but to silence him, especially if he slurred another rude remark about Maura.

Henry half stood and wavered over the table; he cracked a crude grin and stammered, "So you...you don't share your...beaut...beau...oh, hell, pretty sis...sister's hot...no, boiling blood—"

A sharp flick of his wrist emptied Marc's tankard in Henry's face. Henry pitched back in his chair, whipping his head, gasping and sputtering, then froze to the chill of a hovering shadow. He lifted woozy, frightened eyes to Marc's glower. The surrounding clamor made his ears pound; torches, smoke, and grotesque faces whirled frenziedly about him. His eyes squeezed shut, his head lolled backward, and his mouth gaped wide.

"Please, Marc, allow me the honor." Simon's toe met the back of Henry's chair and, with a curt shove, toppled the chair and Henry to the floor. Marc leant long across the table and splashed the remainder of Henry's ale over his silly grin. Henry jerked, spit, giggled, then at long last lay still.

Marc nodded. "Why, thank you, Simon."

"Not at all. I marvel at your restraint!" Simon rummaged through the contents of his saddlebag and produced three stacks of parchment tied neatly with ribbons. "Now, while it's peaceful, we'll have a look at these notes."

Marc scooted his chair nearer to Simon's, leant in close, and whispered, "How old were you, Simon?"

"Old?"

"The first time you—"

"Oh...older than you."

"Really? Tell me."

"I'd rather not."

"Why?"

"Because it was at Maura's suggestion that we—"

"Maura? Oh, I see."

"Marc, don't let Henry bother you, he's all talk."

"No he's not, Simon," Marc returned adamantly. "Women flock to Henry. He must know something special."

"Henry only knows where to stick it. What's special about him is his title—FitzRoy. If you were a poor woman, with no hope of escaping poverty, and in walked a pretty prince who promised salvation for a bit of a tumble, what would you do?"

"I see...but the other soldiers pressure me to go with them to the village and visit a brothel. I wouldn't go, though sometimes I'd like the chance to talk to someone besides lugs like these. And it would be awfully nice if it was a woman."

"I'm certainly no expert. All I can suggest is patience in these matters is not necessarily a bad thing. And waiting to be with someone you're comfortable with, or best yet, you care for, helps cure worries of inadequacy and definitely increases the pleasure. Then again, I've been exceptionally lucky and—"

"Do you love her, Simon?"

"With everything that is me."

"Well put," commented Marc. "That's all I truly need to know."

The men exchanged fond, familiar smiles, then Simon glanced at the dates on the different stacks and noted, "She's organized these...Let's see, here's the earliest one." He passed the folded sheet to Marc. "Read to me. I miss her sweet words."

Marc spread the parchment, squinted a moment at the blurred ink, then steadily began...

"Marc...How can I describe my joy! Simon's been released and will recover from his wounds. I pray for his waking for I so want and need to confess my love..."

"Well, on second thought," sighed Simon as he patted Marc's shoulder. "I'll leave you to read alone."

As Simon pushed up from his chair, Mary happened by and asked, "More ale, Sir?"

"No, but I do have a small request." Simon crouched by Henry, untied the pouch from his belt, extracted a mark, and pressed it to her palm. "Please, take this for all her bother, and would you see we wake by dawn?"

"I'll see to it personally..." she answered and added, "I'm grateful, Sir."

Simon dragged Henry's limp figure close to the wall, rearranged him more comfortably, and blanketed him with his cloak. He settled himself nearby, and glanced fretfully up at Marc. Fully engrossed in Maura's writings, he appeared distressed and somewhat lost. Simon felt a deep yearning for their time long past when Marc's enthused and expectant visage followed him everywhere, questioning, mimicking, and always caring. Simon hoped his innocence was not dead, but only lying dormant, hidden by the thick skin of stoicism needed to survive the rigors of battle. When these wars were done, Marc would be revived simply by returning to him and Maura. Simon squirmed for comfort and, closing his eyes, conjured Maura's comforting image. "Soon," he whispered, "I'll come to you...very soon."

Her answer appeared to him in the form of a letter passed by Marc. "This one," he said, "is addressed to you." Marc returned to the table and Simon read...

"My love, If you are reading this, you are with Marc, and that thought fills me with warmth and evokes the most wondrous memories. I pray you're in a rush, so I will keep this simple. You have all my faith and love, I miss you desperately, and cannot stress strongly enough—please stay shy of Will and your father. Come back to me soon."

Simon clenched the note fast to his chest and cringed, not only to the ache that plagued his shoulder, but also to the one that pained his heart.

Marc nursed his ale and read diligently throughout the night. His blood seethed with rage and despair as Maura and Simon's horrific, yet hopeful tale unfolded before his strained eyes. When he could take no more, he shoved the letters aside and struggled to bury his upset. How much longer he could stay a shell—fighting, killing, obeying with no thought, no feeling? So many times, his frustration and revulsion at the chaos about him had come close to erupting. He knew that with each wretched day his inevitable collapse drew nearer, and the thought terrified him. He chose the letter dated a week past, and in the semi-darkness of the alehouse, felt an overwhelming emptiness as he read...

"Many a night I've pondered your dilemma and always, I reach the same conclusion—you were never meant to be a soldier. I can't convince you of this. Perhaps Simon can, though I doubt it. I can only assure you, the time will surely come when you can bear no more—and when it does, Marc, we pray you will return home to us, for we love you so and need you near."

He crumpled the note, burrowed his head in his folded arms, and wept.

*****

Marc paused by the door to the physician's chamber, and watched unseen as Simon bustled about in busy preparation for the battle to come. As he watched, he reflected fondly on their return from the alehouse. He had felt the joy of a child, racing with Simon and Henry, bounding over streams and hedgerows, and laughing with such hysterics, he'd come near to tumbling from his saddle. Grief jarred his mind back to the present. Simon would soon depart and take with him all the happiness, all the fun. His expression creased with question as he stepped inside the chamber and wondered aloud, "Simon, what are you doing?"

Simon hovered over a steaming pot, ripping a long cloth into squares then immersing the pieces into the pot's molten bubbles. He snapped to the question and smiled broadly. "Marc! You startled me. Come in and sit. I'm making bandages."

"Why dip them in—" Marc leant over the cauldron and sniffed. "That?"

"It's only tallow. It hardens the cloth, then while it's still warm, I'll mold the bandages into makeshift splints. Would you care to help?"

"I suppose."

"Here." Simon passed Marc the linen cloth. "You rip, I'll dip."

Marc moved closer to Simon and broke a confident smile. "That seems fair."

"While we were at Andelys, I felt such pride for you," said Simon. "I feel safe with you near."

"Do you truly?" asked Marc in a surprised voice.

"Of course—you're consistently steady and reliable." With a long wooden spoon, Simon stirred a strip of cloth in the tallow, then poised it over the pot to drain. "Please," he instructed, "make the next few a bit larger. Did you finish the letters?"

"Yes."

"And what do you think of our plans?"

"I'm scared for you." Marc strangled the cloth and spoke critically, "There are far too many obstacles! Obstacles that can kill. Simon, Hugh is a good and gentle man. He'll be kind to Maura. Perhaps if you spoke to him, you'd be assured of her safety and—"

"Marc," Simon cut in brusquely, "Maura shared with me her time with Hugh. He may be good and gentle, except all he sees in her is a step-mother for his daughter, a mother for his future children, and someone to tend his manor while he's away. I see a great deal more." Simon kneaded out the bubbles in the dipped cloth and deftly sculptured the supple wax into an arm brace. "He won't grieve his loss for long."

"Lord Robert will never allow this to happen!"

"Nothing will stop us, Marc!" Simon forced. "If Father refuses to acknowledge the King's decree, we are prepared to use force. It may be our final battle, but Maura and I will fight it together!" Marc's expression took on a daunted look, so Simon tempered his tone. "Besides Rose and the King, you alone know our plan. Swear you'll keep it that way."

"I'll betray nothing." Marc stoically resumed ripping and added in a grunted whisper, "Though I still don't like it."

"Maura wouldn't allow me to read her last letter to you. Did she encourage you to desert?"

"Not in those exact words."

"We argued that matter many a night," said Simon. "And I agree with her to a point—you weren't meant to be here. Still, desertion is not an option, it's certain death. I've been devising a scheme to get you released from the King's service with his blessing, and my plan's been partially realized. On the morrow, when we leave for battle, you'll ride by me as my assistant."

"Your assistant!" gasped Marc. "How did you manage that?"

"I simply asked, and William agreed. He was so delighted with our performance at Andelys, I believe he's considering formally adopting us."

Marc beamed and gripped Simon's shoulders, "How can I thank you?"

"Well, I do need help collecting and packing supplies." Simon rose and strolled through the chamber, sighing as he scanned its over-stocked shelves. "Somehow we must fit all the supplies in this small trunk," said he, lifting its lid. "How many are to fight?"

"One or two hundred."

Simon massaged the back of his neck, and shook his head in doubt. "I'm at a loss, Marc. I've only patched victims of ambushes, never a full battle." He balanced on a chair and stretched up to the top shelf to fetch a ball of stitching silk. "Perhaps with the other physicians' aid we can—"

"Except that..." interrupted Marc as he accepted the silk and set it in the trunk, "there *are* no other physicians."

Bewildered, Simon answered, "William specifically mentioned other physicians."

"The King had but two other doctors and they were slain in our last battle."

"Slain?" Simon froze and gulped his shock. He stood quietly awhile, then he shrugged and firmly stated, "In that case, I suppose we'll be tackling this task blindly. Will Henry fight? If not, perhaps he can be of some help."

"Henry plays at soldiering and does what he pleases," grumbled Marc. "He irks me."

Simon stepped down from the chair and suggested while passing Marc blankets, "Don't judge him too harshly. He's sure to be battling long after you've retired, and has little time left to play. I do understand how you feel, though. Way back, when you were, I'd say, seven, you continuously *irked* me."

"Why?"

"Because you were so damned good! You were Rose's little saint, Maura was her sweet angel, and I earned, unfairly I might add, her dubious title—devil. Maura and I would contrive such marvelous tricks to play on Rose, and if you happened to discover them, you'd immediately rush to her and tattle all. Maura feigned innocence and was never blamed. The punishment always fell on me!" His arm wrapped Marc's shoulders and his tone was benevolent, "A priest is what you should be. I never understood why Father insisted you become a soldier. Then again, I proved such a disappointment, he must have felt you were his final chance for glory."

Marc pressed fingerprints into one of the still warm splints and shook his head vehemently. "Not a priest, Simon."

"Why ever not?" Simon motioned for the splint, then set it by the others in the trunk. "In my estimation, you've always been a candidate for canonization. And if Uncle Odo can take up the robes you certainly—" He paused, noticing Marc's grave expression and finished tenderly, "Well, if not a priest, then perhaps a tradesman with a pretty plump wife who adores you, and dozens of children."

Marc smiled wanly. "I much prefer that image."

"And I promise it *will* happen for you, Marc. First you must survive this terrible time."

"You've known terrible times as well."

"Nothing compared to yours and Maura's."

A complacent quiet followed as the men went about their tedious chores. Simon handed Marc the last packet of suturing needles; he placed it atop the packed contents, shut and bolted the lid, and cracked a thoughtful, almost pleasant grin. "Simon..." he said, "I'll feel honored being your assistant...and also your brother-in-law."

Simon mussed Marc's hair; his broad smile betrayed relief, and he answered with deep affection, "Your blessing means everything to us. Now, help me haul this trunk down to the cart."

*****

The morning sun peaked over the horizon and perked thousands of flower petals that blanketed a tranquil field. A sudden clamorous roar shattered the peaceful scene as William's soldiers swarmed over the field, crushing the pastel carpet and killing the calm. They fumbled about, some donning armor, while others, wielding lances, swords and maces, drilled in mock combat for the true battle soon to come. Half a mile from the sparring band stood a lone, gray tent. Inside, Marc and Simon sat in stiff suspense upon a cot, listening, fidgeting, and awaiting the dreaded battle cry.

Simon anticipated every conceivable injury and, as he sat, he mentally rehearsed his training for punctures, gashes, and broken bones. The dire call, "Philip's men are advancing!" thrust both men to their feet. Fretfulness made Simon tidy supplies and pace the tiny space in scrutiny. The cots were freshly made up and evenly spaced, the cart stood close by the door ready to transport the bandaged back to Rouen, and the pit for the dead had been dug deep and wide. He paused in the doorway and trepidly watched the first skirmish. His eyes locked on the volley of flamed arrows let loose by William's archers. Philip's men launched an immediate parry of darts. The whirring missiles sliced through the brilliant blue sky and fell with lethal accuracy, piercing shields, hauberks, and bodies.

Simon shouldered past Marc and hurried inside the tent. Marc had never witnessed a battle from a distance, so he continued to gape in morbid fascination as dozens of ragged foot soldiers led mounted knights on a cacophonous charge. The armies' savage collision jarred him from his watch and, amid the howling, he caught Simon's pleas for help and hastened to the first casualty. As every cot rapidly filled, and the line of wounded spilled from the tent, Simon soon realized expertise was useless. While he crudely patched and splinted injuries, Marc enlisted the aid of the slightly disabled for swabbing, applying salve or wine, binding and comforting.

By dusk, supplies dwindled, yet the ferocious tumult outside never slackened. Exhaustion and despair overtook Simon; his hands trembled, his eyesight blurred, and an insidious doubt of his skill and sanity took seed in his tired mind. He slouched over a particularly horrendous case. With each stitch another gash spurted blood. Simon flung the needle in exasperation and cried, "How, how can he still breathe? How?!"

"I'll take him away," offered Marc. "There are dozens more needy."

Simon slumped on the empty cot and cradled his head in his red stained hands. He prayed for a moment—one brief moment was all he needed to tame his mind and fingers.

Marc's excited voice ended his prayer. "Simon! There's a lull in the fighting. Reinforcements are gathering. Our chance has come to walk the field."

"Walk the field?" Simon anguished. "I can't...My mind is dead, my fingers are stiff, all I see is red—"

"We must!" Marc sharply insisted. "You are their only salvation. To survive you must block all feeling! We have only an hour, with luck—two."

By the dim light of an oil lamp, they trudged the blood-soaked hills, stumbling and slipping over carnage to answer the groans of survivors. Marc grew anxious with the ample time Simon allowed each downed soldier. Finally, he curtly advised, "Don't treat them here. Decide who stays and who returns to the tent."

Not willing to play God, Simon choked in protest, "No—I won't, I can't!"

"You can and will. Do it and do it fast!" shouted Marc.

A pulsing knot cramped Simon's belly as he stooped to each prone form and dispensed his tragic judgment. Marc and his aides supported the fortunate ones back to the tent. While he awaited their return, rain and hail beat at Simon—God's punishment, he decided. He mopped at his eyes and focused his upset on a red rushing stream circling and splashing the lamp—the sputtering, dying lamp. Suddenly plunged into blackness, Simon cried out in terror, "Marc! Marc! Where are you? Marc!"

Marc's strong grip stilled his alarm. "I'm here, Simon. It's time we return to the tent."

Simon sighed and clutched Marc's hand. Marc didn't budge and, confused, Simon tugged and urged, "Marc, come..."

"Hush!" ordered Marc.

Simon sensed Marc's fear and searched the dark for its cause. "What? What is it?"

"I hear horses."

A shudder crept Simon's spine, thudding his heart, and raising hairs on his neck. "I—"

"Quiet!"

The dull clatter of hooves quaked the ground and Marc's voice shrilled, "Hundreds! Advancing from both sides. Find a horse!"

"What? It can't be, it's dark, how can they fight in the dark?!" cried Simon.

"Find a downed horse!" shouted Marc.

The thundering hooves grew louder, closer. The men crawled frantically through the gore, madly groping, searching. "Simon!" Marc screamed. "Simon, over here...Hurry!"

Simon scrambled over carcasses in the direction of Marc's order. Marc grabbed his wrist and Simon rolled, twisted and tumbled to his side. Shoved beneath a dead horse's sweaty flank, Simon burrowed and curled his body into a tight ball. The armies clashed directly overhead. He clamped his ears and cringed to the screech of clanging metal. A terrible stiffness paralyzed him as visions of his own violent death flashed before his clenched eyes. Marc's advice pounded his mind, '...to survive...block all feeling'. He hugged his knees, thrust his face deep into the horse's flesh, and forced himself to hear only his own raging pulse.

The tumult above stirred in Marc's mind an image of a long past horror. He saw again the licking flames sting his tiny fingers and huge blackened hands rip him from Maura's safe embrace. A blanket swathed his face and he felt he was smothering. The sensation jolted him back to the present. He floundered for air and, wrenching his face from beneath the horse's leg, he squirmed nearer to Simon. His foot slid in the mud; his leg escaped its cover and slicing hooves trampled his thigh.

Marc's agonized scream jarred Simon to action. He darted from beneath the horse; flailing blindly, he seized and tore at Marc's clothes. Marc howled, and writhed from Simon's reach as more hooves jostled his body.

"Take my hand!" Simon wailed, stretching as far as he could toward Marc's cries. "Marc, take my hand!" Their trembling fingers gripped tight; Simon yanked backwards with his entire might, and Marc flopped limply to his side. Crushed together, Simon's body shielded Marc's. And as they cowered under the dead beast's legs, Marc convulsed with sobs to Simon's panted assurance, "You're safe...safe. I won't let anyone hurt you. No one will dare hurt you again...no one."

With the dawn came a forbidding quiet. Simon's red and weary eyes hunted the field for movement. Seeing none, he achingly untangled his cramped body. He gazed down at Marc, lying senseless beneath him, his cherubic face smudged with tears, mud, and blood. Simon tapped his cheek. "Marc, wake up. We must leave here. Please, wake up."

Marc woke with a wailing gasp, his brittle fingers groping the air near his thigh. Simon eased off Marc's boot, and his dagger sliced away his braies to examine the wound. The gash was ragged and deep. A deep breath barely stilled Simon's quaking voice, "I'll carry you to the tent."

"There may be another strike...soon. Leave me, go find shelter."

Simon ignored Marc's advice, hugged his arms round his back, and hoisted him over his shoulder. Unsteadily he rose and, bent with his heavy burden, straggled over mounds of bodies to the tent.

Marc whimpered, scarcely aware, as Simon cleansed and stitched his wound, and then haphazardly secured it with a shredded sheet. The silence, so severe, pained Simon's ears. As he scanned the tent, he saw all the other occupants had breathed their last. He cautiously stuck his head out of the tent and noticed with a stab of panic that the only means of escape—the transport cart and horses—had disappeared.

While Marc twitched in a fitful sleep, Simon rested, his eyes fixed vacantly on a spot of blood staining the tent's wall. He didn't blink as a blazing arrow stuck the canvas. Its flames crept the cloth in an ever-widening circle and leapt to the table, dissolving his bandages to puddles and singeing the remainder of his thread. Marc pried his eyes wide to the stench of smoke, pushed up on his elbows, and nudged Simon with the toe of his good leg. "Simon!" he shouted. "Simon, help me up. We must go!"

"Go!" Simon asked incredulously. "Go where? There's nowhere left to go."

"There is one place left...Take my arm."

What little color was left drained from Simon's face as he realized Marc's plan. He shrank from Marc's reach, batted away his hand, and implored, "No...No, you can't mean. Not there, please not there!"

*****

A corpse dropped with a revolting thud at Simon's feet. Another slammed against the wall of the pit and flopped across his legs. He frenziedly kicked the charred carcass away, gagged at the stench of burnt flesh, and scrambled madly to his feet. He wiped filth from his eyes and searched up to the ridge of the hole, choking, "Wa...Wait...Stop! We're not all dead down here!" Severed heads and limbs rained down from above, striking his head and shoulders, driving him to his knees. He cowered beneath his shielding arms and screamed, "Stop!"

A bug-eyed soldier leant precariously over the rim of the pit. To prove he was no phantom, Simon jumped and waved, calling shrilly, "Fetch a rope, and hurry!" The soldier vanished, and Simon held a hopeful breath. If the soldier served Philip, more bodies would follow, then dirt.

The knotted end of the rope glanced off Simon's skull and he exhaled in blessed relief. He bent and circled Marc's chest with the hemp and tied it securely, all the while babbling excitedly to his unconscious comrade, "Marc, they've come to rescue us! Uncle hasn't forsaken us. They've come!" He yelled up to their liberator, "This man's badly injured. Let your horse haul him out, it will be smoother that way."

The soldier nodded and, after a few frazzling moments, the rope tautened and Marc's flaccid body rose from the carnage. Simon heedfully guided him upward, and watched till his feet disappeared over the ledge. The rope dropped again for Simon; he tested its strength then hurriedly clambered back to the living.

As the soldier's cart plodded down the rutted road, the man muttered over his shoulder, "You gave me quite a scare. I didn't expect any survivors. King Philip takes no prisoners." Simon blanketed Marc's quivering body, and cast a wary eye back over the field. Through the smoky dusk, he beheld the tent's skeletal remains and a dozen or so shawled women roaming the stacks of butchered and blackened soldiers in search of loved ones. Bile burned his throat as he shifted his worry to Marc. He sank down to the cushiony straw by Marc's side and rested a hand over Marc's heart. And to its strong and comforting beat, Simon finally allowed his eyes to close.

*****

CHAPTER TWENTY-FIVE - VEXING COMRADES

𝓕rom beneath her sopping wet hood, Maura raised weary eyes to Pevensey Castle, sentinel for the south coast of England. Many times, she had heard the heralded tale of its past—in 1066, the timbered castle had been hastily constructed following William's victory at the battle of Hastings, and promptly awarded to Lord Robert for his gallant performance during the siege. Long since fortified with stone, the monument to war now served as Robert's primary residence in England. And this stark, horrid place was where she would wed.

Godfrey waved her forward, and she urged E'dain along the flooded lane, replete with perilous potholes and sucking mud. After four days of riding and a continuous pelting by torrential rains, she doubted she'd ever feel dry again. And then there was the problem of E'dain—the sluggish mare frequently balked and tugged the reins from Maura's hold. Her arms ached from their constant wrangling and she was rapidly developing an intense dislike for the ornery creature.

On this bleak day, they had suffered ten hours of riding, and as dusk settled and the rain increased its ferocity, she welcomed the sight of Pevensey's forbidding portcullis and gatehouse. She shuddered along with her chattering teeth while awaiting Godfrey's return from the gatehouse, and grimly reflected on his arrival at Winchester. With Godfrey had come the relentless storms—toppling trees, ripping roofs, and forcing a delay of their departure by four days. A messenger had been sent ahead to relay their plight to Lord Robert. Yet when the weather calmed sufficiently for them to brave the journey, they found all major routes to the south unnavigable, thus extending their trip by an additional two days. Godfrey cast Maura a dismal look as he wearily climbed back into his saddle and clopped across the lowered drawbridge. She followed, striving to cure her gloom with the cheering image of comforts soon to come—a fire, a hot bath, palatable food, dry clothes, and most importantly, the long awaited opportunity to whine her many upsets to Almodis.

She passed under the curtain wall and peered through the dripping gray to the top step of the keep. A fright-induced cramp stabbed her belly as she spied Lord Robert, his fury blatant despite the distance separating them. She steeled herself to the fearsome sight of her Liege hastily descending the stairs and storming across the bailey, skirting and leaping puddles in his frenzied effort to reach her. A dire urge to flee seized her; escape was not an option—Simon would come to Pevensey, so at Pevensey she must stay. The gates thudded close at her back as Robert rabidly approached her side and yanked her roughly from her saddle. "You dare disobey me!" he roared, his face a twisted mask of hate. "You'll pay dearly for your impudence. Guards! Lock her in the buttery!"

Maura strained against his biting hold, wailing, "No, my Lord, *please*, no! I've done nothing—"

Two brawny guards wrenched her arms and dragged her, struggling and howling in protest, past gawking tradesmen, into the keep, and down a long curling stairwell. At the steps' base, a door gouged with a barred window yawned wide. The brutish sentries heaved her inside, then slammed and locked the door. She tumbled and rolled from their mighty thrust; a stone wall prematurely halted her momentum. Sorely, she balanced on scuffed knees and watched in horror as the guards stole away the torch illuminating the stairs. This must be the blackness of death, she thought as she waved her hand before her eyes and saw nothing.

She hugged tight her body and probed her tangled mind. What had she done to incite Robert's wrath?! Had he uncovered their secret? No, only Rose knew, only Rose. The messenger—she had paid him well to deliver her message, perhaps too well! Had he run off? Godfrey would explain their case to Lord Robert, and soon she'd hear boot steps, boot steps coming to set her free! She laughed pitifully into crossed arms. How extremely fortunate she was to be a member of the Royal Family! A full saving breath accompanied her prayer for the nightmare's end, for Simon's arms to surround and wake her, for his loving words to assure her that she was dreaming, only dreaming. But Simon couldn't come now, he was far, far away. Yet he had left her a most valuable gift—the knowledge of her own indomitable strength. She envisioned him near, felt the heat of his body, and heard again his sweet voice. The vivid image tamed her racing pulse. "He *will* come back," she chanted in a whisper. "We will escape this atrocious place, together and alive...He will come...he will...he must!"

*****

In their dank, sparsely furnished bedchamber, Almodis and Robert stood posturing nose-to-nose. Her expression clouded with repulsion as she thrust her palm under his ever stoic gaze and demanded, "Give me the key!"

"Stop this!" he yelled as hotly, rage smoldering his narrow glare.

She flailed wildly and raved, "Maura is a most powerful woman! She manipulates the weather just to spite you. Godfrey explained their peril. How dare you punish her?!"

"Almodis..." Robert paused and struggled inwardly to contain himself. "If you don't cease your nonsense, I—"

"I won't stand for this!" exploded Almodis. "Maura is my friend, my only friend. I will not allow her to be caged like a wild beast. You *are* the beast, you...you vile monster!"

Robert's blow met Almodis' cheek and its force hurled her to the rushes. She gasped shock and placed a whimpered touch on the scarlet mark. "I commanded you to stop," he raged, "yet you ignore me, as everyone ignores me! It is your choice, my bold lady, you will obey or spend eternity in a locked cell." Her abundant sobs dulled his diatribe, and remorse quavered his order, "Acknowledge me, Almodis. Almodis...did you hear? Answer me!"

He squatted near and she shrank from his reach. "Don't touch me, you putrid, shriveled up fiend!" she shrilled. "You'll never touch me again. I despise you!"

"Almodis, you...you hexed me...made me strike you," rued Robert in a tremble. "Come, take my hand. All is forgiven."

She heard none of his wilting dribble; instead she focused on the clink of the buttery key in his tunic's pocket. One hand hid her cheek as her other stretched tentatively out to his. She allowed him to help her stand and promptly feigned a swoon. While Robert fumbled with her weight, her fingers neatly sought and rescued the key. A triumphant shove sent him stumbling. She whisked up a candle and flint and escaped her insufferable chamber and husband. She dashed along shrunken passageways and hugged the steps' pillar as her toe sought the edge of each steep stair descending to the buttery.

Maura's chanting hushed to a peculiar swishing sound. She scrambled up and groped blindly for the door. Her fingers found and strangled the bars and she started to call out, but a horrific memory stifled her plea. Robert's guards—were they coming, stealthily, wickedly, intent on torture?! As if burnt, her hands leapt from the bars. She pressed to the wall, bated her breath, and stared aghast as a band of rats circling her feet scuttled away from the sparks of a struck flint. Maura blinked back stinging tears and focused her fright on bands of faint candlelight filtering through the bars. Her heart faltered to the sound of a key fumbling in the lock.

The door creaked open and Maura sagged in delirious relief as she heard Almodis' call, "Maura? Maura, are you there? Maura?"

Maura shoved from the wall and clasped her friend in a huge grateful hug, exclaiming, "Almodis, praise God, it's you! I feared Robert's guards were—Have you come to release me?" Almodis stayed curiously quiet. Maura pulled away and asked, "You...you *have*, haven't you?"

"Not exactly," replied Almodis.

"I don't understand," said Maura, bewildered. "You have the key. What stops you?"

"Well, Maura," said Almodis as she relocked the door. "I seem to have gotten myself into a bit of a mess. I stole the key from Robert with the foremost intention of setting you free, except I also aim to teach him a lesson."

"Lesson?" Maura echoed pointedly.

"Yes. If he insists on behaving like a spoiled, obstinate child, then I'll have to deprive him of what he craves most—me!"

"Almodis..." gritted Maura. "I'm in no mood for games. Let me out of here!"

"Patience, Maura, patience. I intend to. First, if I'm to defend you to Robert, I must know if it was only the weather that kept you from Pevensey."

Maura's jaw dropped wide at Almodis' accusation and her response shook with fury, "Simon left me eight days past, Rose seven. I suffered four horrendous days at Winchester dodging the guards' crude advances. Then Godfrey and I endured the cursed storms to arrive here as swiftly as possible. And you *dare* question my honesty? Where is the damned messenger?! He should have arrived days ago. Why am I being punished?! Almodis, get me out of here!"

"Maura!" retorted Almodis as she circled Maura's austere expression with the candle. "Don't distort your features so. You look wretched enough as is!"

"God's breath, Almodis!" Maura yelled. "At this particular moment, I don't care how I look!" Her hand shot out and swiped at Almodis' closed fist. "Give me the blasted key!"

Almodis jerked away and strolled casually over to a stout wine cask. She dripped a few beads of tallow atop the cask and secured the candle's base to the wood. With crossed arms, she leant up against the barrel, and smugly replied, "Not just yet."

"You don't believe me?" whined Maura.

"Of course, I believe you. Now hush..."

Maura attacked the door, madly wrestled the latch, then flung her arms in exasperation and spun, poised to rail. Boot steps stalled her tirade; boot steps tramping determinedly, each step louder, closer—then hammering and Robert's strident demand, "Almodis! Unlock this door and come out this instant."

"Only if Maura accompanies me," was her pert reply.

"No!"

"Then I wish you goodnight, sweet Husband. Sleep well and forever alone."

"Almodis, you're trying what little patience I have left. Almodis!"

"Robert...I'll happily obey your pompous blustering, after you've begged forgiveness from me and also Maura."

In perplexed astonishment, Maura's eyes darted back and forth between Almodis' haughty sneer and Robert's framed silhouette. How in God's name had she become a pawn in a domestic squabble? Would the madness never end?!

"Is that your final demand, Almodis?" asked Robert.

"Yes...*Robert*."

He cringed at her flagrant use of his Christian name, then returned staidly, "Then, good Ladies, I pray you enjoy the wine."

Almodis lunged for the door and quaked with furious disbelief at the sight of her departing Lord.

"Almodis!" Maura grabbed Almodis' arm and yanked her close. Her bellow rousted dust from the many casks, "What have you done?!"

"Don't scream at me!" Almodis fumed back. "That putrid old swine! He always surrenders to my schemes." She wrung her hands, and fretted under her breath, "I must rethink my plan. He *will* surrender. He must surrender."

Haltingly, Maura approached and suggested with strained politeness, "Almodis, perhaps you can settle your marital difficulties some other way. Please, don't involve me and hand over the key."

Almodis tapped the prized object to her chin and replied with unnerving calm, "If you wish, though I must warn you, Maura, without my aid, Robert will imprison you again, somewhere not near as cozy as here. You mentioned guards—they will gladly keep a constant watch over you and, as you know, are not overly genteel."

Maura slumped to the ground with a loud, despairing moan. "Why, Almodis? Why is he doing this?"

"I must confess, I'm as fuddled as you." Almodis lowered her cumbersome figure to the dirt and went on, "Something curiously evil has invaded Robert. He's fidgety and quick to temper. His eyes betray a fear I've not noticed before and I sense danger when he's near. He struck me, Maura."

"I'm sorry for his outbursts, Almodis, but I must leave here. Simon—" Maura caught her whine too late.

"Simon?" In a harsh whisper, Almodis chastised, "Are you mad? Is he here?"

"No, no...He's away in Normandy. I can say no more. Please, release me!"

"That can't happen till I've made my peace with Robert. Oh, Maura, don't look so glum. Together we will lighten our misery by imbibing monumental amounts of rotted grape juice. And perhaps in the process, I can coax from you all your spicy secrets!"

*****

Simon started upright in his bed, gasping and batting at an invisible enemy. As the contents of the drab room crystallized before his reddened eyes, he groaned an anguished groan, and raked back his damp, shaggy hair. He had little memory of their return to Rouen. The dour sight of Marc, lying prone on the opposite bed, so quiet and still, thrust his mind back to the battlefield, the carnage, and scores of dead. He rose stiffly, staggered the few feet to Marc's side, and rested two fingers upon Marc's brow; his skin felt oddly cool. Exhaustion hunched Simon's back and he forced his drooping eyelids wide. A linen towel floating in a washing bowl on the table caught his eye; he wrung it, and cleansed his own face, then Marc's, calling, "Marc...it's Simon. Can you hear me? Marc?" There was no answer, no movement. Simon cradled his head in his hands, and struggled to recall the treatment for Marc's injury. A damp chill drew his attention downward. His tunic sagged from the weight of congealed blood. A brushing touch to the stiffening cloth revealed the same rust stain coating his fingers, palms, and forearms. Whimpering, he madly scoured his skin, chafing it raw—still the willful stain endured. The discarded towel colored the water, and he tasted vomit as despair and futility deadened his mind. He had failed so miserably.

The door creaked and Henry's heartening call disturbed his gloom. "Simon? May I enter?" Simon nodded. Henry crept to the empty bed, set his candle by the washbowl, and questioned in a whisper, "How fares Marc?"

Simon shrugged.

"And yourself?"

"There's nothing wrong with me."

"I don't believe you," countered Henry. "I was present when your cart arrived. I thought you both dead, and then, thank the Lord, you moved."

"How long have I slept?" asked Simon.

"From dusk to dusk."

Simon's hooded gaze never strayed from Marc as he faintly asked, "Were you there...at the battle?"

"No. My horse threw me and I wrenched my ankle. I never left the bailey."

"Lucky for you."

"I suppose. Father requests your presence in the great hall."

Simon exhaled raggedly. "I won't leave Marc."

"I'll sit by him," offered Henry as he touched the blood stain on Simon's tunic. Paling, he quickly swished his fingers in the bowl, and asked with dread, "Is any of that blood yours?"

"No," Simon answered shortly. "I said there's nothing wrong with me!"

"Fine...fine. I'll fetch fresh clothes while you wash."

"It won't come off, Henry."

"What won't come off?"

"The blood."

"Then we'll hide it." Henry nudged Simon to break his trance. "Simon, did you hear me?"

Simon hung his head; his breaths shortened with rising upset as Henry patted his shoulder and gently assured, "It's over, Simon. The battle's done."

After Henry left, Simon stripped and dabbed limply at his skin, wondering why the King had asked for him. Most likely to condemn him for not fulfilling their pact and allowing so many to die! Henry swiftly reappeared, draped with elaborate apparel. As Simon dressed, Henry yammered a steady and comforting stream of trivia. He pinched at Simon's ruined clothing, and decided with disgust, "I'll burn these." His concern heightened to Simon's gaunt look and irksome silence, then flared as Simon returned to Marc's side and began mopping his brow with the tainted cloth. "Simon," Henry reminded strictly, "Father has ordered you to the great hall."

Simon gestured angrily for silence and shifted his glare Henry's way. "If he wakes, don't tease him."

"I *do* have a heart," Henry replied, wounded.

"Sometimes I wonder," returned Simon.

*****

Simon trudged down the back stairwell, passed by the Royal bedchamber, and paused behind the dais. William sat before a tall pile of parchments, scribbling his mark recklessly; thick pelts blanketed his slumped shoulders. The quill halted to a rustling sound and, without turning, William commanded, "Stand before me." Simon drew in a fortifying breath, straightened, and strode to the fore of the dais. He genuflected and raised a devastated expression. William's eyes fell again on the parchments and he softly sighed, "Rise, my boy."

The King's sympathetic tone unleashed Simon's torment. He gripped the edge of the dais, his face creased with agony, his voice strained and cracked, "I tried...I tried to help! There were too many. I couldn't keep up...I tried...I..." His confession and resolve sputtered away, leaving him drained and bent.

William rose unsteadily, lumbered round the table, and took Simon's arm. "Come," he simply muttered. Simon trailed William out of the keep and as they stood atop the stairs, the King swept his arm wide over the torch lit courtyard. An enormous tent covered most of the ground. Wordlessly, they descended the steps and stooped beneath the entrance to the canvas dome. Simon marveled at the hundred or so rows of cots, each containing a wounded soldier. The King draped his arm round his nephew's shoulders and lauded, "Yes, my boy, you tried and succeeded. By your valiant efforts, these men will live."

Simon noticed a number of men in physician's garb tending the soldiers and, pointing, asked wishfully, "Those men, are they—"

"They are my daughters' physicians," William interrupted. "Adela seemed glad to be rid of hers. Now, have I sufficiently brightened your spirits?"

Simon managed a weak smile.

"You can advise the doctors shortly," said William, "but first you'll return with me to the hall. I have something for you."

The King ducked back through the door; Simon remained a few moments more. And as he scanned the makeshift hospital, solemn doctors, and flustered servants and squires, a budding contentment began to mend his despair. The evidence stood clearly before him—he *had* made a difference and, charged with renewed determination, he hurried back to the keep to make one final request of his King.

Back in the hall with Simon by his side, William shuffled through stacks of strewn parchment, finally extracting a fully scripted page. He shoved it under Simon's nose and directed, "Read it."

Simon blinked then focused on the elaborate print. The first paragraph annulled the Yorkshire contract. Simon read, "'*...due to improprieties undertaken by the Liege Lord of the intended bride,*' and it orders, '*...The Liege Lord, in retribution, will relinquish to the groom the entire proposed dowry*'." Simon paused and wagged his head in doubt. "Father will not like this."

"He's not meant to," returned William, prodding the parchment. "Read on."

The second paragraph stated William's permission for Simon and Maura's marriage, "*...The couple will be afforded the Crown's protection till King William's death,*" and included the astounding edict, "*...The wedding will be celebrated by Archbishop Lanfranc, at Canterbury Cathedral*!" Raising startled eyes, Simon questioned, "Lanfranc?"

"No one will dare annul a union blessed by the Archbishop. And he loves you dearly. It is fitting. Do you approve?"

"Oh yes, Uncle! How can we ever thank you?"

"You already have, countless times. This is my thanks to you." William tossed a swollen bag of coins before Simon and added with mock sternness, "This time keep a few marks for yourself and Maura, no doubt you'll sorely need them. If you depart at dawn, you'll arrive at Pevensey in ample time to halt the marriage. What is your plan if Robert refuses to acknowledge this document?"

"Fight him."

"Fine, but please don't resort to murder. There is a tiny part of me that still cares for him. I can't spare you soldiers, I can only wish you luck. I've called a family gathering in two hours' time to drink a salute to your upcoming nuptials and—" William paused in perturbed confusion. "What is that furrowed brow about?"

Simon readily spilled his remaining wish, "After he's healed, I ask you to allow Marc to return to England."

"No," William insisted, "I cannot afford the loss of a single soldier."

"I'll teach him my trade," Simon unwisely persisted. "He'd prove an excellent emissary! His heart's not in soldiering."

"I don't want his heart!" smoldered William. "I want his body!"

"One soldier, Uncle!" His vehemence thrust him to his feet. "What difference could it make?"

"All the difference!"

"Please," Simon implored, "release him!"

"I said no!"

"Who will take on my duties?"

"Perhaps Henry."

"No!" Simon sharply interjected. "Marc's better suited."

"Enough, Simon."

"As a reward for his bravery, fealty, expertise—"

"Stop!" the King blared and threatened, "One further word and I'll shred this declaration!"

"But—"

William stretched taut the parchment and Simon shut his mouth to the dreadful sound of tearing. He slumped back into his chair, his chest heaving and heated glare burning into his lap. William released the document, flattened it with his balled fist, and bristled, "Damn you! You're as stubborn as me! It's no wonder you get yourself in such impossible fixes!" To Simon's lame look, he tempered his tone, "I know you love Marc as a brother and feel a need to protect him. I admire your loyalty, Simon, but I cannot honor your request...and that's final. I do, however, have an additional request to make of you."

Simon's glare remained on his belt.

"Are you familiar with Sulien, Bishop of St. Davids Cathedral in the village of Menevia, Wales?" asked William.

Puzzled, Simon momentarily set aside his rancor. "Ye...yes. How do you—"

"In '81, I traveled to South Wales on a pilgrimage to the Cathedral. You had not yet arrived. While visiting, I came to terms with a man called Riset of Wales."

"Prince Rhys?"

"Yes, they are one and the same fellow. He agreed to render forty pounds of silver yearly as tribute to retain his territory and title. Bishop Sulien has since acted as our mediator, and, thus, he could surely use your assistance. The Marcher lords—Lacy, Montgomery, Mortimer, and others, continue their drive westward, and I fear all hopes for peace in Wales are dwindling. Would you consider working with Sulien and the Prince to hold our bargain?"

"Gladly!" beamed Simon. He stood and thrust out his hand to William. Their clasp sealed the pact, and Simon pulled backwards to help his uncle stand.

"Then," said William, "I will consent to keep Marc at Rouen in the room above, and personally see to his recuperation. Now leave me, see to the doctors, tend to Marc, and return in, I'd say, two hours for the gathering. We'll exchange farewells."

A winning smile split Simon's face as he bowed and hastened away to the bailey.

*****

In the tiny bedchamber, Henry watched in wonder as Simon deftly cleansed Marc's leg. "Where were you?" he asked petulantly. "Marc woke and began babbling. I didn't know what to do."

"I spoke to your father, visited with the physicians and wounded, then made a trip to the kitchen."

"Why?"

"To gather supplies for Marc's treatment." Simon lifted a bowl from the rushes, and produced from his cuff a linen towel. Upon it he spread a pungent buff-colored mixture.

"What's that?" asked Henry.

"A concoction of boiled hog's lard, honey, and wine. I'll apply it to his wound to speed the healing. Marc?" Simon glanced to the head of the bed and called again, "Marc? Can you hear me?"

Marc struggled to lift his head and, with his eyelids barely parted, his lips hissed, "Yessss."

"Was Henry kind to you while I was away?"

He managed a slight nod, then dropped his heavy head back to the pillow.

"Henry," said Simon, "try to get him to drink from the cup on the table."

Henry lifted the cup and sniffed; his action provoked a distasteful sneer and shudder. "And what are you torturing him with here?"

"It's only boiled poppy heads in ale."

"My Lord, Simon, why poison the poor lad?"

"It will help him sleep, and that's what he mostly needs."

Henry shrugged and supported Marc's shoulders as he held the cup to his lips. Amazed, he watched the liquid swiftly disappear down Marc's throat and commented,

"Maybe I should have tried a sip myself." His fascination shifted back to Simon, who was now wrapping a bandage around Marc's wound. "Can we eat what's left in the bowl?" wondered Henry.

"Actually, it's quite palatable," said Simon, offering Henry a fingertip topped with the paste.

Henry tasted, nodded appreciatively, and asked, "Did you learn all this from that heathen tribe of heretics you lived with in Wales?"

Simon simpered. "Yes, Henry, from the heathen heretics. I think I'm done."

A quick glance at Marc beheld him sleeping, and Henry noted, "The potion seems to be working favorably. Perhaps you should teach our physicians your magic."

"I already have and, in turn, they've taught me theirs." Simon stretched a reach across the bed and again tested Marc's brow for fever. "He's still cool," he said concernedly.

Henry dismissed Simon's worry with a wave. "Marc's a genuine marvel. He never falls ill, and this isn't the only severe injury he's suffered. I predict he'll be battling again within the week. Actually, Simon, Marc's rather intimidating—Father's prized soldier and dearly beloved by all the troops. I no longer strive to compete with..." Henry dropped his final word snidely, "...him."

"I understand your resentment, Henry," said Simon, cracking a benign smile. "But despite the adulation, Marc still remains a sad, sad soul." His smile broadened. "Henry! I'm certain you have an intimate knowledge of the servants. While I'm cleaning up here, will you go and fetch the ideal nurse for Marc?"

"The ideal nurse..." Henry paused a reflective moment, then beamed and announced, "I know just the one!" as he bounded exuberantly from the chamber.

Marc slept soundly as Simon blanketed him with pelts and wondered, with a doleful sigh, how could he leave him this way? The King had vowed to see to his care personally, only with his many distractions, would he forget? There was less than a week left till Maura's marriage, and Simon didn't cherish the idea of arriving in time to kiss the bride farewell. He could only pray for a swift and complete end to the wars.

The door's creaking cut short his wish, and Simon cocked an ear to the shuffling intrusion. The visitors remained out of sight; he listened and heard Henry hush giggles and gruffly warn, "You'd best behave yourself."

Henry entered, tugging behind him a jittery, pretty young maid, a mass of dark curls framing her flushed face. Her dewy brown eyes passed swiftly over Simon, and her blush deepened. She dropped her shy gaze and clamped tight her mouth to stifle a titter.

"And who might you be?" asked Simon, allowing himself an amused grin.

Henry nudged her forward. "This is Tilly. She's agreed to sit with Marc."

"Well, that's truly generous of you, Tilly. I appreciate your thought—" Simon paused, afraid that one additional compliment might render the trembling young woman unconscious.

"Do you have any specific instructions for her, Simon?" asked Henry.

"No. If you encounter any problems, Tilly, come fetch me in the great hall."

She curtsied stiffly and replied in a breathless stammer, "I'll do...my...my very best, my...Lord."

"I'm certain you will," Simon nodded, then bustled Henry out into the hall to ask, "Where did you find *her*?"

"Tilly is my father's servant, Aggy's daughter, and I can personally attest to her pureness. She's as angelic as Marc. They're bound to get along exquisitely."

"And how has she managed to dodge your gropings?"

"I'm no fool, Simon. No sane man would risk suffering the wrath of Aggy just for a bit of Tilly. Besides, she's been known to wear armor beneath her frock."

Simon wagged his head in wonder. "Henry, you're simply amazing."

"I'm pleased you've noticed. Simon, you've not given me my *word*."

"Your *word*?"

"Yes...You remember, your self-imposed quest to improve my diction."

"Oh yes...Well, when I think back over our week of adventures, one word comes quickly to mind."

"And what's that?" Henry asked expectantly.

"Fulsome...Yes, I believe fulsome amply defines your behavior of late."

"Fulsome..." Henry turned the word over in his mind and flashed a proud smile. "It sounds quite virile!"

"Virile indeed."

"Why, thank you, Simon! And I must admit you look quite dashing in my clothes."

Simon smirked and answered waggishly, "No I don't, I look like you."

Henry gave his cousin a playful shove, and received a rougher one in return which toppled him to the rushes. He scrambled up and scurried to catch Simon, booming his relief, "It's marvelous to have the old Simon back again!"

The late supper made the Royal Family a drowsy, sullen lot. They lounged groggily in their bulky chairs, each seemingly preoccupied with personal thoughts and whims. Simon sat quietly at the King's side, unobtrusively examining the composed group. Adela seemed unusually sedate as she cooed to her chubby son, bundled in the arms of his nurse. William snickered and guffawed in response to Henry's unending discourse of anecdotes and ribald tales. Simon shifted impatiently, and slipped his scrutiny to his knife knocking rhythmically against the side of his empty bowl. He yawned and longed for the salute to be done, for he desperately needed to rest before embarking on his journey to Pevensey.

William glimpsed Simon's brooding, rose stiffly, and tapped the table with his spoon. He cleared his throat and leant forward on his palms to declare, "Simon will depart on the morn and—"

"Thank the Lord!" Adela interjected.

"Adela!" William chided, then sternly praised, "Simon has accomplished a tremendous amount of good while visiting, and we will demonstrate our appreciation with a salute." Sneeringly, Adela barely raised her cup; Henry beamed exaltation and thrust his tankard high as William humbly began, "Simon, to your safe journey home and continued good health—"

"Here, here!" Henry spouted as he and Adela took in great gulps of wine.

"And..." William finished, "to a long, blissful, and fruitful marriage!"

To the King's riveting news, Adela choked violently on her wine, and Henry sprayed his across the table. Simon and William smugly clinked cups and, after sips, chuckled at Henry and Adela's stupefied expressions. "Simon," the King suggested, "we'll leave the clowns and speak further in my chamber."

"I'll join you shortly, first there's something I must do." Simon matched Adela's pernicious glare as he confidently approached Theobald. She bodily challenged his advance and hissed, "Whom are you to marry?"

"I assume you're intelligent enough to discern for yourself the answer to *that* question...Adela. Then again, I may be wrong in my assumption."

"You pompous snot!" she railed. "Maura won't be worthy of a squire after you're done with her! Now get your fetid breath off my son!"

Simon flashed a charming smile at Theobald's nurse, who held the baby out to him despite her Lady's thunderous objections. Strangely, Adela muffled her wrath while Simon bent to kiss the baby's brow, and he pledged in a whisper, "I've no doubt we will meet again."

Meanwhile, Henry, stiff with shock, fumed inwardly. That hateful bitch! Maura had sworn to him she'd ask nothing of Simon. Nothing indeed—only his body, mind, and soul! He had to intervene before the dastardly deed took place, for once her claws were deeply embedded, he would never again see his greatest comrade. Having simmered too long, Henry failed to notice Simon bow graciously to the nurse, blow a triumphant kiss to a seething Adela, and stroll casually from the hall.

Henry's frantic eyes hunted the hall and he squalled, "Simon, wait! Wait for me!" He dashed toward the back stairs and caught sight of his own crimson tunic disappearing behind his father's chamber door. Henry rattled the latch, pounded, and wailed, "Simon!"

"Go away, Henry!" was William's demand.

Mightily bruised, Henry mumbled curses as he slid down the door and pressed his ear to the wood.

"I had an inkling they wouldn't be overly pleased with our news, so I'll offer my personal congratulations and farewells here." Again, William cleared his congested throat and his eyes seemed to rest everywhere but on his nephew. "Our kinship has always been most dear to me." William placed his hands on Simon's shoulders. "We argue, and that's good. We've even managed to teach each other—" His arms dropped dejectedly to his sides and he continued indulgently, "I needn't make a speech to you. We won't meet again. I love you and will miss you. Please take care of yourself and sweet Maura. Send word of your encounter with Robert, and if he so much as slaps you, I'll—"

"No, Uncle," Simon interrupted, "no more harsh words. With God's grace and your blessing, the encounter will prove bloodless." He masked his woe with a radiant smile. "And of course we'll meet again. You do intend to live forever, don't you?"

William lowered his damp gaze to the floor and, from his bed, plucked up two ribboned scrolls. He handed both to Simon with the instructions, "There's one for Robert and one for Lanfranc's signature." They embraced; the King kissed Simon's cheeks, and patted his back, reminding, "You'll have the Crown's protection *only* till my death." Simon nodded and knelt before William. A touch to his head permitted him to rise and, as he headed for the door, the King mournfully confessed, "Simon, I've often wished you were *my*...son. Give Maura my love."

Simon lifted the latch and glanced back one final time, locking away forever his uncle's parting smile. The door opened by itself and in tumbled Henry. "Henry!" William scolded. "I've warned you countless times never to listen at keyholes!"

"I wasn't," retorted Henry, not daring to rise. "Actually, I was listening a bit lower than that."

Simon escaped their haggling and trotted up the back stairs to his chamber.

"Father!" Henry squeaked as William lifted him up by his collar, "you may punish me later. It's urgent I catch Simon. I want to accompany him to England." He jerked from his father's hold and lunged for the door.

"No!" William bellowed, swiping out and yanking him back. "I need you here."

"Why ever for?"

"I...I...I'll think of some reason." William eased his hold and his pensive expression cracked an enlightened grin. "No...Why, yes! You *will* accompany Simon and take all your guards along. He may require your martial expertise." William swatted Henry's backside and affectionately ordered, "Don't tarry, or you'll miss him!"

Henry vaulted the stairs three at a time, speeding past Tilly as she departed the bedchamber and sending her spinning away down the hall. He barged into the chamber, panting and booming, "Simon! I must speak with you, it's urgent!"

"Hush!" Simon scolded in a stern whisper. "Marc's sleeping."

"But Simon!" Henry returned at the top of his voice. "You can't go through with this catastrophe!"

"And what catastrophe are you referring to?" Simon asked mundanely as he busily packed his saddlebag.

"Marrying Maura, you fool!"

"And why am I a fool, Henry?"

"She is not a kind woman."

Simon tensed and glared, "Henry, don't start. I have neither the time nor the patience for your antics."

"I have evidence to back my accusation! Maura...Maura kicked me, hit me, spilled ale on me and it was cold, cursed me, called me a nasty name—"

"And I suppose," Simon interjected dubiously, "you did nothing whatsoever to provoke these incidents?"

"Of course not! Besides, it's not wise to make such an irreversible decision such as marriage so...so rashly."

"Rashly? God's teeth, Henry, I've known Maura sixteen years and have wanted to marry her for the past five. That's certainly not 'rash'."

"You can't allow a mere woman to coerce you into...into—"

"Henry, sit!" thundered Simon.

Henry sat. Simon heaved his saddlebag by the door, and furiously paced, jabbing a rigid finger in Henry's pinched face each time he stormed by. "It seems," he hotly stressed, "you've had a serious lapse of memory. Consider for a moment, Henry, who dragged you to safety after you'd taken that arrow in your shoulder, who spoke to you like no woman has ever spoken to you before—and I doubt ever will again—and who, too politely, ignored your excessively disgusting, yes, *fulsome* behavior when she could have just as easily pounded you to the consistency of hog's meal!"

A moan from the bed stalled Simon's harangue, and he instantly attended to Marc. In the whispered quiet, Henry took a stunned moment to reflect on his time with Maura, and felt an achy yearning for her fiery temperament, her awkward beauty, her lingering farewell kiss. His bluster waned, and his rueful thoughts wandered to his recent behavior. As always, Simon was quite correct, it had been indeed—*fulsome*. With a shrug and sigh, he leant near to catch Simon and Marc's whispers.

"Marc," said Simon, "I'm to leave at dawn. The King refused to allow you to return with me. I did try and I'm sorry."

"Of course...he refused," answered Marc faintly. "I'm grateful for your effort and your...doctoring."

"However," Simon added, "he has sworn to keep you in this chamber till you've healed. Tilly and the physicians will see to your care and comfort."

"I'll like that. Tilly is very sweet." Marc's strangling grip paled Simon's knuckles as he begged, "When you tell Maura about my mishap, do it gently, or else she's liable to come and fetch me. Convince her I will be fine..."

"I promise," Simon answered.

Marc's eyelids fluttered closed to his murmur, "I'm so tired."

Simon squeezed his hand and whispered in his ear, "Never forget her words—when you can take no more, you can always return to us—at Menevia in south Wales."

"Menevia," Marc echoed weakly.

Marc's grip eased and Simon grudgingly rose. He ignored Henry's sulk, snatched up his saddlebag, and lifted the latch.

"Where are you going?" Henry asked. "Marc may need you."

"To the stables." Simon stealthily wiped a tear and muttered, "If I don't leave this room immediately, I may never go."

"Well, then," Henry stood and stated, "wait outside the door. It won't take long to pack my few things."

"Pack?!" Simon asked, aghast.

"Yes, pack. Father's ordered me to accompany you to England. We'll take my full contingent of guards—"

"You filthy liar!" Simon roared. "You're not accompanying me anywhere, ever, ever again!" With a ruffled snort, he flung the door wide, shot one last fretful glance Marc's way and left, slamming the door behind him.

Henry raced after, whining, "Wait! Simon, hear me out. You need me and my guards, and...and, also, I've been invited to your wedding!"

Simon's rage cut short their chase. "Invited to the wedding?! Henry, stop before I have to kill you!"

"It's true. Maura invited me and she did not stipulate, *you may come only if I marry Hugh*."

Simon groaned in exasperation and quickened his pace. Henry sprinted off in the opposite direction, shouting over his shoulder, "I'll send Tilly back to Marc and meet you in the stable."

As he watched Henry vanish around a corner, Simon stomped, then slumped in surrender. "Why me?" he croaked. "Why does he always insist on helping me?"

*****

A giddy Almodis lolled on the dirt, hooting. "Maura, stop! I don't believe you."

"It's true," Maura slurred and, with an emphatic gesture, sloshed wine from her cup. "If...you give them a swift hard kick...right between the eyes, they wilt, and'll follow you anywhere."

"And how did you discover this ingenious technique?" Almodis asked as she floundered to sit.

"I was Lord—no, Lady of the hogs at Dunheved!" proclaimed Maura proudly.

With Maura's fumbled help, Almodis managed to balance on her haunches and clumsily topped their cups. "I wonder if your trick works as well on males."

"Male's what?"

"Humans, silly."

Maura's bleary eyes twinkled mischief as she slurped the potent liquor. "Unfortunately, I've not attempted such a thing, though..." She paused to hiccup and giggled, "there are a few I'd love to experiment on."

"It wouldn't take a kick to make Will...wi...wilt," noted Almodis with difficulty. "He wilts in battle and in bed!" She howled and tipped back upon the ground; her gasping laughter finally slowed, and she raised a woozy expression of concern. "Si...Simon doesn't share that problem, does he?"

"Not that I've ever noticed," Maura replied with a mock seriousness that dissolved them both to hysterics.

"I beg of you, Maura," implored Almodis, "no more...If I don't stop laughing, I'll make myself ill, or worse yet, give birth to this child right on this spot. Oh, you do spin such magnificent stories." Almodis emptied their fourth flask into Maura's cup. "And I especially adored your Domesday tale. My time here has been so dull, and I've found myself at the oddest moments, envisioning you and Simon together...in bed or wherever. I'm positive I've not done you justice. I imagine him a superb lover. He is, isn't he?"

The vision of herself locked in Simon's arms, straining against his damp and insistent body, jolted Maura's blurred mind. She wiped sweat from her brow and admitted with a hungry sigh, "Yes, oh yes, and I do so terribly miss every bit of him."

Encouraged by Maura's confession, Almodis' delved deeper, "Do you fight?"

"Most certainly!" obliged Maura, then hugged herself and proclaimed with rapture, "And after, we reach such explosive compromises."

"No more, Maura. You're depressing me." Almodis stretched out on her side and, resting her cheek on her arm, asked woefully, "Will it ever happen for me, Maura? Will it?"

"I've no doubt."

"I wonder...I'm forever surrounded by louts, fiends, and bores! And there's no escape! After Alan arrived—and I thank you again for sending him my way—we met on a number of occasions, only to talk as you'd advised. I quickly became besotted. He is such an intriguing fellow, and chock full of inconsistencies, shy yet direct, large and gentle, subtle with a dry sense of humor, and so very handsome. For two glorious days, we walked, took in the spring air, and discussed every subject imaginable. And then who should arrive to spoil our budding affection but my irreverent husband. Robert took one look at Alan and promptly reassigned him to the gatehouse. So much for love."

"Robert does excel at spoiling, doesn't he?" Maura frowned, then her tone turned hopeful, "Perhaps, when we leave this pit, I can convince him I'm in some sort of danger, from Rufus, Will, or Simon...and, with luck, he'll agree to allow me my guard. Then... you two can resume your talks."

"Oh, Maura, you *are* wonderful!"

The women clinked cups and Maura soberly atoned, "I apologize for cursing you."

"There's no need. I did deserve it," said Almodis. "I must admit, I do get up to mischief now and then, most times with kind intentions. It was wrong of me to doubt you. Only, you must understand, Maura, I've never before had a close female friend and I find it hard to trust—anyone. Most other women seem appalled by my ways, though not you, which in turn tends to astonish me. You, not unlike Alan, are a bundle of inconsistencies."

"I relish your antics, Almodis." Maura abandoned her cup and slurped directly from the flask. "They're so refreshing in our otherwise pathetic world." Almodis seemed not to hear the compliment; instead she focused intently on something beyond Maura. A tingle climbed Maura's spine, and she warily peeked over her shoulder and saw—nothing. "Almodis," she wondered shakily, "what's caught your eye?"

Almodis shook from her trance and replied, "Nothing. I was remembering—There was one other woman I failed to appall."

Piqued by her friend's bewitched expression, Maura pressed, "Who? You must tell me who!"

A visible tremor took Almodis as she whispered, "*Mabel*..."

"Mabel of Belleme, Will's grandmother and Lord Roger's wife!" exclaimed Maura. "You knew her?"

"Oh, yes, all too well. And I can attest, she was, without challenge, the most vile creature ever to walk the face of the earth! I came to know her through her ties to Will, which were too intimate for my comfort."

Maura crept closer and asked with bated breath, "You don't mean they—"

"I can't say for certain and I never had the gall to ask, but the looks they shared were downright obscene."

"No!" gasped Maura.

"Yes..." Almodis shifted for comfort and continued, her voice thick with distaste, "When we'd visit her gatherings, she would demand, usually during supper, that Will describe in painstaking detail every bizarre aspect of our couplings to the guests. Most lost their appetite, but Mabel and Will and a sprinkling of others reveled in my shame."

"Bizarre aspects?"

"Well..." Oddly Almodis seemed a bit hesitant to divulge her secret; nonetheless, she mumbled, "When he's bored, Will likes to hurt me. You're aware of that." Was it shame that colored her cheeks, wondered Maura, as she watched Almodis create a pattern of intertwining circles in the dirt with the base of her cup. "You mentioned you and Simon fight," said Almodis defensively.

"Argue, Almodis. There *is* a difference. In our loving, we've been known to get a bit rambunctious, but hurt? Never. Love isn't meant to hurt."

"I know that. Nothing Will and I shared physically could ever be construed as love. I only endured his abuse so he would stay with me. I couldn't bear being alone. Finally, I'm beginning to realize that being alone has advantages of its own, most importantly for me—survival. I only pray it's not too late for me to know a tender passion."

"It's not," said Maura assuredly. "Now tell me more about Mabel."

"Once, when Will and Mabel were acting especially fiendish, I screamed at her. I was certain my days were numbered, so on subsequent visits I always brought my hound to sample my supper."

Befuddled, Maura repeated, "To sample your supper?"

"Poison was Mabel's forte. Anyone who displeased her was a likely victim. Then one day Will informed me she'd expired and spoke no more about her. I found his behavior queer, even for Will. As close as they'd been, he had absolutely no reaction to her death."

"You mean her murder!" burst Maura, almost tumbling on Almodis in her zeal.

"Murder?!" gasped Almodis.

"Rose loved to frighten Marc and me with the tale, in our chamber late at night, with only one candle lit."

"And Rose looks awfully frightening herself."

"Almodis..."

"I'm sorry. Do tell me, Maura."

Maura swept back her still damp, matted hair, and avidly began the grisly tale, "I'll try to tell the tale exactly the way Rose phrased it...Mabel terrified Lord Robert. You know, of course, she was his mother-in-law, and he believed, with good reason, that his wife Matilda was a poisoner as well. Robert and Matilda fought like rabid dogs. That's why he spent most of his time in England with Edith. He wisely kept his distance from the Montgomerys. And then came the day when he was summoned to Arundel to attend a celebratory feast in honor of some son's marriage, and he could not refuse. Boldly, Robert traveled to Arundel and managed to survive the feast unscathed. He did notice, though, a guest behaving in a most agitated way, and bolstering his fluster with copious amounts of wine. Lord Roger and Robert left the hall's drama to talk in the quieter bedchamber, only the racket quickly spread there as well. So Robert retired to his own chamber and lay awake, tossing throughout the endless night, awaiting the poison's grip." Maura paused as she noticed genuine fear twitch Almodis' expression. "I won't go on, if you're frightened."

"Don't stop now!" Almodis demanded.

"If you insist...A piercing scream rocked the keep. Robert raced to its origin—the Lord's bedchamber and, upon entering, discovered Roger gone. Mabel's headless torso lay stretched across her bed, her skin still damp from her recent bath, with her head perched on its own upon a nearby pillow, a death scream splitting its face. Beside the bed stood the agitated man, wielding a blood-stained sword, muttering crazily of his beautiful, adoring wife." Maura sat back casually to finish, "It seems Mabel accidently poisoned his wife the week before. Rose loved to scare us with that—"

"Was Will there?!" Almodis cried out, flailing to reach Maura's hand.

"Rose never mentioned Will being there," answered Maura as she helped pull Almodis from her prone position. She fidgeted with her braid and tentatively asked, "Is he here?"

Even in the faint uneven light, Almodis paled. "No, not as yet. If and when he does arrive though, I don't—" She paused, and her eyes darted about the room as she jabbered, "I will catch a rat, yes, a rat! There are plenty to choose from and a cage—I'll have a tradesman build me a cage." She took her fretting to her feet and stumbled in and out of the light. "Will inherited all of Mabel's lethal recipes. Where have all the rats gone to?"

Maura rose uncertainly and joined her friend's hunt. She caught one of Almodis' hands, and asked sincerely, "What *has* he done to you?"

"He wants my baby dead!" she moaned. "At the Tower, he beat me, tortured me, and ordered me to kill my child. If he finds me still pregnant, he'll do the deed himself—Mabel's way!"

"You must tell Robert!"

"I am considering that option." Almodis' jittery fingers traveled her muddied clothes and hair, and came to rest upon her lips. "Even if Robert does discover my sins, I do have some power—while still pregnant. The child is important to him."

"As are you."

"No, Maura, I am dispensable."

"Stay always close by me." Maura squeezed her grip and vowed with an endearing look, "I won't allow Will to hurt you."

Almodis strained a smile and patted Maura's hand. "I do appreciate your concern, Maura, it's just the wine has made me a bit obsessive. Will is much too involved with whoring and shameless boot licking to attend your dismal little wedding." Amazingly, Almodis' calm and guile surfaced again. "Let's sit," she suggested, "sip more of this tongue pleasing potion, and I'm wanting to know—are *you* pregnant?"

"No." Maura sank back to the dirt and let go a grieved sigh. "My flow arrived that last horrid week at Winchester. Which, I suppose in a way, was a good thing. Otherwise, my trip here would've proved painfully messy."

"It hurts you?" grunted Almodis, planting her unwieldy body back on the ground.

"Only the first few days."

"One of the nicer aspects of being pregnant—its absence. I'm so sorry, Maura."

"It will happen."

"You sound more assured of the miracle than before. What has changed your mind?"

Trepidation cracked Maura's voice, "I...I've been debating whether or not to say. I won't endanger you."

Almodis sat up tall and waggled her finger. "You are my ward and I order you to confess."

Maura laced her fingers together, clasped her hands firmly between her knees, then spilled the fragile plans, "Simon's gone to ask the King's permission for us to wed. He'll arrive any day and we'll—"

"Maura," Almodis cut her off with sobering logic, "I must crush your reckless dreams, for that's all they will ever be. Robert will never allow your escape and is, I might add, prepared for just such an event. He's been alerted to Simon's release."

"But," Maura desperately whined, "we will have the King's blessing, and seal, and—"

"A blessing and seal won't dissuade Robert, and William won't spare Simon any manpower."

"Henry will!" Maura wailed.

"Henry's only a child. Maura, you must resolve yourself to marrying Hugh. I know it's difficult—"

"No!" flared Maura; with balled fists and fierce expression, she resolved, "I will battle Robert myself!"

"That I don't doubt." Almodis glimpsed a sparkle on Maura's clenched left hand. She grabbed it, and forced her palm flat, gasping, "You haven't!"

Maura jerked away, crying, "No!"

"You'd best be telling the truth! God doesn't look kindly on bigamists."

"I'm not lying...I'm not!" anguished Maura, great sobs doubling her to the ground.

The cheering wine soured and Maura's melancholy infected Almodis. She supported Maura's limp body and began blubbering herself, managing a few words between sniffs. "Maura, I don't speak to God often, though for you I will make an exception. I'll pray for the success of your mission and will do all I can to aide your cause." She rubbed Maura's back and let her cry on, all the while rambling, "It must be near dawn. Once Robert realizes he cannot manage this household alone, he'll hurry down to fetch me...and you. Be extra sweet to him, Maura, grovel, praise, blindly obey, and never let him suspect a thing."

The sound of boot steps stalled Maura's weeping. The women rose quickly, gulped back tears, and traded winning grins to the approaching candlelight and familiar droning voice, "Almodis...Maura, come out now."

"You've taken your good time, my Lord and husband!" bellowed Almodis.

Maura swabbed tears as she ducked through the squat door, and immediately fell to her knees before Robert. Taken aback by her submission, he muttered an uneasy, "Rise." Still she stayed stooped, then raised awe-filled eyes to her Liege. Robert nodded and stated, "Godfrey has explained your troubles to my satisfaction. You are to be afforded the freedom of the castle, only you *will* remain within the curtain walls."

Almodis, still wary of her volatile husband, kept a safe distance when inquiring, "And what troubles coerced you to free us, my Lord?"

"The cook, servants, tradesmen, even the beasts seem intent on mutiny!" growled Robert.

"It's entirely *your* doing, my gracious Lord," harped Almodis, tossing her braids indignantly. "If you weren't so parsimonious, they'd have the funds needed to purchase supplies. Your stinginess is the cause of everyone's misery."

"This is not the place to settle our discord," said Robert. "Come upstairs and get yourself into dry clothes. You must consider the child!"

"I constantly consider *my* child!" retorted Almodis. The women gathered up their wine-stained and muddied skirts and clambered the stairs after Robert. They stumbled out into the hall and, temporarily blinded by stark torch light, stopped to rub their eyes.

Almodis hugged Maura's arm so severely, she felt herself tipping, and cried out in protest, "Almodis, let go!" As her sight cleared, Maura hugged back as tightly, for there before them, leaning cross-armed against the wall and sporting wicked smirks, stood Will and Rufus.

In vain, Maura strove to support Almodis' swooning figure, and exhaled relief as Robert rushed to help. He swept Almodis up into his arms, and hurled a malicious glare and grimace at the unbidden guests before hastening away down the passageway.

The men regarded Maura's gawking with scornful amusement. She flattened against the wall and inched her way along the jutting stones. Once safely out of their reach, she lurched from the wall and dashed after Robert, her mind screeching, *Pray! Pray till your knees are raw and bleeding—for your Domesday has surely come!*

*****

CHAPTER TWENTY-SIX - AN ACCIDENT

In Lord Robert's bedchamber, Almodis lay ashen and inert across the curtainless bed, blanketed only by a patched wool coverlet. Maura shadowed Robert's pacing as they awaited the physician; she wrung her still frigid hands, and her fretting hinged on hysteria. "Why, Lord Robert, why is Rufus here?!"

Robert never lost stride as he muttered, "He arrived with Will last evening."

"Not when, *why*?!" hurled Maura. She tugged at his floor length tunic as her alarm peaked, "Am I to marry Rufus? Is that why he's here?! Tell me! I deserve the truth!"

"No...you will not wed Rufus," replied Robert with disdain. "You and Simon ruined all hopes of that prosperous union."

"Simon, not I."

"Then I suppose," he noted suspiciously, "you've not heard of his release."

"Release!" she exclaimed, feigning shock. Then she griped, "What a pity. I had hoped by now he'd be eternally encased deep underground."

"I wonder..." Robert's skepticism was interrupted by the physician's arrival. During the course of the brief examination, Maura scrutinized Robert's bated expression and recognized genuine concern. "How is she?" Robert implored.

"Cold and weak," answered the physician. His fingers lightly pressed Almodis' protruding belly and pinched at her wet frock. Worry lined his expression. "Why is she wet and when did she last eat?"

"She threw a tantrum," fussed Robert, "and locked herself in the buttery. It was her own cursed idea and—"

"I don't care whose idea it was!" shouted the doctor, scowling. "She'll have dry clothing, warm food, and rest."

"And the child?" pressed Maura.

"The child's overly active, quite likely from distress." He gave Maura's mussed appearance a quick scan. "Were you with the Lady in the buttery?"

"Yes. But my incarceration was not voluntary."

"What goes on here, Robert?"

"It's not your business."

"The household's health is indeed my business! If you don't cease your ludicrous blustering, you may well lose your child and your Lady wife. Now, have Almodis' servants fetch thick pelts, fresh clothing, and an ample supply of hearty food and warm drink. I'll return this evening and I expect to see the Lady tucked up and nourished!"

The physician left. His demand echoed in Maura's mind, and she envisioned a silver tray set lavishly with food and a goblet brimming with warm red wine tainted with heart-stopping poison! This was far too perilous a situation to keep secret. Her fingers cautiously circled Robert's forearm. "My Lord, I have a request concerning Almodis."

"What is it?" he answered tensely.

"While in the cellar, Almodis confessed a worry—that someone's intent on murdering her."

"That incident occurred over a month ago!"

"She frets whoever tried before may try again...only this time she fears they'll use poison."

"Poison?" As if struck, Robert jerked from her touch. "Why poison?! Why does she think poison?"

"I know not, my Lord. Perhaps we can calm her worries by having her food tasted."

"This is absurd! She suffers from nothing more than a pregnant woman's delirium."

"Granted, my Lord, you may be correct. Yet real or imagined, are you willing to risk her life by ignoring her worries?"

His broad palms pressed the air for silence. "I'll consider the matter. However, *I* have far too much to attend to—the wedding preparations, tradesmen's complaints, judgments—I don't see how I can spare a moment to—"

"I can and gladly will, my Lord. I'll see to her complete comfort and safety."

Her concern curbed his fluster. "That's commendable of you, Maura."

"I care for Almodis."

"As...do I," returned Robert hesitantly.

Maura searched his troubled eyes and was touched by their sincerity and resemblance to Simon's. She shifted her gaze to Almodis and whispered, "I know you do," then promptly abandoned the subject. "Rufus frightens me, my Lord. I'm wary of his motives. When last we met, he was...abusive. I beg of you, please allow me my guard."

"Your guard?"

"Yes, Alan. Almodis tells me you assigned him to police the main gates."

"Why did he arrive before you?"

"He came directly from Normandy and the King. William has extended his term of service to me."

"For what reason?"

"Uncle William is well aware of his son's cruelty."

Uncomfortable with her directness, Robert stammered, "Well, you...your man spent far too much of his idle time sniffing round my wife."

"All men appreciate Almodis' beauty and, of that, you should be proud. Alan meant no harm. My Lord, if you intend to present to Hugh of Ryedale a living, breathing bride, I highly suggest you allow me—Alan."

"If I grant you this wish," he answered curtly, "you will *not*, and I repeat *not* come bothering me with any further imagined complaints!"

Maura hung her head in assent and urged, "You have much to do, my Lord. I'll stay with the Lady and instruct her servants."

"Fine..." Again her instant surrender puzzled Robert and his gaze narrowed. "Where's Rose gone to?"

Maura delivered her lie with great conviction, "We quarreled and I won't have her near. I've sent her to her son Richard's home. I wish to begin my married life... unencumbered."

"I admire your decision, Maura," said Robert, taking on his familiar stoic stance. "You're welcome to any chamber on the floor above and will be relieved to find all the doors bolt from the inside. You may fetch your guard when Almodis wakes."

Maura genuflected, took his hand and rested her cheek upon his fingers. "I'm forever grateful to you, my Lord," she coddled.

"Rise," he muttered, his face tense as he shook from her hold and escaped the chamber.

Maura remained on her knees; with clenched hands, she bowed her head, and prayed aloud so God would surely hear. "I beseech thee, Lord, keep Rufus and Will from me and from the Lady. Protect Almodis and her child and send Simon soon!"

Maura tended to Almodis' needs and left her, at the Lady's insistence, in locked seclusion. The Lords were hunting, so she set about the insurmountable chore of making her chosen chamber habitable. She carted buckets of icy water up three flights of stairs from the buttery well and washed with excruciating haste. Her last fresh chemise and tunic felt luxurious, yet failed to warm. The room was devoid of a fire pit, window or loophole, and its crude bulky furnishings were scant and dismal. She plopped upon the rock-hard mattress, winced to the prick of straw poking through her chemise and skirt, and took in her grim surroundings. Dozens of dangling spider webs swayed to a whistling draft rushing under the gap at the door's base. A family of mice romped in the tipped, rusted chamber pot, and the rushes, long since fresh, were fouled with rodent's droppings and other indistinguishable refuse. How offensively similar was Pevensey to Dunheved, she thought—stark and brutal; except Dunheved had at least one redeeming feature—Simon. She shuddered to the ensnaring cold, swiftly donned her cloak, and escaped the bleakness to seek out Alan.

Most times Maura purposely kept shy of the gatehouse and guards, though as she warily approached the crumbling structure, there seemed to be no sentries about. A quick glance through the slim entrance way revealed a slumped disheveled figure crouched in the corner, dozing. "Alan," she called softly, then ventured louder, "Alan!" He shook from slumber and raised a quizzical face to her beaming one. At once he was on his feet and in her arms. "I've missed you so," gushed Maura, easing her hold.

"I was worried," he replied, with a light touch to her hair. "My fellow sentries told me of your trouble with Lord Robert. Were you hurt?"

"No, only confused." She stepped back and cracked a knowing grin. "I spent the entire night in the buttery with Almodis, and she confided to me your time together."

"Our too short time together," Alan groused, scratching his beard in annoyance.

"Well..." Maura gushed, "I aim to make it longer. Lord Robert has agreed to allow me—you!"

His jaw dropped, then closed to ask, "And how did you get him to agree to your request?"

"I grovel well."

Alan's exuberant hug swept her from the floor and he planted a grateful kiss on her cheek.

"So I see you're fond of the Lady," Maura quipped slyly as he set her down. His scarlet blush confirmed her suspicion and she merrily continued, "Well, she seems equally entranced with you. Though, Alan, I must warn—take care. Lord Robert is leery of your intentions. Above all, be subtle." She grabbed his hand and playfully coaxed him from the gatehouse. A group of returning guards snickered at their antics as Maura boomed her insistence, "Come!"

"Where?" Alan chuckled as he stumbled behind.

"You must help me snare a rat."

"Rufus or Will?"

"Unfortunately neither. One of the nicer kind, with whiskers and a longer tail."

Alan's feelings of futility vanished, and Maura's sense of security returned as they laughed and gamboled hand in hand to the keep.

A short while later Maura tapped on Almodis' door, nudged it open, and called in an excited whisper, "Almodis, it's Maura. May I enter?"

"Yes, come," Almodis dully answered.

Maura noticed Almodis' back faced the door, and her attention was intently focused on her braiding. Maura beckoned to Alan and Godfrey and, on tiptoe, they stole into the chamber to Maura's mysterious announcement, "I've brought you a present."

"And now it is *I* who's not in the mood for games," Almodis answered crossly, and Maura's giggle made her toss her comb and whirl round to reprimand. The vision of her beaming friend, eased her glower to a tender smile. Her admiring gaze promptly settled on Alan. "Alan, how did you convince—"

"It seems," he chimed, boldly stepping forward, "I am once again Maura's guard." Her hand he drew to his lips, and he murmured with an enticing wink, "However, I am not the present Maura speaks of, my Lady. Your gift is here!" He produced from behind his back a clumsily constructed wooden cage; out its small air hole poked a sharp, wiggly nose. "We've christened him Will!" proclaimed Alan.

Almodis' hands stifled her laugh. "I must say," she burbled, "I am immensely overwhelmed by your generosity!"

"Actually," clarified Alan, "Godfrey snagged him. I built the cage."

Gingerly, she took hold of the cage's handle and, at sight of Will's twitchy nose, threw back her head and let out a heartier laugh; her friends vibrantly shared in her cheer.

Alan wiped a giddy tear as his gaze rested once more upon Almodis. Her olive skin radiated joy, yet his worry was drawn to a bruise smudging her cheek. Protectiveness and empathy surged within him, and he linked his arm to hers and gently suggested, "My Lady, would you care to stroll?"

"I would love to," she answered demurely.

Godfrey offered Maura his arm, and the foursome escaped the baleful keep. The meager sunlight allowed them to comfortably roam the battlements. The puddles' glare stung Maura's eyes and she broke from the group and wandered to the ledge. She shaded her eyes and searched out beyond the tumultuous waves. From the west, monstrous black clouds encroached, threatening to blot the cheering light; from the east, only a few brazen ships dared challenge the ensuing tempest and she fretted—which one carried Simon? Only three days remained till her wedding. When would he come...*when*?! She sighed and, chewing on the nub of a nail, shifted her worry to Almodis and Alan. Framed by the mottled sky, their cautious posturing sizzled with bridled passion. Maura's enthusiasm for their budding affection sobered as she realized the extreme peril of their meeting. Then again, the Lords were away, the couple was chaperoned, and they more than deserved their fleeting moment of bliss. A twinge of jealousy stabbed her as she watched Alan delicately stroke the bruise on Almodis' cheek; the Lady's graceful fingers covered his, and her dazzling smile instantly erased his concern.

*****

Supper that evening was a doleful affair. At the dais, Lord Robert sat erect and gruff, flanked by Almodis and Maura. The guards hovered protectively over their charges, their fingers circling the hilts of broad swords, and Will the rat frenziedly scratched for freedom. His cage sat to the fore of Almodis' trencher, the thick slice of bread heaped high with a noxious fishy paste.

"This is preposterous!" fumed Robert. "I absolutely refuse to dine with a rat!"

"Not so preposterous, my Lord," countered Almodis. "Maura mentioned how you were once wary of poison."

Robert turned a fuddled expression Maura's direction, and she innocently explained, "I told her the tale of Mabel, my Lord."

With Robert's attention elsewhere, Almodis chanced a flirtatious glimpse of Alan, who in turn shifted smiling eyes her way. She lowered a wry smile to the smelly stew, pinched off pieces of fish loaf, and dangled them before the air hole. Will's sniffing nose instantly popped forth and his long teeth clicked avariciously.

"No, Almodis!" blared Robert. "I won't agree to this outrage."

"He eats with us or I don't eat at all!" she snapped back.

Robert bristled to her retort and aimed his glare at the center of the room, announcing peevishly, "Why is there no fire?"

"Because there's no cut wood," nagged Almodis. She chirped endearments to her rodent and thrust more crumbs through the vent.

"And why not?" demanded Robert.

"The woodman's ax broke and you refused him funds to purchase a new one."

"I was not alerted to the problem."

"I alerted you, he alerted you, his wife and children alerted you—"

"Enough, Almodis!" railed Robert. He bellowed and his fist rocked the dais. "Remove that cage immediately!"

Maura smiled inwardly at their wrangling. The groan of the hall's doors spoiled her hunger and mirth. In loped baying hounds, four squires, two husky guards and, strutting behind the boisterous parade, came Will and Rufus. They joked and chortled as they whipped off their cloaks and gloves, tossed them to the squires, and jauntily approached the dais. Robert rose with a stern yet cautious air; the guards straightened in defiance; the women, agape and pale, dropped their spoons. Almodis swiftly hid the cage.

"My, my, aren't we a festive crew!" Will snidely observed.

Robert cocked his chin and declared, "You may join us if, and only if, you two can behave yourselves."

"Yes, Father *dear*," Will flippantly assured. "As always, I will strive to obey." He swaggered to Almodis' side and jerked her hand to his lips. She yanked it back and disgustingly swished away his kiss in her washing bowl. Will sniggered, "Mother, you look radiant and so...puffed out. You bring to mind images of the Madonna."

Rufus, heady with power, lumbered up to Maura. She scooted nearer to Robert and cringed to Rufus' sneering yell, "It seems, Cousin Will, we make the ladies nervous!"

"Will!" berated Robert from behind his tall chair. "Come here at once!"

Rufus sat and stole Maura's meal. His squinty eyes devoured her as his fat lips gobbled up the slop. She challenged his glare and fought to still her trembling.

Will joined his father and Robert grumbled, "I won't have that repulsive lout in my home!"

"Father..." Will began smugly, "casting him out would not be wise politically, for you host the next King of England."

"Rubbish!" scowled Robert.

"On numerous occasions, you've admitted the inevitable yourself."

"I care not whom I host!" barked Robert. "He won't disrupt my household or bully Maura."

Will reeked sarcasm as he sneered, "And what makes you suddenly so tender and caring toward the bitch, when just a month ago you were willing to sacrifice her hide to the beast?"

"She alone shows me respect!"

"Respect? How amusing, Father. My spies shared with me an interesting observation—a woman too closely resembling our dear, innocent, obedient Maura was spotted at a siege site north of Rouen. If I recall correctly, you had ordered her to remain at Winchester. I suggest you question her about the incident. But now, my Liege, I'm famished."

"Why did you leave Mortain?" pressed Robert, catching Will's arm.

"I was bored...and you were in no danger."

"I needed you!"

"No, Father...not me, never me." Will captured the chair beside Almodis, hung on her arm and flagrantly goaded, "What ails you, *Mother*? You're so ashen and fidgety. Perhaps your problems lie with the heavy load you carry." His fingers secretly crept her belly and dug deep to his hissed whisper, "If you refuse to rid yourself of your burden, then I'll have to perform the dirty deed myself."

"You harm my child and you destroy yourself," Almodis hissed back.

"And if I allow this birth, I get nothing."

"You haven't been disinherited...yet."

"I aim to make certain I won't be." Will stirred her pie and stuck the spoon brimmed with congealed sauce to her lips. "Why, your food grows cold," he noted with sickening sweetness. "Let me help you eat. After all, your child's welfare is of the utmost importance to me."

She batted the spoon away, splattering cod and soaked crust over the dais, across Will's face, and down his sleeve. "Bitch!" he roared, heaving from his chair. He grabbed a serviette and swabbed furiously at his face and once impeccable clothes, spreading the stain and whining, "Father, your Lady wife ruined my clothes and I was only trying to cheer—"

"Stop your sniveling and move!" barked Robert.

Will stomped to the opposite end of the dais and slumped churlishly into a chair by Rufus. A servant set a trencher before him and dashed away. He attacked his meal and shot a murderous glare Almodis' way...but what was this? Almodis did not return his bile. Instead she rested her mawkish gaze on Maura's guard and the oaf returned her insipidness! Will beamed inwardly as treasonous plots began to take seed in his ever-scheming mind. Ridding himself of the whore and child could ultimately prove, with the oaf's help of course, vastly simpler than he thought it would be.

Rufus' irritation at last exploded to Maura's biting stare. "Stop your gawking!"

"Why are you here?!" she hollered with equal hostility.

He smiled lewdly; pieces of fish clung to his rotted teeth, clotted his beard, and spewed through the air as he spluttered, "I...I missed you, and..." He jabbed a stubby fingertip at her nose. "You owe me money!"

"Money?" Robert whipped his head to the commotion. "What money?"

"Maura has a debt to repay."

"Why would you need to borrow money, Maura?" pressured Robert.

Rufus mumbled darkly in her ear, "You needn't fret, my bold Lady. I won't betray your secrets, at least not here. There is bound to be a better place and time for the grand revelation."

"Maura, I asked you a question!" shouted Robert. "Why did you need money?!"

Her belly lurched to Rufus' foul fumes and her jaw stayed tightly clenched. Simpering, Rufus answered for her, "The Lady is clearly too overwrought with shame to admit her lapse of memory, Uncle."

"You'll get your cursed money!" railed Robert. "And then you'll go!"

"I'll stay for the wedding!" brayed Rufus, rising.

"You'll not hound Maura."

"That's certainly not my intention, dearest Uncle," Rufus replied too smarmily. "I *truly* adore weddings."

"If I command you to go, you go!"

"No one commands me, least of all you...you wrinkled old worm!" Rufus plopped into his seat and stuffed his mouth too full. He chomped on a fish bone, choked, howled, and hurled his bowl into the empty fire pit. The hounds sprang after it, snarling and drooling in their battle to win its contents.

Robert stood, straightened his tunic, and staidly directed, "Alan, escort the FitzRoy from the hall!"

Maura shot up from her seat; her jarring motion provoked Rufus to grab a table knife. Almodis glimpsed the weapon's sheen and shoved clumsily from the table, crying in alarm, "Alan, he has a knife! Stop him!"

Alan unsheathed his sword as Rufus swiped his puny dagger at Maura's face. She ducked and lurched backwards, toppling her chair to the floor and herself into Robert's clutch. Alan smoothly stepped into the crux of the ruckus, leant forward on his sword's hilt, and warned, "I wouldn't bother, my Lord, for my weapon is far larger than yours."

Almodis' burst a cutting laugh. Robert set Maura back on her feet, lifted her chair back up and, hiding his grin, mumbled relief, "Well done, Alan." Godfrey's thin lips curled up their corners, and Will snickered. Maura, though, gripped the edge of the dais for balance and silently screamed at them to stop—for she knew too intimately the dire consequences of taunting Rufus.

Rufus flung his knife and gestured wildly. "You mangy scum! No one mocks *me*! You will all suffer for your insolence." He swept a scathing glare cross the dais, then focused sardonically on Will.

Will swiftly averted his smile. "It *was* amusing, Rufus," he mumbled casually.

"No one mocked you, Rufus," argued Robert. "You ridiculed yourself. Now...get out!"

"Come, Cousin," Will said, sprouting a cloying grin. "We'll visit the village alehouse, where we're certain to find more gracious food and...*company*." He held the door wide for Rufus' storming figure, and cast one final grave look at Almodis before striding after his boys and hounds.

Almodis' hysterics almost pitched her from her chair.

"Almodis, calm yourself!" scolded Robert.

She wiped gleeful tears and gasped, "I'm trying, but...but that was the most hilarious scene I've ever witnessed. Alan, you were absolutely magnificent!"

Alan nodded his thanks and returned to his station, Godfrey shifted slightly his rigid stance, and Maura eased back into her chair with a ragged sigh.

"While Almodis is composing herself," said Robert pointedly to Maura, "You will tell me the reason for your journey to Normandy."

The unexpected query made her gulp and she frantically racked her mind for a placating answer; one that would concur with any rumors Robert might have heard. She stammered to stall her reply, "I...I... journeyed there to...to..."

"I'm waiting," said Robert, irked.

She squeezed shut her eyes and let her mouth rescue her; miraculously, the saving words burst forth, "...to visit Henry."

"Henry?" Thoroughly muddled, Robert asked, "Henry FitzRoy?"

"Yes, my Lord. Rufus loaned me money to finance my trip."

"Why would you want to visit Henry?"

"Henry and I...enjoy each other."

All present gaped at Maura's startling confession. Robert reddened and roared, "You what?!"

"It was a mere tryst, nothing more, my Lord," Maura stressed. "We meet occasionally. Henry heard I was soon to wed and enticed me to spend a fortnight with him at Rouen. I agreed, considering it might be the last opportunity for me to sample the passion only he—"

"Spare me the details!" Robert interjected sharply. "Is there a chance you're pregnant?"

"No, my Lord," she answered accusingly, "that worry was taken care of long ago."

A pall of guilt tempered Robert's scowl; he softened his tone and questioned on, "A mere tryst, you say?"

"Yes, quick and easily forgotten. He may, however, arrive for the wedding."

"I trust he'll make no trouble?"

"No, my Lord."

"Then he will be welcome," said Robert, and he added thoughtfully, "I rather enjoy Henry's company." He stood to leave and imparted to the group his somber wish, "Let us pray that the remainder of the evening proves less exciting than supper. Maura, come morn you will make confession to the Priest for your sins of disobedience and...well...for the others as well."

"Yes, my Lord," replied Maura, bowing her head. She stayed submissive till he had departed, then rose haltingly to deliver her grave portent. "It was foolish to taunt Rufus. Now every one of you is his enemy. And when he strikes, he'll do so brutally and without warning. Never, *never* find yourself alone..."

A ponderous gloom plagued each resident as they retired to their chambers. Maura's vial of vervain, and the calming vision of Alan curled up on a pallet inside her door enabled her to sleep somewhat soundly. Almodis nudged her snoring husband for space on their slim bed and grieved over the hour and means of her death. And Godfrey tossed fitfully on his mat spread outside the Lord's bedchamber door, swatting away clambering mice.

*****

Inside Will's conspicuously lavish bedchamber located down the passageway from the great hall, Will and Rufus whispered plots while reposing upon a canopied feather bed, stacked high with pelts. "In the hall at supper, I glimpsed an intriguing and possibly damning incident," mentioned Will.

"As did I—*your* disloyalty." Rufus stole a fur off Will and draped it atop his portly form.

Will ignored Rufus' barb, poured himself wine, and continued with mystery, "I caught a secret look pass between Almodis and Maura's guard."

"She flirts with anything in braies."

"No, that soulful glance dripped more than lust."

Rufus huffed and rolled away. His impatient wriggling came close to rocking Will off the bed as he grumbled, "What do I care who the whore beds?"

"Oh, but *I* care...I care tremendously," said Will. "If she's stupid enough to spread for a guard, she will ultimately destroy herself. And I've been contemplating a way to hasten that destruction."

Rufus turned attentively. "How?"

"I'll arrange for Father to catch the lovers entangled in a treasonous act."

Rufus nuzzled back into his pillows and mumbled groggily, "I'm becoming quite bored with your petty schemes of revenge. You promised me hunting."

"And we will hunt—tomorrow. Stay by me, Rufus. You are vital to the brilliance of my plan."

"In what way?" Rufus asked, prying one eye wide.

"I won't say as yet." Will finished his wine and scorned, "And I'm growing equally as bored with your atrocious behavior. I did not invite you here to bully Maura, nor to disrupt her wedding! From the paltry union, I'm to receive my first fiefdom—Helmsley Manor will belong solely to me! A promising hideaway in which to carouse, eh, Rufus?"

Rufus grunted.

"You can do what you please with her *after* the wedding," said Will. "The ceremony, however, will proceed as arranged. Do you hear, Rufus?" Will rolled his eyes to Rufus' ingratiating snore, hugged his knees close, and wickedly speculated—how to eliminate Almodis? First, he decided, he must rid her of her lap dog.

*****

"Simon...I'm hungry, and when I get hungry, I become extremely grumpy," warned Henry, leaning impatiently against the door to a sleeping chamber in a monastery located in the coastal village of Dieppe.

"I am well aware of the extent of your grumpiness, Henry. Have patience," muttered Simon. He sat before a wobbly table, hunched over an unrolled parchment, scripting carefully.

"What are you doing that's so damned important?"

"I'm making a copy of the marriage writ and substituting your name for mine," casually answered Simon.

"You're doing what?!" gasped Henry, as he snatched up the document to check Simon's outlandish admission.

Simon grabbed it back and motioned to the opposite chair. "Sit and I'll explain."

"But Simon..." protested Henry in a desperate whine, "I don't want to marry Maura!"

"Heaven forbid," sighed Simon, sticking the quill in the ink well. "Before I explain my scheme, I must thank you for being so helpful on our journey."

"And you were so dubious," scoffed Henry as he lounged on the chair opposite.

"Do you honestly blame me? No, I must say that on this occasion you've definitely proved me wrong. We would never have reached the coast so swiftly had it not been for your intimate knowledge of the back roads of Normandy."

Henry drummed his fingers restlessly on the tabletop. "Simon, stop your drivel and get on with it."

"'*It*'?" Amused by Henry's irritation, Simon continued to nettle. "What, pray tell, is '*it*'? Tell me, Henry, what do you believe to be my father's greatest weakness?"

"His greed," Henry replied without hesitation.

"Excellent. Now, what's your greatest strength?"

With a lusty grin, Henry began, "Why, my—"

"No!" cut in Simon, "I'm speaking in diplomatic terms."

"Oh, my tongue," answered Henry, disappointed.

"Exactly!"

Henry scowled and squirmed. "Simon, you're rambling again."

"I apologize." Simon chuckled and started to rise. "I can hear your grumbling belly from here. We'll eat."

"No, we'll stay awhile," protested Henry. "You've intrigued me. Sit back down and share your scheme."

Simon perched on the edge of his seat and began, suspense hiking his voice, "If I barge into Pevensey demanding Maura, I'll be promptly executed. Yet Father is fond of you and knows little of our friendship. Braced with this document, you will convince Robert of your desire to make Maura your wife. Your flair for the dramatic should make your chore an easy one." Simon dusted the ink, blew off the excess powder, and went on, "Tell Robert that William is rewarding you for bravery, obedience, whatever, by permitting you your choice of a bride. You ask no dowry and will promise in return for her hand—"

"Simon..." Henry interrupted, "I have nothing to give."

"It's a ruse, Henry, only a ruse. Property...you'll pledge property."

Henry pitched back in exasperation. "What property?"

"Choice plots in Normandy when you become Duke."

"Simon!" Henry stood aghast and admonished, "You've gone too far. You speak treason!"

Simon rose in challenge and gestured sharply at the documents. "All this is Robert's punishment for tricking your father. Any lie he hears is of no consequence!"

Henry dropped his glare to the table and nervously fingered the scrolls. "I'm not certain about this, Simon. What if, after the deliberations, Robert refuses me?"

"Father's no fool. Your offerings far outweigh Hugh of Ryedale's. In any event, you won't be present to hear his decision. While he's mulling over your prospects, you and Maura will sneak away. I'll meet you in the stables, we'll bribe the gatehouse sentries, and run."

"It's far too simple," said Henry, wagging his head.

"Perhaps...If you can devise a better scheme by midday tomorrow, I'll be more than willing to listen."

"What of *my* guards?" Henry asked, ignoring Simon's challenge.

"You take two, I'll keep two."

"And if something goes frightfully wrong?"

"Then we'll take up arms."

"We can't defeat him, Simon," Henry stressed.

"I'm painfully aware of that," snorted Simon. "I *can,* however, outwit him." He stacked and rolled the parchments while addressing Henry's uneasy expression, "There is an element of danger involved and I'll understand if you'd rather not—"

"That's not the problem, Simon," countered Henry. "You know how I relish a challenge, especially an intellectual one, and I have every confidence in myself and in you. Then there's Maura—According to you she sees me as a steaming pile of dung. What if *she* refuses to cooperate?"

Simon laughed. "No, Henry, *I* see you as a steaming pile of dung. Maura speaks of you as 'sweet'. When you greet her, whisper that I'm waiting in the stables, and she'll cooperate fully with your direction...well, within reason."

"Isn't that overly presumptuous of you?"

"I know my betrothed well. Come, we'll talk more at supper."

They left the sleeping compound and sprinted under an open trellis on their hurry to the refectory. Driving rain and wind beat at the fragile structure, whipping vines and unearthing bushes. As they stumbled into the sanctuary, Henry breathlessly fretted, "If this tempest keeps on, we won't be sailing anywhere."

Simon jingled the King's gift of coins dangling from his belt. "If need be, we'll use these to bribe the ship's captain. I *will* arrive at Pevensey by tomorrow dusk. I have to."

Henry again wagged his head and trailed Simon into the kitchen, muttering, "How well do you swim, Simon?"

*****

How did I come to be trapped here? Maura repeatedly asked herself as she galloped madly after the hunters through muddy bogs, across swollen creeks, and over stinging brambles. The troop of horses and hounds before her faded in the dusky torrent. Alan turned in his saddle, calling and waving her faster. She kicked her sluggish mare. A whipping gale tried to steal her cloak and, as she wrestled with her hood and shielded her face from the rain, she reflected back upon the whirlwind morning. Almodis and her seamstress had woken her at dawn for the fitting of her wedding dress. How hard she'd fought to keep from snatching the shears from the seamstress and slashing it to shreds! Then Lord Robert had happened by, announcing she was to accompany him on the hunt, followed by her usual pleas of *why*, and his familiar harsh retorts. And here she was, miserably soaked and chilled, with a wall of water cascading off her hood, chasing an elite gang of fools. Her mount's chest heaved and his mouth slavered. This was no hunt, it was a race. Only—a race to where? The party seemed purposely to be evading her. Urgent hoof beats approached from behind and Maura twisted to see Godfrey charging out of the fog. She reined her steed, her alarm spiraling as Godfrey trotted to her side.

"I feared I'd never catch you!" he shouted over the noisy rain.

"What's happened?"

"The Lady has ordered me to accompany you."

"Then who is with Almodis?"

Alan suddenly appeared and demanded to Godfrey, "Why are you here?"

"Robert's men guard Almodis," he explained.

"Are you certain?" Maura asked, askance. "Did you see her?"

"Robert's guards are here! The Lady is alone!" exclaimed Alan; his balled fists clenched his reins and forcefully jerked his horse around. In a flash, he was gone.

"Alan, wait!" Maura screamed too late. "Should we follow, Godfrey?"

"No harm will befall the Lady with Alan at her side," said he. "We'd best ride on as if nothing's amiss. Where have they gone?"

"Ahead...somewhere," she answered, her worried stare continuing down the darkening lane after Alan.

"Come, my Lady, we must find them."

"I want to go back."

"No...We dare not make Lord Robert angry. Come."

*****

In the Lord's bedchamber, Almodis sat propped up in bed, cocooned in her meager blanket and taunted by fears and fantasies. She had tested the door's bolt countless times; it held fast. Will, the rat, had assured her wine safe to drink, yet as she gulped it, the creeping dread returned. Godfrey had disappeared, and he would never willingly desert her! "What joy and terror you've given me thus far," she anguished to her child. Her hands caressed her belly, then hugged her arms. "Will I ever know you, hold you, love you?" To calm her upset, she gulped more wine and forced her frayed thoughts to Alan. A curious warmth enveloped her and she smiled inwardly at the coy image of herself in his stalwart presence—a shy, bumbling, tongue-tied girl. An urgent pounding shattered the bittersweet vision. Almodis bolted from the bed and huddled terrified in the corner.

A loud whisper, "My Lady...My Lady Almodis! It's Alan. Please, let me in!" sent her racing for the door.

Her fingers froze inches from the bolt. She daren't risk deception and asked haltingly, "How...how can I be certain you are who you say?"

"Outside of my brother, Nicolas' forge you touched my hand."

Whimpering joy, she fumbled frantically with the bolt, and cracked open the door just enough to let him slip through. She clung to him, nuzzling against his chest and sobbing, "Why? Why am I alone?"

"You are not alone, and will never be again," he tenderly assured. His broad arms wrapped her quaking shoulders and boldly pressed her closer.

She lifted dark liquid eyes to his careworn face. "I don't want to die!"

"Why do you say such things?"

"Will's threatened me!" she moaned. "He will murder me, my child—"

"No, I will never allow that to happen...never!"

"Alan, how can you stop—"

His lips hushed her panic and hers hungrily answered; she firmed their clutch, increasing the pressure of their first perilous kiss, then she stiffened and cried out, "I've no right to endanger you!"

"I give you the right!"

"No!" she wailed, straining in his hold.

He held tight and murmured, "I am not your enemy, Almodis. Trust in me, let me help you."

Almodis' tumult threatened her sanity; she craved him so, but knew her need could kill! She ceased her useless struggling and surrendered to the bed. Alan stretched out by her side and risked a touch to her hair.

A brushing kiss to his palm began her trembling confession, "I've never known a man such as you, strong though so tender. You frighten me."

"And it's simply amazing and not a little frightening that I lie next to the magnificent Lady Almodis." He caressed her cheek and ached to the misery in her gaunt face and hollowed, spooked eyes. His finger neatened an escaped lock of her hair as he worried, "You're so pale."

"I can't sleep," she choked. "I won't eat. He'll poison me!"

"If he dares harass you again, I'll kill him!"

She searched his tenacious expression and managed a weak grin. "I must admit, I would thrill to his annihilation. But Alan, such a feat would only worsen our dilemma. Don't taint our moment with talk of vermin. I need to feel the strength of your arms once more." Content to lie still in his embrace, she listened to his soothing heartbeat while tracing the rough weave of his sleeve. "I'm certain you've held countless women in your clutch," she remarked with a knowing grin.

"None that I would dream of later. Only your image has stayed to haunt and drive me mad with envy when I think of you and—"

"And who?" she asked tensely.

"Lord Robert."

"Oh no, Alan," she scoffed in a chuckle. "He's but a lump who shares my bed...very infrequently. And while with him, I dream only of you."

His palm covered most of her swollen belly. "Yet he's the cause of this."

"I choose to believe I conceived this child alone." Her fingers laced through his as she hesitantly noted, "You've no doubt heard mention of my many amorous exploits."

"All I've heard I've ignored, Almodis," he murmured, taking her face in his hands, "we've both suffered sad, empty lives. It seems we've been given the opportunity, however brief, to change our fates."

Almodis' belly blocked their attempt to draw closer and they glanced wistfully down at their barrier. "Even *he* keeps us apart," sulked Almodis.

"Oh, no," Alan disagreed with an endearing gaze, "it was he who brought us together, and he surely won't deny us a kiss."

Their eyes brimmed joyful tears as they enjoyed their second lingering kiss. His lips left hers to taste the long length of her neck. The baby's response was a painful lurch, and soured her ecstatic sigh to a pained groan.

Alan too felt the sharp kick and cradled Almodis snugly as she tearfully fretted, "I fear with all that's happened, he'll come early. How patient can we be?"

"I, my sweet Lady," he declared emphatically, "am willing to wait for you...forever."

*****

The mist at last lifted, yet the deluge teemed on. Maura and Godfrey continued to comb futilely through wood and bog for the band of hunters. Maura waved a beckoning hand and Godfrey trotted to her side. "We had best return to the castle before we become hopelessly lost," she wearily suggested. "Clearly, they neither want nor need our company, and I'm concerned about Almodis and Alan."

"As am I," agreed Godfrey.

Side by side, they cantered back to the remnant of road. Maura paused a long moment to mop water from her eyes and froze to the sound of a familiar whir followed by a dull, sickening thud. She gaped in horror at Godfrey's agonized expression. He reached out a desperate hand; she stretched long, but failed to catch his tipping figure as he splashed face down in a puddle, an arrow jutting out of the nape of his neck.

*****

CHAPTER TWENTY-SEVEN - THE DEVILS' LAIR

Maura yanked futilely at Godfrey's writhing torso. She held his head up from the water and, between panicked sobs, comforted, "You're not alone, Godfrey. I'm here and won't leave you. Soon the pain will go...soon..." Her solace ended as death violently took him—blood pulsed and gurgled out his throat, his eyes rolled in their sockets, his body arched for an endless moment, then went limp in her arms.

"Lord Robert!" she wailed to the heavens. "Help us, Lord Robert!" An arrow gouging the ground by the puddle stifled her plea. A second impaled the muck at her side and sent her scrambling for a nearby bush. Godfrey's death grip on her wrist held fast. She moaned, raking at his rigid fingers as lethal darts rained down upon her. One neatly ripped the sleeve of her tunic, grazed her arm, and pinned her cloak to the ground. Shrieking, she thrashed and strained, battling her bindings and the eerie burning that raced her veins, and dulled her sight. Her fight was swiftly lost and she sagged into the muck, gasping a whisper, "It's a scratch...only a scratch...only a..."

"Maura...Maura! Wake up. Wake up!" A gloved hand struck her cheek and the harsh and urgent voice commanded louder, "Wake up!"

Maura's eye lids fluttered, then opened to Robert's sharpening features. "Lo...Lord Rob..." she slurred, floundering to sit.

Her head lolled backward; Robert seized the neck of her cloak and roughly supported her, yelling impatiently, "You'll tell me what's happened here!"

She directed her terror beyond Robert and flinched to the imposing troop of hunters looming above her. A swift glance to her side revealed Godfrey still beside her, his grip relaxed, and his face submerged in the puddle. All arrows save the one in his neck had mysteriously vanished.

"Where's your guard gone to?!" Robert's slap made her cry out; he raised his hand to strike again and threatened, "You'll answer or be punished!"

"He...he..." she stuttered, her lips refusing to obey.

Will swaggered forward and spoke snidely, "I believe he may have returned to the castle to seek out your virtuous wife, Father."

Robert tensed and reddened, his tone turned crazed, "Is that where he's gone?!" He hauled her from the ground and shook her hard. "Answer me!"

"No!" she wailed. Her knees buckled and vision blurred. She hugged his arm for support and groaned as her insides blazed.

"Stop your hysterics!" roared Robert. "I'll discover for myself where Alan's gone!" Robert pried her biting grip from his arm and she dropped heavily to the ground. He swung into his saddle and turned an uncertain eye upon his smirking son. "Have your men return Godfrey's body to the keep. Then fetch Rufus. We mustn't let a similar accident befall the Prince."

In vain Maura strained to hear Robert's speech. Her sight cleared sufficiently to show him on his horse, leaving—leaving her here with this band of blood-thirsty vultures, eager to pounce and rip her to shreds! She struggled to her feet and stumbled in his direction. Miraculously, she found her voice. "Stop!" she screamed, "Lord Robert, don't leave me!"

Robert's already spooked horse reared as Maura clawed at her Liege's mud-caked boot. "God's blood, woman!" he shouted. "Unhand me!" Sharp kicks failed to block her assault and he brandished his crop to strike.

"I beg of you, my...my Lord," she implored with outstretched palms. "Help me...Take me with you. Don't desert me!"

Maura's odd groveling and glazed expression tempered his rage. "Help her up!" he brusquely commanded to his guard, and once she was safely settled before him, his whisper betrayed concern, "Rest back against my shoulder. We'll soon be home."

Robert's swift surrender riled Will. He yanked his guard close and hissed, "You inept idiot. You missed your aim!"

"No, my Lord," his slavish sentry whined, "I'm certain I grazed her arm!"

"Pray her mind stays clouded on their jaunt back to the keep," heeded Will, "for if she dares utter a ruinous word, I'll personally force a stronger potion down your throat. One that will dim your tiny mind forever!"

Maura's consciousness wavered on the return journey. At last the keep's battlements broke through the hovering clouds, and she somehow found the strength to blurt, "It was Will who tried to murder Almodis. He wants your child dead."

The alarming accusation almost rocked Robert from the saddle. He spurred his mount faster, no longer caring what treason he'd discover in his bedchamber. He would save his wife!

Maura chased Robert across the great hall, swiping at his tunic, beseeching, "Spare them! Alan protects her! They are innocent!" She tripped to the rushes beside the dais and made no attempt to rise; her final plea rattled the rafters, "Stop the torture!"

Robert hesitated to her wail, then, with clenched fists and jaw, quickened his pace. His bellow, "Guards!" instantly rallied his troops and Maura's hope for mercy died as boots tramped past her bleary eyes—their destination—the Lord's bedchamber!

The advancing commotion drove Almodis and Alan from the bed. "Run!" Almodis cried, shoving Alan toward the door. "Save yourself!"

He drew her back into his arms. "No...I stay!"

Their clutch strengthened to Robert's bellicose command, "Break the lock!" The force of the guard's kick snapped the bolt like a stick of kindling.

Alan shielded Almodis cowering body. "Your...your Lady wife was threatened, my...my Lord," he stammered in defense. "She was alone...Her guard—"

"Lies dead yonder, an arrow stuck in his throat! Liars!" roared Robert. His fist cut through the air and the men sprang upon Alan. Their ferocious wrestling barely restrainied him, as Robert backed Almodis in a corner and stabbed a damning finger in her face. "The great whore! Yes, my sweet wife, I've heard it all! And now I add the title murderess, for your treason killed Godfrey!"

"No!" Almodis fell to her knees, groping madly at his cloak, wailing, "Me! Punish me! Spare Maura and Alan, this is not their sin! I lured him here. He came to protect me, nothing more." Her rigid grip crept his tunic as she raved on, "Spare your child. I swear he's yours, I swear!" Horrible sobs buckled her body and tipped her to the floor. Alan tore from the Guards' clinch, swiftly gathered her up and crushed her to his chest.

Robert's fingers fondled his dagger's hilt. Alan's neck was exposed, the throbbing veins clearly visible. It would be so simple, so satisfying to cut and watch the blood flow from his body—simple and fitting. Take his life and hers! Kill them all! For then and only then would his torment leave. Torment and guilt were killing him! Repellent images of his past victims flashed before his clenched eyes—Edith's dark eyes, thick with tears, begging for forgiveness; Maura's haunting stare as Rose carried her battered body from the abbey; Simon, lying serenely upon the prison floor, blood streaming from his ripped back, and always nearby—Will's smug smile. Maura's plea 'stop the torture!' jolted him back to the present. He released the hilt, and slumped against the bedpost, embracing it with the weight of his turmoil. "Take...take her," he rasped.

The guards eagerly advanced. Alan frantically crawled from their shadow, dragging Almodis' body along with him to nowhere. She screamed and beat at him to set her free; his gripping devotion held fast.

Robert's raised hand halted the madness. "N...no," he croaked. "You—Alan—get her from my sight! Hide her...far from here. Send word when the child comes."

The couple sat in stunned silence, then Alan swiftly pulled Almodis up from the floor. She lurched away and flung herself at Robert's feet. Her grateful tears smothered his hands. He heaved from her Judas touch and struck the post. "Go before I murder you both! Take the postern stairs. My guard will provide a horse." His mastery wilted and he collapsed across the bed, mumbling, "Leave me! All of you leave me. I'm tired and I need to rest. Leave me...alone."

Amid the raving discord, Maura heard her name. Her hands climbed the leg of the dais and she turned on her knees to the feeble call, and saw Almodis, her arms outstretched and expression hopeful. Alan urged Almodis on and cast Maura a swift, grateful nod. And then they were gone. Heavy boots clomped again, quaking the floorboards beneath her knees. Will had returned and she alone was left to squelch his treachery. She gripped the dais, hauled herself to her feet, and propelled herself toward the hall's doors. Her palms supported the door's framing and barred Will's flurried approach. "Out of my way!" he hollered.

"No," she hissed back.

"I will hurt you."

"You can't hurt me!"

Will clamped her wrists and yanked; all his might failed to weaken her resolve. Her swift kick to his groin hurtled him backward into his mass of guards. He buckled over and wailed, "Tear her from the door!" Two guards thrust her aside, and Will's bellow, "Find the Lady Almodis!" scattered the rest of his contingent. Alone, he stormed across the great hall, his sword poised to kill.

Maura surged and stumbled between the tables. She swiped hold of Will's cloak and leapt onto his back. Her arm wrapped his neck, and she tensed a strangling grip. He howled in agony, lurching and bucking through the dead coals of the fire pit, unable to shake her free.

Strong and gentle arms plucked Maura from Will's back, and the room whirled madly as they slung her over a broad shoulder. Her crazed wriggling only strengthened her captor's grip. Robert's tormented face drifted past her closing eyes and his faint demand, "Lock her in my chamber," blackened her world once more.

She woke sprawled across her Liege's bed and, sitting too quickly, abruptly collapsed back upon the pillows. Her crazed eyes focused on Robert's curiously rueful expression. She brazenly seized his tunic and jerked him near. "Where is Almodis? Alan?" she barraged. "What have you done to them?!"

"I've sent them away."

"What does that mean?" she wailed, twisting tighter. "Away where?"

"I don't know," mumbled Robert.

"I don't believe you!"

"Believe what you like," he suggested wearily.

"Where's Will?"

"Gone."

"Will he return?"

Robert shrugged and, not easily, pried his tunic from her grip. He studied curiously her fevered complexion and wondered, "What's happened to you? You're like a wild beast."

The burning inside her flared again, causing her to moan and croak, "There were more arrows than the one in Godfrey's neck. One grazed my arm and made me feel so queer."

"Show me." He helped her sit and examined the spot where she pointed. A scratch centered a ruby colored rash. Robert ripped the hole larger and could see no end to the irritation. "Perhaps you cut yourself some other way and imagined—"

"Did I imagine this?" she said hotly, thrusting her punctured cloak in his confused face.

"How fare you now?" he asked, removing the filthy garment.

"Groggy...sick."

"Then you'll rest locked in here this night. My servant will bring your supper. Tomorrow, you will not leave my side."

He started to rise, but she yanked him back and blared, "Will murdered Godfrey and poisoned me!"

"Damn your hysterics!" he spat in disgust. "I've no evidence of Will's wrongdoings, only your leery accusations."

"Then why protect me?"

Robert stood and swatted her fingers from his sleeve, as his mask of indifference returned, and he stated with force, "Nothing will interfere with your wedding." He paused a long moment at the door and turned a bewildered, almost caring expression, her way. Did he beg forgiveness, she wondered—he, who had subjected so many to misery and torture? She searched her soul and found only loathing for the rotted shell of a man who stood before her. He dropped shamed eyes and slipped from the chamber.

Exhaustion threatened, yet she dare not sleep! If she slept, she'd dream the nightmare and there was no one to wake her, to save her from the horrors! She was so horribly alone. The candle's flame served as a distraction. She fixed her eyes upon the wavering light and huddled beneath her cloak to ward off the damp chill. The door creaked and a disembodied hand set a tray in the rushes, then swiftly vanished. Maura's sore belly lurched to the scent of fresh bread and cheese. From beyond the closed door came resonant voices. Would Robert keep her shut away till her wedding? If so, how would Simon find her? Where were Almodis and Alan? Were they dead, was Simon?! Her fidgety fingers twisted her ring round and round as she envisioned the worst—his hewn body sprawled upon a battlefield or floating lifeless on the waves. Almodis had spoken the bitter truth, there was no escaping her fate. In two days, she would wed Hugh of Ryedale and live a safe, secure, and empty life in Yorkshire. And there, guarded forever by Robert's soldiers, she would never see Simon again.

Maura had few tears left to weep as she forced her body off the bed and paced, circling the room till dizziness dropped her back upon the rigid mattress. She focused again on the lone candle. Sharp, disturbing shadows danced the walls, lashing out, luring her to close her eyes and sleep. She pinched her arms, chanting, "...mustn't sleep, I mustn't sleep...mustn't..." The flame suddenly flared, illuminating the chamber and driving off her malevolent surroundings. And with its brilliance came the realization that she needn't dream to know the truth. The blazing nightmare flooded her mind, the enshrouding smoke cleared, and at long last the mystery lifted...

Marc, just a babe, lay unconscious in her arms. At her side lay her father, his hand clamped to her ankle, and his copper beard soaked with blood from the gash that had split his throat. Her mother's severed head gaped at her a few feet away, its lips still twitching from the swiftness of death. The man, his face masked with soot, lorded over Maura. His eyes, limpid pools of pale blue, bore into hers and she shuddered at their savagery. The sword fell—She shielded Marc's body with her own, and tensed to the agony to come. But there was no hurt, only harsh sounds of scuffling. Strong arms wrenched Marc from her grasp; a blanket smothered his screech. She lunged to capture him back, but her father's grip held fast, and forward into the pyre she fell. The same arms that stole Marc caught and swept her up, away from the fire, the man, her parents and—death. She gasped in crisp, clean air and peered quizzically up into Robert's eyes, pale blue and brimming with tender relief. Beside them, squirmed a coughing, squalling Marc, and at their back, her home toppled in the ravenous flames...

Maura shifted forlornly on the bed. How could she have forgotten her parents, the fierceness of their love, how they'd nurtured and died for her?! From a hidden place deep inside her heart came her mother's sweet voice, crooning a lullaby. Maura silently thanked the flame, cuddled close to the blanket, and murmured through tears the words to the simple song, odd lilting words she no longer understood. In little time, she drifted off to sleep—a sleep finally devoid of horrors and so full of love.

*****

A bolt of lightning crackled through the blackened sky and splintered a mooring on the dock at Pevensey. The thunderous peal that followed perilously shook the ramshackle structure. Simon tugged strenuously at Henry's arms, while he, like a stubborn mule, sat on the planks and adamantly refused to budge. "No, Simon!" he whined into the wind, "I won't be murdered by this storm, not for Maura's, yours or anyone else's sake. We'll remain aboard ship till it's done!"

"No!" Simon shouted in extreme protest. "It took forever to cross the channel. There's no time left! We'll gallop to the castle, the lightning won't catch us."

"That's very comforting," Henry noted flippantly as Simon dragged him across the planks to his horse, yanked him to his feet, and forced his foot into the stirrup. "This storm is our punishment..." noted Henry frankly, "for missing Mass. It's Easter and we should be at Mass."

Simon roughly pinched Henry's backside and launched him into his saddle. "Since when did you feel the need for religion?" asked Simon dubiously as he swung into his own saddle.

"Whenever I'm near you, I feel an overwhelming need for God's protection."

Simon patted the scrolls tucked in his belt. "We'll review our strategy in the stable."

"The guards at the main gates may demand the names of all who accompany me," said Henry. "Who will *you* be?"

"A member of your guard."

"Simon, you're far too scrawny to pass as my guard."

"Use your imagination, Henry!" shouted Simon over the tempest. "Call your men. Make haste!"

Henry's brusque wave guided the troop from the docks. They raced after Simon's lead, up the river that had recently been a road, leaping fallen tree limbs and dodging lightning strikes. Simon glimpsed Henry's tremulous expression and worried, was he a fool to trust his cousin? He shrugged away his dread, it was far too late for doubts, for at the end of this treacherous path waited Maura. His anticipation surged to her stirring vision and he spurred his horse faster. It was their fate to be together.

With wiggling impatience, Simon watched Henry masterfully bluff the guards and exhaled relief as the gates parted. The band of rescuers trotted gingerly beneath a line of hauberked soldiers, outfitted for war and poised upon the curtain wall. *Am I expected?* Simon wondered as he reined his mount and glanced eagerly up at the keep's walls. His eyes darted from shutter to loophole. The castle refused his craving for a glimpse of her, and he hurried along to catch up with Henry.

The horses huffed as Simon lined them up along the inside of the stable doors. Henry shadowed him, his face twitching trepidation in response to Simon's too rapid review of their plans. "Start your search in the great hall. Convince Father you love Maura and have your father's permission to wed. Tell him if he agrees, he'll be richly rewarded. Do it quickly and, on the ruse of a rendezvous, bring her here."

Henry tossed back his hood and combed through his damp, mussed hair. "I...I've bribed the guards, handsomely I might add. The gates will part for us."

"Excellent."

As he straightened his clothes, Henry's hands shook and his bravado faltered. "Simon," he entreated. "What should I do if—"

Simon cut short his qualms, "If anything should go wrong—*anything,* come directly here." He settled a confident grip on Henry's shoulders, and searched his expression for uncertainty. "Do you have any questions before you proceed?"

"No," said Henry too bluntly.

"Show me your dagger."

Henry exposed his knife, stuck in his belt, and blurted, "And one more...for Maura," as he turned to show another tucked at his back.

"A fine idea. I'm proud of you," praised Simon with an affectionate slap to his cousin's cheek. "Here are the documents. Show Father the false one first, then switch the scrolls and run! I'll wait an hour, no longer, then I'll come find you."

"An hour!" Henry groaned. "But Simon—"

"We must leave before dark! There are few shelters between here and Canterbury. We may be chased, and the condition of the roads makes it imperative we see where we're headed."

Henry gulped a breath and clasped Simon's hand. "I won't fail you."

"Of *that* I'm certain." Simon's bolstering smile and hug partially allayed Henry's worries. Then, flanked by two guards, the FitzRoy strode resolutely from the stable.

*****

In the keep's chapel, Maura's attention to the celebration of the Feast of the Resurrection was often interrupted as she imagined Godfrey's coffin resting in its shallow grave, and wondered gravely—where were Alan, Almodis, Simon? She rose from her knees and abandoned her prayers and the droning priest. Encircled by burly protectors, she wandered glumly to the great hall. There Lord Robert sat at the dais, seemingly entranced by the steep fire roaring before him. She slipped into the chair by his side and quietly thanked the servant for providing her meal. Robert seemed purposely to shun her furtive glances. Maura turned her attention to her cup of wine, hoping the brew would relieve her nausea.

Robert noticed her reluctance to eat and muttered, "How long has it been?"

"My Lord?" she answered.

"When did you last eat?"

"I can't recall." Her spoon nudged cautiously at the bloody slab of meat draping her trencher.

Perturbed, Robert switched their plates. "I've sampled mine and I'm still alive. So eat."

"Where are Will and Rufus?" she asked, continuing her guarded picking.

"I neither know nor care."

Maura set her spoon down and asked without hesitation, "My Lord, did you know my parents?"

The ill-timed query caught Robert mid-chew; he turned wide eyes, swallowed, and answered dryly, "Not intimately."

"Then how did you come to care for Marc and me?"

"No one else would have you!" was his belligerent reply.

"You...you saved us from the fire and the...man." Her moist gaze traveled to the flames and she wondered aloud, "Who murdered my mother and father?"

Robert shuddered at the harrowing memory and stammered, "Yo...your father was...my...one of my better soldiers. I rewarded his allegiance with a manor. Your home was attacked during a Saxon uprising deep in Cornwall. My assistance was called upon and I performed my duty." Restlessness made him squirm and, haltingly, he asked, "What memory do you have of the soldier who struck down your parents?"

"Very little." His dark expression lit slightly to her response, then clouded again as she added, "But his eyes I recall quite vividly."

*****

Will followed Rufus down the passageway leading to the great hall, his mind ever conniving—how to punish Maura for her impudence without resorting to murder? It was a difficult challenge, yet one he could surely meet. He stumbled to Rufus' abrupt halt and exalted bellow, "Henry!"

Henry froze to Rufus' welcome. He waited for the paralyzing tingle to end its creep up his spine, then flashed a garish grin. "Dearest brother!" he gushed, striding forward into Rufus' hearty embrace.

Will's ire erupted at Henry's intrusion. He tugged at the brothers' hug, demanding, "Henry, why are you here?!"

"My, my!" exclaimed Henry, stepping back in awe. He gave Will a sly wink, and continued his enthusiasm, "If it isn't bold cousin Will! I must admit I'm shocked to find you here." His arm fondly hugged Rufus' wide shoulders and, as they swaggered toward the hall's open doors, he turned and flaunted, "If you must know, I represent my father at this grand occasion, although...I've also come to visit for perhaps the last time—"

The men paused inside the door, their figures in shadow. Maura shrank to the two ominously familiar silhouettes, then noticed—a third! Her heart's turbulent pounding lifted her an inch from her seat.

"Maura, my love!" Henry extolled passionately as he strutted forward into the fire's glow, his arms spread wide and beckoning.

It took but an instant for Maura to decipher his drama. Her chair and meal spilled to the rushes as she scrambled over the dais, dashed between the tables, and leapt into her savior's arms. She tightened her clutch to his fervid whisper, "He's waiting in the stable. Follow my lead, squeeze shut your eyes, pretend I'm Simon, and kiss me." Love oozed from her every pore as she crushed her lips to his.

Robert shifted uncomfortably to their unabashed show of lust, then stood and loudly cleared his throat. Their ardor cooled to his third clearing and he nodded. "Henry..."

"Uncle Robert!" boomed Henry, wearing a dazzling smile. "It's simply marvelous to see you again!" Maura and Henry flitted forward, their arms wrapped securely round each other's waists.

Robert grinned at his nephew's exuberance and watched him press a lingering kiss to Maura's palm and murmur with gushing sweetness, "It seems forever since we parted, my sweet love, and I've discovered, I pray not too late, that I...I—" Henry's lovesick eyes darted back to Robert; he dropped to one knee, and postulated in a desperate whine, "Uncle, we must speak on a matter of crucial importance!"

"Of course," replied Robert with surprising mildness. "We'll talk in my chamber."

"I won't leave Maura!" blurted Henry, firming his clutch.

"So bring her."

"I'm grateful, my Lord," said Henry. As Maura guided him past the dais, Henry turned a haughty smirk on Will and Rufus. Inside the Lord's chamber, Henry again swept Maura in his arms and nibbled at her earlobe. A lusty gasp escaped her, then she dissolved with practiced giggles.

Robert settled uneasily in his chair and reminded, "Henry, you mentioned the matter was crucial."

"Oh yes, indeed it is, my Lord! And I heartily apologize. When I'm near your precious Maura, my mind turns to mush." He tasted her lips and spurted, "She's so..." He tasted again and decided, "So...very scrumptious!"

Maura fought to disguise her true chortles by coughing demurely into her palm, then lifted adoring eyes to Henry's, and nuzzled her cheek against his shoulder.

"And...Well," Henry continued, "the matter plainly is—I must have her!"

Robert's fingers impatiently drummed the arms of his chair. "According to Maura you've already done so."

Henry masked his puzzlement with an impish grin. Maura caressed his cheek and turned his face toward hers to explain. "My love, Lord Robert discovered I had journeyed to Normandy. I felt no shame and readily confessed to him our passion."

"But Maura," corrected Robert. "You assured me your passion was temporary and easily forgotten."

"I lied, my Lord," she declared soundly. "I love Henry with my whole heart, soul, and body."

Robert rolled his eyes and dragged his fingers across his bald pate. "Well then, I welcome your presence, Henry. To you, I gratefully relinquish my role as Maura's guardian—and to the both of you, grant my permission to spend these last few days...and nights, together."

Confused, Maura reminded, "My Lord, the wedding's to be celebrated tomorrow."

"The storms have delayed your betrothed. He and his family are sojourning at Berkhamstead and should arrive by the end of the week."

"Lord Robert." Henry straightened and charged, "You insult me! I come not only to *have* the bride, I come to make her *my* bride!"

Maura squeezed Henry's hand and her gaze sweetened with tender admiration. Truly, he was a genius!

Robert asked, slightly intimidated, "Isn't it a bit late to stake your claim?"

"I couldn't get away! I've been battling King Philip at Father's side. When finally I was able to confess my desire, Father consented at once." Henry fumbled inside his cloak for the parchment. He spread it carefully across the bed, gesturing, "My claim lies before you."

"And what of the Yorkshire contract?"

Henry poked at a paragraph, "Father's annulled it here."

Robert rose skeptically from his chair, and made a brief inspection of the flourished document. He didn't read well, yet was able to recognize Henry and Maura's names and his brother's mark. The parchment rolled itself back into a tube, and Robert passed the document back to Henry with his heartfelt apology, "I'm sorry, Henry. I won't benefit in the least from Maura's marriage to a penniless, bachelor knight. I cannot accept this decree."

Henry's eyes shifted restively as he fumbled for his next line. Maura stepped forward to speak; Henry pressed her palm for patience and blurted, "I'm far from penniless, my Lord."

"Explain," was Robert's demand.

"At Father's death—which, if he keeps fighting as he has been of late, shouldn't be long in coming—I become Duke of Normandy!"

Robert's eyes gleamed at the astonishing news and he urged, "Tell me more."

"I ask only for Maura, and if you acquiesce, I intend to bestow on you money, land, jewels, vast political power and more wealth than even *you* can imagine, dearest Uncle."

"And where's the document that proclaims you Duke?" countered Robert.

"You have my word."

"And if that's not sufficient?"

"What a sad soul you'll be if I speak the truth," Henry answered wryly. To Robert's leery expression, he added, "May I ask what pittance you're to receive from Hugh of Ryedale?"

"Quiet!" Robert roared, slumping back in his chair and hiding his distress behind his palms. An excruciatingly long moment passed, then Robert raised narrow eyes to complain shrilly, "Why now, Henry? If only you'd come to me sooner!"

"There wasn't time!" His arms cuddled Maura closer, again they exchanged kisses and adoring gazes. "It wasn't till she had left me to return dutifully to you that I realized how barren my life was without her."

"I've no interest in your over-active urges. I must have assurances!"

Maura could no longer stand idly by. She broke from Henry's hold and boldly argued, "Assurances? Even if Henry exaggerates, he's far wealthier than Hugh! You were willing to risk punishment and my life for a union with Rufus. There's no difference in status between the two brothers, and what's more, you're fond of Henry. He's younger than Rufus, smarter and—"

"Stronger!" Henry staunchly finished. "I will guarantee you this, my Lord, I won't only be Duke, I will be King! And furthermore," he sternly cautioned, "if you don't hand her over to me cordially, I'll take her by force. At a moment's notice, I can amass a rather large army. We have a solid friendship, Robert—don't be a fool and spoil it! Oh yes and, may I add, Uncle..." Henry wrinkled his nose in disgust and pointed to a corner of the room. "I suggest you tend to your rodent problem."

While Robert searched the floor for mice, Henry switched the parchments and noted casually, "They seem to have scurried away." He planted the true document in Robert's hands. "You'll need time alone to consider my overly generous offer. And when we return, I expect to witness your mark gracing Father's declaration." Maura and Henry performed their bows in unison, and left on Henry's gleeful note, "If you have need of us, we can be found in Maura's bed, becoming reacquainted."

Outside the door, a suspicious Will and Rufus blocked the couple's escape route. "What goes on here, little brother?" queried Rufus, askance.

Henry pulled himself erect and gloated, "I've received the Lord's permission to sample the bride before the wedding. Now, if you two don't mind...we'll proceed." They pushed past Rufus, then stopped short before Will's dark and deadly stance.

"We *do* mind, terribly," jeered Will.

"Will," Henry flamboyantly sniped, "don't delay me from what I love most. You're well aware how I relish bragging. If forced to stay, I will definitely feel the need to boast of my recent adventures in Normandy, and they were *so* revealing."

The cousins stood a brittle moment posturing, then Will dropped his glare, stepped aside, and snidely muttered, "We'll meet later."

"Gladly," boomed Henry, laughing. "Shall we make it a tilt?" Henry's snickering echoed through the hall as he, Maura and his guards nimbly ascended the stairs.

Will, snarling curses, stormed to the postern door, twisted the key, locked it, and deposited the key in a purse tied to his belt.

"What are you doing?" bothered Rufus.

"I'm locking their way out. Now, come, we'll wait in my room."

"Wait for what?"

"The stunning conclusion to my scheme."

"I'm starving!"

"We'll feast later. You'll accompany me, now!"

As Rufus humbly followed, he smirked inwardly and considered how he savored watching his insignificant kin fumble through their petty squabbles. Will's stunning scheme could hardly match his own masterful ploy. He'd continue to play the bumbling buffoon till the exact moment arrived for him to unsheathe his invincible prowess and then—all would squirm to his majesty!

Will paused before entering his chamber and beckoned to his squire with a crooked finger. "Come, little one, and listen well...I have a small request to make of you."

Henry and Maura burst into her room. She threw her arms round his neck and vibrantly praised, "Oh, Henry! You were magnificent!"

"I know, I know." He shook from her grasp and worried, "Maura, you look absolutely dreadful! Are you ill?"

Her face was gaunt, her skin gray, her eyes sunken and dark. She self-consciously hid her cheeks, and winced, "I haven't eaten and the strain of waiting has been...hard. Henry, how is he?!"

"As usual, a bit over-anxious, but fine nonetheless." Henry produced the second dagger from his belt and stuck it firmly in her belt. "Take only what you need and hurry! Once Robert reads the declaration I've left him, his wrath will tumble the walls of this hell-hole."

Maura grabbed up her saddlebag from the floor. Her eye caught the wedding gown spread across the bed. She battled the urge to rescue it, then quickly succumbed, snatched up the frock, and crammed it into her satchel.

Henry stuck his head out the door and strictly commanded to one guard, "Search the great hall. If you find someone there, return here, otherwise remain by the postern door. Maura," he called reentering the room, "We need only wait till my guard's positioned—then," he beamed, "to the stables!"

For the hundredth time Simon fought his impatience and let go of the latch. He must have faith and allow Henry time to accomplish his task. He leant back against the stable door and frowned at the torch adorning the opposite wall. Waiting was torture! He viewed Henry's guards, lounging in the straw and chatting amiably, with narrow disdain. How could they be so maddeningly casual? He inspected again all the saddles and bridles, then returned to his frazzling vigil by the door.

Feeling ancient and wounded, Robert sat forlornly on his bed, propped by a bedpost. He tapped the rolled documents against the post and grieved, why couldn't Almodis love him?! He'd given her much—far too much! Emptiness gnawed at his soul and his torment raged on. He forced his thoughts to his most pressing concerns—the wedding; Will's incorrigible behavior; Rufus' impertinence; Henry's astonishing declaration; and Maura's disturbing irascibility. Once more Almodis' tortured face appeared before him, wrenching his gut, and driving him from the bed. He paced, cradling his skull, struggling to forget. What of Henry's ludicrous claims? Always before, a grant of land, a gift of silver, a title, all had helped to dispel the pain and guilt he harbored from his maniacal past. Could they now?! He dropped the documents to the rushes and miserably pondered—*where* had Alan taken her? Was she safe? Was the child?!

At the top of the stairs, Henry and Maura fretfully awaited the guard's wave. When it came, Henry shot Maura an expectant grimace, squeezed tight her hand, and they took the stairs at a run. The postern door obstinately refused to open. Maura pried Henry's insistent fingers from the latch and dragged him across the hall. They sidled between tables and past flaming coals, then stealthily approached the closed doors. Their hushed whispers flushed a dwarfed shadow from its post opposite the huge apertures; it scuttled down the hall and disappeared into a chamber.

Henry leant surreptitiously into the hallway. He peered down one passage, then the other, and huffed a relieved sigh, "There's no one about." One guard led and the other trailed, as the four crept lightly down the passage. The sight of the keep's doors hastened their pace. Maura's excitement spiraled with each cautious step—very soon she would see Simon, escape with him, be with him forever! She couldn't contain her zeal and broke to a run. Henry blubbered alarm as he watched her race pass the guard, "No...no, Maura! Go slowly, Maura!" He charged after her. A door in his path suddenly burst open. He crashed into the thick barrier and was slammed senseless to the floor.

Soldiers barged from the chamber, snaring Maura and the guards, dragging them, flailing and kicking, into Will's lair. They hurled Maura on the bed, and roughly corralled the guards in a corner. Rufus' palm stifled Maura's screams; brandished blades stilled the guards' struggling.

Will leant casually out the open doorway and chuckled at Henry's pathetically sprawled figure. He patted his squire's head and murmured, "You've performed with excellence and, as promised, you may watch."

On the bed, Rufus hugged Maura, easily stilling her pummeling and laughingly warned, "Keep still and no noise. If you disobey, one of Henry's guards will have his throat slashed." Slowly, he eased his paralyzing hold and, before she could protest, slung her weightlessly to her back, caught her hands between his, and yanked them high over her head. He knelt on her forearms, and chuckled to her agonized groans and kicking feet. She bit her lip to staunch her cries—someone must have heard her scream! Henry would fetch Simon! Lord Robert would come! No one would keep her from Simon! No one!

Will avoided Maura's killing glare, climbed the tall bed, and straddled her waist. He removed her dagger and tossed it safely out of reach. His palms flattened the pelts by her temples as he hovered close and hissed, "You won't escape. You will marry Hugh of Ryedale if I have to truss you up and carry you to the chapel! I won't be denied my manor!" He sat back hard, crushing her with his weight, and licked the leer that curled his lips. Delicately, his fingers traced her clenched jaw, walked her neck, and toyed with her tunic's neckline. "It's an unwritten law that a ward submits to her Liege the day before her wedding. Such a fetching custom, don't you agree? At last you will enjoy that which you so foolishly rejected at Berkhamstead!"

Maura tasted bile as his lips nibbled her neck. She twisted in vain and caught the horrific sight of Henry's guard Guy, who had helped guard Simon at Winchester, kneeling in the rushes, a sword poised at his neck. How could she stop her scream, it tore at her throat, deafened her mind! Rufus forced more weight upon her arms. Her fighting eased to the horrendous pain and she suffered more of Will's depravity, "And your homage to me won't end here. We're to be neighbors! While your valiant husband is away at combat, which will be always, we'll continue our wrestling in your marriage bed."

Rufus eased back on his heels and eyed Will's banal performance with amusement. He delighted in Maura's subjugation, though Will's frivolous blather began to bore him. "Will," Rufus snapped impatiently, "get on with it!" Then, he sniggered, "Or perhaps you're unable to rise to the occasion." Will huffed rage while Rufus badgered on, "I truly don't understand why you bother with women. They terrify you! Especially this one, and with good reason. Perhaps it's the crowd that wilts your virility. We could leave you two alone..."

"No!" Will spouted too quickly.

Maura's frantic eyes darted to Rufus, then back to Will. Their haggling had weakened the pressure of Rufus' knees and ever so carefully, she worked her arms free.

"Admit it, Will," snorted Rufus, "Your talents lie in buggery—Oh my!" Rufus' fat fingers hid his sarcastic gasp, "You preferred that kept a secret, didn't you?"

Snickers rumbled from the group. Will whirled round to catch the culprits, but his seething met with abrupt silence. The distraction allowed Maura her chance; she arched steeply and knocked Will off balance. His desperate grab to the bed curtains barely broke his fall as her sharp kicks battered his groin. He swung back on top of her and screamed to Rufus, "Hold her, damn you!"

Rufus sat on her arms, clamped shut her mouth, and flared, "Do it now!"

Will's fury exploded in howled curses. His fists drubbed her face and shoulders, and he lunged for her neck, seized her collar and shredded her tunic to the waist. Maura writhed to the sting of his tongue on her exposed breast, then groaned to his savage bite. She heaved revulsion, gagging and choking into Rufus' palm. Her wild gyrations only made Will's teeth sink deeper and she felt her skin tear.

Henry woke to muffled cries. He pushed himself up with a dizzy slowness and squinted in a clouded stupor at Maura's saddlebag, lying abandoned in the center of the hall. A shake and blink partially dispelled the cloud and another muted moan propelled him to his feet. He stumbled to the chamber door, pounded and squalled, "Maura! Rufus let me in! Rufus!" No one acknowledged his faint effort. The throbbing in his skull made him moan as he staggered down the passage, wheezing, "Si...Simon...must fetch Simon...Simon."

The gleam of Maura's dagger lit Rufus' eye. In a frenzy, he snatched it up, pressed its handle to Maura's palm, and muttered with urgent wickedness, "And now you'll have your turn!" He released her arms and jumped back to watch the fun.

Maura plunged the dagger into Will's shoulder. His shriek rumbled through the keep as he arched in violent spasm, and toppled off the bed. Maura gaped numbly at his lurching figure, miraculously still on his feet, wailing and groping for the knife's hilt. A chair caught his collapse. His squire sped to his aide, steadied his arm, and extracted the blade. The boy then whipped off his own tunic, and pressed the cloth tight to the wound. His master's shame he hid with a pelt.

Will's cry shattered Robert's private dirge. He raced from his chamber, hollering for his guards. They swiftly answered his call and stormed behind him, across the hall, and into the passage. Their charge halted abruptly to the onerous sight of Maura's bag. Alone, Robert approached the door. His fingers splayed over the wood as he leant close and listened.

Rufus left the bed, and stopped his raucous laughter to snarl, "That'll teach you, dear disloyal cousin Will, not to split your allegiance between enemies. If you dare visit Curthose again, I'll skin you alive!"

Robert shouldered the door, roaring, "Rufus, open the door! Let me in! Rufus!"

The soldiers' jeers drowned his order, but Maura heard his rattled plea. While all mocked Will, she slipped from the bed and crept toward the unprotected door. Rufus spied her escape. He shoved aside his men, caught her arm, and wrenched it high behind her back. "Not so fast, my Lady," he snorted. "You're far too valuable to let go." His dagger nipped her throat as he wrestled her to a corner and bellowed, "Lift the latch and let the old fool in!"

Simon twitched to a peculiar scratching noise and cracked the door to peek. He caught Henry's collapsing body, hoisted him inside, and set him gently in the straw. "Henry, wake up!" he desperately pleaded, supporting Henry's shoulders and tapping his chin. "What's happened? You must wake and tell me. Henry!"

Henry rested his bruised cheek on Simon's arm and opened his eyes to rasp, "Rufus..."

*****

CHAPTER TWENTY-EIGHT - AN AUCTION

The chamber door creaked wide. Robert gingerly stepped inside and quickly scrutinized the riotous calm. In a nearby chair, Will sat slumped, shrouded, and miserable. Rufus sported an arrogant grin and stood proudly in the corner. Maura dangled listlessly from his arm, a dagger precariously poised at her throat. The crowd shifted nervously as Robert strode forward. His bold steps faltered at the sight of the blood-soaked tunic draping Will's shoulder. He rearranged the pelts to cover his son completely and winced. "Rufus...are you responsible for Will's wound?"

"Why would I hurt my dearest companion?" Rufus replied with sneering innocence. "No, Uncle, he met with an unfortunate accident—"

"Stop!" Robert roared. "Let her go! I'll pay you your cursed money. End your fiendish games now!"

Robert glimpsed Maura's face. Her tortured expression begged deliverance, and alarm gripped him as he noticed a trickle of blood emerge from under the dagger's point and begin its morbid trail down her neck. *Don't rile Rufus*, he cautioned himself. One jerk of the Prince's wrist would surely kill Maura, and he didn't want her death, he'd never wanted her death! He slouched in submission and spoke as steadily as his trembling allowed, "Rufus, I beseech you...let her go. You'll have your money and can leave here...in peace."

"I'll gladly vacate this pit," replied Rufus, "though, before I go I intend to auction off this wild harpy. And I require more than what's due me. Give me Berkhamstead and she's yours!"

Maura's strength drained, her body grew heavy, the blade dug deeper. Shrill voices hushed to whispers and a black mist cloaked her sight. Sleep...all she wanted to do was sleep.

Robert slowly wagged his head and gestured for patience. "Rufus, I can't—"

"No?" Rufus answered for him and chuckled, "What a pity. And so you'll head the list of those responsible for her death. Only, I doubt you'll be bothered long for, you see, the money she owes me is payment for Simon's release. Even *she* defies you." Rufus turned his glower on Will. "Now Will, Helmsley seems quite important to you, and without Maura there will be no manor. What's your bid to be?"

*****

"Bring that bucket close!" Simon yelled to Henry's guards. He splashed frigid water over Henry's face, gently shook his shoulders, and, frantically, volleyed questions, "Where...where is she? Where's Father? Does Rufus have Maura?! Where does he have her? Henry, tell me!"

Henry pried his eyes wide and floundered to sit. "Si...Simon, I failed, I—"

"Not now, Henry. Tell me where Rufus has Maura."

"In...in a chamber halfway down the passage leading to the great hall."

Simon ordered the guards, "Keep him still and when Maura appears, get them away from here! Once out of town, stop at the first shelter you encounter—barn, cottage, shed. I'll catch you there. No matter what they argue, don't wait for me! Is that clear?"

The guards timorously nodded. Simon carefully lowered Henry back to the straw and dashed away to the keep.

*****

"Will..." Rufus whined, "don't dawdle so. My hand grows weary."

Will lifted his blanched face and blubbered, "You may have Helmsley Manor, Cousin. Only, *please* allow me to live there."

"Now why would I want a manor surrounded by wasteland?"

"I'll continue to serve you and won't ask payment for the luxuries I provide."

"Desperate, aren't you?" Rufus clicked his tongue in disgust. "Someone always ruins your tedious little plots, and your father is about to hoist you out—penniless. However, you're too pitiful to pity. I don't want your measly manor. So her death will be a blot on your conscience as well. That is, if you own one." His lips slavered over Maura's ear. "Well, my feisty Lady, it appears *no* one wants you. That fact makes it simpler to dole out your punishment—"

Simon charged into the chamber. Maura started to his abrupt arrival and the knife dug deeper. She whimpered to a stinging dampness and Rufus' boomed greeting, "Well, if it isn't the one with manners!"

Simon chanced a brief glimpse of his father, and Robert met his confusion with an expression full of relief. Simon shifted his distress back to Rufus and Maura. He lifted his arms high in submission and, ever so haltingly, advanced, speaking reverently, "William FitzRoy, I've yet to give you thanks for my release."

"Don't fool yourself," sniped Rufus. "My decision had nothing to do with affection. You were taking up useful space in my prison. May I suppose you've come to discuss another deal?"

"If you're willing..." Simon dropped to one knee, hung his head low, and added, "Your Grace."

"Take heed his posture and words, gentlemen. I love how he grovels! Isn't it just my luck, though, that the pauper of the family is the only one eager to negotiate?"

Simon kept his meek expression while inwardly struggling for answers and solutions. *What have they done to her?! And why?! Rufus and Will relish this sort of madness. They need no excuse to torture! What is Father's role in this tragedy?!* He glimpsed his father's guilt-ridden face once more. No, it was clear Robert felt as helpless as he. This impasse had to cease before Rufus grew weary and— "I have money, Sire," Simon spouted as he rose, swiftly untying his bag of coins from his belt, and tossing it at Rufus' feet.

Rufus' boot tested the pouch's weight and he nodded appreciatively. "Definitely a promising start. What else might you have?"

"My horse?"

Rufus shook his head.

"My clothes?"

Rufus' titter broke to a chuckle. "I'd love to see them off you, but no, it's not fashionable to dress as a peasant. You'll have to do better."

The drugging cloud returned to steal Simon away and Maura slumped lower. If only they'd let her sleep, the pain would go, Rufus would leave, Will would vanish. She shut her eyes and the trickle of blood widened to a stream.

Simon tensed to her weakening. His panicked eyes darted from Maura to Rufus, then to his father. Robert lurched forward. Simon shot out a hand to stop him and brusquely warned, "No! Don't move!"

The strangling suspense threatened Rufus' fun. This game tired him, his arm ached, and everyone was acting too damned serious! "Where...where's Henry?" he blurted, nervously scanning the room. "I want him here! He'll liven up you pack of morose clods."

Simon almost gasped his relief—so Henry was Rufus' frailty! He brazenly stormed forward, lashing out, "You've battered him! He lies in the stable, senseless from your assault!"

"No!" Rufus cried, daunted, "I never struck him! Bring him here!"

"Fetch him quickly!" Simon shouted to Robert's guard.

"You lie!" Rufus stuttered, his composure wavering, "You beat hi…hi…him, be...beat him because he...took your woman." He burst a wild cackle and steeled his grip. "I'll end your squabble here and now—no one will have her!"

"No, Rufus, wait!" Simon reached out and implored, "I have one final offer to make. Take...take me! I'll gladly pleasure you, battle for you, speak for you! Use me as you—"

"Stop...st...stop!" Rufus stammered. With hooded glare, he retreated a step, and roared, "Bring me Henry!"

"I'm here, sweet Brother." Henry stepped out from behind Simon's back. He immediately sensed Simon's intent and raised his bruised face accusingly.

Rufus sucked a breath. "But I...I never touched you!"

Slowly inching forward, Henry and Simon launched a verbal attack that taunted, jabbed, and wounded. "It makes no difference, Brother," Henry accused scathingly. "You willingly joined in Will's game and are equally as guilty!"

"Take me, Cousin, take me," Simon murmured seductively. His fingers walked Rufus' arm. He inched closer and sighed, "I know you've always wanted me."

Henry's whine grated, "I'll tell Father. I'll tell him all your treasonous acts—lies, thievery, buggery, bribery, murder!"

"Not murder!" wailed Rufus, "I've murdered no one."

"And what is your intent now, you brutish dolt!" blared Henry.

"Now's your chance, Cousin," Simon enticed. "Make me your slave, beat me, make me writhe and howl with agony!"

"You won't escape your treachery," hounded Henry. "It will haunt you forever!"

"Take me, Rufus!" cried Simon passionately. "Take me!"

"Father will lock you away," warned Henry. "You'll share Uncle Odo's cell and the two of you can slander each other for eternity!"

Rufus' eminence began to crumble. His jaw twitched, his lips quivered, his hands shook, and his stormy guise wilted to that of an errant boy. Simon's fingers caressed and laced their way through Rufus' strained knuckles till they firmly circled the dagger's hilt. With a mighty yank, he bellowed, "Now, Henry!"

Henry wedged his wrist beneath Simon's grip. Rufus steered all his vigor to the blade. He whooped in delirious delight as the fray erupted to a contest he would surely win. Robert gestured his guards for restraint as the foursome careened wildly about the room. Locked in a macabre embrace, they stumbled over tipped wine flasks, fallen torch stands, strewn bedclothes, and Maura's dangling body. They crashed into gawking soldiers and crushed side tables to kindling. Will's chair sat directly in the midst of the melee. He burrowed deeper in his pelts and cried a prayer for salvation.

"Your dagger, Simon!" Henry yelled. "Use your dagger. Cut him! He'll let go!"

"I can't reach it!" shouted Simon.

Henry freed one hand and fumbled along Simon's belt, only the lapse of strength immediately gave Rufus an advantage. Simon howled in panic, "No, Henry! Pull back! Keep pulling back!" Together they threw themselves backwards. The space between Maura's neck and the blade gaped ever so slightly. They roared and heaved again. The space widened a tiny bit more...and more...till it eased just enough to— "Push her free!" hollered Simon.

Henry shoved Maura's head down through the lean opening. The blade scraped skin from her jaw, cheek, and forehead as she flopped to the rushes. Henry tripped over her, spilled forward, and hung perilously from Rufus' arm. His feet jostled and tread on Maura, scrambling for a footing. "Guards, take her away!" he squalled. His men shook from their stunned oppressors, dragged Maura from beneath the skirmish, and whisked her to freedom.

Simon and Henry kept their iron grip on Rufus' weapon. "Go with them," grunted Simon. "They can't escape the gates without you."

"No...You can't hold him alone!"

"I can hold him long enough for you to get out the door. Go!"

"Simon, Maura won't leave without you!"

"Do what you must! Go!"

Henry still hesitated. This catastrophe was his doing! To desert Simon now would mean his certain death!

Simon ripped Henry's fingers from the hilt. "Run!" he groaned, shoving him toward the door.

Henry yowled in frustration and raced crazily from the chamber. Simon dove to the rushes as the dagger whizzed inches from his head and embedded itself to its hilt in the slamming door. And then Robert's command roared above the din, "God's blood! Keep him still!"

Simon braced for the prick of a sword, but to his bewilderment, he felt nothing. He flipped to his back, pushed up on his elbows, and gapingly beheld all blades aimed at—Rufus.

*****

A deluge of rain woke Maura and she was amazed to find herself alive and in the arms of Henry's guard. She twisted in his fumbling hold, seeking out Simon, yet saw only empty stairs. Her wriggling intensified and she demanded, "Where...where's Simon?"

"There's no time, my Lady! We must go now!" answered the breathless sentry.

"No!" Maura groaned, lurching from his clutch. She tumbled down several steps, then steadied herself, and scrambled back up the stairs, crying, "Not without Simon!" Her vigor suddenly wavered and an eerie numbness slowed her rescue.

"Don't tarry! Get her to the stable!" shouted Henry, sprinting down the stairs.

"Henry!" she moaned. "I won't leave him, not with Rufus! I won't!"

Henry's response was curt and final, "Silence her."

Maura spun to a hand on her shoulder. The guard's fist neatly met her jaw and she melted against the stairs.

In the stable, Henry held Maura while his men mounted. He grew woozy at the blood oozing from her neck wound and directed to his man, "She'll ride with you. We'll stop at the first Abbey we encounter."

"But, my Lord, your cousin gave instructions to wait at the first shelter—"

"No matter," grunted Henry, clumsily hoisting Maura up into the sentry's saddle. The FitzRoy swung into his saddle and, kicking the stable doors open, bounded into the crowded bailey. The curious tenants scattered from his intrepid figure, as he recklessly galloped toward the gates.

A few folk, roused by the FitzRoy's heroism, broke from the horde and loped alongside him, hollering, "Open the gates for the Prince!"

Framed by the widening doors, Henry turned in his saddle to beam at the adulation and couldn't resist a wave. To his dismay a somber hush descended, followed by concerned murmurs. The peasants promptly ignored the Prince and flocked instead about his guard's steed, straining to touch the unconscious Maura. Henry shrugged off his envy and leant low to press a second bag of coins to the gatekeeper's palm. "There will be three more to let through. Then the gates will close and conveniently break. My father will know of your loyalty."

The keeper nodded in gratitude, and Henry spurred his horse out the gates. His guards raced after him, sending startled villagers scuttling for cover. The gang leapt the town's stone boundary and vanished into a dense, forbidding wood.

*****

"Detain Will's guards!" blared Robert.

Will came alive to his father's command and poked his head out from its cover. "What?" he groused, flinging the pelts aside. He gasped at the perversity surrounding him—his own guards cornered like thieves, Rufus humbled and forced against the wall, Simon lying unscathed and ignored at Robert's feet!

Simon kept a leery eye on his father, while stealthily rising from the floor. Dare he believe his eyes? Nary a move had been made to restrain him! Surely soldiers awaited him in the passageway, ready to pounce and pitch him in the deepest cell—but Robert had yet to name him in any demand! He took advantage of the bedlam to creep backwards toward the door.

"He's escaping!" cried Will, forcing himself from the chair. His hand shielded his shoulder as he hobbled in Simon's direction, hissing pain and anger, "You...you...won't leave here alive! Father! Seize him!"

Robert turned an almost serene expression to his sniveling son and uttered, "No."

"And Will," sniggered Rufus, pointing to Simon, "to add to your misery...behold your mystery knight! My spies stationed at Andelys witnessed your glorious humiliation."

Will stood a dazed moment, struggling to comprehend. Once the shameful truth dawned, his face and body swelled with umbrage and he started down the passageway after his brother. He broke to a teetering run, his mouth rabidly spitting foam, and his fingers, curled claw-like, raking his brother's shoulder. Simon easily jerked away, griping, "Get off me!"

"You won't win! I won't be punished! I'm the legitimate son!" screeched Will, and in a final, desperate attempt at victory, he jumped on Simon's back. Simon stumbled forward, then straightened and slammed Will against the wall.

Simon paused to watch his sibling slump unconscious to the rushes, then he heard the echo of his father's rumblings growing louder. The clanging of swords and hauberks set him racing again, out the keep door and down the wobbly staircase. For a terrible instant he was flung back in time, to the moment of his first escape from his father. Overpowering emotions hampered his progress, and tripped his steps. He tumbled down the last few stairs, twisted on the ground and warily glanced upward. Robert stood alone on the top step. Simon cast his father a pleading look. Robert answered with a nod and a limp wave.

As he dizzily watched his son vanish forever behind the stable door, Robert grasped the railing for support. Without brandishing a weapon or wielding a fist, Simon had triumphed over all—simply with strength and cunning. A flutter of pride lightened Robert's heavy heart, but then the guilt he felt about his past quickly deadened his spirits once more. His fingers dug into his scalp and he wailed a long, grueling wail to the blackened clouds. He craved freedom from this plaguing insanity, to escape like his son from his raving family! His hands dropped limply to his sides and his eyes shone with a faint hope. He'd return to Mortain, immerse himself in the trials of his subjects, join the King in battle, and on his way visit Odo! Yes, Odo would gratefully hear his troubles, empathize and, certainly, offer sincere and expert advice.

Simon sprang upon E'dain and snapped at Henry's dawdling guards, "I thought you were to go with the Prince!"

"He took the others," one guard explained, struggling to his feet.

"How long since they left?"

"Close to an hour, my Lord," answered the other.

Irritation spiked Simon voice, "Then let us go find the FitzRoy."

The ecstatic crowd had begun to disperse when the stable doors burst wide again, and Henry's soldiers galloped into the bailey. They slowed their pace and turned to see Simon standing in the stable door, tugging furiously on E'dain's halter. She, with locked legs, raised head, and flattened ears, adamantly refused to budge. His blared curses and slaps to her rump proved useless.

One guard ventured back to help and offered an arm up. "Will she follow, my Lord?"

Simon swung up behind him, muttering worriedly, "I don't know. She's never behaved like this before." The guard jumped and his steed lurched to Simon's shrill whistle. E'dain pricked her ears and sprinted after them, the groaning gates of Pevensey closing at her back.

The first manor they encountered on the outskirts of town lay in rubble, gutted and abandoned. Simon slogged through a sea of mud on his fervid hunt through the outbuildings for Henry and Maura. His rancor peaked and he wielded a balled fist. "Bleeding Jesus, Henry!" he raved. "Where have you taken her?!" A lightning strike cut short his rebuke, and he continued a silent scourge while sloshing back to the road. *Henry's gotten them lost! How could I have trusted such a bumbling fool with Maura's life? They will never be found!* He lifted his face to the raging sky and railed in anguish, "She'll be dead before I see her again...dead!"

Simon and the guards galloped many more miles and slowed only to the hopeful sight of a steep wooden wall flanking the side of the road. Simon flew off E'dain and fiercely yanked at a dangling bell cord. He waited a moment, heard nothing but wind, then added a yell to the clanging. A hooded figure cracked open the gate an inch and, at sight of Simon's crazed, flailing figure, promptly shut it. Simon caught the movement and attacked the gate with his shoulder, forcing it wide. The young woman cowered to his deafening demand, "Is the FitzRoy inside?!" She didn't respond so he tried again, quieter, and in English, "The Prince...Prince Henry...is he inside, with a maid? Is he here?"

The nun stepped aside and nodded. "They are expecting you, my Lord."

Simon slung a trail of mud and water as he bolted down hallways past gawking novices. At last he spied Henry huddled up against a door at the far end of the hall. Henry snapped to the racket, straightened, and tensed for the explosion sure to come. Yet Simon didn't utter a single disparaging remark, only thrust Henry aside and grabbed hold of the door's latch. He groaned at the unyielding lock, kicked, pounded, and rammed his whole body against the barrier.

"Simon..." Henry duly muttered, "If they won't allow me in, they certainly won't—"

Simon's fist splintered the wood. "Henry, order this door open at once!"

"I tried and they refused!" Gingerly restraining Simon's arm, he assured, "You needn't worry, and she's not alone."

Simon's instant paling scared Henry, and he retreated as his cousin turned his fury upon him. He seized Henry's collar and sputtered dementedly, "If...if she wakes with a...a flock of nuns hovering about her, she'll—" Simon's madness wilted to despair; his fingers bit Henry's shoulders, and he quaked his plea, "Try...you must *try* again."

Henry pried Simon's fingers loose. His expression betrayed terror as he stammered, "Yes, I...I'll do just that...I'll try again." He hurried a few feet down the hall and yelled, "Fetch the Abbess quickly!" then cautiously returned and studied Simon's frenzy from a safer distance. Never had he seen him so agitated. He could practically smell his—was it fear?

Simon pressed tight to the door and listened; he pushed away, tugged at his hair, and returned with a kick and brusque rattle of the latch. To the ceiling, he wailed, "Why? Why, won't they answer?!"

"Because you're terrifying them! Simon, you must calm—"

Henry froze at the sight of a robust looking nun, waddling towards them, her strident voice booming, "What insanity goes on here?!"

"It won't do to scream curses at the Abbess, Simon," cautioned Henry in a sharp whisper. "Control yourself or we'll both be tossed out on our heads." A cloying smile masked Henry's sternness as he bowed deeply, and gushed, "My gracious Lady, the husband has arrived and asks to see his wife. Surely, you can set aside your rules in this very special instance and let him inside the chamber. He is, after all, my father's favored nephew and, in return for your great kindness, the King is bound to favor your humble Abbey with—"

"I will see her now!" shouted Simon, shoving Henry aside.

Henry rolled his eyes, threw up his hands, and sulked away, mumbling, "I did try...I truly did..."

The Abbess regarded the wild-eyed, muddied young man before her with a mixture of disgust and suspicion, though her heart soon melted to his piteous expression. She gently removed his fingers from the latch and muttered through the key hole, "Open."

A fidgety young nun unbolted the door and whined, "She's bleeding heavily, Mother! We were afraid to open the door—"

Simon shouldered past them, drawing gasps from the novices as they herded together in a darkened corner. He snatched up a candle and held it close to examine Maura's wound. "I need suturing thread, wine, bandages, hot water, and blankets!" he ordered. No one moved; he turned to their shocked expressions and fiercely emphasized, "Quickly!"

In unison the young women looked to the Abbess for guidance. She held the door open and ushered them out, requesting evenly, "Get him what he needs and hurry back."

Simon's trembling fingers peeled a clump of hair from Maura's careworn face. Even in sleep she fretted. But, was it only sleep? He warmed her chilled hand against his heated cheek, murmuring, "Maura, I'm here...you're safe." He pressed his lips to her palm, his voice quavering as he stumbled on, "Fa. ..father let us go...he let us go! Maura?" She lay so wan, still, cold. Dread numbed his body. It couldn't be too late! He tossed his soaking cloak in the corner and flung back her blankets.

He started to the Abbess' touch and words. "It's best she stay covered."

"Granted," he said, struggling for control. "Please help me get her wet clothing off."

"My Lord, you must leave before—"

"I am her husband!" he roared. Instantly, he regretted his outburst and softened, "She will fare better lying naked beneath the blankets. Now please, help me."

They pared her chemise and tunic from her legs and belly and Simon silently thanked God for her lack of wounds. Yet, as they exposed her breast and its ragged tear, they both gasped revulsion. Simon whipped his head away, and gagged on his groan. The Abbess rested a hand on his shoulder and soothed, "It's hard to be strong when a loved one suffers. Pray for strength, for her sake and yours."

Simon and the Abbess were straightening Maura's blankets when a gaggle of novices bustled through the door, carrying the items Simon had requested. Their faces betrayed an eagerness to stay, hear all and know all, but the Abbess shooed them from the chamber. As if she knew Simon's thoughts, she set the materials on a side table in correct order of use, and deftly threaded the needle. Simon rinsed and dried his hands. He knelt by Maura's shoulder, accepted a passed towel, and cleansed her neck wound first with water, then with wine. His hope for movement in response to the stinging port was ignored.

The Abbess noticed his frown. "It's good she sleeps soundly. She'll feel no pain from the suturing." After handing him the thread, she lit and set more candles upon the table.

Simon took in a ragged breath, knelt, and pinched the cleaved skin together. His fingers holding the needle shook so violently that he was forced to release her skin, and clasp his wrist to still its shaking—but now both hands trembled. He flung the needle in exasperation, and hid his hands in his crossed arms. "I can't," he cried, "I can't...I'll only hurt her more!"

The Abbess' reply was blunt yet calming, "Of course you can. Will it help if I rest her head in my lap? You needn't bend so low."

Simon nodded. The Abbess threaded another needle, sat on the bed and supported Maura's head. Their eyes met, hers encouraging, as he began to stitch. She continued her pensive watch, wondering if she'd been lied to by this mysterious fellow. Only, what did it matter? His skills were gravely needed and he obviously loved this woman. Amidst all the turbulence, God would surely overlook a small impropriety.

Each successful stitch bolstered Simon's confidence. As he tugged the last tack through, the Abbess snipped the excess thread and grinned approvingly, "Your skill is excellent."

He lowered the blanket, tenderly swabbed crusted blood from Maura's breast. His eyes bulged and jaw dropped as he recognized bite marks. Bile rushed up his throat; he whirled around, retched to the horror, and screamed inwardly, *How could they do something so atrocious?! They truly are devils—devils!* Simon wiped his mouth with his sleeve, and furiously fought for calm for his mind and his belly. He had to stay calm if he was to help her.

Simon turned back to the Abbess' gentle words, "This wound doesn't need closing, only bathing and a bandage and I'll tend to that," she said, passing him a roll of gauze, "while you bind her neck."

Back beside Maura, he wrapped the gauze round her neck, and his worry shifted to the scarlet blotches staining her shoulder and arm. He ruffled with frustration; how could he treat such a mystery?

"What is it?" the Abbess asked, sensing his distress.

"She suffers from more than just her wounds, and I've no clue what's happened to her or what I should be tending to."

To the Abbess, the solution to his quandary seemed obvious. "She'll inform you when she wakes." His haggard eyes brimmed thick tears, and again she knew his thoughts. "She *will* wake. I promise you she will. Please fetch more blankets."

They piled the pelts high. Simon sat at Maura's head and, lightly brushing her hair from her brow, dabbed a gel on the scrapes marring her face. The Abbess dragged a chair close and, once settled, spoke softly, "We've done all we can to help. Her fate is now in God's hands. Before I go though, I believe you've something to confess."

His voice near to cracking, Simon acknowledged, "Some...something terrible happened to her in an Abbey. I feared she'd wake, see your women, and relive that horror. I'm sorry for my rudeness...I—"

"You needn't apologize nor explain. I've heard tell of reputed Abbeys that house pretenders and are ruled by men, not by God. Hell's houses, I call them. Your Lady was fortunate to stumble upon our rectory this vicious night. Perhaps we can help restore her faith. I must know...is my house endangered by your presence?"

"No...I don't—" Overcome with emotion, Simon tumbled tears and words he himself did not wholly believe. "My father...my father nodded at me."

The nun grinned knowingly. "And she's not your wife."

"Is to be, if and when we reach Canterbury."

Her rosy beam brightened the room and his spirits. "Canterbury? I'm highly impressed. The Archbishop is a wonderful man. Is the charming one outside who he claims to be?"

Simon nodded.

"Then we are privileged to house members of the Royal Family. You are his cousin?"

"Yes."

"But you are English."

"Partly."

"And she is?"

"My father's ward, Maura."

"Then we have Henry FitzRoy, Maura, and..."

"Simon."

"Well, Simon," she sighed, as she rose and smoothed her habit, "I am Mother Helena. You won't sleep, but I must. Send my novice if you have need of me. She'll be in the next chamber. I won't disrupt Maura's recovery. When she wakes, only your loving presence will soothe her, and she *will* wake soon." She paused at the door. "What shall I do with—"

"Please send him in." He stood in respect and offered with a bow and great affection. "I am eternally grateful to you, Madam."

She smiled and vanished behind the door; an instant later, she poked her head back in to note, "He's disappeared."

Simon didn't hear. Instead he focused a pleading gaze on the shrouded crucifix bracing the opposite wall. He stretched tall to tug away the cloth covering Jesus, and his strained whisper begged, "Don't take her from me! *Please*, Lord, let her stay with me awhile longer, *please*."

Naked beside Maura, he cuddled her near to share his warmth and searched her face for signs of recognition. Her breath and pulse grew fainter, her skin more frigid, and he shivered from her chill. He knelt to chafe her arms, and her limp hand slipping from his shattered his fragile calm. He fell back beside her, his hands sweeping over her body, desperately clutching her closer. His lips tasted her icy mouth and his torment and tears trickled down upon her ashen cheeks. "Don't leave me, Maura," he sobbed, aching to her stillness. "We've beaten them all and my father nodded to me. Stay with me, my love, don't go...I love you so. Don't go!"

*****

The urgent pounding jolted Rose awake and she groggily wondered why anyone would be calling this late. Perhaps it was best to ignore, she decided, as she shifted away from the intrusion. The rapping sounded again, louder and more insistent. She draped her blanket round her shoulders, and emerged from behind strung tapestries into the hall. Guardedly, she approached the Manor's main doors.

Her son Richard, every bit as dark, lean and fearsome as she, called out, "No, Mother. I'll deal with...whoever."

Her sweeping hand halted his advance. "Return to your bed, you need to rest." She won the race to the door, and trepidly chanced a peek. Alan stood on the stoop, bedraggled and dripping. "By God!" Rose exclaimed, flinging the door wide. "Alan! Hurry, get yourself inside!"

Spotting Rose's son, Alan hesitated, and sputtered from cold and uncertainty, "Rose, I...I am not alone. You do remember..." He reached behind his back and prodded Almodis forward. "My wife."

Rose's jaw dropped and she choked disbelief, "Yo...yo...your wife!"

"Rose, *please*," Almodis implored in a small pained voice, "may we enter?"

Rose shrugged from her shock and tersely directed, "Alan, carry her to my bed."

"Bless you, Rose," Almodis sighed as Alan easily swept her over the threshold, across the hall, and set her gently upon the bed.

Rose helped remove Almodis' drenched cloak and gown while volleying orders. "Richard, fetch dry clothing for Alan, wine, and more blankets for the Lady." Richard, puzzled, stayed where he was, and Rose gently explained, "Alan is the guard who accompanied me on my last visit here. And this is his...*wife*, Almodis."

Alan and Richard exchanged wary nods; Richard briefly acknowledged Almodis, then slowly headed for the trunk gracing the opposite wall.

Alan's hovering bothered Rose, making her blurt, "Go...go help Richard."

Desperate to stay, he resisted. "Rose, I don't need dry clothes...I—"

"Oh, Alan, you needn't fret," assured Almodis with a dainty wave. "Rose won't toss me out...Or will you, Rose?"

"Don't be ridiculous. Alan, you are in the way!"

"You'd best obey our landlady, my love, or face execution, and..." Almodis added with a pert wink, "You're making a puddle."

Alan melted to her sweetness and presently left.

Rage fired Rose's black eyes, huffed her breath, and twitched her stone-like expression as she roughly helped Almodis into a thick wool chemise.

Almodis wriggled beneath the heavy pelts with a cozy sigh and teased, "I know you're dying to ask."

"What mad scheme are you playing at?" burst Rose in a harsh whisper. "And why come here? How dare you endanger my family!"

"I'm far too weary and uncomfortable to relate to you the whole dismal tale. I'll simply say that, at my husband's orders, I'm in hiding."

"Hiding?" Alarm raised Rose's voice. "From whom?"

"Will. He wants me and my child dead."

"Are you pursued?"

"We've not noticed anyone...following—" Almodis' wincing intruded and her hands surrounded and comforted her belly.

Rose's ire switched to worry and she pressed, "What is it?"

"A tightening."

"How long till the babe's due?"

"The beginning of June."

"Then you'll have to stay put—" Rose paused and followed Almodis' syrupy gaze to Alan, newly dressed and peeking through the tapestries.

Almodis sat up and reached long, gushing, "Husband, come!"

Rose's agitation swelled and, to Alan, she huffed disgust, "Have you brought the blankets?"

Alan dutifully passed the blankets to Rose and the cup of wine to Almodis. "Don't look so cross, Rose," chided Almodis, grasping Alan's hand. "We're only trying to make a horrid situation a bit more tolerable."

"How can I agree to this?" Rose hotly contested. "There has to be someplace else you can hide!"

"We feel safest with you," Alan firmly appeased.

"What's happened to Maura?"

"She's still at Pevensey," said he, adding hesitantly, "...unharmed."

"Unharmed?" she gasped. "What do you mean? What of Simon?!"

"When we left, he hadn't yet arrived."

"She was to marry today!" flared Rose. "You are *her* guard! Your duty belongs to her and her alone."

Alan sighed and assured, "I'm confident she...she and Simon will send word of their successful escape."

A bitter silence ensued while Rose struggled inwardly with anger, confusion, and indecision. Finally, she softened her stance and announced, "Supper's leftovers are cold. I can, though, offer you bread and cheese."

"Nothing for me, Rose," Almodis answered as she downed the wine and shifted for comfort beneath the blanket's added weight.

Rose absently fussed with the pelts. "Will you be warm enough?"

"I suppose. Where will you sleep?"

"There's an extra bed across the hall. I'll be near in case you call."

"I am truly thankful, Rose," said Almodis, squeezing Rose's hand.

She flinched from Almodis' touch, and spun to leave, spouting gruffly, "Are you coming, Alan?"

"I'll follow...in a moment."

With Rose gone, Almodis fretted in a hushed voice, "I'm wary of your decision, Alan."

"Where else could we go? This manor's secluded, Will isn't aware that you're familiar with Rose and—"

"I speak of Rose herself," Almodis stressed. "She's hard and intolerant."

"And beneath her coarseness beats a warm and generous heart!" defended Alan.

"That may be so, only—" A sudden moan stole her next word; she crushed his hand, and pressed her cringing face deep into the pillow.

"The pains have returned! I'll fetch Rose!"

"No, stay...I'm afraid."

His fingers soothed the creases from her brow. "We rode far too long today. Rest and wine will calm the baby."

"You'll rest with me?" she begged in a whisper.

His tender smile replied, "I'll eat with Rose, calm her with explanations, then pretend to fall asleep wherever she puts me. When she's still, I'll come visit. Now, Rose insists upon obedience, so you will rest."

He tucked the blankets close beneath her chin. The loving gesture teared her reddened eyes. "Alan..."

"Yes?"

"I wish we didn't have to pretend."

He bent to kiss her brow, the tip of her nose, her lips, and then murmured, "Who's pretending?"

Later, Rose scraped Alan's leftovers into a bowl for her hounds and shook vehemently in response to his dire tale of Pevensey. "You've left her with Will and Rufus?! How can she survive those fiends alone? You should be with her!"

"Lord Robert seems bound to protect her," said Alan. "I don't know him well, but he appears to have softened."

Rose let go a doleful sigh. "Alan, I have no choice. I must allow you both to stay. The child will surely die if it's born this early. The Lady cannot risk further travel. She'll need to stay abed till at least mid-May."

"Mid-May!" echoed Alan. "Keeping her still that long will be impossible."

"I agree, but it must be done. I'm also concerned how this episode may affect my son."

"I don't understand."

"He lost both wife and son in childbirth less than two weeks past. Almodis needn't know of that sorrow, she has troubles aplenty. Somehow, we must convince her of the dangers."

He rested broad palms on her shoulders. "I'll do all I can to help the Lady and you."

Rose shook from his touch and fidgeted with bowls, scraps, and her skirt. "We have only three beds," she rambled. "I'm afraid you'll have to sleep on the floor. I'll fetch you a mat, and pelts, and—"

"No, Rose. I'll find what I need. You get yourself to bed. And what I mentioned before about feeling safest with you—I spoke the truth."

"You always do..." Her fingers brushed his bristly cheek and her fluster came near to easing. "I'm glad you've come," she said, "and no matter how loud I grumble, I'm also pleased to see the Lady. It's been so sad here. Sleep well, Alan."

"And you, Rose."

Alan spread his pallet and pelts by the meager fire that centered the hall. Restively, he listened to Rose's muffled and over-long prayer, and offered a short prayer himself for her shifting to cease. When at last she was still, he left his mat, snuck across the hall, between the tapestries, and into Almodis' eager arms.

*****

His arm in a sling, Will shuffled furiously through a tall stack of formal documents strewn upon a tabletop located in the seneschal's chamber at Pevensey. An ominous shadow fell across the parchments, and Will raised fright-filled eyes to Rufus' almost gleeful face. With a tight gulp, Will asked, "What do you want?"

"I've come to bid you farewell, and felt the need to thank you for a most enjoyable visit."

"Surely you jest," sneered Will.

"No, I mean what I say," Rufus chuckled.

"You were humbled, humiliated!"

Rufus shrugged. "One can't expect to win every squabble. It was a fair match and such great fun! Henry's always a delight, and your brother...He's a shrewd bastard and far prettier than you. You're looking old."

Will ignored Rufus' scorn and continued to shuffle through skins. Rufus watched a perturbed while, then questioned, "What are you doing?"

"I'm searching for the Yorkshire marriage writ," Will replied, annoyed. "Father and I have come to a rather blunt understanding. He's to reside in Normandy, I in England, and we will strive to avoid each other, which suits me fine. The man has definitely outlived his usefulness and is surely feeble minded." He crumpled parchments while carping, "After the 'great fun' of this evening, he informed me that your doltish father has agreed to Simon and Maura's marriage! At this very moment, they're off to Canterbury to solemnize the decree. Father loses little from this atrocity. I, however, stand to lose a great deal. So I've decided to take matters into my own hands."

"What are you on about?" grumbled Rufus' "What matters?"

"As soon as I find the blasted contract, I'm off to Berkhamstead to impart sorrowful news to Sir Hugh of Ryedale." Will risked a meek glance at Rufus. "If you don't mind waiting a little while longer, I'd prefer traveling with your party."

"I have no objections," replied Rufus. "Why are you surrendering with such ease?"

"Surrendering?" Will snorted. "I'll never surrender—not to that loathsome turd."

"Are you describing your father or your brother?"

"Both...and I didn't say *what* news I'd impart to Hugh."

Intrigued, Rufus downed the gulp of wine left in Will's cup, and spluttered, "Ex...explain."

"I've conjured up an exquisite plot." The sound of his own gloating stirred Will's resolve. His voice grew steady and intensely direct as he wondered, "Though I'm not certain you can be trusted with my secrets."

"Come, Will," scoffed Rufus, "I no longer harbor bad feelings toward you. Your betrayal warranted punishment, the nasty deed is done, and our friendship is free to bloom as before. So don't hold me in suspense," he insisted excitedly. "Confess your scheme!"

"Well..." Will started with great mystery, "I plan to tell Hugh this—it seems Maura's adoptive mother Rose has been stricken with a serious malady and Maura, being a selfless, devoted angel, has left to nurse her. Since Hugh is obliged to return shortly to Normandy, I'll simply suggest we not let Maura's untimely absence prevent the wedding ceremony."

"Your wound dulls your mind," said Rufus.

"Dearest Cousin," Will sneered, "surely you're familiar with marriage by proxy? We'll need only a warm body to stand up for the true bride and repeat the vows for the union to be legitimate. Understandably, the groom will be upset that the contract cannot be consummated, and I will swear profusely to deliver Maura to him directly upon his return from Normandy."

"I'm highly impressed," lauded Rufus, resting his broad backside on the edge of the table. "Tell me more."

Will leant forward on his good arm, and prestigiously continued, "Hugh will remain in Normandy for the wars. In time, our mutual prayers will be answered and your father will be vanquished. Maura and Simon's protection dies with him. I'll find them, make the bitch a widow, and present her to Hugh." His finish boomed triumph, "And most importantly, in two days I'll have my manor!"

"And Maura will have two husbands! I pity the poor souls." Rufus chuckled and asked, "What of Almodis' child? I'm sure you're aware that the second son inherits all his father's English holdings."

Will aimed his boasting at the tabletop and resumed rummaging. "Because of Almodis' advanced age, there's an excellent chance that she and the child will both perish in childbirth. If not, they can't escape me forever."

"Such grand plans for such a simpering coward."

Will glowered and hissed, "I'm no coward and certainly no fool. I'll get what's due me if I have to eliminate my entire family in the process!" His scowl slowly brightened as he recognized on the sheet before him the words Ryedale, Hugh, Maura and Mortain. "Ah! At last I've found it! Cousin," he gleefully suggested, "would you care to accompany me to a wedding? Surely, the groom and his humble family will be honored by your illustrious presence."

"I'd love to," answered Rufus, "only before we depart, you'll allow me one final question."

"Certainly," agreed Will, awkwardly donning his cloak.

"What if I've killed Maura?"

Rufus' query doused the gaiety of the moment and Will muttered, "I've taken that possibility into account, and must admit part of me thrills to the notion. It should make little difference. Hugh will be away months, perhaps years. And if his betrothed happens to expire during that time, then he'll receive even sadder news when he comes home." Will laughed wickedly. "With luck, he'll die in combat, *she* will live, and I will claim the remainder of his measly holdings and his betrothed as my property! I'll happily torment her till the end of her days, which I can assure you won't be long in coming." He strutted round the table and warmly embraced his cousin's portly figure. "Sweet Cousin, your vile character stimulates my ruthlessness. By your side, I could perform wonders! Please be mindful of that fact when the time comes for you to reign."

"I will do so gladly, if in turn you take heed of the fact—I see and hear all. Never betray me again!" snapped Rufus, giving Will's cheek a sharp pinch.

Will slapped away Rufus' hand and dismissed his warning with a garish grin. "If we ride through the night, we'll shorten our traveling time. Shall we go?"

Rufus nodded and gestured for Will to lead. Will paused by the door to waggle a finger and add, "And when we arrive at Berkhamstead, I'll expect nothing less than your most *gracious* behavior."

*****

CHAPTER TWENTY-NINE - CAT AND MOUSE

Tree branches clawed at the shuttered window as lightning caused the tiny cubicle to erupt with light, then quake to the thundering tempest. Simon barely noticed the squall. In weary awe, he watched shimmering candlelight dance upon Maura's hair, while keeping two fingers pressed firmly to the side of her neck. The clamor outside peaked, drowning the beat of her heart, and intensifying his panic. *Talk to her*, he said to himself, *she might hear. Memories could bring her back...*

"My love," he murmured, turning her colorless face to his, "lying here beside you has reminded me of our most wondrous times—the magic of Shrove Tuesday, rolling in the cloth behind Arthur's stall, our vow we made amid the pages of the Domesday Book, and the last time we loved. Recalling those moments helped me survive Normandy. Only... can they save you now? Can anything?!" His fingers bit at her cool skin as his despair raged, "Before I left, you had no doubts! 'We will be victorious' you said, 'I'll risk anything to stay with you—anything!' You can't let them win! Fight them, Maura, and come back to me. I love and need you so!"

Sharp threads of pain paralyzed Maura. Rufus loomed above her, his weight crushing, his searing breath torching her skin. Will cackled dementedly, shredding her clothes, drubbing her face, gnawing hungrily on her breast. Her screams proved silent, her fight useless. Slowly Simon's pleas, muffled and choked with tears, seeped through the din, "Fight them...come back...I love...need you—"

Her captors' hold was too strong, her pain too severe! Yet surrendering to the agony dulled Simon's entreaty, resisting it emboldened his words. She mustered her last vestige of strength and tore from the threads. Rufus vanished! She shoved up from the bed. Will disappeared! Seemingly alone, hurting, and so very cold, she cried, "Simon? Don't leave me. Come back. Simon!"

Simon shifted to a vague sound. Thinking it only the storm, he cuddled protectively closer. Then he heard, spoken ever so lightly—his name! He bolted up in the bed and searched her face for a twitch, a flutter, any sign of waking! Her lips parted and breathed, "Simon..."

He exploded with joy, "Maura! I'm here! Can you hear me? Open your eyes and see me!"

He held his ear to her mouth and caught her feeble whisper, "Simon...where?"

"Here, my love, here beside you! You're safe. You needn't fear. Wake up, *please*, wake up!"

Her eyelids fluttered, then parted slowly to the vision of his beautiful face bathed in gentle candlelight. With the saving image came horrendous pain. She arched in his arms, clawing and gasping, "Save me! Simon, make it go! The *pain*, make it go away!" Desperate to help, he crushed her to his chest. Yet past his shoulder, she beheld the mark of her most ultimate torture—*the crucifix*. Her convulsive scream rocked the abbey, jolting the nuns and novices from their beds, and thrusting a dozing Henry to his feet. He burst into the chamber, and stopped abruptly to Simon's halting gesture.

The sound of racing feet encroached and Simon yelled, "Keep them out!" Swiftly, Henry bolted the door, then turned a shocked face on the horrific sight of Simon and Maura wrestling. Despite her blows and groans, Simon kept a steady hold and soothed, "Maura, it *is* Simon. Believe it's me. If you lie still, the pain will ease. Try to lie still. You're safe, no one will hurt you...no one—"

Her flailing ebbed, not in response to his assurances, from weakness. Her head lolled and she grew limp in his arms. "Poisoned...you've poisoned me!" she moaned. "Tricked me. You're not Simon! Not Simon...not—"

"Henry's here, Maura." Simon waved a desperate hand and begged, "Henry, come, speak to her. Convince her!"

"What can I say?" Henry whined.

"Anything! She'll believe it's no trick if she sees your face. You are not part of her nightmare! Please!"

Her misery wrenched Henry's heart; he crept forward and placed a tentative touch on her damp brow. "Maura?" he said with a tenderness that surprised even him.

"Henry?" she whimpered.

He hovered close and smoothed her fevered cheek. "Yes, I'm here, and I would never trick you." His confidence and appeal strengthened, "You've escaped the devils, Maura! They hurt you, that's why you feel such pain. Believe it is Simon and heed his words."

Too gradually, Henry's claims slowed her rapid breaths. She shifted her torment to Simon and her fingers moved with excruciating slowness to his lips. He smothered them with kisses, clutched her close, and shared her grateful sobs.

Henry retreated to a shadowed corner. Huddled there, he felt the shocking sensation of dampness on his cheek. He wiped the lone tear, buried his face in his arms, and prayed for Maura's swift recovery.

Henry woke hours later to an eerie stillness. Once he'd determined where he was, he rose stiffly and cast a wary glance to the bed. What he beheld there filled him with a curious contentment. Simon sat propped up by pillows, with Maura draped over him, her head resting on his chest, her eyes closed and expression at last serene. Simon's loving gaze focused intently on her face, while one hand caressed her shoulder, and the other combed tangles from her disheveled hair.

Simon started to Henry's advancing shadow. "It's only me," he assured, stepping into the dim light. "May I?" He cocked his chin toward the foot of the bed. With a small smile, Simon nodded. Henry clambered aboard, wriggled for comfort, and looked to the window above Simon's head. "The storm's done," he noted mildly.

"For now," said Simon.

"How is she?

"She's past the worst," Simon answered tiredly. "Now her sleep will heal, not haunt. And how is your face?"

"Sore, and a few splinters remain."

"Splinters?" wondered Simon.

"Yes, I did battle with a door and lost."

"Oh...Remind me to remove them come morning."

"I failed you and Maura," sulked Henry.

Simon sat up quizzically. "Failed us how?"

"I fumbled our mission."

"How can you say that?" Simon countered sharply.

"My bumbling almost cost us our lives!"

"No, Henry, your bravery *saved* our lives. As you so astutely stated, we 'escaped the devils'. Your silver tongue enabled that miracle to occur. Moreover, I could never have held Rufus without your added strength. His affection for you gave us the advantage we needed for victory. You didn't bumble a thing."

"When I saw you barreling down the hall," Henry despaired, "I was certain your intent was murder! We couldn't stop at the first manor out of town, it was gutted. Maura needed a dry shelter and immediate tending, she was bleeding and—"

"I heartily agree with your decision...now."

"You seemed terrified of this place. Why?"

"It's nothing to do with you, Henry."

Normally, Henry would have pestered further, only at this particular moment Simon seemed to lack the vigor for bantering, so instead he announced, "Well then, I plucked up Maura's saddlebag on the way to the stables and I have yours here as well. I imagine you both crave clean, dry clothes."

"I appreciate your thoughtfulness, Henry...always believe that. Now, for you, I prescribe more sleep."

Henry curled up in a tight ball at the foot of the bed and obeyed his most trusted physician. When next he woke, it was dawn. Mindful not to disturb Simon and Maura's snuggling, he slipped noiselessly from the bed and snuck from the chamber.

*****

In the doorframe of Maura's chamber, a novice dropped a pail of sudsy water. It fell with a sloshing thud to the rushes as she gaped abashedly at the naked couple entwined on the slim bed. Simon woke to the intrusion and, groping for a pelt, uttered with a guilty grin, "Sister."

She stammered her caution, "The...the Abbess will...will arrive shortly...my Lord!"

"I appreciate the warning," Simon answered, his grin widening. The young woman exited, and he carefully wriggled from Maura's hold to wash and dress. He was tugging on his hose when he sensed the warmth of her gaze. "Maura..." he sighed blissfully. With one foot still bare, he hopped to the bed and lifted her in his arms.

She stayed quiet in his gentle hold, then strained a whisper, "How...how did you escape Rufus? Where are we?"

"Don't try to speak, my love," said he, firming his clutch. Her woeful look begged a kiss which he readily furnished, and she whimpered when he broke away to say, "All you need know now is you're safe, mustn't worry, and with rest and time the pain will fade. Maura," he mentioned cautiously, "we are in an abbey—" Instantly she went rigid, and he rushed to add, "But you needn't fret. The Abbess and her women want only to nurse you." An abrupt knock made her bury her face in the folds of his shirt.

The Abbess entered. Simon cast her a hapless look as she smoothed her habit and veil and started forward. She extended a hand and murmured goodness, "My child, I have no wish to harm you. Let me calm your fear."

Maura burrowed deeper; Simon stroked her hair and soothed, "Maura...this is the Mother Helena. She assisted me while I tended your wounds."

Maura chanced a glance at the Abbess' pacific expression. Her saggy skin glowed pink, smile lines etched the corners of her eyes, and wisps of silver-white hair framed her veil. Maura examined her memories, and decided—this was not a face to fear.

"Simon," the Abbess requested, "it's best I distance myself till she's more confident of her safety. Please hand me a cup. I've brought a more potent brew," she said, filling the passed cup to the brim. "Persuade her to down the entire contents, quickly."

The liquor scorched her lips and tongue, yet Maura's parched throat gratefully accepted each stinging, pain-dulling drop. In scant time, the already muted voices grew more distant, faces blurred, and her pain lulled.

Content that she was asleep, Simon and the Abbess chatted quietly. "Next time she wakes," said Simon, "we must feed her broth to bolster her strength."

"I'll arrange for soup and bread to be brought." The Abbess rose to leave, set the flask upon the table and, in anticipation of an eruption, spoke guardedly, "I will also send a novice to sit by her while you visit the refectory to eat."

"I won't leave her!" retorted Simon.

The Abbess straightened and replied as brusquely, "My charges are young and overly impressionable. They're confused by what's occurred and I won't allow their studies and meditations to be disrupted further. When Maura's pain is done and she's convinced of our good intentions, *you* will sleep next door. And I will have no argument."

Simon swallowed his protest and huffed at the closing door. He dared not anger the Abbess. Maura must have time to heal and if that meant time apart, he had no choice but to accept the strict edict. He settled back upon the pillows and again considered the enigma of Maura's ailments. She had accused him of poisoning; was that a fantasy drawn from her tragic past or a reality of her time at Pevensey? If she *had* been poisoned, there were simple treatments—milk mixed with ash, bruised rue in wine, or chamomile. Yet, he argued inwardly, if she had swallowed a bane there would be other, more drastic symptoms such as vomiting, constant convulsive pain, and quite likely she wouldn't have woken at all. He stared at her for a long while and his pensive gaze focused on her blotchy shoulder. He reexamined the spots on her arm, and was slightly encouraged to discover the irritation had eased. Heaving a relieved sigh, he cradled her closer, and resigned himself to waiting till she awoke for a solution to this mystery.

Throughout the day, Maura did wake sporadically, though only long enough to choke down sopping bread soaked in broth, and gulp another dazing cup of wine. While she slept, consoling voices wove through her mind, allaying her suspicions and tempering her agony.

Henry visited to chat and encourage, though he never lingered long and handled his despondency by walking. Late evening, Maura woke, this time fully alert. Though still weak, she requested her chemise, plumped her own pillows, and refused the cup of wine. "No, Simon," she implored, "I'm tired of sleep."

He beamed at her healthy burst of obstinacy, and offered instead a chunk of bread. "Then will you eat?"

"I'll try." She munched vaguely on the crust and, bewildered, looked to the shadowed corner of the chamber. "Who is she?" she asked with a hint of fear.

"Her name is Sister Mary and she has been assigned to chaperone us," said Simon. "This convent is populated with a Saxon order. If we behave ourselves and converse in French, she can't divulge any of our true intentions."

Maura smiled slightly and shifted for comfort; she failed to find any. "Where's Henry?" she wondered.

"Wandering..." Simon rested beside her on the pillows and kissed the wrinkles from her brow.

She nestled her head onto his shoulder and, despite their closeness, he strained to hear her whisper, "Simon, why did we come here? And when?"

"Henry brought you here last evening straight from Pevensey. I arrived shortly thereafter. He had no choice but to stop here, you were bleeding heavily. What do you last remember?"

"I believed I saw you in Will's chamber, then a cloud seemed to swallow you up."

"I *was* there. Together, Henry and I forced Rufus to release you."

"Wait, I do remember...I woke on the stairs." She raised her head slightly to the illumination. "They wanted me to leave you there, leave you with Rufus. I tried to go back. Henry ordered his guard to silence me. The last thing I saw was a fist."

Simon's retort was swift and severe, "What did Henry do?!"

Precisely on cue, Henry entered, acknowledged the novice with a roguish wink, then strutted over to the bed and nonchalantly flopped himself down. He beamed at seeing Maura awake, then frowned at Simon's tumultuous scowl. "Now what's happened?" he said irritably. "Have you two been quarreling?"

"You ordered your guard to *hit* her?!" assailed Simon.

Henry raised his hands in defense and sharply pleaded his case, "You can't fight me on that point, Simon! I told you she wouldn't leave without you, and you said 'do what you must.'"

Maura cloaked Simon's balled fist and blurted before he could argue, "It's done, Simon. He did what he felt was necessary—" A wince interrupted her chiding.

"Maura, what is it?" asked Simon, placing a worried touch on her cheek.

"It's passed..." she answered faintly and lifted pained eyes to plead, "I don't want you to be upset with him."

"Heed her wise words, Simon." Henry lounged back against the wall and pursed his lips in confusion. "Why are we speaking French? You always demand, Simon, that in your exalted presence, I speak only that barbaric tongue—English."

Simon tilted his head toward the novice, who sat modestly, knitting furiously. Henry's eyes sparked with intrigue. "Oh, I see," he spurted. "I do adore secrets."

"Maura, what's all this?" Simon asked, lowering her sleeve an inch.

"I...I can't say for certain. On a hunting trip an arrow grazed my arm. I think it was dipped in poison. It seems Will wanted me quiet, not dead."

"Is he responsible...for your other wound?"

Maura shuddered to the grisly memory. Her action and Simon's curious question piqued Henry's curiosity and he prodded, "What other wound?"

She answered only Simon, "Yes, and...I'm responsible for his."

"Good for you," Simon murmured in awe. He gathered more pelts to calm her shivering.

"How did you...escape Rufus?" she asked, watching his fussing with affection.

"You needn't know that now," he replied. "You need more rest."

"No, Simon, answer her," pressured Henry. "I've been pondering that mystery myself."

"There was absolutely nothing heroic about my escape. Father's guards restrained Rufus and I simply walked away."

"I disagree!" spouted Henry.

"Disagree with what?" questioned Simon. "You weren't there."

"I think your performance was immensely heroic. Simon pledged to Rufus the ultimate sacrifice for your freedom, Maura." Maura looked muddled and Henry further explained, "He proffered his body for yours."

"Well it didn't come to that, did it, Henry?" carped Simon.

"No...still, Rufus never forgets. In future," Henry earnestly cautioned, "if you happen to meet up with him, I highly suggest you keep your backside covered."

"Henry!" scolded Maura. "Remember where you are!"

"Not to worry," shrugged Henry. He gave the novice a gooey grin, accented by another wink and wave. She colored and dropped her twinkling eyes to her yarn. "She can't comprehend a thing I'm saying," he glibly noted. "I can gush a sling of obscenities and make her truly believe I'm professing my undying love..."

Maura managed a bleak smile and Simon chuckled in amazement. Henry whipped round to their response, cocked his chin, and asked with mock innocence, "What's funny?"

"Nothing Henry," replied Maura, then she asked pleadingly, "Will you please allow us a little time before Simon must leave me?"

"I suppose," surrendered Henry. "Remember...Sister Mary can see all!"

"We will be subtle," added Simon.

Henry left and Simon shifted with discomfort as he softly murmured, "Maura, I need to tell you about what happened in Normandy and what happened to Marc..."

*****

A slim slat of wood separated the lovers, only to them it seemed they reposed on opposite ends of the earth. Simon tossed with agitation and absently traced the wavy patterns on the planks. Henry shifted to his cousin's noisy distress and comforted from the bed across the chamber. "Simon...I'm certain Maura shares Marc's healing power, and I predict that by tomorrow she'll be up and insisting we leave immediately for Canterbury."

Simon squirmed to a sitting position, hugged his pillow close, and said with a disgruntled sigh, "I pray you're correct."

"I always am. Simon?"

"Yes."

"I've discovered something quite marvelous."

"What have you discovered, Henry?" Simon asked distractedly.

"This is a school!" twittered Henry. "The girls are in training and have yet to take their vows of nunhood."

"Nunhood?"

"Whatever it's called."

"I believe it's called *taking the veil*."

"Perhaps I can remove a few veils before I go!"

"Henry..." Simon strangled his pillow and grittingly warned, "If you dare cause trouble here, I'll personally toss you out on your head!"

Henry ignored the threat and harped on, "But when you consider the matter, Simon, what is God actually offering them for their sacrifice? A cold, harsh pauper's existence. When I can offer—"

"Lies, loneliness and too many little ones tugging at their skirts," Simon curtly finished.

"I don't see it that way," pouted Henry.

"I know you don't," Simon snorted, "and I don't believe you ever will." His tone turned troubled as he stretched out on his belly and asked, "Do you ever spend time with your children?"

Henry paused in thought then answered casually, "I don't see them often. Sybil, the serving wench, has two and claims both are mine. They're quite nice, and favor me as well. Then there's the countess who swears all six of hers are mine. By calculation, that would mean I fathered the first when I was twelve. Which is possible, though not probable."

"Doesn't it bother you—the lack of contact, I mean?"

"If I remember correctly," smirked Henry, "there was quite a lot of contact going on."

"I mean with the children, Henry," returned Simon, peeved.

"No, not really. I feel awkward around little ones. Perhaps if I were married and knew for certain the child was my own, I might think and feel differently." Henry rolled to the side of his bed, sat, and asked with rarely heard gravity, "Now you'll answer my query. What, besides her obvious physical attributes, has coerced you to spend forever with Maura? What's so special about her?"

"You wouldn't understand and I'm tired of arguing."

"No, Simon, you won't wiggle out of this one. I demand an answer."

"With her I feel safe, happy, and wholly loved."

"That's all?!" ridiculed Henry. "I get that much from my hound!"

Simon muttered under his breath, "No one else would waste their time."

"What did you say?" demanded Henry.

"I said...my, aren't we having a splendid time!"

"Simon," Henry scorned, "I thought your mind was your own. She's so besotted you that you've ceased to think properly. Consider for a moment the horrendous risks you've taken on her behalf. I never believed I'd ever witness you grovel to a mere woman. Well, by almighty God," Henry declared, standing and raising his pillow high above his head for emphasis, "take heed my vow—such an atrocious calamity will never befall me!" He hurled the pillow at Simon and sneered, "Slave to a woman—how utterly disgusting!"

"Henry..."

"Yes?"

"I'm grateful for the extra pillow," Simon said sweetly. "Now be a good lad and go to sleep!"

Henry let out a war whoop and leapt the short distance between their beds, grabbing back his feather-stuffed weapon and savagely pounding his equally well-armed cousin. Their joyful brawl lasted till the air was thick with down and they were sick from laughter.

*****

A collection of novices, their eyes round with wonder, sat cross-legged at Henry's feet, enthralled by his flowery version of his and Maura's adventures in Normandy. "...And then," Henry flourished, "she shattered my heart with a lingering kiss and left me, risking treacherous seas to free her true love from a deep, dank, rat-infested prison. I gradually recovered from the wound in my shoulder, though the wound in my heart will never fully mend and—"

"Out now!" The young women started to the Mother Helena's roar, scrambled to their feet, and swabbed away tears. "This is not a day of leisure," berated the Abbess. "There are chores to be done and fences to be repaired!" She hustled them from the room and hurled a seething glower Henry's way before slamming the door.

Maura kicked him playfully and chided, "You little liar!"

"Why do you say that?"

"Your story is a bit overdone. Have you forgotten I was also there?"

"Well, I feel forced to elaborate on the more unbelievable parts, such as your unlikely choice of a mate. After all, these girls are so deprived, they need some spice in their—oh so dreary lives. I'll end the tale for them later, perhaps in the stables, but it's so untidy there." He straightened her pelts and gushingly offered, "What else can I do to help, Maura? I'll fetch more food, drink, extra pelts—"

"Henry, stop your fussing!"

"I crave your comfort."

"I'm exceedingly comfortable, thank you." Maura smiled, then said, "There is something you could do."

"What? Anything—"

"Go find Simon for me."

He turned his disappointment away and muttered, "He's off doing chores somewhere."

"And aren't you supposed to be doing chores with him?" she asked, askance.

Henry shrugged and lied, "No."

Maura shoved away her pelts. "Then help me up and we'll go find him!"

"No!" Henry stressed. "You're to stay in that bed till his Lordship decrees you fit to rise."

"Then," she begged ardently, "*please* bring him to me!"

Henry succumbed to her pout. "I'll go, only—don't you like *my* company?" he added in a wounded voice.

"Of course I do, I just—"

"No," he stopped her with a firm gesture, and his hand struck his heart in feigned lament. "Say no more, you'll only wound me further! I'm going...going..." Maura chucked at his drama as he whined and staggered for the door. Bumping into Simon, he quickly composed himself, and stuttered in defense, "Maura seemed lonely and I—"

Simon stopped Henry's sniveling with unexpected praise, "Why do you always expect an argument? I appreciate you entertaining her."

"You do?" Henry asked, surprised.

"Yes. Now it's my turn to entertain, so please go finish fixing the fences."

"Aren't you going to help me?" hoped Henry.

Crawling into Maura's clutch, Simon mumbled between noisy kisses, "You...you didn't help...me."

Henry turned at the door to present them a look of exaggerated anguish. They were busy and paid him no heed, so he shrugged and moped away.

Maura picked at Simon's hair and extracted a feather. "What's this?" she asked with a puzzled grin.

"A bit of madness," he chuckled.

With an alluring sigh, she ran her fingers briskly over his back, up his arms, along his neck and across his lips, and mused aloud, "I wish I'd been there. When you're away all I think of is your lips on mine—"

"Here," he offered, "taste..."

She partook and added, "Your touch—"

"Then feel..." His hand snuck beneath the pelts and, on its journey upward, stopped to tickle behind her knee.

Maura let out a tight gasp as his fingers met their target. They shared lusty snickers and sank back upon the bed. Sister Mary's loud throat-clearing slowed their mounting zeal and, grudgingly, they untangled. Simon bristled with aggravation. "She's so damned quiet, I forget she's here."

"How much longer must we wait?" whined Maura.

"If you feel strong enough to walk by this evening, we should be able to leave tomorrow."

"When tomorrow?" she demanded.

"Maura," he smiled, "have patience...It *will* happen...soon." He stretched to fetch his saddlebag, and extracted a rumpled parchment. "I haven't shown you this rather important writ."

He spread the betrothal document across their laps and as Maura read the words, she marveled, "The King is a generous Lord!"

"When it suits him," Simon agreed. "Before he allowed me this document, he made me agree to serve as mediator for the Prince of South Wales."

"But you enjoy that work."

"To a degree, yet it can be so damned frustrating. I'd much rather tend an infirmary." He watched Maura's fingers trace the scripting of their names, and ventured on, "Actually, I've been considering, if you're willing that is, letting you handle the diplomatic chores."

"Me?" she answered in amazement. "I've no training."

"Neither had I," he mentioned, pride obvious in his gaze. "Maura, anyone who can alter my father's disposition for the better definitely deserves recognition."

"I'm not responsible for his changing," she argued. "Besides, I know no Welsh."

"You're a quick study."

She clasped his hands between hers and zestfully urged, "Say again where we're to go."

"You mean Menevia?"

"No, say it in Welsh."

"We're going to Cymru."

"Kum...ree," she carefully repeated.

"Good. That's the word for Wales. We'll live at Mynyw."

"Minyou?"

"Excellent. And that means Menevia."

"Tell me more..."

He refused with a smile. "You must rest."

"Please..."

Besotted by her beguiling expression, he let the words tumble briskly off his tongue, "Rydw i'n dy garu di."

She opened her mouth to echo the guttural sounds and then laughed. "I can't. What does it mean?"

"I love you."

"I love you, too, but what does it mean?"

"It means 'I love you'."

She looked shocked. "All those words for something so simple?"

"Oh, Maura," he sighed as he touched her scraped cheek. "For us, there's been nothing simple about it."

Her arms wrapped his neck as she promised, "From here on, after all we've suffered, it *has* to be simpler."

Mother Helena burst in, disrupting their caresses with a roar, "He's gone and taken four with him!"

"Damn him!" cursed Simon. "He couldn't have gotten far. Maura, with any luck, I'll return shortly."

"Simon, I believe I know where—"

"It's my fault he's here, so *I* must apprehend him," he said, chasing the Abbess' flurried figure from the chamber.

Maura shook with frustration. She knew that if Henry was to keep his head, she must be first to find him. Her saddlebag lay by the novice's chair and she called out in English, "Sister Mary."

"Yes, my Lady?"

"I'm feeling a bit chilled. Could you please pass me my satchel?"

"Certainly."

Maura yanked out a knotted clump of clothing, rummaged through, and found a heavy tunic. Wincing, she tugged it over her head, kicked the pelts away, and forced her legs to the side of the bed. "Mary," she implored with a pleading look, "could you help me stand?"

"No, my Lady! My orders are—"

"Mary," Maura gently interjected, "I know where to find the Prince. I'm perfectly well and want to walk. Now, *please*, could you help me?" Maura stood on quaking knees, then after circling the chamber with Mary's aide, she felt robust enough to venture out. She snuck along passageways, and at long last discovered the door exiting to the courtyard. The walls of outbuildings served as her crutch as she hobbled her way across the garden. It seemed she'd been shut up forever in a wet tomb, and a whiff of fragrant blossoms gave her the invigorating sensation of being reborn. She squinted up into a timorous sun, rapidly losing its battle with menacing clouds, and marveled at the vibrant blooms garnishing the yard. A large stone structure blocked her way; deducing it to be the stable, she poked her head in the door and shouted her whisper, "Henry! Are you there? I must warn you." She slipped inside, her furtive gaze ever searching. "Simon and the Abbess are after you and I don't believe—"

Maura stopped short and couldn't help but smile at the engaging sight set before her. Henry sat proud and tall upon his throne of straw, and rallied once again by the cluster of entranced young women, he burbled his woeful tale, "I...I begged her Liege Lord for her hand in marriage and he was about to yield to my desire when—"

"Henry, stop and come here now!"

Henry snapped to the summons and gasped, "Maura!" He dashed to her side, and still caught in his role of unfailing lover, hugged her arm and helped her sit. "Are you mad? If Simon finds you out of bed he'll murder us both—me first."

"Henry," she protested, "stop all this bother! I'm fine." She clutched his hands to keep him still. "It's crucial you listen. The sisters must leave and you must appear to be working. Simon and the Abbess are searching you out! They believe you've kidnapped four novices." The young women aimed their fascination on Maura, and she grew annoyed with their mawkish expressions. She delivered what they craved with blunt sincerity, "Maura did not, as suggested, marry the handsome Prince. She instead made the highly intelligent decision to marry his poorer, far less distinguished cousin, Simon. And that is how the story ends. I apologize if I've disappointed you, but Sisters, you must hurry back to the Abbey. You dare not upset the Abbess." Her dire warning finally took root and they scurried away, giggling. Maura thrust a nearby pitchfork in Henry's hands, demanding, "Now start moving those bales and when they arrive—only *I* will speak."

She'd hardly uttered her last command when the door swung wide, and Simon and the Abbess entered, muttering displeasure. Simon froze in his tracks, rubbed his eyes, then peered through the uneven light to exclaim, "Maura, what—" In a flash he swept her into his arms and coarsely ordered, "You're going back to bed!"

Impulsively, she wriggled and explained, "I thought I knew where Henry was, and you didn't let me say. He mentioned this morning something about the stable and how it desperately needed tidying so I—"

"I'll take you back—now!" demanded Simon, ignoring her reasoning.

"No, Simon," she argued, "please put me down and let me stay awhile. Bed won't help the hurt, distraction will. I want to stay."

He slowly set her on her feet and glaringly decided, "We'll stay only till *he's* done."

Henry paused to lift an impish look, then resumed his fervent scooping.

"Simon, you really shouldn't be so judgmental," admonished Maura, as Simon sat on a bale and she settled in his lap.

"I'm not," he contested in a bruised voice.

"Of course you are. At times I'm amazed that I meet your impossibly strict standards." Maura noticed E'dain munching in a nearby stall. She stood and coaxed Simon from his brooding with a placating smile. "Come, we'll see to your horse."

E'dain acknowledged Maura's presence with a fond nuzzle. Simon patted the mare's rump and frowned. "She won't let me ride her anymore."

Maura's fingers wove through his; she leant close, nibbled his ear, and murmured, "You'll never know that problem with me." Her comment replaced his worry with a blush. "I had nothing but bother from her as well. I thought she specifically hated me."

"No," said he. "She's normally a good-natured soul. She doesn't seem ill."

Henry stabbed at the straw in the adjacent stall, keenly listening.

Maura ran her hands down E'dain's neck, over her back, and down her flanks. When she probed the mare's underside, her quizzical expression relaxed. "I should have guessed. Her teats are swollen and her belly's distended. Simon, she's pregnant."

"That's impossible!" Simon exclaimed, grabbing the stall's wall for balance.

"No, Simon," Maura grinned, "not impossible."

"I've always keep her separated, especially when she's in season. It has to be something else!"

"By the size of her belly, it didn't happen recently," noted Maura. "I expect she's seven, maybe eight months along."

Henry overheard Maura's alarming discovery. His face twitched as he mentally counted back the months. Then he gulped and stealthily scooped his way to the opposite end of the stable. The Abbess followed suspiciously.

"Eight months? Where was I?" Simon struggled to recall and sputtered pieces of his memory, "We...we were in Yorkshire...Richmond, solving a dispute and—"

"We?"

"Yes, Henry and I. He was in particularly rare form. I had to banish him from the meeting for—" He stopped, flashed crimson, and whirled to shout, "Henry!"

Henry froze and squealed back, "Don't yell at me! It...it wasn't my fault!"

Maura swiped hold of Simon's sleeve, stalling his attack. "Before you execute him, let him speak. What happened, Henry?"

"I'm beholden to you, Maura. Well—" he started with extreme caution, brandishing the fork in case his explanation failed to pacify. "Simon asked—no, ordered me to leave the talks, so I went strolling. These two," he said, pointing to E'dain and his stallion, Fulk, "were corralled in separate paddocks. They kept cooing to each other, and seemed lonely, as was I, so I allowed them a visit. I intended to separate them before they became too amorous, but then the guards came to escort me—"

"Why guards?" questioned Maura.

She got no answer. Gesturing furiously and spewing curses, Simon broke from her hold and stormed for Henry. "You bleeding liar!" he ranted. "You're a greedy, spiteful, spoiled baby and I'm sick to death of your pesty tricks! A nursemaid, that's all I am to you, a milksop of a nursemaid! Never again! To Hell with you Henry, to Hell with—" Too irate to continue, he sputtered broken profanities and whirled away.

"Nursemaid!" raved Henry as he seized Simon's tunic, jerked him back around, and thrust the pitchfork deep into the earth. "You self-righteous turd! Always blustering, always moaning, no one or nothing's ever superb enough for you. We'll show Maura who's the true baby here!" He slapped at Simon's face, inciting, "Prove how fierce you are, Simon. I dare you!"

Their escalating fray drained what little strength Maura had left and she uttered faintly, "Stop."

"Enough!" the Abbess trumpeted so all could hear, "I demand you both halt your disgraceful behavior this instant! You," she aimed her scourge at Simon, "and your Lady will leave as soon as she regains her strength, which I pray is very soon. And you!" she railed, turning her wrath on Henry, "will go within the hour." She gathered her wits and her skirts, and thundered out. The door slammed shut at her back, quaking the rafters, and plunging the stalls into a gray gloom.

Maura raised troubled eyes to Simon's chastened expression.

Henry remained a safe distance behind him; his surly scowl betrayed disappointment as he assaulted a pillar with kicks and grunts.

"If you two are emissaries for the Crown," Maura commented with wagging head, "then I fear this Kingdom is in grave, grave danger. Talk to him, Simon."

"Why me?" countered Simon.

"Because you are older and, I pray, wiser."

Henry stopped kicking to fume, "Why am I blamed for everything?!"

"Not everything," Simon muttered, turning to face his adversary.

"I thought you needed my help," sulked Henry.

"I did, only at times you seem to *want* to be yelled at."

"And at times, I do...when I'm certain you don't mean it! Lately, Simon, I've not been so certain."

"God's blood, Henry! With everything that's happened of late, I don't know what I've said or yelled. I apologize if I've wounded your feelings."

Henry hung his head ashamedly and mumbled, "And I'm sorry about E'dain. I meant no malice."

Maura shut her eyes in relief and considered for a moment the true cause of this uproar. Jealousy had claimed Henry, forcing him to use drastic measures to keep his closest companion's attention. Good or bad, any notice was preferable to none. Dizziness visited her again, and she supposed it was far past time for her to return to her lonely bed. "I'll leave you two—to talk," she said.

"I'll go with you," said Simon, his hand cupping her elbow.

They walked to the door, where she stopped him with a kiss and a request, "Stay with him awhile. He needs you as well. Simon, he's terribly bored, but...don't give him menial chores to do. If he has to leave, ask him to perform a task that befits his rank."

"A task that befits his rank," echoed Simon thoughtfully. Promptly an idea emerged. "I'll send him on to Canterbury to lord over the preparations for our wedding!"

"*That* he will thoroughly enjoy," said Maura tiredly.

His fingers pressed hers. "Thank you for calming us. Are you certain you'll be—"

"I'm quite capable of finding my way back...only, you must hurry. We have scant time left before you're barred from my bed."

He begged a second kiss, received his wish, then returned to Henry. Side by side upon the straw throne they sat. Henry tugged on the grass and griped, "What were you two muttering about?"

"She says you're bored."

"She's correct, again." He handed Simon a blade and noted, "You seem unduly upset about your horse."

"I've a bundle of anger inside me...simmering. You provided a spark and it flared. It was unfair of me to blame you...yet, I must add, it *is* a long walk to Wales."

"Consider E'dain's blessed event as the beginning of your burgeoning family," assuaged Henry. "On your wedding night, you'll make Maura pregnant and by the close of the year, there will be two additions to your clan."

Simon smirked, chewed on the blade of straw, then arched a brow. "You're quite certain about...the wedding night?"

"Definitely, and I'm never wrong."

"Well, I know of a way you can help that miracle come about."

"How? Tell me!" urged Henry, squirming in anticipation.

"Ride to Canterbury and assist Lanfranc with the wedding preparations."

"What a splendid idea!" burst Henry. "I'll ensure perfection!"

"And Lanfranc will be delighted to see you." Simon fondly mused, "Do you remember our treks to Canterbury?"

"Oh, yes, with the greatest joy!" spouted Henry. "They were our only legitimate means of escaping Uncle Odo." Henry's enthusiasm faltered and, ruefully, he asked, "Simon, why are we battling so? Twice this month, we've almost come to blows. In our entire history that has never happened before."

Simon let go a woeful sigh. "I have no answer for you, Henry. We've played our cat and mouse game since first we met, and lately it's gotten a bit exaggerated."

"I've no recollection of ever meeting you. I only remember you always being close by. It's been comforting."

Simon softened to Henry's memory and answered with deep affection, "We met when you were but one year old, and your sweet mother brought you to Dunheved to pass you about and boast. I couldn't fathom what all the fuss was about. All you did was bawl, burp, drool, and smell bad."

"I haven't changed much," chortled Henry.

"You stole my toys and bit the tip off my hound's ear!"

Henry thought to himself, *I'd love to steal your toy now,* but admitted only, "I'll miss you."

"I hope you'll want to visit," encouraged Simon.

"Where? You've not told me where."

"Menevia, South Wales."

"Where you were before—"

"Yes."

"It'll be great fun to visit, disguised of course." Suddenly solemn, Henry added, "When Father dies, you'll need my help again."

"Indeed we shall." Simon clasped his shoulder. "Now get yourself to Canterbury. With luck, we'll join you there tomorrow, late afternoon."

The cousins shared an atoning hug, then parted company. Henry gathered together his belongings and half his contingent, and left the Abbey to a chorus of the novices' exalted farewells. Simon, having coddled Henry too long, lost his chance to bid Maura goodnight.

For the lovers, the night proved desperately long and lonely. To be so close yet forced apart was torture. Maura lay awake reflecting on Simon's account of his time in

Normandy. She anguished over his depiction of Marc's wounding, and drifted off to a vain wish that her sweet brother would be here to witness their glorious union. Simon in turn lamented over Godfrey's tragic end, and composed a fleeting prayer for the wellbeing of Alan, Almodis, and her child. As he lapsed into a fretful slumber, the astounding vision of his father's nod returned to grant a slip of hope for their tenuous future.

*****

Sharing Maura's saddle, Simon pointed over her shoulder, announcing vibrantly, "There! Past the next hill."

She reined Henry's stallion and peered past the mound to the jutting gilded spire of Canterbury Cathedral. A brisk, tepid wind whipped her flame-colored hair, and blackened clouds tumbled their way. "We must hurry," she shouted, "or be caught in a downpour!"

Simon hugged Maura's waist and, to her sharp kick, Henry's horse, Fulk bounded forward, with E'dain huffing behind, and Henry's guards struggling to keep pace.

The colossal cathedral and the Archbishop's palace, housed within the city of Canterbury's protective walls, boasted no battlements or soldiers. Two large timbered structures also graced the hallowed ground—Lanfranc's infirmaries, Simon explained as they trotted up to the city's open gates. Pilgrims, peasants, clergy, and an assortment of beasts loitered about the entrance and reluctantly scattered to let the impatient party pass. Once inside the wall, Maura marveled at the surrounding gaiety—tradesmen, servants, squires and maids, all clearly happy at their work. She directed her awe to the top of the cathedral stairs and beheld a regal Henry, waving. Maura tugged on Simon's sleeve, pointed, and they avidly returned the Prince's greeting. Grooms dashed to their side, helped them dismount, and escorted them to the church. With hands tightly clasped, they scampered up the stairs and through the arched doors. Maura twirled to the sanctuary's majesty. Doves perched on and swooped among the towering arches, golden-framed portraits embellished the walls, and lancet windows stained in the most vivid colors turned the last vestiges of sunlight into dancing rainbows. Maura clutched Simon's arm excitedly, gasping, "Oh Simon, it's truly magnificent!"

"Lanfranc hordes beautiful things," commented Simon. "I wouldn't be at all surprised if he decides to add you to his collection." She dragged him to a huge framed painting and reached out to caress the paint's bumpy texture. Simon studied the portrait and remarked on the scowling model, "He's most likely a former pope, which one, I do not know."

A hand on his shoulder spun Simon round, and there stood Henry, a wily grin curling his lips. "All is ready!" he gloated, weaving his arms through theirs. "Come, Lanfranc is overly eager to meet you, Maura."

The Archbishop, his robes flapping wildly, flew down the altar steps, and loped along the center aisle, gesticulating and booming all the way, "Simon! Henry! Where have you gone?"

Maura watched Simon's tremulous expression beam radiant at the sight of the Bishop. "Simon, my lad!" Lanfranc exclaimed with glee. "How absolutely marvelous to see you again!"

Simon disappeared into Lanfranc's huge hug; when freed, he stepped back, genuflected, and kissed the Bishop's ring, muttering, "Your Grace."

"Up, Simon, up! None of that formality, not on this very joyous day!" His admiring gaze settled upon Maura, as he raised her hand to his lips, and sighed, "Maura...your legend is well known here, my sweet Lady."

His thick accent intrigued her, as did his welcoming presence, shaggy gray hair, and smiling brown eyes. "And I've heard only the greatest praise for you, Your Grace," she charmed and rose up on tip-toe to kiss his swarthy cheeks.

Lanfranc blushed and tittered, "Come, let's make ready. I'll perform a quick though sacred ceremony and we'll spend our remaining time together—celebrating! Henry's truly outdone himself. He personally supervised the selection of food, music, and wine!"

Simon snapped his head to a rash of giggles. He tugged and protested, "Maura? Where?" as her hand was torn from his and a dozen maids spirited her away.

Fuddled, he started after them; Henry restrained him and wryly assured, "She won't be gone long, and when she returns, you'll be dazzled." He regarded Simon's rumpled appearance with distaste and complained, "Why do you always look as though you're off to slop the hogs?"

"Maura likes how I look," Simon mumbled in defense, sticking his shirt tail into his braies.

"She's no judge. Have you taken a close look at her lately?" belittled Henry. "Now, it will be difficult, but come. I'll see what I can do to pretty you up."

Simon sheepishly tagged behind and felt a twinge of consternation flutter his belly. He'd imagined the ritual would be simple and quick; how clearly wrong he'd been. Then again, it had been *his* idea to involve—Henry.

Maura self-consciously held a towel to her injured breast and swiftly climbed into the steaming tub. Immediately, she baptized herself with a duck beneath the soapy bubbles, then emerged to wilt as sturdy hands rigorously scrubbed her scalp. Maids skittered about the chamber, jabbering as they gathered clothing and toiletries. "Is this the frock you spoke of, my Lady?" inquired a young maid.

Maura's eyes opened to the dismal sight of her crinkled wedding gown. "Yes," she frowned.

"No matter, my Lady," bolstered the maid. "We'll dangle it atop a boiling cauldron in the kitchen. That'll smooth its creases."

The rotund matron washing Maura's hair chirped, "Your betrothed is a bit scruffy, but nonetheless quite nice, my Lady. It seems you've met before."

Maura smiled inwardly and murmured, "Many times."

"And are you pleased?"

"Very," Maura sighed as she rested back upon the tub's wall and admired the chamber's opulence. A fire blazed in a tiled hearth set between the bed and the door, intricately sewn tapestries adorned each wall and curtained the bed. She marveled at the rarity gracing one corner—a tall looking glass. After her soaking, she wrapped herself in a robe and perched herself upon the foot of the lofty bed to comb out tangles and dry her hair by the fire's warmth. The bustling din made dwelling on the upcoming ritual impossible. She paused in her combing to trace the raised embroidery on the bed curtain, and pondered with a luscious shiver, would they love here this night? Her musing was disrupted by the matron's finger, daubing a flesh colored cream on her scrapes and gash.

Maura removed her robe to dress, revealing to all her many bruises. After an initial unified gasp, a troubled hush descended. The matron broke the disquiet by chatting merrily while massaging pungent oils into Maura's skin; the heady aromas refreshed her senses and helped quell her apprehension. She stepped into a silk chemise and her skin tingled to its sumptuousness. Maura noticed a girl child sitting on the floor by the fire, deftly weaving marigold blossoms into a gold braided circlet. She started to a tickle and was amazed to see two women poised over her legs, rolling on linen hose and securing them above her knees with lace garters. The pampering overwhelmed her and, feeling a bit spent, she sat and braced herself against a bedpost. A cup of wine presently appeared with the guarantee, "This will help calm you, my Lady."

The gown was hauled in minus its wrinkles, and Maura felt encumbered by its ponderous weight, draggling sleeves, and long train as it was draped about her. While wincing to its lacing, she happened a glimpse of herself in the glass and sucked an exalted breath. The ice-blue brocade gave her usually wan complexion color, and her eyes sparkle. The flattering material clung to her breasts, tapered her waist, and flared to ample folds just past her lean hips. She delicately stroked the peach colored threads bordering the gown's yoke and cuffs, and twisted and turned every which way to appreciate her astonishing transformation.

Like butterflies, the women flitted about, straightening Maura's frock and combing and fluffing her hair. A mint leaf disappeared between her lips, a gilded girdle cinched her waist, golden slippers adorned her feet and, lastly, the circlet was set like a crown low on her brow. A few final neatening touches followed, and then the women, clucking their approval, left her alone to suffer...the waiting.

Henry eyed his creation skeptically, fingered his beard, and twisted his lips to a sour scowl. "Won't do," he decided, and resumed sifting through a pile of select garments.

Simon huffed and wriggled from the rejected tunic, and threw it upon the steep discard pile. "God's blood, Henry," he flared, "make up your blasted mind! I do not intend to spend the entire day dressing!" He scratched furiously at the cut hairs that chafed his neck and griped, "Thanks to your inept snipping, I'll be twitching all throughout the ceremony."

"A perfectly normal reaction to getting married," noted Henry dryly. He picked up a royal blue tunic and passed it to a page, speculating, "Perhaps this one will work."

The page leapt puddles circling the tub, and handed the garment to Simon with a tiny bow. Simon wondered how long the lad would have to keep up Henry's preposterous show. He smoothed the lavish material between his fingers and admired, "I like its sheen." Swiftly donning the tunic, he spread his arms, twirled once, and asked with bated breath, "Well?"

"It doesn't do a thing for your knobby knees," opined Henry. "Once we decide on braies and hose, I'll know better."

Henry continued his rummaging while Simon perused a mass of vibrantly colored outfits hanging from a strung rope. "Why does Lanfranc need such a varied wardrobe?" he asked absently.

"They're not for him," said Henry. "These clothes are for visitors attending state occasions where proper fashion is critical. You would know little about such things. Now, shall we try light braies and hose with dark laces or—"

"Not laces!" moaned Simon.

"Of course laces!" returned Henry, aghast.

"Tell me true, Henry," said Simon scathingly, "do you endure this grueling ritual each and every time you dress?"

"Heavens no," scoffed Henry. "I know exactly what suits me. It's you who's so damned difficult—Or dark braies and hose with light laces?" He strolled over to the bed and spread out the garments as they would be worn. His face pinched to the weight of his ponderous decision and he threw up his hands in defeat.

"Give me the blasted braies!" growled Simon, snatching up the black pants from the bed. In a rabid flurry, he hopped into the braies, tugged on the hose and, struggling with the laces, cried out in frustration, "What do you do with these cursed strings?!"

Henry knelt and offered, "Allow me. I swear, Simon, you are absolutely hopeless."

"What is the point of wrapping ribbons round one's legs?"

"No point. They're used only for show and not in the least bit practical."

"Sounds like you," sniggered Simon.

Henry simpered and sneered, "Very droll, Simon," then gestured for his cousin to turn so he could appraise the whole stunning effect. Simon waited in prolonged suspense for Henry's blessing, and when it came it took the form of a rather vague nod. He brushed tiny blond hairs from Simon's shoulders and remarked disparagingly, "There's little I can do to dispel your peasant look, for alas, it's in your blood."

"Insult me and you insult yourself," scorned Simon.

"Not true! You're strictly peasant stock," countered Henry haughtily. "My mother possessed *true* royal blood." His coarseness subsided and he patted the bed for Simon to sit. "And now comes the most torturous part of all...waiting. You're dreadfully pale, Simon." He poured wine and commanded, "I suggest you imbibe this before you faint."

Simon downed the cup in one gulp and reached long to beg, "More..."

Henry obeyed and his look turned benevolent as he asked, "Would you like me to stay and sit with you?"

Simon raked madly at his newly fringed hair and threw back his second cup. He plopped down hard upon the bed, let out an anguished moan, and hiccupped, "*Ple...ase.*"

*****

CHAPTER THIRTY - WEDDINGS

Henry and Simon were first to be summoned to the Chapel. Simon stood idly by the altar, fidgeting and scratching, while Henry assisted a pretty maid with flower arranging. Reaching to pluck a stray hair from his shoulder, Simon glimpsed at the end of the aisle a vision in blue. He whirled around and sucked an exalted breath. Maura froze to the equally entrancing sight of Simon and blinked away her doubt. Then, beaming ecstatically, she hiked her skirts and sprinted the entire length of the aisle, leapt the two steps to the altar, and threw herself into his eager arms.

Titters erupted from the maids and Henry snapped to the commotion. For a curious instant, he wondered—who was the ravishing maiden kissing Simon? When Maura briefly broke away to acknowledge him with a wink and blown kiss, his cheeks flamed so hot he could feel beads of sweat popping out upon his brow. He dropped his embarrassed gaze to his boots, now piled high with spilt flowers.

Lanfranc, in celebratory vestments, glided gracefully to the altar, trailed by a train of church inhabitants who, together with the maids, filed into pews. The Bishop paused beside the enmeshed couple and gruffly cleared his throat, noting with a grin, "There will be *plenty* of time for that sort of thing later. My dear children," he stated gleefully, taking their hands, "come with me." He led them to the altar's wooden railing and set two pillows upon the stone floor for the sake of their knees. Simon and Maura clasped hands and knelt before Lanfranc, exuding such excitement, that the Bishop felt the need to calm. "Henry," he called, "come close, my lad. In jittery times it's comforting to have a friend nearby." Henry kicked the flowers aside and knelt opposite the couple at the railing.

The loquacious Bishop, sporting a contemplative grin and gesturing happily, first addressed Maura, "My most favorite times, my dear Lady, were always visits by these two ruffians. As different as night and day they were—Simon so steadfast, Henry so carefree—yet also so close, they knew each other's thoughts. Henry's interests lay elsewhere, though Simon's love of medicine sprouted early. Many a night I'd find him slumped and snoring over a stack of medical volumes in my chamber. And then there was his never-ending quest to find some man or beast to mend. How pleased I made him when I decided to build my hospitals, and what a prodigious role he has played in their success. By far his greatest jubilation was boasting of his family...particularly you." To the delight of the congregation, each time the Archbishop diverted his gaze, Maura and Simon stole an amorous glance or shared a sweet kiss. But alas, they held one kiss too long and Lanfranc caught their mischief. He chided them with a look, then reflected on, "After your tragic separation, when Simon had returned to England, he journeyed here often for solitude and to share his sorrows. Time and time again, he adamantly swore he'd discover a way for the two of you to be reunited. I believed that impossible and told him so. Then Henry arrived yesterday with the glorious news of your betrothal! Why I ever doubted you, Simon, I'll never know, for you are, without challenge, the most determined soul I have ever had the extreme privilege to know."

Maura leant near to kiss away Simon's blush. Lanfranc lifted their adoring, eager faces and admitted, "I've been known to rattle on forever, so let us proceed. Though, let me add how miraculous it is to solemnize a marriage blessed by mutual love. It's literally been ages since a rarity such as your union has occurred, and I don't recall the proper litany, so I'll improvise as we go along. Now, first I will need the document stating permission for your joining from your Liege Lord." Henry fumbled along his belt, extracted the parchment, and presented it to the Bishop. Lanfranc spread the scroll across the altar, and his inspection of the script was accented by a host of oohs and aahs.

Lost in Maura's beauty, Simon fingered the blossoms in her hair. Her blissful smile cracked his trance and she exclaimed in a whisper, "You look absolutely magnificent!"

"It is entirely Henry's doing," Simon mumbled peevishly, scratching his neck. "He gave me no choice. While I bathed, he ceremoniously burned all my clothing. It was either this, or marry naked."

Their eyes gleamed to the intriguing notion. Lanfranc snapped to their muffled chuckling, folded the papers, and nodded in wonder. "I'm greatly impressed. The King obviously cares deeply for the both of you. Now, I'll have the land grants."

Simon shook his head. "There's no land involved."

Lanfranc turned his bewilderment to Maura. "Then there must be a statement of dowry."

"No, no dowry," shrugged Maura. "It's all gone to Hugh of Ryedale."

"Oh dear," said Lanfranc, "this is highly irregular, and I must say I'm a bit muddled as to what I'm—"

"Can't you just bless them and have done with it?" Henry sniped impatiently.

"Henry!" admonished Lanfranc. "I don't believe you have the training or disposition to teach me my place!"

Henry huffed, leant on the railing, and let his perturbed gaze wander the chapel. Yet his eyes were perpetually drawn back to the lovers. Staring at them, he drummed his fingers upon the wood and inwardly wrestled unbidden emotions. Their rapt expressions miffed him; their felicity in each other nauseated him; their secret looks repulsed him! To pass the interminable moments, he fantasized Maura professing her lust for him. How clearly he could envision himself snatching her from Simon's side, stealing away to a forbidden place, stripping off her fancy frock, and having at her! Now uncomfortably aroused, he shook away his dream, wiped his brow, and focused again on the Bishop.

Lanfranc recited his melodic prayers, his one palm resting on Maura's head, the other on Simon's. He motioned for them to lift their clasped hands and motioned a blessing first in a tiny cross, then larger to cover the two, and finally one huge enough to encompass the entire congregation. Then he beamed and trumpeted, "To complete the marriage of your bodies and souls, you may seal the sacrament with a kiss!"

The crowd struggled to contain their exuberance as Simon and Maura murmured vows of love; Simon kissed her ring, Maura his, and their lips and bodies crushed together in a smothering embrace. Henry looked away and dismissed the stab in his belly as hunger. Lanfranc clapped his hands to regain their attention and extolled, "Go my children! Be fruitful and happy together!" They remained on their knees a moment more to offer prayers of thanks to God, their King, and the Archbishop for their wondrous gifts of freedom and protection.

*****

Rain dripped like tears through the fissures separating planks in the roof of Berkhamstead's chapel. Hugh of Ryedale stood before an ancient priest and faced a pale, trembling maid, whose every response needed prompting by the cleric. Will hugged Rufus' arm for support and wiped sweat from his brow. It had been a painstaking chore convincing Hugh to agree to this queer union. And now each of Will's labored breaths stabbed his chest and a burning hurt surged from his shoulder down his arm. He must persevere! Only the blessing and the signing of the marriage documents remained till Helmsley Manor belonged at long last to him.

Will sighed raggedly as the priest ceased his droning. He dug into his coin pouch, extracted a mark for the maid, and waved her away. Rufus assisted him to the altar and eyed his uncontrollable hacking with disgust. Will regained his composure, unrolled the parchment, and pointed to the spot designated for Hugh's mark. Hugh and Rufus loomed close, making Will feel a bit like a trapped mouse set to be pounced upon. As the groom scratched his name, the script blurred before Will's eyes and he stood dumbly, frantically blinking to restore his sight.

Rufus placed the quill in Will's palm, wrapped his fingers around it, and guided his hand to the appropriate place, grumbling, "Get on with it, Will."

His name—that's all that was needed—his name and it was done! Yet, as the ink scribbled over the parchment, a fleeting incertitude rocked Will's resolve. He swiftly squelched it and, with his last vestige of strength, pressed his father's stolen seal into the heated wax. He seized Rufus' sleeve, and thrust a congratulatory hand out to Hugh. Hugh warily offered his in return, but hesitated as Will's triumphant grin twisted to agony. He caught Will's collapsing body, and wondered at his strangled croaking, "God damn her! Damn the filthy bitch..."

Rufus shook his head at Will's pathetic figure and, to Hugh, muttered, "Well...it appears there will be no celebratory feast *this* night."

*****

The doors to the Archbishop's great hall burst wide and the wedding party swept gaily into the resplendent room. Maura and Simon paused, overwhelmed by the rousing chorus of cathedral residents awaiting their arrival. The Archbishop excitedly urged them on, "To the dais with you, and once there, thrill them with a kiss!"

Henry gamboled behind them, hollering orders, "Bring on the food and drink!" Servants skittered between embellished trestle tables, delivering platters of roasted pheasant, peas, and onions, served upon thick trenchers adorned with dried apples and pears. Wine, ale, and mead flowed freely into tankards as the elated throng crowded onto benches.

A raucous salute of hoisted cups accompanied the lovers' kiss, after which Maura and Simon turned to admire their backdrop of towering stained glass. A sudden lightning strike sent vivid sparks of color cascading over the panes, and a hush followed the rattling thunder. Lanfranc thrust his cup high and exclaimed, "Even the Lord booms his mirth!" Relieved laughter rumbled from the congregation, then all bowed their heads to the Bishop's blessing.

Strains of sweet music filled the hall as the diners ate and chatted amongst themselves. Maura politely answered questions from a cleric concerning her unusual and varied education. To Simon, Lanfranc emphasized the rarity of their consensual marriage with harrowing tales of forced unions. All the while, Simon and Maura's fingers knitted together, teasing and petting. Henry, when he could tear his eyes from Maura, regarded the crowd below with satisfaction. His special demand that no distinction be made to class had been carried out to perfection, and all celebrated with equal vivacity.

The meal ended and the servants bustled forth to clear, dismantle, and stack the trestle tables. The musicians settled themselves on benches at the far end of the hall and, at Henry's waved cue, they began to play a brisk tune. Henry's pleasing voice sang to the rafters, flushing birds from their nests and couples out onto the swept floor. Simon and Maura watched amused as Henry rushed the flock, snared a pretty maid from her partner, and whirled her madly about the room. The horde hooted in approval and mimicked the Prince, stomping, leaping, and spinning to his sprightly tune. Simon chuckled and murmured, "Care for a spin, my sweet?"

Maura hugged his arm and gushed, "I'd love to..." and her eyes twinkled passion as she added, "but we must save some vigor...for later."

"We'll tread lightly," he answered and, laughing, they ventured into the core of the gaiety.

Henry strutted up beside them to comment on their lively stepping. "This brings back hysterical memories, eh, Cousin?"

"You mean painful memories, don't you?" replied Simon.

Maura spun under Simon's arm and asked, "What are you two talking about?"

"At Uncle Odo's, dancing was an intricate part of our training," explained Simon. "And guess who was always assigned as my partner?"

"It wasn't Henry, was it?" smirked Maura.

"I could never escape him or his cloddish feet!"

Henry lived up to the insult and stomped on his cousin's toes. Simon wailed and hopped in a circle to the crowd's chortling, and Henry's sneering retort, "He's jealous because I got to play the Lady."

"You?" snorted Maura, "I find that hard to believe."

"Why?" Henry asked, pitching his voice high. "I'm clearly more graceful and, I dare say—" He paused to flutter his lashes, then finished, "—infinitely prettier!"

"Graceful, my arse," snickered Simon as his boot's tip met Henry's behind.

Henry whooped and darted amongst the crowd, pinching and startling the women. He paused before the band and his exuberant gesturing roused their tempo and the dancers' spirits.

Wrapped in Simon's arms, Maura swayed to the music, and remarked, "I've never seen him so happy."

"He thrives on excitement and attention." Simon's lips tickled her neck and he asked, "And you, my love—are *you* happy?"

Her eyes sparkled happy tears as she attempted to sputter a response, yet her radiance sufficed as an answer. They sensed scrutiny and, looking about, were surprised to see the floor clear save for themselves. The crowd shouted encouragement and Maura suggested, "If we're to show off, we'll do it properly. For a start, you'll feel freer without this," she said, tugging at his tunic. She reached round and gathered up her gown's train, hooked it through her girdle, and sighed, "That's much better." Simon tossed his tunic to Henry and Maura knelt to remove his laces. He chuckled to her tickling, and the audience whistled as she tied a ribbon round his brow. The lovers, emboldened by the effusive retinue, swirled, dipped and pranced to a nimble tune. And shortly, Lanfranc and the others followed their lead, each vying for the fanciest footwork.

Along with the frenzied combination of a driving beat and ample drink came the games. The men stalked and heckled the blindfolded bride. Fervently her fingers sought out Simon and, to the men's lusty taunting, her laughter boomed hysterical. When she finally removed her blindfold, Henry's leering snicker greeted her. A drunken reveler blabbed Henry's secret of bribing the men to kidnap Simon from the hall. Maura promptly chased Henry out the door and returned victorious with her man in tow. Squealing women instantly snatched him away, tied taut the blindfold over his eyes, and spun him furiously round and round. However, to their groans of disappointment, he sniffed out Maura's luscious scent, and followed his nose straight into her arms.

After an especially tempestuous jig, the lovers drifted from the party and ambled back to the dais. Henry's zeal faltered at their departure. He trailed them with a sly gate, and narrowly watched Maura bunch up her skirts, and sit upon Simon's lap. Again, they murmured secrets, shared voracious kisses, and Henry's jaw fell slack as their eager fingers vanished beneath each other's clothing. Stunned, he sat unnoticed a short distance away and continued his spying. A firm hand on his shoulder accompanied a strict warning, "Thou shall not covet thy neighbor's wife!"

Without a twitch, Henry muttered, "Surely, I'm allowed to admire beauty."

"Admire, perhaps, lust after—no." Lanfranc slipped into the chair beside Henry's.

"And what could you possibly know of lust?" snorted Henry.

"I don't claim to be an expert such as yourself, nevertheless, I am after all—a man." Lanfranc followed Henry's ogling to the entangled couple, and sighed, "They're not exactly subtle, are they? I don't believe their wedding night will be a novel experience for either of them." Henry didn't appear to hear so Lanfranc nudged him and suggested, "Before they slip beneath the table and cause a riot, I think the time has arrived for the women to take her away. Be a good lad and fetch the matron." Henry, stiff and silent, rose to obey, but Lanfranc didn't appreciate the naughty glint in his eye and offered a silent plea, *Please Lord, don't let him cause trouble.*

Maura caressed Simon's damp chest and squirmed as his fingers toyed with her garters. She broke from their kiss to pant, "Let's sneak away. No one will notice. There are scores of beds to choose from...upstairs."

He tasted her mouth once more. "Beds...upstairs," he sputtered. "Oh yes...we'll sample them all. It's been so long!"

"Twenty-one days," she clarified and then enticed, "I crave you so, over me, filling me—"

"Stop!" he whined, "You'll drive me mad! We'll go, we'll go—" They slipped from their seat and Simon moaned as Maura again was plucked from his hold. This time he wrestled to keep her, but his fight was swiftly humbled by the giddy, determined maids.

Henry restrained his cousin, chuckling, "It's all part of the game! They must make her ready for you."

"From what I could tell, she's overly ready!" Simon hotly contested, ripping from Henry's hold. "Where are they taking her?"

"I haven't a clue," laughed Henry. "And to have her, you must find her. If you're not quick enough, someone else may find her first!" Henry eyes sparked mischief as he dashed after the maids; Simon sprinted at his heels; the other men struggled to catch up, and yapping hounds loped behind. Only Lanfranc, the band of musicians, and a few snoring souls remained in the hall. The Archbishop grinned at the rakish revelry, and hummed along with the melody while contentedly sipping wine.

Upstairs, the maids scampered down passageways and slipped into different chambers to fuddle the men. Maura, locked in the vise-like grip of the matron, glanced warily at the merry chaos unfolding behind her. The matron and a younger maid hustled her into a chamber at the far end of the hall. There, dozens of tapers glittered the cozy room with an unearthly glow. Two tables flanked the slim, curtained bed, one set with a platter of cheese, bread and dried fruit, the other holding a flask of wine and two silver cups. The maid filled the cups, then parted the bed-curtains, flung back the pelts, and showered the silk sheets with scarlet petals.

Maura watched the maid with fascination, her mind swimming with anticipation—though also with an elusive dread.

The matron unlaced Maura's gown and noticed her shivering. "Are you chilled, my Lady?"

"Ye...yes..." stammered Maura.

"Not to worry," Matron said, winking, "he'll soon warm you. We envy you this night." She helped Maura squirm out of the gown and suggested, "Out of the chemise as well. While rummaging through the trunk, I discovered something more revealing and ever so lovely. This chamber was the Queen's favorite and she kept her personal items always close. Prince Henry told us she considered you her daughter, and we thought she'd be delighted to look down from Heaven and see you wearing this..."

At sight of the linen chemise, Maura whispered fondly, "Matilda was a sweet mother," and stepped into the translucent slip of a frock.

The ivory material clung snugly to her every charm and hung temptingly low off her shoulders. She chafed the bumps that covered her bare arms and hardly heard the matron yammer, "The King and Queen would visit often. They were hearty lovers, always fondling, kissing—"

The sound of encroaching ruckus silenced the matron, and the young maid squeaked, "They're coming! They're coming!"

Inches from Maura's chamber door, Simon tumbled to the rushes. He swiped at the boot that tripped him, and missed. Henry, staggering from hysterics, crashed into the door, crowing, "I won! I won!" Simon chuckled in defeat as he slowly sat and brushed grass from his hair and clothes.

The matron hurried Maura to the bed, removed her circlet, and chirped, "Drape the curtain across you. Your husband may not win this race!" Yet she voiced Maura's fear too late.

Henry barreled through the door, and surged toward Maura with such urgency, she hadn't the time or room to dodge him. Simon's laughter suddenly ceased; he scrambled to his feet and burst into the chamber, shouting, "Henry, no! Wait!"

Henry's arms circled Maura's chest and he yanked her up from the bed. About to kiss her, he froze to her pained cry. His shock intensified as she doubled over and sagged back to the bed. Matron's and the maid's condemning glares bore into him, making him twist and whine in anguish, "What? What have I done? Maura, how did I hurt—"

Simon raced up behind Henry, nudged him aside, and took Maura in his arms. The women hovered close, their eyes round with fretting. Maura at last raised her blanched face and said faintly, "I'm fine..."

"Did he reopen the wound?" fretted Simon.

"No, I don't believe so."

"Wound!" gasped Henry. "What wound?!"

"It's not your fault, Henry," said Simon. "I should have warned you."

"Oh, my Lord!" Henry wailed. He fell to his knees and gripped her hands between his, beseeching, "Forgive me, Maura! I...I didn't know. I swear, I meant no harm. I could never hurt you. Please say you forgive me!"

She ached to his moist, pleading gaze and, touching his cheek, consoled with a tender look. "There's nothing to forgive and ever so much to thank you for! The ceremony was absolutely glorious, Henry. And now, I want to be with my husband—alone."

Henry bowed to her goodness, kissed her hand, and rose to leave. The maids ambled away, mumbling good will, and Henry paused at the door somberly to wish, "Sweet dreams, my Lady."

Outside the door, he slid crestfallen to the rushes, and pressed his ear firmly to the wood. A rustling at his back interrupted his surveillance, and he turned to see a not so young, rumply dressed, towheaded woman. Her large dark eyes lured him up from the floor, and his moping look brightened as he hurried to catch her.

"Will he be all right?" Maura asked.

Simon dismissed her concern with a shrug. "He won't sulk for long."

Maura caressed Simon's brooding face. His expression betrayed such apprehension that she grew uneasy, and implored, "Simon, you mustn't fret so."

"Tell me true, do you hurt?"

"Yes, I'm a bit sore, but it's nothing we can't overcome—if we're cautious." Her lips skimmed his neck and her fingers tugged at his shirt; he succumbed to her urging with a rapturous sigh and drew the garment over his head. He peeled her shift lower, but she stopped him and pleaded, "No...not yet—"

"Maura...why?"

"I don't want you to see what Will's done."

"Then the shift stays," Simon appeased, helping her between the fragrant sheets. He swiftly shed his clothes and slipped in beside her. Their lips gently joined and his touch sparked a shiver; it raced over her skin raising bumps to the surface. She stiffened and he wondered again at her hesitation, "What frightens you, my love?"

"That this is a dream and I'll wake alone!" she despaired.

He smoothed her mussed hair and murmured, "This *is* a dream! Our most wondrous dream and it's finally come true. We'll never wake alone again...I love you so."

"And I love you," she choked and, melting to his intense gaze, removed the shift.

Simon gathered her close, shut his eyes, and took a sensuous moment to savor the tranquil quiet, the rich scents, and the sumptuous feel of her skin against his. Her starved kiss stirred him, and his feather touch discovered a pulsing warmth had replaced her chill. "Cautious..." he murmured, stretching with her across the bed, "we'll take care to be cautious—"

"And gentle," she breathed, molding to him, "ever so gentle..."

His lips soothed her wounded breast, traveled lower to tingle her belly, and came to rest in the soft down between her legs. She moaned a blissful, "Oh, Simon," and reached down to weave her fingers through his hair.

Henry entered the stable and casually checked every empty stall. A glimpse in the last one revealed the maid on her back in the straw, her skirts hiked high, and her expression mundane. She limply raised her arms, asking, "Is this what you're wanting, my Lord?"

He folded his arms and leant back thoughtfully against the stall's fence. Normally, he preferred a bit of tickling and teasing before it came to this, but, after his overly frustrating evening, he really shouldn't be so particular. Her legs parted for him. He dropped to his knees, threw off his tunic, and wondered politely, "Do you have a name?"

"You needn't know," she answered flatly.

Henry looked puzzled, then shrugged as he lay over her and awaited her touch. Strangely, her arms stayed stiff at her sides. His mouth roughly covered hers. She jerked away, spitting and sputtering, "Do...don't!"

"I want to!" he loudly argued, bracing himself up on his arms. Though peering closer, he wasn't so certain. A coating of grime soiled her pocked skin, the few teeth she possessed were chipped and stained, her girth was too ample for his tastes, and she stank. Then again, he considered, it would be a sin to waste such a willing vessel simply because of an unpleasant odor and spurned kiss—he'd suffered far worse. With a labored sigh, he freed himself from his braies, wedged between her legs, and rubbed against her belly. She remained still and rigid beneath him, her eyes squeezed shut. No response from the girl was tolerable, but—resting back on his haunches, he stared in abhorrent shock at his state of detumescence. Head in hand, he wailed to himself, *This can't be happening! I'll run and hide. No one can know! Yet she knows and, if I leave, she will surely betray my failure! How can I possibly survive that nightmare?!*

Maura spread Simon back upon the bed and worshipped his body with strokes and kisses. Her mouth tasted and surrounded, stoking and swelling his passion. She mounted him and moaned to the thrill of her breasts filling his cupped palms. He reeled from the feeling of her wetness moving over him, her lush hair hanging long, tickling his chest, the divine look of ecstasy flushing her face. She lay over him; he clutched her and strained a confession, "What I feel with you is so strong, sometimes...it hurts."

"I know, my love," she murmured, "I feel the same." They slipped to their sides, and she hugged him with her legs, her fevered kisses begging as she guided him inside her body.

The bewildered maid pushed up on her elbows and studied Henry's trouble. As she considered leaving, he contrived a swift solution to his torment. Easily, he envisioned Maura sprawled beneath him, panting with desire, igniting his passion with sizzling caresses and lewd comments. Her slippery thighs eagerly parted and, crying an exalted cry, she welcomed his now hardened body deep within her belly. The maid gasped as Henry shoved her back into the straw. She remained mute as he drove into her; yet in his dream, Maura was anything but quiet. She moaned, howled his name, writhed and encouraged his powerful pulsing, smothering him with lavish kisses as he masterfully ravished her.

The sheets barely rippled as Simon and Maura glided together; nuzzling, petting, praising, they celebrated their love with endless kisses and caresses. He stroked the spot where their bodies met, creating in her shudders of coursing bliss that urged him closer, deeper. And as their passion neared its peak, they abandoned their vow of caution. Their coupling took on frenetic, desperate temper. She flipped to her back, pulled him over her, and their frenzy culminated in one long, eruptive moan. For a good while, neither moved from their fierce hold. Then, damp and blushed with sensual heat, they stretched, sighed with pleasure, and wound contentedly back together again.

The maid listened intently to Henry's spiraling breaths. Adept at her profession, she knew exactly when to pull away. Henry's eyes flew wide and flailing madly, he found himself alone at an excruciatingly dreadful moment. His seed spilled into the straw and his face wrenched with rage. "Why?!" he howled, clamping his hands together to keep from striking her.

"I don't want your bastards," she spat, lowering her skirts.

In a terrible instant, she had ruined his ultimate fantasy! While he groaned his anguish to the rafters, she took advantage of his distress to rummage through his money pouch. But his eye caught her crime. He snatched the bag from her greedy grip, and she paled as he raved, "You flaming whore! I've never paid a woman and don't intend to start with a putrid sow like you. Get from my sight before I wring your fat neck!" She stole a few escaped coins, scrambled from beneath his heaving shadow, and dashed from the stall.

Her wicked cackling echoed as he lurched from the stall. "Bitch!" he screeched. "Putrid, vile bitch!" He hurled his coin pouch at the slamming door. It exploded against the wood and shot coins through the air; one glanced off his brow, making him yowl and rail, "They're all bitches...all flaming bitches!" In a crazed fury, he attacked the door with his feet and fists, shrieked many more curses, and finally collapsed in the straw. But his body and mind refused to calm, and he continued to writhe and rip at the grass. "She can't do this to me," he croaked, "...I won't let her torture me! I can't let her...I refuse to love—Maura!"

Simon retrieved Maura's shift and swabbed away her dampness, making her chuckle and sigh, "We've never loved like that before."

He tossed the shift from the bed and beamed, "I wholeheartedly agree! Yet we say that every time."

"Because every time it's true!" Maura knelt and scurried on her knees about the draggled bed, shutting tight the damask bed curtains. "We'll never leave here," she vibrantly decided. "We don't need food or drink or sleep—we'll survive solely on love!"

"And die ecstatic!" he added with zest, showering her with petals.

As she stretched for a pelt at the foot of the bed, he couldn't resist a pinch to her backside and, yelping, she threw the fur over their heads and attacked him with tickles. They played together in their secret cave, laughing and squealing. Eventually, their enthusiasm brought on exhaustion. So, snuggled tight, they murmured of their delight with the wedding celebration, each other, and the world...and at last surrendered to the most illustrious dreams.

Henry lay coiled in the straw, shuddering with aching emptiness and cold. All around him, beasts snorted and stomped, as one lone tear trickled down his cheek.

*****

"It's a wondrous morning!" Henry boomed, flinging wide Simon and Maura's chamber door. "The sun is in the heavens, the birds are chirping, and I do hope I'm interrupting—" He stopped short as he beheld the empty bed, then approached cautiously and fingered the crumpled sheets and crushed petals. He noticed a wisp of a frock lying at his feet, snatched it up, and buried his nose deep within its pungent folds. Secretly, he stuffed the cloth down the front of his tunic and, relishing his naughtiness, left to find them.

Henry's hunt led him to the door of Lanfranc's chamber. He knelt and gaped through the keyhole at a bewildering, possibly criminal scene. Lanfranc and Simon sat hunched over a body, he supposed was Maura, lying on a table—perhaps dead. He barged in, crying, "What's happened? Is she—"

Maura's figure jerked to his abrupt entrance. Simon and Lanfranc regarded his fluster with annoyance, Simon asking, "Is she what?"

"What are you doing to her?"

"Simon's removing her stitches," replied Lanfranc.

Maura waved her arm invitingly, and mumbled, "Henry, please come."

"Does it hurt?" Henry asked warily.

"A little," said Maura. She blindly sought out his hand; he caught hers and squeezed it firmly. Their medical jargon and picking sickened him, so he focused his concentration instead on her hand. The ivory skin was spattered with peach freckles and her nails were chewed to the nub. Envy again stabbed his belly as his fingers played across her palm, laced between her knuckles, and smudged her ring.

Maura struggled to keep still. Whatever Henry was doing tickled, but his curious antics did help ease the stinging and pinching at her neck.

"Done," sighed Simon.

"Excellent work!" praised Lanfranc. While Simon fetched a fresh bandage, Lanfranc helped Maura sit and inspected the gash, noting, "With Simon's expert handiwork, I expect there will be little scarring."

Henry unwillingly released her hand. He felt useless watching Simon wrap the bandage and announced, "Well, I'm off."

All heads whipped his way, and Maura blurted, "So soon?"

"This dripping sentimentality bores me," he returned snidely. "I crave a diversion."

"Such as?" Simon asked.

"I don't know," shrugged Henry. "I fear if I stay here one moment longer, I'll turn as sickly sweet as the lot of you."

"Heaven forbid!" wailed Lanfranc.

Maura wondered at Henry's awkwardness and uneasy gaze as he grasped the door handle to leave. "I...I wish you both...luck," he muttered.

"Henry, wait!" she cried. "At least let us walk with you to the stable."

"No need," he said, firming his grip on the latch.

Maura's expression begged Simon to intervene, and he called, "Henry, wait for us!"

Wordlessly, Henry led his friends to the stable, then ignored them while saddling his horse. Maura urged Simon forward with a pleading look; he cleared his throat and stated far too formally, "Henry, we wish to thank you, truly, for—"

"Spare the niceties, Simon," Henry curtly intruded. "You never wanted me here."

"Wh...what?" sputtered Simon.

"So, I ended up being useful to you," Henry sniped, "and now you're all agush with gratitude. Well, I fear your platitudes come too late."

Simon bristled, and Maura pulled him aside to whisper, "Let me speak to him. I believe he's still upset over last night and only *I* can convince him that he did no harm."

"I pray that's the only problem." He kissed her for luck and left them alone.

Henry continued his saddling, and Maura appeared on the opposite side of his mount, straining a smile as a peace offering.

"What do *you* want?" sneered Henry.

"A smile..."

He scowled and continued his angry adjustment of the girth. When next he looked up, she was gone. He leant round his horse's rump and yelled at her departing figure, "Maura, don't go!" As she turned her disappointment on him, he noticed, to his chagrin, that even in the drabbest tunic she was lovely; her color was high, her braid slightly askew, and tears sparkled her sad eyes. A desperate longing nipped at his heart and his lips betrayed,

"I'm disgustingly jealous! I've never felt this way before and I despise myself! Please allow me to go. I have to get away!"

"Oh, Henry," Maura cried out indulgently. "I couldn't bear it if you left angry!" She hugged his arm and praised on, "You're so precious to us. We envy you! You own everyone's love and respect, and all the women you meet fall instantly in love with you."

"Not *all* the women," he noted forlornly, cocking his chin.

"Please be happy for us! We owe you so very much."

For a moment, Henry swept aside his nicked feelings, and promptly realized his mistake. He was intentionally wounding the two people he loved more than anyone else in the world, simply because of his pride. His posture softened, and his impish grin admitted, "I've no wedding present for you."

"You've been present enough," she answered with relief.

"No, it's time I started answering for my foolishness." He loosened the girth on his saddle and yanked it off Fulk's back, proclaiming, "He's yours!"

"No, Henry, you mustn't," she countered vehemently.

"I do what I please. Besides, how can I visit you in Wales if you never arrive there? He's a gentle brute, especially when ridden by the perfect wo...rider." He patted the stallion fondly and added, "He may enjoy watching his child grow."

In thanks, she kissed the side of his mouth. He cringed to her nearness, but resisted retreating. "Simon awaits us outside," she said, weaving her arm through his.

Maura stayed away while the men talked. Henry hid his awkwardness behind a bawdy smirk. "So, I trust you performed the deed properly last night?"

"You'll need to ask Maura about that," laughed Simon.

"She looks sufficiently plucked to me."

Simon turned pensive, and shielded his eyes to ask, "What do you believe will happen...when your father dies?"

Henry gestured for his guard to dismount, swung up into his saddle, and staidly replied, "Rufus will get England, Curthose Normandy, and I'll be snubbed completely."

"It's a pity. You've more sense and courage than the whole lot of them."

"Don't cry for me, Simon. In time, I'll have it all."

"Where will you go?"

"I'm considering visiting my sister, Cecily. You remember her. She's the Abbess of a daughter-house in Caen and doesn't receive many visitors. She seems to enjoy my visits." Henry's eyes shifted briefly to Maura and he added with a wistful smile, "The only other woman who suffers kindly my prattle. And after our recent adventure, I feel I deserve a bit of peace. When next we meet, it may be under tragic circumstances."

"Let's pray your father lives many more years." Simon offered his hand and affirmation, "We'll miss you."

"You're an immensely lucky man, Cousin, and she's a fine, fine Lady." Henry gripped Simon's hand too tightly and issued a gritted warning, "You'd best treat her well, or I'll steal her from you in an instant—" He stopped his ill-timed belligerence, and ended tenderly, "Take care, be happy, and kiss the colt and the baby for me." Then he tossed his new money bag to Simon.

"Henry, no," protested Simon.

"Don't argue," said Henry. "I sail from Westminster and Rufus will lend me money." He was thoughtful a moment, then stated, "For such a boring old man, Cousin, you lead an exceedingly thrilling existence."

"And you—" Simon hesitated.

Henry pressed, "And I what?"

"No longer need help with your diction."

Henry hooted in victory and galloped away.

Simon reached out to Maura. Swiftly, she came to him and wrapped his waist with her arm. He smiled after Henry's shrinking figure and remarked, "He's not a babe any longer." Then, looking to Maura, added glibly, "...And it seems you've got yourself a stallion."

"Indeed, I do," she replied, eyeing her husband lustily.

"Oh, Maura, please!" Simon moaned, rolling his eyes. "Henry's correct, we *are* sickly sweet."

"Henry's guilty of dripping a few honeyed words himself," said Maura.

"What? Tell me!" he excitedly pressed.

"Begging for my hand, he called me 'scrumptious'."

"God's teeth!" Simon laughed. "Never let me forget that jewel. I'll need it for future ammunition." They trudged the many steps to the palace, and Simon warned, "Now, I must humor Lanfranc, and listen politely to his dissertation concerning the most recent medical findings from Salerno."

"Is that where he's from?"

"No, but there's a magnificent Medical University there and he corresponds regularly with the physicians. What will you do?"

"May I come along?"

"If you wish, though he does rattle on—forever."

"Will it please him to have me there?"

Simon snorted in assent.

"Then I will listen—forever."

*****

Following a late supper, Maura left Lanfranc and Simon at the dais to chatter on, and returned to their chamber to pack. While attempting to stuff her wedding gown into her saddlebag, she paused a moment to ponder the past few tumultuous weeks. The last few glorious days had all but blotted the more despicable moments, and she smiled at her most heartfelt memory—the Abbess' tear-stained, beaming face bidding them farewell. The door creaked at her back and, without turning, she reached for two light woolen, unbleached tunics lying on the bed. "Simon," she said merrily, "the matron brought me these tunics. I think they'll suit you fine. What do you—"

Her next word caught in her throat as she turned to his alarming paleness. The tunics slipped from her grasp; she rushed to him, seized his hands and implored, "Simon, what happened?!" He stayed painfully silent. Maura feared he would faint and carefully helped him to the bed. She sat, again took his hands, and pressed, "Simon, tell me what's wrong."

"It's...It's nothing to do with you," he strained in a whisper.

"It does if it hurts you!" she countered. "Are we safe?!"

"Yes...Give me a moment to find the words, then I'll tell you all."

She waited as patiently as her growing panic would allow. His expression, white and fierce, was like that of a lost, abused child. Everything inside her ached to his misery and again she urged, "Simon, *please!*"

He squeezed her hand, and explained with quiet anguish, "After you'd left the hall, Lanfranc asked of my father. I've never discussed with him the cause of our rift, I suppose because of the shame I felt...the shame I feel." He inched nearer to her, his voice and hold tensing. "I described to him that last horrible night at Dunheved. How Father had condemned me for Odo's arrest. And when I was done, Lanfranc told me the truth..."

"What truth?"

"I had nothing to do with Odo's imprisonment. Lanfranc alone discovered his scheme to usurp the Pope and had alerted the King months before I'd ever uttered a word about his trip to Rome."

"Then why did Robert blame you?"

His fingers dug his brow as he sifted through the too few clues. "I know that Father met with Odo immediately before our confrontation at Dunheved. It must have been there that Odo convinced Father his arrest was entirely my doing."

"Robert wouldn't have believed Odo's word over yours!" said she.

"Robert never allowed my word!" he flared. "Even if he *had* let me speak, it would've made no difference. Robert worships Odo, does his every bidding no matter *how* criminal, and would believe his word over God's!"

"But why destroy your bond with Robert?" questioned Maura. "What would Odo stand to gain from such treachery?"

"Vengeance!" spat Simon. Rapidly his despair tumbled forth, "When...when first we met, he...he addressed me as Father's 'carnal blunder', and that is the kindest thing he has ever said to me. Father purposely sent me to Odo's for training to cure the badness between us. It only made it worse. I endured his cuffing and taunting, everyone suffered under Odo's rule. It irked him that his meanness had no effect on my skills, and his attacks turned more brutal." Simon's upset thrust him to his feet; one fist muzzled the other as he paced and muttered bitterly. "Henry turned eight years old the day he arrived at Rochester for instruction in, of all things, the priesthood! It was his first separation from his mother. He was miserable and one night he cried to me about something, I don't recall what. I was comforting him when Odo burst into Henry's chamber, accused us of sodomy, and started beating Henry with his staff! I wrestled the pole from Odo, struck him once, then cracked the staff. After that, he never hit Henry again, though he was determined to ruin me."

Maura left the bed and reached out to him. "Simon, Odo's lie almost caused your death!"

"That was his plan! He wanted me gone, my mother gone, anyone my Father loved had to go! And you weren't spared his wrath, he despised you as well."

"Why me, Simon? What did he know of me? I've never seen him."

"Oh, yes you have. I'll never forget the time." He slumped to the memory, and Maura lured him back to the bed. His voice lost its heated edge and took on instead a grim, haunting tone. "You'd been with us near a year and had finally started talking, though brokenly. You followed me everywhere, I wasn't sure why and, God knows, I didn't mind. But Odo did. He visited at Christmas and insisted that Father keep Marc, and cast you out. He claimed you were damaged, a daughter of the devil, and a costly burden." Simon sank across the bed on his back; Maura stretched out beside him and stroked his brow. "Luckily," he said, gazing into her eyes, "that was one request Father refused to do. On Christmas Eve, we were playing our games near the dais, too near for Odo's comfort, and yet, he ordered only you to leave. You gaped at him with such terror that Marc started to bawl, and I felt so queer. Then you ran screaming from the hall. We finally found you the next morn, huddled behind the grain stores in the buttery. It took me half the day to coax you out and, till Odo left, you wouldn't let go of my shirt sleeve."

Maura racked her mind; still the memory he'd described remained hidden. Carefully, she risked the question, "Now that you know the truth, will you confront Robert?"

"No!" His anger blazed anew. He shrank from her caress and lurched to the side of the bed. Madness again claimed him, making him strike the bedpost and rave, "It's too late! He's with Odo now, I know he is, I can feel it. I can hear Odo spewing more lies, more hate, more—"

"Stop, Simon!" She caught his arm and stressed, "Odo didn't ruin you! He can't, no one can!"

"But I loved my father!" he choked, crushing her hand between his.

"And he never truly stopped loving you! He left you with a nod. If there was ever any hate, it's gone now."

"Odo is the Devil, Maura—not Rufus, Will, or Robert, only Odo!"

"And you've beaten the Devil, Simon! You've beaten them all. I know it seems impossible, but you must try to forget." Her fingers bit his shoulders as she warned, "If you don't, rancor will gnaw forever at your insides and rot whatever tender feelings you have left! Believe me, Simon, I know of what I speak..." He sagged into her embrace, and his fury sputtered and died to her petting and soothing words, "Let me comfort you, my love. I'll protect you. No one dare harm you—not in my arms." Yet cuddled close, he continued to shift with torment, and she fumbled for a lulling thought or word. "Simon," she said wishfully, "let's take time to travel on our journey to Wales, and we can stay awhile with Edith." He cast her a quizzical look, and she explained, "It's time she and I made our peace, and we must visit Rose." He agreed with a solemn nod. Ever so slowly, she felt his tumult ease and his body grow limp, but before he slept, she asked, "I can't recall Odo, my love. Would you describe him to me?"

"He...he favors Robert," Simon mumbled groggily, "only larger, more hair. He has the same eyes, my eyes..." His voice faded, but his grip held firm.

Maura's cheek rested upon his brow as she struggled to recall her veiled past. Would she ever remember? Did she want to remember? She nestled closer; her lips touched his cheek and, certain of his slumber, she allowed herself a tear for Simon, and one more for the countless other victims of his family's treachery.

*****

CHAPTER THIRTY-ONE - NO LONGER LOST

Dawn arrived at last, boasting a cleansed sky and a peeking orange sun. At the base of the palace's steps, Simon and Maura mingled with the Bishop and their new-found friends. Expressions betrayed both gloom and cheer as all gathered exchanged kisses, fond wishes, and bittersweet farewells. Simon swung up into the saddle behind Maura and hugged her waist as she steered the prancing Fulk onto the lane leading out of Canterbury. E'dain, packed with a number of medical journals and what few belongings they possessed, trotted behind.

The couple spent the remainder of April and the first half of May touring the south of England, visiting old haunts and searching out new wonders. They raced the plain of Salisbury, scaled and romped upon the stones of the Giant's Dance, and took a full day to invigorate themselves with a soak in the medicinal springs of Bath. Farther south, they came upon the outline of a monstrous giant etched into the hilly landscape northeast of the village of Cerne Abbas. While there, they devotedly partook of a touted cure for barrenness—a wish and offering deposited at the fertility well at the foot of the hill, then a night spent lying and loving upon the Giant's erect phallus. And with cluttered feelings, they returned to the seashore bracing the southwest tip of Cornwall, to rediscover the beaches where they'd frolicked as new lovers. They braved the frigid waves, galloped Fulk along the endless shore line, and strolled the sand bridge to the island abbey of St. Michael's Mount, Lord Robert's newest acquisition.

Lush growth spirited by spring storms carpeted the lane leading into the borough of Dunheved. As they passed beyond the town's vined walls, the malignant shadow of Dunheved Castle fell upon them, chilling all warm images with a sense of foreboding. Clashing emotions ripped at Maura's insides, making her bury her face into Simon's back and tauten her grip on his waist. He sensed her turmoil, and reined Fulk a moment to kiss and stroke her hands. He wondered if this fortuitous venture to see Edith was nothing more than a horrendous mistake. He felt her tenseness somewhat subside, and he urged Fulk ahead.

The sun, in a myriad of veiled colors, was resting large and low on the eastern horizon when they arrived at Edith's cottage. Simon slipped to the ground and, seeing Maura's gaunt pallor, suggested, "I'll go in first."

She nodded and strained a smile. "And I'll stable the horses." Once on her feet, Maura's head reeled and her knees buckled.

He caught and held her close, fretting, "What is it?"

"It's nothing," she assured. "My legs are a bit numb from the long ride. Now, go tell Edith we're here," she urged, easing from his hold. "I'm far too nervous to wait."

There was no reply to his repeated knocking, so he opened the door wide enough to poke in his head, and called softly, "Mother..." then louder, "Mother, are you here?" He sniffed at a musty odor hanging in the air as he wandered across the tiny room to the stable door. He opened the top half and Maura's pinched expression greeted him. "She's not here," he said. His upset mounted as he checked the empty stalls and searched her tiny toft of land behind the cottage. No garden had been planted and no beasts graced the pens. He caressed the side of the huge stone oven bracing the back wall of the cottage and felt no warmth. Then, he rejoined Maura in the hut. "By the look and feel of things," he said, tracing a circle in the dust that topped the trestle table, "she's been away for some time."

"Perhaps she's visiting family or friends," hoped Maura.

Simon shrugged and brooded, while Maura climbed the woven ladder to the loft. "She's left a good amount of foodstuffs," she called down. "There's cut wood and ale. We could stay awhile to catch her return."

But he didn't seem to hear and continued his fretting, "Her family refuses to see her. All her friends live here in Dunheved."

"She may have gotten lonely and moved in with someone."

Her statement piqued his confusion and he asked, "What did you say?"

"Maybe she's found herself a lover," she answered wryly.

"My mother?!" he exclaimed. The notion seemed to plunge him into a deeper dole.

Maura mussed his hair and gently teased, "She is capable of such a thing. After all, how do you think you came about?" Her joking failed to cheer, and she stressed, "Simon, don't fret so. I'm certain she's come to no harm."

"My father harassed her last November. What if he's come again—"

"If he's accepted what we've done, why would he bother her?"

"He's been known to be slightly unpredictable..."

She cupped his hands in hers and carefully suggested, "Once we get the horses fed, we'll visit the market and ask after her." He nodded and crouched to check the temperature of the coals.

In the early morning mist, only a spattering of market stalls had opened, none of them Edith's. The imposing keep continued to haunt Maura, wickedly beckoning. Suddenly, she let go of Simon's hand, and the crowd parted to her struggle as she hurried to the castle.

Simon panicked to her sudden absence and, fervently searching, shoved his way through unyielding bodies. He glimpsed her hooded figure hastening along the curtain wall, and screamed, "Maura, no! Stop!" Yet by the time he'd sprinted across the drawbridge and through the deserted gatehouse, she had already reached the keep's top stair.

The thick door slammed against Maura's back. Winded, and blinded by blackness, she rested a moment to catch her breath, then, trance-like, forged ahead. No guard questioned her presence as she resolutely strode the passageway leading to the great hall. Instead, they stepped from her path, as if no time had passed since she'd last wandered these halls. She hastened by the Lord's bedchamber, her fingers stroking its door and the stone wall as she nimbly padded the open stairway to the chambers above.

Simon's bellow, "Maura! Stop!" rattled the hall's rafters, though fell on deaf ears as invisible hands lured Maura along the dank tunnel to her chamber's door. Her fingers met and fondled the latch. Simon grabbed hold her shoulders, spun her around, and beseeched, "Don't do this! Why torture yourself? Mind your own words and forget! Forget and come away!"

His plea failed to stop the door; it swung open on its own to reveal a tidy, cozy chamber, crowded with a bed, chair, washstand and trunk. Up against the bed's lone pillow sat a soiled, ragged doll. Maura pried from Simon's grasp and lunged for the doll. A touch to the bed shattered the cheering image! She buried her face in the doll's skirt and suffered again the horrors! Will's icy eyes laughed at her from behind the tapestry; bloodied bedclothes tangled her legs, forcing her still as chainmail shredded her skin; she smothered beneath the guard's hugeness and gasped horrible breaths. "No!" she wailed above the screams in her head. "Make them go, Simon! Make them go away!"

Simon whisked her from the hell, kicked open his chamber door, and set her carefully upon his bed. She cleaved to him and sobbed, "I...I needed to know if the nightmare was real. To forget, I had to know the truth!" As she warily lifted her head and took in her new surroundings, her fingers lovingly stroked the familiar blanket, and she snuggled deeper in Simon's embrace. Quiet and contemplative, they stayed awhile, remembering this spot as the site of some of their most cherished moments.

As they approached the main gates of Dunheved to leave, Simon recognized a face in the guard's shelter. He waved and shouted, "Guy!" A lanky, ginger-haired man returned his wave and trotted to his side. Simon clasped his hand and addressed Maura, "Do you remember Henry's guard, Guy?"

She studied the sentry, then answered fondly, "Of course, I remember. You were at Westminster."

"Yes, my Lady," replied Guy. "I'm grateful to see you both well."

"Why are you here?" wondered Simon.

"Henry FitzRoy's orders. He's posted one of us at each of Lord Robert's principal residences. If we hear of any mischief aimed at you or your Lady, we're to race to Menevia and warn you."

Simon and Maura traded astounded expressions, then Maura took Guy's hand. "We appreciate your loyalty, Guy. When you see the FitzRoy, tell him of our love."

"I certainly will, my Lady," he murmured.

A walk through the forest that blanketed the valley below the castle unleashed a glut of emotions, both glorious and malign. They strolled the path to the river, and roamed the magical forest that was once their secret world. Too soon, they stumbled upon the main road and headed back to town. Sinuous and pitted, the road branched and at its split, a broad clearing lay strewn with the charred remains of a good-sized building. Maura paused; her strangling grip and harrowed expression told Simon they had come upon what remained of Robert's Abbey. He carefully guided her away, muttering, "A fair retribution..."

Back inside Edith's cottage, each struggled silently with wrenching thoughts as they listlessly prepared a meal. Soon they abandoned the food and cuddled upon a mat by the fire. Gradually remembrances of the joyous times spent at Dunheved began to flow from them, times so easily overshadowed, though so truly precious. And before long, the spell of those memories ignited their passion. They ripped clothing, toppled stools, and scattered stacked wood, coming together again and again in a desperate attempt to exorcise their horrific past.

*****

The next morning two shadows crept over their still bodies. Maura woke to a nudge and sleepily pondered how Simon could be snug up against her back and also standing above her. Her heart faltered as she beheld—the skirt. Without daring to look up, she yanked a pelt over her bared breasts, and whispered sharply, "Simon!"

He stirred to her call and the cool air on his now exposed skin; nuzzling closer, he mumbled, "Later, Maura. You've milked me dry. Please, let me sleep." His eyes flew open to the stab of her elbow and the sound of a resonant voice clearing. He sat with a start, taking the pelt with him. Maura jerked it back and stayed flat, while Simon raised guilty eyes to his mother. "Mo...Mother," he squeaked with a parched effort, then gulped, "Arthur?" at the stout figure by her side.

Edith stood slack-jawed with her hands on her hips, glowering down at her flustered son and his lover.

Arthur cringed at the standoff. He cupped Edith's elbow and gently suggested, "Come, my dove. We'll give them some time to tidy the room and themselves up a bit."

"Thank you, Arthur," sighed Simon.

"It's no problem, lad." Arthur steered Edith's stiff figure toward the door and turned on them a smirk. "It's wonderful to see you two haven't lost any of your enthusiasm."

With that, Maura moaned and burrowed under the pelts.

The door latched. Simon slowly came to realize the levity of the episode, and repressed a chuckle while speaking to the mound beside him, "You'll have to come out sometime."

"I won't, ever!" cried Maura in a muted whine. "I'm completely mortified! Simon, she hates me. I didn't even have to see her face to know she hates me!"

"She doesn't hate you. She was only reacting to a rather awkward situation."

Maura peeked from between skins to counter, "She does so! Edith blames me for everything bad that's ever happened to you. I'm sure Arthur's told her about your punishment and imprisonment. She blames me and hates me!"

Simon stepped into his braies and knotted the cord at his waist. "When last I left her, she sent you her love. Why would she bother to do that if she hates you? Come out, Maura. They'll return soon and we need to tidy up..." He surveyed the mess and scratched his head. "I don't remember knocking over the stools."

Maura tossed aside the pelts, leapt up, and scampered naked across the floor, dipping to fetch odd pieces of clothing on her way. Once she'd found and donned her hose, she began a frantic search for her chemise.

Simon lounged on the table's bench, sporting only his braies and an immensely silly grin.

She stopped askance and, glancing behind her, asked testily, "What are you gawking at?"

"I like that."

"What?" she ordered.

"Just the hose."

"Simon—help me!"

"Are you perhaps looking for this?" he asked, producing her chemise from behind his back.

She lunged for the garment, but he was quicker and easily dodged her swipe. Crouching, she tried to hide her nakedness behind a too tiny pelt and bargained with barely controlled fury, "If you give it to me now, I'll parade for you later."

"I'm afraid you'll have to fetch it," he teased, dangling it just out of her reach.

"Simon, please!" she whined as she tossed the pelt and chased him around the table. "Give it to me or I'll...I'll—"

"You'll what?"

"Spank you!"

"Promise?"

"They'll be back soon!" she shrilled. "*Please!*"

He darted from behind the table and leapt the fire pit. His heel caught an escaped log and he landed with a splintering crash upon the wood pile.

She snatched away the chemise, yanked it over her scowl, and snapped, "Serves you right!"

"You're a hard woman, Maura," he croaked, rubbing his backside.

The latch rattled and Arthur called, "Is it safe?"

Maura scurried across the room to fetch her tunic, setting the stools upright on her way. Her head popped through the tunic's neck hole as Edith and Arthur gingerly stepped inside the hut. Simon scrambled to his feet and Maura came up behind him, lacing her fingers through his.

Edith's austere expression softened. She rushed forward to hug Simon, and her hands patted his reddened cheeks as she gushed, "You look healthier than I would have thought! Arthur's told me of your trials and I didn't know what to expect or if I'd ever see you—"

"Mother..." He squirmed from her fussing. "I'm fine."

Edith's glare lit briefly upon Maura, then darted away as she muttered pointedly, "Maura...I must say I'm a bit shocked to see you."

Arthur cheerily intruded, "Well, Maura, you certainly brightened my morning!" He stepped forward to engulf her in an embrace. She relaxed in his abundant hold and smiled to his whispered clue, "Edith believes you hate her."

Maura cleared her throat and cocked her head toward the stable door. "Simon, I'm sure Arthur would love to see our new horse."

"Yes indeed!" Arthur agreed with a wink. "And lad, I can certainly use your help unpacking my cart." Simon looked puzzled, and Arthur took his arm. "Come, we'll leave the ladies to talk."

The men gone, Edith's irritation swelled, quickening her breath and firing her eyes. She strode purposefully to the table, pulled herself erect and, at last, challenged Maura's benign gaze. "I am thankful that you are...well. Though, once again your wanton behavior with my son has caused him, and countless others, great tragedy. Yet you refuse to learn reason. Do you want to die? Do you want *him* to die?!"

"Edith, stop—" Maura raised her hands in defense.

Edith slammed her fist on the table, unleashing a cloud of dust as she roared, "Answer me!"

"Of course not!" Maura stood her ground, and answered with emboldened calm, "We only want to be together."

"At the expense of—"

"As far as we know, nothing."

"How can you say that?!" raved Edith.

Maura huffed and squatted to rummage through Simon's saddlebag. She yanked out the parchment, flapped it open, and thrust it at Edith. "I say it with this!"

Edith squinted at the tiny script, and curtly passed it back. "I...I can't read it. The words are too small."

"It says..." Maura paused to draw a bracing breath, then continued, "that over a month ago we were wed at Canterbury by the Archbishop Lanfranc, with the King's blessing and protection."

Edith's hand struck her breast as she wailed, "Robert will murder you both!"

"He's seen the betrothal document and didn't dare fight us," countered Maura. "The only devil who seems determined to murder us is Will, and I believe I've slowed his plans of revenge."

As Edith struggled to regain her verbal edge, Maura's startling revelation gradually sifted through her panic. She hung her head and mumbled, "Now I am ashamed."

"You needn't be." Maura chanced a step forward and tenderly assured, "How could I hate you? Simon explained what happened to you when we were forced apart. We all lost everything on that terrible morning! I believed you furious with me. I always seem to lead your son down perilous paths."

"And he willingly charges those paths after you." Her strife gone, Edith sagged wearily down on the bench. "I knew years back you had a hold on him that no one, not even I, could break. And if I could have...I wouldn't have."

"I never stopped loving him or you," admitted Maura.

"You bring him such joy!" Edith's eyes brimmed tears as she extended both hands to confess, "I've missed you so."

Maura bent again to retrieve something, then happily joined Edith's embrace at the table, blubbering, "I've missed you as much." She sniffed, sat back, and presented Edith with the doll. "Do you remember this?"

Edith's hand hid her smile. "Where—"

"We made a trip to the castle."

"It must have been terribly hard for you...I've never been able to—" Edith's fingers combed through the doll's tangled hair and brushed dust from its face. "I made you this for your sixth birthday," she wistfully recalled.

"What we pretended was my birthday."

"The anniversary of your arrival at Dunheved. You were quite a challenge that first year, and then—"

"I discovered how truly much I was loved," Maura warmly finished. They hugged again for a long while, and when their clutch finally eased, Maura remarked, "I adore your cottage."

"Obviously!" Edith chortled. "You put it to fine use last night."

Blushing, Maura smudged the dust and asked, "Where have you been?"

"Winchester. About two months ago, Arthur dropped out of nowhere and asked me to marry him!"

"Oh, Edith!" Maura exclaimed. "How marvelous! And—"

"I'm considering his proposal. Only, I do cherish my life here in Dunheved and I made it quite clear to him I would not leave. Then, without so much as a grunt, Arthur asked me to accompany him to Winchester to help cart his belongings back here." She sighed as her fond gaze roamed her home. "I've been alone near five years, and most times prefer it that way."

"Surely there is a void..." prompted Maura.

"Yes, I won't deny it."

"That Arthur would gladly fill," Maura returned quickly. "Simon says he's loved you forever."

"He's a fine man and quite determined." Edith stood, switching thoughts with a worry, "Where's Rose?"

"She's at Richard's manor. We plan to visit tomorrow. You'll join us, I hope."

"I'd love to. Does she know you're wed?"

"She knows what we intended, though not that it's done."

Edith looked skeptical. "And she approves?"

"Wholeheartedly!" Maura beamed proudly and thrust forth her hand.

"I see," said Edith, favorably scrutinizing Rose's ring. "Well, if Rose has bestowed her blessing, I suppose I've no cause to object to anything you two get up to."

Arthur and Simon liberated the pigs from their cages. As the hogs raced squealing about their new home, Arthur snagged Simon affectionately around the neck. "You've done it! I'm proud of you, lad! She's a sweet thing and—" he arched a brow to note, "from the peek I had this morning, quite a prize!"

"And I'm highly impressed with you!" Simon lauded, hanging on the fence.

"Your unflinching spirit inspired me," said Arthur.

"You mean my damned stubbornness!" Simon corrected. "Has she accepted?"

Arthur sadly watched the runt's futile effort to catch his siblings and wagged his head. "Not as yet, but I believe she's weakening."

"She's always cared for you, Arthur," encouraged Simon.

"Yes, but is that enough?" Arthur's expression clouded with concern. "Edith was terribly upset by your show of this morning. We'd best go see how the ladies are faring."

They paused in the door and gaped at the women chatting cordially while tidying the room. Edith regarded their gawking with disdain. "We *are* still alive," she sniped, "so you can shut your gobs and help."

Arthur lumbered forward, sputtering, "Yes...yes, my dove, right away, my dove."

Simon laughed sharply at Arthur's instant surrender, but stopped with a yowl as Edith pinched his ear and chided, "Why didn't you tell me your grand news?"

He wriggled from her grasp and grumbled, "You weren't exactly in a mood to listen!" Then, he asked expectantly, "Well?"

"I couldn't be more pleased!" Edith acclaimed, catching him in a hug.

Simon extracted himself from his mother's clutch, and knelt beside Maura as she stacked wood for a fire. He stole a kiss, and murmured, "You are a marvel."

Maura gladly abandoned her chore to enjoy a longer kiss, and heard Edith call to Arthur, "Fetch the pork and dried vegetables. To celebrate, I'll whip up a *scrumptious* stew!" Simon and Maura broke apart, laughing at the memory of Henry's drama, and Edith whirled round to demand, "What's funny?"

*****

Arthur expertly steered his squeaky cart along the road to Richard's manor home. Edith, exhausted by a full night of reminiscing, slept, her head resting in his lap. She woke abruptly to the sound of thundering hooves and Simon's harsh command, "Stop!"

Maura, looking petulant, reined in Fulk. Simon slipped off his back and leapt into the back of the cart. "What is it?" Edith groggily asked.

"Your son is a coward," Maura sneered in jest.

"No, my dearest dear," Simon scowled, crossing his arms. "I happen to value my life."

Edith grinned at the old squabble, and settled back in Arthur's lap. Arthur waited for Maura's retort, yet none came. Instead, she blew them a haughty kiss and streaked away. Fulk veered sharply off the lane and vanished into the wood.

The cart didn't budge, so Simon tapped Arthur's shoulder and asked politely, "Is there a problem?"

"Would somebody please tell me what's happened?!" he insisted.

"It's nothing, Arthur," said Edith. "Maura thinks we're dawdling, and you don't want to be sharing her saddle when Maura's in a hurry. It's a sobering experience."

It took a moment, and finally Arthur uttered, "Oh, I see—Maura wants to go faster, and goes a bit too fast for you, Simon. Yes, it all makes perfect sense." He shook his head in wonder, chuckled, then jiggled the reins. And as his shaggy pony trudged ahead, he pondered the tempting thought—if Edith did accept him, and he joined this curious bunch, how thrilling his life would quickly become!

Fulk wove deftly at a full gallop through a cluster of oaks. Maura tingled with exhilaration atop the magnificent mount. A brush of her hand along his sweaty neck sent him flying across a clearing and soaring up a sheer embankment. She reigned him at the summit, and beamed down upon the walled manor home nestled at the base of the plateau. Fulk sensed her anticipation and, without a prompt, cantered down the slippery, rock-strewn hill to Richard's manor. He charged through the open gates and Maura sprang from the saddle. An astounded servant chased and caught the bucking beast, and wrestled him to a tethering post. Once he'd secured the stallion, he ran to fetch Rose.

Maura hollered, "Rose! Rose!" as she tripped up the steps to the manor. She reached the top stair and pounded fiercely on the door. The door creaked open and her call, "Rose!" echoed throughout the timbered hall, but only steam swirling from a cauldron greeted her. She quivered to the comforting aroma and hugged herself, recalling her merry visits here as a child. This had been her second home and, thankfully, little about it had changed. She strode to the fire pit, wondering loudly, "Is anyone here?"

Almodis woke to the sound of a misplaced voice. She expected Rose or Alan to be flanking her bed and grew fearful at their absence. The sight of rustling tapestries made her heart flutter. She pushed up on her elbows, gripped the bedclothes, and asked, "Who's there?"

Maura started to the faint question, then flung back a tapestry. The women gasped surprise and squeaked joy as Maura rushed round the bed to hug her dear friend. Their exclamations tumbled together.

"My Lord, Maura, how did you—"

"Almodis, I never thought you'd come—"

"survive the fiends? Where's—"

"here, but it makes perfect sense. Where's—"

"Simon?"

"Rose, Alan?"

And as one they both proclaimed, "I've been so worried about you!"

Tears of laughter spilled down their cheeks, and Almodis was first to compose herself. "Rose and Alan are searching the buttery for a cradle."

"Are you having pains?" wondered Maura excitedly.

"They come and go. Rose and Alan have forced me to be still for the past six weeks! As huge as I am, I can't imagine how this babe might not be big enough to survive birth. Where's Simon?"

"He's dawdling."

"And?" pressed Almodis with bated breath.

Maura gleefully burst, "Lanfranc married us five weeks ago!"

"Oh, Maura!" Almodis said, hugging her again. "What a fool I was ever to doubt you. And Will?"

"I've clipped one of his talons," boasted Maura. "He won't be troubling anyone for quite awhile."

"Bless you, bless you! You truly *are* an angel. And Robert?"

"He chose not to fight us. Simon believes he's sulking in Mortain."

"Rufus?"

"He came too close this time, Almodis." Maura solemnly lowered her collar to expose her scar. Almodis gasped a shocked breath and reached out to the purple gash.

"Somehow," said Maura, "Henry and Simon yanked him off me."

"Henry?" Almodis repeated, bewildered. "From the gossip I've heard, he's a pesky rascal, not much good for anything but—"

"I disagree!" Maura interjected sharply. "He's a damned *brave*, pesky rascal! We never would had gotten married if it hadn't been for Henry!"

"Where have you been all this time?"

"Traveling," Maura said in a breathy sigh.

"From your enchanted look," Almodis chuckled, "it must have been an exquisite ride. Now, where's Simon? I must congratulate him."

He's with—" Maura paused as she envisioned the potentially volatile confrontation.

"With whom?"

"Uh...Ar...Arthur," stammered Maura.

"Arthur!" spouted Almodis, bringing her hands together. "Oh my, what a grand reunion we'll have!"

"And...Edith."

Almodis' jaw dropped. "She's coming here?!"

"Rose and Edith are like sisters!" explained Maura. "Of course, when I mentioned visiting Rose, she wanted—"

"No, Maura, don't fret," Almodis heartened, "I'll quite enjoy speaking with the Lady Edith, my husband's mistress for how dreadfully long?"

"Over twenty years."

Almodis cracked a smug grin. "Perhaps meeting her will help ease my guilt over my indiscretions."

"Maura! Maura, where have you gone to?!" Rose's strident voice thundered across the hall, tumbling over Alan's excited one. Maura rushed from Almodis' side, and surged from behind the tapestry to revel in their fervid hugs and kisses.

*****

Almodis' lips twisted as she studied the diminutive, yet fierce looking woman standing at the foot of her bed. She hadn't expected Edith to be attractive. But then, she thought, why ever not? She was after all Simon's mother.

Edith boldly returned Almodis' narrow stare, and her eyes soon strayed to Almodis' round belly. She felt a strong stab of envy. Almodis was so young, lovely, exotic. Even her swollen face became her.

Almodis forced a grin and cracked the icy silence. "I'm honored to meet you, Edith." Edith started to bow, but Almodis stopped her with a gesture. "No, no you deserve my homage as much as I deserve yours. I have a peculiar sense we've met before, that somehow we're related."

"Our children will be," Edith remarked, her hands clasped firmly before her. "Simon speaks kindly of you."

"Without his dear friendship and loyalty, I doubt I'd be alive."

Edith's dark glare paled. "Last evening he said the same of you. When will your child be born?"

"Supposedly the first of June."

"Then, my Lady, if you'll pardon my boldness, why are you bedridden?"

"The babe's been teasing me for ages, and Rose has commanded I stay confined till—"

"Surely," Edith objected, "if the child's due in only two weeks, he can come now with little danger. And, I can rightly imagine you long for this pregnancy to be done. The more you're up and about, the quicker it will happen."

Edith's revelation caught Almodis by surprise. Her fuddled expression brightened as she hoped, "Are you saying...I can escape this bed?"

"I fail to see why not."

"Oh, Edith!" exclaimed Almodis. "I fretted over how I'd react to your unheralded arrival, yet now I'm truly beholden to you! My gracious lady," Almodis stated triumphantly as she kicked away the pelts, "I would be highly pleased if you'd agree to accompany me on a stroll about the bailey. I'm wanting to hear of your life before and after Robert. And please, you may call me Almodis."

"I'd be honored to walk with you, Almodis." Edith smiled warmly, and offered a helping hand. "I must admit, ever since Simon first mentioned you, I've fantasized our confrontation and saw it as not so congenial. Now that it's happened, I find I'm curious about you as well."

Almodis grabbed Edith's hand, straining and grunting as she floundered up from the bed. She waited till Edith had draped a cloak over her shoulders, then hugged her arm and wobbled out into the much craved fresh air.

Rose and Alan escorted Maura, Simon, and Arthur about the property, Rose acting as guide. "With Alan's expert guidance," she announced proudly, "we've managed to transform the manor into a habitable residence once again. Richard's away so often that the manor and outbuildings had fallen into a disgraceful state. All that has changed, and there's an excellent chance of reaping a plentiful harvest this autumn! Now, what would make my life perfect would be—"

All eyes shifted anxiously to the unlikely couple descending the manor's stairs. Rose's cheer soured and she started for Almodis. Maura grabbed her arm and blurted, "She'll be fine, Rose. Edith is with her."

"But Maura—"

"It's time to let go," Maura said, patting her hand.

Alan sprinted to Almodis' side and gripped her hands. "Almodis, should you?"

"Oh Alan!" she beamed. "I'm now free to have this child! Edith has given her permission." They cleaved together and, at Almodis' request, "Let me stroll with Edith awhile," they parted. She blushed Alan's cheek with a kiss and promised, "And when I return, we'll have a most splendid feast to celebrate our many blessings."

*****

By the next sunrise, Simon found himself retracing the path to Dunheved. He turned in his saddle and smiled at the blithe troop following. However, the morning had not begun so cheerily. Upon waking, he'd found himself inexplicably tangled in a fierce war— Almodis bellowing her demand that she be allowed to attend the delayed Mayday celebrations in Dunheved, Rose screeching her ferocious objections, and he forced to bestow a final judgment. At times, he thought, medical knowledge could be a rather bothersome thing. Now, seeing Almodis' merriment, he knew he'd made the correct decision. After all, she did seem in robust health, and he hadn't the heart to deny her a bit of fun after she'd been shut up for so long. He held Fulk still to let the cart pass by and hoped Rose would eventually forgive his disloyalty to her. The ladies sat cramped tightly in the rear of the cart, jabbering gaily. Simon thrilled to Maura's happiness, though also worried how harshly their upcoming departure might upset her. Then again, they needn't leave immediately. They'd at least wait for the child to arrive.

Although treacherous storms had blighted the first half of May, this third week was blessed with warm bursts of sun and only a hint of showers. The doors of the village huts were adorned with bulging wreaths of flowers and fluttering ribbons of every hue. The jubilant group unloaded Maura's trunk at Edith's, shed their wintry clothes for lighter cloth, and bustled off to join the entertainment. Rose, Arthur and Edith headed for the food stalls to greet old friends. Alan and Simon trotted off in the direction of the more physically demanding events. Maura and Almodis dallied behind, Almodis all aflutter over Alan, her baby, and herself. Maura didn't attempt to comment, yet listened with loving amusement to Almodis' yammering. "Maura, I never believed I would anticipate simply talking with a man! Alan's enjoyed such a rich, varied life. Did you know his family is Jewish and because he decided to serve the King instead of pursuing his family's metalwork business, his father disinherited him? Which is so hypocritical, don't you agree, since the King has afforded the Jews special protection. He's only remained close to his brother, Nicolas. Oh, Maura, you know all this, you're humoring me. He speaks so fondly of you, and considers you his dearest friend." Almodis linked Maura's arm, and hugging her near, spoke with rampant excitement, "Everything about him is immensely intense, but ever so gentle. He's fiercely protective, which is his nature and profession. We drive Rose mad with our cooing. His touch alone thrills me! The feelings I have for him frighten me at times, only—that's foolish, isn't it?"

"Not at all," soothed Maura.

"The babe's so testy, we've yet to come together properly and have created new ways to share pleasure. And he possesses the most exquisite body! I cringe to think how I'll look after this child leaves me. We sleep together—Rose gave up that battle weeks past. I've asked her about my confinement after the birth, about how long we need wait till—"

"You asked Rose *that*?" Maura interrupted, amazed.

"Oh yes, and she seemed perturbed at first, then replied bluntly but politely, 'when your bleeding's done'."

"What a brave woman you are, Almodis!" Maura returned.

"And I'm tremendously proud of you! What a monumental victory you both have achieved. You have defeated the most powerful family in two countries. A promising start to your divine future, don't you agree?"

"Oh, yes!"

"And I'm highly impressed with Edith as well, though surprised she allowed Robert to fool her for so many years."

"She loved a different Robert," said Maura.

"So I hear and, for that, I'm grateful."

It seemed an odd response, even for Almodis, and Maura asked, "Why?"

"If he hadn't changed, I might have wanted to stay with him." Almodis stopped to catch her breath and murmured, "I wish you didn't have to go."

Maura took her hand and somberly stated the inevitable, "Our protection is temporary, Almodis. You've discovered the perfect hiding place, and we'd never risk jeopardizing you. It would be suicidal for us to settle in Dunheved. We must find our own home." She masked her sorrow behind a full smile and encouraged, "Now, come along! The fun can't begin without you."

Almodis firmed her grip on Maura's hand, wiped a tear, and waddled on.

Simon hung on the fence and halfheartedly watched the wrestling match, while listening to Alan's burbling, "Almodis is so stimulating, keeping her amused is exhausting—"

"And?" helped Simon.

"Something I never want to quit." Alan stepped back as a wrestler crashed into the fence before him. Unruffled, he reached down, lifted the dazed man up, shoved him in the direction of his opponent, and continued, "She's a changeling—one moment the most intelligent, calculating, spoiled, ingratiating woman I've ever encountered, other times she's a helpless clinging child, so innocent, and so needy. And when she flashes those doe eyes, pouts her lips and purrs to me, I...I—"

"Blubber?" Simon offered.

"Like a baby. She listens to me. Makes me feel special." He crossed his arms, admitting with a rapturous sigh, "There's no escaping it, I'm hopelessly smitten..."

Simon smiled inwardly as Alan praised on. Clearly he loved Almodis! Never had Simon seen him this animated, and he reveled in Alan's joy. Then a sobering thought intruded—what was to become of this peculiar couple after the child was born? He swiftly shirked the worry to focus again on Alan's tribute and heard, "...She's aggravatingly wonderful!"

Simon chuckled and deduced, "So it seems we're both firmly ensconced in domestic bliss."

Alan started and stated vehemently, "Domestic! Almodis? Never! Unruly bliss, perhaps."

They laughed and then noticed the wrestling field was empty and the onlookers impatient for more brutality. Alan nudged Simon. "Would you care for a good-natured tussle?"

"Are you certain? You may regret the challenge," bragged Simon.

Alan smiled a derisive smile and, waving Simon onto the field, sneered, "After you, my skinny little friend."

At the sweets stall, Almodis' eyes gleamed at the sight of plump oozing pastries; suddenly, she hugged her belly and paled. Maura had just opened her mouth to fuss, when Arthur appeared, suggesting, "Almodis, let me take you a few stalls down where I saw a mass of pretty, glittering baubles. Maura, Rose is looking mighty dreary. Perhaps you can cheer her."

Maura nodded and answered, "I'll try." She watched them saunter away, then hurried to Rose's side and snuggled up against her. "Why are you sad?"

"I'm not sad, angel, only tired. Where have Alan and Simon gone?"

"They're off shooting arrows, or wrestling."

"Then why aren't you with them?"

"I'm dreadfully out of practice, besides I want to be with you." Maura grew curious at Rose's narrow stare and blurted, "What's afflicted you, Rose? You're so intense!"

"I'm trying to decide what's different about you."

Maura shifted uneasily and said, "Will and Rufus no longer hound me! That alone has done wonders for my mood."

"No. It's a great deal more than that. I'm not yet able to put words to my suspicion, but I will...soon."

"Maura, come!" shouted Almodis, returning with Arthur in tow. "We must find Alan and Simon. As Arthur has so eloquently stated, 'they're engaging in feats requiring extreme courage, massive brawn, and boundless stupidity'! We dare not miss such a tempting prospect."

Maura eagerly searched Rose's face for permission. Rose clicked her tongue, and urged her on her way, muttering, "You'd best find them before they do themselves injury."

Arriving at the wrestling arena, Almodis elbowed her way to the front of the rowdy crowd and Maura followed, apologizing for her friend's rudeness. Almodis grabbed Maura and gasped at the vicious drama being played out before them. Alan, the obvious victor, had a flushed, gritting Simon clamped in a choking hold. Almodis gaped at

Maura's lame reaction to her husband's murder and cried, "We must stop this atrocity! It isn't fair. Alan is a great deal larger than Simon. He'll surely kill—"

Maura's laugh interrupted Almodis' panic. "Don't fret, Almodis, they're only playing. To compensate for his lack of bulk, Simon has mastered the art of—" They snapped their heads to Alan's groan, and saw him clutch his bottom, and sink to his knees in the dust. Simon leapt nimbly away to an explosive cheer. Maura beamed and finished, "—nasty fighting!"

Almodis flamed red, spat curses, and surged forward to avenge her man. Maura yanked her back, insisting, "He'll be fine!" Almodis sulked, and watched with guarded interest as the men clutched each other, and thrashed about the pen. Simon had shed both shirt and tunic, his bronze skin and sinewy muscles rippled and glistened in the sun. Alan's sweat-soaked shirt clung to his brawny form and his fierce expression evoked an enticing terror. Dreamy, enthralled looks slowly crept across the faces of all the women present.

Two nearby women distracted Almodis with their zealous English clucking. She nudged Maura and curtly asked, "What are they saying?"

Maura ignored her to watch Simon careen over Alan's shoulder. She cringed to his mournful groan as Alan dove on top of him.

"Maura!" Almodis demanded, "*What* are they saying?"

A bulky spectator blocked Maura's view. Perturbed, she cocked her ear to the chatter and muttered, "They think the wrestlers are handsome and plan to speak to them after the match."

"They plan to what?!" Almodis bellowed, again flashing scarlet.

"Please, Almodis," Maura complained and begged, "let me watch." But she turned to find Almodis gone and, searching, spotted her between the women, flailing and flaring at them in rabid French. The women looked on aghast. Maura caught hold of her crazed friend, and dragged her, ever ranting, from the throng. She shook her to contain her ire. "Almodis, don't be ridiculous! Do you actually think Alan would dare pay heed to another woman when he knows you're near?"

Before Almodis had a chance to consider the obvious, she let out a small cry. Her stormy face turned terrified, and she slumped against Maura, almost knocking her to the ground. "Maura..." she whispered in alarm, "there's water running down my leg and I can't stop it! Help me sit."

Maura felt faint, but she swiftly gathered her wits and cautiously guided Almodis to the village well. "Brace yourself against the stones and don't move!" she instructed in a quaver. "I'll fetch Simon."

"Wait!" called Almodis, snatching up Maura's hand. "Before you go...I...I have a confession to make."

"What?" Almodis stayed silent, so Maura probed louder, "What?!"

"I...I've had pains all day. Perhaps that's why I've been so cross."

"Almodis!" roared Maura.

"Don't yell at me!" whined Almodis, then she dismissed Maura with a wave and warning, "I suggest you hurry."

Maura dashed back to the wrestling field, propelled herself through the crowd, vaulted the fence, and threw herself between the two grunting men. "Stop!" she yelled. "It's time!" The audience gasped their shock and, as Simon and Alan bounded after Maura, grumbled their discontent.

Over the next few interminable hours, Almodis employed the men to accompany her as she hobbled for what seemed miles, round and round the cottage. Inside, the women prepared for the birth. They fashioned a cradle from the lid of a trunk, plumped it full of straw, and covered it with the softest pelt they could find. Edith measured and snipped a length of thread, Rose ripped sheets to swaddle the child, and Maura warmed water for its bathing. The air crackled with excitement, but also with Rose's petulance. Edith addressed her curtness, "If Almodis doesn't fluster me, why does she rile you?"

Rose snapped back, "Because she's always causing trouble, ordering me about, ignoring what's best, constantly quibbling—"

"And a part of you loves her for it. She wouldn't upset you so if you didn't care for her. I see you two as very similar."

Appalled, Rose stammered, "Edith! I...I..."

Edith smirked and said, "I've never known you to be speechless. Come now," she comforted, squeezing Rose's shoulder, "attend to the miracle we're about to witness. I know you feel this child is partly yours."

A nervous smile stirred Rose's lips. Maura intervened; she wound her arm round Rose's, led her aside and asked, "Rose, I've been meaning to ask you."

"What is it, angel?"

"Simon and I are at odds—"

"You're fighting?"

"Oh no" said Maura, "it's only a case of conflicting tales concerning my parents. It seems Avenal told Simon my father was killed on the north border of Wales. Lord Robert claims he was murdered in Cornwall. We thought if anyone knew the truth it would be you, since your husband..." Maura faltered, not certain how to continue.

Rose patted her hand. "You were wise to come to me. My husband died defending *your* father on the north border of Wales."

Maura lifted her bewildered gaze and further wondered, "Why would Robert lie to me?"

"Perhaps he's forgotten."

"Or he's purposely lying."

"Oh Maura, leave the past be. Think instead on your promising future."

Maura nodded and, together, they rose to Edith's request, "Ladies, I need help with this cauldron."

Simon braced himself as Almodis wrapped her arms round his neck and hung her entire weight on him. When her pain eased, she raised weary eyes to his smiling ones. "I don't much like this."

"I have yet to meet a woman who does," answered Simon.

"How much longer?"

"There's no way to tell," he said, then praised, "You're doing wonderfully well."

"And you're a sweet liar," said she. They continued their walk and Almodis weakly atoned, "I'm sorry."

"For what?"

"Causing trouble."

He waved away her concern. "So the baby's born here, what does it matter?"

"I didn't mean to cause your mother upset. She's been kind to me. She didn't have to be."

"My mother doesn't waste her kindness. She's thrilled the child will be here soon and so am I! This sibling may grow to like me."

"He will know of you and if possible spend time with you. Of that, I'll make certain!" She stopped with a gasp and dug her fingers into his arms. In awe, he watched her immerse herself in her agony. This pain stayed with her longer and left her shaken and pleading, "Oh, Simon, they're coming faster and getting much worse. I want to go back to the cottage." He took her arm to start back; she hesitated, drew him close and kissed him. "I haven't thanked you for picking Alan to guard Maura."

Simon blushed a bit and smiled, "I only pick the best."

"I agree—" Another pain struck which she bravely suffered, then she fretted, "You'll be close by, in case anything should go amiss?"

He seemed surprised by the question. "Of course, I will, but it won't. Come, you'll be more comfortable inside."

Almodis settled herself on a mat in a darkened corner of the hut, and held everyone at bay while quietly enduring her pains.

Fascinated, Maura studied Almodis from the table's bench. She secretly compared her friend's stoic performance to Adela's hysterical one, and shook her head to the wonder of it all. Alan, full of new fears and feeling inept and awkward, couldn't take himself far from Almodis and waited in the stable. Simon sat outside on the lawn with Arthur, intent on letting the experts inside handle the seemingly uncomplicated event.

After a desperately long hour, Almodis suddenly came alive with vigor and spouted excitedly, "Please, call Alan! I need to hold to someone, someone I won't easily hurt." Alan approached and at Almodis' assurance, "It won't be long now," the color returned to his face. He knelt beside her and held her tightly, while she strained and grunted the baby from her body.

The child's head soon appeared. Edith dipped a dampened cloth inside its mouth, and asked Almodis for one more push; the child dropped into her hands. "A boy!" she cried, and marveled, "A very big boy!"

A collective "Aaahhh..." resounded from the group. Rose joined Edith on the floor, tied and cut the cord, and gathered up the afterbirth. Edith swaddled the sputtering, kicking babe, dabbed his tongue with honey, and passed him into his mother's groping hands.

Almodis looked a bit startled, then tearfully giggled at her son's peculiar appearance. Alan placed a proud kiss on her cheek and on the boy's brow, then grew misty-eyed at Almodis' request, "Would you consider acting as my son's father? There is no one I'd rather have guide him."

I'd be honored," he humbly replied.

Maura hung out the door and announced, "It's a boy, and he's wonderful!"

The two men leapt up and hugged each other, Simon asking, "How fares Almodis?"

Maura turned back to the room and answered with an astonished laugh, "She's arguing with Rose over getting up!"

*****

The beasts were housed in outside pens and the stable turned into a makeshift dormitory for the men. The long night held novel sounds and Maura tossed fitfully to Simon's absence, the babe's mewling, and Almodis' cooing. She sat and happily crawled to Almodis' beckoning finger. The babe suckled contentedly at Almodis' breast and she whispered, "I hadn't expected to perform this duty, and yet my genius son seemed to know exactly what to do. In but a few hours, he's taught me much."

Maura gently stroked his coal black hair. "He's so beautiful. What will you call him?"

"I need to discuss the choices with Alan, though I've settled on Adam, after the original Adam, of course. This one will be the first Mortain to escape the treachery."

The boy's tiny fingers circled Maura's thumb. "I'm so proud of you, Almodis. I pray if ever my time comes, I can be as brave."

"I'm certain of it," said Almodis. "Can't you sleep?"

"No, too much excitement, I suppose. And I miss Simon."

"No one is standing guard. Go to your rightful place by his side, and..." her eyes sparkled mischief as she added, "while there, send Alan back to me." Maura hesitated, and Almodis begged, "Maura, if you don't go soon, we'll only end up blubbering again."

A giant moon lit the stalls with a silver glow. Alan and Simon chuckled at Arthur's grating snore, and Alan noted, "It's amazing how quickly one becomes accustomed to sleeping with someone."

"Yes," Simon wistfully mused, "sleeping alone is not unlike having a part of your body hacked off."

"Oh, Simon," Alan moaned in disgust, "that's dreadful. But it is near enough to the truth to make me act." He rose and swatted straw from his clothes, announcing with gumption, "I'm going in!"

"I wish you luck!" Simon said, offering his hand and adding with a sly wink, "Send Maura to me, will you please?"

Maura and Alan met at the door. After embarrassed titters, they excused themselves and squeezed past each other through the slim opening. Alan joined the child in Almodis' embrace. Maura, clutching their quilt, leant against the wall and gazed sweetly down at her eager husband. She tossed the blanket to his side, sank to her knees and draped his body with hers. He covered them both and sighed, "That's much better."

*****

A whirlwind week passed, highlighted by Adam's christening and Arthur and Edith's wedding, and although tightly packed, the extended family resided comfortably together. Too soon the day arrived for Simon and Maura's departure. Simon hid his woe by working steadily throughout the morning, packing the cart with assorted beasts, trunks, food, ale, bolts of cloth, and whatever else he could force beneath the binding ropes. And to the tail of the cart he secured E'dain's new companion, Maude the cow.

Maura was so sick with grief she wasn't able to help Simon, and handled her woe by wandering. Upon her return, Edith took her aside and, together, they delightedly watched Simon play with Adam. "Simon is a changed man," Edith whispered. "He's no longer lost, and *that*, Maura, is due entirely to you. I've no doubt you two will do well in Wales, only—it's late in the year for planting and..."

"What is it, Edith?" Maura tenderly pressed, sensing her struggle.

"One thing you'll never cure him of is stubbornness. He refuses to accept this." Edith placed the money bag in Maura's hand and griped, "It's *his* money! He insists on giving it to me and I don't need it. Arthur has saved up quite a bit, and Robert doesn't tax me. Please Maura, take it, and keep our secret till you reach your new home."

Maura wiped her damp cheeks and sputtered, "I...I don't know what to say. How can I—how can we thank—how can we say good-bye?!"

"You won't," Edith laughed through tears. "Sooner than you expect you'll see our old wrinkled faces at your door."

"I pray so," sniffed Maura as they clasped hands and turned their attention once again to the brothers.

"The boy has the blackest eyes," said Edith distantly. "I believe that's a good omen... Come," she said, rising, "it's time you left. Everything's packed and the others are waiting outside."

Throughout the wrenching farewells, everyone held up fairly well, till Maura, that is, came to Rose. They couldn't speak, they could only sob, and their sobbing unleashed a rash of tears along the line of well-wishers. Simon gently plucked Maura from Rose's clench, kissed Rose himself, then helped Maura up into the cart. She buried her grief in his lap and, as Fulk lumbered forward, Simon turned to wave one last wave.

The group reluctantly dispersed but Rose stayed awhile on the lane. Her tears mingled with spitting rain as she wrung her hands, and watched the cart disappear from view. Edith joined her and urged, "Come in, Rose, you'll catch a chill."

Rose jerked from her touch, anguish choking her lament, "What will happen to them, Edith? How long before tragedy visits again? And now that the child's come, what will become of Alan and Almodis? The thought of young Marc lying broken and alone in Normandy cracks my heart. They fool themselves into believing all's well. But all's *not* well and never will be!"

"Oh Rose, you slight them!" admonished Edith. "They are well aware of the dangers. Alan and Almodis have a curious, rare bond, and are more than willing to suffer the consequences of their union. Our children were raised with strong souls and minds. And that strength has clearly served them well. We shouldn't be doubting them, we should be praising them!"

Rose's melancholy began to lift. She swabbed at her puffy eyes and, for a long pensive moment, squinted down the road. "Edith!" she suddenly blurted. Her dark eyes lit and her tone turned expectant. "I know what's different about Maura!"

"What?"

"Come!" She squeezed Edith's hand and pulled her toward the door, bubbling with suspense, "I'll tell you inside where it's warm!"

*****

CHAPTER THIRTY-TWO - A MIRACLE

The blustery sea foamed and the cold cut to the bone as Simon reined Fulk alongside the timbered long house that centered the commote of Mynyw. Maura shivered violently beneath her cloak, raised her drawn face to the bleak surroundings, and wondered at the eerie sense that she'd visited this place before. Beyond the crumbling rock wall circling the huts, Maura spied the immense cathedral veiled behind a drifting fog. Squawking sea gulls swirled round its sacristy and infested the gray sky above her. She lowered her eyes and directed her scrutiny to the weighty discourse taking place between Simon and a plump older woman. She grew worried at his grieved expression and sulking posture. He left the woman and slowly climbed up into their cart. "Rhodri died...six months past," he uttered brokenly.

"And what of Gael?" asked Maura.

"She's still here. She's moved to the next lane." The news of Rhodri and sight of Maura's sickly complexion fueled Simon's festering panic. He swallowed to the touch of her cheek on his, and slapped Fulk's back with the reins.

Gruffydd, a sturdy eight year old lad, sat earnestly whittling in the doorway of his modest cottage. To the sound of squeaking wheels, he snapped to alertness and brushed a shock of damp auburn hair from his brow. He rose cautiously, his sea-green eyes bulging and tiny features pinched with confusion. His puzzlement quickly switched to glee; he tossed his wood, screeched, "Mam! Mam! It's Simon! It's Simon!" and tore away down the lane. Simon dropped the reins, jumped from the cart, and met him half-way. Delightedly, he scooped the youngster into his arms.

Maura looked on with a strained smile, recalling Simon's loving tales of Rhodri and Gael's remarkable son, Gruffydd. She pulled herself to the side of the cart, though stopped as she caught sight of another advancing figure. An attractive woman of modest height and slim figure strode determinedly, her steps quickening with her ever-widening smile. She wiped her hands on her stained skirt, her face on her sleeve, and gasped, "Thank the Lord! You've come back!" Simon set Gruffydd down to engulf the woman in a smothering embrace. And as he did so, a sharp pain stabbed Maura's belly. She squeezed shut her eyes as doubts and nausea pained her mind. She had come to accept the fact that Simon had known intimately only a few women during their years apart, but she wasn't at all interested in meeting one of them. A small voice intruded on her jealousy, "Maura..."

Maura opened her eyes and was greeted by the most engaging, lovely face. Gael's features were as delicate as a child's, yet her limpid green eyes betrayed tremendous strength. Her wavy, sand colored hair, hung like a crimped shawl about her shoulders, and bobbed as she thrust out her arms, and gushed, "I knew when next we saw Simon, you'd be with him! I feel we're already dear, dear friends." Her eyebrows met in a worried frown. "You're drenched and weary. Come inside. I've a hot stew brewing, and we'll fetch you warm clothing."

The mention of stew dizzied Maura; Gael noticed her difficulty and shouted, "Simon! Come help." Gruffydd saw to the stabling of the beasts, and Simon and Gael helped Maura inside. Exhausted and nauseous, she lay cradled in Simon's hug, upon a bed of pelts. Her aching head stayed still while her eyes traveled the comfortable room. Garlic, herbs, and dried flowers dangled from the rafters. A bulky table and rolled mats served as the only furniture, and scented rushes jutted betwixt the pelts and pillows covering the floor. Gruffydd's carvings and toys lay strewn everywhere. A furious wind droned through slits in the shutters, and Maura cuddled closer to Simon. Her tired mind caught only a spattering of Simon and Gael's words, yet from their somber tone, she guessed they spoke of Rhodri.

"How did he die?" pressed Simon forlornly.

"No one knows, Simon," sighed Gael. "To me, it stank of poison, accidental or deliberate, I'll never know. He died bravely and we buried him on the hill where you two would go to talk."

Simon wiped away her one tear. "And how have *you* been?"

She sniffed, "I'm fine. Gruffydd took longer than I expected to recover, and now that you're back it will be easier for him. For both of us, loneliness has been the hardest obstacle. The villagers, though, have been loving and supportive."

"Why have you moved?"

"They may be loving and supportive, but they weren't willing to let a Saxon woman be their pennaeth. And I understood their hesitation completely. They continue to seek my guidance and, for that, I'm grateful." Gael rose to her knees and peeked into the bubbling cauldron. "The stew's hot, if you're hungry."

"No, thank you," said he.

Gael studied Maura's wan complexion; she lay so still, her eyes tightly shut. Gael shifted thoughtfully on the pelts, remembering the glowing description Simon had given of his love. Never did she recall the term *frail* ever being used. Her puzzled gaze fixed upon Simon's hand stroking Maura's cheek, then she looked into his careworn face and asked, "What can we do for her?"

"For now, leave her be. This is the first time she's slept calmly for days. She's eaten little, said less. We can't force help. When she's ready, she'll ask."

Gruffydd tumbled into the room, panting, "A meeting's been called to discuss Simon settling here."

Simon stiffened to the announcement and repeated, "Discuss?"

Gruffydd rested on his mother's knee, while she explained in a miffed voice, "Since Rhodri's death, dissent has racked the village. Of course, Gruffydd's too young to lead, and we haven't picked a guardian to act as pennaeth. Most dwellers are becoming more and more suspicious of anyone entering the commote, and of each other. I swear, Simon, the Normans need not attack this village, they need only wait for it to destroy itself!"

*****

At the far end of the long house, trestle tables arranged in a square surrounded a fire. Another fire blazed at the opposite end of the house, making the room stifling. Inside the main door, adults and children filed by Simon. By some he was welcomed with handshakes, hugs, and kisses; others blatantly snubbed him. Maura hung heavily on his arm, and answered their murmured greetings with a nod and faint smile. The children swarmed to the opposite end of the room to play, while the adults settled themselves onto benches flanking the tables, and the debate promptly began. To Maura, everyone spoke at once and too rapidly, but Simon and Gael seemed to have no trouble targeting questions and hurling back answers. The guttural, incomprehensible language irritated Maura, made her head pound, and the scant stew she'd eaten rumbled and lurched about her belly. Her anxious eyes darted about the tables, struggling to keep up with the bantering, striving to discern a mood.

"We've come to find some peace and start anew," Simon began wishfully. "This was the one place I felt safe and accepted."

Bishop Sulien, a balding elder draped in monk's robes, stood to speak. "I invited Simon to return. Before, when he was a respected member of our community, his medical knowledge—acquired, I might add in Myddfai—proved a tremendous help in the infirmary. And now that he's also become an experienced and effective emissary, I, for one, need him desperately."

"An emissary?!" bellowed a ruddy faced man named Hywell. "An emissary for whom? The same Norman pigs who trample our border, torch our commotes, rape our women!"

"My uncle, King William, has little control over the Marcher barons!" countered Simon. A few sharp jeers burst from the group, making him bristle with distress. He dug his fingers into Maura's palm, and vehemently continued, "He encouraged me to return here, to work with Sulien and Prince Rhys to preserve your independence. He has no quarrel with your Prince! They made their peace long ago."

Gael stood and spoke with great conviction, "Simon lived with Rhodri, Gruffydd, and me for a full year. Besides his wife, Maura, I am his greatest advocate. I'm shocked you felt the need to meet here tonight! There is absolutely no cause to distrust Simon. This commote is intent on refusing help of any kind, and we suffer for our stubbornness. Having Simon and Maura settle with us will only bolster our strength and well-being! I call for everyone present to join with me in welcoming them, and I would like to hear your agreement." Approving exclamations followed and she triumphantly finished, "Then it's settled—"

"I disagree!" interrupted a lone man with a slow growl.

Gael's fingers strangled her skirt as she met his brash glower. "Owain!" she spat, striking an indignant pose. "Why am I not surprised?"

"I am entitled to an opinion, aren't I?" Owain goaded.

"If it were my decision," she hissed through bared teeth, "I'd say never—"

"Let him speak, Gael," cut in Sulien.

In surrender, Gael crossed her arms and slumped back in her chair.

Owain rested one thigh on the table. His moss-brown eyes bore into Simon as he tersely claimed, "I question your allegiance."

"My allegiance is to peace and peace alone," Simon retorted.

"Hah!" scoffed Owain.

"By the fire in your eyes, Sir," Simon said smoothly, "I doubt you're familiar with the concept."

Enraged, Owain slammed his fist on the table. Gael jumped up and accused with a rigid finger, "You and only you are the cause of strife in Mynyw!"

Sulien rose to the simmering war and pleaded, "No battles. Not here, not now! Owain, has your question been answered to your satisfaction?"

"No!" barked Owain. "Simon, I've heard tell you're not completely tainted with Norman blood, which vindicates you—a bit. But," he added snidely, "what of your lovely wife? What talents does the Norman *Lady* have to offer us?"

Owain's irony boiled Simon's blood. He struggled to hold his anger, and his voice quaked his answer, "For the past five years, my wife has fought fiercely to survive our family. Believe me when I say she has less allegiance to the Norman dynasty than do I. She owns an impartial calming way and, many times, I've seen her influence the most ruthless men to think twice before they acted on their cruelty."

Owain arched a brow to sneer, "And *softened* their actions, I suppose."

"Yes," Simon gritted.

Maura cringed to the scores of piercing glares aimed at her and her mind screamed, *What are they saying, thinking?! Why don't they want us here? Who is this hateful man and why is he badgering Simon?!* The room spun madly and she buried her head in her crossed arms, but still the snide faces haunted her, shouting, taunting, accusing.

Simon shook her. "Maura?" he whispered frantically. "What is it? Maura, look at me! Answer me!"

The stew burned her throat on its swift journey upward. She shoved his hands away, lurched from the table, and staggered from the room. The chaotic meeting collapsed as Simon raced after her. Gael tried her best to restore order. The annoyed villagers pushed from the table, wagging their heads and muttering concerns of contagion. Before long, only two remained in the hall, guarding their respective tables. Gael hurled a seething glare Owain's way, and he postured back a haughty smirk.

Later at Gael's cottage, Maura instantly fell into a fitful sleep; Simon knelt and fretted at her side. Gruffydd continued his carving, and Gael paced, spitting frustration, "Owain's been here a month, which is a month too long for my liking. He came down from the mountains. He's a raider, a spy, an instigator!"

"And how did *he* get accepted?" snorted Simon.

"We had no choice! He was sent by Prince Rhys to protect us from saboteurs and infiltrators. Damn him! Wait till the Prince hears of his hateful behavior toward *you*. Maybe then he'll banish him back to the hills where he belongs!"

"Gael," pleaded Simon, his voice slurred with worry and fatigue, "no more fighting." He sank down beside Maura, and mumbled, "I'm...We're awfully tired of fighting."

"Simon..." She knelt by him and trepidly asked, "If you're not allowed to stay, what will you do? Where will you go?"

Simon did not want to hear or admit the dreaded answer, but muttered anyway, "I hear Ireland is so panicked by the wars here, they will murder anyone who doesn't know their language. Will, Curthose, and Rufus have spies throughout England and Normandy. It would take little time for us to be discovered."

"Scotland?" offered Gael.

"They hide King Edward's great nephew, Edgar Atheling. He is a weak contender to the throne of England and would not be keen on hiding another enemy of the crown."

"You are not the King's enemy!" stressed Gael.

"Once Uncle William is dead, I surely will be..."

*****

Maura sat serenely in the tall dewy grass, watching the rising copper sun bleed the sky. Everything seemed calmer this bright morning, including her belly. She'd left the others still sleeping, and had wandered to the cliffs to wrestle with her discomfort, doubts, and disappointments. To cheer herself, she sang softly and plucked a bunch of yellow blossoms.

"A pretty song, my Lady."

Maura started and rose clumsily to Owain's comment. She struggled with an answer, then realized he'd spoken to her in English! Embarrassed, she mumbled, "I thought I was alone." Maura studied him awhile. He was an intriguing fellow and his feral guise reminded her of Rose's tales of wood sprites. She liked his rumpled leather tunic and patched baggy braies. His unruly chestnut hair and scraggly beard merged together and hung low beyond his shoulders. At her ceaseless gaze, his guarded expression faded to reveal a questioning, almost daunted look and a thought jolted her. This man was bluffing! Irritation prompted her demand, "Why do you hate us so?!"

His hands braced his hips as he snidely replied, "I've been battling Normans for years. It's hard to be forced to be cordial to them."

"Then I should despise *you*," she returned sharply.

"We've made no attacks on the Normans!"

"My parents were murdered by the Welsh!" Her bluntness struck deep and, while he fumbled for a retort, she humbly explained, "We ask not for your kindness or friendship, we ask only for a home. There is nowhere else for us to go. We are outcasts. Surely, you've known that dilemma. We are more than willing to share our skills, contribute what we can, and work for peace. Will you alone crush our simple wish?"

Owain took a moment to examine Maura. She appeared not much different from a Welsh woman, though she did seem overly peaked. He fancied her appearance and soon found himself comparing her to Gael; why, he hadn't a clue. His study done, he wagged his head, crossed his arms, and snorted a nervous laugh.

"I don't appreciate your humor," Maura said uneasily.

"Few do," Owain replied.

"And I don't know your name."

"Owain."

"I'm called Maura." She lifted her hand. He started to raise his, but stopped and instead shrank from her touch.

Owain bristled inwardly. He'd never allow a woman, least of all a Norman woman, to break his resolve! His gruff, unyielding scowl returned, and he let fly his wrath, "For all I care, you can have this bleeding town and all its niggling fools!" He stormed away and, she watched, in wonder, him disappear over the bend in the cliff.

Simon caught Maura at the commote's wall. He brusquely took her arm and steered her toward Gael's hut. His tone betrayed annoyance as he declared, "I haven't time to discuss where you've been. I've been called to the long house. They've made their decision about our staying."

She flinched to his manner and said, "I'll go with—"

"No!" he flared, "I won't let them attack you. Not again!"

In strained silence, they continued their walk and, upon reaching Gael's door, Maura asked cautiously, "Are you certain you'll be all right?"

Simon nodded, and then his chest heaved as he confessed, "I'm so worried about you. We haven't spoken in days! When I woke this morning and found you gone, I...I—"

"Believe me," she said, grasping his hands, "I'm fine! Once the meeting's done, we'll talk."

His voice trembled, "Will...will you swear to stay in the hut till my return?"

"Yes...I promise I'll stay." They grabbed hold of each other and held snugly, while Maura comforted, "They won't turn you away, Simon. They love you, I love you." With a swift, brushing kiss, he left her, and hastened to his inquisition.

Maura twisted with discomfort upon the pelts, chastising herself for neglecting Simon. He was in despair, and she was so absorbed with her own petty grievances that she'd failed to see the severity of their situation. The result of this meeting would dictate their future—and a precarious future it could instantly become. Her nausea surged at the sickening image of a lifetime cursed with hiding, constant uncertainty, and turmoil. She rushed out the back door of the hut to retch into the dirt.

Gael entered through the front door, and called, "Maura? Are you here?"

Maura wiped her mouth, stood with difficulty, and reentered the room. She felt miserable and useless, yet, nonetheless, she offered, "May I help with something?"

"No, you look wretched. You should rest."

"I'm fine," Maura curtly countered.

"Then don't rest!" Gael snapped back.

"You spoke up quite boldly for my husband last night!" flashed Maura.

The barb was too full of aggravation for Gael to ignore, and she turned and flared, "And why shouldn't I have?"

Shocked by her own insinuation, Maura sank down on the pillows and started to weep, slowly at first, then quickly she lapsed into hysterical sobs. Gael awkwardly knelt by her side, wrung her hands, and implored, "What is it, Maura? Simon's crazed with worry over you. You must tell us what's wrong!"

"I feel so lost, so separate!" sobbed Maura. "I don't know how to help Simon, let alone help myself. What I just said to you—it was as if someone else, someone horrid, was speaking. And Gael," she groaned, "I'm so sick!"

Gael sat back to ponder Maura's misery. The vision of herself as a terrified girl first entering the village came to her and evoked caring words. "Maura," she began shakily, "I believe I know a little of how you must feel. When I first arrived here, I was but fourteen years old, newly married, and knew not a word of Welsh—I barely knew my husband. At first I resisted help, and was as heartsick as you. It was a terribly hard time. Though eventually, with time and my husband's help, I came to feel accepted, even loved by the villagers."

"I'm so sorry about your husband," Maura sniffled. "It's clear from the way you speak that you loved him deeply."

Gael's somber gaze drifted and she quietly mused, "Our love held great respect and companionship. Now," she said, brightening, "we must determine what ails you. What are your symptoms?"

A curious comfort replaced Maura's dole and she sat back to say, "I'm nauseated one moment, famished the next, always exhausted, and too quick to temper and tears. Do you work in the infirmary?"

"Oh no. At times, I do tend to the women's needs. When did you last bleed?" Maura started to the question, and Gael asked again, "Your flow, your course—whatever you call it, when did it last happen?"

Maura searched her mind; the date eluded her, and she shrugged and muttered, "It never comes when it's due."

"Well then," Gael said, "this time it's not come for a reason—you're pregnant."

"No!" Maura gaped and stammered, "No...no...I can't be!"

"Maura..." Gael grinned and wryly commented, "I do hope after two months of marriage, there's at least a possibility."

"No, you don't understand."

"Then explain."

"When I was last pregnant, I was hurt inside and—"

"Last pregnant?!" gasped Gael. "What are you saying? When were you last pregnant?"

"It's been almost five years," sighed Maura, bowing her head.

Round-eyed, Gael blurted, "Was it Simon's?"

"Yes."

"But he never mentioned—"

"He never knew," cut in Maura. She swallowed her sorrow and admitted, "The child died."

A disturbing silence fell which Gael lifted with an awed murmur, "Then this truly *is* a miracle." She beamed and clasped Maura's hands between hers. "Believe it, Maura, you are pregnant!"

The magical words rang in Maura's mind and elation raced through her veins, making her sputter tears and doubt, "I want so much to believe, but I'm afraid!"

"Don't be!" said Gael. "And..." Her exuberance sobered as she assured, "Simon and I were never anything but dear friends. Never, never doubt his love!"

With that, Maura's tears dribbled faster. Gael shed a few herself as she laughed, and suggested, "When Simon returns, ask him to walk you to the hill. He'll know the spot. You can tell him there."

Simon burst through the door and stopped short at the astounding sight of the women clasped in a tight hug. They broke apart, raised eager faces, and chorused, "Well?!"

"We can stay!" he exclaimed, then added, "The consensus was unanimous!"

"Oh, Simon!" Maura cried, lunging into his arms.

Gael held back and wondered, "What about Owain?"

"He wasn't there," answered Simon. "Rumor has it he's gone."

"Gone?" she repeated, then sighed, "Thank the Lord!" Yet the slight regret in her tone did not escape Maura. Gael stood and fidgeted with the girdle of her tunic. "Maura," she reminded, "weren't you mentioning a walk?"

"Oh, yes! Simon, would you take me to the hill?"

Her radiance almost blinded him, and he muttered, askance, "How did you know I planned to take you there?"

"I didn't, *really*...Gael thought—"

He grasped her waist and hustled her out the door. She turned and stretched out her hand to Gael, mouthing, *Thank you.*

Gael pressed Maura's fingers and chuckled, "Off with you..." and, winking, added, "Gruffydd's to stay the night with a playmate, and I'm planning on visiting a friend till very late, so don't stay out too long." Gael leant, cross-armed, in the doorway, her smile full of satisfaction as she watched them stride in an excited clutch down the lane. The thought of Owain briefly intruded, but she snubbed it and considered instead how blessed she and the commote were to have Simon and Maura.

The summit of the hill spanned a wide plateau. Upon reaching the crest of the path, they waded through a sea of wild flowers, and crossed an emerald carpet to a grove of gnarled oaks. The dense thicket shielded the crumbled remains of a cottage. Pensively, they stepped between, ducked under, and wove among the ruins. Maura lightly stroked the rotted timbers, and easily imagined their home being raised from the rubble. A sharp squeal escaped her as Simon grabbed her from behind and spun her around, insisting, "You'll tell me now!"

"Tell you what?" she teased.

"Ever since we left Gael's, you've looked about to burst. Tell me why!"

Her hands covered his cheeks as she gushed, "We think I may be pregnant!"

"We?"

"Gael and I," beamed Maura. Simon whooped and spun her round and round. When at last he set her down, she noticed something in his ecstatic look that made her guess, "You knew!"

"I only suspected," he confessed.

"How?"

"The usual symptoms, and Henry predicted it and he's never wrong, and...your body feels different."

"It does?"

"Yes...it's...rounder in places."

"Show me," she prompted, her eyes gleaming with anticipation.

"Here." His hand closed over one breast, his other hand covered the other. "And here."

"Why didn't you say?"

"I was afraid to raise your hopes, and wanted you to discover first for yourself."

They wandered from the cottage and sprawled in the silken grass. Simon rolled to his side and said, "You seem to feel much better."

Her cheek nuzzled his shoulder and she smiled. "Now that I know its reason, the sickness won't bother me."

"I'll brew you something to tame your ornery belly. And," he added as his arm swept the ruins, "what do you think of our new home?"

"It's simply magnificent! I can envision it all with exquisite clarity—the fire, our mat, our quilt—"

"No mats!" Simon returned stridently. "I'll build us a bed and stuff the mattress thick with the most supple feathers and," he sighed as his leg draped her hip and pulled her near, "when we sink into its folds..."

"And you sink into mine..." she purred.

"Lord!" he grunted, then nipped her neck and moaned, "I'm dying to get you alone."

"We are alone," she breathed and crushed her lips to his. Their kiss exuded great passion and hope, yet the chilled touch of an unwelcome wind separated them. Simon sat back on his heels and cast a troubled glance at the sea. "I don't like the look of the water. We'd best get back."

Maura pushed up and twisted to see black malevolent clouds stirring and chopping the waves and creeping ever closer. An assault by stinging rain and dust drove them to their feet. They hurried through the tousled flowers to the head of the path, and there they paused as a dreadful portent invaded them both.

Maura clung to Simon; her voice heaved panic and wailed above the wind's howl, "No one will take this child from us, will they?! Swear to me they won't, Simon, swear to me!"

Simon firmed their clutch and glared out across the raging sea. The courage in his pale eyes challenged the tempest and he swore, "No...never!"

Alone and snug in the tranquil hut, they slipped beneath their quilt to rejoice in each other and their glorious news. Later, as Simon slept, Maura found parchment and quill. She sighed blissfully and caressed her belly as she settled back beside him, and continued her writings to Marc.

*****

To be continued in the sequel:

A Plague of Devils

NOTES

The historical question that looms over my novel is, did Robert, Count of Mortain and Earl of Cornwall, in fact, have an illegitimate child? I don't know. I have read practically everything ever written about Robert, and, in those writings, I discovered much. Robert's first marriage to Matilda, daughter of Roger of Montgomery, was tenuous to say the least. They fought so fiercely, verbally and physically, that their priest threatened to annul the marriage if their battling didn't stop. I have also wondered about the close bond between Matilda and her mother, the poisoner Mabel of Belleme. Did this relationship frighten Robert? What effect did it have on their marriage? Knowing what I know, and also realizing that having an illegitimate child during the late 11th century was not that uncommon, I created Simon and Edith. I have based Simon on a real individual—Simon de Crépy, William the Conqueror's foster son and mediator. I made the decision not to use the true Simon in my book because de Crépy seemed a bit boring. Not that I'm criticizing the fellow. Like my Simon, he despised violence and war. He became a monk after he refused William's offer of a daughter in marriage, and was a hermit in later life.

There is no record of Robert having a second legitimate son with his second wife, Almodis. In the sequel to this novel, <u>A Plague of Devils,</u> I take care of this problem by creating a situation in which Robert's second legitimate son would not appear in future history books.

Rufus' great hall in the Palace of Westminster was built in 1097, not the late 1080's. I describe this as happening earlier in order to emphasize Rufus's responsibility for the illustrious room. His great hall has survived and can be seen to this day.

As for Maura's betrothal to Rufus, William did not arrange a marriage for any of his sons, and he mentions this problem in my book. Robert, William's brother, was rapacious when it came to land and money and, as such, I imagined him making a last ditch effort to connect himself with the next King of England and/or Duke of Normandy using Maura, his ward. This betrothal in my novel was not legal and lasted all of six weeks.

The first recorded physicians of Myddfai were mediciners to Rhys Gryg, in 1234. Rhys Gryg was Prince of Deheubarth, grandson to *'The Lord Rhys'*, who was grandson to Rhys ap Tewdwr. Rhys ap Tewdwr is a main character in the sequel of this book. In the sequel, Simon becomes Rhys ap Tewdwr's Court physician, and head physician to St. Davids Cathedral and its village, Mynyw. Court physicians were already common in Wales before <u>The Laws of Hywel Dda</u> was written in 930. Druidic and Galenic medicine seem to be a basis for the Myddfai remedies, and Roman medicinal plants may have been used in their concoctions as well. Thus, in reality, Simon would not have been called a Physician of Myddfai, but would have used remedies similar to theirs'. I've used their title with his name to show reverence to the Welsh family of physicians whose influence was known far and wide throughout history, and still remains so today.

I have studied the family of William the Conqueror for the past thirty years. From the inconclusive and contrary research I have read, I believe I have created believable identities and personalities for all the characters involved in the everyday lives of this iconic family. Contrary research does not necessarily hinder the creation of believable characters; instead it tends to make them richer, more colorful and multi-faceted. I do hope you agree.

ABOUT THE AUTHOR

M. (Maggie) Garfield was born in Alexandria, Virginia. An author, historian, editor and educator, she has lived and traveled throughout the world. Presently, she lives in Lafayette, Colorado.

Maggie's greatest joy is her family. Her second joy is writing for adults and young adults, who wish to learn and dream of living in a time of history that was frequently tragic, challenging, and fulfilling, yet always fascinating.

*****

BIBLIOGRAPHY

Arano, Luisa Cogliati. The Medieval Health Handbook. George Braziller, New York, 1976.

Aries, Philippe. A History of Private Life, Revelations of the Medieval World. Cambridge: The Belknap Press of Harvard University Press, 1988.

Ashley, Maurice. The Life and Times of William I. New York: Cross River Press, a division of Abbeville Press, Inc. 1992.

Barrow, G.W.S. Feudal Britain. London: Edward Arnold Ltd., 1956.

Breverton, Terry. The Physicians of Myddfai. Carmarthenshire, Wales: Cambria Books, 2012.

Bridgeford, Andrew. 1066 The Hidden History in the Bayeux Tapestry. New York: Walker Publishing Company, Inc., 2006.

Bowen, John T. and Rhys Jones, T.J. Teach Yourself Welsh. London: The English Universities Press, 1960.

Brochard, Phillip. Castles of the Middle Ages. Morrison, New Jersey, Adapted U.S. Silver Burdett: Librairie Hechette, 1980.

Brooke, Christopher. From Alfred to Henry III 871-1272. New York and London: W.W. Norton & Company, 1961.

Brooke, Christopher. The Saxon and Norman Kings. Fontana/Collins, 1963.

Brown, R. Allen. Castles, A History and Guide. New York: Greenwich House, 1980.

Brown, R. Allen. The Normans. New York: St. Martin's Press, 1984.

Brown, R. Allen. The Normans and the Norman Conquest. Woodbridge, Suffolk: The Boydell Press, 1985.

Burke, John. Life in the Castle in Medieval England. New York: British Heritage Press, 1978.

Charles-Edwards, T.M.; Owen, Morfydd E.; Russell, Paul, Editors. The Welsh King and His Court. Cardiff: University of Wales Press, 2000.

Chibnall, Marjorie. Anglo-Norman England 1066-1166. Oxford: Basil Blackwell, 1986.

Chibnall, Marjorie, Editor. The Ecclesiastical History of Orderic Vitalis, Volume II, Books III and IV. Oxford: Clarendon Press, 1969.

Costain, Thomas B. The Conquerors. New York: Doubleday & Company, 1949.

Crouch, David. The Normans. London: Hambledon Continuum, 2007.

Davies, John. A History of Wales. Penguin Books, 1990.

Davies, R.R. The Age of Conquest, Wales 1063-1415. Oxford University Press, 1987.

Douglas, David C. The Norman Achievement 1050-1100. Berkeley: University of California Press, 1969.

Douglas, David C. William the Conqueror. Berkeley and Los Angeles: University of California Press, 1964.

Evans, Gwynfor. Land of My Fathers. Yllolfa, 1974.

Ford, Boris, Editor. Early Britain, The Cultural History. Cambridge University Press, 1988.

Gantz, Jeffrey. The Mabinogion. Penguin Books, 1976.

Gies, Joseph & Frances. Life in a Medieval Castle. New York, Hagerstown, San Francisco, London: Harper Colophon Books, 1974.

Gies, Joseph & Frances. Women in the Middle Ages. New York: Thomas Y. Crowell Company, 1978.

Given-Wilson, Chris and Alice Custeis. The Royal Bastards of Medieval England. New York: Barnes and Noble Books, 1984.

Green, Judith A. Henry I. Cambridge University Press, 2009

Hartley, Dorothy. Lost Country Life. New York: Pantheon Books, 1979.

Haskins, Charles Homer. The Normans in European History. New York: Barnes and Noble Books, 1995.

Herm, Gerhard. The Celts. New York: St. Martin's Press, 1975.

Higham, Robert and Philip Barker. Timber Castles. Stackpole Books, 1995.

Hollister, C. Warren. Henry I. New Haven and London: Yale University Press, 2001.

Jones, T.J. Rhys. Teach Yourself Welsh. NTC Publishing Group, 1992.

Kerr, Nigel and Mary. A Guide to Medieval Sites in Britain. London: Diamond Books, 1992.

Kightly, Charles. A Mirror of Medieval Wales. Cardiff, Wales: Cadw: Welsh Historic Monuments, 1988.

Kightly, Charles. A Traveller's Guide to Royal Roads. London: Spectator Publications, 1985.

Labarge, Margaret Wade. A Small Sound of the Trumpet, Women in Medieval Life. Boston: Beacon Press, 1986.

Le Goff, Jacques, Editor. The Medieval World. Collins & Brown, 1990.

Lewis, D. Geraint. Welsh Names. Scotland: Geddes & Grosset, 2001.

Leyser, Henrietta. Medieval Women, A Social History of Women in England 450-1500. London: Phoenix Press, 1996.

Lloyd, J.E., Sir. A History of Wales. Golden Grove Editions, 1989.

MacDonald, Fiona. A Medieval Castle. New York: Peter Bedrick Books, 1990.

Matarasso, Francois. The English Castle. London: Cassell Books, 1993.

Mennell, Stephen. All Manners of Food. University of Illinois Press, 1996.

Morgan, Gwyneth. Life in a Medieval Village. Minneapolis, Minnesota: Lerner Publication Co. by permission from Cambridge University Press, 1982.

Nelson, Lynn H. The Normans in South Wales, 1070-1171. Austin & London: The University of Texas Press, 1966.

Peacock, John. Costume 1066-1966. London: Thames and Hudson, Ltd., 1986.

Pelner Cosman, Madeleine. Medieval Wordbook. New York: Barnes & Noble, 1996.

Pine, L.G. They Came With the Conqueror. London: Evans Brothers Limited, 1966.

Poole, A.L. Domesday Book to Magna Carta 1087-1216. Oxford University Press, 1955.

Pounds, N.J.G. The Medieval Castle in England and Wales. Cambridge: Cambridge University Press, 1990.

Power, Eileen. Medieval Women. Cambridge University Press, 1975.

Pryor, Francis. Britain in the Middle Ages. London: Harper Perennial, 2006.

Pughe, John, Translator. The Herbal Remedies of the Physicians of Myddfai. Edited by Derek Bryce, Felinfach, 1987.

Rawson, Hugh. Wicked Words. New York: Crown Publishers, Inc., 1989.

Renn, D.F. Norman Castles in Britain. John Baker, Humanities Press, 1968.

Rhys, John and David Brynmor-Jones. The Welsh People. London: T. Fisher Unwin Paternoster Square, 1900.

Rowley, Trevor. A Traveller's Guide to Norman Britain. London: Spectator Publications, 1986.

Rowley, Trevor. The Man Behind the Bayeux Tapestry. Gloucestershire: The History Press, 2013.

Rowley, Trevor. The Norman Heritage 1066-1200. London: Routledge & Kegan Paul, 1983.

Rowling, Marjorie. Everyday Life in Medieval Times. New York: Dorset Press, 1968.

Shorter, Edward. A History of Women's Bodies. New York: Basic Books, 1982.

Slocombe, George. Sons of the Conqueror. London: Hutchinson & Co. Ltd., 1960.

Smith, Charles Hamilton. Ancient Costumes of Great Britain and Ireland. London: Bracken Books, 1989.

Stafford, Pauline. Unification and Conquest. London: Edward Arnold, 1989.

Steane, John M. The Archaeology of Medieval England and Wales. The University of Georgia Press, 1984.

Steane, John M. The Archaeology of Medieval English Monarchy. London: B.T. Batsford Ltd., 1993.

Stenton, Doris Mary. English Society in the Early Middle Ages. Penguin Books, 1951.

Stephenson, Carl. Medieaval Feudalism. Ithaca, New York: Cornell University Press, 1942.

Strickland, Matthew, Editor. Anglo-Norman Warfare. Suffolk: The Boydell Press, 1992.

Talbot, Charles H. Medieval Medicine. London: Oldbourne, 1967.

Thompson, C.J.S. Magic and Healing. New York: Bell Publishing Co., 1989.

Thorpe, Lewis, Translator. Gerald of Wales, The Journey through Wales and The Description of Wales. Penguin Books, 1978.

Toy, Sidney. Castles, Their Construction and History. New York: Dover Publications, Inc., 1985.

Turvey, Roger. Twenty-one Welsh Princes. Wales: Gwasg Carreg Gwalch, 2010.

Turvey, Roger. Pembrokeshire, The Concise History. Wales: University of Wales Press, Cardiff, 2007.

Van Houts, Elisabeth M.C., Editor. The Gesta Normannorum Ducum of William of Jumieges, Orderic Vitalis, and Robert of Torigni, Volume I. Oxford: Clarendon Press, 1992.

Van Houts, Elisabeth M.C., Editor. The Gesta Normannorum Ducum of William of Jumieges, Orderic Vitalis, and Robert of Torigni, Volume II. Oxford: Clarendon Press, 1992.

Vander Zee, Barbara. Green Pharmacy; A History of Herbal Medicine. New York: Viking Press, 1982.

Venning, Timothy. The Kings and Queens of Wales. Gloucestershire: Amberley Publishing, 2012.

Walker, David. Medieval Wales. Cambridge: Cambridge Medieval Press, 1990.

Warner, Philip. The Medieval Castle. New York: Barnes and Noble Books, 1971.

Williams, A.H., M.A. An Introduction to the History of Wales, Volume I. Cardiff, University of Wales Press, 1949.

Williams, A.H., M.A. An Introduction to the History of Wales, Volume II. Cardiff, University of Wales Press, 1948.

William, John. Brut Y Tywysogion: The Chronicles of the Princes of Wales. Cambridge: Cambridge University Press, 2012.

Williams, Moelwyn. The South Wales Landscape. Hodder and Stoughton, 1975.

*****